CW00486422

Also by L. J. Hutton

Fantasy:
The Power & Empire series:
Chasing Sorcery
The Darkening Storm
Fleeting Victories
Unleashing the Power

The Menaced by Magic Series:
Menaced by Magic
No Human Hunter
Shards of Sorcery
The Rite to Rule

Historical:
Heaven's Kingdom – prequel
Crusades
Outlawed
Broken Arrow

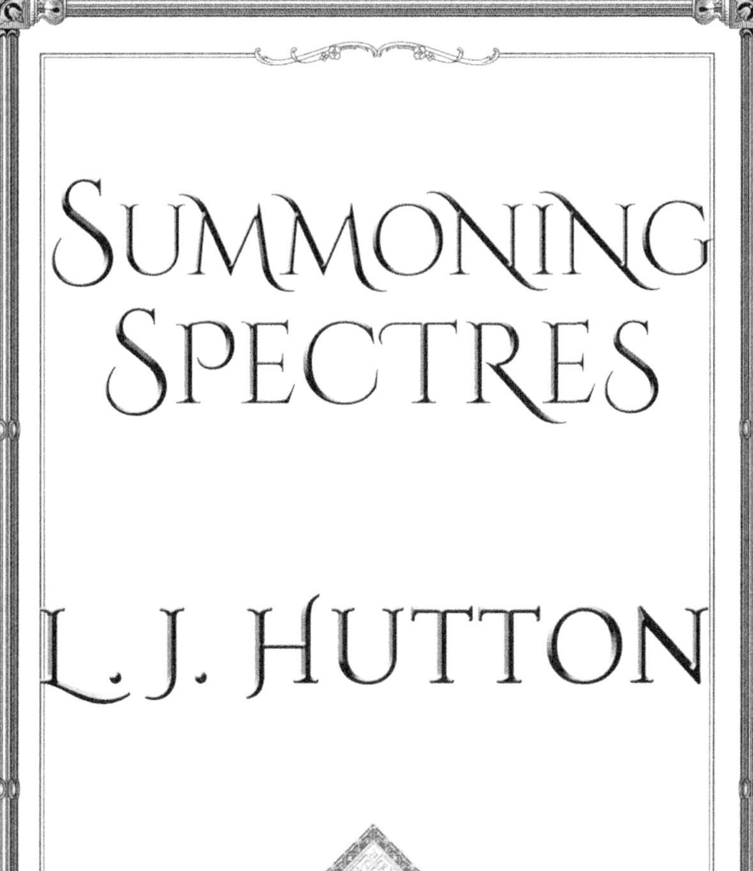

Summoning Spectres

L. J. Hutton

ISBN 13: 9781719988155

First published 2013
This edition 2021

Copyright

Acknowledgements

As ever there are people whom I need to thank – no writer works in a vacuum!

Firstly, thanks to Karen Murray for her stalwart support right from the very first page of this series. She has been the best first reader a fledgling writer could hope to have, always encouraging but never backwards in telling me when things weren't working. Everyone needs someone who can put things into perspective from a distance and she has done this admirably.

My husband John has had to cope with a very absent wife during the writing phases but has somehow survived! And of course my lovely lurchers, Blue, Raffles and Minnie have been companionable sleepers at my side while I've worked. I don't think I would have stayed sane without them.

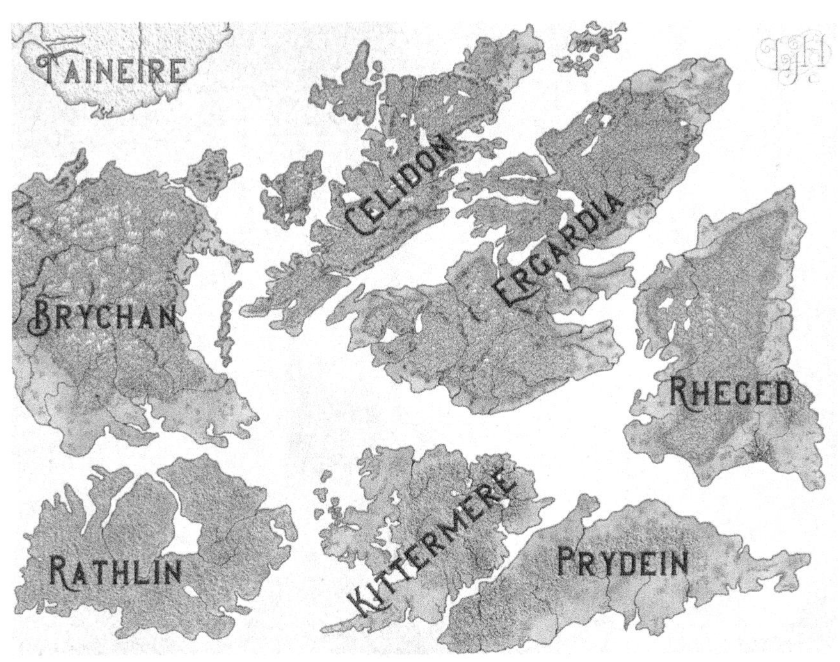
TAINEIRE
CELIDON
BRYCHAN
ERGARDIA
RHEGED
KITTERMERE
PRYDEIN
RATHLIN

Cava
Cava Skerries
Elotta
Teeth of Auskerry
Auskerry Island
The Gullet
Gura Vaii
Turnu
Sgurr Beg
Novo Selo
Sgurr Mor
Bali Mare
Salu Mare
Tokai Palace
Kuzmin Palace
Bruighean
Ralja Palace
Mereholt
Eldr Forest
Wyrdholt
The Assynt Highlands
Kotor
Ada
Endrod
Mol
Arad
Bocsa
Lovrin
Tisza
Tarhos
Mako
Palic
Caj
Selo
Pahi
Curug
Ilia
Kovin
Lupa
Javor
Mij
Kula
Backa
The Salton Sea Flats
Siria
Bors
Cluj
Raks
Danj
Surcin
Sabac
Sip
Suho
Sombor
Drinjacar
Janja
mouth of the Sava rivers
mouth of the Drina rivers
mouth of the Jana rivers

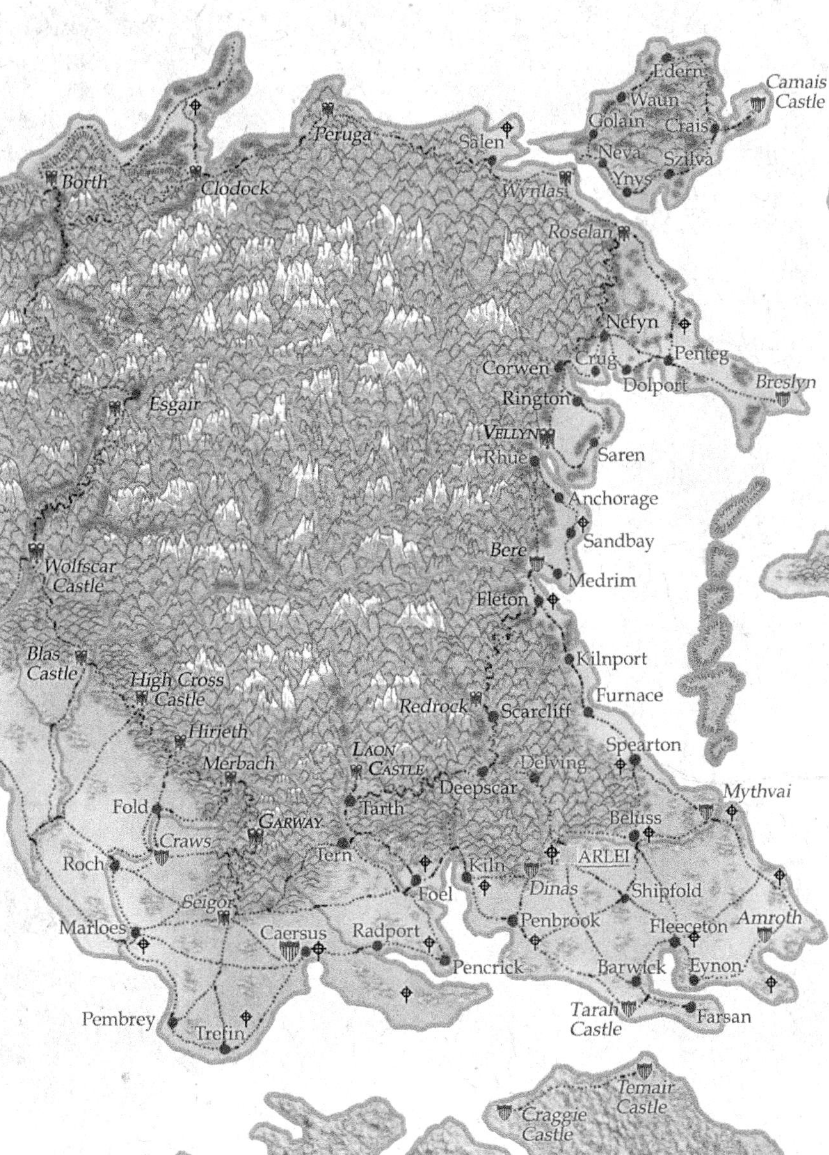
Edern
Camais Castle
Waun
Golain
Crais
Neva
Szilva
Ynys
Peruga
Salen
Wynlas
Borth
Clodock
Roselan
Nefyn
Crug
Penteg
Corwen
Dolport
Breslyn
Esgair
Rington
VELLYN
Rhue
Saren
Anchorage
Sandbay
Bere
Medrim
Wolfscar Castle
Fleton
Kilnport
Blas Castle
High Cross Castle
Redrock
Scarcliff
Furnace
Hirieth
Spearton
LAON CASTLE
Merbach
Delving
Deepscar
Mythvai
Fold
Tarth
GARWAY
Beluss
Craws
Tern
ARLEI
Roch
Kiln
Foel
Dinas
Shipfold
Seigor
Penbrook
Marloes
Caersus
Radport
Fleeceton
Amroth
Pencrick
Eynon
Barwick
Pembrey
Trefin
Tarah Castle
Farsan
Temair Castle
Craggie Castle

Chapter 1

Rescue and Revenge

New Lochlainn: early Spring-moon – early Earrach

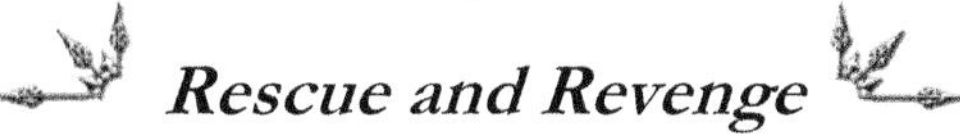

During the early days Labhran and the Knights spent travelling in company with the retreating section of the DeÁine army, they spent the whole time feeling like they were walking on eggshells, dreading that they would be found out and revealed as frauds. Their nerves were not helped by the realisation of how close they had come to making a mess of things right at the start. It had seemed so logical for the Knights to pose as prisoners, with the ordinary men-at-arms acting the part of sullen DeÁine soldiers under Labhran's command – certainly Labhran's past experience was of Donns relishing making slaves out of their enemies, so it had been a reasonable assumption.

Mercifully they had joined the main body of troops returning to New Lochlainn as the light was fading, and so it had only been with the coming morning that they had realised that this part of the army, at least, had taken no prisoners. It was just luck that they had not had chance to speak to anyone else in the force yet. Yes, there were some special prisoners up with Masanae and surrounded by a full company of very nasty household guards, but that was it. Having met with other officers the next morning, Labhran had consequently hurried back as fast as he could without causing comment, to tell the Knights to shed every recognisable vestige of uniform.

"Get rid of it! Burn it on the camp fires if you can," he had hissed at them.

The eight Knights had feared they would be in for a very cold time as they frantically stripped off, while the others kept watch and prayed nobody had seen them in the dawn light. However, that very day they had come upon the grim remains of the massacre of King Edward's army. The bitter cold was a mercy then, for it had stopped the corpses rotting and the stench was nothing like it could have been. Keeping to the wings of the returning force, the covert troop managed the grisly task of scavenging pieces of DeÁine uniform from the dead slaves who had come to grief at the hands of the Islanders.

There were nothing like the numbers of these as of the native dead, but the Knights managed to get enough pieces of outer clothing to enable them to blend in. The fact that several items were stiff with dried blood worked in their favour if not their comfort, since most of the men around them sported some kind of injury. With Labhran then concocting a tale of how this was all that was left of his larger company, the others having fallen in an ambush sprung by a few renegade Knights, they managed to establish their credentials to the, thankfully, incurious men around them. If they were not talking much to those around them, it hardly stood out because nobody else did either. As for Labhran himself, he stalked about the camp as if he owned it, exchanging snide sounding comments with other equally haughty young Donns, most of whom soon seemed to be regarding him with some awe. At least it kept them away from his men for fear of Labhran's displeasure.

"It's the battle ribbons," Labhran explained to the others, tapping at what seemed to be just ornament on the one shoulder of his jerkin. "For most of this lot, this foray into Brychan was the first real encounter they've experienced. They don't hand these out for a border raid!" Then added, "Thank the Spirits, because it's stopping any of them being tempted to call me out in a duel!"

"What? Here?" Friedl asked incredulously. "And with wounded all around? Surely not!"

"Oh yes," Labhran answered wearily. "They're like a pack of dogs – always wanting to move up in the pack order! And with the easy victory they've just had, it's not like they're worried about an enemy harassing their retreat. In fact they're more pissed off that there wasn't more blood and guts! So keep your heads down if one goes past! We don't want them venting their indulged, spoilt tempers on one of us!"

In this way they toiled across the snowbound Brychan landscape. In seven limping days they made it to the River Mer and the deserted town of Roch. Five more took them to the massive bridge across the Blane Water, frozen to a fraction of its normal torrent by the icy conditions higher up its course. Only another four took them to the Water of Sgair and the border between Brychan and New Lochlainn, and by now the Islanders were noticing the increase in pace.

Partly this was due to the falling by the wayside of the severely wounded, left to die for want of food, warmth and medical attention. Such wanton waste of life appalled the men of the Order, but there was nothing they could do about it. Unlike the others (accustomed to such treatment) they found it hard to rejoice that there were fewer mouths to feed from the pitifully small supplies. On which score they were also thankful for being kept well separated from the unfortunate slaves travelling behind them, who similarly fell in increasing numbers, so that their distress at the sight of such cruelty did not give them away. They privately feared some of their Order's Brychan sept might be prisoners amongst the driven drudges, but never having met anyone from that sept there was no way of knowing by sight alone.

"Will it get any better than this?" Oliver asked Labhran when they could talk under the cover of darkness. "Most of those slaves are starving to death, and we'll not be much better if we have to go all the way to Bruighean on such short rations in cold like this."

Labhran could say nothing to allay their fears, but almost as soon as they were out of the Sgair's valley the snow disappeared altogether – another reason for the quickening pace – and it became noticeably warmer. Out of habit the little band gathered wood as they went now, for they travelled through light woodland and along wide roads edged with mature hedges. This too nearly undid them, for the DeÁine soldiers and slaves turned out to be singularly inept at fending for themselves. The slaves did nothing without being told to do it by one of the drivers, and the first night that the Islanders snuggled around their cosy fire, they found themselves gaining an outer circle of soldiers, all trying to get warm too.

Labhran was forced into another piece of fiction, explaining to grumbling fellow officers that these men were scouts used to marching away from the main army, his apparent experience making this unquestioned, to everyone's relief. On the second night around their camp fire some of the biggest men from the neighbouring unit, clearly used to barging in and stealing what they wanted off the weaker slaves, tried to muscle the Islanders out of the way and got a nasty surprise. The Ergardia men-at-arms were well versed in some very dirty unarmed combat techniques, and the bullies of the camp rapidly learned to leave them alone.

Keeping a low profile was turning out to be a major headache at a level they had never expected, and one which was only made worse by the rescue party's inability to get close to the Abend's prisoners. Time after time Labhran made sorties accompanied by one or another of the rest of the group during the night-time camps. Yet it was clear that Masanae had her prizes very well secured. If the main body of the troops were ragged failures, those surrounding the queen of the Abend (in all but name) were alert and lethal. There was no getting past their guard, and the Islanders finally agreed that they would have to stop trying, or they were going to give themselves away and wreck any later chance of making a rescue attempt. It was made worse by the need for Labhran to walk openly through the camp with the characteristic overt swagger of a Donn, for acting covertly would be so out of character for any Donn as to raise suspicions even faster, but it did mean he and the men with him were constantly in view.

"There's nothing for it," Labhran told them resignedly. "We're going to have to stick with this lot until we get to somewhere where Masanae decides to make a longer stop. We'll have more chance of breaking Wistan and Kenelm out of a cell, or guarded chamber, than taking on a whole troop of guards on the road."

"I suppose we should be grateful that we haven't heard the boys screaming," Hamelin admitted mournfully.

The night air had occasionally been punctuated by terrible screams. At first the Knights had feared the worst, but when they could bring themselves to actually listen to the screamer they had all agreed that it was not a young boy's voice. Later they had discovered purely by chance that it was probably King Edward who was being tormented by Masanae, and although none of them had much sympathy for him, it still did not make pleasant hearing. More intriguingly, around the time when they crossed the border, Labhran overheard some of the Abend's guards talking, and learned that there were two women amongst the prisoners. Two women who by all accounts were driving Masanae crazy. Whatever her reasons were for taking them captive in the first place, she quite clearly did not want them to arrive at their destination damaged, because although they fought her at every turn, she always stopped short of killing or severely maiming them.

In a hurried conference in the depths of night, the Islanders agreed that they felt morally bound to try to rescue these two as well as the boys. It went beyond chivalry, although only Labhran was even able to pretend any detachment about leaving women to fend for themselves in such hostile circumstances. Oliver had voiced what they had all thought in some form, that if Masanae was keeping prisoners alive then it was for some purpose of her own, and that was likely to involve something very nasty.

There were therefore mixed feelings when the men eventually halted one day at the top of a low rise, and looked down for the first time onto the great plain of what had once been Attacotti-held West Brychan, and was now New Lochlainn. Barely half a day's march away loomed a massive citadel sitting astride a large, low spur of rock which once upon a time must have been part of the foothills they were just leaving. Beyond it on the floor of the plain sprawled an untidy city, very little of which seemed to bear any signs of permanence. Wooden buildings tumbled shabbily through a maze of twisting small streets, with the only ones paved being the wide thoroughfares running out from the citadel like spokes from the hub of a wheel. However, the towering citadel had every appearance of being utterly impregnable.

"Take a good look, gentlemen," Labhran said, his voice dripping with loathing. "Before you lies Bruighean – heart of Imperial DeÁine power in these islands and the most vile, vice-ridden and corrupt place you or I will ever lay eyes on."

It was hardly an inspiring statement and did nothing to cheer the men around him. The sight of Bruighean alone was enough to depress them without Labhran's gloomy additions. Rarely had they seen such a completely alien building. To be sure there was what the Knights assumed was a curtain wall around the whole edifice, and then something resembling a central keep-like cluster within it. However, the likeness was only in the most general of terms. On the side facing the mountains where they stood, the outer wall ran in a straight stretch between two huge towers at each end, and was only punctuated by a small tower at the centre guarding a small gate. The towers were each three times the size across of a large Island keep, and rising to at least six floors. Each great squat barrel was made of something which had no seams. If there were blocks of stone held together with masonry in their construction, then they had been faced with something which had a completely smooth finish, and which gleamed a sickly white even in daylight. At the top of these towers, instead of crenellations, rose fluted roofs of blue tiles rising to a point at the tower's centre, looking for all the world as though massive trumpet-shaped flowers had been placed upon the circular walls. The roofs projected out from the walls to some distance too, although what possible function that could serve was beyond the Islanders.

The rest of the curtain wall's circuit ran in a loop making about two thirds of a circle. In this orbit were six more towers, also circular, but around half the circumference of the two end towers. Not that that made them small by anyone's stretch of the imagination. The main gate also lay in the centre of the curved span, dominated by a twin towered construction of oval shape which was of a size with its neighbours. Yet all of these were dwarfed by the edifice in the central space encompassed by the walls.

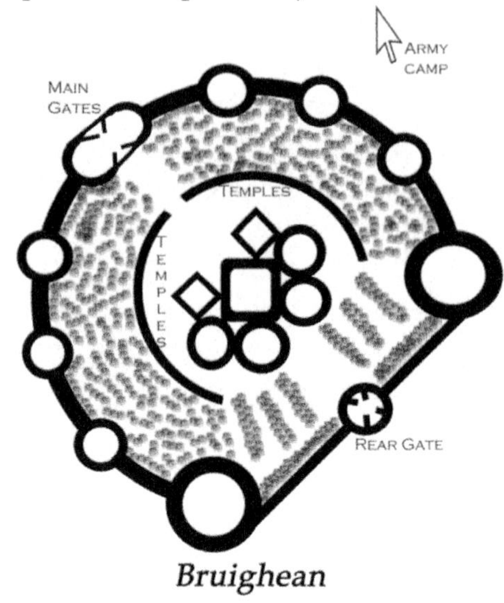

Bruighean

In one sense it was one complete building, but it was made up of several distinct parts. At the back, nearest to the Knights, were a further four circular towers, only in this case they were so close that they touched one another like a chain. Although they were each the same width as the corner-towers of the walls, their greater height made them look slender instead of squat. Built in an arc, they then had a lower, square tower at each end of the curve and also partially filing the internal space they created. Although none of the observers could see the far side, Labhran told them that there was yet another, even lower but wider, square tower connecting those two square, end-towers they could see. According to him, there was also no kind of open space in between any of the towers either, and even from this far back they could see more blue roofing covering every available gap.

Somewhat lower down the rocky spur than the multiple keep, but not as low as the base of the curtain wall, there was another semicircle of buildings echoing the shape of the outer circuit. It was a shock for the Islanders to realise that, although these looked puny against their massive neighbours, they were in fact at least three substantial floors high. These alone looked as though they were used for normal habitation, having windows and doors all along their length. In the rest of the buildings the Islanders could see no window of any size.

"By the Trees, it must be gloomy in there!" Hamelin said, wrinkling his nose in distaste.

Labhran gave a snort, which was about as close as he had come to laughing for a very long time. "Well it saves on heating! This monster was built using the Power in the first DeÁine conquest, and its design reflects the way their main concern traditionally had been how to keep buildings cool, not warm. But it's typical of the DeÁine that they think the scenery around here isn't worth looking out on anyway. All the corridors and main rooms are lit by dozens of oil lamps. The slaves make do with the dregs of the oil or poor quality candles and grope around in the semi-dark for most of the time. Unless, that is, it's a bright day outside and some light trickles in through the air vents. It's pretty grim for them because the lamps were designed to run on the oil from a fruit which grows in abundance in all the places the DeÁine lived in before, but it can't grow here. Instead they use fish oil and it really stinks when it gets old!"

"Oh yuk!" Freidl groaned in disgust. "Black as the inside of a cow's belly *and* smelly too, what kind of delightful place is this?"

"We are going in, I presume?" Oliver asked Labhran, and got a curt nod for an answer before their guide bothered to explain,

"Yes, but not into the citadel itself. We're going over there." His finger pointed to a huge sprawl of tents to one side of the dilapidated city. "That's the army camp. ...Oh, and a word of warning! When queuing for your meals at the mess tent don't expect meat. There isn't any for the likes of you."

"Oh happy thought," Bertrand sighed morosely. "And why might that be?"

Labhran let another troop pass them before waving them back on the road as he enlightened them.

"There's a huge number of mouths to feed down there. But more than that, the proper DeÁine come from a country where it's very hot most of the time and it's nearly impossible to keep meat for long. Certainly not in the quantities needed to feed whole armies. So they have an ingenious solution. The rabble aren't allowed to worship the higher DeÁine gods and goddesses, so they have two of their own, and very conveniently these two forbid the eating of animal flesh. So the long-term slaves' families have never known meat – although they are allowed fish from the rivers. Of course those taken into slavery have, and that's why every sheep and chicken in Brychan in the path of the DeÁine army got slaughtered and devoured. Not just because the slaves were on short rations! That was probably the first meat they'd had the chance to get their hands on in a very long time."

"Excuse me, sire." One of the soldiers named Toby came to Labhran. "I can see that we have to go into the camp. It would look pretty odd if we didn't. But do we have to stay there?"

Labhran quirked a questioning eyebrow, prompting Toby to reply to the unspoken query.

"It's just that these woods are heaving with rabbits! Maybe the slaves don't know about cooking conies, but I do! There're loads of big birds about too. And there's plenty of other stuff to forage here as well. Without the snowfall rotting them over this way, there are still plenty of nuts and roots which are fine to eat."

Toby had turned out to be the group's finest cook by some way, so if he said he could make a meal out of what surrounded them nobody doubted him. Labhran thought for a moment then gave his judgement.

"I don't think we can stay out of the camp altogether – far too suspicious! But we can come out on a daily basis. In fact it would be a relief to me to not spend too much time in the young Donns' company. I have no wish to be drawn inside Bruighean! Not under any pretext! Nothing's going to ruin my cover quicker than being forced to accept an invitation to dine with one of the Donn families, because word of 'my demise' at Gavra is sure to come out then! So I shall do my best to remain mysterious, and come out with you under pretext of some mission I can't talk about. If you set snares, will you have time to cook what you catch before we go back into camp each night?"

"I have my ways!" Toby answered him mysteriously with a wink. "No problem there!"

"Thank the Trees for that!" Bertrand sighed with relief. "We can get some decent food in our bellies once a day at least. I wasn't fancying trying to do any quick escapes after weeks of no proper grub! I don't run any too fast when I'm that empty!"

Even Labhran had to smile at the squarely built Knight's words, but quickly added,

"By the way, watch your words, everyone! No swearing on the Trees or the like! Remember that nobody will know what that means, and it'll sound strange enough to make them ask what you're talking about, and you don't want that! …Oh, and the other thing, Toby, …leave the ducks alone! If you get caught cooking one of those, even I won't be able to save you from some very nasty punishments."

"Great Maker, what's so special about ducks?" Friedl asked in disgust before Toby could.

"They're reserved food back in the DeÁine homeland, apparently," Labhran told them. "I don't think they're anything like the same breed we have here, but as far as the highborn are concerned a duck's a duck and not for the likes of us."

However, that was not the end of ducks for the Knights. After a week of skulking around the citadel in between food forays to the hills, they were no closer to getting to the prisoners. The best source of information turned out to be one of the archers. Cody had clearly had a misspent youth, for after one afternoon of watching the bored slave soldiers playing a gambling game with dice, he joined in and proceeded to take everything but the shirts off their backs.

There after Labhran excused him and his friend Trip any duties in camp, leaving them to circulate amongst the multitude of games on the go at any given time, thereby pumping their fellow gamblers for information. Amongst the slaves a fair few spoke a rough version of Islander – enough for Trip and Cody not to stand out, and sufficient for them to have plenty of men to question. By this means on the sixth day the covert group learned that the next was a holy day to the DeÁine goddess Ama. For this first day of Earrach, and this day alone in the year, the lower orders were allowed to present themselves at the shrine inside the citadel's walls.

Labhran was eager to seize the chance, but it was Toby who came up with the method. He had stood watching the camp kitchens on many occasions, tutting at the way that everything was just dumped into cauldrons with every herb and spice the cooks could afford to use, and stewed up together. The aroma was often pungent and inviting, but the taste rarely lived up to expectations. What he had noticed as a result was that some ducks had been brought into the kitchen tents that very day, and a little further prying by himself and two others had revealed that the priestesses were amongst those allowed the rich meat. Yet even this precious meat was being wasted in another spicy stew, albeit made in a separate container.

"Go and get me some ducks, lads," he said with glee. "I'm going to cook those lovely ladies a Toby special!"

While the three other archers went hunting, Cody and Trip managed to get him some rare citrus fruits, although they declined to say how, and early the next morning Toby disappeared for several hours with a hijacked cook-pot and an escort. When he returned surrounded by his friendly entourage, it was bearing the hot pot from which the most mouth-watering smells were wafting. The three Ergardia Knights – Kym, Lorcan and Teryl – told Labhran that they had learned to keep quiet and out of the way when the enlisted men started on one of their schemes. He was nonetheless worried, but managed to contain himself through the morning, although it was a revelation even to him how Lorcan's scruffy little sergeant managed to get his hands on a proper platter in a squalid army camp.

"Evans has his ways," Lorcan said with a wry shake of the head. "Whenever I've asked him, he just says that if he doesn't tell me then I can't be blamed by my superiors for what he does, and I'll have a clear conscience when I go to sleep. He obviously doesn't lose any sleep over what he does, so either the Trees approve or he's in for a rough time in the hereafter!"

However, there was no time to waste, for the six archers and six men-at-arms had formed up as a guard of honour, two of them bearing the heavy platter shoulder-high between them. The Knights hurriedly fell in, behind them for once instead of in the lead, and with Toby brandishing a purloined carving knife and fork, the party set off for the shrine. Some guards at the great gate of Bruighean were dissuading some of the grubbier supplicants, but the sight of Toby's troop convinced them that, however odd it was that a bunch of soldiers would wish to worship the earth-mother figure of Ama, they were sincere.

Cody was softly calling directions from his place as one of the bearers, and Labhran realised that the archer had found out the quickest route without ever having to check back with himself. The rest of the troop could now see that, dwarfed by the massive buildings around them, the whole of the inner space of Bruighean was a maze of single storey buildings, whose grubby roofs they had thought to be the ground when looking down on the place from the hills.

Within minutes the group had reached the middle circle of buildings, and turned around their circuit until they came to where a large set of double doors had been thrown open. A strong smell of incense drifted out, and over the chatter of the crowds around the entrance they could hear singing. Quite where Trip had picked up such a comprehensive set of abusive phrases in such a short space of time was beyond Labhran, but the archer was now scattering slaves to the left and right, having moved to the front of the procession. Oliver risked flicking a glance Labhran's way and saw the former member of the Covert Brethren wore a twitch of a smile beneath his slightly surprised expression. Clearly he was amazed that they had got this far so easily.

Then they were inside the temple shrine and Oliver found himself staring about him in amazement. Every inch of the walls was covered in intricate mosaics, some in geometric designs, but others showing the great Ama fulfilling her role as the goddess of fertility in some very creative ways!

"Great M…!" spluttered Hamelin behind them as his eyes found a depiction of Ama cohabiting with several men, then blushed furiously.

With such pornographic images all around, it was even more distracting when half a dozen scantily clad young girls drifted forward accompanying a more matronly figure hardly any better dressed. The younger Knights were beginning to find the whole experience a trial of a totally different kind to the ones they had encountered so far. Leaving a completely disconcerted Oliver in the file, Labhran slipped forward, expecting to have to do some explaining. He nearly tripped on one of the layered rugs to go flying when he was shocked to hear Trip speaking to the older priestess in fluent, but heavily accented, DeÁine. Just about recovering his composure in time, he heard Trip saying,

"…and we all called her grandmother. Wonderful woman! Brought all us orphans up after our parents had been killed in the big battle. Me and Cody here, and Toby, and Waza and Newt behind there. So when our troop came back here instead of the far south, and we heard that we could pay our respects in the shrine, well, …we all thought we should come along. ….Say thank you, like, for grandma. …We couldn't think what would be proper, so Toby here cooked you grandma's special recipe. …We used to have it with chicken, of course, but for you we thought only ducks were right."

He was the picture of deference, his tatty woolly hat clutched in his hands before him, and giving little bows as he spoke. By the time he ran out of words, the smell of Toby's duck was filling the surrounding space, and the matron's frown had softened to a smile. She waved them forward and led them deeper into the complex. Labhran stepped to the front to beside Trip, only once having to prompt the men into an obeisance before Trip could. At one turn of a corner Trip managed to quickly say to Labhran,

"Gran really was a slave before Moytirra," in explanation, before they turned the bend and were back behind the priestess.

Trip had been very clever in his choice of the named men, Labhran also realised. Every one of them was in his late thirties or forties, and therefore old enough to have been potential orphans of slaves who had fought at Moytirra. The story had clearly carried conviction, for they arrived in a long hall where a low rectangular table was surrounded by floor cushions, on which sat several elderly women. At the head of the table was a wizened old crone with skin like tanned leather, and with only wisps of white hair falling around her shoulders. Her breasts had shrivelled to folds of skin and were clearly visible through the stole which was the only thing covering her apart from a swaddling of cloth like a baby's diaper. The guiding priestess gestured the platter forward to where a space was being cleared on the table before the crone. Once it was there, a girl drifted forward and lifted the cover, while another came with a small silver plate and another with a cloth and silver fork. The girl with the cover then reached out a hand as if to pull a leg off the nearest duck, but Toby was quicker.

He had guessed that the girls were about to feed the near-senile old woman, and had also spotted her lack of teeth. With amazing speed and dexterity he shot in and began carving wafer-thin slivers off the duck, carefully removing any bits of skin, and then slid several onto the knife and placed them with a flourish on the plate, put down the carvers and stepped back. The priestesses were temporarily nonplussed. Clearly having someone carving for them was a novelty, let alone it being a man. However, the girl with the fork quickly speared one of the slim slices and placed it in the already open mouth of the crone. The tender, marinated duck hardly needed chewing, and disappeared in the gummy mouth in a slurping gulp as the old woman licked the delicate sauce from her lips. Within a minute the plate was empty and Toby was carving more for the eager old lady, who surprised everyone by clapping her hands in delight and saying something which was unintelligible to the soldiers. For a moment their guiding priestess was totally flummoxed, but then bowed deeply in acknowledgement even if her smile became distinctly strained.

"What was that?" Oliver whispered in Labhran's ear, as Toby proceeded to demolish the rest of the ducks for the others at the table.

"I don't quite believe this," Labhran answered, sounding as stunned as the priestess looked, "but that's the old high priestess and Toby's obviously hit the spot, because she says we're to stay for the main ceremony."

"We're not that bad, are we?" Oliver wondered, glancing at the scowls of the second rank of priestesses who were stood in attendance, and were clearly not going to get a chance to taste the mouth-watering dish. "I mean they must expect that they'll get a few worshippers who aren't all dressed up in silks and things."

"It's not that," Labhran told him in a strangled whisper, which sounded as though he was having to struggle not to laugh out loud. "This feast? It's all about fertility. The crone just said that if any of the young women about to take their vows – and they do that at various stages in the levels of the priesthood – want to test their …ehmm …fertility, then if one of the lads takes their eye they can go ahead!"

Oliver forgot himself and his eyes shot open as his head spun to check if he had heard Labhran right. The former Covert Brethren spy had his hand over his mouth smothering any laughter, but by the twinkling in his eyes this was the funniest thing he had heard in a long time. Quite why it tickled him so much was less than clear to Oliver, but by the time all twenty-one of them were seated on cushions at the back of the temple space a couple of hours later, the word had gone through the troop.

"Can we really?" Teryl, the youngest Ergardian Knight, checked hopefully, unable to believe what he might be doing in the course of duty. "I mean, we're not supposed to decline an invitation, are we?"

"Decline at your peril …and ours!" Labhran told him, still struggling with his composure and wiping the mirth from his eyes. "It's an enormous honour you've been given! I think that other priestesses would undo the offer if they could, but the high priestess' word is law – even if she is getting a bit senile by now."

Further discussion was halted by the start of the ceremony. What Oliver had not been expecting was to be struck by the beauty of it all. The temple around the shrine was decorated with glazed tiles of stunning geometric designs, and the ceiling and uppermost quarter of the walls were a filigree of the finest white plaster-work he had ever seen, some cut-outs acting as lanterns for tiny candles slipped into the spaces behind them. The whole place twinkled as if lit by tiny captive stars.

Something about the space around the central shrine gave all sounds a delicate echo, and as the young priestesses came into the temple singing a drone-like chant, it built in volume to an intricate web of sound. When the women were all assembled around the four sides of the shrine, the chant changed subtly and they began to dance in a sinuous, weaving motion. Myriad tiny candles were hung from the ceiling, and stood in tall multi-bracketed candelabra which filled the temple's central space, and these became more fluttering as the dance increased in pace, their flames wafted by the swirling fabric of the garments. The outer edge of girls were the youngest and dressed in white, but the closer to the shrine the dancers were, the more richly coloured the silks of their wrapped gowns became. The whirling kaleidoscope of colour became quite mesmerising after a while and Oliver lost track of time.

Suddenly he realised that the chanting had stopped and the dancers were still. A regal woman of middle years stepped forward first and scrutinised the ranks of the highly born DeÁine who filled the front rows of cushions nearest the shrine. Clearly she was looking for a particular man, and having found him she pulled him to his feet and off towards a side room, totally ignoring the acid glare of the woman sitting next to him who had the air of being his wife.

"That wasn't popular!" Hamelin commented from the other side of Labhran.

"If I remember right from way back, that man's family sent the priestess when a girl to the temples rather than let him marry her," Labhran softly replied. "It was quite a scandal! It was said that he was destined for someone of greater political standing and his now wife's family were it. Well it looks like even sending his lover to the temple hasn't stopped her having her revenge on the woman who had her incarcerated here, because she still has him once a year!"

"What a system!" was Hamelin's stunned comment, but not only on Labhran's story. Other girls were coming forward now to make their choice, and some of the DeÁine men were being none too gentle in response, and not all waited to be asked. One pulled a girl down onto the cushion where he had been sitting and took her there in front of everyone, oblivious to her cries of pain. All the Islander men struggled not to intervene. It went against everything they believed in. Some of their disgust when other DeÁine men followed suit must have shown on their faces, because to their surprise some of the girls began to drift their way. For Teryl and Kym this was a hoped for delight, as it was for Friedl and two of the younger men-at-arms. However, Oliver then found himself being approached by a slender figure and felt his ardour draining away.

"Oh Spirits, Labhran," he whispered in dismay, "she can't be more than thirteen! I can't do this, she's a child!"

"You can't refuse!" Labhran whispered back urgently. "Find somewhere quiet and then …well do as much or as little as you can. But you mustn't refuse her *here*! It would be the ultimate humiliation for her, and even worse, she would be thrown out and sold to a brothel. You don't want that for her do you?"

The stricken Oliver gave a minute shake of his head, before rising to his feet and graciously bending over the girl's proffered hand, then allowing her to lead him away. He was more than a little surprised when the girl led him past several empty, curtained niches, and right to the back of the long corridor leading from the shrine. Through a door and onwards they went until she pulled him into a dark room. Suddenly she let go of his hand and he was alone, but only for a second. Someone seized a handful of his hair and began kissing him. Whoever this was, though, it was definitely not the girl who had led him here. This was someone much older and more experienced, not to mention taller and more voluptuous although still slender. She was also downright eager, but only for a moment. In a heartbeat she changed and he found himself fighting a savage she-cat in the pitch-black darkness. As he grappled with the writhing claws, he was eternally grateful for the Ergardian men-at-arms, who had given him some much needed practical training along the way. Oliver's fighting until then had been of the chivalrous kind, and had had everything to do with Knights fighting knights. Never in his life had he fought a woman before!

As his superior muscle began to tell, he was finally able to throw his spitting assailant down, finding the cushioned bed more by luck than design. As he straddled her and pinned her down he heard her hiss,

"Sacred Martyrs! Get off me you fucking bastard!"

"By the Trees! …Hold on a second!" he gasped. "You're no priestess! Not swearing on the Martyrs!"

"*Hmmph*! And you're no groping DeÁine either," the husky voice beneath him retorted. "Haven't heard one of them mention the Trees. Who in the Islands are you?"

He felt a movement through the cushions and the scraping of a flint, and then an oil lamp flickered into life held by the shaking hand of the girl priestess, revealing a dark-haired woman of about his own age below him. She turned and propped herself up on one elbow to look him in the eye as he rocked back on his heels. Normally her striking looks would have been the cause of her getting noticed, but at the moment she was sporting several cuts and bruises, one of which was a splendidly purpling black-eye.

"Great Maker!" Oliver spluttered. "Who in the Islands did that to you!"

"A nasty bitch called Masanae," the woman spat in fury.

"Masanae? One of the Abend." Oliver was thinking furiously. "Are you one of the women she brought here as a prisoner?"

"That's right." The woman turned and spat savagely. "The bitch dragged us all the way from Brychan. When we got here she was so fed up with us she temporarily turned us over to these shrivelled crones! Spirits, I hate fucking nuns! Poor Aoife here has been our servant in this stinking pit. She was going to be ritually deflowered even though she's only a kid. …Couldn't have that! So my sister helped her …*ehmm* … so that she would pass later inspection …having been groped once already to make sure she was a virgin. Right up our Breizh's line of work, that was! And then I persuaded Aoife to smuggle me down here to pose as her once the lecherous bastard had followed her." Then she peered hard at Oliver. "So if you know who I am, who are you? No DeÁine like I said. But why come here and hurt her in that case?"

Oliver rolled his eyes in despair. "Do I look like a rapist? Of course I wasn't going to hurt her! She picked me, not the other way round! But the leader of our group said that if I refused, even though she's no older than my youngest sister, then our cover would be blown and even worse, Aoife – as I now know she's called – would be sent to some brothel instead. I was planning on trying to talk *her* out of it once we were alone!"

"Group? Cover?" Heledd said suspiciously. "What are you up to then?"

Oliver warily got up off Heledd's middle and sat himself on a cushion, well clear of her hands if she decided to lash out again. "We're here to rescue the two boys who are with you. The two Masanae has as prisoners."

"What boys?" Heledd demanded, on her guard again. "There are no boys!"

"What?" Oliver was horrified. Had it all been for nothing? "The two boys who came from Rheged! The one's who were fetched by Quintillean! Did he go on ahead? Why hasn't he come west with Masanae?"

"No kids prisoners with us," Heledd said, still suspicious. "And who's this Quintillean? We've not heard of anyone by that name. The only other prisoner travelling with us – although I think she has more already stashed away here – is that useless cock Edward, and Masanae can cut his balls off bit by bit for all I care. It's about time he got some of the suffering he's handed out to others!"

A quavering voice came from by the lamp. "Quintillean's the head of the Abend," Aoife explained to Heledd. "He's always in cahoots with

Masanae, according to the older women here. They've been wondering where he is, too."

Heledd scowled as she realised that there was something more going on here than just her and Breizh's kidnapping. Oliver did his best to explain why he had ended up here too, and by the time he had got to the ritual slaughtering of innocents, Heledd was sitting up and taking serious notice.

"We honestly didn't realise that you two were prisoners until we'd been travelling in Masanae's guard for some time," Oliver apologised. "Once we did, we'd already factored in the fact that we'd have to get you both out as well."

"Well thanks for that at least," Heledd grudgingly conceded. "I don't much fancy being filleted for that bitch's lunch. …But you said your experts thought that the …us sacrifices …were chosen for being pure. Why in the Islands would they choose me and my sister then?"

"Because you're the king's sisters and so you can't have been allowed to be spoiled by anyone until you're to be married," little Aoife supplied, as if this were the most normal thing in the world. "That's why I let you take my place. I thought I was saving you. She won't want you once your virgin's blood is spilt."

"Virgin's blood?" Heledd hooted with laughter. "Blessed Martyr's tits girl! I haven't been a virgin since I was only a bit older than you! By choice as well! And sure as the Underworld burns, we're not related to that prick Edward either! I was taking your place because I've had more men than I can keep track of – and enjoyed myself mightily in the process, I can assure you! One more was hardly going to make any difference, and anyway, I was going to make sure he was going to have the roughest ride of his life if he tried!"

"Oh thanks," Oliver said weakly.

"Well how was I to know she was going to pick a pretty one!" Heledd retorted, making him blush. "Why *did* you pick him?" she demanded of Aoife.

Aoife now blushed too. "Because I thought you might've changed your mind and left me to it, and he looked nice. He looked angry when the young milor Monreux mounted Saffy without taking her to the rooms first. It was like he didn't like seeing her hurt. So I hoped that if I picked him he'd at least be nice to me."

"Oh you poor kid!" said Oliver, getting up and wrapping her in his arms in a hug. "No! I would never have hurt you!" Then a thought occurred. "Does this young …what did you call him? Milor?"

"It's his title," Aoife explained. "His father is the head of the family. They're very important. Nobody stands up to them except the royals. He comes here for every festival – not just this one. We were told it would be an honour to be deflowered by him."

"Honour, my arse!" Heledd snorted. "Dirty bastard just likes raping women!"

Although Heledd's forthright language kept making Oliver wince, he totally agreed with her.

"Hmmph! So he *does* do this often! I think young milor Monreux might need a lesson in manners! Whatever else, though, I'm not leaving you here, Aoife! Stay close to …what's your name, by the way?" he asked the other woman.

"I'm Heledd," his attacker told him. "My younger sister's name is Breizh. Once upon a time we had a brother who lived with us. One night when Masanae had softened Edward up for us, we got to him in our prison wagon. He confessed that he'd killed our Ben." Her voice choked up. "You just wait 'til our Berengar gets hold of him!"

Oliver felt his blood run cold. "Who's Berengar?" he asked faintly.

"Our older half-brother," Heledd told him. "He's a Knight! He thought the world of Ben. He's going to go mad when he finds out."

"Oh Trees!" Oliver groaned, rubbing his temples as his head spun with the added new complications. "Let me just check. Was your Berengar fairly senior among the Knights. An ealdorman, perhaps?"

"That's right! How did you know? Have you met him? Is he coming here too?"

"I've not met him. And I'm sorry, but he won't be here any time soon. You see," he coughed to cover his sudden indecision, wondering whether he should tell Heledd about Berengar's elevation to Grand Master. Maybe not. "You see, he's been left in charge of rather a lot of Knights since the DeÁine invaded. We heard from some other Knights that Berengar's co-ordinating an attack by the Knights. But I believe he might be struggling to get through the snow at the moment."

"Oh!" Heledd's voice drooped sadly for a second, but soon picked up. "Well they won't pin him down for long. Not my brother! And then you just wait and see who gets it in the neck!" Then something occurred to her. "Are you a Knight, then?"

"Yes. My name's Oliver, but I'm from Prydein, not Brychan. I've come with my own Knights and some others from Ergardia. That's why we didn't get snowed-in with the Brychan Knights."

"Oh. …Where will you take us then? Now you've rescued us?"

There was nothing like mentioning the Order to raise people's expectations of what you could achieve, Oliver thought wearily. How to let her down gently and explain that the rescue would not be immediately?

"I have to get back to the others now," he said carefully. "Explain to me where your main quarters are in this building."

Aoife rather than Heledd was able to give clear directions, and then Heledd produced a bloodstained robe to allow the girl to continue the deception. Oliver turned his back while Aoife changed, making Heledd smile at his gallant conduct, then let the girl in her besmirched robe lead him away. Crouching in the room out of sight waiting for Aoife's return, Heledd hugged herself. Finally things looked like they might be getting better. She must get to Breizh as soon as possible and warn her to expect visitors, and Oliver had said they would take Saffy too. They must find the ravaged child and do what they could to get her ready as well.

Meanwhile, in the temple Labhran was getting increasingly concerned. All but one other man had returned, including Hamelin – dragged back by a disgruntled older woman who complained bitterly to Labhran over his lack of performance – and still no sign of Oliver. When Cody reappeared, who had been the last to be pulled out of the crowd by a comely woman of his own age, even the non-DeÁine speaking members of the party could see that the priestesses were getting eager to move them on. Clearly they had no desire to have a party of rampant males at their cloistered hearths for any longer than necessary, and the covert Knights were outstaying their welcome. All the other men had already gone.

"Where *is* he?" Labhran fretted. Getting to his feet he walked to the leading priestess watching them.

"I'm so sorry," he said deferentially. "Our friend was aware that your girl was very young and that this might be her first time. He was …ehmm, …disgusted at the way some of the priestesses were treated with such little respect. I believe he wanted it not to be too traumatic for your young oblate."

The older priestesses stared at him with hard eyes. They clearly wanted to believe his words but did not quite have such faith in human nature. Then suddenly Oliver appeared at the curtained exit from the shrine. The others saw him bend over the little girl's hand and her smile as he walked away. Suddenly all the older women were beaming at him, and Labhran grasped his arm and hustled him out before any further misadventure could happen. Even so, Trip made his obeisances at the appropriate points, and the ordinary soldiers followed him, forcing the Knights and Labhran to do the same. Yet even this worked in their favour, for as the priestesses closed the outer door behind them, Labhran heard one say something about how nice it was to see men who had been brought up properly for a change.

"Are you lot trying to make me old before my time?" he demanded as they hustled Oliver away with as much speed as was practical in the congested lanes. "And since when have you been fluent in DeÁine, Trip? You might have helped out earlier!"

"Sorry, sire," Trip said with genuine regret, "but it wasn't as easy as that. You see I haven't heard DeÁine spoken since I was a kid. My family were refugees after Moytirra. Because my dad was good with horses we relocated to Ergardia, and that was where I was brought up. DeÁine was spoken at home because no matter how she tried, my grandma couldn't seem to get her tongue around the Islander language. The thing is, she died when I was twelve and after that none of us bothered with anything but Islander. If you'd needed me to do what I've just done when we set out, I wouldn't have known where to start. It's only been travelling on the road and hearing it on a daily basis that's brought the DeÁine back to me. And the more I hear, the more I'm remembering. I still wouldn't trust myself to carry it off for long. My limit is soldier's language from the camp, and domestic bits and pieces I can dredge up from back at home. Beyond that I'm stuffed."

"Oh I see," Labhran relented. "Well whenever we get chance I'm going to give you some speedy tuition. Always better if you don't have to rely only on me in case we get separated."

Hamelin and Oliver exchanged furtive glances. Separated? Was Labhran planning something they knew nothing about? The troubled former spy was definitely taking on a haggard air the longer they were around Bruighean. The sooner they got him away from here the better.

Once safely deep in the maze, Labhran stopped and turned on Oliver.

"What in the Maker's name happened in there? How hard was it for you to deal with one little girl? We haven't got all night, you know! It's going to take some time to find where the boys are. Now come on!"

"No! Wait!" Oliver cried urgently. "Stop!""

"What?" demanded Labhran irately, clearly reaching some sort of crisis point.

"There are no boys," Oliver frantically told them. "The boys aren't here! Quintillean never came this way! He didn't meet with Masanae, and she only has the two women and Edward. No boys …of any description!" Labhran and the others stared at him in horror.

"That's why I was so long," Oliver explained desperately. "When they got here, Masanae sent the two women to these priestesses to be watched over. I'll explain more later when we have time, but the thing is, those two women are clearly going to end up as sacrifices. Masanae has some ritual planned, although they don't know what. But do we want to wait to find out? And we can't possibly leave the two women now. And not just because of Masanae," he added quickly to prevent Labhran making any sarcastic comments about chivalry. "We have to rescue them because they're Berengar's sisters. You remember who Berengar is, don't you?"

He did not want to mention the words 'Grand Master' in this place, even though they were alone in the night, but the name was clearly enough. All the men looked at one another in horror.

"Shit! That complicates things!" Bertrand muttered with feeling.

"Yes and no!" Oliver was quick to carry on. "We've been thinking along the lines that we have to break into some prison to get the boys out. Well now we just have to get back into that temple complex to get Heledd and Breizh out. Oh, …and by the way, I've promised to get my little girl out and her friend who was the first one raped at the shrine. They're with the other two and we can hardly leave them."

Labhran glared furiously at Oliver. He clearly disapproved of such a kind-hearted but un-thought-out gesture. But before he could reprimand Oliver, Hamelin had stepped in and the other Knights were nodding their approval as he said,

"Yes, we get them out and soon. Masanae must be getting ready to move by now." The others looked queryingly at him. "Think about it," he said. "We've been here nearly a week. If she was going to do the sacrificing, or whatever, whilst here, she'd have done it by now. What do you think are the chances of Quintillean coming here now? I'd say nil. He must've gone by the northern route with the boys. That means that Will Montrose will have to do the rescuing of them. I don't know about you, Labhran, but in the light of what we know now, I'd expect Masanae to move on to meet Quintillean somewhere else, and pretty soon too."

Labhran was surprised at Hamelin's tactical thinking, but could not fault his reasoning. "So you're thinking that the best thing that we can do is get the women out here, where we know we've got a chance, because she could be on the road any day and back with a heavily armed escort?" he postulated.

"That's right," Hamelin responded. "Let's go with what we've got now, because it might get worse sooner rather than later."

"Back to the temple, then," Labhran sighed resignedly, and led the men back the way they had come.

"Are you alright?" Oliver asked him softly as they walked at the head of the line. "You've been very stressed in the last days. I know we must be a huge liability to you, but we are trying to help, you know."

Labhran's shocked expression told Oliver that their leader had no idea of how much his inner demons had been troubling him. "I'm sorry," he sighed. "It's just very hard for me to be back here."

"You must be worried that someone will recognise you from the past," sympathised Hamelin from behind.

"It's not just that," Labhran confessed. "I had to do things when I was here before. Things that have haunted me for years. And being back here where it all happened keeps bringing bits back. Bits I thought I'd finally allowed to disappear into the back of my mind. Awful things." He ran his hand over his face and the two younger Knights could see, even in the weak light of the occasional suspended lamp in the covered warren, that he was very pale.

Hamelin moved up to beside him and gripped his elbow. "It will be better this time," he said firmly. "We'll make it better! You won't be stuck here for years like before. We're going for the women Oliver's found and we're getting out of here tonight." He gave Labhran's arm a gentle shake. "Tonight! Alright? Not next week or next month. Tonight! No more deceptions in the camp, no more pretending to be a DeÁine soldier after tonight. You'll be back to being our guide, not covering all our backs."

To Oliver's relief Hamelin's words had an effect on Labhran. He drew a ragged breath but then squared his shoulders and nodded, and slowly his colouring returned to something more like normal.

"You're right," he was just saying when they heard the sound of marching boots coming from a converging alley. He froze and threw up a cautioning arm to the men behind who halted too. As they also heard the approach of what was clearly a sizeable group, the men flattened themselves against the walls of the alley in the deepest shadows they could find. They were only a twisting lane away from the temples now, and several of the alleys met just a short way ahead at a small square.

From out of the gloom strode the young DeÁine nobleman Oliver now knew was Monreux. However, there were fewer men with him than the echoing footsteps had hinted at – a bodyguard of six and no more. Then the hidden men heard the sound of approaching sobbing from beyond the square. Into the oily light came two huge men, dragging the sobbing form of Saffy between them.

"Castrati," Labhran whispered to Oliver and Hamelin, who immediately caught on that these must be castrated men who served the women's temple. They looked fearsome and by bulk alone would overwhelmed any woman, but the front Knights could see that the pair were vastly overweight, and most of their size was blubber.

"What's happening here?" the watchers heard the young Monreux demand imperiously.

"Unclean," one of the castrati grunted, as Saffy caught sight of her rapist once more and began whimpering in terror.

"Ah! Been a naughty girl, have we?" Monreux sneered sarcastically. "Not a virgin when you went to take your vows! Tut tut! So it's off to the pleasure baths for you!" He had clearly orchestrated the situation, and had deliberately blackened Saffy's reputation in order to get her out of the temple for his own warped pleasures. He turned his attention to the two guards. "You must have many more duties tonight, especially with it being the feast night. Let me take her there for you."

The two castrati were clearly not overly blessed with brains, and thought nothing beyond saving themselves the effort of walking further. They shrugged their shoulders, shoved Saffy towards Monreux, and waddled back the way they had come. Before Labhran could call for restraint, the men with him had surged forward like avenging hounds of the Underworld.

One minute Monreux was laughing nastily and ripping Saffy's gown to expose her to the leering gaze of his men – who no doubt got their chance at such women once the lordling tired of his latest acquisition – the next his world disintegrated in violence. The men of the Order jumped the bodyguards, and Labhran realised that he had forgotten how efficiently quiet they could be in the years he had lived apart from the world. His memory was largely of open fighting. Only in his last frantic race north to

Gavra Pass had he been around large numbers of his fellow Covert Brethren, and they had, by definition, been better trained to slip into places unnoticed and to avoid confrontation, than killing silently.

With lethal, practised ease the bodyguards died from broken necks with not a cry being uttered or a drop of blood spilt, leaving Monreux staring around him in horror. Bertrand surged forward and swept the sobbing Saffy into his arms, swathing her in one of the bodyguard's dropped opulent capes as he did so.

"There, there, little one," he said gently, as he whisked her away from the carnage, her head buried in his shoulder so that she did not have to see the corpses. "No need to be frightened anymore. You're safe now."

That was the last thing young Monreux was. He found himself at the centre of a circle of the most frightening men he had seen outside of the veteran combat troops out in the camps. The young man standing in front of him might have been better bred, but something about the way the dark-haired man was looking at him was worrying.

"Like raping little girls, do you?" Oliver snarled. Monreux looked blank, so Trip translated.

"Strip him!" Oliver ordered, and without bothering to undo buttons or belts the men cut the clothes off Monreux within seconds, leaving him suddenly naked and shivering in the cold. It had happened so fast and was so unexpected that Monreux had not even had the presence of mind to call out. Now Oliver was nearly nose to nose with him and holding a wickedly sharp dagger to his throat, and as he swallowed he felt the blade nick his neck. A puddle of piss appeared at his feet, soaking the tattered remains of his clothes.

"Pathetic little thing isn't it?" Oliver sneered, lowering the knife to lift the DeÁine's wilted member. "Got you into all kinds of trouble. You wouldn't be here without that thinking for you. Better off without it, eh?"

Monreux felt someone close behind him even as he tried to step back. Someone who stuffed a cloth into his mouth as he opened it to scream when Oliver's other hand seized his cock and the blade sliced upwards. The gag was removed to allow the castrated youth to vomit.

"Where does this piece of dirt live?" Oliver demanded of Labhran, who had never seen the young Knight so angry. "Close or too far to carry?"

"Other side of the compound, I'm afraid," Labhran answered, thinking that the Knights had been going to return the young noble to his family still alive, and dreading that he might have to be the one to kill him, since he now knew that Islanders were on the loose in the citadel.

"Oh well, we won't be able to slaughter him like the animal he is on their doorstep," Oliver grimaced. "Shame! It would have been nice to give the arrogant bastards a nasty shock with their breakfast. Right lads! Nearest butcher's shop, then!"

"Saw a place with meat in it on the way in," Toby supplied.

"Remember it!" was Cody's terse acknowledgement, and he led the way. Between them the Knights and their men carried the bodyguards' corpses with them. Oliver and Hamelin had Monreux slung between them, his piss-sodden clothes draped over his bleeding groin to mop up. In moments they were at the small stall and Cody had the lock picked. It was clearly nothing more than a lock-up stall sandwiched between other buildings. Nobody slept above it, or at least nobody with access via any internal stair. Lifting down the few pathetic cuts of meat from off the hooks in the ceiling joists, the Knights hoisted the dead bodyguards up like slaughtered pigs, heads down and suspended by hooks through the ankles. Monreux had passed out from the pain long ago, and was now spread-eagled on the butcher's block. Although Oliver had hoped to impale him on it, there were only two rather ancient-looking knives in the place, and the men did not want to leave any of their own, so they made do by tying him to the block at each corner. With another swift cut of his knife Oliver completed the castration, and calmly turned away after placing the severed genitalia in a conspicuous position on the man's stomach.

"You can't let him live," Labhran said sickly in protest, drawing his own knife with a hand that threatened to shake. *Not again, please the Rowan. Not another body on my conscience. Not here, not now, where it'll join with all the others.*

"You think he'll live through that?" Oliver demanded. "He'll have bled to death by dawn!" He pointed to the already spreading pool of blood on the block, and Labhran's hand let the knife drop back in its sheath with a sharp exhalation of relief. "He won't wake up again, more's the pity after the suffering he's caused. But I want it made clear that he died in suffering, and that the punishment was picked to fit the crime! He died on the feast of the All-mother after assaulting a woman!" He gestured to Bertrand who threw across to him the tattered dress Saffy had worn. "This is a priestesses robe, right? It'll be recognised as such, yes?"

Suddenly Labhran saw where he was going with this. "When the ones thrown out of the temple get to the pleasure baths, the robes go back to the temple! Nobody normally knows the new girls came from the temple – and inquiries are heavily 'discouraged'! So to most folk here this looks like a priestess was abducted, and Ama has taken divine retribution!"

"You've got it!" Oliver managed a savage smile. "See? Hamelin told you it would be better this time! Now then, let's get back and rescue the others!"

To Labhran's surprise Hamelin got Cody to lock the stall again, but when Bertrand stayed behind with Theo to guard Saffy he realised there was a plan, and so he kept quiet. These men were so used to working in teams it sometimes threw him, having been alone for so long.

Back at the temple some nifty blade-work by Cody and Trip got the side door open, and the men crept inside. Someone was getting a strip torn off them by the sound of an irate woman's voice coming from a room not far away. Trip slipped stealthily that way, and returned silently chuckling to tell them that the two who had handed over Saffy were having their carelessness explained in no uncertain terms by a dragon of a priestess.

"Don't think they're any too happy about the loss of the robes either!" he added. "They'll be even unhappier come the morning!"

However, few other people seemed to be about, but once they reached the temple it was clear that this was not because they were all in bed, but because more of the rituals were being gone through in the central space. Totally absorbed in their chanting, the priestesses were oblivious to the intruders, but it made things difficult. Oliver had thought he would be able to walk straight across the shrine floor to the room he had occupied with Heledd and Aoife. Instead, they had to negotiate the warren of side corridors until they finally got beyond the shrine after getting lost twice. Once there, though, Aoife's instructions proved to be good, and they quickly found themselves up in a totally different part of the temple. Oliver tried the door he had been directed to but it was locked.

"It's me, Oliver!" he risked calling softly through it. "Unlock the door."

"We can't, we're locked in!" Heledd's voice came back.

Cody and Trip stepped up to the door, tinkered with the lock for a second and then the door swung inwards.

"Crap workmanship," Trip said sagely. "Wouldn't keep a cat in!"

"I'm so glad you're on our side," Friedl said admiringly, as he went to keep a lookout at the turn in the corridor.

"Hmm, …you don't know the half of it!" Kym told him as he came to watch the other way. "Nothing stays shut for long with that pair around!"

In the meantime, Heledd and Breizh had been offered capes brought from the bodyguards against the chill of the night.

"Where's Aoife?" was the first thing a worried Oliver asked. "She's not in the temple is she?"

"No, I'm here," a little voice said, and Aoife wriggled out from under the rough cot bed, which was all the two sisters had in the room.

Oliver breathed a sigh of relief. He had dreaded the thought that the little novice might have been dragged off to the ceremony, for they could never have got her out of there unnoticed.

"Have you seen Saffy?" Breizh asked urgently in turn. "We can't find her anywhere."

Oliver took in their concerned faces and replied gently,

"We've rescued her already, but she's in a bad way."

Before they could ask more, Labhran stepped forward and demanded,

"Where's Masanae? Have you seen her today?"

"No sign," Heledd replied. "I don't think she bothers with things like feasts."

"Oh she does!" corrected Labhran. "Even the Abend don't risk offending the gods! We must be careful in case she's here."

Silent as ghosts they slipped back the way they had come. The biggest risk was near the outer door. The berated guards had gone and the priestess too, but they were still perilously close to the main shrine area. Things were obviously picking up in there, going by the chanting. Cody and Trip led the way forward to deal with any locks, while Oliver and Labhran slunk along the corridor towards the main shrine until they could see in, keeping watch while the others scurried past. From the depths of the shadows, the two could see that all the priestesses were now on their knees, and all facing to the central pedestal of the shrine. Luckily the women had their faces cast down, and rhythmically bowed to touch their foreheads to the carpet as they chanted. The difference from when Oliver and Labhran had seen it last was that there was now a figure lying on top of the carved shrine, arms and legs splayed. Stripped naked, the head was lolling backwards so that the face was out of sight from their angle.

"Is that her?" Oliver mouthed silently to Labhran, even so not wanting to actually say Masanae's name this close to her.

Labhran nodded, clearly worried. What happened next shook Oliver to the core, and he realised Labhran must have guessed this bit was going to happen. A white mist rose from the recumbent figure's mouth and hovered over it. The priestesses were working themselves into a frenzy by now, and suddenly one leapt to her feet and ran towards the tomb, arms outstretched and an expression of religious ecstasy on her face. The misty form turned, and then lightning fast it struck like a snake at the centre of the girl's body. With a shriek the girl jack-knifed backwards, spasmed and then fell to the floor in a rigid pose. Oliver expected the priestesses to come to their senses and run from the room screaming, but instead only one got up and that was to hurl herself with similar masochistic ardour at the thing above Masanae.

Utterly nauseated, Oliver looked away to see Friedl gesturing from back at the turning. The two watchers left the vampire-like soul-sucking with relief, and hurried to where the others waited in the cool of the night air. As Cody sealed the door behind them Oliver turned to Labhran.

"What in the Islands was that all about?"

"That was one of the Abend feeding its Power-based self," came the bitter reply. "The life-force of others fuels the Abend's ability to work with and control the Power. Disgusting isn't it? I can't tell you much more than that, either. But I think it might be that the chief witch was topping up her powers in there ready for whatever she had planned for the two we've just rescued. I doubt she'll squander it willingly, though, because the religious fervour those priestesses were filled with carries its own kind of energy, and it's one which she couldn't replace just by sucking some poor slave dry. To get that much again she'd need many times the number."

"Never mind that. Let's get out of here fast!" was all Oliver could think of, although his stomach was still churning.

They hurried through the deserted tangle of enclosed alleys and lanes to the shop, never encountering another soul. Whatever reign of terror the DeÁine perpetrated on their own people, it was sufficient to avoid the need for a patrolling night-watch. At the butcher's stall Bertrand and Theo melted out from the shadows with Saffy, who was hugged with sobs of relief by Aoife.

Cody unlocked the stall once the two girls were past it and lifted the shutters. An iron grill covered the front of the opening, leaving it open for all to see, but probably originally intended to stop starving slaves from stealing meat as they passed. Now, though, it displayed a different kind of meat, and by locking the door again the Knights had ensured that passers-by would get a good view of what the stall contained. Saffy's dress was also hung, ghost-like, above the bodies, and was shimmying in the faint night-breeze. Moreover, the door was sturdy, and without a key it would take some breaking down. There was no way the Monreux family was going to be able to keep this quiet.

"Like your style, boys!" Breizh whispered, this being the first thing she had said so far. She was grinning furiously and clearly approved of the punishment the Knights had handed out.

Just short of the gates, the Knights halted and tucked themselves away in amongst a pile of water barrels waiting to go out and be refilled.

"No point in waking the guards by trying to force our way out," Lorcan explained with a wink to Breizh, who had just been about to complain at the delay. "We'll slip out when the screaming starts!"

Not that they had long to wait. The workers within Bruighean were used to rising early, the first signs of life being scabrous urchins who appeared with brooms and began sweeping the streets. Since they did the main roads first, they were not the ones to discover the grisly tableau. That honour fell to a nearby baker. His hysterical screaming was swiftly joined by others, and within minutes the great inner gates were thrown open and a troop of soldiers appeared at the run, heading for the sounds of chaos. Evans flitted from the shadows like a dark bat and into the gateway, to be followed by Kym and Lorcan.

Kym then swiftly reappeared and waved them forward, Cody in the lead with Trip beside him. In the gloom of the huge archway, they were directed by Lorcan into the recently vacated guardroom, and the door was closed except for a crack at which Evans kept watch. Moments later a soldier tore back into the gatehouse, but not to their hiding place. Instead he flung the opposite door open and screamed to those within. The sound of more running feet told of other guards being summoned, then Evans was out and across the gap, returning instantly to call them to join him.

"That's why the other lot went first," he explained, pointing to a small doorway in the second room. "This is the postern gate. They wouldn't want to leave that unguarded except in an emergency."

Easing the key in the lock, Cody gave a nod to the four men-at-arms who stood right by him. He flung the door open and the four piled through at speed. There was the sound of a scuffle and then all went quiet.

"All clear," a voice called softly and they all crept past the bodies of two more sentries and out into the early morning.

Chapter 2

Fresh Hope

New Lochlainn: Spring-moon – early Earrach

When Jacinto awoke in the manger it was to feel better than he had in a long time. The presence of the horses and their calm state had assured him that nothing untoward was going to happen, and that if it did they would pick up on it and give him enough warning to prepare himself for the worst. He had therefore slept for the rest of the day and all through the night, which did more to ease his suffering than anything else could have done. If he dreamt of the horrors he had seen, his exhaustion guaranteed that it never woke him, nor that he remembered any dream come the morning. It was the smell of cooking which finally roused him, and he was already out of the manger by the time a guard brought him a portion of the food. They had made some kind of flat bread cooked on a griddle and seasoned with spices – simple fare for on the road, but it tasted fit for a king to Jacinto, who wolfed it down while it was still hot.

He was left to his own devices for a short while as the guards cleared away their things, but then two came and marched him into the lodge. It was a mark of how much better he felt that he kept to his feet instead of being dragged in. If it lacked the old Jacinto's arrogant saunter, being more of an inelegant hobble as his skinned heel smarted painfully, it nonetheless gave him a tiny scrap of dignity. Not that it lasted long once he came into sight of Eliavres and Anarawd. It was all he could do to stop a puddle forming at his feet.

In his worst nightmares he had never thought he could be so terrified by just two figures, yet in their own way they were every bit as gut-wrenchingly alien as the huge army he had faced. Tall, and pale beyond any person he had seen before, it was the eyes which chilled him most. Irises clear as water made the blackness of the pupils more stark, and in those dark centres Jacinto could have sworn he could see something indefinable swirling deep within. The one who had wreaked such havoc the day before, while still tall, was the slightly shorter of the two and more solidly built, whereas the even taller one was thinner and angular. Then it struck him where he had seen such looks before. Edward! The king of Brychan had DeÁine blood in him! Jacinto shuddered, shaken to the core by the realisation that he had been assaulted by one of these creatures already. If that was what someone of mongrel stock could do to him, there was little chance of him surviving the attentions of the more powerful of their kind.

He was relieved when the guards flung him into a wooden chair left by the lodge's departed owners. It saved him the trouble of collapsing. At first his captor's questions were simple, phrased in precise and uninflected Islander so that he could understand. Who were the boys Quintillean had with him? They must be special, so who were they? What of the two women Masanae had with her? What was so special about the king's sisters? The two seemed perplexed as to how he would know nothing about persons who must, by their reasoning, be highly important people in the Islands. That Jacinto knew nothing of the major houses of any Island beyond Brychan was something they had trouble grasping, and he was repeatedly badgered over this. When it came to Heledd and Breizh, though, the more he insisted that Edward had no sisters the more the second strange being seemed delighted.

Once it was clear that Jacinto truly knew nothing of these people, the two had a long conversation in their own tongue which Jacinto could make nothing of. Managing to keep his wits about him he followed the rapid flows enough to pick up odd words, and that his captor was called Eliavres and the other Anarawd. It took all of his control not to break down and blubber in fear at that point, when the memory of lessons with the Knights came flooding back and he realised that he was sat in the presence of two of the most fearsome DeÁine in the Islands. From the same source, he knew he should know what Kuzmin, Ralja and Tokai were, but the memory refused to come. Whatever they were talking about, Kuzmin was clearly the important one and was connected to Masanae and Quintillean. Names which again he linked with the Abend, and made him shake at the thought of the mess he had somehow got himself into.

Stupid, stupid bastard! he chastised himself. *Why did you have to be so idiotic as to ignore Berengar and Esclados? Could you not have followed them when they left Garway? Wherever they are it isn't sat in a chair about to be turned into a statue that crumbles like old biscuits! How dumb was I to run to Edward? Edward of all people! Even then I should have picked up that it was all wrong by the way all of the soldiers thought I was mad to go to him that first night. Why didn't I run like they told me to? Stupid, stupid me*!

But to his amazement, instead of frying him to a crisp where he sat, the pair then turned on their heels and strode out of the room.

"Don't you want to deep-search him?" Anarawd asked idly as they walked to where their horses were already saddled and waiting. "Wring his pathetic little brain and be done with it?"

"Why expend the energy?" Eliavres said with a shrug. "He's so terrified of us he'd have told me anything he knew long ago."

"Why keep him then?"

"Because he was the pet of that equally pathetic king of the Islanders that Masanae has prisoner. Why she took him and hauled his sorry body all the way to Bruighean is beyond me. Masanae normally likes her meat young and pliant when she plays with it, and bores with it as fast. She must've kept him for some reason, and this one might just know what that is. Not knowingly – if he did he would have let it slip by now. It's buried where he doesn't know the importance of what he's seen or heard. I don't have time to mess around with her secondary plots and schemes now, but I won't forget this either. When we get back with the Scabbard, I want to know what else she's up to."

He turned to the guards. "The Hunters will escort us from now onwards. You are to return to Bruighean. Take the prisoner and put him in the cells there to await my return. Not the lowest ones! He's to be fed, cleaned and kept unharmed! Do you hear? I want him alive and well enough to question when I get back. Not some half-dead skeleton spitting through the remains of his teeth and crawling with vermin. You will all answer to me personally if he's not fit to stand questioning!"

The threat alone was enough to ensure that, however much the guards might have seethed inwardly at the thought of having to care for someone they saw as nothing other than a rebellious slave, they would comply. So as the two Abend rode off west again to head towards the palace of Mereholt, Jacinto was dragged into another room where an un-emptied bath of water stood cooling, and he was unceremoniously dunked in the dregs of Eliavres' bath. When that water became filthy, he was transferred to the even colder water of Anarawd's and scrubbed again.

If the guards were none too gentle, Eliavres' words had ensured that they were not as rough as they would have liked to be, for Jacinto would have been the means to vent their anger had they not been under orders. It rankled mightily with them that they had had to fetch and heat this water – such a menial task – while the Hunters sat and watched. From a cupboard somewhere they dug out clothing which Jacinto could get on. It fitted where it touched, the boots pinched, and there was no underwear, but with three thick layers of clothing now over most of his body, Jacinto had the first ray of hope that he might survive this winter yet.

On the ninth day of travelling with the guards, he saw looming in front of them a huge citadel, and by the end of that day they were within its walls. Later on Jacinto was to realise that he had arrived on the very same day as Labhran and the rescue party, but at the time he knew nothing of this. Instead of going to the sprawling army camp, he was marched into the confines of the citadel itself and put into a cell. To his astonishment he spotted Edward in the cell opposite. The former king was in a bad way. His face was battered to a pulp, his one arm seemed broken, the other hand mangled, and he could barely crawl across the floor to lap his food like a dog from the plate shoved under the iron bars.

Feigning ignorance, Jacinto asked, "What did he do?" of a slave who brought food the next day and looked like he might be an Islander.

"Set himself up as a DeÁine ruler," the slave whispered. "Probably going to be given to the queen as a peace offering. After the feast of Ama, that is. The queen's preparing for it now, like all the highborn ladies."

That was all Jacinto got, but it was interesting to see that while he got proper food of a kind, even though it tasted revolting, it was substantially better than the slops dished out to Edward. It was also nerve wracking just sitting around for so long, but by the time a week had gone by Jacinto was rested and, if nothing like what he classified as fit, at least feeling alert. Alert enough to be watching his captors for any sign of weakness he might exploit. Too run down to be anything other than subservient when the guards first saw him, Jacinto now had the presence of mind not to make it clear how much he had recovered from his ordeal. When anyone was around to watch him, he remained listless and disinterested in anything but the other prisoners, and then only in a vague sort of way.

On his seventh day in the cell the slave who spoke Islander was back but this time with soldiers, although not the ones who had brought Jacinto in. They stopped at Edward's cell and the lead guard let fly a stream of DeÁine. Jacinto might not have understood the words, but the tone clearly indicated that orders were being given. When Edward failed to even look up the slave was prodded forward to translate.

"Tonight the priestesses celebrate the feast of the Great Ama, All-Mother, the giver of fertility, the womb of our people. Tomorrow the All-Father, Phol, will be praised for his seed and the coming year will be blessed. You have been chosen to be sacrificed to the Seed-Giver. You will be taken away and prepared to go to the temple."

Edward lay there and never batted an eyelid, but Jacinto's mind was whirling.

"You've got the wrong one!" he called across. "He's for Eliavres. I'm the one Masanae brought in."

The slave looked at him as though he had gone mad, translated his words to the guards and then hissed urgently,

"You'll be killed at the altar! Quiet!"

But Jacinto winked at the slave on his side which the guards could not see. "Would you sacrifice such a pathetic specimen to the All-Father?" he demanded. He was praying that this worked. If he could get to a temple, not be confined behind bars, he might be in with a chance. What he was gambling on was the fact that he had always been considered well-endowed, and he knew from bitter experience that while Edward was brutal he was not the specimen of manhood that Jacinto was, and also that this must be a fertility god they were talking about. "Strip him and see!" he called out again. Then undid his pants and exposed himself to the guards. "The God Phol wants a male sacrifice? Am I not more male than him over there?"

Completely confused, the guards conferred amid much scratching of heads and shrugging of shoulders. They looked at the beaming Jacinto and down at his groin. Then one of them went into Edward's cell and hoisted down his garments to look up moments later shaking his head. A flurry of more words and then the slave was at the cell door as it was unlocked, saying,

"You're mad, you know that! *Aach*! Come on, off to the baths with you!"

The guards marched the two of them off through a maze of corridors and stairs to a lower level, and then shoved them into a steam-filled chamber, rattling off a stream of instructions to the slave and then shutting the door on them. The slave grabbed his arm and pulled him into the damp recesses of the room farthest from the door.

"Strip," he commanded wearily. "If anyone enters, for my own sake I have to be seen to be preparing you. The door's locked on the outside and guarded, so there's no point in knocking me over the head."

Jacinto divested himself of the now lousy rags and willingly set to work with the soap which the slave handed him. His locks had been getting shorter with each new phase of captivity, and now the last remnants disappeared as the slave applied the shears. This time though, Jacinto was glad to see them go. His thick, wiry hair had become a breeding ground for fleas and lice, and he was glad to be able to scrub his scalp with the astringent soap and feel nothing but hair again.

"You're a fucking idiot," the slave now hissed urgently in his ear. "Why in the Islands couldn't you keep quiet? The chances are Eliavres would've forgotten he put you there, but the guards wouldn't dare forget that he gave orders for you to be fed and kept well. You could've stayed safe for ages."

"Safe but not free," Jacinto answered. "Do you know what they're doing? The DeÁine, I mean?" The slave shook his head. "They've marched into Brychan! Even now the DeÁine army must be in Arlei. My old commander is up in the hills, and someday soon he'll come out of all the snow those demons sent, and he'll come out fighting. When that day comes I want to be there. I owe him that. That and a lot more, but it'll be a start if I can watch his back in battle."

"You're a soldier?"

"I'm a Knight! Or at least a squire."

"Oh Sacred Trees! The DeÁine in Brychan? Oh curses!" The slave looked truly distraught. He turned and walked away then paced back again. "I'm coming with you."

"Thank you," Jacinto said gratefully, but then another thought came to him. "But it'll be bad for you if we get caught. Can you fight? I won't be able to look out for you if things get rough."

"I'm not just a slave, …I'm one of the last Covert Brethren! I was too far away to join the others when they made the dash north eight years ago. Instead I got stuck here. I've been waiting for messengers to start coming looking for us from Brychan. But if what you say is true then there won't be anyone. I'm waiting for nothing!" He paused then stuck out his hand. "I'm Saul. That's not my slave name. I won't tell you that in case we get separated. That way, I can go back under cover without you betraying me if you get caught."

Jacinto shook his hand. "I'm Jacinto. And I have to make it out, because *I* don't have anywhere to go back to to hide."

The guards were evidently used to the amount of time it took to transform a louse-ridden slave into a clean offering, for shortly afterwards the door swung inwards and they were summoned out. Jacinto was supplied with a towel to dry himself and was then given a simple tunic, trousers and slippers in a plain white cloth. They were not as warm as the homespun woollens he had left behind, but in the close atmosphere of the citadel warmth was not the problem it had been on the road. However, once outside he would need something more substantial again, but for that he would have to trust to Saul's guidance.

Once again he was led through the warren-like building until he was thrust into a small room lit by a single torch. Three of the walls – including the one he had entered through – were solid, but the fourth was an interlace of stone fretwork. On the other side of the lattice he could see more torches shining in a larger room.

"That's the main shrine," Saul said laconically. "I have to go now, but I'll be back later."

With that he turned and left, and the door was slammed shut behind him. Jacinto fought down the urge to run to the door and test whether it was locked. He knew that it must be, and the more he acted the docile, passive sacrifice the more he would lull his guards into a false belief in his placidity. He wanted them fully off guard when the moment came.

Going to the stone lattice he peered through. The priests beyond were going through some kind of complex ritual, no doubt in preparation for the coming celebration. In the distance, Jacinto could hear the sound of melodic chanting, and assumed that the shrine to Ama must be close by. So that celebration was going ahead as normal. He calmed himself and made himself listen carefully to the muffled women's voices. There were a lot of them, he decided. So if the priests followed suit, then the whole of the room beyond would be stuffed with priests once the main proceedings got started. That meant that he had to make his move before he got into the shrine room, for if the place was packed, he would find it hard to move unhampered. Besides, he had no idea whether these priests had any training in the martial arts. Monks at home did not, but that was nothing to go by here.

Very carefully, he began to do some of the exercises which had been second nature to him back in the castles and preceptories of the Order. He was not stupid enough to think he could do what he had done back then – he was a far cry from the toned man of rippling muscle he had once been – but he did know that getting the blood pumping would speed up his responses considerably. Although it pulled and tweaked at his battered body, he was relieved to find as he gradually limbered up that he was not so badly out of condition as his traumatised mind had feared he might be. All the walking and riding had ensured that he was not entirely stiff, and if he lacked the power he had once had, he was still faster than the guards might expect an ordinary man to be.

As the night wore on, and the women's voices dipped and then rose again an hour or so later, Jacinto realised that it could be a long wait. Evidently these ceremonies had various parts and they all took their time. Somewhere around what he assumed must be the middle of the night he heard the voices become more hysterical. Whatever they were doing was working them into a frenzy. It was also doing something to the air in the temples complex. The hair on the back of his arms was standing up as the air began to crackle around him, soon to be followed by an unpleasant sensation as though ants were crawling all over him. Not long afterwards Saul appeared with some water for him.

"No food I'm afraid. You're supposed to be fasting and they'll check for signs of crumbs and the like before they take you out of here. They'd cut my throat on the spot if they found any."

"What was going on next door?" Jacinto asked softly.

"Masanae," was Saul's hurried and terse response. "You picked one Underworld of a night to try this on!" Then hurried out again before the guards had to fetch him.

Jacinto had not intended to sleep but must have dozed for a while, only to wake in the early hours by the sound of a commotion going on in the distance. Already limbering up and alert once more, he nearly pounced on Saul when he appeared at the door.

"Come on!" Saul hissed urgently.

As Jacinto followed him out he could see the guard lying with his throat cut and the blade beside him.

"Leave it!" Saul snapped as Jacinto's hand went for it. "I have another for you."

They turned the corner, and now Jacinto could see two other guards in a compromising position even in death. Saul had done his best to make it seem like a falling out between the guards.

"Strip!" Saul ordered him, and as Jacinto shrugged his way out of the sacrificial robes, produced serviceable slave garments for him. The moment the robes were off Jacinto, Saul picked them up, threw them into the chamber, and then shut and bolted the door again. "No point in making it too obvious," he said with a grimace. "Now follow me, keep your head down and try to look downtrodden!"

Keeping one eye on Saul's back as he hurried along, Jacinto tried to watch for signs of suspicion in others. However, all was in chaos with people running anywhere and everywhere in apparent disorder. Outside the temples it was even more chaotic and Jacinto had to practically walk on Saul's heels not to lose track of him in the throng. Saul was taking a weaving route but with great purpose.

Soon they were at the great gate, but that was blocked by guards attempting to hold up the flow of seething people. Some were trying to come in and being turned back, while others were trying to get out and having to be forcefully dissuaded. Just as Jacinto thought their luck had run out, Saul turned aside and dived in through a side door. When he emerged a second later, Jacinto saw that he was carrying a bundle of linen in his arms and as they ran into three soldiers in the confined gatehouse room, Saul let loose a babble of DeÁine, thrusting the linen out towards them.

The guards' expressions turned from watchful to irritated in a second, and the nearest came forward as if to bundle them out, already chivvying Saul in an exasperated voice. Jacinto did not need to know the language to tell that the guard was saying that this was not the time or place to be worrying about clean linen. It was his last thought. Saul's long knife took him under the chin, up through the mouth and into his brain as the linen was flung upwards in a distracting flurry. Needing no prompting, Jacinto made as if to scramble for one of the pieces of cloth and used it to disguise the punch to the throat he made to the next guard, breaking his windpipe. As he finished the kill with the knife Saul had given him, Saul himself was already on the third man, and if the attack was less clean it was no less effective. Jacinto sprang back to the door and dropped the bar to secure it.

"Quick," Saul called softly from the other door and led Jacinto into a short passage to a picket gate in the wall. Two more bodies lay there but these were already cooling. Saul's voice sounded shocked as he said,

"Someone else has made their escape tonight!"

He peered cautiously out of the picket, then when the main force at the gate was distracted, quickly shoved Jacinto out into the crowd and shut the door behind them. Holding Jacinto's sleeve, Saul led him off into the tangle of streets which made up the ramshackle city around the citadel. Whatever had happened was enough of an event for even those outside of the citadel to be hurrying to speak to their neighbours, or to try to find out more, and so they hardly stood out by moving at a steady jog amongst the milling bodies. For a heart stopping moment they were halted by a party of four guards, but Saul gave some kind of explanation while gesturing wildly towards the citadel, and the party left them to hurry off on a mission of their own.

"What was that about?" panted Jacinto, as they swiftly ducked into the next alley, and cut across to a different road leading away from the towering mountain of stone behind them.

"Household guards," Saul breathed quietly, as they waited for a troop of horsemen to go past before stepping out onto one of the wider streets. "I told them half the citadel's guards were dead! They've gone running off to find out if their master still lives or not."

The further out they got, the poorer the dwellings around them became, until they almost stood out for being too well-dressed. Then suddenly they were beyond the last of the houses. Saul took a lane to the left and before long they spotted horses in a field.

"We'll need those," Saul said. "You ride, of course?"

"Of course," was Jacinto's instinctive response, but now he thought to clarify it in a way he once would never have done. "Not well, though, I'm no natural horseman."

"That's alright, you're not going in to battle, just stick on the beast so that we can travel faster."

Saul dug around under the roots of an old lightning-blasted oak and came up with a couple of rope halters. "Left in case of emergencies," he informed Jacinto. "There were always plans. These will have to do for now. At least we won't attract attention by being too well furnished in our equipment!"

Jacinto turned to stare at him with surprise, then realised that the spy had a smile on his face and was being sarcastic. It made him smile too as he realised that if nothing else, for the first time in a long while he was free. They caught two horses and mounted up.

"Which way?" Jacinto asked.

"South-west for a while maybe, but by the country roads. We daren't use the old highway going south. Whatever went on in the citadel, they'll soon have guards out scouring the roads. In fact, I think we should go straight west for a bit. Escaped slaves always head east for the mountains. If that's what it was, then the eastern roads will be hit first. The more we go off into the farmlands, the safer we'll be too."

In the chill morning light they rode off at a steady pace, just two servants delivering horses from one farm to another. Turning to look back, Jacinto commented,

"I can't believe how little snow there is on these slopes of the mountains."

Saul was surprised. "How little? Seems a fair amount to me!"

"Well it's nothing to how much there is on the other side," Jacinto said bitterly. "The passes are full to the brim, and come the first storm there'll be the avalanches of the century, because there's no way that much snow can be stable. They'll be lucky to be able to get the castle doors open up in the mountains, let alone get out of them."

They were so taken up with their discussion, and watching for pursuit, that they never saw the man until he stepped out in front of them.

"We'll be taking those horses," he said in a villainously thick DeÁine accent. Jacinto had no idea what had been said, but he understood the sword in the man's hand. With a snarl he launched himself off at the man, only to brought down by another assailant who dropped from the tree branch above onto him. Jacinto swore and fought back only to find himself surrounded by men. He was nonetheless about to head-butt a man coming at him from the front when a voice called out,

"Hold it Trip! He swore in our language. He's not DeÁine!"

"No, by the Trees I'm not!" Jacinto snarled as the man stepped smartly back. Then he heard Saul speak,

"Donn Valdemar? Is that you?"

In response, a tall man with pale skin and fair hair stepped forward around some of the others. "You know my cover name?"

"Who seeks the seeker?" Saul replied enigmatically.

"Quester! Who has the power?"

"He who knows!"

"Let him go!" Labhran ordered instantly. "He's Covert Brethren! Sweet Rowan! I had no idea anyone was still left here? How did you come to be left behind?"

"I was with Eriu's entourage over at Ralja Palace when the trouble exploded," Saul explained. "I rode with her household to get back to

Bruighean, but too late to join the rest of you going north. I waited, expecting to find someone coming to make contact. Nobody came and then the purges started. I was demoted from household servant, and by then trying to get away was …well it was impossible in the first couple of years. After that I started trying to find people, but the more I looked the less I found. I realised there was no-one to help me escape. So I stayed, hoping that soon someone would come back and I'd see signs that the old networks were becoming active again. It never happened."

"Sacred Trees, I'm so sorry," Labhran breathed. "So long, and all alone! I'm so sorry!"

"Well you've found him now," Hamelin consoled Labhran coming to lay a hand on his shoulder. "Who's this chap with you?" he asked Saul.

"I'm Jacinto," he replied for himself, "and I was a squire in the Brychan sept before the world went mad"

"Who with?" Oliver asked, coming to stand by Labhran on the other side to Hamelin.

"I was attached to an older Knight called Esclados under Ealdorman Berengar," Jacinto answered, trying to pull himself a bit more upright to stand to attention. Something which he was suddenly able to do a lot more easily when Waza and Newt let go of him.

"Sorry, sire," they mumbled but not very contritely. If folks would go skulking around foreign parts of the Islands dressed like slaves, then it was hardly the two soldiers' fault if they were a bit rough on him.

"Berengar again," Lorcan said. "We keep falling over his name again and again at the moment."

"You know where he is?" Jacinto asked eagerly.

"Not exactly," Teryl admitted. "We're from Ergardia, and these others are from the Prydein sept. We all came at the behest of Grand Master Brego to rescue two boys. Since then, though, it's all gone a long way from what was planned."

"But I'm afraid that will have to wait," Labhran said sternly. "And I'm sorry, but you'll have to walk like the rest of us, we need your horses for someone else. Dusty? Waza? Bring those two nags will you?" And he led the way off the road into a small copse of trees.

To Jacinto's astonishment he saw four women sitting on the ground in a clearing in the middle. Or to be more precise two women and two girls. A bulky Knight was gently washing the face of one of the girls who lay slumped in the arms of one of the women.

"Did you get them?" he asked looking up at Labhran. When he got a nod for an answer he sighed in relief. "Good! Because Breizh is going to have to ride and hold Saffy in her arms. If Heledd and Aoife go on the other horse, they can swap Saffy and Aoife when Breizh's arms get tired."

"What happened to her?" Jacinto found himself asking, the sight of the girl bringing back memories of Cwen's family. Not so many months ago the condition of the girl would hardly have registered with him, but now he found himself wanting to know.

Lorcan replied softly so the girls would not hear him. "In the temple. Some sort of ritual deflowering. Aoife picked Oliver here, so she got nothing worse than a hug and got rescued before anything worse could happen. Poor little Saffy there was raped by some rich bastard!"

"I hope he rots," Jacinto hoped, realising that his perceptions of such things had changed dramatically and forever in the last few months.

"Oh don't worry! Milor Monreux died a very unpleasant death!" Hamelin assured him. "We made sure of that!"

"Monreux!" Saul gasped. "Not the oldest son?"

"If you mean an arrogant bastard with a swagger, lots of mouth, and a nasty penchant for little girls, then yes," Oliver said in clipped tones.

Saul gasped again, then chuckled. "By the Gods, is that what all the screaming was about? No wonder the place was in uproar!" His grin got wider. "The times I've wanted to gut that evil little shit! Even his own family tried to distance themselves from him. You know he got chucked out of the army by the Donns? What a disgrace for one of the Monreux's – soldiers to a man until him! They'll be torn in two. Nobody will weep for his passing, but they'll be smarting from the affront to the family name."

"Not for long," Labhran told him, passing over a water flask. "This bunch used Saffy's bloodstained novice robes and made it look like Ama herself struck him down!"

Saul looked from Labhran to the others as if not sure that he could believe what he was hearing. "Blessed Temples! That's a neat trick! Was it you lot who got out through the picket gate ahead of us?" He got nods in confirmation. "What of these two boys you spoke of?"

"We're not the only rescue party," Oliver explained. "Someone else took the northern route. That was before the trouble happened in Brychan. The Abend have been out in the Islands." Saul gasped in horror, and Jacinto too, for he had not know of the Abend's ventures beyond Brychan to be able to tell Saul of this. "I know, chilling thought isn't it. Rheged's had Tancostyl causing chaos over there, Calatin is somewhere in Prydein – and I hope my old Grand Master, Hugh, is giving him grief. Where Eliavres is is anyone's guess, but Master Brego thought Brychan. Quintillean came to Ergardia, would you believe the cheek of him.

"It did him no good, but in the process he took two boys hostage. Both of them are from the ruling family in Rheged, but one's only about eleven or twelve, and the other's a simple soul who's lived his life in a monastery. So neither is fit to even begin to cope with what's coming their way. On top of that we had evidence brought from Celidon that Quintillean and Masanae are probably planning some grim ritual. When we left Lorne they were still trying to work out what it was.

"Our mission has been dogged by misfortune. We got caught in the mother of all storms and got shipwrecked. Then when we finally got to Brychan it was to find the DeÁine marching in, the Knights snowed-in in the mountains, and Masanae heading back this way with two sacrifices. It wasn't until we reached Bruighean that we found out that it was Heledd and Breizh, here, and not our boys. Where Quintillean is with *them* is anyone's guess. He must have gone by the northern route, so we can only hope that the others going that way will catch him."

"Not anyone's guess," Saul was able to correct him firmly. "Quintillean passed through here at speed the best part of a month ago. He only stopped to pick up more triads of Hunters, then left again. I only know because he didn't go to the royal court but stopped in the temples. He could've had hostages with him, but I don't know for sure. Masanae was in Ama's temple last night…"

"We know, we saw her." Oliver saved him the trouble of explaining. "Any idea where Quintillean was going? This is bad news. It means Will must have failed."

"I think I can help there," Jacinto broke in. "I was held prisoner by Eliavres and another called Anarawd – he's Abend too, isn't he? While they were questioning me about these two women," he gestured to Heledd and Breizh, "…who by the way Masanae thinks are King Edward's full-blooded sisters, they mentioned several names. I don't understand DeÁine, so I'm sorry, I can't tell you word for word what they said. But they mentioned Tokai, Ralja and Kuzmin a lot and in connection with Quintillean and Masanae."

"The royal palaces," Labhran sighed. "Flaming Underworlds! The cursed places will be stuffed with guards. And worse, …if Quintillean was at Bruighean …when?"

"About the ninth of last month," Saul supplied.

"…So over twenty days ago, that means he could already be at Tokai and we could be too late."

"No we couldn't!" Oliver leapt in as Jacinto said at the same time,

"…Not Tokai. He isn't going to Tokai, it's Kuzmin that's important."

Labhran and the others looked from Oliver to Jacinto and back.

"What do you mean?" Labhran demanded of Oliver first.

"Masanae! You've forgotten Masanae's as much a part of this as Quintillean. He won't have started without her. There was a reason she hauled Breizh and Heledd all this way and remember, even back at Lorne we were speculating that Quintillean might be after a sacrifice for each of the Treasures."

Labhran breathed a huge sigh of relief, and Oliver and Hamelin once again exchanged private glances at the worrying way that Labhran expected the worst so much that it blinded him to what was possible.

"So what's this about Kuzmin?" Oliver carried on, determined to keep positive.

Jacinto frowned. "Well as I said, I don't speak DeÁine. But it was clear that Eliavres and Anarawd were shaking their heads over Tokai and nodding a lot over Kuzmin. And I hate to worry you Prydein folk, but I think your Island is where those two are heading."

"Oh Sacred Trees!" Theo groaned. "Not two more on top of Calatin!"

"No!" Saul corrected him. "Calatin's dead!"

"Dead!" Labhran exclaimed. "How? Are you sure?"

"How? I don't know. …Sure? Yes I am. There were ceremonies said for the passing of his soul in the temples at the coming of the new year. He was the oddest of the Abend, but he was Abend nonetheless and the proper observances were made."

"Master Hugh!" Freidl grinned. "I bet it was him! If anyone could give one of the Abend a thrashing it would be him."

"And it would explain why Eliavres and Anarawd are heading to Prydein," added Theo. "If Calatin couldn't get the Scabbard, they must be going for it themselves."

"Is there any way we can warn Master Hugh?" Oliver asked the assembly in general.

"I doubt it," Jacinto answered regretfully. "They packed me off up here the best part of two …no, three weeks ago. Even if some of you rode like the wind, you'd never catch up in time."

"And you may not be too late to save those two boys," added Saul pointedly. "Anarawd was at Tokai for months and months before he came to Bruighean. Yet Quintillean never knew he was in the citadel at the same time as him. He may think Anarawd is still at Tokai. If this is some scheme that Quintillean and Masanae are pulling off on their own, then Quintillean may not want to go anywhere near Tokai. If he knows he has to wait for Masanae, he could well have gone around the Salu Maré!"

Labhran's head came up and Oliver was relieved to see a fresh sparkle in them. "Great Maker, Saul, you're right! I was thinking of him making for Tokai in all events – either to do what he's planning there or to catch one of the boats across to Kuzmin. I never thought he would go for Ralja, that's too much the province of the royals. But if he's trying to exclude others of the Abend, then he would avoid Tokai at all costs. And if it's something really perverted to do with the Power, then he wouldn't want the priests in the Houses of the Holy at Tokai looking too closely either. How long do you think it would take him to get to Kuzmin, if he avoids cutting the corner off by getting a boat across from Ralja?"

Saul thought carefully. "I reckon he'd be getting there about now. He could've done it faster, but if Masanae is so far behind and he needs her, then there wouldn't be any rush. If you want to follow him, of course, there's no reason why *you* can't go the faster route to Tokai and take one of the ferries across. That would get you there in under a fortnight."

Labhran shook his head. "Not on foot we wouldn't!"

"Who said anything about on foot? You're an hour's walk from the main stud farms. March in and demand horses for your men who are chasing escaped murderers! Pick prime horses and you could be at Tokai in eight days."

"Let's go for it!" was Oliver's instant response. "If we're all riding we can take it in turns to hold the two little girls. How well do you ride?" he asked looking at Breizh and Heledd.

"Born to it," Heledd said with confidence. "Our father was first a head ostler and then the farrier at Breslyn. We grew up in and out of the stables."

That settled the argument, and while Bertrand helped Breizh up onto one of the horses and handed a shaking Saffy up to her, Kym, Lorcan and

Teryl were off at the run with the men-at-arms and archers following Saul's lead. The Prydein Knights followed a little more slowly with the women and Jacinto, but Labhran had hurried to catch up with Saul. By the time the Prydein party caught them up, horses were already being led out onto the road near the stud by Topher and Mitch, two of the archers, closely followed by Toby, Newt and another archer named Busby.

Labhran had clearly not lost his touch with playing the irate commander whatever his private torment, and within the stud's main gate, people could be seen hurrying to and fro as Labhran stood imperiously in the centre of the court, with arms folded and a sneer on his lips. In short order the whole group were mounted up except for Freidl and Bertrand, who had stayed back out of sight with Jacinto and the four women. Their horses were brought to them by Jens, Dusty and Colum, who had managed to befuddle the poor grooms into thinking that they had had fewer horses than had been signed for.

With Saffy clinging to Bertrand's jacket, cradled in his arms and swathed in his cloak, they set off at a brisk canter, Aoife up behind Heledd and hanging on for grim death. The raped little novice had formed a strong attachment to Bertrand and seemed to feel safest with him or Theo, something which surprised Heledd and Breizh since these were the two biggest and most muscular Knights. They had expected Saffy to want nothing to do with any men once she had the option, but put it down to Bertrand having been the one to pluck her out of the grasp of her tormentor.

Whatever the reason they were soon glad of it, for the Knights set a stinging pace, and both women realised it would have been punishing trying to hold Saffy's bruised and battered form while coping with the rhythm of the horses. As it was they frequently swapped Aoife between them. The young girl had no experience of riding and had to be held in front of them, having almost come off several times when first sat behind Heledd. She was hard enough work, and she was far from the dead weight Saffy posed.

After the first day they managed to get Saffy to go with Busby for a while, who was another solidly built man with great arm strength, being an archer, and the day after she agreed to ride with Colum for part of the day. She was definitely happier with the older, more fatherly men, and so Teryl, Kym, Topher, Mitch and Jens, as the young men of the group, stayed well away from her even in camp out of kindness. Maybe it was seeing Aoife sitting between Oliver and Hamelin at every opportunity, but Saffy was less bothered by those two, although neither pushed their company on to her. To Bertrand's great relief she slowly began to perk up, for as the one with the most medical knowledge, he had been worried that she might be bleeding internally. By the fifth day, though, he was fairly sure that it was simply severe bruising. Unpleasant and painful for her, but not life-threatening. The mental scars would take a lot longer, but the Knights felt there was little they could do to help, and time was everything if they were to save Wistan and Kenelm. All they could do was keep the four women safe, and hope that sooner rather than later they would be able to stop and find them a refuge.

With Earrach being the month known for its spring showers, all were grateful that when they came they were only light and infrequent at that. It allowed them to make good time, and avoided the misery of setting camp and then having to try to dry sodden clothing by a camp fire sputtering in the rain. In such a way they made it to the last high ground before the slope down to the shores of the Salu Maré in the eight days Saul had predicted. What they had not expected was the sight of utter confusion around the palace. For a heart-stopping moment the lead riders of Labhran, Oliver and Saul thought they were looking down on a whole contingent of the Imperial guard, but only for a second. There was no sign of the vivid clothing beneath the distinctive armour. Instead, these seemed like ordinary people going in and out of the palace gates.

"What in the Islands is going on here?" a bemused Labhran wondered. "Who are all these people and why are they here? Surely they're not sacrifices?"

"Not likely," Saul agreed, "there'd be more panic if there was even a hint of that and with such a crowd to fed the hysteria."

"Only one way to find out," Oliver said with his usual optimism, and heeled his horse forward, swiftly followed by the other men.

"Curses," Labhran muttered to Saul. "I do wish they wouldn't keep doing this to me! They barge in where the Martyrs would fear to tread! No bloody idea of what they're getting into. I'll be grey if I survive this mission."

Saul laughed. "Maybe, but think on this. Perhaps it's the fact that they don't behave as expected which has given them their success so far? You and I would've tiptoed around because we're used to having to go unnoticed for long periods. It doesn't matter to them if they're recognised, because they don't expect to ever be here again. Cheer up, Labhran, your errant Knights might yet carry the day!"

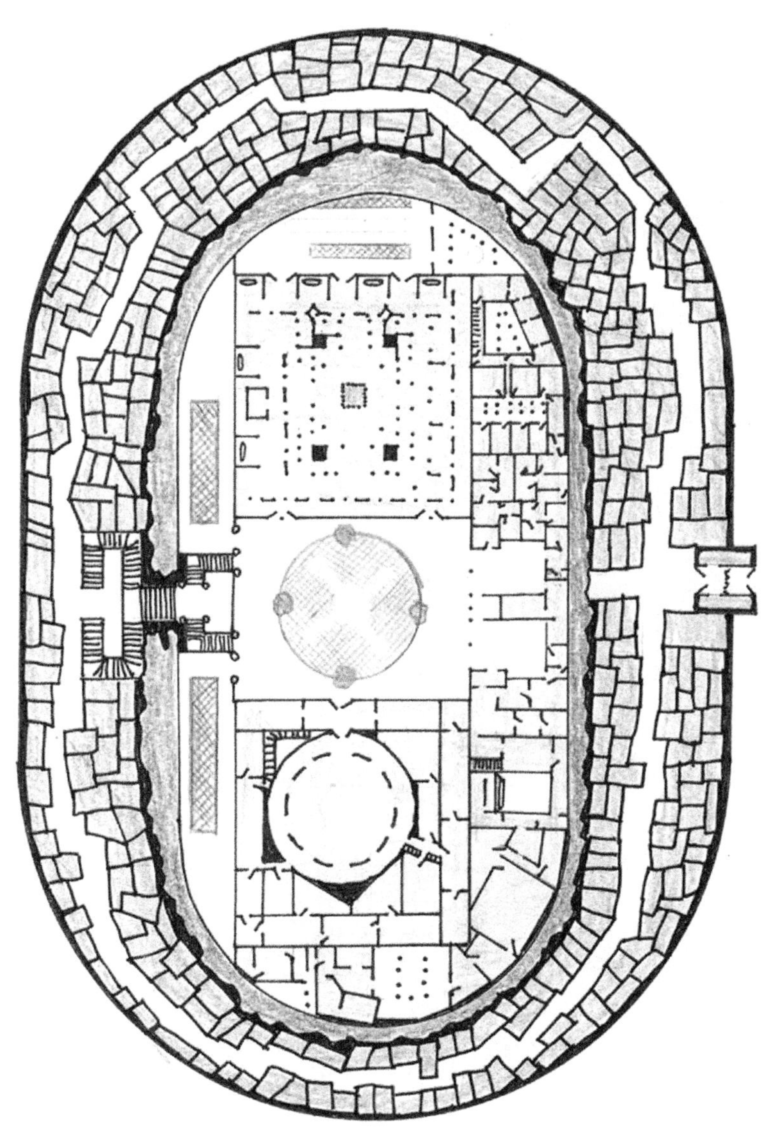

Chapter 3

An Enemy Stronghold

New Lochlainn: Spring-moon

On the evening of the third of Spring-moon, with something like a sniff of real spring in the air, Will led his makeshift army to the gates of Turnu. The townspeople had the gates locked and barred, which Will could hardly blame them for – who would want to be raided and ravished by a ragged bunch of thugs masquerading as your own army? Unfortunately he had no choice but to pass through the town to get to the great stone bridge which crossed the River Vaii, and he needed that bridge. Sioncaet, now starting to really enjoy this venture, rode forward to the walls and let rip a long string of commands in DeÁine. There was a long pause and then a sullen looking official appeared at the battlements.

"Is he DeÁine?" Will asked Sioncaet very softly.

"Oh I think we can safely say he's near pure bred," the minstrel replied equally muted, so that only Will could hear. "They wouldn't leave one of the few major towns they have in the north in just anybody's hands."

"Right, then," Will murmured, "tell him that we haven't come to raid the town for supplies. Tell him that I shall send you across with the first batch of fifty soldiers, and that the rest of them will follow in groups of the same. You'll take them straight through the town, across the bridge and onto the opposite bank where I can see you. Tell him that a new group will only enter once the one in front is safely out of the town and assembled where I can see them."

Sioncaet looked sceptical. "That doesn't ring true for a Donn, Will. It makes it sound like you think they're against you when a real Donn wouldn't think twice about that."

"I know," Will said patiently, "and that's why you're going to tell him that I don't want this bunch of half-wits getting stuck in his delightful taverns when I want them on the road. Tell him to get his provosts – or whatever you have in a DeÁine town – at all major road junctions to stop anyone from absconding. Tell him that if I don't see the same number of men coming out as went in, I'll be in like the Wild Hunt and make him wish he'd never been born – whether or not he's commandeered them for road-mending duties, or they made off of their own accord! Will that do?"

"Oh yes!" Sioncaet answered with a grin. "That's far more like it!" And with that he rode forward and began a heated exchange with the official on the wall.

Not long after that a clanking of chains began, and then the portcullis to the town gates began to asthmatically wheeze its way up into the gatehouse.

"And that needs a good coat of looking at," Will muttered with despair as he rode to within a few yards of it, and chivvied the first batch through in Sioncaet's wake.

As he sat there, keeping one eye on the opposite bank as the evening wore on, he got a good look at the state of repairs and tried to make sense of it all. Why anyone would let it all go to rack and ruin, if there was enough of a genuine threat to build defences in the first place, was illogical. Yet the portcullis was full of rust and the mortar in the walls had all but disappeared in places. The more he looked the surer he was that the original town and its defences had been built by Islanders, but were long out of use under DeÁine rule. So the gates had only been shut this time in a half-hearted attempt to prevent the town being ransacked. It must have been the first time in a very long while too.

With the last batch of soldiers ahead of him, he finally rode in himself, giving a curt nod and wave of the hand in dismissal to the official who stood glowering at him, but not daring to say anything. The place itself made even the simplest of towns in his home island of Rheged look sumptuous. The buildings were being held together by grime more than anything else, the roads were in a dire state and running with sewage, and the people looked haggard and haunted. It tore at Will to see common folk so misused, and he cast a backward glance to see if the DeÁine official was close enough to hear him if he spoke to people. Then he spotted a burly blacksmith who could never have been DeÁine, going by his pure Attacotti black hair and eyes, and freckled skin.

Shooing the soldiers on ahead of him, Will edged his horse close to the man and leaned close enough to be able to speak quietly. The man's eyes held nothing but contempt, and Will felt sure that he would have spat in his face if he had not feared the retribution.

"Listen!" Will hissed urgently in Islander. "If anyone asks what I've said, tell them I was trying to recruit you for the army." The blacksmith's eyebrows rose in astonishment, but Will did not give him time to speak. "Get that bloody portcullis oiled and in working order! I'm from Brychan! If we succeed, the Underworld is going to break out around here, so get some trusted men – not the ones who are brown-nosing round the arse of that fucking DeÁine – and make sure you can really shut the gates, and that the walls won't fall down the first time someone leans on them. You're going to need them if we succeed in lighting a fire under the Abend!" And with that Will heeled his horse forward leaving the blacksmith in open-mouthed shock behind him.

Luckily Sioncaet had already got the men setting up camp, and soon a third town made up of tents had sprung up at the opposite side of the bridge between Turnu and Gura Vaii. The next morning Will and Sioncaet set about negotiating levies of food with the official in Gura Vaii. The main difference between the two towns was that Turnu was located where it was to guard and maintain the seven-arched bridge across the River Vaii, whereas its neighbour was a few miles away on the shore and was the major fishing port on the north coast. As it was bypassed by the road down to Bruighean, albeit closely, it rarely got visitors – who mostly stayed in Turnu instead – and much of the time Gura Vaii got left to conduct its own business. The leading men were none too pleased at Will's demands, but Will had shrewdly guessed that the idle DeÁine officers who sporadically marched men down that main road would seize goods in Turnu; whose DeÁine 'majordomo' would then seek to recoup his losses with interest from Gura Vaii. By telling the folk of Gura Vaii that he suspected the Turnu leaders of profiteering, and that an investigation was forthcoming, Will got them on his side. When he added that he would only be taking what his men actually needed, instead of adding exorbitant profit-making levies on top (as had happened before), they were only too eager to co-operate.

The result was that in the morning three days later, the army set off westwards with every man carrying a full pack, and some spare rations packed onto half a dozen mules – which the town had been happy to hand over when Sioncaet had written them a bill of sale, to be handed for compensation to the next tax collector who came their way. They had even had a couple of recruits from Turnu sneaking out to join them, who kept giving Will sideways glances but carefully kept quiet just in case what they had clearly heard from the blacksmith turned out to be false. It was a cold and chilly start to the march westwards, for the brief hint of spring had disappeared for a while, but it was peaceful and at least there was no snow.

Will commented on the absence of the white stuff to Sioncaet, and got a smug grin in reply before he said,

"I was right! The cursed witches *did* drive everything to the mountains! Look ahead," and he pointed to a grey lump on the distant horizon. "That's Sgurr Mor and it's high enough that at this time of year it should be showing up white against the grey of this sky. We can't be any further from those highlands than Tokai Palace is, and I've been there at about this time of year in the past and been able to see the white domes on the distant horizon. Now look at it! You can barely make it out from the sky. I know the cloud is low today, but it's not that low that it's brushing the tops of the highlands."

Will nodded thoughtfully. "Well at least we won't be trying to camp in the freezing cold, because snow or no snow, don't you think it's milder here too? I know we're nearer the sea and that always makes a difference – even somewhere mountainous like Celidon – but it's more than that, surely?"

Sioncaet paused and sniffed the air thoughtfully. "It's probably because we're lower here than we've been for a long time on our journey," he decided. "We're also nicely tucked behind the highlands from any south-westerly wind even though, going by the way the clouds are moving, that's the direction it's coming from."

"Well I'm not complaining," Will said hastily, "long may this continue."

For the first week they marched through fertile farmland, and Will took the opportunity to requisition what extra he could in the way of supplies, never taking more than the farmers could spare. Sioncaet had been right, most of these folk had never seen a full army and even less of pure bred DeÁine, and so nobody voiced any suspicions about his behaviour. As far as the men were concerned, as soon as they were on the fourth day out of Gura Vaii and far from observation, Will began running exercises as they marched. Some men would go ahead with him and lay ambushes for the others as they came up under Sioncaet's command. It was far from the extensive training Will would have wished to give them, but he did manage to start getting some sense of battle tactics into them.

For one day, while they were in the rolling, craggy moorland of the Sgurr Mor, Will actually staged two mock battles. One was a set face to face battle, and the second time they besieged an ancient and ruined fortified tower-house. It was hardly a DeÁine palace, but at least the men got a feel for what would be expected of them. Throughout, Will rode up and down and through their ranks giving orders, or telling them in no uncertain terms what they could have expected if a real enemy were facing them. By that evening he fell into their tent utterly spent and not much reassured, but to Sioncaet's eyes there was a huge improvement.

"I've never seen a slave army work so well together," he reassured Will. "Most of the time they're rounded up, driven by slave-masters riding fearsome beasts-of-battle to where the fighting is to take place, and then herded forward straight at the enemy. It's up to them whether they fight well, or are just so downright terrified that they lash out indiscriminately and ineffectively. The Donns work on overwhelming their enemies with the first wave so that they're already tired by the time the veteran troops come up to fight. By your standards these lads may know nothing of tactics, but against DeÁine slaves you might be surprised at how much of an upper hand they'd have."

"Thanks," Will groaned around a massive yawn, "but in that case we'd better start praying that there are no veterans at Tokai Palace, or we're in big trouble and fast!"

Sioncaet handed him a mug of spiced herb tea from the pot which had been brought into the tent, then sat on the edge of the camp bed Will had flopped onto.

"I don't think you need to worry too much about that," he said with slow thoughtfulness. "I'm trying to remember things that I saw in the past but, do you know, I don't think I can ever recall there being veteran troops at any of the palaces unless the royal family was in residence. Most of the time, the real hard core of the army is stationed around the citadel of Bruighean, which is because there the Donns really do train *them*. They spend days and nights rehearsing battle tactics, and having mock battles between the armed companies belonging to the different Donns. Other than that, the big slave-training camps are way down in the south."

"What about the Abend?" Will asked, propping himself up on one elbow to fix Sioncaet with a harassed look as he slurped the scalding hot drink. "Do the Abend get an armed escort, or are they deemed to be capable of looking after themselves?"

Sioncaet mulled the issue over as he sipped his own tea. "Funny you should ask that… It's a good point, and for once I think things are more in our favour than they might once have been. Once upon a time, when we first came back and occupied this side of Brychan, you're right – the Abend did have an armed guard at all times because of the threat of rebellion. Even now, were one of them to venture into the far south where there are lots of small towns around the waterways, and lots of places for rebels to hide, then they'd probably want to take much more than one triad of Hunters as protection. But up here it was soon clear that the scattered farming communities posed little threat.

"I can't recall a single report of anyone being waylaid or ambushed north of the Brychan Mere or the Eldr Forest even in the early days. Since the fiasco defeat by the Order's Knights at Gavra, the Abend have been given short shrift by the Donns, and I think they'd be laughed at outright if they requested an armed escort just to come up here. And the Abend do hate to be ridiculed. That in itself would make certain that they'd never ask."

"Ahh," Will mused, "which also makes more sense of why Quintillean had his thugs of Hunters round up this lot of innocents. It might not have been just convenience – the need for some easy battle-fodder to distract the Knights at Borth. But do you think he actually might've had no other alternative? Had no real troops to call upon?"

"I think that's very likely," Sioncaet confirmed. "It doesn't mean that we won't encounter Hunters when we get to Tokai, but at least with them we'll have the advantage of seriously outnumbering them, even if they do have near inhuman strength."

That gave Will something more to worry about over the next couple of days, and his mind rattled around along with the rhythmic clattering of his horse's tack and hooves, mulling over what to do if they met Hunters. Four days' march on from the second practice battle, and with the Salu Maré only another day away, Will came to a decision. They had had to stop to build a pontoon bridge to cross a large river in order to be able to continue marching on down to Tokai, and he took the opportunity to assemble all the men in a natural hollow amphitheatre above the river-valley woods. When he was sure they were all present and paying attention, he got Sioncaet to call them to order.

"Pay attention all of you," he then barked in his best parade-ground voice, which carried across the gathering and was bounced back off the rock walls. "I know none of you have ever served with the DeÁine army before. What it may surprise you to know is that you're not going to now!"

Many men looked around in bemusement. What was he talking about? "Up until now I've had to drive you hard and fast, and I make no apology for that. You have to learn how to fight effectively. As to why you need to fight . . . my name is General William Montrose, and I'm no DeÁine Donn!" That really set the cat amongst the pigeons and he had to wait for the babble to die down. "But I really *am* a general in the army of Rheged, and Sioncaet here and myself are one of several rescue missions who were launched into this side of Brychan to recover children kidnapped by the Abend."

Will had deliberately decided to describe both Wistan and Kenelm simply as children, knowing that it would be less contentious than revealing their status as members of the ruling family of Rheged. The more Will saw of this oppressed land, the more he believed that it would only stir up resentment if these folk thought that the rest of the Islands would move heaven and earth to recover two royals – however young – yet leave thousands of ordinary Islanders to suffer under the heel of the DeÁine without seeming, from their viewpoint, to lift a hand to help. So having hopefully got some understanding, he now needed to get them fully onto his side.

"You all saw the Knight's great castle guarding Borth," he continued, "but I would guess that that's the first time most of you have ever got that close to the border. For that reason you won't know that the far south is even more heavily guarded, but not just by the Knights. The DeÁine guard their own side as fiercely to prevent escape as well as invasion, and so in the east we've heard nothing of what happens over here since the defeat of Gavra Pass."

"What's that?" someone called out as the men exchanged bemused looks.

"You didn't even hear of that?" Will asked in astonishment, and received a multitude of shaking heads in response. He looked at Sioncaet in frustration before bracing himself for what looked like being a longer session than he had anticipated. Keeping it very simple, Will told them of the way the Knights had infiltrated the DeÁine citadel, and had found out about the Abend's plan to march an army through the northern hills beyond the reach of the Order's coastal fortresses of Borth and Clodoch, and the Knights' response. He told of the fierce battle where the Abend had thrown their acolytes into the fray, wielding the Power and bringing arcane forces into play against the all too human forces of the Knights.

"But against all of that – the overwhelming numbers and the magic of the Abend – the Knights stopped them," he told a spellbound audience. "Most of the Knights of Celidon died that day, and Gavra Pass doesn't exist as a pass anymore after all those rock falls, but the Abend lost the majority of their apprentices that day too, and the casualties in the main DeÁine army were horrendous."

He took a moment to draw breath and to let that sink in, then carried on. "I hope you can see that against such opposition, there was no way we could openly strike into this side of the mountains to try to free you folk over here. It was taking us all our time just to stop the DeÁine advancing any further after we first halted them. But after Gavra they were weaker, weaker than even we dared hope, in as much as it's now been possible for some of us to come and scout westwards.

"I had no knowledge of you men until we saw you camped by the castle, but let me tell you this, Quintillean only wanted you so that you could slow down any pursuit by the Knights which came after him. He left you there to die at the hands of the Knights and he didn't care! That's something that would *never* be allowed to happen in the rest of the Islands, and that's something that *I* would never allow to happen! Without knowing whether you all served the DeÁine by choice, I couldn't allow you across the bridge and into a position where hidden saboteurs might do damage to the castle. But equally I couldn't leave you there to be massacred by the Knights – and make no mistake, the Knights are superb soldiers to a man, and they would've wiped you out once that evil mage had left."

He paused again and let what he had said sink in while he got his breath back. Making his voice carry over an assembly of nearly three hundred men was hard going.

"So what are we doing here, you might ask?" he continued. "Well, we're heading for a bloody big palace that's south of this river we're trying to cross. We're going there because that bastard wizard who left you die in the cold and at the hands of the Knights is heading there too, we think. When he gets there he's going to kill those children in some nasty ritual that we can't even guess the details of. He's going to kill them, because he thinks that by doing that he can get control of some very important objects. Those objects are magical and they'll make him even more powerful in the Power he can wield. The objects are hidden for now, but if his ritual works – and it may well – they won't be for much longer. And if he succeeds, what you've suffered until now will pale by comparison with what the pure-bred DeÁine will become capable of inflicting.

"So my mission has two parts. The one is to rescue the children, and the other is to stop Quintillean doing his magical ritual. Sioncaet here came with me because he really is DeÁine, and I needed someone who could speak the language, but I promise you he's on our side. I say 'our' side because this affects you and every person this side of the mountains, too. You could walk away and leave me to fight on alone with Sioncaet. There are near three hundred of you and two of us, so I couldn't stop you. But if you do that, you'll be throwing away the best chance of freedom you'll have in years, if ever. If the mages of the DeÁine – those they call the Abend – win, then nobody will be safe ever again. You think things are bad now, but I make no empty threat to fool you when I say things can and will get worse."

"Worse than this?" someone called out in disbelief. "We're already starving most of the time!"

"Well you'll starve even more unless you become mindless slaves creeping around and never daring to raise your eyes, or dare to think of what you might like for yourself," Will told them. "Does that sound cruel? Does that sound unbearable? Well it is, but it's no more than the truth. If you resist alone they'll kill you, make your wives and children slaves, and bring in slaves from the other lands they conquered centuries ago to farm in your place. If anyone has any doubts, take the time to talk to Sioncaet while we march, because he's seen how the DeÁine can trample a whole race into the ground. That's why he's fighting with us. So that it doesn't happen again here.

"So I'm asking you to fight with me. We're going to get as close as possible to the palace. It's called Tokai Palace. Then we're going to do some scouting around. We don't think that there are any of the hardened DeÁine troops posted here, so the only soldiers you're likely to meet will be no better trained than you, and with little more practice either. The really nasty ones to watch for are Hunters like the ones who herded you north. The difference this time is that I can tell you ways of getting around them.

"For now though I'll tell you this. They get their incredible strength and speed from some special drugs the Abend give them, but those drugs come with a price! The Hunters burn out! Their bodies are only made the same as ours. Once upon a time, before they got taken away to the camps, they were children just like we were. There they were trained and fed the Abend's deadly potions to make them into killing machines, but none of them live even into middle age, let alone get old. Their bodies wear out and break down with the strain.

"So the trick is to run them ragged! Ten or twelve of you to one of them is not being cowardly! Keep them moving and stay out of reach. Harass them, taunt them, don't let them rest and don't let them have the time to take more of their potions! Did you ever play tag in the woods as lads?" A fair percentage of heads nodded. "Then play tag with them through the buildings or in the countryside. Run as fast as you can in short bursts and then let someone else take over when you can where there's cover. Only when they start swaying on their feet with exhaustion should you even think about getting close, and then not alone.

"Don't try to be clever. Cut the main vein in their neck, arm or leg and get away. Leave them to bleed to death, don't get close. If you can do it by firing arrows into them, then do it that way, you'll need a lot but they'll still die, and that's all you should be aiming for. Forget taking revenge on them for what they've done to you while they're breathing, you can piss on them when they're dead!"

He paused and looked around again. That bit about revenge had hit a nerve as he had hoped it would. He had been wary of hammering that overly hard in case it sounded as though he was being too manipulative. Far better to just drop the word in and wait for them to make the connection themselves. He took another deep breath and launched into his final speech.

"So that's it. It's up to you. You can sit back and do nothing, and then hope that the worst doesn't come to pass. Or you can follow me as you've been doing these past days. You've all seen enough of me in that time to have a fair idea that I can deliver what I promise. I've fought in battles since long before many of you were born, and I've been a soldier for even longer. If you've any doubts about that, think about what it was like marching north being flayed on by the Hunters, against what things have been like on this march west. I may have driven you hard, but you've had food and I've always stopped you at places where you've had firewood and water to heat up. And hopefully you've learned a thing or two on the way too. So tonight we'll make camp here, and tomorrow those of you who want to carry on will start helping me make a bridge across that river. But make no mistake, with or without you, Sioncaet and I are going on, even if we have to fight our way into that palace on our own and against overwhelming odds. *I'm* going on because for me there's no choice. I won't be a slave and I won't leave someone else to be one either."

And with that he turned his horse and rode down to where his tent had been pitched, closely followed by Sioncaet. Once they had dismounted, Sioncaet worriedly spoke up.

"I hope you know what you're doing, Will. That's a huge gamble you've taken there. What if they turn on us? We're really in a mess then!"

But Will shook his head and gave a weary smile. "Don't worry," he said, giving Sioncaet a reassuring pat on the arm as he passed him going into the tent. "These are good men and they're not stupid. Oh I'm sure a few will sneak off into the night, but not many, and what can they do? They can't cross the river and warn the men at Tokai because there's no bridge for miles and miles, and it's too cold and running too fast to be swim-able. And I'd rather we sorted out the ones with no heart for a fight before we get to it. The last thing I want is for some troublemaker to start eroding what little confidence they've got just as we're face to face with a triad of Hunters, or up against a bunch of promoted slave soldiers, all champing at the bit to prove they're as good as veterans at protecting the palace."

"I hope you're right," Sioncaet sighed despite Will's confidence, "I really hope you are."

Yet in the morning, to his amazement, Will really had been right. One or two seemed to have disappeared back the way they had come, but the vast majority got up and started with the routine of getting the camp sorted as though nothing had happened. The only difference was that there was far more talking going on. As the day wore on, and Will got the job of building a makeshift bridge underway, there were often times when someone would warily question some instruction or other. But it dawned on Sioncaet that every time Will had an answer, and a good one at that, and that every time he did that it built a bit more confidence in him to the men. The men clearly did not doubt him when he had said what would happen if the Abend won. All they were doing was checking that he really had the experience to lead them, and that they had not been duped in their earlier assessment of him.

By the time the bridge was ready on the morning of the third day, the morale of the men had risen to a new high, and it was with real enthusiasm that the little army began to cross the river. Once everyone was on the other side, Will had them disassemble the bridge again. The wood was stacked neatly, but it was the ropes and leather straps which they needed to carry onwards with them, for they had little to spare once the lashings had been made. It all took time and Sioncaet was starting to worry about that, but Will was not to be rushed.

"Many a battle's been lost by some idiot not thinking about the supplies and the basics of the job," he told Sioncaet with a wag of a finger. "If it all goes pear-shaped in a hurry, we might want to have an escape route. That bridge will go back together in a fraction of the time it took us to do all the work of cutting the wood to make it. We can make a dash for this spot, lash it up, cross the river and be leaving any pursuers fuming on the south bank unable to touch us – vital if we have many wounded to carry. If we retreat into that Sgurr Mor, I can run any DeÁine troops ragged, because I know that kind of terrain and they clearly haven't bothered learning it at all."

It was the kind of thinking which marked such a difference between Will's idea of soldiering and the DeÁine Donns for Sioncaet, and all the more of a revelation since he had never been involved with an Island army before. No Donn would give a second thought to the fate of his men if they were defeated. That was some consolation when they turned around the last inlet of the Salu Maré and saw the massed pointed roofs of Tokai gleaming bright blue in the late spring sunshine. Most of the cover in between their vantage point and the palace was little more than tall bushes, and so it was possible to see the camp of a large slave company sprawling to one side of the great gate.

By now Will had picked out several promising men to be his aides, having stripped some of the earlier sergeants of their rank and promoted more able men. He had these chosen men beside him as he lay flat on a grassy hummock covertly watching the road and the gate. The circuit of the main walls went in a great oval, as he knew from Sioncaet, but his immediate concern was the single massive gateway into the complex.

"Watch carefully," he instructed them. "Do you see any men making regular patrols? Are there too many tents for the number of men you can see? If there are, then there are likely to be men out on patrol. Good for us in one way because there'll be fewer to fight. But maybe not so good if that patrol came back unexpectedly, and joined in the fight from our rear."

One man cleared his throat nervously. "General? I think there are women and children in the camp. See over there? By that big tree? Aren't those women?"

"Well spotted!" Will praised him. "Maybe not everyone in those tents might be a fighter. …So let's hear your estimations as to how many men there are down there."

He gave them a moment to look and think, then began to ask for numbers. In general they were a little optimistic as to the numbers they might have to fight, but not dangerously so. Will then pointed out the unspotted men on the walls and some shadows under the gate. None of these were making any real attempt to watch for attacks, and Will suspected that nobody had ever told them why they should be up on the walls except for show. However, they could still raise the alarm even if they were inept at fighting. For that reason Will had decided on a night attack. It was still only springtime, and night fell early enough to give them cover of darkness without having to wait for the depths of night.

"A good spring shower is what we want," he said wishfully to Sioncaet, as they waited beyond the first ridge of higher ground. "Something to make any sentry want to huddle under his cape, and enough cloud to cover the moon and keep it properly dark."

As if by order a squally shower blew in just at dusk, and come nightfall it was as black as Will could have wished. He led his men forward at a steady walk down the slope towards the roadway, and then along the side of it amongst the scrubby bushes. There was no way he wanted to make any heroic dashes where men might fall, and where the noise of pounding feet would give them away. The men were under strict orders: get right into the camp and disable the men. Knock them out, tie them up, but only kill if absolutely necessary. Sioncaet wondered at this, until Will whispered to him that he feared that there might be some whom his men would know amongst the slaves.

"If they think they've *got* to kill and then come face to face with a neighbour from the past, how do you think they'd cope?" he posed the question to Sioncaet. "They'll falter. They'll hesitate, and no fault in them for that. They didn't sign up as volunteers for this. They're here because Quintillean gave them no other choice. But that won't stop that friend or neighbour calling out and giving us away.

"On the other hand, knowing that all they have to do is immobilise someone means our lads won't stay their hand. Like I've said before, Sioncaet, you keep the commands simple, and with lads like this you keep them to what they can reasonably hope to achieve. Nothing will give them more confidence like a bit of success." He did not add that he feared that equally, nothing would make all his work fall to bits quicker than if these men failed at their first attempt at resistance. He was not a praying man, but tonight Will was keeping his fingers crossed like rarely before.

To his great relief it all worked like a charm. The men slid into the camp like ghosts, and with only minor scuffles the camp was subdued. As his aides slipped back to report in, it transpired that the only real resistance had come from a batch of slaves from the lands to the south. Although born here, these men were from families so indoctrinated by the DeÁine that they believed everything they were told. Luckily, though, these were not the men with families with them. Those were all native Islanders, whose families had been thrown off what meagre smallholdings they might have farmed, and had no choice but to tag along in the wake of the army. For these folk the appearance of Islanders offering a way out was an offer of salvation they had never expected to see, but one which was seized with both hands. Three men actually came forward to Will and told him where the DeÁine officers and slave-masters were within the palace complex. The masters within the external camp had been amongst the southern slaves, and were already tied and gagged.

With Sioncaet leading to provide a spokesman should he be needed, Will and a handpicked group slunk up to the gate then stood up and marched in taking the guards by surprise. Anyone who did not throw down their weapons when Will ordered them to was summarily killed. For these men there could be no half measures, as from this point onwards the attack had to roll through the lower palace in one smooth wave. Nonetheless it was gratifying for Will to see that four of the eight gate guards dropped their swords without a moment's hesitation when spoken to in their own tongue. Behind him, men dragged the bodies of the other four and the two slave-masters into the guardroom, then waved additional men to follow them in.

It was surprising to Will to discover how few servants were in the outer dwellings and halls. The palace was made up of two oval compounds, one within the other. The upper one was densely packed with the elite buildings, while the lower one was almost like a miniature town. Since there were no windows or apertures of any kind in the outer wall, the lower circuit had something like a street running around it onto which the apartments and halls gave out. Sometimes it was covered by bridges linking one set of rooms on one side to ones on the other at upper levels, but mostly it was open to provide much needed ventilation and light. Big enough to accommodate several entourages, it was this maze of potential ambush points over three floors which had worried Will at the planning stage. However, Sioncaet had told him that the trusted servants travelled around with their master to provide constant service wherever they went, and that within the walls they would not be guarded. Yet having only ever travelled here with the court, even he had not anticipated how few would be left to look after such a huge sprawling place like this.

With Sioncaet having been able to draw a rough map, Will had planned to completely secure the outer circuit of rooms before moving in to deal with the inner sanctums. However, nothing had prepared him for the sight of the maze of buildings in the lower court, and he was infinitely glad that the lower circuit was not looked down upon by windows from the upper one. That would have been lethal for ambushes. A single street wound its way left and right of the gate, but not in anything like a straight line. Ahead was the solid high wall of the upper enclosure.

"The temples and the royal apartments are up there," Sioncaet said pointing up to the top of the wall.

"What's beneath the upper buildings?" Will asked, looking at the height of the wall, and estimating that the top of it must be at least another three storeys higher than the roofs of the lower buildings.

"Nothing."

"What do you mean, nothing? Surely there must be cellars or something or why else would you build it that high? You could have a whole labyrinth built into that much earth and still be higher than the roofs of this lot. This monster isn't built on any natural rocky knoll. The land by the water's as flat as a pancake."

Sioncaet sighed. "It's built like that because it's a smaller version of the Imperial Palace in Lochlainn. That *is* built on rock in the foothills of an enormous mountain range, so it's on several levels. But all the copies the Exiles build are replicas right down to the elevations."

Will looked at him as though he was mad. "You're surely not telling me that the daft buggers brought in all the earth that must be under there just to make it look right?"

"I'm afraid so."

"Barking mad, the lot of you!" Will muttered in disbelief. "What a waste of effort! The bloody thing isn't even assault proof!"

Stung to respond, even though he no longer really thought of himself as DeÁine, Sioncaet demanded, "What do you mean not even assault proof? The inner gate is on the opposite side to this one! Nobody's ever taken a DeÁine palace before"

Will rolled his eyes in exasperation. "That's probably because nobody's ever *tried* before! But take it from me, this thing would crack like a rotten nut under siege from one of our armies. Look at it! The outer wall is low enough that you can see the point where the inner elevation stops being a bank and becomes the upper compound wall. A few good trebuchets would undermine those walls from outside in no time at all! Any commander worth his salt would know that he only had to take the outer gate. After that he could do what he liked inside it.

"By the Trees! If we'd known there were three palaces this vulnerable thirty years ago, we might've made for them and avoided giving the DeÁine top-dogs luxury kennels to hide in. Oh I'll admit this is very good for imposing your mastery over a bunch of farmers who've never held a sword, but it's all show and no substance."

Sioncaet looked unconvinced, but was prevented from arguing further by one of the men bringing a huge slave up to them. The man was one of the southern slaves with skin like black velvet and a physique which dwarfed the Island men around him.

"We found him chained in a filthy cell off the gatehouse," Will's man explained. "The other slaves in the prison said he was in there for refusing to stop worshipping his own god. Nothing more. He hasn't killed anyone or done anything really bad. He was tortured and all sorts, can you believe. Just for that! They even cut out his tongue, but he wouldn't stop. What do we do with him?"

Will looked at the slave by the flickering torch-light. Even in the semi-darkness the signs of the man's suffering were clear, and he seemed severely battered about.

"Let him go," Will ordered.

"Is that wise?" Sioncaet asked.

Will looked up into the man's face. "Can you understand me? I know you can't answer in words." The man gave a tiny nod of his head. "Good. Then you have two choices. You can leave now and go where you want. I won't stop you, but in that case I can't guarantee that you won't be recaptured. …Or you can join us. I don't care who you worship as long as you don't do it in the middle of me giving orders, or put any of my men's lives in danger by doing something like drawing attention to us when we're trying to sneak up on someone. You don't kill unless I say so; you don't steal; and you don't fight any of us. You can get as drunk as a rat when I give the say so, but you work for your rations like anyone else. Sound fair to you?"

The slave gave a wary but more definite nod. Will turned back to his aide.

"In that case take him off to the others and let him show you around this place. And get him some clean clothes instead of these rags. There must be something in this oversized wardrobe of a place! …Oh, and by the way, see if one of the other slaves in here can tell you what his name is. His real one, not whatever they called him." He looked back to the slave. "I can't give you back your tongue, but if I can I'll give you back your true identity. You may be far from home but you can be yourself again."

The smile which broke over the slave's face brought a lump to Sioncaet's throat. *Such a little thing*, he thought, *and yet it means so much. We never learned that. And Will's done it again. That man will follow him through thick and thin now.* He shook his head in sorrow at the failings of his own race and refocused on Will, who was already receiving reports back that the men on lookout duty on the walls had all been subdued without raising any alarms – those who had not surrendered at the first chance, that was.

Will was ordering all his army to come within the walls, along with the newest additions, their families, and the prisoners. The poor souls who had been persecuted by the DeÁine highborn, and then forgotten, were released from their gloomy incarceration to make way for the newer prisoners – although Will's men at least had the decency to sweep out the rotten dregs of straw and put new in, before slamming the doors on their enemies. So by the time Will came to do head counts, he found he had gained another hundred men willing to fight, plus several dozen who were in no fit state to go far but were willing to help in any way they could. Many of the wives were already making habitable quarters out of the nearest rooms, and somewhere Will could detect cooking smells beginning to waft through the place.

The basics sorted, Will now turned his attention to the inner part of the complex. As Sioncaet led him through the twisting turning street to the opposite side, Will gazed about him with an expression of disbelief even in the dim light of hurriedly lit torches.

"Your folk aren't people," he finally declared to Sioncaet. "They're human sized rabbits! This is a warren not a palace!"

"Oh come on," Sioncaet remonstrated. "Some of your towns aren't much better! Look at Cabrack. It's hardly what I'd expected as the capital of Celidon. A muddle of houses thrown together and only one decent straight paved street."

Will threw his hands up to gesture at the frontages around him. "But this was planned like this! Cabrack's different. There's only so much land between the mountains and the sea, and folk have gradually used what space they can out of necessity, not choice. This? Someone with the brain of a squirrel actually thought this was a good idea! And others who must've been even dafter built the bloody thing! Brick by precise brick, if what you said is true about it being an exact copy. Why in the Islands would you *want* a place to be like this?"

Sioncaet relented and had to laugh at Will's bemusement. "Oh it's precise all right." Then a mischievous grin appeared on his face. "In fact, you should know that Ralja and Kuzmin are exactly like it."

Will stopped in his tracks. "*Three? Exactly?* You are joking!"

"Not a bit of it. All three palaces were built to the same plan. Same layout, same size, same elevations, …same everything. The only difference is that the Imperial palace is exactly five times the dimensions in every direction! It's all about showing reverence for the Emperor. Imitation is the best form of flattery. And if you went to Sinut you'd find more exactly the same at our town of Carta, and continue to travel eastwards to Elin and there are more. Every odd-shaped room, every column, every bit of garden all recreated to the closest possible detail, …all the same in every respect, just smaller than the original."

Will shook his head in despair. "What a waste of effort. Barking mad! The lot of them!"

They had reached the opposite side of the inner oval to the outer gate to find several of Will's men holding four muscular slaves captive. The four were, according to Sioncaet again, there to keep the unclean of the lower level from going into the inner sanctum except in their roles as the most menial of servants. Apparently the servants who attended the priests were a whole separate section, of far higher station, and who never descended to the lower level unless it was to accompany one of their masters.

"If I were you," Sioncaet told Will, "I wouldn't try to go into the upper level in the dark. If you think the lower level is confusing, the upper one is a nightmare. There are suites of rooms which can only be accessed by one door, but which look out through stone lattices onto courtyards or corridors. You don't want a dagger in the dark to get you or one of the men, and be unable to chase the attacker because you have three more rooms to get through before you can even get to where they were."

That seemed like good advice, and so with the men suitably quartered and sentries posted, Will had the main gate shut and barred and settled down for the rest of the night. With the new dawn he led a party of the steadier men up the twin flights of stone steps to the upper level. A hundred of the original army stayed below with the new additions, with stern instructions to begin proper patrols along the walls and to search for hidden weapons. Not that Will expected to find any, but he needed something to keep the less-able soldiers occupied and feeling useful. One hundred men each for himself and Sioncaet to command – without decent men to delegate to – was going to be extremely hard work, and far from the way things Will would have wished when it came to searching a hostile encampment. When they emerged onto a high open terrace they received their first surprise, although not the sort they would ever have expected. In front of them was not a bunch of armed men but a peaceful garden, and Will gave a chuckle. Now it was Sioncaet's turn to be confused.

"Whatever is there here to laugh at?" he asked, perplexed, as were the men.

Will pointed to the green sward ahead of them. It was nothing like any garden in the Islands would be. A perfect circle of clipped grass surrounded a central pool, with four rills as wheel-spokes coming off it to four smaller pools. The rest of the court was paved in stone, but around the walls of the buildings were a multitude of pots with plants growing in them. At the edge of the grass circle four trees had been planted marking each quarter.

"Trees!" Will said still chuckling as if no other explanation were needed, but Sioncaet and the others still looked blank.

"I can see they're trees," Sioncaet said patiently. "What's so odd about having trees in a garden. Even in the Islands you have those!"

Will sighed and rolled his eyes. "For all the years you've lived with us, Sioncaet, haven't you learned to identify our plants better than that? Yes, they're trees, but they're not just any old trees, are they? They're Trees! *The* Trees!"

Understanding suddenly dawned for Sioncaet and he gasped. There in the heart of a DeÁine palace were four of the Sacred Trees of the Islands.

Very carefully tended and trimmed so that they bore little resemblance to their wild cousins, to be sure, but there stood an oak, a birch, a yew and an ash. The yew was to their left, neatly formed into a tight column of green but right in front of the temple. On the far, eastern side stood a clipped birch, its weeping branches delicately swaying in the breeze. Opposite the yew on their right stood a severely trimmed ash, but it was smack in front of the main door to the royal residence within the palace, and an equally constrained oak was immediately in front of them on the western side.

"And you thought that there was no more fight in this part of Brychan," Will chuckled. "There's proof of ongoing resistance right in front of you!"

"So long I've waited to hear someone speak like that," a voice as crackly as autumn leaves came from the side. A little old man came from out of a side garden, his gait stiff from years of working out of doors, with skin as brown as a nut and wrinkled by the weather. "So clever they thought they were. 'There should be trees!' they told me, all high and mighty. 'Plant trees!' So I did. The ones they gave me died. No good in these cold parts. So I go and get others. They didn't know any difference. Our only sacred Tree they recognise is the Rowan. I didn't dare plant one of those, but the others were easy. And every day I prayed as I tended them that one day things would change."

"What's your name, grandpa?" Will asked gently. "You must have been here a long time." The trees were no young saplings yet this man had planted them.

The battered hat dipped and came up again. "Must be over thirty years now."

"By the Trees, before Moytirra!" Will was appalled. "That's a long time to keep the faith."

The hat dipped again. "Aye, that it is, but I never doubted, not old Obad… No, …not that name now. Not that name ever again." He straightened his bent back with a slight grunt to look up at Will with a smile. "I was Sam before, …I'm Sam again now."

Will turned to his men and detailed ten of them off. "You guard old Sam here come what may!" he ordered them. "And listen to what he says – you'll learn a thing or two! Get him to take you around those gardens and look for any vantage points we can use, and any hidden doors!"

"Palace is empty," Sam volunteered, "but them priests is all of a twitter! Another babe born to one of the acolytes who that nasty big bald brute took to his bed. Head priest isn't pleased, no he isn't, but he can't stand up to that one alone."

"The Abend?" Sioncaet guessed. "One of the Abend was here?"

"Here a long time," Sam confirmed. "Months and months."

"Anarawd?" wondered Will, lifting a quizzical eyebrow to Sioncaet, but Sam answered before him.

"That be the one. Up to something, he is, but he's gone now."

"Thank the Trees for that!" Will breathed. "No new ones arrived? Like Quintillean?"

But Sam shook his head, and Will and Sioncaet allowed themselves a little optimism that they might just have stolen a march on the head of the Abend, to be one jump ahead of him for once.

"Right lads, let's start clearing out this stone warren!" Will commanded. "Work in teams of four. Don't split up. Don't let yourselves get separated. Take it steady and be thorough. Make sure each room is truly clear before you go on to the next one. Check under tables, behind doors, under beds and in cupboards. I don't want any of you getting a knife in the back! I know Sam said the palace is empty, but let's check that first."

With Sioncaet directing men across the court, past the birch tree, to where three columns supported arches to a gazebo, and around behind it to a back door into the nobility's suites, Will took the larger half of the men through the palace's front doors. The huge double doors gave into an outer hall as big as many Island manor houses' great hall. But beyond it was the biggest domed space Will had ever laid eyes on. They had seen the dome from far off, but it never occurred to any of them that it might cover a single room. Tiny pieces of stone, enamel and glass had been worked to make mosaics over every inch of its surface. Coming in through the vast double doors of beaten copper, Will and the lead men realised that there was an inner circle of stone arches. The men fanned out left and right until Will could see that they had reached the point opposite him. He gestured for the men to look upwards, for he could see that the arches supported some kind of balcony – a balcony which would provide an ideal firing platform for anyone defending the place to start taking out his men. However all he was greeted with was shaking heads.

Taking a deep breath he stepped out into the main space and was staggered by the size of it. If anything this mighty hall was taller than it was wide, and it was wider than any room Will had ever heard of. If the Imperial Palace was five times this size it was a vast place indeed.

Somewhere there must have been many series of tiny windows, too small to have been spotted from the outside but enough to let light in, for the early sun was bouncing off the mirrored tessera to light the space. There seemed to be two more doors leading out of the ceremonial room, and Will led some men to the right hand one, sending others to the left. From what Sioncaet had said the left-hand door led only to seven rooms and the servant's stairs, whereas the right one not only served another eleven on this floor but also the main staircase. He was much relieved that nobody was showing signs of a spirited defence, since given the way sets of rooms were accessed by only one door at a time, any defender could have held the first door then fallen back to the next, and so on. To have to take a place of this size room by room could have proven very costly in lives.

Once it was clear the ground floor was clear, Will left a contingent to watch the doors and tramped upstairs. He had expected the balcony to run off the first floor rooms yet they did nothing of the sort. Where the rooms came up against the domed room there were just blank walls. Curiosity piqued by the odd layout, Will left most of the men checking the apartments and went up to the top floor. Suddenly he was in a very different space. Below it had all been massive and imposing, but now he was in rooms with sumptuous hangings and soft furnishings instead of polished hard woods and leather seats. At which point the purpose of the balcony became clear – it was for the women of the court.

Away from the main stairs and the one for the servants, there were two short sets of steps which led down to the balcony where seats were arranged a little back from the edge. It took no effort for Will to imagine the ladies of the court sitting and having their own discussions up here while the business of ruling went on below. Separate, they were still close enough to be able to hear what was going on if they wished to. Abandoned on a distant cushion Will spotted an embroidered glove, which some poor servant had no doubt got into trouble over the loss of. When he picked it up the scent of its former owner still clung to it, musky and exotic.

Yet there was little to detain any of them here. Back at ground level he found three of the men carrying out the body of a servant.

"Caretaker," one of the men said laconically. "Whatever possessed him to try to take all of us is beyond me, but he came screaming out of a tiny cupboard of a room under the servants' stairs waving an axe."

It struck Will that up in the balcony he had not heard even a hint that a fight was going on, however brief. He made a mental note to bear that in mind if he had to fight in one of the other palaces. Men could be screaming for help from reinforcements and never be heard. He must make sure someone was in line of sight of other groups at all times. For now though all was quiet, and when Sioncaet rejoined him in the garden it was to report that although they had met with around a dozen servants, who had defended their masters' possessions with fanatical but somewhat pointless aggression, they were now subdued or dead.

"Is it odd that this place is so quiet?" Will asked him.

"A bit," admitted Sioncaet, "but it might be nothing more than the fact that we're approaching some of the big religious festivals. These spring ones tend to get celebrated in Bruighean, whereas the end of year ones in the autumn are all held here. We got lucky. Had we come here in six months time, we would've been fighting our way into every room, and the place would be packed with servants who would've thrown themselves onto our swords even if they didn't know how to use one themselves."

Will snorted and shook his head at what he saw as such total folly.

"That's going to be the nasty one," Sioncaet continued pointing to the twin sets of doors into the temple. "That's always fully manned and the priests and priestesses aren't just dumb servants acting out orders because they don't know better." He lifted his voice and addressed the men. "Be careful when you go in there! The people inside will be pure-bred DeÁine, or very near. They'll be stronger than you because of that. Not as strong as the Hunters or the Abend, but don't take chances. And they know this place like the back of their hands. It's a maze in there, and unlike the palace with its central space, those two upper floors are full of rooms used by priests, and the first floor has a different layout to the second. Never, ever go into a room alone, and if a room's locked don't force it – there're some nasty things supposed to be hidden away in there that even I don't know about, but they're supposed to be to do with the Power. So be very, very careful!"

"Right, then. Let's tackle the vipers' nest!" Will called out. "Remember, lads, these might be priests but they're dangerous! And no being nice to the ladies! This lot are as dangerous as the men!"

He waved the main body of men with Sioncaet to the two sets of doors into the main temple. With a third of the men, Will headed back to the gazebo and turned left this time. Four men disappeared into a small suite of two rooms ahead but quickly reported them empty, which left the door immediately on Will's left. That led nowhere either.

"How do you get into this confounded place?" Will growled in frustration.

Between the two rooms was one of the lattices Sioncaet had spoken of. It looked like a master weaver had made the design for a stone mason to copy, loops and curls of stone making small openings, some of which a hand might pass through but little more. Through it they could see another suite of rooms lit by lamps rather than windows, but clearly they must be got at through the temple, for there was no way in from outside.

Marching his men back outside and around into the temple by the next door, Will kept them by its right-hand wall, briefly gesturing in acknowledgement to Sioncaet, who was stood in the centre by a shrine, already directing men through a multitude of the most intricately carved columns any of them had ever seen. The columns supported seemingly endless arches of patterned stone, so tightly packed that the vaults of the arches became the ceiling. It was like a forest of green, gold, black and white marble – mesmerising and disorientating.

"No-one here either," Sioncaet reported moments later as he and the men converged on Will at a small door in the west wall. "The quarters are through there, although that's one part of the palaces I've never been in."

"First time for everything, then!" Will responded cheerfully. He reached out and tried the door latch but it was locked. "*Humph*!" Will waved the men behind him out of the way, went back a few paces, then charged the door like a bull. His broad shoulder hit it with a thump and it flew open, unused to such treatment. Before Will could collect himself a young woman ran at him. Expecting an attack Will brought his arms up to defend himself only to find himself clutching a small child.

"Flaming Underworlds!" he gulped, totally thrown, and shoved the child back towards her.

She pushed the child back at him and rattled off a string of words.

"She says she wants you to take him," Sioncaet translated. "It's yours!"

Chapter 4

Unlooked-for Friends

New Lochlainn: late Spring-moon – early Earrach

Will stared at Sioncaet in horror, then back to the baby the young woman was thrusting at him once more.

"Mine? Mine! You've got to be joking!" he spluttered. "I know I've dipped my wick a bit, but I've never come west of the mountains before! I may not remember the *names* of all the women I've bedded, but I do remember their faces and I've never seen this one before." He looked her up and down even as he took another step back to avoid the baby again. "She's not my type, but for a skinny little wench she's pretty. Not the sort you'd forget in a hurry."

However Sioncaet was already engaged in another rapid exchange with the young woman and held up his hand to halt Will's panicked words. "Ah! ...Now I understand! It's alright, Will, she's not implying that you're the father – although if I may say so, you were a bit quick on the defence there. Had much experience of that kind of accusation?" he asked innocently, but with a knowing wink to the men around them, who promptly guffawed at Will's embarrassment.

"A bit," Will admitted sheepishly.

Sioncaet grinned, then stepped between him and the woman, gently pushing the baby back into her arms and drawing her forward into the midst of the men. Her eyes flickered all over the place, as if she was expecting them to jump on her and was trying to watch all of them at once. Whatever Sioncaet said to her, it slowly appeared to reassure her that she was not about to be raped on the spot, then he spoke up to inform the men,

"This is Rahana. What she just told me was that Anarawd had some kind of surgery here last year using the Power. Whatever it was, against all odds it's made Anarawd fertile again. Since then he's taken to raping the younger priestess of mixed blood, but not solely for his perverted pleasure. Rahana says that he intends to use these children he's fathered as sacrifices in some kind of ritual. That's why she wanted Will to take her son. She wanted us to take him away so that he'd be safe."

Suddenly Will was very different. "Poor little chap," he said gruffly and gently lifted up the gurgling child in his two massive scarred hands to look into its face. "Another innocent victim. What is it with the Abend that they're fixated on slaughtering little kiddies? Fucking perverts!" The baby giggled and smiled, kicking its feet in the air as it dangled secure in Will's strong grasp. "How could anyone harm you?"

"I think he likes you," Sioncaet teased, expecting Will to shy away again.

Will did nothing of the sort, carefully handing the child back to its mother and putting a protective arm around her and guiding her towards a couple of the older men.

"Look after her. Take them both outside to that garden gazebo and wait there. Treat her with respect but keep your wits about you. Get two of the lads we left outside to stand close to you. There's always the chance, grim though it might sound, that she might be using her child as a ruse." He eyed her skimpy clothing. "It doesn't look like there's anywhere to conceal anything, but don't turn your backs in case she has a knife hidden somewhere. Get someone to find her a cloak, though, she'll freeze out there in that bit of flimsy stuff."

As the men led Rahana away, Will and Sioncaet hurriedly conferred.

"So Anarawd was here and scheming while the others were away," mused Sioncaet. "Taise was right. He had his own agenda. No wonder the head priest was angry. The priestesses are supposed to remain pure in every way. Their celibacy should preclude sex with everyone, including the Abend not just the lower orders."

"That won't necessarily mean that the priests will welcome us with open arms, though, will it?"

"Oh, Spirits forefend, no! They'll see us as the great unwashed desecrating the holy ground. However much they might rail at the way the Abend use them, they are at least of the pure race. All differences between them will be forgotten for the time it takes to rid themselves of us."

Will muttered something darkly under his breath then waved the men forward. Using the hand signals he had taught them, he directed them down the passage in front of them to check the doors leading off it, all in silence. All that could be heard was the tread of their boots, and even then they were attempting to move as quietly as possible. Through a door immediately to their left, Sioncaet discovered a stair to the upper floors, although Will would not allow him to take the lead going up.

"You're too valuable for us to lose," he told his friend in a tone which brooked no argument. "Ordinary soldiers are one thing, but who knows what's up there! Stay behind me at all times!"

With that Will set off, hugging the wall and leaving the centre clear, indicating to the men to do the same. His caution paid off. With a maniacal shriek, a white-robed figure appeared out of the gloom at the top of the stairs and hurtled down at them, screaming and brandishing a pair of wickedly curved swords. The attacker had expected the men to be in the centre of the stairs, was fooled by their stance at the side, and all Will did was stick out his foot to trip the figure. It lost its footing, flew outwards and dived to the bottom to land with a sickening crunch. For good measure one of the men plunged his sword into its back, but the body never even twitched. Someone beyond the door reached in to grab it by the collar-folds of the swathing robes, and hauled it out of the way into the temple.

The men made as if to move on, but Will was holding up a hand to pause them. As he did so another figure appeared followed by another. Will ducked down, lunged upwards with his blade and took the front figure in the gut. As it folded over, its fellow attacker tried to halt its own headlong dash to avoid falling over it. A luxury which Will never allowed. Loosing his sword still impaled in the first, he sprang up and with both hands seized the front of the second's robes, hauling him forwards and straight over the top of the falling first. In a screaming tangle the two fell to be dispatched by the men at the bottom again.

Will held out his hand and someone passed him a sword, and in similar fashion got rid of two more attackers in less than a minute. When the sixth and seventh robed madmen appeared, he gestured to the nearest men to take over, rolling his eyes at Sioncaet down below with an expression of contempt on his face. Clearly he was not impressed by their lack of originality.

As the third pair fell Will held up his hand again, gestured, then held up three fingers and mouthed as he dropped them, "three, …two, …one, …go!"

He took off like a scalded cat, taking the last few steps two at a time with his men streaming after him. Skidding round the turn at the top of the stairs, he barrelled into someone coming at him, used his sword guard like a knuckle-duster to smash into their teeth, then shoved past them leaving the killing to the man behind. Now the fighting got bloody. In the close confines of the claustrophobic rooms it was knife work, lacking the room to swing swords. Sioncaet managed to edge closer to Will, then was torn between disgust at the way Will so casually handed out violence, and admiration for the way everything was done with such economy of movement. Never wasting energy, Will made every blow count, and if he could side-step someone for the men behind him to deal with, he did.

What shocked Sioncaet was the way that Will fought dirty. His own experience of fighting had been first with the elegant forms of the DeÁine style of swordplay, and then with the restrained but effective style of Knights such as Labhran and Maelbrigt when undercover. But that had inevitably been acts of self-defence and assassination. At Gavra he had come upon the fighting late, and so had assumed that desperation and battle weariness had created some of the more brutal encounters he had seen.

Somehow it had never occurred to him that the rough bar brawling he had seen in the odd tavern could be a style all of its own. Now though he was watching it elevated to an art form in Will, and it was proving singularly effective. Many a priest clutching their groin, eye or broken nose, blindly reeled in the wake of the muscular general as he ploughed onwards, only for them to be skewered by those following him whilst they were distracted.

They cleared a long suite of rooms heading back above the temple in this way, and a runner came to Will proclaiming that the rooms to the right of the stair were also now subdued, if rather bloodied. For a second there was another lull, but before anyone could draw breath, five more murderous priests appeared waving what looked like glowing orbs in their hands. Even as Sioncaet screamed, "Power!" Will dived forward and pulled the solid oak door ahead shut and stabbed his dagger into the latch to hold it. A second later there was a massive thump on the door followed by four more, and for an instant the wood almost seemed to glow. Everyone leapt back, weapons in hand, expecting the door to shatter – but it held.

"Good Island oak," Will said smugly, "can't beat it!"

He spotted several heavy oak chests in the rooms back the way they had come, and ordered the men to drag them in and stack them in front of the door. With several layers of oak reinforcing the door it seemed well protected.

"They might have another way out," he declared to Sioncaet and the men, "but at least they won't be coming up on our backs. Two of you stay on watch in this room, and two more in the room beyond but out of direct line, just in case they do break through with some witchy thing. If we had a decent Forester with us, I've no doubt he could mutter some incantation over that oak and increase its protective powers, but as we don't we'll just have to trust to the wood."

Since Sioncaet could provide no clue as to whether there were other ways into the suite they had just sealed off, Will turned his attention to the rooms in the other direction, which turned out to be more sumptuous and looking down over an enclosed garden. This too must have been in the aged Sam's tender care, for drooping artistically over a long thin pool was a weeping silver birch, while three neatly clipped yews stood like sentinels at the doors into the temple at ground floor level. The first six rooms all ran in a line along the garden frontage and were deserted. However, the door to the seventh was closed, and when approached stealthily it was reported that there were sounds of movement within.

Will got everyone way back out of direct line of the door, flattening them against the walls of the adjoining rooms. With the speed of a striking snake, he flipped the latch and used a sword point to push it open, even as he turned and dived flat away from it. As he hit the floor, a bolt of Power flamed through the doorway ripping holes in the ones further along as it expanded, coming to a halt when it hit the end stone wall with a terrific explosion which took most of the wall with it, and showered the stairwell beyond with rubble. Without waiting for any more, Will was up in a crouch then dived through the door, rolling and coming to his feet with his dagger at a priestess' throat even as he spun her so that she was between him and the rest of the room. As men poured into the room, Will realised that the women were standing were surrounding a bed. A bed with rather a lot of blood on it, and a weak and distraught young woman in it.

"Stay your blades!" Will roared.

"Hold your Power!" Sioncaet echoed him in DeÁine, shouldering his way to the front. "These men will not harm you if you don't attack them!"

"So you say!" a heavily pregnant young woman snarled and lifted her hand.

Will felt the tingling in the air, shoved his captive to another man and floored the pregnant woman with a single punch to the jaw, catching her as she fell and lowering her gently to the floor. The women all screamed, then looked startled at the way that Will had broken her fall so that she did no damage to her child. Whatever they had been told about Islander armies, it certainly had not prepared them for that.

"As I said, they won't harm you," Sioncaet repeated firmly. "What's happened here?"

A fragile white-blonde, looking far from well herself and clutching a sickly-looking child, came forward.

"Amaranth gave birth this morning. We can't seem to stop her bleeding." She suddenly broke down in sobs. "She's going to die!"

Again Sioncaet did not expect Will's decisiveness when he translated this back to him. Without missing a beat Will turned and barked to the men behind,

"Any shepherds amongst you? …Anyone used to delivering difficult births?"

There was a shuffling and the sound of feet, and then two men appeared at the door. The older one knuckled his forehead and introduced himself as Clem, a stockman from the Assynt Highlands, the younger as Orly, whose father had been the physician in the town of Paks in the far south before the invasion, and who still practised covertly.

"See if you can help her," Will ordered them and got Sioncaet to translate.

The woman began wailing again at what they seemed to see as a violation of their friend, but Will brooked no argument, and the others were firmly dragged back from the bed into the previous room – this time with their arms securely pinned to their sides to avoid any directing of the Power. Will went with them, getting Sioncaet to explain to them that he could feel it when they started to draw the Power, and that if he felt so much as the hairs on his arms start to tickle he would have all their throats cut, although not the babies, of which it turned out there were three.

The argumentative woman whom Will had floored was called Tabith, and the oldest child belonged to her; a robust toddler who to her utter disgust took an immediate shine to Will. The ill-looking one was the frail blonde Seline's own child, while another woman cradled a tiny new-born baby whose mother had died only a week ago. Now Amaranth's baby had been stillborn, and they had been hoping that if she lived, Amaranth would consent to look after the orphaned infant. However, these priestesses seemed clue-less over caring for such a small child, and it was already sickening. As its carer tried to pour something into its throat from a small jug, one of the men dashed forward and snatched the child out of her arms.

"Sacred Trees, woman! Not like that! You'll choke the poor little bugger!" Then tutted in disgust as he realised what they were trying to feed the baby on. "Great Maker, it's a wonder the babe's made it this far! Freezing cold cream, I ask you!" He turned to Will. "Beg pardon, General, but one of the Islander women had a nanny goat she brought in with her. If you'll let me, I'll take this little 'un down and get it some warm milk, and give it to some who's brought up kids before. Not some frigid, sour-faced crone!"

Will waved him on, and made Sioncaet translate his stinging rebuke to the priestess word for word. At that Clem came out looking shaken and pale.

"You'd best come in and see this, sire," he told Will, "and those women had better see too. If you wouldn't mind translating, Mister Sioncaet?"

They all filed back into the room until one of the priestesses saw what lay on the sheets and started screaming. Even Will felt his stomach lurch as he stared at the monstrosity.

"This was a second foetus," Orly explained, wiping his bloody hands on a cloth and gesturing to a matted, twisted bundle of skin, hair and teeth. "The afterbirth got stuck with it. She was in such a bad way because her body was still trying to give birth to that thing." He took several ragged breaths. "I've never seen the like, sire. It's like something from the Underworld!"

The women were all stunned, and the men who could see it were swearing or praying as their inclination took them. It truly was the grossest thing any of them had ever seen. With wiry black hair sprouting from everywhere, it was impossible to tell whether it was curled into a foetal ball or actually shaped like that. There seemed to be no limbs, but a wicked slash of a mouth revealed two rows of small but razor-sharp needle teeth which already looked half rotten. No head, no eyes, no indication that it bore any kinship to a human being.

"The Power," Sioncaet said softly. "Anarawd must have used the Power when he was with her. When he fathered them both. If you opened up the one which was stillborn I'm afraid you'd find its organs would be deformed or missing. It had only the outer show of being a proper babe. This one's only worse in having the outer form as well." When he translated this, for the first time they saw the abrasive Tabith wilt. She stared down at her swollen belly with horror, and no translation was needed to know what had happened and what she now feared.

"Did he use the Power when he was with you the first time?" Sioncaet demanded, indicating her healthy, normal son who was once again gazing up at Will while holding on to his jerkin's hem, and getting his hair absent-mindedly ruffled. She shook her head. "But he did this time?" She nodded and her eyes filled with tears, then broke down in heaving sobs.

"Can you get rid of her child for her?" Will asked Orly very softly. "Not now, of course, but later when we've got more time."

The young trainee physician looked a touch faint at the prospect, but having taken another glance at the gross, solid ball, the sharp teeth, and the jutting pieces of thin and lethally sharp bone, he nodded. "I think so. I'd appreciate the chance to talk to some of the women down below first, though. There might be village wise women amongst them who'll know more than me. But yes, with the right herbs, I think so."

"Will she live?" was Will's next question nodding to the unconscious woman on the bed.

Orly shrugged. "I don't know. Most of the blood wasn't hers, so that's good. On the other hand she's utterly spent, and she doesn't look as though she was particularly strong to start off with. Carrying that thing and its twin must have taken it out of her, even being a DeÁine, especially in the last few months. All I can say is that she now has a chance."

"Then you stay here, and while you're at it, have a look at that Seline girl. She hardly seems any better." He turned to the other women and nodded to Sioncaet to start translating again. "I want to know the plan of this place. We've saved the life of your friend. And if you help us now we'll do what we can for Tabith and Seline."

The three oldest priestesses curled their lips in disdain and said nothing, but a strange-looking girl with white hair but dusky skin, proclaiming some slave ancestor, stepped forward. Will knew she was saying "I'll show you," even before Sioncaet opened his mouth, but he never got to hear the words. As the girl stepped forward he felt a tingling on his left side, and spun round to see the oldest priestess' eyes swirl faintly. With great speed for such a bulky man, Will pivoted and struck with his knife, driving it hilt-deep through one of her eyes even as a glow formed around her. There was a bang like a thunder clap had gone off in the confines of the room, Will letting go of the knife handle with a yelp, as a blast knocked them all from their feet. The priestess burst into puss green flames, spontaneous combustion ripping her asunder from the inside outwards, her skin blackening in seconds.

Thinking that the flames would spread, all the men leapt backwards, two hauling Will back with them as he clutched his burned hand. The other two older priestesses moved the other way, pouncing on their colleague and beginning to glow in their own right, but the men were ready now. A thickset man hefted his sword like a spear and launched it, taking one through the middle while five knives found their mark in her, and more knives took down the other woman before she could fully form the orb of Power which began to glow about her. A second explosive wave rocked the rooms and blew out the frames of the already shattered windows. The nearest men got some nasty singeing, but when the acrid smoke from the sulphurous flames cleared none of their own had died.

"Throw those bodies out of the window," Sioncaet croaked, "and use your gloves! Don't touch them!"

Then the women began crying in earnest. For a second it was not clear why but then someone lifted up the blackened, burned body of Tabith's little boy. He had tried to get to Will and been indiscriminately cut down by the blast of Power. As Tabith howled her grief, it seemed to finally bring it home to the priestesses just what Anarawd had been proposing to do with these children. The white-haired one whose simple act of defiance had precipitated the dreadful slaughter, came and touched Will on his good arm and gave a simple bow.

Cradling his painful hand, Will gestured the men to fall in behind their new guide, Neena, and followed her himself a few back from the front. Archers now formed the front ranks with bows nocked and at the ready. Many priests died stuck like hedgehogs with arrows, which then had to be cut out for reuse, slowing their progress down. However, by the time the sun had reached its zenith the first floor was theirs. The floors of many rooms ran with the blood of priests but were safe. Will had found an indoor pool of blissfully cold water and remained there with his hand immersed in it, until Sioncaet came back with a priest by the scruff of the neck clutching a small orb-like device. Whatever he was snarling to the priest was putting the fear of the Underworld into him, because when Sioncaet told Will that the priest was going to heal him, the man was practically on his knees nodding pitifully.

With Sioncaet holding Will's arm out to expose the hand, the priest began to draw in the Power and the orb glowed. Will's other hand came up and the point of his dagger touched the priest's throat, drawing the faintest pinprick of blood and making him swallow convulsively. With a shaking hand the priest held the glowing orb over Will's hand and slowly the angry blistering began to subside. The priest seemed bothered by the way that Will's lips drew back over his teeth in a snarl of pain as he began and got worse – this clearly was not supposed to happen. So as soon as the worst of the damaged was repaired, Sioncaet told him to stop just as Will was doing the same.

"Any pain now?" Sioncaet interrogated Will. "Any funny tingling? Numbness where there shouldn't be? Too much feeling?"

Will flexed his fingers experimentally. "Still hurts, but only like I'd brushed against an oven or something. It's like a normal light burn. I tell you what, though, Sioncaet, I think the exposure to the Helm left a taint. I felt so sick when he used that thing I thought I was going to throw up over him, and I felt …still feel …shaky. Dithery, not like shock or cold. The only time I've ever felt like that was when I had some bad mussels one time. Sacred Root and Branch, that was bad. I puked, shivered and sweated for a whole day and night, and I came out in the most amazing rash when the hallucinations subsided."

"You are a bit flushed," admitted Sioncaet. "Maybe you're somehow allergic to the lesser pieces now? We must ask Taise if we ever get the chance."

"Well for now we're going to leave a substantial guard at the two doors to the second floor stairs, and send the rest of the lads down for food and a break. Great Maker I could use a goblet of wine," Will said with feeling. "What a morning!"

"Don't you want to press on?" Sioncaet wondered.

"No. These aren't experienced troops. Let them catch their breath and realise what they've achieved. That last floor is going to be wicked."

"Yes it is. Neena said something about there being a Power-filled room up there."

Will groaned. "Bloody marvellous! Just what we want. Not only mad men chucking the stuff about like lightning bolts, we have to have a room with a mind of its own! Oh joy!"

As it turned out Will's idea of a break was substantially shorter than Sioncaet had envisaged. As soon as food had been brought up from some lower store rooms and the first batch of men fed, they went to relieve the guards. While this went on, Will and Sioncaet went down to look at the temple garden. They found a side cloistered area, with a pretty circular pool and seats around the wall.

"I know we can't move that poor girl Amaranth," Will said, gratefully subsiding onto a cushion and taking a pull from the wine flask someone had brought him. "But I think we should bring the others down here. It's out of the main building, and if those priests up above start chucking lightning bolts about, who knows what damage they might do? How many of them do you think Anarawd raped?"

Sioncaet sighed and took his turn at the flask. "Who knows? ...Possibly all of them. He might've found a way to reverse his infertility, but he couldn't guarantee theirs, could he?"

"Even those old crones who tried to fry me? Sacred Root and Branch, he must have a cock of steel now if he could get it up for them! One look from those eyes would freeze your nads!"

"Well probably not them," chuckled Sioncaet, reassured that Will was still his earthy self after encountering so much Power – after all, this was the man who had been going slightly mad after his exposure to the Helm only months ago. "They were a bit old to carry a child even for DeÁine. Probably there to make sure that the young ones didn't get a taste for men and start corrupting the younger priests. They wouldn't have been able to stop Anarawd. Not with his ability in the Power, anyway. But they could stop their own from copying him."

"Stop them? They'd kill any man's ardour at fifty paces!"

Having gratefully gnawed their way through some hard bread and cheese, washed down by the wine, Will felt a lot more like himself again, and ordered the women brought down. With Neena remaining as their guide, there were still fourteen women clustered in the little cloister. Tabith was in a terrible state. So much so that it occurred to Will that she might miscarry, and with that in mind he ordered Orly to come down and stay with them, leaving Clem to watch over Amaranth, for whom they could do nothing more.

As Will and Sioncaet trudged back upstairs, negotiating fallen plaster and rubble as they stepped through the blast holes, Sioncaet realised how tired Will was starting to look. Not just a bit short of sleep but bone-weary, and decided he had to put his foot down or there would be nothing left of his friend.

"We should rest after we've secured this place. All we can do is wait for Quintillean to turn up now, and you need a rest. You haven't stopped since we took this lot on at Borth. There's only so hard you can drive yourself, Will."

"I know," Will groaned, stretching to un-kink his weary muscles rather than arguing – in itself a sign of how worn-out he felt. "By the Maker, I'm not getting any younger!"

They reached the men and made their way to the front where Neena waited for them. With great care they ascended the stairs and went into the first room. Neena assured them that there was no sign of the Power being used just yet, but in a large hall-like room there was a short but bloody battle with more of the fanatical priests. For the first time Will's men suffered serious casualties loosing twenty men, although the DeÁine's losses were higher. It hit Will's men hard since it was the first time any of them had seen any of their own cut down in a fight, and everyone was in a sombre mood as they gingerly moved on to the next suite of rooms. On Will's instructions Neena was taking them through the lesser rooms first. He wanted the priests to throw men away over rooms of no consequence, rather than going straight for the Power-filled room and find themselves confronting many priests all channelling its warped energy.

As they came back to the garden side once more, they found a room where a young priest was hurriedly trying to burn papers. He was swiftly dissuaded, and when questioned revealed that this was the message room, with its bird coops beyond on a balcony overlooking the garden. There was no time at present to deal with the room's contents, but Will set a strong guard on it, vowing to spend some time there later with Sioncaet to read the stuff for him.

In the centre of the floor, directly above the temple's shrine they finally came to the Power-filled room. Will would have guessed something was wrong over a room away. Each time they had come near it in adjoining rooms he felt queasy, even though there was no direct access. Now he was practically retching, and was leaning heavily on two men as they stood outside its door.

"I don't think I'm going to be able to go in," he told Sioncaet. "You're going to have to do this one alone. If I come I'm only going to be a liability."

Sioncaet felt far from confident at taking Will's place. This was hardly the sort of thing he excelled at, but equally he could see that Will was saying nothing but the truth. Their best fighter could barely stand unaided this close to the room. Gritting his teeth, Sioncaet therefore squared his shoulders, put on his most confident expression and stepped up to the door.

Before his hand touched the latch, the air swirled unnaturally and his vision seemed to swim, but it was too late to stop. He had flipped the latch before he could stop himself and the door swung open. Yet Sioncaet was not the first through the door. Out of nowhere a huge wild cat appeared and bounded through ahead of him. With an ear-piercing yowl it launched itself at the cluster of priests who had all brought their right hands up in unison, palms facing Sioncaet and the men. As the spitting bundle of fury sprang at them at throat height the line of hands wavered, and whatever they had been conjuring with them. With a blinding flash the building shook, plaster fell, and some large holes appeared in the walls in direct line. Wise to what might be happening after their previous encounters, the soldiers were already on the floor as the blast ripped through and outwards from the room. But they were on their feet quicker than the priests, who had obviously had little practice at this kind of thing, and what happened when it went wrong in a confined space.

In a flash the men were on the priests, with more reinforcements coming in until they had to stop for lack of room to move. Leaving the fighting to the soldiers, who were of a mind for blood in revenge for their fallen comrades, Sioncaet struggled his way to the pool at the centre of the room. There, perched on the opposite rim out of the way of the worst of the fighting sat the wild cat. If Sioncaet had not known better he would have sworn the cat was grinning. Shaking his head, thinking he was beginning to suffer the same effects as Will, Sioncaet looked over the rim into the water to find himself looking at a beautiful mosaic map of the Islands.

"Impressive isn't it?" a sibilant voice purred.

A shiver ran down Sioncaet's spine. Fearfully he risked looking up and found the cat staring straight at him. *Oh Sweet Lotus, I've lost it! Am I seeing things? Hearing things*? Sioncaet wondered. *I really am mad if that cat just spoke to me.* Something of his thoughts must have been clear in his face, for the striped feline tapped the water with a delicate claw and repeated itself, adding,

"Yes I can speak, but that's because I'm not a real cat."

"Really?" croaked Sioncaet, struggling to find his words for once.

"Vanadis sent me," the cat said with an airy wave of his paw, as though that explained everything. Sioncaet groaned and buried his head in his hands, he was going mad! Not a real cat? A hallucination of his own making or of the room's? But then a memory crept to the surface.

"Vanadis? As in the ancient goddess?"

"Goddess? Oh no! Not that!" and the cat gave what ought to have been a laugh but came out rather more scratchily through the cat's mouth. "No. We're all that's left of the ancients. She met your friend MacBeth. She promised him we would watch over you, since that was the only way she could stop him following you and go to fulfil his destiny."

"Destiny? Ruari?"

"Indeed. In fact you're all woven into the great scheme of things now. We've been watching you too, Sioncaet."

"How nice. And you are?"

"My name is Urien. This cat is my disguise, my familiar if you like."

"And are you an ancient too?"

The cat inclined his head, which was about as near as he could get to nodding. "I am. I was once a great warrior. To appear in my real form costs me much energy – although that is improving. The wild cat is much easier, and by taking this form I'm allowing another to use more energy to aid others of your people. Besides, the likes of Quintillean and Masanae would recognise me if they saw me again."

Sioncaet's reeling mind grappled with this, although he was aware that several men were now standing in open-mouthed amazement staring at the cat. Not his illusion alone, then. That was reassuring in a worrying sort of way. Worrying in that it meant that he had to take the cat seriously, whether it was what it said it was, or a summoning of the Power by the priests. Then the niggling irritant at the back of his mind popped to the fore, and he suddenly knew where he had heard the names before. Moreover he remembered seeing a very knowing hare not long ago.

"Great Maker! You're the ones who helped defend the Islands before, aren't you? The ones the Abend think they killed. You live!"

The cat scratched its ear with a forepaw – possibly the nearest thing the shape could do to a man rubbing his ear since it was a very half-hearted scratch. "Not live, exactly. And they nearly did kill us. Our real forms are far beneath the ice on Taineire, and the bindings which keep them suspended and whole are fading. That's what we needed MacBeth for. But even though he helped us, I doubt we shall ever take real form and walk the earth again. I know Aneirin and Vanadis hope so, but Cynddylan, Peredur and I have our doubts. Very grave doubts. I don't think Owein's totally convinced either."

His form wavered and he gave a feline growl. "This costs me dear, so listen now! This pool shows the DeÁine Treasures and their locations. As you see, we destroyed several of them the last time. The two glowing ones on the side are far away, but they do link the ones you hide to their corrupt Emperor. If you break this room you help break the link. Break all three rooms and you limit the connection to the homeland. The Emperor will know the pieces move, but won't be able to reach out to them anymore."

"He can do that? Here? Now?" Will's ragged voice sounded from the doorway where Sioncaet turned to see him draped over two men's shoulders, very haggard but alert.

"Yes he can! He wants those pieces back more than anything, because he too is weaker without them. With all of them he would be invincible to you, but since we destroyed some that's no longer so. But he could still seriously harm you. These rooms are his conduit, his relay station if you like. Without them he can't function over such a distance."

Will grimaced. "What do we do? Break the pool? The room? Pull down walls? What will do it?"

"Drain the pool with buckets. The water isn't just water after this many years, and it's potent, so empty every load in a different spot. And for the love of the Islands don't encircle this place with it! That would only dilute the effect, not remove it. Then smash the walls. Every brick on the inside of this room was invested with as much Power as the ancient, potent Abend could pour into it. Get rid of them! Again as far away as possible. Smash them. Never let anything be built with them again."

"What of this ritual Quintillean plans?" Will demanded. "Lives are at stake here. We can come back to this room later."

"No!" screeched Urien desperately trying to stuff as much force as he could through the cat's vocal chords. "The room must come first! Break it and you're already part way to stopping Quintillean. Anyway, you're in the wron…" He flickered and wavered. "He won't come here because of the prie…" His voice became fainter. "*Aach*! I fade! You need to go t…" But he was gone.

Will's language ought to have stripped a layer off the walls all by itself. When he ran out of invective he stood panting and glaring at the pool. "Bastard Abend! Why do they always have to complicate things!"

"We have to do as he said, Will," Sioncaet placated his friend. "You heard him. It will help Kenelm and Wistan. It's not wasted effort."

"I know," snarled Will. "But it's what those two youngsters are suffering every day which chews at my gut! We may save their lives, but what state will they be in when we do?"

However, with no immediate destination to aim for, there was nothing for it but to do the job at hand. For the rest of that day, Will let the men rest and tend their wounds. Come the morning, however, he had them using every bucket in the place to drain the pool, sending each pail far out, first by men on foot and then by riders. No man took more than one bucket full, even though the pool was deeper than it seemed. When it came to dismantling the room, Will rotated men too. One brick alone ever got carried out by a man, then they took a break doing sentry duty or one of the mundane tasks within the camp. Only then were they allowed back to the road outside of the gates where men with hammers and picks were breaking the bricks into chippings. The shards were shovelled into bags which were taken out and scattered across the distant fields. Unable to stand being in the room, Will took charge of this while Sioncaet dismantled, making sure that only certain fields were used so that even in such a fragmented state they did not inadvertently ring the palace.

It took two whole days to pull down just the one room, for each brick was a nightmare to hack out. Once done, Will still found he felt sick up there. So they took the outer row of bricks down, so that the space only existed as a gaping round hole in the middle of a circle of open rooms, each of only three walls. And still Will felt sick. So the radial walls came down too. On Sam's suggestion, men went and got fresh spring water from a spout further up the shoreline. Good clean, fresh Island water which they refilled the pool with and then emptied again.

Luckily that seemed to do the trick, and Will could walk in without so much as a hair twitching; which was good since the men who had done the last of the dismantling pointed out that they had come to the roof timbers' supports. Any more walls to come down and they would have had to take the roof down first to avoid it falling on them. It was also good because the men were ailing. The exposure to the Power wore at every one of them, and all complained of dizziness and stomach upsets to the extent that, although it infuriated Will, he could not in any conscience expect them to march on straight away, and he was reluctantly grateful that no sign of Quintillean had surfaced. Several days' rest once the temple's Power-room was cleansed was the only option, but at least the men did rapidly recover now the dreadful miasma had gone.

After much deliberation, Will and Sioncaet had decided against dismantling the pool. There was always a chance that it might still reveal where the pieces were. When it had been refilled with spring water, the symbol which represented the Helm, according to Neena, suddenly moved the moment it could float. It was not the pouring of the water which moved it, for it shifted only a short way and then settled on the bottom again and did not move throughout the rest of the refill and draining. Clearly the Helm was in Brychan and moving westwards towards New Lochlainn.

Somewhat odder was the sudden flaring into light of the Gauntlet. They would have missed it had Sioncaet not been sitting on the rim with a couple of the men awaiting Will. It only happened for a short burst and then was gone, but the symbol was warm to the touch when Sioncaet tentatively poked it. It had not moved, but something had surely happened to it or around it, and so with that in mind they had refilled the pool with the spring water. Will could feel nothing of the Power in the room afterwards, not even when he stuck his hand in the water, so it seemed likely that it was safe. Now all they had to do was see if anything happened.

In the meantime there was the problem of what to do with the priestesses. When the bodies of the temple's defenders had been hauled out, the soldiers had been horrified to find that a good third of the masked and swathed fighters had been women. What distinguished the seventeen living from them was that they had all suffered at the hands of Anarawd. Apart from Tabith, eight of them were in various stages of pregnancy, which complicated matters enormously. Will felt he could hardly expect them to ride with him, but equally he was less than enthusiastic about the prospect of leaving them behind. And that was not only out of fear of them raising some kind of alarm.

From what Sioncaet told of life amongst the DeÁine, if even a normal patrol came up and found them, the women would be assumed to have been complicit in the fall of the Houses of the Holy, and would be slaughtered on the spot. On the second day after finding them, Tabith began losing blood, so with the aid of three wise women from the encampment Orly administered a potent cocktail of herbs, and tried not to show how nervous he was about terminating this pregnancy. Will paced the corridor outside the room with as much anxiety as if he was the father himself, but as he reminded Sioncaet, it was the saving of Amaranth which had brought the women round before, therefore losing Tabith might well set them against him once more.

Everyone breathed a little easier when a wane Orly came out to announce that Tabith was as well as could be expected, but that the foetus had been another aberration. Such evidence was hard on the remaining priestesses, and those in the very early stages of their confinements immediately asked for the herbs to be given to them. For three of them it was harder. They were further along making it more risky to terminate. Tabith, Orly admitted, had been already miscarrying so it had only hastened things along. Sioncaet found himself shouldering the burden of advising them because of the language problem, but he found out something else surprising along the way which he was quick to relay to Will.

"We have two of Taise's friends, or at least her fellow acolytes from the same cell, amongst our ladies," he told Will on the third night, as they enjoyed a bowl of savoury stew, in an apartment which Will had taken for their use beside the main gate.

"One of the ones who betrayed her?" Will was suspicious.

Sioncaet rocked his hand in a balancing motion and grimaced. "Kind of depends on whose version of the story you hear, I'm afraid. I know Taise said that they left her to rot in the Abend's cage. That none of them lifted a finger to help her through fear and to save their own skins. That may yet be the truth, but I'm inclined to believe these two in some measure. You see, they say that they were all split up. That they had no idea who had lived or died. These two, who are called Leifi and Selra, didn't even know each other had survived until Anarawd brought them here about two years ago, and they haven't seen any others.

"I don't think they know that Sithfrey still lives. They aren't priestesses either. Not even ones in training like Tabith and Seline were before Anarawd seduced them. They were former acolytes to Magda! This was just one more prison for them when they first arrived, but they thought they were lucky, because for the first time they were shut up with other women for company and re-met each other."

He paused before saying carefully. "They thought they were lucky that Anarawd took an interest in them."

"Lucky?" Will was flabbergasted. "How in the Islands does getting raped by an Abend pervert constitute lucky?"

"Because each of them heard separately that the men from their little group, …coterie, …whatever, …were taken away and tortured for weeks and then killed when it turned out that they knew nothing of the Abend's betrayal at Gavra. Taise by this time, as we know, had been taken to where Anarawd couldn't get to her, so Selra and Leifi thought she'd probably died too. They think they survived because they were the last to be interrogated, and just got lucky that around that time the Abend found out that it was Bres, in his role as acting king, who'd fouled all the plans.

"They're not so naïve as to think Anarawd felt sorry for them, let alone cared in any way. But they do think he held a grudge against Quintillean and Masanae, and so whoever those two were against might be of use to him. A case of my enemy's enemy must be my friend – or, if not friend, at least useful inferior ally. The bad news is that they're two of the three Orly and the wise women don't want to risk doing abortions on."

Will groaned. "Curses! Why does everything have to get so complicated?" He stared moodily out of the window at the gate. "If they were little more than prisoners, then we can't in any sort of conscience leave them here to the mercy of any stray Donn, or arrogant pure-bred, to come along and incarcerate again. Flaming Trees! Are we destined to get held up at every turn in trying to save Kenelm and Wistan?"

He rested his scarred knuckles on the sill and leaned his forehead against the cool glass. Leaving him to think, Sioncaet picked up a cittern and began to strum a tune on it. It had been a huge solace to him to find both citterns and lutes tucked away in the palace, and now he retreated into his music for inspiration whenever he could. Letting the music flow he found himself strumming a soulful ballad called 'the Seafarer' – a tale of a lord-less man doomed to wander. Its rhythms echoed the rocking of the waves against the shore which suddenly provided him with a solution.

"Boats!" he exclaimed stopping abruptly.

"Boats?" queried Will, jolted out of his reverie.

Sioncaet was sitting bolt upright with his eyes bright. "Yes, boats! Think about it Will. Where will Quintillean go if not here? It has to be a place which lends itself to his purpose. Remember what Urien said about there being two more rooms like the one we found? That has to be the old temples at Ralja and Kuzmin. This place's duplicates in every way!

"Well what if Quintillean is going there? Ralja's a bit unlikely because there'll always be lots of courtiers there. But what about Kuzmin? He could use the Power-room there, and there aren't even any priests to argue the toss with him over what he's doing. That's what Urien was trying to tell us – there are no priests!"

Will nodded thoughtfully. "I can go along with that idea."

"In which case we don't have to ride or march, and neither do the women – we can even take Amaranth carried on a litter. There are ferryboats tied up down at the waterfront! We send the soldiers over first, of course. But the thing is, Will, the ferries aren't really proper boats. They're more like huge rafts and as such they're not very seaworthy. Across the water from here there are some islands. The big rafts follow immense chain ropes which cross the Salu Maré going from island to island. If a storm blows up, they put into one of the islands and wait it out, because they can't move in high waves – especially ones coming sideways on to them, as often happens on the Maré. So there are refuges on those islands. Big ones. After all you can't expect the great and the good to rough it on a raft in a storm."

Will's grin broke like sun through clouds. "We take everyone in stages to the islands, then we leave the women and children on one and send the rafts back to it with a reasonable guard – their husbands where possible, of course. That way we can send for them to retreat if necessary, but more importantly nobody can take them prisoner behind our backs. Brilliant, Sioncaet!"

They were putting the idea into practice by getting the rafts lined up the next day down at the loch edge when a sentry dashed up to Will. He had run all the way down to the shore from the palace and was panting.

"Sire! …Sire! …There are men coming! …Riders!"

Will turned, vaulted onto his horse with more speed than grace, and heeled it hard back towards the walls. With Sioncaet on his heels, he tore around the walls and round to the gate, cursing the fact that the gate faced the other way to the waterfront, forcing him to do a whole half circuit of the defences. Already he could see in the distance a small blur on the road which must be the approaching party, but from down at ground level he could see no more. Throwing the reins to someone, he raced up the steps to the wall top and peered over to where a worried young man was pointing.

"There, sire. I can't be sure, but there are at least twenty of them, maybe more." The young former slave gulped. "They look dangerous."

They did have a very competent air about them, but as they got closer

Sioncaet placed a restraining hand on Will's arm. "Don't jump to conclusions," he warned.

"You don't think these are really household guards?" Will screwed up his eyes and squinted hard. "That looks awfully like real DeÁine uniforms and insignia to me."

Sioncaet was also staring, giving faint shakes to his head and spoke distantly. "I know, …I know." He raised a hand to shield his eyes to see better. "But something's not right." Then as they got a little closer he realised what it was. "They're riding all wrong!"

The blank look on Will's face forced him to explain. "Household guard don't normally ride hard and fast. Even if they're with the army going into battle, they go at the speed of the foot soldiers until they actually come to engage. More often they ride for ceremonial duties. So they ride with short stirrups. Cloaks draped to cover their boots so they appear to be floating on the horses.

"These men are riding like Islanders! All for comfort, practicality and speed. Long stirrups." They got a bit closer and he actually laughed. "And they're riding with the reins in their left hands! The right is free for their swords. They're Knights, Will, they're Knights!"

And with that he was off, bounding down the steps, and was on his horse and out of the gate before Will had even reached the base of the stair.

"Sioncaet! Wait!" Will bellowed anxiously, then threw himself onto his own horse and set off in pursuit, calling to the guards to form up and follow as fast as they could.

From their viewpoint, Labhran and Oliver had seen two riders hurtling into the palace and feared the worst. The last thing they wanted was to have to fight their way in against hideous odds. It confused them mightily when they then saw one of the riders come back out at an equally headlong race, and head straight for them, the other appearing moments later in hot pursuit and calling out to the one in front. On the wind they then heard faintly the name 'Sioncaet' called and Labhran gave a whoop of joy and clapped his heels to his own horse to ride to meet his old friend. In his turn, Will heard Oliver calling 'Labhran' and slowed his horse to lean over its withers and allow his racing heart to calm down.

The reunion was one of great relief that everyone had survived so far, especially when Labhran's party told Will and Sioncaet of the fall of Brychan. Within the safety of the palace walls, the two groups caught up on each other's progress over a hearty fish supper, aided by wine brought up from the palace's capacious wine store. For Will and Sioncaet it was some consolation to have Kuzmin confirmed as Quintillean's destination, while for Labhran's party it was to know that preparations of the rafts to cross the water were already taking place. It was also a great relief for the Knights to find that there were women who could take care of the two young girls they had so carefully brought with them. Saffy would now travel with the still weak Amaranth and Seline, and be cosseted in a way which had just not been possible on the road.

In the morning Will gratefully accepted the help of the Order's enlisted men to help get things underway, while Sioncaet led the Knights up to the dismantled Power-room. The guided tour he gave them of the whole palace complex brought it home to the newcomers just what a mammoth task it would be to get into its twin across the water. None of them had expected quite such a warren of rooms, despite what Labhran had warned them of. However, Will now came up with the bright idea of making a practice assault here on Tokai.

"You said these palaces are all identical," he reminded Sioncaet, who now had Labhran backing him up confirming this. "So let's give the lads a chance to try a proper assault before we expect them to do it for real."

With the former slaves' families already making the first wave of evacuees to the islands, the men who were to fight were lined up in and around the gatehouse, even hanging out of upper windows to allow them to watch.

"This is what we're going to do," Will bellowed to them, every bit the general again. "We're going to kit you lot out with stuff from here to make you look like proper DeÁine troops. Each of the men who arrived here yesterday will command a unit. Listen to them! They're all trained for this! When we move out tomorrow they'll be dressed like slave-masters and officers, but for now they're going to show you how Island troop take a shit-hole like this! …Sarg'nt Evans? Carry on!"

With undisguised glee the men of the Order appeared at the gate. With the Knights mounted and flanking the men to protect them, they tore in. But instead of breaking left and right to follow the winding street, they went straight for the dead-end wall. Evans began whirling a metal contraption on the end of a rope, as did Waza, Newt and Busby. They let fly and the things flew upwards, opening into claws which imbedded themselves at the top of the rough slope at the base of the upper level's wall. At the same time Toby, Cody, Trip and the three other archers let fly arrows which had similar heads. These flew up and over the top of the walls to catch on the edge. Without a break, they all ran forward and grasped the first ropes to use them to run up the rough, near-vertical slope like it was a stair. The arrow grapples had had lighter weight ropes attached, but these were pulled through to be used doubled, and the men were soon climbing like murderous spiders straight up the wall. The eerie thing was that they hardly made a sound. In no time at all the first men were over the top and standing guard over the rope tops.

The former slaves stood agog at the speed of the assault, but were even more astounded when Will informed them that they were going to learn how to do the same.

"These men will set the ropes for you, have no fear of that, but you will climb them too!" he commanded, and for the rest of the day the men practised and practised. The Order's men replaced the valuable grapples with spikes to save straining them for too long, but the ropes stayed. With Kym, Teryl and Lorcan helping, Will swiftly weeded out those of his men who had no sense of balance or were just downright clumsy. They had enough to choose from to find fifty men who could climb with speed. Another fifty were found who could climb, albeit slower, who would make up the second wave. Oliver and Hamelin, with Kym and Teryl, would go to lead the assault as the youngest and fittest. The rest would split into two groups and take the long way round under the command of Will, Labhran and the remaining Knights. It grieved Jacinto that he was still in no state to take to the ropes, for nothing made it clearer how far from well he was that he could not even attempt to do this – something he had once done with complete ease.

In the meantime Labhran and Sioncaet went to investigate the message room. With enough people to help Will, Sioncaet finally felt he could turn his back on him for a few hours. Enough to allow him to spend some time alone with his other friend and accomplish another job at the same time. Labhran might look fine if a little tired, but Sioncaet knew only too well how adept Labhran was at concealing his nightmares, and still harboured a deep anxiety for Labhran's sanity. He could almost have cried with relief at the way Labhran talked freely of the time within Bruighean. Clearly the resourcefulness and steadfast support of the young Prydein Knights had made all the difference.

It was sad that the feeling of optimism did not last. He had thrown one piece of paper onto an increasing heap of useless ones when the next one brought him up sharply. The name of Quintillean as the sender was enough to alert him, but its contents made him cry out in horror.

"What's wrong?" Labhran demanded. "Sacred Trees, Sioncaet you've gone as white as a sheet."

With despair written all over his face Sioncaet held out the message for Labhran to read for himself, then watched his friend go pale too.

"The army from Sinut," Sioncaet coughed weakly, having already done some rapid calculations looking at a carved calendar on the opposite wall. "It might've already got to the Isle of Arieda! Maybe even as early as the end of Spring-moon. Oh, Trees! That was two weeks ago nearly."

Labhran's expression was desolate. "Which means we can expect another army to reach the southern coasts of the Islands by the end of Beltane, or not long after." He inadvertently sobbed. "Spirits preserve us! We have six to eight weeks left at the most if they land on Prydein. Only a couple more if they come to Brychan. There's no hope left now. All we can do is save the boys and then head back to Ergardia with all haste."

Haggard and depressed, they went to find the others and broke the bad news. Neither of them knew whether to be glad that their friends were not so downcast. If they had no idea of the true awfulness of what was coming, who were Sioncaet and Labhran to increase their despair? With the younger Knights it could be put down to the resilience of youth, but Will's optimism was harder to understand. All he did was ask how many Islanders there were in the south of New Lochlainn, then went and stood staring at the mosaic map in the pool as the best that they had.

Later he sent for Oliver, while Sioncaet and Labhran were still half-heartedly working their way through the residue of messages.

"I'm not giving up," he declared immediately.

"Good!" was Oliver's instant response.

Will had a stick and began pointing to the map. "Over one hundred thousand. That's the estimate of how many new troops will arrive. If Berengar's half the soldier I've heard he is, then he'll make the army camped in Arlei pay for every inch of ground they hold. I can't get an army together in time to help him and deal with this new threat, so I have to trust him."

"An army?" Oliver was quick to pick up on the words.

"Yes, an army! You didn't see how quick these lads were to fight once they were given a chance. I reckon I can get maybe as many as twenty thousand from the southern towns if every man and boy fights. All right, maybe fifteen is more realistic. The thing is, if your Master Hugh can get the Prydein sept armed and ready, …if Master Brego knows and can get Ergardia and what's left of Celidon and Ruari's men from home into the field, …well we might – just might – be in with a chance of defeating them."

Oliver did some quick maths of his own. "We'll be heavily outnumbered. …Could be as bad as two to one." He scowled at the map. "It would help if we knew where they're likely to land."

"Prydein? Is that possible?"

"In distance, yes. In real terms? No. The south-east coast is all tiny coves with high cliffs which are death to ships who don't know the way into the harbours. That's why so many fishing villages have survived in the face of Attacotti raids. But come west and all of a sudden the cliffs go and there's just miles and miles of shallow saltwater marshes – equally useless for invading over!"

"Good!" Will said thoughtfully. "Because I don't think they'll land here in New Lochlainn, either. I reckon they'll want to see some proof from the Abend that they really can produce the goods. Not to mention ensuring it's safe here. Tactically I'd say that southern Rathlin will seem like a safe bet to them. It's not too hard to land on, it's largely unpopulated, but it's close enough for them to march north and steal the show if all is as they expect."

"What do you want me to do? I assume you do want me?"

"I want to try to send a message to Master Hugh first of all. If it comes in your name then he'll take note. Does he know your handwriting?"

"Yes."

"Even in that bloody cramped code of yours?"

"Yes, I'm sure he'd know it."

"Good. Because I'm counting on there being a bird in that coop which knows its way to get to Calatin."

"So if we send a message there…"

"…then Hugh will get it. Yes."

"What about Master Brego?" wondered Oliver.

"I'm sending Sioncaet back the way we came as soon as we have the boys," Will told him. "He's risked his life enough already. With your lads I have enough help and I'll keep Labhran with me to translate." He held up his hand to stop Oliver's protest. "I know. You had a few heart-stopping moments with him. But even Sioncaet's said how much better he is after coming out of the end of his escapade with you lot. If he pulls it all back, if he saves the folk of Brychan, how much better do you think he'd be then? Anyway, I need someone to impersonate a real Donn, not my fumbling attempts. I'll be the aide this time and do the tactics, and he can prance around in the frilly clothes!"

Together they went in search of Labhran and Sioncaet, both of whom were sceptical in the extreme once they knew what was wanted. Taking the lead they went out onto the high balcony and pointed to a long aviary divided up into sections.

"Not pigeons but ravens," Labhran said dryly pointing to the rows of black feathered birds. "But not just any old ravens, oh no. These are *talking* ravens and they're a bloody nightmare!"

"They can take your finger off," Sioncaet added glumly. "There's no way I'd try to handle one of them. Vicious big bastards they are."

He nearly fell over when Oliver gave a chuckle, began pulling on his armoured gloves and winked at Will. "You want to bet?"

He marched over to one of the cages, flipped the latch, reached in and with remarkable speed came back out with a raven clasped in his hands, its beak clamped shut in the process. "Worked in the hawks' aviary as a squire," he revealed with a mischievous grin. "Once you've handled a sea eagle, a raven's rather small fry!"

Will's hoot of laughter was clearly not appreciated by the bird, which fixed him with an evil eye and wriggled, but to no avail.

Labhran ran his fingers through his hair and wondered what it would take to get this young Knight to take danger seriously. "Alright, clever clogs," he said witheringly. "And now what are you going to get it to say that won't have it shot the minute it flies in?"

Oliver changed his grip, held the bird well away from his face but where he could look it in the eye, and said firmly, "I'm a fucking ugly duck, I am!"

Three hours later there was a very irate raven marching up and down its cage muttering "I'm a fucking ugly duck, I am," in Islander – possibly the first time ever that that language had passed its beak.

The young priest who had been captured was brought up at nightfall and made, with Will's dagger to his throat, to weave the Power-bound command to send it to Calatin's last known location. Thanks to Saul, they knew there was no chance of the war-mage himself being there, but Oliver was also hopeful that since Calatin was dead, Master Hugh might well have despatched Duke Brion to the Underworld too. He could not be sure, but he and Will felt it worth trying and the raven was released into the night sky.

That night the whole band of Islanders assembled to toast the venture.

"Tomorrow we embark for the islets in the Salu Maré," Will declared. "Two days to get everyone to the end isle, then one great push to get everyone across as fast as possible and all together."

"Here's to rescuing Kenelm and Wistan!" Heledd raised her glass, she and Breizh having declined to remain with the women however much Labhran had fumed at them.

"To Wistan and Kenelm!" they all toasted.

"And may Quintillean and Masanae not summon their spectres!" Jacinto added from the heart, to which everyone gave their assent. The best part of four hundred men were going in, but they would be no match for the Abend's voracious feeding spectral selves if they had time to release them.

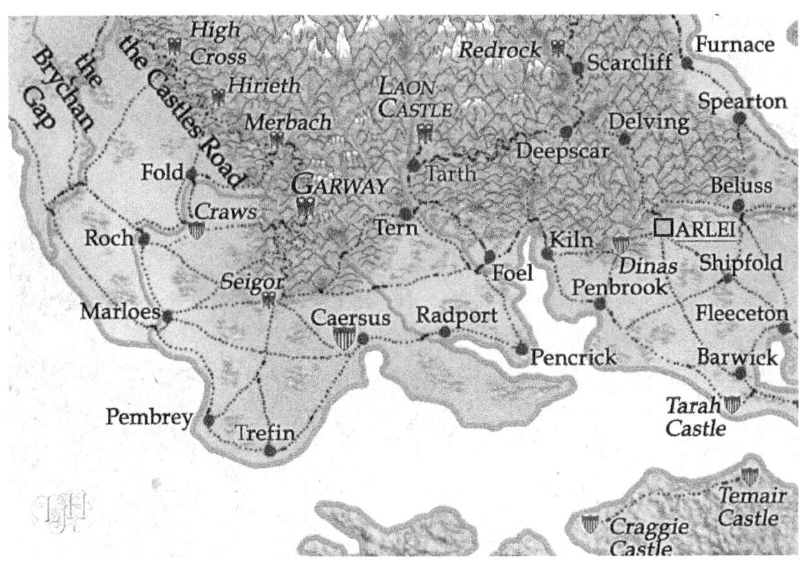

Chapter 5

Not As Planned

Brychan: early-Earrach

Helga smiled with the kind of contentment a cat shows after a good mousing. Three weeks to the day after the unknown assassin had made an attempt on her life, she was fully in control of this south-easternmost corner of the Island known as Brychan. Quite where most of the local population had fled to was unknown and, in her eyes, unimportant. The talented young member of the Monreux family had continued to prove his ability by successfully securing this area to her satisfaction, and had earned a glowing report from her sent back to his family superiors, who were with the main invading party at Arlei. Meanwhile, only a morning ago the ships she had sent for from the New Lochlainn ports had arrived. Those few Islanders her force had taken prisoner were immediately herded off to be chained to the oars in the galleys – for the traditional vessels of the Attacotti were still in use in the New Lochlainn coastal waters – thereby freeing their guards for better uses, like conquest. At this time of year the galleys had been brought back into service after their winter in dock, and provided useful troop transports and prisons at the same time.

Currently, several were accompanying those few sail-driven DeÁine ships available at such short notice, in taking more of the Jundis Minors across to the coast of Rathlin. At the same time, Helga was pursuing her own plan to clear an overland passage as near as possible to Rheged and its wealth, and overall it was all going remarkably smoothly. Moreover, from what she had worked out from the words of the young captain she had tortured, the DeÁine Scabbard was at some backwater on Kittermere called Draynes – a desolate spot unlikely to be defended at all. Barring exceedingly bad luck, she was therefore sure that she could succeed where Calatin had failed, and another of the Treasures would be in Abend hands once more. The current members of the DeÁine arcane elite would succeed where their predecessors had failed, and the exiled masses would return to the DeÁine homeland – or at least those who longed to could, and they did not include Helga.

She preened herself and went to meet young Donn Monreux, newly returned from Rathlin, who made his usual deep bow over her hand accompanied by a knowing glance which carried sexual undertones. Helga was still wondering whether to allow him the privilege of sharing her bed, but was reluctant to allow anyone the chance to leave her so open to attack. It would never be one of the physical kinds, she was sure. He was far from being that much of a fool, for he had made it clear how well he understood that she could blast him to cinders in a heartbeat. It was more the barrack-room gossip she feared. One slip of the tongue, rumours spreading, and she would be forced to dispense with him – but he was far too useful at present to risk that.

She sighed inaudibly, then demanded crisply,

"So tell me, Donn Monreux, have your scouts found anything yet?"

His smile was a wisp of a thing, quickly smothered by stern functionality. "No, Great One, not a soul. As my earlier message said, there are signs that many people passed through the pitiful thing they call a castle at the place named Temair. However, they're long gone – and not in the direction we're heading in either. They seem to have run away into the moors and marshes, where no doubt they'll die of pestilence soon enough. There's nobody in our way at all."

"Excellent!" Helga purred.

The four hundred seasoned troops of the Jundis Minors would make short work of any rebels scurrying out of those distant hills, and surely there could not be more than a handful of people living in such desolate conditions. "I shall join you over there shortly. Prepare accommodation for me."

"Great One, there's even less over there than in this miserable place," Donn Monreux warned her. "We've yet to find a single bath even here! There's no hope of finding one on the whole of the other island!" He knew how much this particular member of the Abend loved to immerse herself in the warm waters of the marble baths in the DeÁine citadel of Bruighean, and their other palaces. She had consequently been tetchy enough here at Tarah Castle on not finding anywhere to bathe in warmth. He hated deprivation enough himself, but he had no desire to be doing rough campaigning with a bad tempered witch at his heels. "You could remain here until we've pushed further into the interior, then join us when you can make a single journey to the opposite coast," he suggested hopefully."

"I think not," Helga replied frostily, "I *will* join you to direct things."

Vir Monreux groaned in his soul, but kept his mouth shut until he was out of the room. His aide was waiting for him.

"Bad news, Donn?" he ventured to ask seeing his young lord's face like thunder.

"The worst!" Donn Vir Monreux growled. "The witch-bitch is coming with us!"

"Phol's scrotum!" his aide swore.

"Yes," Vir Monreux agreed, but added sternly, "and in the interests of our souls reaching the Immaculate Temples Above intact, tell the men that there's to be no mention of Phol or Ama. I doubt that Her-in-there has any affinity with either of the fertility deities – with or without appendages! In fact, no swearing of any kind while she's crawling all over us with her creepy spells! Too much danger of saying the wrong thing. Impress it on her bodyguard, and on the great Volla's breath, keep the rest well away from her!"

"I thought you were keen on her," the aide asked cagily, prepared for a quick exit if he found he had overstepped the mark.

Vir sniffed in revulsion. "Sweet Lotus, no! I just watched the way she looked down her nose at that other Abend, Geitla, coupling with everything male, and decided that if I wanted to keep her at arm's length the best way to drive her off was to flirt with her. Take her to my bed?

Urgh!" He shuddered. "I demand my women pleasure *me*. That's what I pay pleasure slaves for, not to do the work myself. I have no intention of sweating over a cold fish like her!" And he shuddered again as he turned on his heels and marched off.

The aide shrugged and went to do the real work, mentally cursing haughty officers and their strange ways.

Two days later Helga was privately wishing she had listened to Donn Monreux. Even swathed in exotic furs, she was freezing in the bleak hall of Temair castle, and likely to continue to do so, given that there was not a thing to burn except the castle itself. Even with her talents, in order to make a blaze which could warm a room she required some kind of fuel for her Power to ignite.

Unwilling to linger, she ordered an immediate march to secure a distant port which would open her way to take Kittermere, eager to get the job finished now. Of course she realised that she could not take it with a mere four hundred men. But she was confident that if she could get that far, then the more senior Donns at Arlei would not be able to resist the chance to stamp all over some more of the dreadful Islanders' homelands.

As the four Jundis Minors formed up in marching order and left Temair, ahead of them, four solitary men watched them from up on a distant hillside.

"Hounds of the Wild Hunt!" a dark-haired scruffy man sitting on an equally shaggy hill-pony muttered. "The bloody foreign women were right! Those are DeÁine troops! Quick lads! Ride like the Dark Lord Jolnir was on your heels! We have to warn Magnus!"

The others turned their mounts with him and dug their heels in, the four Attacotti scouts disappearing before the DeÁine soldiers had even noticed them.

The riders knew they did not have far to go to reach others who would relay the message on if they fell. One of Magnus' clan chiefs was patrolling in the north, and chieftain Colm Ap'brien was a wily fighter and shrewd tactician who would see the dangers without having to be lengthily convinced. When the four hill-men galloped into his camp he was just thinking about turning back to Kylesk the next day, having found nothing worth worrying over. By the time he had heard the news, he instead had his men breaking camp and on the move under cover of darkness. Several riders were sent back in a hurry to warn not only Magnus but the other clan chiefs.

Although he had not said a word to the men around him, Colm was worried about Magnus. The charismatic leader of the Attacotti was always volatile, but since the strange women had come and gone he had become wildly erratic and unstable. That, in part, had been why the main clan chiefs had departed under the pretext of checking out the story. Better to get well away than find themselves being ordered to slaughter one another by a morair (as they called their premier chieftain) who had lost what little grasp on sanity he had ever had.

Now, though, Colm was hoping and praying that Magnus had merely been afflicted with a temporary illness. Mad as a Spring-moon hare he might be, but he was lucky in war. Against the Islanders he had had no more, nor greater, successes than any other of the other war-band leaders. Against the dreaded DeÁine, though, he had succeeded against the odds time and time again. And at times when he never should have, too. Colm hawked and spat a lump of phlegm into the dirt for luck, making the sign to ward off evil as he did so. 'Lucky' was the kind of leader they needed now – Magnus' luck – and he dug his heels into his shaggy pony's side as he led his men back towards a prime ambush point he knew well from long ago. Pray that Magnus is up off his sick bed, he thought over and over, and will ride to aid us. For if not this ambush would only be a delaying tactic, and Colm and his men would have to flee into the hills until they could join with two or three other clans.

Oblivious to the fact that they were being shadowed, Monreux and the Jundis Minors continued to march for all of the next day and into the one beyond. Colm's scouts were reporting that the cursed foreigners were setting a blistering pace and showing no sign of faltering, and it was certain that if they intended to fight, the two groups would meet at the end of this day or early into the next. As a result Colm drove his men at a frantic rate until an ancient hill fort appeared on the horizon, and that was when he breathed a sigh of relief which was not only to do with reaching a defendable spot. To one not used to the terrain it all looked quiet, but these were Colm's homelands and he could tell that the banks and ditches of the hill were filled with men by the arrival of the camouflage bushes which had sprouted within days on the ridges. As he urged his pony round to the fort's far side, and up the ramp which led to the heart of the ramparts, he saw a familiar figure striding towards him. Magnus!

Vaulting from the pony and throwing the reins to a waiting lad, Colm strode up to his overlord and greeted him warmly.

"May the Goddess be praised! It's good to see you," he exclaimed, unable to keep the relief out of his voice. "We thought you to be on your sickbed!"

"I was," Magnus growled. "One of those cursed witches took my treasure I've guarded all these years. The one I took from the Islanders as a lad. I felt it being torn from me! Like a piece of my scalp had been ripped off in battle! The first couple of days I could barely stand. I nearly ordered the death of the other two wenches who got dragged back to me. But the one is with child, and you know how superstitious the men are about women near their child-bed. I daren't lay a hand on her if I wanted to." Then he gave a wolfish grin. "It was the other one who got me on my feet, though. Or on my back! Ha! Nothing like a warm handful of lusty wench to revive a man's spirits, eh?"

Colm laughed readily with his leader. This was the Magnus of old. Always tupping some girl or other when there was no fighting. The Goddess only knew where he got the stamina from. These days, Colm found it tough enough keeping up with his new young wife after his first wife had died. May be because, he admitted in private if not in public, he had married this one only out of necessity, and in his heart he still mourned the woman who had shared his life for decades. His heart was not in casual couplings any more, and the rest of his body followed it in its reluctance. How, then, Magnus still got through so many women given that he was of a similar age was astonishing. However, with equally characteristic speed Magnus' mood had already switched back to the matter at hand and solemnity.

"The thing is, Colm, while she was warming me up, the dark-haired lass kept on about the dangers coming. She soon changed her tune about her companions, but about this she never faltered. Made me think! Maybe there was something in it. So a week later, when my head cleared, I thought to ride this way. Seamus told me you'd ridden out, and that made me think you must feel it was worth checking on, but what put the seal on it was a galley.

"One of the ones Dunall runs, which he puts up for the winter on the north coast, was just coming out to test her sea worthiness for the new season, and saw DeÁine ships going back and forth up by Temair. The captain flayed his slaves day and night to get to me, arriving as we were about to leave. I've sent orders out for more men to join me immediately. I sent riders after Greum and Tormod too, for they'd only been gone a day, and they're here now. Raghnall will take longer to get here but I've no fears that he will come."

Colm felt the weight of dread lift from his shoulders. Greum Caimbeul was a fierce fighter with many men in his war-band, as was Tormod Ap'caoig. Good men with experience as well as courage. With Magnus at their head they would fight hard. Raghnall Friseal was the man most of them would vote for to become the next morair if Magnus fell, and for that reason if nothing else Colm was glad that word had also gone his way.

"How many men?" he asked Magnus, as they walked to the camp hidden on the far side of the great flat-topped hill. "I've sixty men all told with me, but many are lads. I never came expecting a great fight. The DeÁine march in four files, so there can't be less than three hundred and probably closer to four, if not even a few more."

"I brought seventy out of Kylesk," Magnus informed him. "Luckily we passed through Greum's clan-home on the way, and so we've near a hundred of his men-folk. Unfortunately Tormod was on his way home still, so he only has the forty he came hunting with."

"A little over two hundred and seventy, then, if you don't count the boys for whom this will be the first blooding," Colm reckoned aloud. "Not good odds, Magnus. Every one of the DeÁine is a seasoned fighter. No slaves march with them."

Magnus tossed his black mane confidently, his one blue and one brown eyes glinting red in the lowering sun. "Ha! I have no intention of giving them a fair fight!" he snorted. "Hit and run, Colm! Hit them and disappear into the hills. I want all your archers at the ramparts by dawn. Let's even the odds!"

With the first watery light creeping up at their backs the Attacotti rebels were ready and waiting. They did not wait long. Around a shoulder of high land the DeÁine troops appeared, marching in rigid formation, not bothering to scout ahead and clearly not expecting any kind of attack.

"Almost too easy, boys," Magnus' distinctive rich bass voice sounded softly in the silence, and his good humour was echoed by well muffled chuckles. "Wait for it now! ...Let the first lot get so you can see the whites of their eyes! ...We don't want to warn the ones out of range that they're under attack. Can't have them fighting back, now, can we?" There was more muffled laughter. Their morair was in good humour, things must be going to be all right. "Steady now …!"

The nail-soled shoes of the leading Jundis clattered rhythmically on the stony ground of the wide track they were marching down, but aside from that the countryside was the picture of peacefulness. The birds were up and singing, well used to the presence of the men swathed in muted plaids whom they ignored, even as they flew clear of the strangers on the track. The first shaft of sunlight crested the hill-fort and straight into the eyes of the marching men. One instinctively lifted his hand to his eyes to shield them and got reprimanded by his sergeant (or whatever passed for one in the Jundis Minors).

"Silly bugger," Colm breathed and Magnus nodded. That man might just have spotted the waiting trap, but now he was squinting and blinking with the rest of the troop.

When the leading men were within a few paces of coming into the shade of the hill-fort Magnus raised his arm. Group leaders among the clans tensed, watching for his signal to pass on to their men. As the front ranks of DeÁine stepped into the shade and blinked, Magnus' arm dropped. The first volley of arrows sailed out, goose-feather flights singing their song of impending doom as death fell out of the sun on the DeÁine. Armour protected many men, but the screams of pain signalled where the arrows had found a mark. Without a word of command needing to be said, the Attacotti were reloading and loosing at will now, the more experienced archers careful picking out targets while others simply laid down blanket shots.

From within her litter at the rear, Helga heard the commotion. For a moment she was nonplussed as to what it could be, but then a runner came back and told her.

"Forward!" she screamed at her bearers. "Run!" and the litter bounced and jounced as the eight men carrying her broke into an ungainly jog.

"Great One, this is too close!" Monreux's voice called out to her in warning.

Helga's bearers halted, but she slipped gracefully from the litter and strode on forward, already drawing the Power to her. As soon as she felt she had sufficient, she formed a ball of fire and launched it at towards the enemy. It impacted on the ramparts sending earth flying into the air, another already in flight as the air began to clear. The second ploughed a furrow through the packed earth, but a third arced higher and fell amongst men who disappeared in a flash of flames.

"Fucking arseholes! What was that?" yelled Colm as he spat soil and wiped his streaming eyes clear of grit.

"Someone shoot that bitch!" Magnus bellowed. "Kill that fucking witch dead! A quart of mead to the man who does!"

Every sharpshooter amongst the archers turned their attention on Helga, then stopped in shock as their arrows hit an invisible wall and clattered off it yards in front of her.

"Bastard Bitch of the Wild Hunt!" Magnus swore.

"Oh Great Goddess!" someone cried out, an aged veteran of many battles. "It's one of the war-witches!"

The rise of panic amongst Magnus' men was almost tangible.

"Stop!" he shouted, batting men back down with his fists as they rose to flee. "Kill the fucking men! They're not witches! They have no magic! Kill the men!"

Some returned to fight and scored hits, and while some of the Attacotti did flee, others saw their fellow archers striking targets amongst the ordinary enemy and steadied. However, the invisible shield now began to move forwards to cover the soldiers and fewer arrows got close enough to penetrate. Three more of the fire balls flew into the ramparts, but Magnus' men were too spread out by now for the fatalities to be great.

"Fall back!" Magnus ordered. "Into the hills, lads! ...Scatter and reform at Clows Top!"

The Attacotti broke and fled, shooting as they went. It had all happened so fast that the men of the four Jundis Minors had hardly got an arrow off of their own. Now they tore after the fleeing men but were quickly recalled by the squad leaders, who had no wish to have to account for missing men to one of the Abend.

In the centre, a shaken Vir Monreux still cast about him looking for the enemy and where they had come from. Nothing in his training had prepared him for this kind of fight.

"Should we chase them, Great One?" he asked Helga anxiously, thoroughly scared. With her in this mood he could end up as ashes if he failed to do her will, whatever the military advisability in the circumstances.

Helga was tying off the streams of Power she had drawn, furious at such an affront but equally unsure as to how to proceed. She had never encountered fighting like this either – except to some extent at Gavra Pass.

The only other time she had openly fought the Islanders had been at the great battle some thirty years ago, but then troops had also been drawn up in formation in the kind of battle she had been led to expect. This kind of hit and run tactic was new to her, but she dared not show uncertainty in front of young Monreux, for that would undermine her hold over him. Taking a gamble she waved a hand in what she hoped would be read as a nonchalant fashion.

"Leave them!" she said imperiously.

"Then I must attend to the wounded," Monreux told her, feeling that at least here he was on familiar ground. "We must kill the ones unable to march before going on. We cannot leave them for the enemy to torture."

Nobody had ever told him about treating battle wounded – his training said that if they could walk they were sent back along the lines, but if not it was not the Donns' business. After all, there were always other slaves who could be trained up. So the wounded who could walk did so, even if some then fell by the wayside. Others had their throats cut, and the Attacotti scouts watching from the hills shook their heads in horror and reported back on the heathen practices of their enemy.

In Brychan, Magda stood with uncharacteristic stillness in front of the fire in her room as Geitla and Tancostyl entered. It was the second time in as many days that they had met up. Only yesterday they had all felt two quite separate surges on the Power. One came from somewhere to the north-east. Only a brief burst and very small, but it was there. To the west it was more as though something had gone. As though a link in the Power had been disrupted, cutting it short and leaving a void. Whatever either one was, it was a very different feeling to that which they had picked up this morning. That had quite definitely had Helga's signature about it even if they had no idea what their fellow Abend was up to. Both Tancostyl and Geitla had agreed with Magda that the other two flashes were like nothing they had ever felt before, and the threesome had been united in their concern.

As Magda had predicted, the other two Abend had long since tired of each other's company, but were still on close terms – which was just as well given that only the three of them were here to make a decision. One look at Magda was enough to convince them that something once more was seriously wrong.

"What's happened now?" Geitla asked with genuine concern. Without the constant harassment of Masanae and Helga she was a lot easier to deal with, Magda realised. No pouting, no temper tantrums, no sulking.

"I've had a message from Eliavres," she told them as they settled into comfortable chairs. "A message which is both good news and worrying at the same time. Even as he rode west he met with Anarawd coming to find him. The good news is that Anarawd has been simply following some half-baked scheme of his own."

"Following his cock more like," Geitla observed darkly.

"Oh poppet! You do have such a dirty mouth!"

"Yes she does!" Tancostyl interrupted with a smirk. "And a wicked tongue to go with it!"

Geitla gave a simpering smile and ran her tongue slowly over her upper lip. "You know where I am! Any time…!"

Ah, thought Magda, *why didn't I see that before! Anarawd does love using the Power when he fucks his little girls. That's what Geitla's been after! No wonder she's more stable now. She craved that like I hunger for my boy. Dear Jolnir – as you are now – soon my poppet, soon…!* But she dragged her mind back to the present with some effort and focused again.

"Whatever he's been up to," she admonished the pair opposite her, "he had the presence of mind to know it concerns all of us when he found out that Quintillean had spent some time at the Houses of the Holy at Tokai. Not, unfortunately, for the good of his soul, but using them to track the Great Volla's armour, or what's left of it now. That's no worse than we might expect of him. But what horrified Anarawd – and Eliavres when he was told – is that Quintillean has summoned the rest of our Exiles' army from Sinut!"

"Great Volla!" Tancostyl growled as Geitla gasped,

"Sweet Lotus, is he mad? To spoil it all now?"

Magda wrinkled her pert little nose. "I know, I know! After all the care we took to bring the most malleable of our pure-ones with us! The Great Ama knows how even *they've* tried our patience with their inflated ideas of their powers. And these others have had years without our guiding hand to subdue their grander delusions!" She made a moue with her reddened lips and gave a delicate flick of her hand. "No matter to him! Oh no! Quintillean thinks he knows best! *Phaa*! …Proof, as if we needed it, that he'll leave us scrabbling in the dirt if he can get control of the Treasures. Eliavres says that Quintillean and Masanae are planning some ritual at

Kuzmin, although they're not there yet. And even more worrying is the news that we've barely two months left before we can expect to see the Sinut army at the coast."

"Two months?" Tancostyl was appalled. "So this is no new scheme then?" He stood up and prowled the room, his expression getting bleaker with every step. "Curse Quintillean! Eliavres said he was sent on a futile trip chasing remnants of the Power all over Brychan. Quintillean must've known that the Gorget wouldn't be found there."

"Indeed, sweetling! My dear boy says that Anarawd told him that this room of the priests shows quite clearly that the Gorget is on the tainted island of Ergardia."

Tancostyl's face as he turned to Magda would have frozen the marrow of a lesser being. "On Ergardia?"

"Oh yes! And apparently Quintillean went there. He took several triads of Hunters and seems to have left them hunting the Gauntlet on Celidon while he went after the Gorget."

"How many Hunters?" a furious Geitla wanted to know. "Curse him! May the Lotus eat his flesh away and the Seagang rot his bones! Many of those Hunters were mine! For all Masanae and Helga get so sniffy about me not training acolytes, I put more hours into the Hunters than either of them ...or even both together."

"My boy doesn't specify how many," Magda admitted, "but it sounds like it was a lot." Now she also had a shrewd idea of why Geitla had spent more time with the Hunters – they were the nearest ones to the Abend who could handle the Power, once the acolytes were discounted. "As for acolytes, Anarawd agrees that *we* should pick the next member of the Abend. Since neither Eliavres nor Anarawd have any primed and ready, they believe I should scour the coteries for suitable candidates. No offence, dearest Geitla, but they fear that your known tendency to get close to your own students would render them open to blackmail or worse. And we really don't want to leave Quintillean or Masanae room for that, do we?"

"No we don't!" snapped Tancostyl. "And I know someone else who'll not be pleased about the coming of the Sinut pure ones – Eriu! I bet she'll be furious when Eliavres tells her."

"Ah," Magda lifted a cautionary finger, "but he hasn't gone on to Bruighean! He and Anarawd felt it likely that the Sinut fleet will land along one of the south coasts. With that in mind their first thought was to go after the Scabbard. Anarawd knows where it is, but Eliavres wasn't going to let him go alone. But neither of them wanted any of these arriving highborn to seize the Scabbard and take control of it. Imagine what it would look like if that lot decided to take it straight back to the Emperor without waiting for us! They could sail back to Sinut, pick up whatever they might perversely want to take back from those Lotus-cursed shores, and sail eastwards again to Elin. Once they've picked up those who stayed there, and told them their version of the truth, they'll be in an unassailable position before they even start back for Lochlainn"

Tancostyl picked up a heavy oak chair and threw it with such force at the stone wall that it shattered into pieces. Both women could feel the Power surging up within him as his anger grew to explosive proportions. An angry war-mage was something to behold and the air around him was becoming incandescent with surging Power. Magda began backing away from him, moving clear of the force before it was unleashed and drawing Power of her own as a shield. But Geitla had a different way of averting danger. She dropped her gown in a second and urgently ripped his breeches off him. The two of them coupled there and then, right in front of Magda, who barely had time to weave a full shield of her own drawing when their joint climax released a blast of Power which ripped the door off its hinges, blew out the window, and incinerated everything in the room but the three Abend to cinders. Magda grimaced at the devastation and the holes in the ceiling and floor, but had to admit that had Geitla not done what she did, the damage could have been worse.

As the panting couple separated, she dusted the bits off herself before asking,

"And what, besides *that*, do you intend to do?"

Tancostyl stood up, indifferent to his state of undress but coherent once more. "I shall go to Bruighean," he announced forcefully, "and I shall take the Helm with me! We must play the highborn ones off against one another. If Eriu and that dim-witted son of hers hold the Helm through me, it'll matter less if the others get hold of the Scabbard. I've only lingered this long because Helga was out of the way. But she must return soon, and it would be better if I was gone by then. I've no wish to tempt her into trying one of her quaint poisons on me in the night!"

He turned and marched out of the room without giving anyone chance to object. Magda was expecting Geitla to immediately offer to ride with him. Such an addiction to the Power must be fierce to resist. Yet when she turned to look at Geitla she was still lying where he had left her, an intoxicated smile on her lips and a glazed expression in her eyes. Despite her natural revulsion Magda forced herself to look harder. Something was definitely not right. Surely Geitla's belly hadn't been so distended when she'd dropped her gown? Peering closer Magda realised that there was a glow under the stretched skin as though a ball of Power had entered Geitla and was filling her womb.

"Geitla! Let it go!" Magda commanded urgently. "Let that Power within you go!" Yet her words might as well have been uttered to a corpse for all the effect they had.

By the next day, when Tancostyl was about to leave, Magda forced him to the chamber where Geitla had been taken and where she still lay inert, except for the eerie glow inside. The two of them stood staring at her.

"I've tried all I know and there's no response," Magda told him. She felt no great sympathy for the other woman's plight, but if she remained in such a state it left herself in sole control of Arlei and, even worse, alone against Helga.

With substantially more brutality, Tancostyl reached out on the Power and jolted Geitla with it. Nothing happened. In itself that was worrying for the Power should've convulsed even a dead body. Instead it was as though Geitla had simply absorbed it. But equally surprising, it was Tancostyl who recoiled.

"Great Lotus! That's disgusting! Something grows within her!"

Magda's eyes flew to his in horror. "Something *growing*? Do you mean like a growth, or a child?"

"It lives," was all Tancostyl would say.

She reached out in a drawing of her own and carefully probed more deeply than she had bothered to do so far. Within Geitla, behind her own veil of Power, was a seething ball of Power which seemed to be consuming the witch from the inside outwards, as if the Power were taking Geitla and forming her flesh into something else. Something alien yet familiar.

"Recruit *two* new members," Tancostyl said without any sign of grief for Geitla's imminent passing. "The stronger the better. And make sure they're wholly ours! I ride for Bruighean. Keep me informed through the Power!" and was gone.

But Magda was slower to leave her dying fellow Abend. As Tancostyl left, a smile spread across her face and she clasped her hands together in joy. Clearly this was nothing emanating from Tancostyl, judging by his surprise, so it must be externally created.

"Jolnir, my love? Is that you?" she whispered ecstatically. "Have you come back to me? Have you found a way?" *Take your time, Helga*, she thought, *and by the time you get back there might be a big surprise for you*!

Unfortunately Tancostyl had other ideas, and even as he mounted up and set off with a bodyguard in pursuit, he was drawing a fine sending and aiming at where Helga had last been.

"*Get back to Arlei*!" he sent to her. "*Geitla has overreached herself and is dying! We all need you back at Arlei. For your own miserable sake – even if you care nothing for us – you should come, for you know as well as I that Magda cannot hope to control the Donns alone. There is news*!" And by the time he left her that he could feel her anger shift from him to Masanae and Quintillean.

"*May the Great Ganna suck their brains dry*!" her thoughts snarled. "*They shall pay for this*!"

Tancostyl broke the link and rode on – smugly content that Helga's self-serving nature would guarantee her return.

However, that was easier said than done. Helga was still stuck in the wilds of Rathlin as Donn Monreux sorted his men out after their skirmish with the Attacotti. As she paced to and fro, fuming inside but forcing herself to keep some vestige of calm on the outside, a new weaving on the Power appeared.

"*Helga? Was that you*?" a thought pattern which was unmistakably Eliavres' came to her.

With immense effort Helga force calm into her thought and answered. "*Yes it was*."

"*Are you on Rathlin? The island to the south of New Lochlainn*?"

"*If that's the name of the benighted place, then yes*."

"*Ah! Then Anarawd and I are on our way towards you onboard a ship*."

Helga mentally distanced herself and considered this news. Of course, she realised. If Eliavres and Anarawd were heading for the Scabbard, then it was small wonder that they were trying to keep as much on land as possible. Should she tell them that she had intelligence that it was at Draynes? Then thought on Eliavres' mistake in thinking one of their Treasures was in southern Brychan, and the derision he had incited from the other Abend who had marched in on his say so. He would never let her live it down if she had been misled! No, she would keep that knowledge to herself for now.

"*You're after the Scabbard*," she sent back bluntly. She had no intention of being coy about the matter even in her deviousness.

Her abruptness incited a similar response. "*Yes we are,*" Anarawd's thought ground unwelcome into her head. "*Have you been told why?*"

"*Yes.*"

"*Then you'll hardly need me to draw a picture. Have you encountered resistance there?*"

Helga ground her teeth. No getting around that now. "*Yes I have. Some kind of pestilent random warfare. Irritatingly effective when it comes, although in the long-term I doubt it will linger in the face of proper cleansing by our troops.*" The usual procedure in the face of such opposition was to simply wipe out the civilian population so that there was nobody left for the fighters to recruit from, and the two war-mages knew that.

"*Marvellous, dear heart, but that hardly helps us at this point, does it?*" Anarawd was acerbic. "*Ideally we could do with marching across this desolate rock. Can we do that without sending up such fireworks on the Power, that any novice acolyte working with the Sinut force will feel it halfway to Arieda?*"

"*You mean you want me to clear a path for you?*" The tone of Helga's sending made it clear that she was prepared to fight over doing such a menial task.

"*Tsk!*" Eliavres tutted. "*Get off your dignity, my dear! We're asking no such thing! In fact that would be the worst thing you could do. We want to slip in and seize the Scabbard without anyone amongst our former fellow exiles spotting a thing, not broadcast it to the skies! Anarawd knows that it's on the north coast of Prydein.* (At which point Helga wondered how he could be so certain but carefully kept her silence.) *So there's no point in sailing around the south coast, but the passage through the inner sea is rough, as Tancostyl found to his peril. We were simply trying to ensure that we got to the Scabbard in a fit state to seize it, in case we need to blast our way back out again. So I ask again. Can we go overland? Is it possible? Or should we sail on to Kittermere and rest there before trying to seize the Scabbard?*"

Anarawd felt Helga's aggression slip away and once again felt a sneaking admiration for the way Eliavres handled another of the Abend. He really was far more subtle than they had given him credit for. Had that been Tancostyl or Quintillean, Helga would have been fuming and spitting hard enough to send massive shock waves rippling out on the Power. Instead her ire had dissipated to something hardly worth any observer's notice. Any acolyte with the Sinut fleet would certainly not have the experience to unravel such echoes and make anything of them, which was good.

"*No,*" she was saying. "*If you want to go unnoticed then you'd best sail on. To pass through the hills would require substantial use of the Power.*" For her own part congratulating herself on playing the game rather better than Eliavres had. Time would tell which one of them was right, but she was sure she would come out of it unsullied whichever way it went.

"*Very well, then,*" Eliavres thought in even and placatory tones. "*What do you want, Helga? Anarawd here wants to go back to Lochlainn in style. Me, I want to stop here and rule my own small kingdom, not be a small fish in a very big lake. What do you want?*"

Cautiously Helga carefully phrased her reply. "*I want the east of these Islands. I want wealth. I want to live in comfort. I don't want to be forever on some quest to repent for a fault that wasn't mine, grovelling to get back into favour with an Emperor I've never met, who may go back on any decision or promises he makes by the time we get back to him.*"

Anarawd felt the bitterness roiling around her and realised how astute Eliavres' summation of the younger Abend had been. Having never seen the splendour of the Imperial court in Lochlainn, there was nothing to entice the likes of Helga and Eliavres back. However, Eliavres was already negotiating and doing a successful job.

"*There's nothing in that I would argue with,*" he was thinking back at her, as if they were discussing nothing more than who got the prettiest new slave. "*Then let's agree on this. If you'll go back as Tancostyl was shouting at you to do, it would help us greatly if you'd then bring as many of the Donns as you can round up to secure the way back for us.*"

Nice choice of words, Anarawd thought, 'shouting'. It made it sound as though Eliavres was all sympathy in the face of a bullying Tancostyl.

"*If you do this for us,*" Eliavres was continuing, "*then I don't see why you shouldn't then use the same troops to carry on and secure your own objectives. That way you get a big enough force to comfortably do what you want, and we can travel back the rest of the way with ease. Will you do that, Helga? If we support you, will you go and get troops to meet us for when we bring the Scabbard back from Prydein?*"

There was a pregnant pause while Helga thought, but Anarawd got no sense of building anger.

"*Very well,*" her thoughts came back to them. "*For now I shall return and find additional fighters. We may need to throw a few Seljuqs at these rebels to soften them up anyway.*"

"*Excellent!*" Eliavres purred in his most amenable way, projecting gratitude and warmth as Helga broke the connection.

"You're going to do that?" Anarawd asked him, once he was sure all Power links were gone.

"Too right!" Eliavres chuckled. "Oh come on, Anarawd, what do you think Helga's chances are of getting the Donns to move further east in pursuit of some plan of hers? They'll move to come and get the Scabbard, because now that Tancostyl's brought the Helm home they can see it's possible to retrieve the Great Pieces. They want that. They want that for themselves! Magda is subtle enough to dangle the threat of the Sinut highborn before them so that their arrogance will make them want to be the ones who go home covered in glory. They'll come here alright, but they won't move just for us. Not these days, they won't. So I'm using that."

"And using Helga too?"

Eliavres smiled wickedly. "Well doesn't she deserve that? All that scheming with Quintillean and Masanae? She has to pay the price sometime. And what in her defence does she have? We turn our backs for five heartbeats and she's already siphoning troops off for her own little plans and schemes. We'd never have heard a word about *that* if she and Tancostyl hadn't had another one of their spats on the Power. She certainly wouldn't have told us of her own volition. Magda's left alone trying to hold all that we've gained with just a few Donns. We two are acting in all our interests. Tancostyl's gone to Bruighean – where I hope he doesn't undo all my good work with Eriu. And the Divine Ama only knows what's wrong with Geitla! *Tsk*! And just when she was working with us too! I can't feel her, can you?"

Anarawd pulled the Power into him and reached out with great delicacy only to jerk back with a shudder. "Great Seagang! That's horrible! It's like something's feasting on her through the Power!"

"The Emperor?" wondered an appalled Eliavres. The last thing any of them needed was the Emperor's heavy hand interfering.

However Anarawd shook his head emphatically. "Oh no! It's not him. It's nothing like his pattern. It's something much more perverted than that."

"Oh joy," Eliavres sighed drily. "Even more perverted than the Emperor! What delight! Any idea what it is?"

But Anarawd was completely in the dark.

So was Magda, and she was in no mood to be polite when Helga came back to her with imperious demands. With biting sarcasm and abruptness, Magda made it clear that she would do nothing with regard to summoning

Donns or making arrangements for further forays onto Rathlin. If Helga wanted that, then she would have to do it once she was back on Brychan, and preferably back in Arlei. Magda had her hands full with everything else. For a start it was clear that Geitla was undergoing some form of fundamental change, but what it was was beyond Magda, and she had no intention of informing Masanae and Quintillean just yet.

Instead she focused on finding a new member for the Abend. Her intuition told her that Geitla's body could be being used by some entity, even if her soul was gone, and with any luck it would be Jolnir or Calatin. As yet it was too early to say which for sure. But it was definitely someone with a great skill in the Power, someone also familiar, and that meant there would be no problem with it continuing a role within the Abend.

As for the other position, much as it grieved her, she had to acknowledge that what they needed most was another war-mage. Whoever took over Geitla, there was no guarantee that their Power would manifest itself in that particular way, even if they had once been capable of such mass destruction. If they did then it was an added bonus. However, four war-mages were an absolute must if they were to make the best of this opportunity to reclaim the Islands. Quintillean might have an over-inflated opinion of his place within the Abend, but he would fight with the others if need be. Tancostyl was theirs for now, and in that respect was well able to stand up to Quintillean in brute force, even if he was no match in the more subtle ways. Eliavres had acquired her own aptitude for negotiating the ways of power and influence while still having a healthy ability when it came to death and destruction. What they needed, Magda decided, was another Eliavres. Someone not given to fighting everything in sight as Tancostyl did, thus giving Quintillean opportunities to manipulate weaknesses. And certainly not another eccentric like Calatin.

A week later she had whittled away the inexperienced and the insufficiently talented, and was ready to make her decision. Her attention had been caught by the very acolyte Anarawd had mentioned to Eliavres. The good thing was that he appeared to be a very different personality from his former mentor, whatever his destructive gifts or training. Yet there was another candidate, too. A woman! One with abnormal talents in such things and none in the more usual areas the witches regularly excelled in. Yet who to choose? Staring down at Geitla's recumbent and swelling form, Magda completed her daily inspection of the dying witch and left the room with a cursory nod to the slaves who attended to Geitla's bodily needs. Nothing to be done there today.

Instead she walked to a small chamber on the south side, where a pleasant solar had become her favourite place for examining the acolytes. The two candidates were already there waiting for her, each tense and expectant but neither talking to the other, and standing at opposite ends of the room. That was good. She did not want to elevate two who were friends with one another before they joined the higher ranks. That would complicate matters far too much!

The woman was coarse-featured and muscular. That in itself surprised Magda, for the woman could not possibly be totally pure-bred DeÁine with her flame-red hair and bulk. She had the height to be sure, but that was all. Yet she certainly had an aptitude when it came to drawing in Power and using it for violence. Of all the candidates except the man standing opposite her, this one could handle the destructive side with the greatest dexterity and in the largest quantities. The only thing which made Magda cautious was that the woman appeared to have very little talent in other areas. She would have loved nothing more than to have a true war-witch amongst them, and to see the male Abend's faces when they had to fight alongside her, but she was not totally convinced.

As for the man, the only thing holding Magda back from offering him the position was the fact that he had studied for so long under Anarawd. Would that mean he had odd ideas about how little he needed to co-operate with the rest of the Abend? Anarawd was bad enough, going off on one of his schemes usually just when he was wanted. To have two like that would be disastrous, as they had found with Calatin's eccentricities. In his defence the acolyte had shown little loyalty to Anarawd for having abandoned his training and leaving him in the lurch. It would not have hurt Anarawd to have at least formally handed his students to others when he was in disgrace, rather than leaving them in limbo. What surprised Magda more was the revelation that Geitla had picked up the threads as best she could in Anarawd's absence.

Suddenly she had an idea of what might settle her mind one way or the other.

"Come with me," she commanded, and led the two of them back to Geitla's room. "Give me your assessment of what afflicts this Abend," she demanded, gesturing the woman forward. "You first, Harimella."

The large woman walked forward and pulled back the sheets and blankets, then lifted Geitla's gown to expose her midriff.

"Curious," she muttered, passing her hand over the distended flesh.

However, she offered no insight or explanation, seeming more interested in Geitla's full figure in a sexual way than in whatever Power structure was churning away within the recumbent witch. Inside Magda sighed. No, this one would never do outside of a war situation. As a sledgehammer she was perfect, for subtle work useless. She must be brought on and nurtured in her talents, and if she was that interested in other women, then Magda could think of ways of passing some hours very pleasurably with her. But as a member of the Abend? No.

"Barrax, what do you think?" Magda asked gesturing Harimella back and the man forward.

His reaction was completely different. Magda felt him draw the finest, delicate trickle of Power and reach out with great finesse to probe the surface of the abomination. His eyebrows rose in surprise at whatever he felt there although he remained silent. Opening Geitla's legs he inserted fingers inside her and appeared to be examining her internally.

"This is most odd," he said without emotion or arousal, looking up to Magda. "Geitla has attempted to seduce me into using my Power on her on several occasions. Normally just touching her in this way would incite a response, but she's completely oblivious to my probing. Even stranger, it's as though her womb has been sealed off with a weaving of Power. I can feel it with the tips of my fingers. There's no way I'll risk pushing against this barrier, because I can feel a serious warding within it. If I did, I would most likely lose my fingers if not my hand or arm. And it's a male weaving."

"A male weaving?" Harimella was looking at him with dense incomprehension on her face. "How can you tell that?"

Barrax quirked and eyebrow at Magda which seemed to say 'how could you consider this one for elevation when she doesn't know something as basic as that?' *And he's right*, Magda thought.

"Harimella, my sweetling. Would you be so good as to leave us for now. Come to my rooms this evening and I'll offer you something you may find interesting."

Harimella's expression flickered brief disappointment, then her eyes travelled down over Magda's figure and a smile broke out as she left. *Oh yes! We shall have fun tonight!* Magda thought with relish. That one would willingly accept a different kind of partnership unofficially, and officially Magda would take her under her wing and begin some serious training with her. Most remiss of Helga to have let such talent slip without being channelled. Possibly because Harimella did not seem the sort to take to Helga's sadistic scheming.

When the other woman had gone, Magda turned her attention back to Barrax, who was currently washing his hands at the pitcher and bowl by the window.

"Any other observations," she asked guardedly.

Barrax thought as he towelled his hands dry, and threw the damp cloth onto a pile of others awaiting washing.

"Hmmm, ... Very curious weaving, that one," he pondered. "I've never felt the like, but then I assume neither has anyone else. It seems to be for a very specific purpose. If I were to venture a guess, I would say that another life-force was using the Power to weave a container for itself within Geitla. It seems to be attaching itself to her in all fundamental functions, so it will presumably be able to keep her body functioning as normal once it has full control." He frowned. "What's more concerning is the fact that Geitla's own signature is now very faint. Mind you, I don't think she's passed on to beyond the veil yet. It doesn't feel like that at all."

"No, it didn't to me," admitted Magda. "I think she's still alive in some form."

"And some form is probably right. It's as though she's being dragged forcibly into becoming mere energy. Divorced from her body, if you will. This other is now taking control of the physical side, and I suspect within days we'll find the body of Geitla will awake with a totally different personality inside it. A male personality." He paused and appeared to be weighing up whether he should say what was in his mind. After a moment with the two of them in a locked gaze, he exhaled heavily and spoke again.

"I believe I've felt that presence before. A long time ago when I was in the early stages of my training. It was a senior acolyte who undertook much of my initial higher training. His name was Othinn. …I heard he had some kind of accident, then he was gone. …Is it possible it's him?"

Magda breathed a sigh of relief. Barrax! Of course! That was where she had heard his name before. Now her memory had been jogged she remembered Othinn talking about his favourite trainee when they were in bed, back in the days when Othinn had been nearly normal, her lover, and before his obsession with becoming Jolnir. It also explained Barrax's antipathy at being abandoned by Anarawd, because it had been the second time he had lost his personal tutor despite having risen so far so fast.

"Yes!" she said with more eagerness than she had planned. "Othinn went over into the Power and his physical body wasted and died. But his spirit was long out of the body when that stopped functioning. The soul has lingered, riding the tides for several years. I've spoken to him, or at least his essence, many a time." It was such a relief to speak to someone who accepted the possibility without thinking her mad. "When he first became energy he was intoxicated with it. I believe he tried everything he could think of to find out what his powers were. Whatever they were, I'm convinced they weren't what he expected. Of late I've felt him ever closer. It's as if he wants to come back."

"Then be careful," Barrax warned her, "because I can feel a death-wish in there as well! He may have seen an opportunity to reunite with a physical body so that when that gets killed, he'll pass over properly this time."

That jolted Magda. It was the one thing she had not considered. She had assumed that Othinn/Jolnir was coming back to her. A hope that he had finally understood that together they were far more than the sum of their separate parts. That he was still following his own selfish desires was not a happy thought, but one which she admitted she should have considered.

Seeing the conflicting emotions flitting across Magda's face, Barrax stepped closer to her and drew her into his arms, intending words of comfort but unable to disguise his physical delight at getting this close to a senior Abend.

"My, my, poppet," Magda breathed huskily, and snuggled closer prompting a further reaction. "I think we should celebrate your *elevation* to the Abend, don't you?" She had not felt this way about a male acolyte since losing Othinn, and it was a surprisingly welcome return. Harimella would wait. This was far more intense, and she led Barrax away to a separate tower room where some time later rippling surges of the Power caused masonry to shake, and loose roof tiles to cascade down into the yard below.

"Bloody witches," muttered a slave as he went to find a broom to sweep up the slate shards from the cobbles. "All they do is fuck and fight!"

He should have added 'and scheme', for as Magda broke the news later that evening it had varying responses. Her highly controlled conversation with Eliavres and Anarawd brought her their wholehearted approval. If Eliavres was less than thrilled that it had turned out to be Anarawd's former acolyte who had been chosen, he was wise enough to say nothing, and he openly commended Magda on the process by which she had made the selection. Together they had contacted Tancostyl next. As a fellow war-mage he would have to work with Barrax if in no other area. To the trio's surprise he accepted Barrax's elevation without question or rancour.

"*Excellent news*," he observed in an almost distracted way.

"*What's wrong*?" Eliavres asked before they broke off contact. "*You seem to be preoccupied*."

Anarawd would have said 'worried', or even 'stressed' might describe what they were feeling better, but as ever Eliavres had the tactful touch.

"*The rivers*," Tancostyl's distracted thoughts came back. "*They're already over their banks and there are still great chunks of snow and ice coming down on them. My horse has had to plough through water near up to its belly twice already. It's to be hoped this passes swiftly!*"

He broke the connection abruptly.

"*Dare we ask Helga to control the weather again*?" wondered Magda.

"*Sweet Lotus, no*!" Eliavres exclaimed. "*She may have the ability, but she'll rush the job and we could well end up with a bigger mess than we have already*."

"*I agree*," Anarawd seconded him. "*We shall just have to put up with a little inconvenience for a while. I doubt Helga will be overly pleased at Barrax's selection, and she might take her revenge in spiteful ways which do more harm than good*."

Helga, already back at Tarah Castle, was indeed not pleased. However, she was shrewd enough to recognise that she would do well to side with the majority of the Abend for now. She was too isolated to fight them when they were united, and she suspected that whatever Masanae and Quintillean were up to, it would bring little benefit to her personally. Against that, Eliavres and Anarawd had given initial backing to her own schemes, which was not to be gone back on lightly. Grudgingly, she therefore gave her consent which cemented the preliminary elevation officially. Five members supporting a nomination, when there were only two other left to vote, overrode even a leader of Quintillean's long-standing. She would not join the others breaking the news to Masanae, though. Her reactions would be judged and analysed, as she knew from past experience of the head witch, and she wanted no weakness to be displayed for further exploitation.

Masanae's reaction was one which brought secret delight to Eliavres and Anarawd. It was a very long time since either of them had known the controlled witch be so startled, but that was as nothing to Quintillean's reaction.

"*You've done what?*" his thoughts shrieked back at them.

"*Well you've been out of contact for so long,*" Eliavres responded calmly. "*Things are moving on a pace here without you, Quintillean, and we had no way of knowing when you were likely to come back. We needed another war-mage to replace Calatin, and you've done nothing to show us that you had any intention of taking the matter in hand.*"

Sweet Lotus, that's a nice move! Anarawd thought to himself. *That's dropped it straight back in Quintillean's lap! He's the leader, he really should've done something about it the minute we knew Calatin was gone. He's not left himself any room to wriggle this time.*

"*We've learned that some of our fellow DeÁine from Sinut are on their way,*" Eliavres added with withering sweetness. "*We certainly don't want to greet them and their tame acolytes under-strength, do we?*"

Anarawd winced at that, but with pleasure. It was good to feel Quintillean stuck on a hook of his own making. He could not ask how they knew about Sinut without revealing that he had plotted behind the rest of the Abend's backs. Eliavres had him with his back to the wall, and at this point Anarawd was secretly glad that he had backed Eliavres and not Quintillean, for it was nice to be on the winning side for the first time in a long while. And although Quintillean did posture and protest, it was clear that he could do nothing about being so neatly outmanoeuvred. Yet as the three broke the link and brought Barrax into their circle for a celebratory first meeting, Quintillean was linking to Masanae.

"*We must hurry!*" he told her insistently. "*Where are you?*"

He knew she was getting ever closer, but could barely conceal his relief when her reply came from much closer than he had expected.

"*I'm at Ralja,*" she told him with icy calm. "*I shall cross by ferry tomorrow and should easily be with you the day after.*"

"*We must hurry!*" he repeated, in itself a bad sign. It was not like Quintillean to be so agitated.

"*Be calm!*" Masanae ordered him. "*This was never going to be easy. As it is I've had my own prime sacrifices spirited away from me, and as you keep saying, there is little time. Certainly no time for me to go chasing round the countryside looking for them. I have the king of Brychan with me. He's a poor specimen, but he'll do for the binding.*"

"*What of the third and fourth?*" demanded Quintillean, still barely in control. "*We must have four!*"

Grinding her teeth in exasperation Masanae snapped back,

"*I've brought plenty of sacrifices! The spare ones will just have to do! Adapt, Quintillean! We must make the best of what we have or not do it at all. I'm fully aware that we planned to obtain control over the cursed Island weapons too, and that may not happen now. It's regrettable, but have we seen hide or hair of these things in all of the centuries since the great defeat? No! So if time and events are conspiring against us doing the whole ritual, then at least we should get total control of our own Treasures as soon as possible. Therefore there's no more time to dither around finding precisely the right sacrifices! I believe we should act decisively with what we have at our disposal. Don't you agree?*" She decided to prod his ego hard. "*Or are you losing your nerve?*"

"*No!*" he snapped back. "*We do it the day after tomorrow! I will have control!*"

You? Have control? Masanae thought to herself when the link was gone. *Oh I doubt that! We shall be the ones who return in glory with Volla's lost Treasures, not you alone. They are what's important now, not some spectre of the past which haunts you!*

Chapter 6

The Care Of Others

Ergardia: late Spring-moon

"Blessed Martyrs! Look at the size of that thing!" Ivain gasped in awe as he and Hugh rounded the end of the loch and he caught his first sight of Lorne Castle.

"Pretty impressive, isn't it?" Hugh said with a smile for his protégé's wonderment. "No hostile army has ever entered those walls – not even in the first DeÁine invasion."

"That's a proper castle!" Tiny Arthur declared approvingly from his spot in front of Hugh on the hired horse.

"A little loyalty to Prydein would be nice," Hugh chided him with good humour, responding to Arthur's excitement. "I know our castles aren't quite on the same scale, but this is the headquarters of the whole of the Order, you know. We don't do so badly in comparison to the rest of the Islands. And while we're on the subject, young Arthur, no running riot around this place! This is no homely castle. There are places where you might come to serious harm – not least because with so many men within, there not everyone will know who you are, and they might arrest you for being a spy!"

Hugh had little hope that his warnings would do any good. Even after his dreadful ride to catch up with Hugh, it had only taken a few days for Arthur to bounce back to his usual ebullient self. Luckily the diminutive street urchin had taken an immediate liking to Ivain, and the young king had responded in kind, which meant that Ivain was able to distract Arthur when Hugh needed him out of the way. However, Arthur had somehow already wheedled Ivain's life-story out of him, and was now as determined as Ivain that his monarch should no longer be kept in the dark about important matters. So most of the time it was easier just to tell the two of them, rather than trying to fend off two such determined young folk.

An exhausted Haply and Grimston had ridden into Bittern a couple of days after Arthur, just as Hugh was about to set off for the coast, but had shown similarly determination over not letting their young wards out of their sight again so quickly. For both Knights there had been the additional and unexpected reward of discovering Ivain alive and well, and neither had attempted to conceal their delight at the reunion. So they had staggered on board the ship and done their recovering during the voyage, content to have their two favourite charges in their sights once more. Aside from them, a mere two lances of men had come as an escort, since Ergardia was hardly hostile territory. However, Commander Breca had asked to come along as Hugh's aide, confessing that he wanted to continue to do what he could to help Ivain as well. Since Ealdorman Hereman was well able to cope without his capable second-in-command now that the fighting was over, Breca and the ever loyal Pauli were also amongst the small party riding up to the great castle.

At the nearest jetty Hugh hailed the castle, and by nightfall they were settled in the capacious guest quarters being well fed on excellent food. For Hugh it felt strange to be in a near-deserted Lorne. He would have been worried had he not been told when they landed at Firthton of the recent goings on on Ergardia. Commander Dana had apparently passed through there two weeks ago on the fifth, with a huge number of Knights from Rheged, and the grange commander had confirmed that Dana was riding to make the muster. That Brego had called a full muster of all Ergardia Knights was evidence enough for Hugh that he too had received Berengar's warning. Nothing less would have warranted such an action, as those left behind to defend Ergardia were all aged veterans whose fighting days were over, or boys little older than Arthur. The Rheged Knights were those who had returned from fighting in the east, and were now undertaking the defence of Ergardia's east coast from where they could go to the aid of their old homeland if necessary. Remembering Jaenberht's message of the total collapse of the regular army on Rheged, Hugh was deeply relieved that so many of its Order men had survived against the odds.

Even here in Lorne, only a skeleton defence remained. Brego would never leave Lorne completely undefended – its incredible library carrying the sum of all Island knowledge was enough in itself to justify a sizeable guard, whatever else happened. But by Lorne's standards this was a fraction of those who would normally be here. However, Hugh was assured that Brego himself was due back and soon, having only gone as far as Elphstone to consult with Master Arsaidh.

"He'll be back by the end of the month, have no fear, sire," the senior captain had assured him. "Probably sooner knowing the Master!"

More intriguing was the news that two DeÁine had recently been at Lorne, and had been allowed into the inner sanctum of the library. For once Hugh had some sympathy with Arthur, for he found it frustrating in the extreme to be kept waiting in the dark with only cryptic remarks to make guesses from. Despite being a Grand Master on his own Island, the men of Lorne clearly recognise no authority except Brego's, and without his consent they were reticent to tell Hugh anything of consequence. All the visitors could do was talk to the head librarian about the great bow which Ivain carried. The researchers were all fascinated by the thing, and even more so by Ivain's assertion that he had felt something very odd happen on the fifteenth when they had only just landed. Carefully recounting the experience while a scribe took notes, Ivain found it hard to put the experience into words.

"It was the oddest tingling," he told them. "I had the Bow in its case slung across my back. Most of the time now I'm vaguely aware of its presence, but before then I had no inkling that it had any sort of power or energy – not even after we worked out that it was something special. It was other people who said that they had a weird crawling sensation over their flesh when I used it. Me, I felt nothing – and that was how it was on that morning. There was nothing out of the ordinary. Then all of a sudden, in the afternoon, it was like it was alive and had woken up! There was this strange vibration. You know how a hound sometimes quivers with excitement? That shiver which runs right through them? That was how it felt as though the Bow was behaving! Like something had called to it!"

The researchers all looked at one another.

"I wonder," the head scribe mused. "Could another of the Island Treasures be responsible for that?"

The researchers all swiftly disappeared into the warren of the library, muttering about sympathetic reactions, and leaving Ivain and the others none the wiser.

It was therefore with considerable relief three days later, on the twenty-fourth, that the trumpets rang out signalling Brego's return. With strict instructions to Haply and Grimston to hold on to Arthur for all they were worth, Hugh led his small party down to Brego's office to wait for him. It seemed to take forever for Brego to appear, and it was all Haply, Grimston and Ivain could do to stop Arthur from climbing the huge dragon carved into Brego's office doors. Hoisting him onto Ivain's shoulder so that he could examine the dragon's face was the only way that they managed to keep him out of mischief, for the street-urchin was fascinated by the great fabled creature.

"I'd love to ride one of *those*! Look at how big his wings are! I bet he could carry me even faster than Scythian!" he was declaring excitedly to his friends, when the sound of marching boots announced Brego's presence moments before he appeared around the corner of the corridor.

He stopped in his tracks at the sight of his old friend trying to loosen Arthur's grasp on the dragon.

"Great Maker! You're recruiting them a bit young aren't you?" he commented in surprise.

Hugh turned to his old friend in time to see the shock turn to eyes twinkling with amusement.

"Brego! By the Trees, it's good to see you!"

Hugh strode to meet Brego and clasped his hand warmly, taking in the fact that Brego was mailed and armed.

"You have the Bow?" were Brego's first words. "It's safe? It's here?"

"Yes it is," Hugh replied, thinking nothing illustrated how much must hang on this than the way Brego had forgone all formality and hospitality to ask of this before all else. "We have it. Or rather Ivain has it. May I introduce King Ivain," and he gestured Ivain forward to shake Brego's hand. As Ivain stepped forward and Haply and Grimston hauled Arthur firmly back into their grasp, Hugh added. "And he's the only one who seems to be able to handle the thing without feeling ill."

Brego's eyebrows raised in mild surprise then ushered them into his office. His servant, Angus, hurried in behind them and immediately disappeared into an antechamber. Someone must have deputised in his absence, for almost immediately he reappeared, still in his travelling clothes, but bearing a tray with hot drinks and refreshments on it. Tiny Arthur's eyes lit up at the sight of the thick slices of rich fruit cake and Breca had to grab the scruff of his jacket and haul him back from making a dash for the plate.

"That's for the Master," he hissed urgently. "You've had your lunch already!"

"I could find room for a bit of that!" Arthur declared longingly, the habits of scavenging food whenever it passed his way having lingered.

Luckily Brego was more amused than the scowling Angus. "Where did you find this one, Hugh?" he chuckled.

Hugh gave a short summation of Arthur's connection with the Knights, doing his best to hint at the massacre of several of Arthur's companions at the hands of Duke Brion without being open about the extent of the atrocity in front of Arthur. Brego's equally suppressed response nonetheless signalled that he understood exactly what Hugh had tried to convey.

"I think we might need more cake," was all he said to Angus, whose disapproval was melting into sympathy too. "I see there's been more going on in Prydein than I'd heard of. You'd better tell me all."

Galling though it was for the Prydein folk to recount their story first, they hid their impatience and did their best to brief Brego as fully as they could. When they got to the news that Alaiz had been sighted he was delighted, but that rapidly faded with the news of Alaiz' pregnancy.

"May the Trees protect her!" he prayed fervently. "I had no idea – please believe me in that, Hugh. I would *never* have let her out of the castle if I'd had any notion of her condition."

Ivain coughed. "Excuse me Master Brego, but there's something more I have to know. You see Alaiz was more like my sister than my wife. I'm not such a fool as to believe it's my child she's carrying. I know beyond a shadow of a doubt that it isn't. But I do love her like a sister. Please tell me, do you know who the father is? Please set my mind at rest that it isn't some fop of a courtier who blinded her with empty promises."

Brego and Hugh exchanged shocked glances.

"You know it isn't *yours*?" Hugh said in surprise. "Why didn't you say so when you first heard about it?"

Ivain gave a bitter laugh. "Because I've belatedly realised that we've all done enough damage to Alaiz as it is. I might've been a bit slow catching on while I was fighting the court at every turn, but I'm not entirely stupid! The last thing I wanted was for this to become common knowledge on Prydein. There's little I can do to make right the miserable years she suffered at court going through our farce of a marriage. But the least I could do was make sure she would continue to be treated with respect, not be ostracised and persecuted for finding some happiness. And before you ask what I think will happen, Hugh, the answer is that I'll worry about that when the bigger problems are sorted. But the last thing I care about is what that two-faced bunch of nobles think! If Alaiz wants to go her own way, then the likes of Amalric, and those he was sucking up to, will just have to swallow the bitter pill – given the way they behaved over Brion, it won't be the only one!"

Brego gave Ivain a long appraising look. "I hope you're sincere in your concern for Alaiz," he cautioned, "because I'll be much displeased if I find that this has rebounded on the man concerned. Your wife spent a lot of time here in the company of one of the Knights who came with her, despite our best efforts to minimise their contact."

"Oliver?" guessed Hugh immediately, imagining how the tall, dark and handsome Knight might have caught Alaiz' eye because of his similarity to Ivain.

"No," Brego sighed. "To his credit Oliver foresaw the potential complications of Alaiz' relationship and confided his worries to me. No, it was Hamelin – his closest friend – whom Alaiz fell for. He – and *only* he – could possibly be the father of her child."

Hugh groaned. The honest and kind-hearted Knight was someone whom it would be much harder to sway from Alaiz's side. Far harder than

Oliver, who could have been made to see political necessities. Yet Ivain stunned him with his next words.

"Then they shall have a manor provided for them. Somewhere they can live away from the vicious backbiting of the court and the pointing fingers and the whispers behind their backs. I liked Hamelin enormously the little I saw of him when he, with Oliver and the others, dragged Amalric back after Calatin had imprisoned him at Trevelga. I can't imagine him seducing Alaiz just to brag about it later on. If he truly cares for her, then it's the least I can do for her to let her be happy with him."

"But she's your *queen*!" Hugh groaned, his heart sinking into his boots at the thought of trying to sort this additional mess out. For all that he had chastised Amalric for putting Alaiz's role before the woman, he had not expected Ivain to totally sweep it away with such little regard. At the moment an heir was what Prydein desperately needed to give the people a sense of continuity and stability. Without Alaiz how was Ivain to do that with any decorum?

However, Ivain was having none of it. With great firmness he looked Hugh in the eye. "Yes she is! But she was forced into that when we were both children younger than Arthur here. How could we possibly have known what would be expected of us? It was callous and unfair to tie her to me for life in the first place. Surely a simple betrothal which could've been broken would've been enough? But to keep that bondage going when the political necessity had long since gone was cruel and pointless, and I won't be a party to it anymore. Do you understand me, Hugh? I'm eternally grateful for everything you ever did for me, but on this matter I won't be swayed. If we both come out of this and there's anything of Prydein left to rule over, then it's going to be by a very different kind of kingship. If necessary I'll simply declare Alaiz dead in the mayhem and let her escape that way, but I won't force her back into a cage again. I couldn't live with myself if I did. Sacred Trees, I'm fighting hard enough to stay out of a cage of my own which everyone's made for me. So I'm going to be the best kind of king I can be. Not some half-strangled shadow of my grandfather! And that has to start with how I treat Alaiz."

Hugh sat looking stunned as Commander Breca gently reminded his superior,

"He's changed, Master Hugh. Ivain's his own man now. I've seen that, and so have Haply and Grimston. That's why we were so committed to helping him. He has to rule as a man, not some bound and tied child, and that means making his own decisions. While you were freeing Prydein, we've found that Ivain's an able commander in his own right whilst over in the west."

"But what of an heir?" Hugh asked weakly. "That was the start of all our troubles."

"Yes it was!" Ivain declared. "And now I can't believe that nobody told me to simply nominate someone. Or better still, several! That way the throne would never have been compromised. But since I intend to return Prydein to having a Jarl and a body of nobles who *elect* our leader, an heir isn't an issue! And I'm sure I can find someone capable, just in case I don't live to see it through," and his gaze strayed to an oblivious Arthur, occupied by cake.

Hugh looked as though he might just faint. Brego went to a cupboard in the corner of the room, extracted a glass decanter and gestured to Angus to find glasses.

"Sounds a sensible idea to me," he told Hugh, as he poured him a stiff drink. He placed the decanter within reach of the others and went back to his seat. "I'll leave that there. You might need another after I've told you my news!"

With that he proceeded to tell Hugh of all that had gone on at Lorne. Of the arrival of Taise and Sithfrey, and their work in the archives with Andra. Of how he had despatched folk to the other Islands in search of the Island Treasures, and to rescue Wistan and Kenelm. And how he had proclaimed the revival of the sept in Celidon on receipt of earlier news from Brychan.

"I believe we have to fight," he told his stunned audience as he came to an end. "That's why I've sent Dana to muster every man I can afford to take across to Brychan. Others have gone ahead to Celidon and will do what they can to get that Island ready. If Brychan falls, I've no doubt that the Abend will see Celidon as their next target, for that's the obvious way to neutralise us here on Ergardia. We know that the Abend can't personally come onto this Island and still hope to use their powers, but that won't stop them sending a slave army our way. An army which can walk in with immunity to Ergardia's own power. I won't let that happen, but the first step towards that means denying them the crossing to Celidon. And I won't abandon Brychan to its fate either."

After a moment to allow everything to sink in, Hugh took another swig of uisge before changing the subject slightly. "Berengar's an interesting choice of Grand Master, don't you think?"

Brego grinned for the first time since they had met. "And a good one, I'd say! For the life of me I could never understand why the Brychan sept elected Rainer. Maybe they thought he'd be good for them in that quagmire of a political system they have over there? Who knows? …Another lesson you might want to study," he added, looking to Ivain with a wink. "But I'm much relieved that it's Berengar who's in charge now it's come to a fight."

"You've met him?"

"Oh yes! Not for long enough to know him like I know you, Hugh – or even like Maelbrigt – but enough to tell you that he's a first class leader in the field, and that his ability's teamed with a healthy dose of common sense. He's not an arrogant man either. He's not the type to underestimate his enemies. Ruari MacBeth thinks highly of him too. And while I know you've had reservations in the past about Sionnachan, he rates Berengar's capabilities as a leader very highly as well – and he's well placed to comment having fought alongside Brychan's Master of Foresters, and therefore in part with Berengar, after Gavra."

Ivain leaned forwards. "So Brychan's defence is being led by the man who stands the best chance of succeeding?" Brego nodded, pleasantly surprised at the way the young king was keeping up with things and showing an intelligent understanding. "In which case how do things like the Bow help?" Ivain asked him cutting to the heart of the matter.

"Ah," Brego sighed. "That's what I've been up to ask Arsaidh about. If the Forester's records are right – and we have to remember that they've been copied out a few times over the centuries – then the answer, Ivain, is 'a lot'!"

"Are they magic?" asked Arthur. He had surprised Hugh by sitting quietly through all of this, a frown of concentration on his small face as he consumed an enormous amount of cake whilst trying to make sure he missed nothing of the planning.

"In a way, yes, I suppose they are," Brego answered, unable to refrain from smiling at the way Arthur had subconsciously pocketed several slices for later on. Old habits clearly died hard no matter how his circumstances had changed. "Arsaidh tells me that all these pieces are best used in conjunction with one another. Which makes it all the more important to track them all down. But equally interestingly, his records imply that the pieces will select the one who is best suited to use each one. And that's something which you folk have thankfully confirmed for me already. You're clearly meant to be the one, Ivain."

Ivain looked shocked. "It *chose* me? Why me?"

"That I can't begin to answer," Brego admitted. "However, Arsaidh assures me that you, and only you, will be able to shoot that Bow without some pretty unpleasant side effects. I doubt it would kill anyone else, but they'd feel distinctly unwell. More to the point, whatever unearthly powers the Bow possesses would fail to manifest themselves for anyone else. And before you ask, as far as we can tell it stays that way until you die. If you were to be killed then the Bow would choose someone else. If you were desperately wounded, but hung onto life, it seems likely that the Bow would transfer itself temporarily to someone both you and it were comfortable with."

"Sacred Trees," Commander Breca breathed. "That makes it sound as though it's almost alive! Like it has a free will of its own?"

Brego sighed and shrugged. "Don't ask me to explain. I'm just telling you what Arsaidh's records say. I think 'alive' might be pushing it a bit too far, but yes, it does seem to interact in a way that no weapon we're capable of creating can."

"So what you goin' to do about them nasty wizards?" Arthur piped up, his voice muffled around a mouthful of cake. "Can Ivain's Bow stick an arrow in 'em? Kill 'em and their magic too?"

The adults all struggled to hide their smiles. There was something strangely endearing about the fierce way Arthur stuck to the idea of fighting the DeÁine, never getting distracted too far from the point.

"Well that's the question, isn't it, Arthur," Brego told him gravely. "I think Hugh and I have some serious planning to do now."

"I got me armour with me!" Arthur declared stoutly, scrubbing his hands clean down his front as if he might be asked to go and fetch it straight away. "Haply and Grimston brung it for me. You say the word Mister Brego and I'm ready!"

"Sacred Root and Branch! The boy has armour?" Brego was aghast. "You don't mean to tell me you intend to take him into battle, Hugh?"

"I *been* in a battle!" Arthur told him before Hugh could explain. "I sat on Scythian wiv' Master Hugh and we chopped them evil rebels to bits! Beat 'em proper! 'Specially that Brion! He was piss-scared when we beat him!"

Hugh groaned and slid a touch lower in his seat as Brego fixed him with an appalled glare.

Grimston cleared his throat. "Don't look like that, Master Brego. You don't know Arthur! Try as you might you won't keep him out of a fight. He's defeated all of our best efforts! In the end we decided that, since we couldn't stop him coming along, the best thing we could do was make sure he was properly kitted out. Some idiot nobleman had already had the armour made, so our armourer only had to adjust it to fit Arthur properly. We bought it along because we know what he's like. You could tie him up in the dungeons here, and he'd still pop up out of some piece of baggage just before you rode into battle two Islands away."

Brego gave a disbelieving shake of his head but declined to argue the point. However, he successfully kept Arthur out of his office for the next couple of days by the simple expediency of arranging training sessions for every hour Arthur was awake. By the end of the next day Arthur was so tired he was falling asleep in his dinner and had to be carried from the dining room by Ivain and put to bed.

Yet even Brego had not the heart to keep Arthur away when a long line of soldiers appeared on the shores of the loch the next evening. Under the strict supervision of Haply and Grimston, Arthur was allowed to accompany Brego and Hugh down to the great landing stage, which not so long ago had seen the mass embarkation of troops. There they waited as the ferry brought a tall, thin Knight across, with an escort carrying two items slung in makeshift slings. As the ferry docked, the tall Knight stepped up onto the quay and made a crisp salute to the two Grand Masters.

"Yaroman of Celidon, reporting sire," he said. "I come on the instructions of MacBeth and Maelbrigt."

That made Brego start. "MacBeth *and* Maelbrigt? They're together?"

"Yes, sire, they are. It's a long story, but before I tell you, can we get these two things to some safe place?"

"What are they?"

"The Sword and the Shield, sire!"

There was a collective gasp from all those on the quay.

"They found them?" Brego demanded, unable to keep the delight from his voice.

In response even the normally sombre Yaroman could not resist grinning. "Aye, sire! That they did!" Then his face fell. "Mind you, we paid a high price to get the Sword. Two of the very best left on Celidon paid for it with their lives. Forester Knights Aldred and Bosel were killed after a terrible fight with DeÁine Hunters while trying to get a ship to bring these back on. We'd had to separate our force because of lack of boats to get us to a proper port."

He sighed. "After that, I marched south with the greater force. Maelbrigt and the survivors of the attack sailed down to Sarn Castle in a ship they finally got from Noth. When I got to Sarn, Captain Heaney told me that they'd arrived the same day that MacBeth turned up on one of the North-folk's boats. When Maelbrigt retrieved the Sword he got a strange little creature called a squint too. The ancients seem to have bred or somehow made them to live in between time. They connect people to the weapons – but don't ask me to explain how because I don't know. Heaney says that this squint managed to tell them that there ought to be a squint for every one of the Island Treasures. He also said that MacBeth and Maelbrigt were most insistent that you'd find one with the Bowl, and that there's a Knife too."

"Did they?" Brego was intrigued. "Well, now, that's something even I didn't know until a few days ago! And Arsaidh didn't tell me all of that – about the squints that is. He only told me about the Knife. Apparently I won't know where that is until we've activated the Bowl, but if there's something to help then that might make it easier."

"They're funny things," Yaroman continued as Brego led the way into the heart of the fortress, several men behind carrying the huge weapons. "A squint's a bit like a very odd looking squirrel, and about the size of a large child or a very small adult."

"Sacred Trees!" Hugh gasped. "The creatures from the old legends? I haven't heard of them since I was young enough to be told stories by my nurse!"

"Well you'd better start believing, sire," Yaroman told him, "because they're pretty useful little chaps. I suspect they might understand the Treasures even more than the ancients do. And on that score, MacBeth seems to have picked up a ghostly apparition of one of them. It was she who told him to get the Shield back to Celidon and send it on to you here. According to her, Maelbrigt is the rightful user of the Sword, but the Shield hasn't chosen its bearer yet. Maelbrigt and MacBeth have continued on the ship to follow her instructions.

"Apparently the ancients have problems of their own and this ghostly lady thinks that MacBeth can help them. From the message he's written it would seem that he believes that if he helps them, then they'll be able to help us more." He dug into an inside pocket and produced two sealed letters. "But both Maelbrigt and MacBeth wrote to you themselves before they left. They were long gone by the time I got to Sarn, so I'm telling you all this through Heaney."

However, he was just handing over the letters when the men carrying the two Treasures yelped and dropped them with a clang onto the stone floor. As the sling of blankets fell away everyone saw that both pieces were glowing eerily.

"Cross of Swords!" Hugh gasped, as Brego hurriedly signalled his men to sheath the half drawn swords.

But the most dramatic reaction came from Ivain. The young king gave a gasp and dropped to his knees.

"It's happening again!" he cried out. "What happened before! It's the same tingling."

Haply and Grimston leapt to Ivain's aid, but equally as quickly had to retreat.

"Lost Souls!" groaned Haply, turning a sickly colour. "*Aagh*! I can't touch him without wanting to heave!"

Grimston tried a second time, but had to let go of Ivain's arm as he gulped convulsively. "No use," he gasped. "Can't do it."

At which point Arthur scrambled to Ivain's side and helped him to his feet without suffering any ill effects.

"By the Trees, look at that!" Commander Breca exclaimed. "Do you think it's because he's a child? Is it his innocence which protects him?"

Hugh shook his head. "Sadly, I doubt that Arthur's got much in the way of innocence left after the childhood he's had. Youth may be the reason, or rather more worryingly, maybe the Bow has chosen Arthur as Ivain's replacement if he gets killed?"

Master Brego looked appalled. "Surely not! He's a little lad! He can't be expected to lead men into battle!"

However, the unearthly glow surrounding the Shield and Sword was subsiding, and as it did Ivain swiftly recovered. By the time they were all congregated in Brego's office, the Sword and Shield propped up on either side of the great hearth, he was able to tell them more of what he had felt. With one hand close to the Bow, which currently rested on the massive stone mantle-shelf, he tried to formulate his thoughts.

"Knowing a bit more about things this time, I think the best way to explain what happened was that it was like the pieces were calling out to something. It's like the pieces were trying to reach something or someone. If you hadn't said that the Sword had picked Maelbrigt, and the Bow me, I would say that they're trying to call to the right person. But it can't be that, because if that was the case then I shouldn't have been affected. And I can still feel the residue on the Bow now, even though I wasn't in contact with it when they went all strange."

"The Sword wasn't as glowy as that Shield," Arthur observed.

"Wasn't it? I didn't spot that," Haply said.

"Me neither, even though I was practically on top of it," admitted Grimston. "But then again I was focused on Ivain, and the world was spinning around me."

"Well it weren't!" Arthur was adamant. "So mebbe it has somthin' to do with them squints? You said that this mister Maelbrigt had one wiv' him, an' he's the one what belongs to the Sword. So mebbe that's why it didn't glow so much?"

Brego stared at Arthur in astonishment. "Sacred Trees! He's right!"

Hugh permitted himself a smug moment at Brego's disconcertion. "Never mind, Brego, you'll get used to it after you've been around Arthur for a bit! He does have a knack of getting to the heart of things."

Brego shook his head in despair at the way the world he knew seemed to be galloping off a cliff in a hurry. If six months ago someone had told him that he would have had DeÁine scholars in Lorne, young women fighting dressed in the uniform of squires, and now a young boy at council meetings, he would have thought the speaker had lost his mind. Yet all three had happened and he was pretty sure he was still sane. He shook his head again and then opened Ruari's letter, handing Maelbrigt's to Hugh to read first. By the time they had exchanged letters and read the other's, Brego was convinced that Arthur had guessed correctly. It certainly seemed as though the pieces were calling out to the missing squints.

"Why now, though?" he asked once he had relayed the information to the others.

Ivain took a deep breath, having read the letters over Hugh's shoulder. "Well Master Brego, this is only a guess, but – given that you sent so many search parties out – do you think that it might be that another of the Treasures has been brought back out into our world? By the sound of it MacBeth found the Shield on exactly the same day that I found the Bow, and Maelbrigt found the Sword about five days before us. That means that three of the Treasures came into the world about the same time – when neither Maelbrigt nor I would've been aware of what was strange in comparison to the way these things normally are. If you discount your Bowl, and this Knife that you've been told of, the only two left to find were the Arrow and the Spear. Do you think it coincidence that this strange pull I've felt has only happened twice?"

Hugh and Brego looked hopeful.

"Oh that's a comforting thought," Hugh admitted.

"You mean you think my plans have born fruit?" Brego wondered, almost as if he dared not hope for as much.

"Well it's either that or the DeÁine are using their Treasures in some way," Ivain speculated, "And unsettling though the experience was, I didn't feel anything threatening."

"Then I think it's time to start making war plans!" Brego declared.

To Arthur and Ivain's disappointment, the planning seemed to take more time than they had hoped. At least Ivain was kept at the heart of things, for Brego wanted to keep him close in case he could provide further insights into how the Treasures worked. Arthur, however, was shunted off to more classes. Classes it only took him another day to figure out how to mainly get out of. His tutors foolishly told him that they would see him at the same time the next day, and so he swiftly worked out that if he told one that he had to rush off to another class they would let him go. By this means he cut down his classes by half on the second day, and within the week he was hardly turning up to any. For a boy used to exploring hidden ways, Lorne Castle was a place of wonderful excitement. Arthur climbed half-forgotten attic stairs, up ancient chimneys, and out onto tiny ledges and bits of shingle roofs. He made friends with the birds who nested undisturbed in the eaves, and the colony of squirrels who had avoided expulsion from one of the lofts.

His undoing came when Haply and Grimston tried to find him about ten days later. Having spoken to soldier after soldier who each sent them off on some wild goose chase to another equally bemused person, they realised that Arthur had outwitted even the Grand Master of the Order.

"He's off somewhere, sire, but where we'll only find out when he comes back," Haply sighed as he and Grimston stood in front of Brego's desk, resigned to the punishment detail they felt sure would be coming.

However, Hugh came to their rescue. "I warned you, Brego! The lad's a law unto himself. And there's no use shouting at him. He'll just take off into the wilds. You have to remember that although he's a little boy to us, he's very used to taking care of himself. He's got no discipline because it's utterly alien to him. No parent has ever made him do things. He's like a wild animal who's brought himself up. Kindness gets you much further than all the berating in the world. I've just got used to keeping him close and explaining everything to him. He's very bright. If you can tell him why he has to do something he'll do it and willingly. I know you think you don't have the time to keep spelling every last thing out to one small boy, but he does repay you with the most remarkable insights sometimes."

Brego gave him a withering glare, but waved Haply and Grimston away. "Go and find him," he sighed. "Hugh's right. I should've let you two carry on looking after him. You clearly know the little wretch far better than me."

"He's not a wretch!" Ivain protested.

Brego sighed again. "No, I suppose he isn't. It's not his fau.."

"…I ain't no wretch!" an indignant little voice interrupted from up the chimney.

As Hugh and Brego groaned, realising that these last couple of days it had been warm enough to not require a fire in the day, a laughing Ivain went and stuck his head up the wide chimney. Two bright eyes shone in the sooty gloom. Clearly Arthur had found a nice warm ledge and had made himself quite comfortable.

"I think you'd better come down," Ivain chuckled, carefully pulling the wool rug away from the hearth as a soot-covered Arthur nimbly dropped down, and showered the floor with black residue. "Stand there and don't move! You can't cover Master Brego's office with soot and ash!"

Brego resignedly hauled himself to his feet and went to stare down at the grubby figure.

"Don't look at me like that, Mister Brego," Arthur protested. "What was I supposed to do? You don't tell me nothin'!"

"Because it's no matter for small boys," Brego tried to explain with as much patience as he could muster.

"You sez that," Arthur sniffed, wiping his nose on his sleeve and spreading the grime even further across his face, "but what'd 'ave 'appened if I'd knowed nothin' back home? Master Hugh's Knights would've been slaughtered in their beds, that's what!"

"He's right, sire," admitted Haply. "It was Arthur and his gang who warned the men within Trevelga that Brion planned to trap them in the city and kill them all. He's been the saving of countless lives. He's surprisingly astute for a little lad at picking up what's important."

Brego clenched his jaw, held up a pausing hand, turned on his heels and marched into Angus' anteroom. There came the muffled sound of several thumps as if a cushion were being hit very hard, then Brego re-emerged, looking calmer but massaging his right-hand knuckles. A rather startled Angus stuck his head round the door to look at his master's departing back, as if not quite believing what he had just witnessed.

"One of you get this ragamuffin something to wear which won't wreck the furniture," he growled to Haply and Grimston, and Grimston shot out of the room while Haply went to stand beside Arthur in case restraint was necessary. "So what are your thoughts then, young Arthur, since you've clearly been to great pains to find out what's going on?"

Brego's pained expression was matched by the way Arthur screwed his small face up in thought. "I 'finks you got the wrong end of the stick keepin' Ivain wrapped up here," he said with great deliberation. "You sez he's safe here, but you don't know them other Treasures is safe, do you? Mebbe he could feel where they are? If he goes out and follows his feelin's, he might be able to go right to 'em. And if you sends lots of men with him, I reckon you got more chance of gettin' them *all* back safe. And what about them squints – whatever they is? Why weren't there no squint with the Bow? Or with the Shield? You been talking lots about them writin's you been decipherin', and how the Bow got moved. So that might explain why it ain't got no squint. But you sez that Mister MacBeth found the Shield where it always was. So why ain't he got no squint?"

Brego sighed. "We have no idea, Arthur, and we talked about that a lot evidently before you started listening in to us, which is why you haven't heard us discussing the matter. That doesn't mean we haven't given it our serious consideration. However, you do have a point about Ivain…"

Yet before he could go any further Ivain gave a ragged gasp. "Oh Trees, it's starting again! That weird feeling!"

They all spun to stare at the three weapons at the fireplace, Arthur and Haply supporting a now very queasy looking Ivain.

"It's different!" Arthur yelped.

"Yes!" Ivain croaked.

"How?" Hugh demanded. The fact that Haply could still hold Ivain was evidence, but of what?

"They'm glowing white!" Arthur said, pointing at the Sword whose blade now glowed with a bluish white light. "Last time it was a gold light. Like sunshine! This is like moonshine!"

"Sacred Trees, he's right!" Brego gasped as Ivain nodded his head weakly, and added,

"And it feels totally different!" He drew a ragged breath. "*Aagh*! Trees! …This is painful! …Wasn't like this before!"

"Someone make a note of the time!" Breca suddenly suggested, then realised he was the closest to Master Brego's desk and grabbed a quill pen as he looked up to the hourglass.

As quickly as it had come the peculiar sensation passed, the weapons returned to their normal dull appearance and Ivain straightened up, albeit shakily.

"Sacred Root and Branch that was weird!" he gulped. "When it started it felt like I was about to come under attack. Then it somehow changed. The Blessed Martyrs only know how, but it felt like whatever that force was has had its focus changed. It was still there, but it wasn't pointing at me anymore."

"Midmorning on the sixth of Earrach," observed Breca, writing carefully. "We shall have to see if any reports come in which shed any light on this."

"And what if they don't?" fretted Hugh.

They were still trying to unravel the strange event the following day when the sentinel trumpets rang out again. Someone else was returning to Lorne.

Once more the Prydein contingent stood on the castle quay with Brego beside them. As the chain ferry slowly crossed the stretch of water from the loch's bank they could see two figures standing separate at the front. One was a tall, lean, clean-shaven, blonde-haired man with hawk-like features, while his companion was a touch shorter but more solidly built, as dark as the other was fair, and with a neatly trimmed short beard.

"Who are they?" Arthur asked in a stage whisper – which meant everyone could hear him.

Brego glanced down to where the boy stood between him and Hugh. "The one on the left is Ruari MacBeth."

"Is he the one they sez is going to be the next Grand Master on Rheged?" Arthur immediately wanted to know.

Brego rolled his eyes to Hugh. How in the Islands the lad had already managed to get hold of that?

"Yes, that's right," he answered resignedly. "And the other is Maelbrigt – a leading Forester from Celidon. You might find it harder to wheedle answers out of him!"

"He's the one wiv' the Sword, ain't he," Arthur whispered backwards to Ivain, clearly resorting to someone he thought was more approachable.

However, before Ivain could respond, the ferry clanked up against the quay and the two leaders stepped ashore to greet Brego. With only a shake of the hand as a preamble, Ruari announced,

"We have to talk! Something's going on with the Treasures!"

"We know," Brego replied. "This is King Ivain of Prydein. He has the Bow, and he was right here when it started acting up the last two times."

Maelbrigt stepped over to Ivain and clasped his hand in greeting. "Then I'm very glad to meet you! Did you think the third time was different to the last two."

"Your Sword was glowin' white instead of yellow," Arthur told him as he craned his neck to look up at the two tall men at such close quarters.

Maelbrigt looked down and realised just who had spoken. "Did it? Were you there too?" His manner was sufficiently different to Brego's to have Arthur telling him the whole sequence of events in a frantic scramble of words.

"This is Tiny Arthur," Ivain explained when he could get a word in edgewise. "He was the leader of a group of street urchins in Trevelga. They warned the Knights of an intended massacre and he's been with Master Hugh pretty well ever since – even in battle, since it seems impossible to keep him away!"

Maelbrigt's laugh was of relaxed good humour and without the touch of resigned despair of Brego. "Did you indeed, Arthur? Well I think I might have to introduce you to two boys called Rob and Jakie if you ever come to Celidon. You three should get on famously!"

His easy manner had Arthur grinning cheekily back up at him instantly. Then Squint appeared on the quay and Arthur's mouth fell open in astonishment.

"*Woah*! Is that a squint!" he asked in wonderment.

Guthlaf walked Squint towards the boy, broad grins breaking out on everyone's faces as they watched the encounter. It was hard to say who was the more surprised of the two – Arthur at meeting a legendary creature, or Squint at finding himself facing a human smaller than himself. Squint's ears wiggled furiously, and he whistled when Arthur tentatively reached out a hand and stroked the exposed fur at the neck of the enveloping cape. Clearly entranced by the softness, Arthur's eyes were like saucers, and for once the youngster was too enraptured to talk.

Squint, however, suddenly looked up at Ivain and whistled again. He waddled forward and reached out a paw to touch him. Then he trilled sadly.

Ivain immediately caught on. "I'm sorry, no, I don't have one of your friends with me. I don't know what happened to him, but I fear it isn't good. The place where the Bow was originally fell prey to a natural disaster. There was a land slip and the whole thing ended up under water. The Bow got moved centuries ago and nobody recorded if there was a squint then."

Ruari sighed. "We sort of knew that. One of the ancients called Vanadis told us that. I think it was more that Squint hoped that if he got to you he would sense where his friend might be." He looked down at Squint and put a consoling hand on the dejected creature's shoulder. "But I'm guessing you got no sense of where he is at all."

Squint gave a mournful whistle and shook his head.

"Don't you worry, Mister Squint," Arthur said stoutly. "You leave it to us, we'll find 'im for you, don't you fret!"

Hugh and Brego groaned at the way Squint perked up at this, but before either of them could chastise Arthur, it was Ivain who tactfully intervened.

"I don't think we should get Squint's hopes up too far, Arthur. This isn't like finding a lost dog."

"No, I'm afraid it won't be," a young Knight came forward to say, "but we can work on it together if you like, Arthur? I'm Raethun and I have some ideas of how we can do it. Would you like to help?"

Arthur's face lit up. Here was someone who finally did not want to talk down to him or pat him on the head. It was also rather nice that Raethun was not so very much taller than him so that he did not get a crick in his neck looking up all the time.

"Oh good," Brego sighed with relief. "Then you can keep an eye on Arthur while we plan the rescue of all the rest of the Islands!"

Ruari and Maelbrigt raised amused eyebrows. "Been a bit of a handful has he?" Maelbrigt guessed.

Brego's shudder was enough of a reply without further elaboration.

"Well I think that's a very good thing to be working on," Ruari said, bending down to look Arthur in the eye but in an encouraging way. He looked up at Brego. "Because, you see, you're going to have a squint of your own, Brego."

"Me?" gasped the Grand Master. "Oh Trees! I hadn't thought of it in that way! I suppose it's all to do with the Bowl and this Knife which is supposed to appear?"

"It is," Ruari confirmed, "but Vanadis surprised us all by saying that you're the one who'll use the Knife. We'll explain more when we get settled, but suffice it to say that you'll be the one travelling to where the Treasures will be used with the Knife. Someone else will be back here with the Bowl, and the connection between the two will allow huge amounts of some kind of energy to be focused to counter the DeÁine Treasures."

Brego and Hugh looked to one another. "Then I sincerely hope it's you, Hugh, who gets to use the Bowl," Brego said from the heart. "By the Rowan, I hope it isn't Arsaidh, because he's so frail it's likely to kill him in the first breath, going by the reactions we've seen Ivain have!"

"Reaction?" Ruari queried.

"When the Treasures started glowing," Haply spoke up. "It was all right the first time, but poor Ivain was in agony the last time."

Maelbrigt looked astonished. "Really? It was uncomfortable, to be sure. Pretty unpleasant, actually, but painful? No. …Oh wait a moment, I have Squint! Do you think that's one of the benefits of having a squint?"

"Now there's a thought," Ruari mused. "What if this last time it was one of the DeÁine pieces which was being used? That would explain why Arthur thought they glowed a different colour. Maybe it would feel like an attack on the holders of the Island Treasures? Then Squint's presence somehow moderated it for you, Maelbrigt. That would make sense and why the ancients were so adamant that we should have squints with us before we tried to combat the DeÁine Treasures."

"We have other news," Maelbrigt added, having nodded his agreement with Ruari's assessment. "We managed to get the sailors who carried us to Taineire to land us at Borth on the way back. The Brychan Knights are working wonders under the circumstances! Two Ealdormen, Phineus and Errol, have joined forces at Borth and are sealing the northern route against any possible army coming out of New Lochlainn that way. They found us passage east on a ship bound for Celidon, but before we left they told us that Berengar, with Warwick of the Foresters, have been hard at work. A bird came in telling of a battle Warwick fought with some of the DeÁine on the sixteenth when we docked by Roselan on the nineteenth. He won decisively! Almost no casualties and a full Jundis wiped out, by all accounts!"

Everyone was immensely cheered by this.

"Have they found the old routes?" Brego demanded eagerly.

Maelbrigt's grin was an answer even before he spoke. "Oh yes! And Berengar's really using them by the sound of it!"

"And there's more," Ruari enthused. "We had to leave the ancients after we'd cleared the ice from around those strange machines of theirs. We couldn't wait to see if they really worked, because by then we were running out of food and fuel. By the Trees, it's cold up there! Anyway, we'd just had to hope that it would be enough. So it was a surprise of the nicer kind when we were riding into Carndhu to catch a boat from Celidon to Ergardia and Vanadis appeared again."

"This is your mysterious lady?" Hugh wondered.

"That she is. She initially summoned me because she could see that we'd have to help them before they'd be able to help us. By some amazing fluke of luck what I did with their help worked. Don't ask me how, because I haven't a clue. Once we were inside their caverns, Vanadis and some of the others told us what needed doing, and we just provided the physical presence. But it's meant that they're really back in action again. Apparently they were once able to do this manifesting thing so well that they could touch things. Unfortunately they can't quite do that anymore, but they can appear for increasingly long periods of time. Long enough to be able to start giving us some decent information, instead of cryptic clues and them fading halfway through and leaving us in the dark guessing at hints – which is very good!"

"It certainly is," Maelbrigt agreed and with obvious relief. "I've already been getting some tuition from Aneirin over what and what not to do with the Sword. Other ancients will be along to coach the other users too – they have particular affinities apparently."

"Who's mine?" Ivain wondered.

Raethun was scanning through a grubby set of notes he had retrieved from a pocket. "A former warrior called Peredur," he told Ivain. "He was really helpful, as was his partner – another warrior called Cynddylan who links to the Arrow. Whoever gets the Shield has another willing ancient called Owein, but the Trees help the poor soul who gets the Spear, because that's linked to a real misery called Urien. Quite a nasty piece of work, I reckon, if pushed." He flipped the page over. "Master Brego, you'll be on your own, I'm afraid. There should have been one of them called Elphin, but he died while we were there."

"Not much of a loss," Guthlaf added. "He'd gone a bit crazy over the years, and somehow managed to nearly kill everyone by going off into some kind of trance."

Raethun circled a finger at his temple to signify insanity and nodded at Guthlaf's words. "Oh yes! He'd totally lost the plot! Luckily the lady Vanadis is the one who connects to the Bowl and she'll do her best to help you. Which, going on what we've seen of her so far, will probably be pretty useful stuff. The really big problem we've got is the need for a squint for every weapon." He put a comforting arm around Squint. "Sadly, poor Squint here is the only one of his kind we've found so far."

"Yes, we really must ask Master Arsaidh if he has any ideas on this," Maelbrigt said forcefully. "It's the one area the ancients were really sloppy over organising. It's possible Squint's friends are drifting in some kind of eternal limbo, but the ancients have never tried to rescue the poor little beggars. We're all agreed that that has to be a priority after the time we've spent with Squint – and for all sorts of reasons."

They had finally reached Brego's office when the air by the fireplace began to shimmer.

"Here we go again," Hrethel called out, being the first to spot it. "Look out everyone, incoming ancients!"

A warrior form appeared with a wry smile. "I know I'm linked to the Bow, but you don't have to shout a warning as though I'm an arrow about to hit you!" he chastised Hrethel, who smile and shrugged. "Hello everyone."

He got no further before an excited Arthur shot forward and waved his hand through the spectral form.

"*Woah*! You're thin air!" he chortled excitedly. "How'd you do that, mister? Can you show me?"

"Oh Arthur," Hugh groaned as Peredur looked down in amazement.

The apparition-warrior's smile was a touch strained as he disappointed Arthur that he could not say a spell and do the same for him.

"Shame," Arthur sighed with amusing gravity, retreating to Raethun and Ivain shaking his head. "Could'a been really useful, that."

"Don't worry, he's one of a kind," Brego told Peredur. Then added, "Thank the Trees! I don't think the entire Order could cope with more than one Arthur!"

Peredur's ghostly face still managed to look vaguely relieved at that. However, he swiftly returned to his original purpose.

"First of all I came to thank Ruari and Maelbrigt and those who came with them to Taineire," he said. "We're seeing definite improvements all the time since you cleared the ice for us. I don't know that we shall ever get back quite to the point where we used to be when we first entered the cocoons, but we shall certainly be able to keep an eye on things and be around to advise you without draining all our resources in only a few minutes. I also wanted to prepare Master Brego. Vanadis will be coming to give you all the help she can soon. We must begin your training as soon as possible, and speaking of that, I thought I should come and introduce myself to Ivain. I've waited so that Squint could be present when we try to test your affinities, Ivain. He won't necessarily be the squint you'll end up by working with, but it's a good opportunity for you to see how it feels with one around rather than having to work things out by yourself."

"Wonderful!" Ivain enthused. "When can we start?"

Chapter 7

A Change of Roles

Prydein & Ergardia: Spring-moon – early Earrach

Far away back in the south, others were also hoping a plan would appear. Below the castle at Draynes on the Kittermere coast, the *Craken* swayed gently at anchor as its passengers disembarked down a narrow gangplank. Talorcan had run nimbly along it without so much as a waiver, but Swein staggered as he stepped onto dry land once more.

"Steady, lad," Tamàs said kindly, putting a helping hand under his elbow. "Don't want you pitching on your nose in front of all these folk!"

Before them, the quay was lined with soldiers of the Order, all curious as to where an Order warship had appeared from out of the blue. Swein felt a huge responsibility falling on him as he clutched the oilcloth bundle which contained the Arrow, and he hurriedly tried to stand in what he hoped was an assured manner. It was quite one thing to travel with Berengar and Esclados as a simple civilian along with Cwen, under their protection and with no expectations made of him. It was quite something else to turn up on another Island in the company of a renowned DeÁine killer like Talorcan. A Knight who never seemed to have heard of the word 'jitters', let alone felt them.

No wonder Alaiz had found him intimidating, Swein thought. However much he thought Talorcan one of the sexiest men he had ever met, he was also one of the most unnerving. Thankfully all of Talorcan's lance were much more like Esclados and the men he had met in the Brychan sept of the Order. The big sergeant, Barcwith, gently teased him, but without offence or malice and often in collaboration with the other man-at-arms, Galey. The other archer apart from Tamàs, Decke, was distant with everyone and spent more time apart than in the company, while young Ad – nominally Talorcan's trainee page – had been full of youthful enthusiasm for Swein's new role.

"You'll be fine!" he had cheerfully reassured Swein. "If Tamàs can teach *me* to be a good archer, he can certainly teach you!"

However, aboard the sea-tossed *Craken* there had been no chance to practise any kind of archery, yet now Swein feared he might be about to be put to the test. The only good thing was the squint Dylan's presence. For it was really more Dylan whom they hoped would lead them to the Bow. It was therefore startling to hear the alien creature give an ear-piercing whistle and see him scurry off at speed, even as Talorcan was explaining things to the local Knights. Tail stuck straight out like a rod behind him, Dylan showed a remarkable turn of speed as he made a beeline for the castle up on the hill.

"Flaming Underworlds!" Barcwith swore. "After him lads! Don't let him get out of our sight or we might not find him again!"

He pounded off up the street with Galey hot on his heels, the two of them charging through the gap in the crowd which Dylan had made. Talorcan heard their cries and turned to run after them with the Prydein Knights beside him, leaving Swein and Tamàs to hurry in their wake with Decke and Ad. In the bailey of the castle Dylan never faltered, but turned and hared straight for an obviously older keep on an ancient motte. Behind him, the leading Knights were calling to their friends to let Dylan go where he would, and so the main door was opened and Dylan disappeared inside. When they all caught up with him, gasping for their breath, it was to find him staring dejectedly down into a pit in the keep's dungeon.

"Great Rowan!" the leading Prydein Knight exclaimed. "Like an arrow to the target! That's right where King Ivain found a great bow!"

"This was where it was resting?" Talorcan demanded.

"Oh yes! Must've been down there for centuries! I tell you, it was the weirdest thing when Ivain pulled it out. Everyone but him felt this peculiar tingling sensation. Of course, we'd no idea it was this Island Treasure you've just told me about, but that would explain a lot."

"So where is it now?" Talorcan asked worriedly.

"Oh don't fret," another of the Knights reassured them. "Ivain and Commander Breca were heading back to the other castle we liberated at Osraig, but on the way they heard news from the monks at Blessed Mungo's. Some folk had passed through there looking for this thing, so Ivain and the Commander put two and two together and they've taken it across to Ealdorman Hereman at Mullion."

"That was us hunting for it the first time," Talorcan sighed. "Curses! To have been so near and yet so far! Oh well, at least it's safe. I suppose we'd better sail for Mullion, then."

But Swein held up his hand. "Wait a moment, please," he said anxiously. "Look at poor Dylan! He's distraught! We need to find out what's wrong with him first."

Talorcan turned to look at the squint and was horrified to see the little creature down on all four paws peering down into the gloom and keening softly to himself. Tamàs was kneeling beside him murmuring softly to him, and stroking the fur between his dejected ears in an attempt to console him.

"I don't what up with him," the older archer said softly to Talorcan, "but he's real upset."

Swein suddenly remembered Cynddylan's words. "Oh no!" he gasped in dismay. "I know what it is! Don't you remember? Cynddylan said that there should be a squint for every one of the Treasures? But that some had already come to grief? Is that the problem Dylan? Is your friend dead?"

Dylan gave a long and mournful trill before returning to his keening.

Talorcan's shoulders slumped. "Oh Trees, I'm so sorry Dylan." The normally acerbic Knight was instantly kindness itself, going to crouch down beside Dylan. "Did you think you'd find something like the chapel where we found you?" Dylan gave a sad whiffle of confirmation and Talorcan put an arm around the strange sloping shoulders to hug him in consolation.

"I think I can explain," Galey said gently coming to bend down so that he too could look Dylan in the eye. "There must've been a chapel once upon a time. Unfortunately, Dylan, there was a land slip. A whole section of the valley caved in and whatever remained of the chapel ended up completely under water. We've seen it on the first time through here. It's awfully deep water. The local men managed to rescue the Bow, but they wouldn't have noticed a squint who was already only halfway in this world. I'm so sorry, Dylan, but they wouldn't have rescued him because they wouldn't have even known he was there. He must've died with the Guardian. And while this isn't much consolation, it must've been very quick."

Then a thought occurred to Swein. "But would he have actually died?" he wondered. "I mean, …if he wasn't quite in this world …would he have necessarily died here?"

Galey immediately caught on to what Swein was saying. "Sacred Trees! Could someone show us where the original chapel was from here?" he asked of the roomful in general. "We saw the valley and a village before we had Dylan with us, but not where the chapel was. If it's like the other we found the Arrow at, it would've been a bit out of the village. I know the valley was on an inlet from the sea which had flooded it even more deeply. Is it close to here? Can we get to it from the sea end?"

"It's not close," someone replied, "but not a long sail either. We can show you on the charts where it is. You'll be able to get to it up to the last half mile or so. After that you'll have to go in a rowing boat because there are submerged buildings that'll rip the bottom out of a big ship, but you can get there alright."

Dylan's strange face had lifted up and he was looking from one speaker to another, making them fairly certain that he understood what was being said. He still looked mournful, as though he was less than sure that they would find his companion alive, but it had halted his grieving for now.

So two days later, the *Craken*'s boat was being rowed up the submerged valley by Barcwith and Galey while Swein, Tamàs and Dylan sat in the stern looking down into the murky depths. Talorcan, Decke and Ad sat in the bows – Talorcan and Decke already having taken a turn at rowing – as Ad navigated under Talorcan's supervision from a map the local Knights had drawn up. Dylan's beaky nose quested back and forth only inches above the surface of the water, making a faint chattering noise as if talking to himself under his breath. Suddenly he gave a proper whistle and Tamàs immediately asked Galey and Barcwith to stop.

"Oh I see it!" Swein gasped after a second longer. "We're right over it! We're right over the chapel! It looks like the dome caved in and buried the inside of the chapel with rubble. It must've smashed the pool to bits. That must be how come the men were able to get the Bow out." He placed a gentle hand on Dylan. "What do you think? Can you feel the Guardian?"

Dylan's response was an instant and unequivocal 'no' even though it was done with a whistle, accompanied by a single shake of his head.

"What about the other squint?" Talorcan asked edging his way forward to lean carefully out to see for himself.

However, this time Dylan's response was more ambiguous. He seemed perplexed, tilting his head on one side then on another as he made little whistles.

"I wonder," Talorcan pondered. "Is the other squint somehow trapped on the other side? The other side of the veil, that is? Is he there but out of reach of Dylan now that he's fully here with us?"

Along with everyone else Dylan seemed to mull the idea over, then gave a tentative nod, but seemed very downcast by the prospect.

It was Tamàs who worked out why. "Oh Trees, then is he lost over there? Was this like a way-marker for him? A doorway? And without it he can't find his way back out of the strange place he's in?"

Clearly this was it, and everyone felt very sombre at the thought of an endearing creature like Dylan permanently lost in limbo. However, here and now there was nothing more that they could do. Promising Dylan that if they found a way to rescue his friend that they would return, they rowed back to the *Craken* and set sail for Mullion.

On the fourth day out of Draynes, they moored at the quay at Mullion beneath the gaze of the great castle and made their way up the hill to pass through its massive gates. In the great hall they were warmly received by Ealdorman Hereman, but were frustrated to learn that Ivain and the Bow were long gone, heading for Ergardia and Master Brego.

"*Now* what do we do?" Swein asked Talorcan as they were at breakfast two mornings later. "Do you have any plans? I mean it's all very well waiting here now that we've got the Arrow safe, but who are we waiting for? Master Hugh? Or the other one, Master Brego? Do you have to obey this Ealdorman Hereman, or can you go your own way since he's not your own Master?"

Talorcan was about to make one of his normal swift ripostes, chiding Swein for foolish questions, when the memory of Alaiz flooded back. How time and again he had wished he had thought a little more before speaking after he had seen the way she flinched at his words. Swein was not Alaiz, but Alaiz herself had told him to be kind to Swein, and that the pale young man now sitting by him had suffered torments of the most savage kind. She had boldly admitted comparing notes with Cwen, and the two of them deciding that there was little to choose between the brutal childhood he himself had suffered, and the dreadful experiences Swein had endured. On the voyage he had inserted carefully phrased questions into conversations, and had been forced to admit that maybe Swein's life to date had been even more dire than his own. At least he had been rescued by the Knights, and shown how to turn his life around while still young – something which had only happened for Swein in the last half-year.

"Why do you ask?" he carefully said instead.

Swein swirled his mug of caff. "Well it's only a thought, …but if we're here for some days, I thought it might be an idea if I tried to use the Arrow to see if I could sense where Dylan's friend is. I know I mustn't use it as a weapon yet. But this wouldn't be the same, would it?"

Talorcan weighed up the situation. He had the Arrow. The Bow was already in Brego's hands with any luck. A few more days was hardly likely to make much difference either way in terms of how fast they could get to Ergardia. And if they could rescue another squint it would surely help the cause.

"Alright," he said, keeping his tone measured. "We'll see what Hereman can do to find us a safe place for you to try. I think we should try it well away from the castle just in case something strange happens. It wouldn't do for us to demolish this place after Hereman's only just liberated it! And we don't know what effect your using the Arrow might have on the men. You heard them say that everyone felt queasy when Ivain used the Bow just as an ordinary weapon. He wasn't even trying to tap into its energy then. So we don't want to jeopardise men's sanity by being careless."

When the predicament was explained to Hereman he was completely sympathetic, and all for trying to trace Dylan's fellow squints.

"There's a small lookout tower about a mile away," he suggested. "It's useful for watching the Sound from, but it's not vital to our defences. It would keep us warm and away from prying eyes without risking anyone's neck."

"Our?" queried Talorcan. "With the greatest of respect, sire, should you be putting yourself in the line of fire, so to speak? If something does go badly wrong, you're the most senior person on this side of the Island and too valuable to lose."

Hereman gave a wry smile. "Thank you for the reminder – not that I needed it. I meant that I'll be nearby. I was thinking that I and several others could wait on the land-ward side of the tower. The door's on that side, and if left open we should be able to watch you and observe what goes on from a safe distance. That way, if things do go wrong, there'll be someone left to record the events to make sure that the same doesn't happen again. For that reason I would suggest that Tamàs stays with me, too. As the reserve user for the Bow he shouldn't be in there with you either."

Such common sense could not be faulted, and so the following morning a small group rode out to the old watchtower. A worried and unhappy Tamàs remained a short distance outside with Hereman, along with Decke – whose religious sensibilities would not allow him to witness such arcane goings on – and Ad, who would have loved to go in and was as miffed as Tamàs to be excluded. From a distance they saw Talorcan halt at the door and wave the others through. Given the trouble his DeÁine blood had caused before, he had decided that it might be better if he too remained away from the centre of things, but was risking being nearby. Moreover, they had reasoned that if Dylan and Swein could not do what was necessary, there was little point in having large numbers of others present, for what could ordinary folk do under such circumstances? Barcwith and Galey were going in simply to witness the events, and to provide some expert protection in the unlikely event of some malevolent physical manifestation which they could tackle.

Clean straw had been strewn in a thick layer on the floor against the worst of the cold, and the four of them sat down around the Arrow, the three men sitting cross-legged while Dylan plumped down on his haunches. Hereman's Foresters had suggested that Swein might try the Knights' prayer to the great Birch from which the Arrow was made. In the absence of any other ideas as to how Swein might harness the energy of the Arrow, he cleared his throat, leaned forward and placed a hand upon the Arrow's shaft, then carefully enunciated that section of the prayer.

"Great Birch, tree of air and water. Heal the wounds of those who fight. May the wind that passes through your branches heal us from evil spirits, and drive away malignancy summoned against us. Great Birch in you we trust,"

"In you we trust," intoned Barcwith and Galey automatically, not even thinking about it.

Dylan had already begun to reach out to place his paw over Swein's just as he began speaking, but, as the response was made, squeaked and dived to pounce with both paws on Swein's hand. The Arrow flamed into golden light and Dylan let out a long trilling set of notes, and the whole tower felt as if it shifted on its foundations in a clockwise direction. As if from very far away, another squint was heard whistling its response and Dylan's ears flicked rapidly in excitement. The other, distant squint seemed even more agitated, its chirps and whistles ranging ever higher in sound. Then abruptly there was another shifting sensation and Dylan gave a long low whistle and sat back looking up. The air above the Arrow swirled into a white column and seemed to solidify even as Decke's first arrow sang through the air, passed through the apparition, and imbedded itself in the wall opposite the door.

"Please don't try to shoot me," a voice said in Islander. "I'm not DeÁine and you can't hurt me, anyway, because I'm not really here."

Barcwith's frantic gestures to those outside were not in time to halt Decke's second arrow – one which Barcwith had to dive flat to avoid – but it did halt him stringing the third to his bow.

"Thank you," the voice said, and coalesced into the form of a man wearing a strange uniform. "Would you mind telling me what you were trying to do?"

However, before any human could speak, Dylan was chattering away in his strange way at the figure hovering a foot off the ground. If the Islanders had no idea what was being said the stranger clearly did.

"Oh, I see! …Well it's very commendable, gentlemen, but I don't know what good it will do."

"*Humph*!" Barcwith snorted. "In that case, who or where was that other squint we heard? Swein's efforts certainly got a result there. You can't dismiss that!"

The figure shook his head as if bemused. "It's obviously an Islander thing, this obsession with rescuing the squints. What you heard was Squint. He has no other name, but he's attached to a Forester called Maelbrigt who's the holder of the Sword. Some of Maelbrigt's young friends are also trying to work out a way of communicating with the lost squints. That's why Squint got so excited when he heard Dylan calling. A young Knight called Raethun thinks that if we have two, or better, three, squints all calling together then the lost squints might find a way to come through a remaining portal. He's aiming at using the Bowl on Ergardia, since it's the one which is most anchored in this time and place by virtue of the Bowl being a natural pool in the Ergardian mountains. Raethun and Maelbrigt were most insistent that I come to you and tell you this immediately."

Going by the faintly exasperated expression on the warrior's face, he was unused to being relegated to the task of spectral messenger. Shaking his head he turned as if to walk away but simply disappeared. Yet before anyone could move or speak, another figure appeared looking a little flustered as if having had to appear in a hurry.

"I do beg your pardon," it said. "You caught me unawares. I'm Cynddylan."

"Oh! The hound!" Swein exclaimed.

"Yes, the hound," it said with a smile. "I'm sorry Aneirin was a bit brusque with you. As the Sword user he's not used to having to stoop to carry messages, but then I think he thought this would all be happening very differently."

"In what way?" Galey wondered curiously.

Cynddylan sighed. "His homeland was Celidon – the most isolated of the Islands in many ways – and even in our current form he never ventured very far afield. So the way the world has changed since our time has rather taken him by surprise." Then a mischievous grin appeared on his face. "Sheep on a windswept hillside look much the same in any century! On the other hand, Peredur and I have been watching Prydein, Kittermere and Rathlin off and on over the years, and have observed a lot of changes. I think we're a bit more prepared for what Islanders are like now. We think it's very healthy that you're making such creative attempts at using the Treasures. Peredur's with Squint now trying to reassure him. You see you caught him at Lorne Castle with Maelbrigt and the others. For a moment Squint thought Dylan was one of the lost squints, and was terrified that he might have missed some kind of window to get him out."

"Oh no, I'm so sorry, I never meant to distress anyone!" Swein apologised.

"Don't be sorry!" Cynddylan hurried reassured him. "We never had to use the squints, so even we didn't know that in this here-and-now the squints could communicate with one another – or at least not for certain. This is very good news! Especially operating over such a distance." He paused and stared off into the distance. "Ah! I have a message for Swein and Dylan from Maelbrigt, Squint and Raethun. They say that they'll let you know through us when they are ready to try another attempt at reaching the lost squints. That way you'll be able to co-ordinate your efforts."

"Are you in touch with Lorne Castle right now?" Hereman's voice came from the door, where he stood shoulder to shoulder with Talorcan.

Now it was Cynddylan's turn to look bemused. "Er, …yes, I am."

Hereman tried to make the request as respectful as possible. "In which case – although I know that you must be one of the ancients, and unused to such menial tasks – could you relay a question to Master Hugh of Prydein? He should be there by now with King Ivain who has the Bow. Would you ask him what he wants us to do about finding Alaiz? He'll know who this is. Talorcan, here, and I have been talking about her, and whilst we acknowledge that she made a courageous move in going to find Magnus – that's the current Attacotti leader – to try to bring him over to our side, we're now very worried for her safety. Will Master Hugh let me take men over to Kittermere in force? Let us find a ship to take us to Rathlin to find her? And what does he, and Master Brego, want to do about young Swein and Dylan? Do they want them to continue on to Ergardia? Or should they remain here for now?"

"And please excuse me for asking," Swein quickly added. "But when you've done that, could you see if you can find my friend Cwen? She's with Alaiz. As you can move about without being seen, would it be too much to ask you to see if you can find her? I just want to know they're both alright. You don't have to this manifesting thing if that's too taxing. Just take a look. …Please?"

Beside him Dylan gave a twitter and looked longingly at Cynddylan too.

"Good grief," Cynddylan sighed, rolling his eyes but with good humour. "With the two of you pleading how can I say no? Very well! Let me relay these messages back to Lorne, and then Peredur and I will cast about on Rathlin and see if we can find these women for you."

At Lorne, Raethun had just been crouched over the Sword with Maelbrigt and Squint, when they had felt the tug of Swein using the Arrow.

"What's that?" Raethun gasped as he felt the Sword tingling beneath his fingers.

"I've no idea," Maelbrigt was replying, when Squint began whistling and chirruping with increasing urgency until he was almost beside himself.

With surprising speed Aneirin appeared and communicated something hastily to Squint before disappearing again.

"*Humph*! Nice to see you too!" muttered Tobias witheringly to the space where Aneirin had been. "It would've been nice if he'd told us what was going on so that we could comfort Squint! I don't know about anyone else, but Aneirin is starting to seriously piss me off. It's like he only tells us what he thinks matters. It never seems to occur to him that if he told us everything it might be a good deal more use. That way we'd be prepared for these strange happenings far more."

"I know what you mean," Raethun agreed. "I know you and Ewan and I are only young, but it's a bit much treating Maelbrigt like he's the rawest recruit."

However, before Maelbrigt himself could comment, the air shimmered again and a slightly flustered ancient appeared.

"Which one are you, then?" demanded Ewan brusquely. "Or are you going to flit in and out and leave us guessing again?"

The figure stopped with its mouth open about to speak, shocked at the vehemence of Ewan's words and the glowers from the assembled men. Maelbrigt hurriedly stood up.

"I'm sorry, you're Peredur aren't you?" The figure nodded. Maelbrigt sighed. "I'm afraid Aneirin has been and gone with his usual abrupt manner leaving us to deal with a very shaken Squint without telling us a thing." He gestured to where Arthur and Raethun were stroking Squint's fur while the little alien sat on the floor shivering.

Peredur groaned. "Oh heavens! I really must get Cynddylan and Owein to join me in having a word with Aneirin! This really isn't helpful! Let me tell you that some of your folk have found and used the Arrow. They have another squint who they've called Dylan. Like you, they thought it was awful that he believes his friend who was once with the Bow is now lost in some other place. While they were waiting to hear from someone, they tried to use the Arrow to locate him. It was Dylan Squint heard, but he must've thought it was one of the squints on the other side."

"Oh poor Squint!" Raethun gasped and hugged his furry friend. "What a nasty shock! …Never mind, though, it's good that at least one of your friends is here and safe now."

"Yes, it rather rattled Dylan too," admitted Peredur. "Cynddylan's with them now. I have to say that you've surprised us all. We had no idea that squints could communicate in this world via the Treasures, but it's very good news. Well done Squint! And all of you too! This is all very hopeful."

"Indeed it is," came another voice out of thin air and then Cynddylan appeared beside Peredur.

"I came to ask you something, actually," Cynddylan addressed the gathering. "The Arrow is out in the world and its squint with it. The thing is, it's on Prydein. It landed at Draynes eight days ago and has since made its way to Mullion on board one of your warships, the *Craken*. The one who will use the Arrow isn't part of your Order, but he's with a Knight called Talorcan and his lance. They're currently with an Ealdorman called Hereman at Mullion and they wanted to see if I could relay a message to someone called Master Hugh."

"That's me!" Hugh stepped forward.

"Oh good! They thought you'd be here by now. The thing is, they left someone called Alaiz behind to try to convince the Attacotti leader to join forces with you. Apparently someone they referred to as 'Ivain's mother' is this Magnus' mistress now, and the two women know one another."

"Oh no!" Ivain had gone white. "Magnus? My mother's stayed willingly with *Magnus*? That's awful!"

Hugh went and placed a sympathetic hand on Ivain's shoulder. "I'm so sorry. I hoped you'd never have to know this, Ivain, but he was your mother's lover long before your father was. It was one of the reasons why we watched her so carefully after his death. We feared precisely this – that she would go back to Magnus."

"But Alaiz?" Ivain groaned. "She's pregnant! What if Magnus mistreats her?"

"I think that was Talorcan's worry," Cynddylan interrupted. "He and Hereman would like your approval, Master Hugh, for some of your men to go back and seek out this Alaiz. Talorcan dearly wants to go himself, but he can't because one of his archers has been selected by the Arrow as the reserve bearer, and he won't split his lance. For what it's worth, I've already told him that was the right decision. The young man who has the Arrow is called Swein, and he desperately needs the help of experienced soldiers to guide him at the times when I'm not there."

"He won't get any better than Talorcan's men," Brego told him proudly. "Hand-picked, every one of them, and a huge amount of experience. I know them all and would vouch for their courage and steadiness in any situation."

Cynddylan smiled. "That's good to know. They seemed that way, but sometimes appearances can be deceptive."

"And you can relay my approval," Hugh added. "If you'd be so kind as to tell Hereman that I still want the muster to go ahead in the east and to be brought westwards. However, he can use as many men as he can spare from those he has at Mullion to go and rescue Alaiz. It was a courageous thing for Alaiz to do, and I now know that it was at Master Brego's request. But if I were a gambling man I'd bet good money on her pleas going unheard by either Magnus or Gillies."

He looked back to Ivain. "I'm so sorry, but I wouldn't trust either to make a reasoned response. Those two are both people who follow their own indulgences regardless of the consequences to others. Your mother was good to you, Ivain, but she was a hopeless wife to your father. She would never have been half the queen Alaiz is even now at such a young age."

"What can I do?" Ivain moaned miserably. "I can't bear just sitting up here doing nothing when all this is happening."

"But we can't endanger the Bow," Brego remonstrated.

"May I make a suggestion?" asked Peredur. "You have the Sword and the Shield here, and soon Master Brego will have the Knife. Master Hugh, you can't possibly hope to ship all your men up here to Ergardia, and anyway the threat is in Brychan. What were you planning?"

Hugh looked to Brego and back. "We were going to repeat what we did before Moytirra, thirty years ago. My men would cross from Mullion to Kittermere, landing somewhere south of Ceos, then march around the edge of the great sea-marshes to a sheltered part of the west coast. Brego would have every fishing vessel and craft capable of crossing the open sea from the southern coast of Ergardia sail across to northern Brychan, to ship his own men across to then make the march south. Those same boats will then hurry south and repeat the process, sailing us from Kittermere either to south-east Brychan or, if the DeÁine have that, then onto the north coast of Rathlin facing the Brychan shore. It's the other side of the island to Magnus' strongholds. We'd just by-pass him. Of course last time, there wasn't really an Attacotti rebel force to worry about at our backs. But we think he won't risk taking on a heavily armed huge force like ours anyway."

Cynddylan nodded thoughtfully. "It's a good plan. So why, then, don't we send the Bow south to join that force and have the Bow and Arrow march together? You see, the Arrow has its squint, which one of your people rather quaintly named Dylan. If Ivain joins Swein, then Dylan can help both of them. But there's another problem. The Spear has appeared in the south as we told Ruari and Maelbrigt, and they've no doubt told you. What's new is that now we can sense it going further south. We can't seem to pinpoint it, but we're trying hard to track it. It may be that it's on Rathlin – or even western Kittermere – and is trying to avoid pursuit. All we can tell is that the right person has it. If you send an army that way we can try to locate it with Dylan, even though three of the great weapons is asking too much of one squint to actually help use. But in the process you could also find your young lady. This Magnus person might resist a small force but not your assembled army. You can fulfil both aims at the same time!"

"Then change my order to Hereman, please, Cynddylan," Hugh requested. "Tell him that we're going to start moving as soon as the men coming from the east are west of Trevelga. My ealdormen will know what to do if you tell them we're repeating the Moytirra muster. We must find a fast ship to Prydein, Brego."

"Not you, Master Hugh," a female voice said and Vanadis appeared. "You must stay here. I sense it now. You are the one who will use the Bowl. You and Master Brego have a bond already. I can work with that, but you must remain here while he takes the Knife with the men of the north."

"But Ivain…!" Hugh protested.

"Someone else must go," Vanadis insisted.

Brego looked around the room. Maelbrigt was looking at the Sword and then at Ivain and was clearly feeling torn, but knew that Squint would be needed to help the Shield bearer. However, Ruari stepped forwards.

"Then I'll go. Of all the Islands, Rheged is farthest from danger from the DeÁine. And anyway, Master Brego's already done a great job of getting those I brought back from the east into places where they can watch eastern Ergardia and Rheged at the same time. If the war reaches them, then there'll be little left of the Islands to defend. It'll be a case of trusting to Ergardia itself to keep the Abend at bay and fighting a raiding war from up in the mountains here. My men don't need me to show them how to do that!"

Brego and Hugh cautiously nodded their consent.

"It's good," Brego admitted. "As you're acting head of the Order in Rheged, you have my backing to use that authority if need be."

"And mine," echoed Hugh. "All my Ealdormen have fought skirmishes with the Attacotti for years, but I'd be much happier with a man of your experience of proper battles at their head if I can't go myself. Take care of my people MacBeth."

"I will," Ruari promised. "And I'll take care of Ivain. When should we leave?"

"As soon as possible," Vanadis suggested.

Brego pulled a message slate to him and began writing. "I'll send word to have the fastest ship in the harbour waiting for you at Firthton," he said.

"Then if you can provide me with fresh kit, we'll ride tomorrow," Ruari confirmed.

"I'd better go and get ready, then," Commander Breca said with a grimace. He could imagine what kind of pace this hardened warrior would set and it would not be easy. However, he had no intention of leaving Ivain to travel alone, and was none too surprised when he saw Grimston and Haply heading his way too.

"What about me?" Arthur's voice piped up. Suddenly he sounded very young, all his bounce fading away as he watched his friends about to leave. "Aren't you taking me?"

As his lips began to quiver, Raethun saved the day. Bending down to hoist Arthur up onto a stool so that he stood looking himself and Ewan in the eye, Raethun said,

"You have to help us find the squints, remember? And Master Hugh's still going to be here. While Master Hugh plots up here with Master Brego, we're going to be doing some planning of our own!" He gave Arthur a hug to emphasis his words and the youngest fighter in the room managed a wobbly smile. "You won't be left behind Arthur. And when *we* ride out to battle it'll be with lots of squints at our side," and Arthur beamed to Squint, his fears forgotten at the prospect of finding a whole new gang to lead made up of legendary creatures.

Brychan (East)

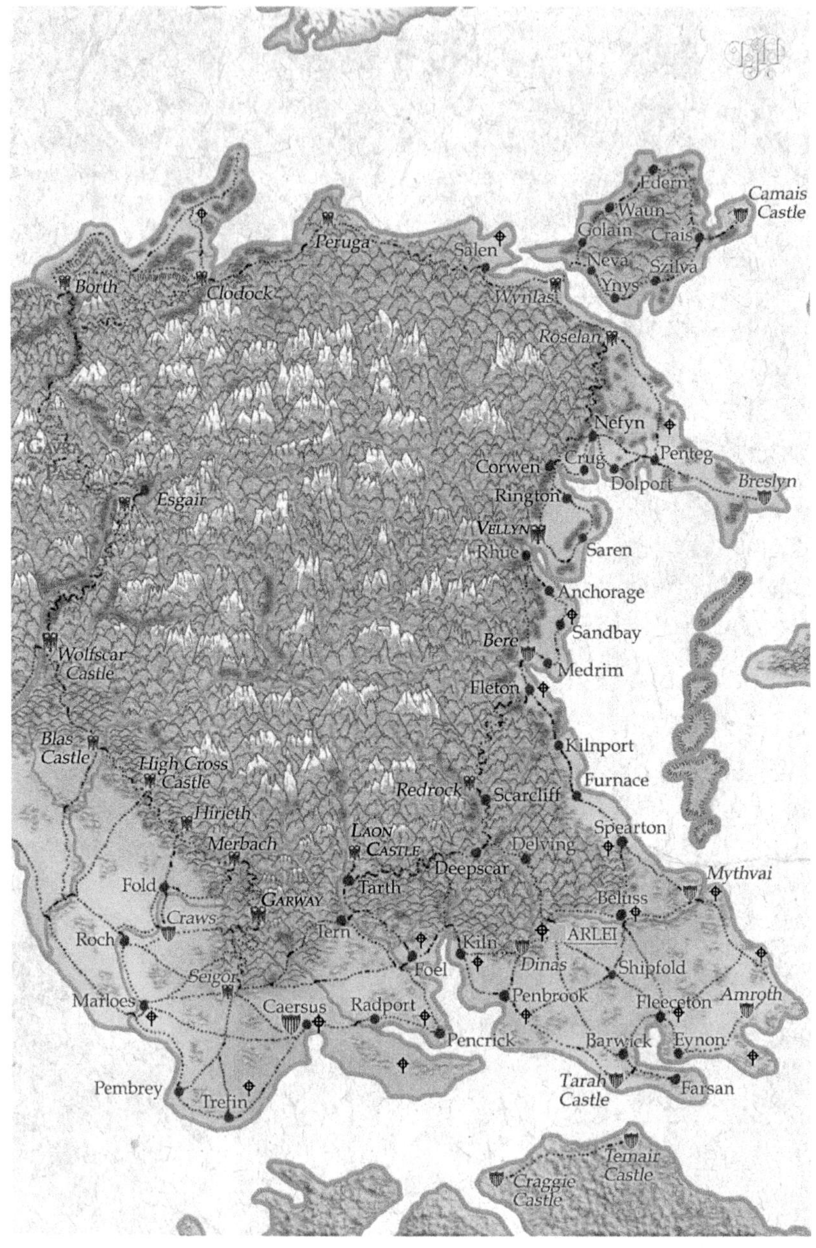

Chapter 8

Retrieving The Lost

Ergardia & Brychan: early Earrach

If Ruari was packing again almost as soon as he had arrived at Lorne, Brego was not far behind him. Deep in the archives of the Order at Lorne lay all the information Brego needed to order a full mobilisation of his men. It was not something which took lengthy planning – that had all been done decades ago, when there had been time to do it and someone with foresight had predicted that such a day as this might come.

"It's good timing," Brego commented to Hugh and Ruari, as they stood together looking at the map of the Islands together. "Pure luck, of course. Spring's well on the way and there are merchant ships already at the southern harbours. I've sent a bird with requisition orders already."

"Can you do that?" Ivain asked in astonishment. "We'd have complaints going on for months – no, make that years – if we tried that on Prydein! The nobles and the merchants would never let us hear the end of it, and we'd never get the ships!"

"Oh we would," Hugh contradicted him gently. "Why do you think they hate me so much, Ivain? It's because I've issued that order twice in my life already. Once as the Prydein second-in-command when we went to fight at Moytirra, and once when Gavra took place. The second time we didn't actually use it, because the DeÁine had retreated to New Lochlainn in chaos by the time we'd made our muster. But in those dark days when it seemed all too horribly likely that they were trying to invade, I had to prepare. That's why they pushed so hard for Amalric to be Grand Master. They thought he would never issue that order, or if he did that they'd be able to bully him out of it.

"When I gave way and put him forward to take over – while I travelled the Islands going back and forth sorting out the mess left behind after Gavra, and trying to save the Covert Brethren – I smugly thought they were wrong. I foolishly believed that I was the one who'd judged Amalric correctly. Now I know I couldn't have been more wrong. They were right.

He'd never have sent that order and the DeÁine would've walked in unopposed."

Ivain stared back at Hugh open-mouthed. It all made more sense now he knew this.

Brego smiled at him. "So, yes …I can! And I, too, have done it before. It's in the merchants' interest to comply. We take their goods and store them for them. If the cargo's perishable we use it and pay them later. We're only using the ships for transport. We're not using them as actual warships. In return the merchants get our protection, and they know this only happens in the direst emergency when they're also in danger. …Or at least the ones with any brains do!"

Ruari was scanning a long and detailed list thoughtfully. "This is such a bloody good idea," he mused. "We really must get something like this going in Rheged when I finally get round to dealing with my own sept. What a blessing to know how long it takes to move the whole sept at different times of the year. When did you say you thought Commander Dana would get to Culva with the muster?"

Brego consulted a slate with jotted notes on it, already showing signs of having been wiped and reused several times recently.

"I'd think the fifteenth would be a reasonable date to count on that."

"Eight days from now," Hugh supplied.

"Yes. The orders will be there waiting for him."

Ruari looked back at the list. "So where will he go from there? Straight down Celidon to Belhaven?"

Brego nodded. "All ships summoned from the southern ports should be at anchor there by the time the first of his men get there on the twenty-eighth or -ninth. That means the first shipment can embark on the thirtieth. In this instance that will mean the horses. They need the quickest crossing, so I've instructed my quartermasters to grab every deep-drafted merchantman they can lay their hands on for that run. I want at least three-quarters of our horses to go across in that voyage. The only men to go will be those who have the experience to lead a long string of horses each. We'll ship the men and equipment in two more waves directly to the Brychan coast too, but each one a bit further south."

Ruari ran a finger down the list, flipping the scroll to continue. "Ah! …Oh dear, at this time of the year the first wave would previously have landed at Breslyn."

"Yes it would've," admitted Brego, "but after what you reported of its devastation, they're going to have to go into the inner channel and land at Anchorage instead. It's not ideal but it'll have to do. Thank the Trees we'll be past the equinox, because the passage through the rocky islets to get to Brychan's east coast can be wicked in high seas. It's protected their eastern towns from Attacotti raids in the past, and the big merchant men who trade up and down the inner passage usually access it from the south, down by Mythvai. We don't have that luxury. Our captains will have to make the run through the narrow channel which separates the northernmost islet from the Breslyn peninsula. It's a pig of a place to navigate through, but it's got to be done.

"I propose to land the second wave south of them at Kilnport. That at least will mean the ships can go through the isles one channel further down, which will be easier to do. A third load of men and equipment will land even further south at Spearton. They can go the southern route via the gap at Mythvai!

"By my calculations, and those on the sheet you're holding, if the first wave with the horses land at Anchorage on the fourth of Beltane, they'll be able to get to Kilnport in plenty of time to meet the ships which should land there around the twelfth of the month. That won't be exhausting the horses too much. They can then make a steady progress, and hope to meet the third wave when they land at Spearton on the twenty-second. To be honest, they should be there well before them, but it'll give them time to secure the area and rest the horses again. That's the southernmost point on the great road leading to the north of Brychan which we can really hope to barricade off and hold against all comers."

"What of the Brychan Order?" Ivain asked. "Do you know where they are?"

"Aye," Ruari agreed, "it'd be useful if you could forewarn Berengar. Let him know you're coming and arrange a meet – although if the Abend are nearby I suppose we can't really ask the ancients to act as messengers. That might dangerously tip our hand, and way too early if we're to have any success against those bloody mages! We'll just have to disregard them and hope our own efforts are good enough."

"We can make a good guess about Brychan, though," Hugh told them encouragingly. "We know from what you said, Ruari, that Ealdorman Warwick sealed the road north at Bere. So it's a pretty good guess that there'll be a substantial force left there to hold it whatever comes. Berengar won't risk pulling too many men from there, and Maelbrigt – who's met this Warwick – says Warwick won't take chances either. Brego and I are gambling on the fact that whoever's in charge at Bere will have some way of getting a message to Berengar, even if it's only by hawk. That's the point when we can let him know help is on its way."

"Why are we bringing everyone from Prydein as well, then?" With a frown of concentration Ivain tapped the map around Arlei. "You said that an army of twenty thousand marched in and camped here. You're taking that number from Ergardia alone, not to mention the men of Celidon under …er, Baderon of Castle Sligo, was it you said had gone already to them?"

Brego nodded. "Yes, Baderon has already set things in motion on Celidon. I'll admit I wasn't foreseeing quite this situation when I sent him! The good thing is that he's another of the more experienced men."

"Oh yes, Baderon's good!" Maelbrigt said, nudging the door shut behind him as he came in clutching five mugs in one hand and a large pot of caff in the other. "Sorry I'm late, but Raethun's having a bit of a set to with Angus over some cake Arthur liberated!"

Hugh groaned and Brego rolled his eyes in despair.

"Are you sure you want to offer to foster him?" he asked Maelbrigt. "I've never met such a troublesome child!"

"You didn't know me at that age!" Maelbrigt replied with a grin. "I could've put Arthur in the pale! At least he's using his head. I was just plain trouble!" Then he became serious. "But at least I understand how it feels for him. I've been there and it isn't nice. I won't be judging him in the way other people might, and I hope I can explain things to him so that they'll make sense, instead of handing out mindless orders he doesn't see any reason not to try to get around. So yes, I do want to foster him if we ever get back to Celidon and peace. And I also know that he isn't ready to hear that yet. Leave him to me, Master Brego."

Ivain looked at Maelbrigt with new insight. He had found Aeschere – the only Forester he had ever had more than a few words with – rather distant, and had assumed that all Foresters were like that. Maelbrigt's cheerful common sense had already prompted him to ask several questions he would never have asked Aeschere. Now, listening to him talking about what had clearly been a troubled childhood, Ivain wished there was more time. He desperately wanted someone to talk to himself. Someone who might just understand the mess his own upbringing had been and be able to offer some advice. Standing back from the others, he sighed regretfully.

"Something wrong?" Maelbrigt asked softly, having been close enough to him to hear, due to putting the caff and mugs on a side-table where they would not end up marking the precious maps.

Ivain smiled ruefully. "I was just wishing I'd been fostered by someone like you." Maelbrigt quirked a questioning eyebrow. "If Arthur's life has been dreadful, mine was bad in a totally different way. You wouldn't believe the stuff I *don't* know, Maelbrigt! I'm doing my best…but honestly? …Honestly, I think I'm drowning, and I'm scared stiff that from nothing more than ignorance and lack of knowledge I might end up getting a lot of men killed."

He sighed again more deeply. "Don't get me wrong, I think the world of Master Hugh. I can see now that he tried to curb the worst of it all for me. To at least let me have some kind of childhood. But these few months I've just spent with only Pauli to watch over me, and make sure I didn't fall over my own feet, were such a revelation. I was actually allowed to make my own mistakes, and I learned more from them than years of being lectured to. Hereman and Breca have been amazing. They've given me more freedom than I've ever had in my life. Not to be stupid with, but to learn. At every step there's always been someone there with me. Someone who could tell me if I was going wrong. But at least they let me *try*. Now I feel like I've been wrapped back in wool-felt and put back in the box. On the other hand, I'm fearing that Master Hugh thinks he can pull me back out and use me as a figurehead, and yet that I won't make any mistakes. I'm scared stiff!"

Maelbrigt felt a sudden rush of sympathy for the young king. "I'll have a word with Ruari for you," he promised. "He's actually a very good trainer. You won't know this, but he brought a young monk all the way through war-torn Rheged with him to get here the first time. I don't think even you could be as naïve as Andra was! He'll be very understanding if he knows there's a problem. The only time he gets a bit short with people is if he thinks they're being deliberately obtuse or idle. Given how much you want to learn, I'm sure he'll do all he can to help you."

Ivain managed a strained smile. "Thank you! Then for what it's worth, I'm very glad you're going to be looking after Arthur. I don't think he could want for a better person to make up for what he's missed. I've been feeling very guilty that I'll be leaving him behind. I don't think Hugh means it, but Arthur's in danger of feeling like a parcel that just keeps getting passed from one person to another, because they don't know what to do with it. I know that feeling and it isn't good!"

"So do I!" Maelbrigt agreed. "I didn't have it in the full glare of the court's gaze like you, though, Rowan be thanked! With me it was a family who didn't want the problem kid after my mother died. They never grasped that they'd been treating me like dirt for years before that, so I was hardly going to be a meek little soul. Then I got shunted on to a monastery, and they couldn't cope with me either. It was sheer chance that I ended up with a soldier from the Order. Thank the Trees I did! Without that, I'd probably have ended up swinging from the gallows as a thief or worse by now. I really do understand what it's like to be in Arthur's shoes." He looked at Ivain again and saw the longing in his eyes. "And when this is all over, even if you're forced back into a kingship you don't want, I promise I'll come and see you and bring Arthur with me."

It was heart-rending to see the way Ivain's eyes lit up at that. *Sacred Trees, to be so deprived of friendship*! Maelbrigt thought, appalled.

Ivain in turn made a promise of his own. "I'd like that, and you could even make it official. I'm determined that Prydein should have far more Foresters. I'd be very glad if you, and any others you think of, would come and train more men for the Prydein sept. We were hopelessly lost when we realised just who Calatin was. We were just plain lucky that it wasn't worse and we can't, and shouldn't, count on having that luck again."

"In that case I'll gladly come!" Maelbrigt promised.

Ruari had been watching the exchange out of the corner of his eye, and was already thinking he must ask Maelbrigt what it had all been about, when he saw Maelbrigt look up and surreptitiously wink at him. Maybe there would be no need to ask after all.

"We'll be leaving first thing in the morning," he informed Ivain coming to claim his mug of caff before it got cold. "And in answer to your earlier question, we're taking that many men because we intend to clear the DeÁine out of the Islands once and for all. And that includes New Lochlainn!"

"And I think I, too, should leave now," Brego added. "I want to be at Belhaven as soon as possible. We're going to have to assume these ancients will be good to their word and continue to keep us informed of one another's movements. As it is, Hugh, I think you should ride with me at least back up to Elphstone. If I'm to have this Knife, then I think it should be now. I don't see me having time to come all the way back for it if things turn nasty. From the north of Ergardia to southern Brychan isn't a quick journey even at the height of summer. Now the snow's gone, we should be able to make Elphstone in five days if we ride hard. After that it would be good if I could find a ship to take me straight to Celidon. The northern seas shouldn't be too bad now and it'll save a lot of time. Even so, I may not make the second shipment of men. I may have to go with the third wave and hope Dana can hold things together until then."

"Excuse me, but I'm sorry, I don't understand," Ivain spoke up plaintively. "If I've heard right, Dana is only a commander. Surely you have other ealdormen? Wouldn't they be in command?"

Brego's surprise was well camouflaged, but it brought it home to Maelbrigt how true the young king's words had been. People really did expect him to know all this stuff, and yet nobody ever explained it to him.

"It works like this," he quickly stepped in before Brego could unwittingly knock Ivain's fragile confidence. "There are other ealdormen. Apart from Master Arsaidh up at Elphstone with his Foresters – who really are a separate entity – there's an ealdorman up in the far north at Mearns near Wyke, another in the west at Dunathe. One at Erefort guarding the channel up between Celidon and Ergardia. And then two more at Clavaness and Speyfort waiting to co-ordinate any defences needed against Attacotti attacks. They're all experienced men, and if Dana was anywhere else but at Lorne he would hold the rank of Ealdorman equal to them. He's nominally called commander here because Master Brego, as Grand Master of the Order in Ergardia, is officially the castellan of Lorne. It's the same at Elphstone where Sionnachan is commander, because Master Arsaidh is the castellan, even though Sionnachan leads all the Foresters of Ergardia if they go to war. In the current situation Dana will be deemed to know what Master Brego was planning more than anyone else, so the others will look to him for directions, even though they might all confer and come to a collective decision over actions. Does that help?"

Ivain's instant grateful smile was answer enough, even though he thanked Maelbrigt with restrained words for others to hear.

"You're going to have to do that a lot," Maelbrigt softly warned Ruari as they left the office together. "The poor lad's worried sick he's going to make a pig's ear of the whole thing, and nobody bothers telling him anything."

"I'd heard something to that effect from the Knight who's been travelling with him, and Commander Breca," admitted Ruari. "They're both adamant that they're coming with him for the very reason you've just said. Both of them are horrified at the way he's been kept in the dark for years."

"I'm glad you're already onto the problem. I did promise that I'd speak to you about it. I think he's a bit in awe of you. Let's face it, the Prydein Knights haven't really seen action in the same way that you or I have over the years. Breca's about the best they've got along with Hereman, but it's only in the last couple of months that they've been allowed anywhere near Ivain. I suspect that together they've been playing a frantic game of catch up."

"I'd got that impression too," Ruari agreed. "It was the way both Pauli and Breca kept pushing how quickly Ivain's been learning, and how willing he's been to take criticism. I think the lad's built up a lot of good will – which, given who that's been with, makes me inclined to do all I can to help him too."

"The things royal families do to their kids!"

"Tell me about it! Every night I'm still haunted by Wistan and Kenelm's faces. It should never have been left to me to be the one and only member of the family who looked out for their safety, Maelbrigt. Flaming Underworlds, I always was here, there and everywhere! The chances of me ending up in a shallow grave somewhere were always pretty high. It's like it's only a roll of the dice of fate that I was still around to realise that they were at such risk this time, and look how little I've been able to do to protect them!"

The air in front of them swirled and coalesced into Vanadis' shape. "You malign yourself, Ruari," she chastised him gently. "You've done a lot for them. Just because others failed in their duty doesn't diminish what you've done. Without you, Will Montrose would never have gone after them. He wouldn't have been *able* to after what Tancostyl did to him. That's down to you for saving him. Now, I must speak with Hugh and Brego!" and she disappeared again.

"Well that's told you!" Maelbrigt said with a grin to Ruari, who shook his head resignedly.

"Is it me, or is it really disconcerting the way they keep popping up out of thin air just when you least expect it?"

Maelbrigt laughed. "No, it irritates the living daylights out of me when Aneirin does it to me! He always seems to think he has the right to interrupt any conversation or situation. Sacred Trees! He caught me in the privy the other day!"

"I hope you told him to piss off!"

"Too right! And do you know what it was for? Something about how the bloody Sword should be stored! I told him I'd looked after enough swords in my time and none of them had gone rusty or dull-edged, and if it was that flaming fragile it wasn't going to be much use after all. I think he took the hump at that, because I hadn't seen him for a while, thank the Trees, until yesterday when Squint had hysterics. I was really grateful to see him when we first met the ancients, because I thought he'd be giving me lots of information. But do you know, I don't think he's ever fought with a sword himself! What in the Islands the ancients *did* fight with is beyond me, but he has no idea about basic drills and exercises. To him it's just a lump of metal to channel energy through."

"It's funny you should say that," Ruari said thoughtfully, "because I was in Brego's office last night when Vanadis showed up for one of her visits. She as good as admitted that they chose these specific weapons because they thought we – the Islanders – would go *back* to what she called 'such basic weapons'. Isn't that curious? It was something to do with recognising the limitations of our craftsmen once the higher skills her people once had had died out."

Maelbrigt frowned. "Curious is right. That certainly explains why they seem to know so very little about the pieces as real weapons. It's as though they'd seen things like them as family heirlooms without ever handling one in earnest."

"In which case, what you've been doing with Raethun, Ewan and Tobias is probably a very good thing! If I'm heading off to find these others, I'd better make sure I have some expert bowmen and fletchers with me, and a few experts with spears wouldn't go amiss either, just in case I end up as military advisor to all three! Somehow I don't see Urien being a fat lot of help if that's the case."

"No, I don't think he will. And being the least obliging of all the ancients, he's not going to easily admit that he knows nothing, either. Flaming Underworlds, Aneirin's touchy enough on that score, and if Urien's supposed to be worse, Rowan preserve us! Do you know, I think I'll go and see the armourer here and see if he can recommend two or three men who really know how to use a shield to the best effect. I don't think Brego would mind me keeping a specialist lance back for whoever gets the

Shield. If they've started to work out tactics already, it's going to make that other person's life a lot easier."

Together Ruari and Maelbrigt went in search of the castle's armourers and soon had a list of men to choose from. Meanwhile, Brego and Hugh were getting instructions from Vanadis about retrieving the Knife. It was the first time in a long while that either of the senior men had had to learn so much so fast, and they were writing everything down in the desperate hope that it would serve if memory failed them.

Come the morning, Lorne Castle witnessed yet another set of departures. Maelbrigt took Arthur up on the roof to where Taise had previously waved him goodbye, and together they saw Ruari and Ivain off, using a small hand mirror which Maelbrigt had found to flash a signal of their presence to the riders. From a gap in the trees along the loch Ivain pulled up and waved vigorously back to Arthur, while Ruari threw them a salute before riding on. A few minutes later Brego and Hugh rode off with a smaller escort but at greater speed.

"Don't worry, Arthur, they'll all be back soon enough," Raethun consoled his new young friend from the other side of him to Maelbrigt.

"Everyone's always leaving places," Arthur said in a small voice, once more acting his age and unable to keep the tough mask in place.

"Well we're not going anywhere just yet," Maelbrigt said firmly and gave him a hug. "And when we do you'll be with us."

"Promise?"

"Promise!"

While Ruari and Ivain rode with all speed for the port of Firthton, Brego and Hugh made equal speed in their journey to Elphstone. If Arsaidh was surprised at their reappearance so swiftly after Brego's last visit, he was even more startled when they told him why. In the solar where Andra and Sithfrey had been entertained, the three leaders conferred.

"I shall have to come with you," Arsaidh insisted. "I should've foreseen this sooner, but now there's no time to continue copying out instructions for you for once you get to the Bowl. We've made a start since you were here, but my scribes are nowhere near finished. I'll just have to read them out to you, translating them as we go."

"I don't mean to belittle you, Arsaidh," Brego said carefully, "but are you really up to that ride?"

"I'll have to be!" the ancient Forester responded with characteristic pragmatism. "I will bring my master scribe with me, though, just in case it's the undoing of me. But I don't think I'm quite that decrepit yet!"

Neither of the two Grand Masters felt quite so certain when they all set out the next morning. Arsaidh was bundled into a litter swathed in heavy furs to keep his frail form warm, and to provide some cushioning against the worst jolting of the journey. The site of the Bowl was barely half a day's ride from Elphstone Castle itself, but that was more than enough for a man of Arsaidh's age on a chilly spring morning. They rode through the mountains to the west of Elphstone, and taking a clearly defined pass between two lofty peaks, they came upon a scene of calm and tranquillity.

A natural depression in the landscape contained a mountain pool, its edges wreathed in rushes. If Brego and Hugh were surprised to not find a chapel with a man-made pool as the others had described, what they saw was impressive in other ways nonetheless. Instead of stonework forming a rim to a formal pool, it was there in the form of a huge circular arch in the middle of the water. At present, the circle merely formed a frame through which they could see more of the mountains beyond, although what might happen later they could not guess. There was no sign of anything within it except for the shallow covering of its lower edge by the pond's water. The upper section was battered and weathered by the mountain storms it had endured for centuries, yet it still seemed to be stable, for now.

"Well now, isn't that something!" Hugh breathed to Brego. "Do you think this was done when the DeÁine were first driven out?"

"It looks even more weathered to me," admitted Brego. "What do you say, Arsaidh?"

The ancient Head Forester was being helped to the ground by two of his men, and grasped a stout staff before hobbling over to them. "Oh I think we can definitely say it's older than that. Don't forget, when the ancients drove the original Abend out it cost them very dear. We knew that from our records, but everything the ancients have said to us since they've reappeared has backed that up. Somehow I don't see them having the ability to build something like this *after* they'd fought the Abend of old. This has to have been here already. When the crisis came, the Island Treasures must've been pushed hurriedly into their hiding places even as those ancients who survived raced for their cocoons in the north. I know you've said that they told MacBeth that they used to be able to perform physical tasks when they first went into that hibernation, or whatever it is, but this would take more than that to make. This is the work of master craftsmen and it'd take time. You can't just throw a circular arch together.

"And look at the stone itself. …It has to be granite. Yet look how it's worn down. If you think about Elphstone castle, most of that's granite and that's well over six hundred years old. Yet our castle walls are nowhere near as eroded as this arch. This must've been standing for at least double that time and more likely even longer." He sighed. "I haven't been up here for years and now I realise I should've. We've been very remiss in our custodianship. All these rushes and reeds! They should never have been allowed to grow so high!"

"Could Sionnachan not have come and done that?" Hugh remonstrated gently. "He's a lot younger and fitter. It wouldn't have been a hardship for him."

Brego frowned. It was clear that Hugh still had reservations about the Foresters' second-in-command. However, before he could comment, Arsaidh was waving a mitten-muffled hand in the negative.

"No, no, Hugh, you mustn't blame Sionnachan for this. It's my fault alone. After my brother Cullin died, I felt Sionnachan had enough on his plate to take over the running of the Order in the field. Or at least that's what I told myself. Too late I now realise that it had more to do with me not wanting Sionnachan replacing my beloved younger brother in every respect. I wanted some corner of what Cullin and I had done together to remain ours. …Very stupid! Very stupid indeed! I of all people should've known of the dangers of keeping things to myself. I'm not immortal, and none of us have the luxury of knowing the time of our passing over to the Summerlands in advance."

"I wouldn't call that a luxury!" Brego remonstrated. "I'd rather not know the date of my death! Sacred Trees, it'd be awful to go through life waiting for a certain day to loom on the horizon! I'd call that a curse not a blessing."

Arsaidh bobbed his head and gave a wry smile. "Very perceptive Brego, but that wasn't quite what I was getting at."

"No, I know it wasn't, but your reaction was only human, Arsaidh. You shouldn't berate yourself for missing your brother."

"Grief is one thing. But Cullin's been gone a very long time," Arsaidh said firmly. "Long enough that I should've started thinking about the long term consequences of my actions. So you must be fair to Sionnachan, Hugh. Had I ever brought him up here and shown him what needed doing, I know he's conscientious enough to have made sure it got done. But, having never given him the slightest reason to wonder if he should be taking any action up here, you have to allow that he cannot be blamed for not guessing it."

He turned to two of the scribes who stood just behind him. "I want you two to record everything you can of what we do here," he instructed them. "And when you get back to Elphstone, you're to write it all out and give a copy to Commander Sionnachan at the earliest possible moment, do you understand? He cannot be kept in the dark any longer. Too much hangs on it, and there's no possible reason why he shouldn't know."

He then began to hobble around the edge of the pool, beckoning Hugh and Brego to follow him, which they did closely followed by the scribes and others of their party. They had not gone far when the two leaders heard him tut to himself.

"What's wrong?" asked Hugh.

Arsaidh shook his head in despair and gestured to a thicket of reeds ahead. "There should be a stone pathway right there, but the reeds have grown all over it. Once upon a time I could've scrambled over them but not anymore. You can just see the tops of the two standing stones which mark either side of the path."

Brego turned back and waved several men forward. "You're going to have to clear those reeds," he told them. "It doesn't have to be a perfect job, but we do need a path wide enough for the Master to walk along."

The men looked at the thick mat of shoots and their faces fell. However, nobody said a word of protest. One man went back for a couple of hand axes they had brought to chop firewood with if necessary, and with those and their swords they set to work. It was tough going. The roots were thick and entwined, with little room to swing a blade to get a good cut. However, things got a bit easier once they had found the start of the causeway out into the pool. The flagstone walkway was sufficiently high enough out of the water that the worst of the roots had not got a real grip on them. In fact the reeds proved to be oddly helpful, for they were so densely packed along the sides of the causeway that there was no chance of anyone slipping into the cold water. Suddenly one of the men called back that they had found a larger than usual slab of stone.

"Excellent!" Arsaidh declared. "That's the main platform," he called to the men. "Clear out to the edges of it and that's all we need. It doesn't go any farther than that anyway, and this path is quite sufficient."

A few minutes later one of the men called back that they were done and they came back, scarlet in the face from their exertions, filthy, and covered in bits of leaf from off the dead fronds which had not begun to sprout spring growth yet.

"There's something that looks like a big nest out there," the last man said as he passed the three leaders. "What in the Islands made it is anyone's guess. It's too big even for a swan or a goose, and it's not made the way any bird I know nests, it's too loosely knitted. There's nothing there at the moment but it doesn't look disused. I'd be careful if I were you. Whatever it is may come back."

"Oh wonderful!" Hugh muttered to himself under his breath as he followed Arsaidh and Brego out onto what amounted to a stone platform. "As if we hadn't had enough strange creatures as it is!"

"Maybe it's a dragon's nest?" one of the scribes whispered fearfully to him from right on his heels.

Hugh shot him a withering glance over his shoulder, quelling any further speculation, but privately hoped that that was one creature from out of legend which would stay firmly out of their reality. With so many dry and dead grasses around them, anything breathing fire was likely to roast them where they stood before they could run for cover. Then he mentally kicked himself for even thinking such things. Daydreaming like this was unproductive when there were so many other things he should have been thinking about. *Get a grip on yourself, de Burh*! he told himself firmly, *you're as bad as Arthur and without the excuse of his age! He'd be thrilled to bits to meet a real dragon, even if it did toast him, but you've got other things to think on*!

Maybe it was because he had been thinking of Arthur, though, that he spoke as he did shortly afterwards. No sooner had they arrived on the platform than the air shimmered and Vanadis appeared before them.

"Well done, gentlemen," she said, nodding a greeting to Arsaidh, who for the first time in Hugh's knowing of him was openly surprised. "Have you seen the squints yet?"

"Squints?" Brego replied. "No. Neither hide nor hair of anything."

Vanadis took what looked like a small but rather ghostly carved whistle from out of the folds of her robes with great concentration on her face. Clearly it was difficult for her to hold an object even now after all of Ruari's work to make the orbs work better.

"Blow this like you would a whistle," she instructed Brego handing to him.

As his hand closed over it he felt it become more solid. It could have been made of bone or horn, although from what creature he could not hazard a guess. With great care he blew it gently. It made a soft trilling noise, but one which did not carry very far. Vanadis was just telling him to blow it again, harder, when there was a rustling in the rushes behind where the mysterious nest was. Hugh and Brego's hands immediately went to their sword hilts, then froze as two snouts peeped out from the rushes. Two pairs of tiny eyes blinked at them from behind a shielding screen of stems.

"Squints?" Hugh breathed to Brego.

"Looks like it!"

Vanadis drifted their way and some sort of conversation went on in high tones mostly out of the register of the men's hearing. Very timidly, the two creatures crept out of their hiding place and into view. They barely brushed the reeds aside, being not quite in the Islanders' world, which explained why the nest only looked part trampled down.

"Scared Trees!" Arsaidh gasped, but so did Brego and Hugh.

"Well I never!" Brego exclaimed. "They're nothing like Squint!"

Whereas Squint and Dylan were like large squirrels in general outline, these two were more like beavers. They had the same bony snouts as Squint if not as long, but the head itself was bigger and broader. Their front paws were more muscled, and the rear legs ended in webbed feet more suitable for swimming with. To finish with, the tails were short, flat, paddle-shaped rudders rather than the other squints' long whippy tails. Yet in coat they were also different to one another. One was a sleek jet black, while the other was white as snow.

"Who goes with which?" Hugh managed to pull his shocked mind back enough to ask Vanadis.

She gestured to the black squint. "This one goes with you, Brego, with the Knife. The white squint stays here, or close by, with you, Hugh. Keep close to the Bowl! I warn you ...once we start using the Bowl you'll have to camp up here. It's too far for you to keep riding to and fro from Elphstone all the time. I may need you at a moment's notice and this squint should always stay close to the pool."

"We'll need names for them," Brego added. "It'll get awfully confusing back at Lorne if we have Squint, Squint and Squint. They'll never know who's talking to who."

Hugh pointed to the black squint. "Sooty!" he declared, then gestured to the white one, "and Snowy!"

"*Sooty* and *Snowy*?" Brego demanded in disgust. "Where in the Islands did you think those names up from?"

Hugh winced. "Alright! …I've been spending too much time around Arthur! …But you've heard what Maelbrigt said. They don't have much concept of what a name means, and nobody's ever given them one before. Whatever it is will have to be short, snappy and simple, and one which can't be easily confused by us, let alone them."

Arsaidh was standing back looking amused at this exchange, while Vanadis wore an expression which hovered between faint bemusement and despair.

"Names …names…" she sighed in resignation, shaking her head. "…Very well… Sooty and Snowy it is," and she turned and spoke to the squints in their language again, then gesturing each squint in turn to Hugh and Brego.

Snowy was by far the more timid of the two, sidling nearer to Hugh but never closer than an arm's length, and with eyes downcast to the floor except for nervous, darting glances up at him. However, when Brego called Sooty's name, he waddled over with great speed and stood looking up at Brego with inquisitive, dark, round eyes. His curiosity made his short, round ears flicker upright, and everyone could now see that they lacked the other squints' fringes too. Carefully reaching out, Brego tried to stroke his fur behind his ears as he would have done one of the large wolfhounds which lived at Lorne. Yet Sooty shot back even as Brego's fingers felt a strong tingling sensation.

"Oh! Of course! They're not fully in our world yet!" he exclaimed. "I should've accounted for that!" He turned back to Vanadis. "How do we do it? Get them into this world, I mean? With Maelbrigt and the others we were told it was accessing the chapel that was the trigger. What works here?"

"It's both simpler and more difficult," the ghostly lady told them. "We have to invoke the Guardian of the Bowl first, then he and …*Sooty*," she grimaced, "will call to the Knife's Guardian."

"I have something which I think is the ritual written down here," Arsaidh said, fumbling with a long scroll. "Shall we give it a go?"

"The sooner the better," Hugh answered. "If I've got to camp out up here I'd rather like a few more creature comforts than one bedroll!"

Brego nodded. "Good point!" He beckoned three of their escort over to them and told them to ride back to Elphstone with all speed and bring everything they could think of to make Hugh comfortable for at least one night. After that there would be plenty of time to bring further supplies and equipment in, for little could happen until Brego got to Brychan.

The three riders gone, Arsaidh came to stand beside Hugh. "I'll read this out phrase by phrase. You repeat what I say as near exactly as you can. We'll just have to wait and see what happens. And you, my lady Vanadis, will have to correct me if something's become corrupted in the years of copying it out."

She inclined her head graciously and came to stand beside him, both of them just behind Hugh.

"Come on Snowy," he called to the squint. "You'd better come over here by me."

However, the squint shied away even further rather than drawing closer. Vanadis tried calling to it in the trilling language she had used before, but the squint only retreated further.

"Oh dear, this isn't good," Hugh sighed. "It isn't going to be easy if the poor little soul is scared of me. Can you find out what's wrong, please, Vanadis?"

The ancient's leading lady drifted forwards and began another conversation with the white squint. Whatever it was saying back was barely audible to the others for it whistled and chirped in what was hardly above a whisper. When Vanadis turned back she seemed torn between irritation and compassion.

"She's scared," Vanadis explained.

"Not of me, I hope," Hugh hurriedly asked. He turned to face the white squint. "I won't hurt you, really I won't!" he said with heartfelt earnestness.

"It's not exactly you," Vanadis grudgingly admitted. "It's rather that while she and her mate are in this state they can still feel the other squints who're on their side of the divide. They were together because the two pieces are together. But they can hear the lonely calls of the other squints."

"We told you!" Brego snapped. "We said that they had feelings and that you'd misused them! Well here's your proof!"

Vanadis had the grace to look at least a little ashamed. However, she was clearly not going to admit to anything. "Apparently they both felt Squint and Dylan leave their reality, but she says that that only made the remaining three squints more panic-stricken."

Brego squared his shoulders and looked fiercely at Vanadis. "Right! Well in that case you'd better summon some of your friends here," he said, very much the Grand Master and expecting to be obeyed. It certainly made Vanadis raise her eyebrows.

"And exactly what do you intend to do?" she demanded frostily.

"We're going to rescue those squints before we pull these two through," Brego declared. "Call your friends, please! We shall need them to liaise with Squint and Dylan." He took in the way her lips had pursed in resistance and glared back at her. "You can help us here and now, or we shall ride back to Lorne, fetch Squint and Maelbrigt with the Sword and the Shield, and do it the hard way. It's up to you. But what's *not* negotiable is leaving those other squints behind!"

"I agree," Hugh declared firmly, "and you shouldn't need either of us to tell you that Maelbrigt and Ivain do too. And going by the fact that they've made one attempt already, so do Swein and Dylan."

Vanadis shot them a furious glance and then disappeared from view.

"That was a little high-handed," Arsaidh said mildly, with a twitch of a smile.

"*Phaa!*" Brego snorted. "High-handed? Don't you believe it, Arsaidh! It's nothing to what they've tried to do their very selves! We've learned very quickly that if you just obey, they find you a dozen more hoops to jump through, and most of them without really understanding why themselves."

A moment later the air around them shimmered and three figures appeared. Peredur, Cynddylan and Owein all looked positively eager, and it was only then that the men realised that Vanadis was there but far more faintly, as if registering her disapproval by not deigning to materialise fully.

"Upset her sensibilities, have I?" Brego said brusquely, nodding to Vanadis' shade.

"Just a touch," admitted Owein with a grin. "But what's this about rescuing the squints?"

"This white squint can hear them," Hugh told them without preamble. "She's frightened to come into our world because she can hear them calling out in fear and she thinks they'll be lost for good if she comes. They've already been panicked by Squint and then Dylan coming over."

The three ancient warriors looked to one another. It clearly bothered them much more than Vanadis to realise that the squints had been aware of their lost state.

"Very well, what are we going to do?" asked Owein in a way which made it clear that he, if no-one else, was only too willing to help.

Brego turned to Sooty. "Can you call out to the lost squints and actually tell them things?" he asked. The black squint looked perplexed. "What I mean is, could you tell them to come towards you?" Sooty gave a rather doubtful whistle. "What we'll do is get Dylan to call with his Arrow, and Squint to call using the Sword. We know they can do this even here. Then if you and …are we really going to call her *Snowy*?" He looked at Hugh who sighed and shrugged.

"Alright. I must admit Snowy isn't really a name for a female." He looked to the white squint. "I'm sorry, we assumed you either had no gender or were all males. Would you prefer Daisy? It's a pretty little white flower."

The white squint blinked rapidly several times then gave a small tweet of pleasure.

Brego shook his head. Clearly he thought Daisy was hardly any better than Snowy as a name, but since the squint herself had shown a preference for it he could hardly object now.

"Very well. Sooty and Daisy will then call together. The lost squints should be able to navigate towards them if they know that Dylan is far away from us, but Squint isn't that many miles away. The squint who had the Bow should go towards Dylan first because of all the squints, Dylan surely must be the closest to where the lost squint once was. After that he'll have a straight line to follow to get to us" Sooty and Daisy were not looking hopeful. "I know it's a lot to try to get across, but can you tell that squint that when he gets near to you two and Squint, that he'll feel the Bow too? That Ivain has the Bow out in the world and that he's not so very far away?"

That seemed to make sense to Sooty and Daisy for they went out to the edge of the stone platform and huddled together facing the huge circular arch.

"Now what I need you to do, please," Brego addressed the ancients, "is to go to Squint and Dylan. Tell them we shall all start calling at the same time. If one of you is with me, would the other two know pretty much instantly what's being called out here?"

"I see where you're going with this!" Owein said enthusiastically. "Yes we can!"

"I'll go to Dylan now!" Cynddylan said eagerly and winked out of sight.

"I'll go to Squint," Peredur responded as quickly. "That way, if I need to go to Ivain I'm in the right direction. I know this kind of communication is fast, but distance still slows things down a bit when so much is at stake. This is my squint you're trying to rescue, so I'm with you all the way!"

Brego turned to Arsaidh and surreptitiously signalled his relief that some of the ancients, at least, were obliging.

Meanwhile Owein had drifted over to the two squints at the water's edge. "You know it would be helpful if you'd join in," he called to Vanadis. "Daisy is your squint and you have the caring of Sooty now that Elphin is gone. They could both do with your support." Then he turned to look over his shoulder at Brego as Vanadis materialised beside him. "Peredur and Cynddylan say they're ready."

"Good!" Brego said, rubbing his hands together, both against the chill in the air and in eagerness to be at the task. "Now then, can you tell Dylan to start calling out 'Arrow'?"

In an instant Owein said, "It's being done."

"Can you feel anything?" Brego asked Sooty and Daisy. Sooty was clearly not sure, but Daisy quickly trilled positively. "Good then can you call out 'Bow' and see if one of those squints you say you can hear responds?"

Even to the men's ears the sound Daisy was making changed, and then Sooty echoed her until they were in unison. Daisy suddenly gave a very excited squeak.

"I don't need you to tell me that one just acknowledged that," Brego said, smiling. "Now then, Daisy, tell him 'Arrow' then 'Sword' if you can. Owein? Would you ask Peredur to get Squint to start calling out 'Sword'? So the squint will hear 'Arrow', 'Sword' and then 'Bow' in that sequence for him to navigate by."

A heartbeat later Owein affirmed that Squint was now calling too. Sooty was calling out in a steady pattern which was underpinning another pattern woven by Daisy and for what felt like far too long nothing seemed to be happening. Brego stood as still as a stone, but Hugh and Arsaidh could see that the hands which he clasped behind his back had their fingers crossed.

"Come on," whispered Hugh. "Follow the sheepdog! Follow the leader and come home! You can do it!"

Behind him, Arsaidh suddenly beckoned the scribes who had come with him forwards and had a hurried, whispered conversation. Brushing past Hugh and Brego, he led his four scribes forward, and in unison they began chanting in an ancient tongue. Whatever they were saying made Vanadis jump in surprise, while Owein half glanced their way and gave a grin of approval and joined in. After a moment recovering, Vanadis too began chanting with Arsaidh as he read off one of the scrolls which a scribe on either side of him held out, the other two scribes reading over the shoulders of their colleagues. As the Foresters began to repeat themselves, Vanadis took over and led the chanting in a different sequence. Slowly the centre of the stone arch began to go opaque until it looked as though a cloud had become trapped within its stone orbit.

Suddenly Daisy's ears shot upright and she gave a tremendous whistle. There in the swirling mist within the circle a small figure was becoming visible. In a flash Owein was calling something out and then Peredur was back with them and calling out as if he were calling a much loved family dog to him. From out of the circle a rather dazed and flickering squint appeared. The Foresters on the pool's bank cheered and Brego and Hugh clapped one another on the back in relief and joy. They had done it! The first of the lost squints was back.

"I'll go tell Squint and Maelbrigt," Owein said happily, "Then we can try for the others."

"No, I'll go!" Out of nowhere Aneirin appeared. He looked at the quivering squint, who hardly seemed able to believe its luck after all this time, and was being chirruped over by Sooty and Daisy. The more close contact the lost squint had with the two of them the more distinct it seemed to be becoming. "I'll go," Aneirin repeated. "You stay here Owein. Your own squint is out there somewhere and needs you." He shook his head and looked to Brego and Hugh. "I fear I owe you all an apology," was all he said before disappearing, but that was more than either leader had ever expected to hear.

Hugh quirked an eyebrow at Brego. "That was a turn up for the books, wasn't it?"

Brego nodded but refrained from commenting further due to Vanadis' presence. "Well done, Arsaidh," he said instead. "I haven't a clue what it was you said, but it certainly seemed to help."

"One of these texts suddenly made sense to me, that's all," Arsaidh said modestly. "It just came to me that this pool must be some kind of doorway. A portal. But that it must have to be activated in some way, since up until then it was just fresh air. It was the bit I'd read about making 'clouds of water' that dropped into place, and I realised that there must be some way of making a sheet of water within the arch, however ridiculous it might seem to us."

"I knew that," admitted Vanadis. "I just never thought of it being used for anything but summoning the Knife and the two guardians." She sighed. "You all think far more creatively about these things than we do. We must stop thinking we know everything about these pieces. We've only ever accepted what their makers had the time to tell us. *Aach*! All that time we had when we should've thought through more of what we were told. How foolish. How terribly, terribly foolish."

Both Masters had to bite their lip to not say something cutting at this statement of the obvious.

"I think we should get this squint to Ivain as soon as possible and into this world, don't you?" Hugh said instead. "That way he can't lose his grip on his location and get lost again."

"I'll take him to Ivain now," Peredur agreed. "Sooty? Would you come with us so that he can hold onto you on the way?"

The black squint trilled his agreement, and with Sooty on one side and Peredur on the other the three of them disappeared through the arch. It was not many minutes later that Sooty reappeared on his own.

"Peredur and the squint are with Ivain and your friend MacBeth," Owein confirmed. "I think we should try to get the squint for the Spear next. I'm getting a feel for this, but if we call my squint for the Shield next, then I'll have to leave off what I'm doing to care for him. That might mean events overtake us and the last squint never gets called back."

"Good thinking," Brego agreed. "All right, let's call the squint for the Spear. Should Urien be here?"

"I am," a voice was heard and then the figure of Urien appeared.

The normally taciturn one of the ancients was unusually subdued and compliant. When Brego got Daisy to start calling to the squint for the Spear he added his voice to the call, Owein assuring them that Squint and Dylan were once again calling in the same sequence since they believed the Spear to be in the same southern part of the Islands as Dylan. This time it happened much faster, but the sad creature which crawled out of the mists was in a terrible state. It looked as though it had pulled its own fur out in its distress, and its eyes were glazed and unfocused. How it had responded was beyond anyone's guess. It must have come to their call more by instinct than anything, moving in the wake of Ivain's squint. Of all of them Urien was the most deeply shocked, and later on the men speculated that he may never have imagined that any harm could come to the squints in their state of limbo.

"Do you think the poor little thing is quite sane?" Arsaidh whispered to Hugh and Brego. However Vanadis heard them and drifted over looking shocked and distressed herself.

"It may not be," she admitted. "Urien just told me, and Owein agrees, that it's possible that someone who was not the rightful user of the Spear has tried repeatedly to use it. Urien felt something, but never enough to be able to pin it down when we were in such a state ourselves. He's very distraught himself, but as near as I can make out, when the rightful user got it something like two weeks ago he felt it was as though the Spear had been pulled away from another. It wasn't anything like when Ivain got the Bow, which is the only other we've found without either us or the squints present. That was quite gentle in comparison from what we can gather."

"I hate to say this," Hugh added regretfully, "but that damage to the squint won't have happened in just two weeks. I'm sorry, but it won't. I've seen something like it before. I wish I hadn't! It was a corrupt and stupid nobleman down in the south of Prydein. He had some prize hunting dogs for sale and I went there to look at them. As luck would have it I went with Amalric, and he kept the man talking while I started going along the kennels.

"The first few animals I saw were in wonderful condition, but then we got to the bitches he was breeding from. They'd been kept in isolation in stone pens. They were like that poor little squint. Bald where they'd licked at themselves and full of sores, but it was the look in their eyes which makes me think they're so much alike. That dazed and tormented glazed expression only comes over time. Bless him, that squint has suffered for a very long time." He did not add that he had beaten the nobleman to within an inch of his life in his fury at the dogs' state, and had then brought them all to the preceptory to be revived. That might not go down too well just now!

Vanadis and Owein were horrified. All of the Knights' warnings were coming home to roost like the DeÁine's rooks, black and unwanted but there nonetheless. No words needed to be said to see that they were heartily wishing that they had responded as quickly as the Knights had to the potential damage. If they had not been able to imagine it, it was no less shocking for all that when they saw it in the physical reality of the keening squint curled in a ball between Sooty and Daisy.

"I have an idea," Hugh said. He walked carefully over to the three squints and squatted down beside the injured one, looking up at Daisy. "I know you've been here with Sooty all these years, but would you think about something for me, please?" The white squint trilled her willingness. Hugh had more than redeemed himself in her eyes by now.

"This poor little soul can't go anywhere for some time," Hugh said carefully. "I also think that if we make him have any more contact with the Spear in our reality it may kill him. He's too shocked and damaged. Daisy, would it be possible for you to change affinity? Would you be very brave and try to make contact with the Spear when we find whoever has it? It would mean you wouldn't be so directly linked with Sooty, but when we've driven the DeÁine out you'd be able to be together in our world, and your link might not be the same when you come into our world anyway. If you think you could do that, then I could bond with this squint here and now. We could bring him straight into our world and look after him."

Vanadis gasped. "But what of the Bowl?" she asked anxiously. "This co-ordinates all the pieces! What if he's not able to do what's needed?"

Brego had joined Hugh in looking down at the traumatised squint. "Lady, I see where Hugh's going with this. I think you need to remember that the link between the Knife and the Bowl might well have been damaged beyond repair when you lost Elphin. After all, you yourself told Ruari MacBeth that you and Elphin were yourselves only substitutes for the original warriors from your ranks, after they were killed fighting the Abend. Your own links must therefore be weaker, surely? If Daisy can help us get the Knife into this world, then Sooty and I will have to manage the best we can with whatever help you can give us. But that might be the case anyway. As long as Owein and the others are willing to come and give us messages in a crisis, then we should cope."

"Gladly," Owein immediately responded.

"Good," Hugh said with a smile of thanks. "Then if we can get the Knife without Daisy coming fully into our world, she could go with you, Urien, and help the Spear user. They'll be in need of a squint fairly quickly I should imagine. On the other hand, I know you said I should stay up here, Vanadis, but nothing's going to happen until Brego and Sooty get to the coast of Brychan at least. That's going to take weeks no matter what happens on Brychan in that time. That's time for this squint to be cared for and start recovering. If all he has to do is make connections, by then he may be up to it. There's a world of difference between that and expecting him to travel again to another user, fall into this world under who knows what kind of circumstances, and then maybe have to fight quite quickly afterwards. Daisy is in much better shape to cope with that. Could you do it, Daisy? Could you bond with the Spear instead of with me and the Bowl?"

The white squint stared at Hugh with huge eyes, then whistled softly to Sooty and some kind of conversation went on between them. However there was no mistaking the nodding motion to Hugh which came at the end of it.

"Brave girl!" Brego praised her. "Urien? Can we get this poor soul through into our world with your help, please?"

The ancient warrior solemnly nodded, and with Owein and Vanadis began chanting.

"Oh! I know this too!" Arsaidh exclaimed and began to join in, hurriedly rolling the scroll along until he could point to the relevant spot for the scribes to read from and join in with him. Once more the combination of ancients on their side of reality and the Foresters on theirs seemed to make the difference.

"Reach out and touch him, Hugh!" Vanadis called in a frantic gasp between chants as Arsaidh's finger approached the end of a section on the scroll.

With great care Hugh reached out to the least damaged part of the wounded squint and forced his hand to push on even when the tingling sensation became unpleasantly painful. A sudden flash and a squeal of agony from the squint announced his arrival in the Islanders' reality as Hugh was thrown backwards. Brego shot forwards and began to murmur soothingly to the squint, even as a couple of the Foresters raced across from the bank with bags of emergency medicines and bandages. Crawling back to the squint Hugh reached out a hand and touched the bleeding skin as softly as he could. The moment he made contact, the squint's eyes opened and looked at him.

"It's alright," Hugh told him gently. "You're going to be safe now. You'll never be lost again."

Chapter 9

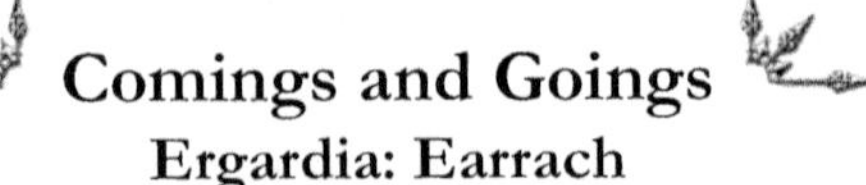

Comings and Goings

Ergardia: Earrach

The retrieving of the squint for the Shield turned out to be different again. For a start off Brego and Hugh agreed that Dylan, down in Prydein, should tell the squint to go away from him rather than come towards him. Nothing would be gained by dragging the poor creature half way across the Islands if it was still somewhere close to where its weapon had been stored. Even in the hazy other-world, where time and space seemed to blur, that was bound to take time. Instead it was Squint who was calling strongly, for he was right by the Shield in Lorne Castle. Owein and Vanadis called out with Sooty and Daisy, but for what seemed like a very long time, although, when asked, Daisy conveyed that she could hear the other squint responding – it was just taking him longer. Momentarily at one point, in one brief chirping sentence, she managed to tell them via Owein that this squint was panicking badly, fearing that they would give up on him and leave him there all alone.

"Reassure him, Daisy," Brego said calmly. "Call out to him and tell him we're *definitely* staying until he gets here."

However, when he appeared, this squint shot out of the cloudy circle like an arrow from a bow, straight to Sooty and Daisy, quivering and whistling. He was not in the appalling condition of the second lost squint, though. And once they got through to him that the only reason they could not make the transfer for him to leave his ghostly state was because the Shield user had not been found, he calmed down and they could see that he was actually quite well.

By now Hugh had the ravaged squint over on the pool's banks, where the Foresters were still salving his wounds and putting dressings on the worst of them. Hugh was sat on a couple of bedrolls with the squint's head cradled in his lap, all the time talking softly to him and stroking those few spots on his head where he had not scratched himself raw. It seemed to be working, for if the squint was not actively responding, he did at least seem to be calming down and shivering less.

"I think what we should do now," Brego announced, "is leave Daisy with Owein's squint here. That will mean that there are two of them together until such time as the other users are found and they can each bond with them." He had far fewer qualms over Owein than any of the other ancients, for Owein himself had instantly gone to his squint and begun reassuring him that he would not be left alone again. Of all the squints, if one had to be left until last this was the right ancient to do that with. "If we have a rest for an hour and then try to get the Knife, that will be all we could possibly do at the moment anyway."

Arsaidh added, "If someone could go to Elphstone and request another litter for me to travel back in, Hugh could take his squint back there right now in the one I came in," which Brego and Hugh agreed with immediately.

For once Vanadis did not hesitate or question. She disappeared and then returned moments later, saying that another litter would start out immediately from Elphstone and should be with them by dusk. So while his squint sat on the nest of rushes with Daisy, Owein joined Vanadis in chanting at the water's edge with Arsaidh until a be-whiskered face appeared in the centre of the arch's circle. Carefully priming Hugh and Brego, Vanadis then got them to repeat three sequences of words. Words which were utterly meaningless to both of them, but which had Arsaidh gesturing frantically to his scribes to copy down.

The change in the circle was abrupt when it came. From swirling mist to a sheet of clear, bright water, the change was instant. Now everyone was looking at the arch but seeing something that should have been impossible, for they seemed to be looking down into a second pool at right-angles to the one they stood by. An ancient face appeared in its midst and once again challenged all those present. However, this time it was Vanadis who spoke up, telling the Guardian in brief, terse sentences what had happened. The injured squint was carried forward and set alongside Daisy, and the Guardian's face was filled with horror at the state of the lost squint.

"We had to do it," Hugh told the disembodied face. "I know he's not the squint you should've had, but it's the only way around the problem. Once we've finished here today, he'll have time to rest and be cared for."

"You do realise that it may not be enough," the Guardian warned them. "I know the Bowl is the most stable of all the pieces we made – and that's because it's anchored in the very earth of Ergardia – but it still takes some strength to use it."

"We'd rather guessed that," Brego admitted, "but from what Vanadis has said, having lost what amounts to three of the ancients who were intended to help make the bonds, it seemed to us that we should send Daisy to the Spear which has, in an odd way, been less compromised. By giving it a new squint, who hasn't been driven to the brink of collapse by whomever this person was who tried to use it before, it surely must strengthen the Spear. That in turn means that all of the Island Treasures which might be used actually within a battle situation will be up to full strength."

Hugh looked up from where he sat beside his squint. "It makes tactical sense that way. There'll be no weak link in the chain of Island Treasures actually facing the DeÁine, and if the Bowl is weakened, then that weakness is shared by all the other Treasures. In effect we'll not be trying to plug a gap in our defences, only in our co-ordination – and the ancients can help with that to some extent."

The Guardian nodded his be-whiskered head in acknowledgement. Maybe the stability of the Bowl had something to do with it, but going on what Ruari and Maelbrigt had said, he was by far the sanest of the Guardian's so far. For once there was no arguing, and he turned and summoned the second Guardian for the Knife. This one, too, gave every appearance of having listened in to what had been said already and understanding the depths of the problem.

"He can't speak directly to you yet," the first explained, as the second remained hazily out of focus, "but he tells me he understands what you've done and why. All he wants to know is if the original squint will be with the Knife-wielder?"

"Oh yes, Sooty will still be with me," Brego confirmed. "We wouldn't mess around with things except in the direst of need, and Sooty is well able to come with me to lead our forces in retaking Brychan."

And so the lengthy ritual began. As had happened with Maelbrigt, a series of questions had to be answered. However, this went far more speedily since Vanadis was there to tell Hugh the correct response at every turn. It was a good thing, because the questions were far greater in number, and even Arsaidh admitted he would have been utterly lost as to the answers of a good half of them. Yet they eventually got through all of them and only one remained – the name of the Bowl.

"This is it," the Guardian announced. "Once you give the name I shall be gone. I have to say that it'll be a relief! If I haven't really been aware of time passing, I've also felt distinctly stretched over what must've been the last few centuries. I was old when I entered this place. I shan't be sorry to pass on, now. Good luck! I hope you succeed in your battle. If it's possible to do such a thing from the afterlife, I shall be watching you and praying for you."

"Thank you," Hugh said gratefully. "What must I do when I've said the Bowl's name? The others said that they had to pull the weapons out of the water, but here that's impossible. I can hardly shift the arch!"

"Not at all!" the Guardian responded with a grin. "What you *will* receive is a chalice. When you open the arch – as you must do when you want all of the pieces to fight together and be effective – then the natural pool itself becomes charged with the energy you need. If you take the chalice and dip it into the water, you'll be able to use it as a scrying bowl. With it you'll be able to see afar. If you wish – and here's the catch with being so compassionate to the squint – and *if* he can help you, you'll be able to look to each of the pieces in turn. If he *really* recovers, you'll be able to look down on the battlefield from a great height as if you were an eagle soaring high in the sky. That way you'll have an understanding of where each of your pieces is and also the enemy's."

"And if he doesn't?"

The Guardian's expression was regretful. "Then I'm afraid much may depend on your strength of will and your resourcefulness." Then he cheered up. "But on that score I am very hopeful! What you've done here today is something none of those who made the pieces and the squints, and who sent us here, would ever have dreamed possible. It never occurred to any of us that the chapels we made wouldn't stand until the day they needed to be opened. If it's any encouragement to you, we also thought we'd be needed far sooner than this! You've obviously proved to be far tougher to overrun than the DeÁine expected now that they've fewer weapons of their own to use. So take heart from that!

"Now, we must conclude this ritual and allow the Knife to be taken. Unfortunately, gentlemen, you're going to have to get wet! Hugh, you must wade out to the stone arch first. When you say the name, be prepared to plunge your hand right into the circle and grab the chalice."

"One moment!" Hugh cried, "I've had an idea!" He turned to the Foresters and called, "Could four of you lift this squint onto your shoulders and bring him into the water with me? If I can, I'd like to have one hand on him when I take the chalice. It might help him to bond with it. And if he can do that then he might also recover better."

The Guardian beamed at him in approval, as four men ran and gently hoisted the squint up onto their shoulders, a fifth man running to help them by supporting the frail creature's head. With great care they bore him over to Hugh.

"Here! Take my walking stick!" Arsaidh said, grabbing Brego's arm instead, and thrusting his staff into Hugh's hand as he stepped down into the chilly water.

Carefully probing the bottom of the pool, Hugh walked out.

"It feels very tangled underfoot," he called back to the bank, "but as long as you're cautious and lift up your feet it's almost as though there's a lower pathway here. I think the main problem is the roots of the rushes. They must be over stone pavers of some kind."

When he got right close to the stone arch, he carefully handed Arsaidh's staff to the nearest man who was supporting the squint, and then reached up to take one of its paws. The bearers had to shuffle forwards and turn a bit further to allow Hugh to still be close enough to grasp the chalice when it came, but finally they were ready.

"Then this is goodbye, and good luck!" the Guardian said. "Tell me, what is the name of the chalice?"

"Calic!" Hugh responded without hesitation, having been primed by Vanadis already.

The elderly face faded with a smile and behind where he had been there appeared a beautiful golden chalice. Hugh plunged his hand in to grasp it but needed to get even further in. Without hesitation the Foresters bearing the squint stayed with him, moving ever closer until Hugh had to take a deep breath and plunge into the strange water. Only the hand holding the squint's paw remained on the outside, but then his outstretched other hand closed around the stem of the chalice and he began to draw it back out. As he emerged, dripping, the squint blinked and then for the first time seemed to truly focus on the world around him.

Pulling the chalice out to himself, Hugh reached up and placed it on the bandaged stomach of the squint, who let out a long soft whistle, as if relieved to find that it was not the Spear after all. The chalice itself had begun to change from glistening gold to something resembling stone the moment its first edge had left the water, and now looked utterly unremarkable to any number of old chalices kept at Lorne or Elphstone.

"I think I'd better have a look at Angus' store cupboard!" Brego joked, as he came forward with a thick blanket for Hugh as he squelched his way up onto dry land. "Good grief, we could've had that all the time and never known! Here, wrap this round you."

"It's not too bad while you're in there," Hugh responded through chattering teeth, "but coming out in this wind is bloody freezing!"

"Have a blanket ready for me, then," Brego told him as he stepped past him to go out to the pool.

Already the second Guardian had appeared and was waiting for him with an encouraging smile, and although there was another series of in-depth questions to be got through, they managed them in short order with the help of Vanadis and Owein. This Guardian, too, appeared to have all his mental faculties, which later on had Arsaidh dictating lengthy notes to his scribes on the effects of having the Guardian, squint and chapel separated for lengthy periods of time, and also on the effect of having the Bowl and Knife's people close to one another, not isolated.

"Not that we're ever going to put any creature back into that Maker-forsaken other-world," he commented to Hugh for now, as they sat beside the squint on the litter, which was on the floor, allowing them all the comfort of the pile of soft furs as Hugh steamed before a blazing fire. "But I will write all this down for historical accuracy, and in case the ancients hid other things away that we're not aware of yet."

However, at this point Brego had got to the naming of names, and both other leaders had their fingers crossed as Sooty waddled out to join Brego. Clearly this need to be in the water was why the ancients had made these two squints different to the others, for Sooty began swimming in circles around Brego as the Guardian asked for the name.

As Brego called out "Seaxwulf!" in a clear voice, and the Guardian faded, Sooty had no reservations in diving into the strange vertical pool and taking a black-handled knife in his mouth from deep within the pool. Taking a deep breath, Brego plunged his head and shoulder into the same water and embraced Sooty as he swam back to him, and taking the Knife by the hilt and keeping the other firmly on one of Sooty's paws, drew them both out. No sooner were they all clear than the water went opaque and then dissolved altogether, leaving everyone looking at an arch which was a wonder of engineering, but otherwise unremarkable. Through it they now saw only mountains again.

Bundling Brego into more blankets, the men began to get ready to ride out, while he dried as best he could by Hugh's fire. The chilly spring afternoon was well on, and nobody wanted to hang around getting even colder with the oncoming night. Owein had already agreed that he would stay as long as possible every day with Daisy and his squint, which was as yet unnamed. Since the Foresters who had been sent to acquire camping gear would be back soon, Brego decided they should stay at the pool side with two of the men who were still there. These men would remain as observers, but also to reassure Daisy and the other that they had not been abandoned by the humans either. Unfortunately the men would not be able to share food with them yet in their hazy state, but the cheery blaze seemed to be something which the two squints could feel and appreciate the warmth from.

Urien too had remained visible and co-operative, and once they were on the way home, Brego and Hugh told Arsaidh that they thought it possible that Urien's irascibility had been connected to the fate of the squint and the Spear. It was very clear that he was far less irritable and unpredictable already. Certainly far more willing to listen than in the brief irate appearances he had made to them up until they began rescuing the squints.

"Go on then," Brego said with weary humour to Hugh. "Tell me what daft name you're going to saddle that poor squint with!"

Sooty was sharing the litter with the other squint for now, since Arsaidh had announced he would ride until they met with the extra litter, having declared a deep longing for his own bed after all the excitement.

"I think I'll leave that to Arthur," Hugh declared. "He'll be delighted to have a squint to look after, and given the way he developed such an affinity with Maelbrigt's Squint, I think he might just pick something which will appeal to the poor soul. He's already calling Squint 'Timmy' sometimes – although he's the only one who does – and Squint seems to be happy enough with that. He'll be pretty miffed to have missed all the fun as it is, and he'll be even more aggrieved to have missed meeting Ivain's squint."

Arthur was indeed put-out to find that Brego and Hugh had decided to rescue the squints without him, but he was bright enough to have understood what had happened when Peredur had appeared the first time and hurriedly got Squint to the Sword. After that he had sat cross-legged beside Squint and Maelbrigt by the Sword, encouraging him all the way. He was less pleased by the arrival of Aneirin, despite realising that Peredur had to take his squint straight to Ivain. Peredur conveyed the need to bond, but also Arthur's disappointment, to Ivain and Ruari after he had caught up with them on their journey. So when Ruari asked Ivain what he was going to call the squint, Ivain asked Peredur to take the squint briefly to Arthur and get him to pick a name for him.

"That was a kind gesture," Ruari commented as the odd pair disappeared. Two days earlier they had embarked on a ship at Firthton, and had nothing to do now but sit on the deck enjoying the warm spring sun.

"I know what it means to be constantly left behind," Ivain explained. "I want Arthur to know that I haven't forgotten him, and this way he gets to bond with another of the squints. Have you noticed how good he is at that? It's not just the weapons he seems to have an affinity for."

"Yes, it's curious, isn't it? I can't begin to explain it, but then I suspect that lies more in Maelbrigt's area of expertise as a Forester than mine."

However, Maelbrigt more than had his hands full at that point with a very excited Arthur. The appearance of Peredur with a new squint had had Arthur dancing on the spot with delight.

"Ivain says that you should choose a name for him," Peredur told the bouncing youngster with mock solemnity. "What do you think his name is?"

Arthur walked up to the still slightly dazed squint and stared into his eyes. Squint, too, trundled over and whistled gently to his long-lost friend. Both squints seemed deeply relieved to see one another.

"Hmmm…," Arthur pondered. "I 'fink he's an Eric. Is that your name, mister squint? Are you Eric?"

Peredur looked to Maelbrigt and rolled his eyes. *Eric?* he mouthed silently. Struggling to keep a straight face, Maelbrigt simply quirked an eyebrow at Peredur before asking,

"Are you sure, Arthur?"

Yet it was the squint himself who seemed to provide the answer. He gave the most cheerful whistle yet and put his nose as close to Arthur as was possible in his still hazy state, much to the youngster's delight.

Maelbrigt shrugged to Peredur. "I think we can take that as a 'yes', don't you? Whether Arthur's picked up on a name the squint already knew, or whether the squint just likes the sound of the name, Eric it is!"

"Eric!" Peredur muttered under his breath with resignation, then more clearly called out, "Come on then, Eric. We'd best be getting back to Ivain with you."

The air beside them shimmered and then Aneirin appeared.

"Oh? I thought you were with the Bow?" he asked Peredur.

"We are. Ivain just asked if we'd come here for Arthur to give the squint a name." Then a mischievous twinkle appeared in Peredur's eyes even as he took Eric by the paw. "Apparently he's called Eric!" and then they disappeared.

Aneirin looked at the empty space and shook his head. "Eric? Oh well, given that your Master Hugh has for some inexplicable reason called the Bowl's squint Sooty and the Knife's squint Daisy, I suppose I shouldn't be surprised. I've come back to tell you that any moment now we'll be calling for the second squint. Ah! Here we go! Squint? Would you start calling again?"

And they all focused their attention on the Sword once more.

On the deck of the ship Ivain felt the energy rise again.

"Should we try to help?" he asked Peredur, but the ancient shook his head.

"No, the first thing we have to do is get Eric fully into your side of the world. If we start trying to help the others, Eric might only get lost again, and that would never do!"

Together they worked their way through a process dictated by Peredur until Ivain reached out and was able to fully grasp Eric's paw, even as he held the Bow with the other hand. As before, the act was hardly painless, and Eric's howl was echoed by Ivain's muffled swearing, as he cradled his stung hand to his chest several feet away where he had been thrown by the force of Eric's entrance into the real world. As Breca and Pauli helped Ivain to his feet, Haply and Grimston went with Ruari to aid Eric.

"He seems to be fine," Haply told everyone, as the one who was normally considered the animal expert by his colleagues. "Mind you, squint anatomy is a bit out of my normal area of expertise!"

However, Eric was sitting up and breathing if looking a bit dazed.

"Here you go, lad, have an apple," Grimston said, fishing a slightly withered but still sweet russet from out of his pocket. "It's one of last year's I'm afraid, but it's still tastes good even if it isn't quite as crisp as it once was."

Eric took it in his forepaws and began nibbling at it with enthusiasm, his ears semaphoring his pleasure.

"I think we'd better reserve any store of apples on boards for Eric's use!" Ruari observed. "He's certainly enjoying that one, and after centuries in limbo it's the least we can do for him."

They were in the middle of discovering that Eric was also very partial to walnuts, when Peredur gave a gasp and went as pale as it was possible for someone who was virtually a ghost to go.

"What's wrong?" asked Ruari. "Something's happened, hasn't it!"

Peredur looked distraught. "It's the squint for the Spear! He's in a terrible state! Owein says he may be insane. Apparently, he's pulled all his fur out and is covered in sores where he's chewed at himself. Oh no! We did this to him! You saw the problem straight away, so we should've too. Oh Eric, I'm so sorry!"

Everyone felt their hearts go out to the sad soul back in Ergardia, and as a consequence were all much cheered by the next news, which was that Hugh had managed to change the squints' affinities. Daisy would now be with the Spear's user, and Hugh would care for the sick squint at Elphstone, and maybe even at Lorne, for the time being. It was therefore with substantial relief that they heard of the successful recovery of the last squint, and also of the Chalice and Knife.

Although Peredur was still not able to stay with them all of the time – the orbs were not quite up to that yet – he did return the next day with further news. Having told Owein of Arthur's ability to interact with the squints and his choosing of Eric's name, Owein had risked a trip to Lorne himself with Daisy and his own squint, who had been duly named Moss by Arthur.

"Apparently Moss is as pleased with his name as Eric," Peredur told Ruari as they watched Haply and Ivain grooming Eric in a sheltered patch of sunlight on the deck. The squint seemed to be revelling in all the sensor delights of his new world, and would take all the fussing and attention they could give him. "The ailing squint reached Elphstone with Hugh and Brego last night, and is recovering with the help of some of your healers. I'm not sure why, but they've given him some kind of herbs to calm him and he's spending a lot of time sleeping."

Grimston strolled over. "Sounds like the kind of thing I've seen Haply do with animals," he admitted. "They're no different to us in that respect. When they're ill they need rest and preferably sleep. If he's spent what must feel like an eternity being overwhelmed by a feeling of being lost, and yet never being able to turn away from it, it must be bliss for him to just stop everything and rest."

Back at Lorne, Hugh was busy trying to pick up the threads of leadership in the north. He had separated from Brego at Elphstone, for Brego was currently riding further north again to where a ship waited for him at the port of Logir. Having the ancients to relay messages for them was really starting to pay dividends for them now, and even the ancients themselves were beginning to understand how much difference it made to be able to inform someone within an hour of a new developments, rather than waiting for days or even weeks for messenger birds to make their way to and fro. For instance, knowing that Ruari and Ivain had landed safely at Mullion and only the day after he himself had returned to Lorne, was a huge relief to Hugh. He also no longer needed to assume that the muster would begin moving and hope he was right – he knew it for certain. Moreover, Peredur and Cynddylan had already spoken to Thorold and Piran and reported back.

However, he was forced to confront a misjudgement of his own within days of his return. The more he had spoken with Brego and Arsaidh, the more he realised that he had severely misjudged Sionnachan, but coming to terms with that and dealing with the man himself were two different things. Having Maelbrigt still with him at Lorne was a boon the day Sionnachan, Sithfrey and Andra returned. The two Foresters greeted each other warmly and without restraint as soon as Sionnachan set foot on the Lorne quay, thus allowing Hugh time to compose himself for the coming encounter. He had deliberately taken his time getting down to the quay when the newcomers had been announced to allow others to get there before him, which gave him time to observe the arrivals unseen.

The DeÁine, Sithfrey, was easily spotted by his height and pallor, but what surprised Hugh was the easy manner the Foresters had around him. They disembarked from the ferry and streamed past their leader to find quarters and food, but all of them exchanged some kind of words with Sithfrey and in clearly friendly fashion. As the quay cleared, Hugh saw a much shorter figure, whom he guessed must be the monk Andra, clutching a carefully wrapped bundle – a bundle Sionnachan was gesturing to, and which Maelbrigt was looking askance at and then visibly congratulated Sithfrey.

Unable to contain his curiosity anymore, Hugh stepped forwards out of the shadows of the doorway.

"What have you got there?"

"Master Hugh," Sionnachan said cagily. His voice, which had been warm and relaxed instantly dropped into cool neutrality. "I didn't expect to see you here."

Hugh bit back the automatic riposte which sprang to mind and forced himself to smile. It was vital that he build bridges with this man. If he himself was to use the Bowl to co-ordinate the fight against the DeÁine, then everything the ancients had told him pointed to a need for all the Islanders being united without disharmony amongst them. He was also honest enough to recognise that he had been the one to instigate the hostility between Sionnachan and himself. That meant that he must be the one to attempt to mend matters and give Sionnachan a chance.

"I didn't expect to be here myself," he responded lightly. "I thought I was just bringing King Ivain and the Bow over to Brego for safe keeping. Unfortunately events rather overtook us in all sorts of ways."

"Really?" Sionnachan looked to Maelbrigt for confirmation and the other head Forester sighed and nodded.

"I'm afraid so, Sionnachan. You heard about the fall of Brychan to the DeÁine force?"

"Oh yes, that message came in before Master Brego brought Andra and Sithfrey up to meet me. So he was able to tell both Arsaidh and me about that. What's happened since then? The last I heard you were off in the wilds of the north."

Maelbrigt shuddered. "'Wilds' is about right! Great Maker it's cold on Taineire! Not a place I'd go to willingly again, but in this instance we did the right thing. Ruari was summoned by the ancients to help free them from what amounted to being a tomb of ice. I'll tell you more of how later on, but for now, suffice it to say that we succeeded. Since then the ancients have been trying to tell us how to use the Island Treasures," he looked about himself cautiously, "but to be honest, they aren't the help we thought they might be."

Sionnachan looked quizzical. "Are they being difficult or what?"

"I wouldn't say difficult – mind you, with some that's really only since we rescued the squints and proved to them that we were right to be worried stiff for the poor souls. Up until then, though, there were really only three ancients who were actively making an effort to teach us things.

No, it's more that they only ever seem to have used the different pieces to channel energy through. They don't quite understand them themselves, I fear. It's certainly been the case that we've found out as much by trial and error ourselves than by their teachings."

Sionnachan gave a small smile of satisfaction. "Then I think we might have a surprise for them when they find out what Sithfrey did! This," he gestured to Andra's bundle, "is the DeÁine Gauntlet!"

As the main party walked up to Hugh's newly-allocated office, Sionnachan told them how Sithfrey had apparently changed the Gauntlet in some significant way. The way that Sionnachan gave Sithfrey every credit for what he had done emphasised to Hugh that Brego and Arsaidh, who knew Sionnachan far better than he did, were right – the second-in-command of the Foresters was an honourable man who did not seek glory for himself. Swallowing his pride, as they passed through into the office, Hugh managed to say softly to Sionnachan,

"I hope you can forgive my blunt speaking the last time we were together in the same room. All I wanted was the best for the men of Celidon, and now I recognise that you did too. It was just that we saw things in very different ways."

For a second Hugh expected Sionnachan to rub his nose in it by pointing out how much better off they would be at this moment in time if his advice had been heeded, and the Celidon sept had been supported rather than mothballed. Instead, the fiery-coloured man, who towered over Hugh's slender frame, simply bobbed his head in acknowledgement. If it was less than Hugh had hoped for it was nothing like as bad as it might have been either. However, by the time Maelbrigt had finished explaining why Hugh was temporarily in command of Lorne while Brego sailed for Celidon and then Brychan, Sionnachan was more relaxed.

"These ancients seem to have been quite specific over who gets what," he said thoughtfully. "It's odd, then, that they can't tell us in advance who will get the Shield, or who has the Spear and where exactly this person is."

Maelbrigt grimaced. "That's what I mean! They know so much in one way and then you turn a corner, something new crops up, and lo-and-behold they know nothing! Hugh and I have been talking, and we think that it's dangerous to rely on them too much. When they have gaps in their knowledge they're bloody big ones. That in turn makes us wonder how much they actually understand of what they're telling us..."

"…and how much they've just learned by rote?" Sionnachan finished for him, and got a warm smile for catching on so swiftly.

"That's it exactly!" Maelbrigt confirmed. "That's why we're quite glad that Ruari's gone with Ivain to meet this Swein who has the Arrow. Ruari's good at thinking on his feet, for one thing. If he has so much as a whisker of a shadow of doubt, he'll not take anything at face value. He'll also be good at getting the ancients who are with him to come and tell us what they're up to. At the moment the Bow and Arrow have Cynddylan and Peredur as their advisors. They're two of the original co-operative ones. The other one is Owein, and he's still lurking around up here because he's attached to the Shield. It's lucky it's worked out that way so that we have those three split between our two separate prongs of attack. They don't seem to mind flitting back and forth with messages because they kind of get the point of it all.

"Aneirin's the one I've been stuck with. He's alright at times, but he's not the help I would've hoped for. We think it's something to do with the fact that he's regarded as the senior one apart from Vanadis, and she's in a class of her own, it seems. Urien is the ancient who links with the Spear. Oak preserve the poor soul who has to work with him. I'll tell you Master Hugh's theory about why he's so awkward later – it makes perfect sense, but means he's going to be difficult for the foreseeable future. Aneirin and Urien were almost hostile to us at first and they've still got some catching up to do, while Vanadis may have been the one to see the need for Ruari, but she certainly doesn't like it when we take the lead."

At that moment the door of the office burst open and Arthur charged in, hotly pursued by Raethun and Ewan.

"Sorry, Master Hugh!" Raethun gasped, clearly having made a grab for Arthur before he could enter and missed by the way he stumbled in. "Arthur! How many times have we told you! You *must* knock before charging into Master Hugh's office. Not every person he's in a meeting with will want to see you."

However Arthur was far more interested in Sithfrey. Coming to stand in front of the seated DeÁine scholar, he fixed him with a steely glare.

"You'm like that wicked wizard Master Hugh and me trapped!" he declared belligerently.

"That's right, Arthur," Maelbrigt intervened before Arthur could dig himself in any deeper. "Sithfrey *is* DeÁine, but that doesn't automatically mean he's a bad person." The youngster's expression shifted to confused wariness. "Don't forget that Duke Brion was an Islander and he was wicked, wasn't he? That doesn't mean that all Islanders are bad, does it? Well the same applies to the DeÁine. They're people just like us. Yes, their leaders are downright evil, and the majority of the ordinary folk are far too willing to take what they're told without question – but maybe we'd be no better after centuries of slavery.

"But amongst them are some who do see things differently. That's like my friend Sioncaet whom I've told you about. And there are some who have the intelligence to see things differently once they've got away from the Abend and the nobles. Sithfrey was one of those. He wasn't any too keen on me when we met! I had to thump him a few times first!" Arthur's expression changed to one of satisfaction – clearly getting thumped was more like it. "But now he's done something which may help us all."

"That's right," added Sionnachan, catching on to what Maelbrigt was doing. "He was very brave, Arthur. He risked me getting things wrong and killing him, even though he only meant to save one of my men who was dying. Even better, because when he acted it was out of a genuine desire to help, he's changed one of the DeÁine weapons in a way that Maelbrigt and I are going to have to try to work out."

Arthur's small brow furrowed in concentration as he thought this through. Then his head came up and he drew a deep breath.

"Oh Trees, this is going to be another one of *those* questions," Raethun sighed under his breath, but audible to Sionnachan who raised a questioning eyebrow Maelbrigt's way and got a wry smile in answer.

"If you done sommat to that DeÁine thingy…" Arthur started off slowly, speaking to Sithfrey and Sionnachan, "…then when did you do it? …Cos back when we got here, Maelbrigt's Sword went all funny and the Shield did too. Poor Ivain was took quite bad, and even his Bow went all pale and moonlighty. …What date was that? …You got it writ on a piece of parchment Master Hugh," he directed the Master with all innocence, oblivious to the niceties of not telling a superior what to do.

As Sionnachan smothered a chuckle, Hugh dug through the mass of paperwork accruing in piles on his desk already and found the date and time. "It was the sixth of Earrach," he told the new arrivals, but before he could go any further Sionnachan had sat bolt upright in his seat.

"The sixth? That was the date! That was the day Sithfrey used the Gauntlet!"

"Yes it was," confirmed Andra.

"Well done, Arthur!" Maelbrigt praised his young student, then turned to Sionnachan. "He does have remarkable insight."

"So I see! I think we might have to think about recruiting you into the Foresters, young Arthur!"

The lad's face lit up at the prospect, and was therefore quite content to sit beside Sionnachan while Maelbrigt sent for Squint, and together they called to the ancients. When Aneirin appeared and they told him of what had happened he gave Sithfrey a very strange glance, then confessed that he had no idea what might have happened and that he would need to consult with the others. In a heartbeat he was gone again.

"*Humph!*" Sionnachan snorted. "That wasn't much help, was it?"

"No," Hugh agreed. "You see now what Maelbrigt meant about working things out for ourselves."

"So they didn't tell you that one of the DeÁine Treasures had been used? Or that it must've felt different to them from the other times the Treasures have been connected to the Power?"

"Never said a word," Hugh sighed. "Not even to Maelbrigt or Ivain, let alone the rest of us. I think you and Maelbrigt have more chance of figuring out the workings of that change. I'd be grateful if you'd put your heads together on this while we wait for word to come from Brego."

"Any idea where he is at the moment?"

There was a general shaking of heads. Raethun tapped the large map which had been strung up on the wall of the office.

"He caught the evening tide at Logir six days ago on the twentieth. At the moment his ship should be rounding the northern point of Ergardia. With any luck he'll make Belhaven in time to leave with the second wave of troops."

Sionnachan looked back to his old friend Maelbrigt. "What about you? When will you go to fight?"

"I honestly don't know," Maelbrigt confessed. "I've been hanging on in the hope that the user for the Shield would become known. If I catch a swift ship from Firthton, I could be in Belhaven in two weeks if wind and tide are with me. The last shipment of troops for Brychan won't be able to leave there until nearly the end of Beltane, by the time the ships have been back and forth. By my reckoning I've got until the eighth or ninth of Beltane before I need to leave here. But then I really do need to go. If the Shield wielder hasn't appeared by then it'll just be hard luck. I'll have to go. I can't have Brego going into battle unprotected against the Abend when I have something which may tip the balance."

"Oh, absolutely not!" agreed Sionnachan. "I was just thinking, that's all…"

Maelbrigt felt a smile welling up inside. When Sionnachan said he was thinking it usually boded well for some fiendishly sneaky plan appearing later on. In that respect he was very like a much older Arthur. As it was the redheaded Forester leaned back in his chair and stared at the ceiling for a moment before declaring,

"You know, it might not be a bad thing if none of our other Treasures went by the same route as Master Brego. The Abend will be looking for something that way. I'd guess they'd be thinking more of one of their own Treasures, but the fact remains that they'll be looking. Let's face it, they'd have to be pretty disinterested if they missed Sithfrey's work. They must surely have felt something and know something happened with one of their Treasures, and that it wasn't one of them doing it. If you and I sailed for Rathlin, not Brychan, and joined with MacBeth, we could sweep up on their rear with the Island Treasures. That way, if we plan for that, it'll mean that if the Shield doesn't find someone, you won't be the only Treasure coming out of the north."

"He wouldn't be the only one," protested Raethun. "Don't forget that Master Brego has the Knife."

"I hadn't forgotten," Sionnachan said evenly, "but you yourselves have said that the ancients haven't told you a fat lot. How does this Knife work? You see I'm worried that it might turn out to be only a communication device, or at best something which you point at a target to focus the power of the Bowl. But what if, after all the changes in ancients and squints, you can't harness that? It could leave Maelbrigt very exposed."

Hugh had to admit that, put that way, Sionnachan had spotted a loophole he had missed. "It's a reasonable concern," he conceded. "I think in the time we have available we must think this through very carefully."

Maelbrigt nodded. "I agree. And given Sionnachan's reservations I think it only fair to work out a plan for if the Spear has gone beyond our reach. I know we have a squint for it now, but Daisy isn't the Spear's original squint and she can't seem to track it down to anywhere beyond a broad sweep of land. Trees, it would be nice if we had a clue as to who had the flaming thing!"

Chapter 10

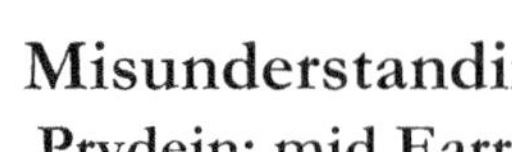

Misunderstandings

Prydein: mid Earrach

By the time Ruari and Ivain's ship swooped up to the Prydein coast on the brisk winds, Peredur reported to them that Hugh had left the squint resting at Elphstone in the care of Master Arsaidh, heavily sedated but very slowly improving. If nothing else the Foresters' salves were soothing the outer damage and he appeared to be healing, aided by the plentiful good food he was being given whenever he awoke. Even as they docked at Mullion to see a slim, white-haired young man with another squint waiting for them, surrounded by Knights, Peredur confirmed that Hugh had arrived back at Lorne that very day and was now with Maelbrigt and Squint.

"MacBeth!" Hereman warmly greeted his new leader as he led the party down the gangplank. "Your reputation precedes you! Welcome to Prydein. Not that you're going to see much of it, I'm afraid! We've started things moving because we're desperately short of ships to carry men between here and Kittermere. However, I'll tell you all about that when we get up to the castle. For now, may I introduce Swein to you all. He's the one whom the Arrow chose, and this is his squint, Dylan."

Ivain stepped forward around Ruari and took Swein's proffered hand. "Hello, Swein! I'm so glad to meet you! I'm Ivain, and this is Eric. I'm guessing we're going to be doing a lot of learning together."

"Oh *you've* got a lot to learn," a sardonic voice came from to one side, and Ivain turned to see a tall, dark Knight standing with his arms folded and a look of utter contempt on his face as he stared at Ivain.

"I'm sorry? Do I know you?" a mystified Ivain asked.

"This is Talorcan," Swein said hurriedly, somewhat embarrassed by Talorcan's surliness. "Don't worry, he's like this a lot," he added very quietly so that Talorcan wouldn't hear him.

"No, *we've* not met," Talorcan overrode Swein, "but we both have someone in common."

Ivain was even more confused. "We do?"

"Oh yes! A very nice lady by the name of Alaiz!"

A moment of panic hit Ivain. Had Brego been wrong? Was *this* really the father of Alaiz' child? "Alaiz? Yes …yes she is nice. And very special, wouldn't you agree?"

"Oh *I* would! But you seem to have changed your tune! *You* seemed to think it was perfectly alright to pack her off to Magnus in the first place. But oh …wait a minute! No, *you* wouldn't even have noticed that, because you were off chasing every bit of skirt in the royal palace when she left. Did you even notice she'd gone? Or did that only enter your spoilt head when someone else pointed out that the queen of Prydein had had to make it across a war-torn country in the guise of a farm lad?"

Talorcan raised a hand theatrically to halt any interjection on Ivain's part. "Oh no! Of course you didn't. How silly of me! Alaiz said that when she got to you and Master Hugh, you were going to incarcerate her in some nunnery for the duration of the crisis. Didn't quite work out that way, though, did it? So while you were out getting your arse whipped by all and sundry for being the useless big girl you are, your *wife* is risking life and limb to help all the people of the Islands!"

"You hold on a minute!" snarled Haply as Pauli demanded,

"Who the fuck do you think you are?"

"How dare you!" barked an equally angry Breca, attempting to pull rank on Talorcan and yank him verbally into line.

Unfortunately Talorcan was too angry to notice, and was ploughing on even as Barcwith and Galey grabbed an arm each and Barcwith hissed in his ear, "Shut up you idiot!"

"Very sorry gentlemen, but you see me and my men have spent *many* weeks with Alaiz. Weeks in which we've come to hear of a very different side of the story to the official version you've no doubt been told! Oh yes, it's different alright! The girl who was kept as good as a prisoner by royal command while he went around enjoying the …oh, what shall we call them, Ivain? The rights of kingship? Is that grand enough for you? 'Did his growing up with the ladies of the court,' was the way I seem to remember Alaiz saying it. Well here's news for you! She's pregnant and it isn't yours, and a good thing too!"

"You bastard!" Ivain bawled, his voice carrying over those of his friends who were already shouting back in his defence. All doubt was gone from his mind now. This arrogant, and clearly cruel, thug had taken every advantage of Alaiz' innocence and sweet nature. "How dare you rape her!" he screamed, and before Pauli or Haply could grab him, Ivain had launched himself at Talorcan and threw a punch which smacked Talorcan right on the nose.

The crunch of bone was barely audible over the shouting, but Talorcan shook himself like a fighting terrier and, despite being half blinded by the tears in his eyes from the pain, launched himself at Ivain. Ivain's recent training had improved his fighting enormously, but it was nothing in comparison to the years of battling it out with every kind of foe that Talorcan had had. In the flailing limbs, Ivain swiftly ended up as the one on the floor with Talorcan's fist in his face, after a head-butt which did even more damage to his nose than he had done to Talorcan's. Ivain managed to writhe enough to knee Talorcan in the groin, and heard a gratifying grunt of pain. It did him little good, though, as Talorcan head-butted him again as he folded up. Almost equally matched in height and build, Talorcan's only advantage was his experience, but that was substantial.

Never afraid to fight dirty if the need arose, Talorcan sank his teeth into the hand Ivain had over his face forcing the young king to let go. Talorcan then punched Ivain hard, although not as hard as expected since Ivain managed to twist enough to let the punch half slide off him. As he squirmed to the side, Ivain managed to jab his elbow into Talorcan's face and felt a satisfying impact. That at least had landed and done some damage. It did not last and he got punched in the ribs as a response. As Talorcan drew back his arm for another vicious punch there came a hysterical high pitched shriek.

Ruari, Breca, Haply and Grimston, all piling in with Barcwith and Galey to separate the two fighters, missed it, but it was Swein who called out a desperate warning. Eric was beside himself, repeatedly shrieking in a high monotone, as the side of the ship shattered into bits. The Bow exploded into existence sitting in the air wreathed in gold flames just above Eric's head.

"No, Dylan! Not the Arrow!" Swein yelled desperately, throwing his arms around his own squint. "It's not the right time! No! Don't give him the Arrow to use."

Realising the danger, Tamàs was by his side in an instant reinforcing Swein's words, and it was seeing this out of the corner of his eye which alerted Haply and made him dive for Eric.

"No Eric!" he cried urgently. "This is just an accident!"

Luckily Ivain came to his senses and gestured for Pauli to get him to

Eric, even as Ruari lost his patience with the thrashing Talorcan and hit him so hard he knocked him out momentarily.

"It's alright!" Ivain panted, putting an arm around Eric as he clutched a handkerchief to his nose with the other to try to stem the blood. "It's alright!"

"Talorcan, you fucking idiot, what do you think you're doing?" a furious Ruari demanded of the dazed Knight as his dazed eyes opened fractionally, and as Breca turned to his ealdorman and furiously demanded,

"Who is this brawling fool?"

"His name's Talorcan," Hereman answered. "Actually he's from Ergardia, not here." The implication from Hereman's tone was that he would have knocked Talorcan into line a lot earlier had he been one of his men.

"I'll deal with this," Ruari said firmly to the assembled men.

As Talorcan sat with his head between his knees, trying to stem the flow of blood from his nose, Ruari walked over to Eric and knelt down in front of the still quivering squint.

"Listen to me, Eric!" Ruari said firmly but calmly. "I know you sensed *DeÁine* then, but this one isn't one of our enemies." Hereman and the Prydein Knights all looked astonished at this revelation. "He was brought to us when he was a child, do you understand me? When he was not much older than Arthur. There aren't many people here who've fought the DeÁine as much as him. He's not a pleasant man, but his life would make anyone ...difficult!" He reached out and ruffled the squint's fur. "But you're a very clever lad for summoning the Bow like that! Well done!"

Eric gave a confused whistle but seemed to be mollified. The Bow had practically thrust itself into Ivain's hands, but thankfully now lay in its more normal guise on the quay stones at Ivain's feet, quiet and unresponsive. Ruari got to his feet and gestured men to Talorcan. "Take him away and put him in a secure room under guard." He caught sight of Hereman's clear disapproval and thought to make himself clear. "Not the cells! Just somewhere we can keep him out of trouble until I can have a *strong* word with him."

He threw Hereman a glance which he hoped would convey the thought that he would explain further in private. "Ealdorman Hereman? I think we'd better get to this castle of yours before any more excitement overtakes us!" he added for the general audience.

As they turned to follow a Knight who led them uphill, Ruari was about to tell Ivain quietly that he would be having strong words with him too, when Ivain surprised him.

"I'm sorry," the young king said quickly through his soggy handkerchief, which was doing little to staunch the blood from his nose. "That was so stupid of me! I thought I'd learned better by now. Blessed Martyrs! I've had enough practice at court of being called a fool. Usually dressed up in more flowery language I'll admit, but the intention was the same. I'm so, so sorry. I should have thought about Eric's reaction first."

This rather took the wind out of Ruari's sails. It would be hard to berate his young charge when he had already seen for himself the danger he had nearly put them all in. Forcing himself to speak more calmly than he might have to another raw recruit, Ruari asked,

"Why did you do it, then? What was different this time?"

"Alaiz!" Ivain said straight away. "I *was* an idiot! I'll admit to that! She saw far more than I ever did how we were being manipulated by the court. And it made her miserable. Very miserable, and I was too blind to see it until everything went crazy and when I saw her away from the court, when she'd already escaped from Magnus. I wouldn't have argued with him – that prick Talorcan – over that. It was the fact that he's cold-bloodedly taken advantage of her when she was most vulnerable that I can't stomach.

"Flaming Underworlds, MacBeth, I know I wasn't perfect. I wasn't even halfway good! But I did what I did out of ignorance, not malice! There's a world of difference between that, and seeing an easy prey and taking advantage of a woman in the full knowledge of what you're doing. Hamelin I could have coped with, but not this one!"

Suddenly Ruari began to laugh as he realised just what Ivain thought Talorcan had done to Alaiz.

"What's so funny?" Ivain demanded, feeling rather aggrieved to have someone he had hoped would take him seriously mocking him.

Ruari picked up on the hurt tone of voice and draped a friendly arm over Ivain's shoulders. "Ah, son! It's not you! …Well actually it is, but not in the way you think. I understand now why you're pissed off with Talorcan, but the thing is …it's not him."

"What's not him?"

"The one who got your wife pregnant. That really was Hamelin. In fact I'll go as far as to say that I know it *couldn't* have been Talorcan. The Maker only knows what's got up his arse and bitten him this time …Flaming Trees, that wasn't the right thing to say either!"

"It wasn't? Now I'm really confused!"

"Look …Talorcan is as bent as a butcher's hook, alright?"

"Bent?"

"Queer. Limp-wristed – no that's hardly right either given the mess he's made of your nose! Look, he shags other men. Never been known to go near a woman – and plenty have tried! Does that explain it for you? In all the years I've known of Talorcan the one thing that everyone will tell you is that you keep him well away from any rather pretty *male* recruits. And I don't mean he rapes them, either! It's just that when he wants to be, however surprising this may be to you, he can be quite the charmer. Talorcan's a fierce fighter, and like you he had a pretty appalling childhood, although in a different way. Think of what Arthur might be like in twenty years time after a lifetime of fighting and you're getting close to it.

"What you also don't know is that he's nothing if not honourable. Actually I suspect that that's the problem. If, against the odds he's befriended your wife, then it would be totally in character for him to see himself as needing to be her champion, and defend her against someone who he sees as a useless tit of a husband."

"Useless tit? Oh thunk you very b'much!" Ivain groaned around his rapidly swelling nose.

"Don't worry, I'll sort him out for you," Ruari promised. "Just do me a favour and steer well clear of him until I do!"

Ivain stared balefully back at him through two rapidly swelling eyes, and Ruari reflected that the young king was not going to be seeing much of anything for the next few days while the spectacular black eyes he was going to get subsided. The ever watchful Pauli had been beside them, and now took it upon himself to take charge of Ivain for Ruari.

"Come on lad. Let's find something to put on this mess and try to stop that nose from bleeding before you cover us all."

"I don't subbose you 'ave one of those b'wonder cures like the 'angover one?" Ivain asked thickly through swelling lips – still remembering the way his head had spun as the volcano of Pauli's home-made cure had exploded inside him. The way he felt at the moment, a cure like that might blow him apart for good.

"Sorry, my friend. You'll just have to get better the hard way this time," Pauli told him. "But I bet there's an icehouse somewhere near the castle, if only for preserving the local fish with. We should be able to ease the swelling a bit. But you're going to have the most spectacular bruises! Princely purple's going to have nothing on those!"

Ruari chuckled as Pauli led Ivain away, closely followed by Haply and Grimston with Eric between them. Inside the keep Hereman took Ruari with Breca up to his office, summoned refreshments, and then closed the door.

"Would you mind enlightening me now as to why you were so lenient with Talorcan?" he asked politely, as befitted speaking to his new commander. However, Ruari had enough experience to hear the undertone of frustration and hint of criticism.

The new acting-head of the Prydein sept nodded and went to sit on a thick seat pad in the window recess where the sun was streaming in. "Great Maker, this is good!" he sighed. "Sorry, Hereman. It's just that in the east it was always so wet and misty, I don't think we saw the sun for more than about two days in three years! And since then I've been freezing my arse off in icy wastes for months. It's bliss just to be warm again! ...But as to Talorcan ...this possibly wasn't all his fault."

"It wasn't?" Hereman was clearly dubious.

"From what I've seen with Maelbrigt and Squint," Ruari explained to the two senior men, "Ivain and Eric are now very much intertwined. Now in Maelbrigt's case, he's a very experienced and stable man, and so we've never seen Squint exercise much in the way of influence over him. Out on that quay Talorcan hit a raw nerve with Ivain, and Ivain's emotional reaction would've fed back to Eric. But rather more importantly, I suspect that Eric picked up on the fact that Talorcan is half-DeÁine, and his emotional response might well have fed back to Ivain without Ivain being aware of it. He's already just said to me that he doesn't know why he suddenly flew at Talorcan."

"Talorcan ...a Knight ...is half-DeÁine!" Breca was appalled. "How in the Islands did that happen?"

However Hereman was gazing at the ceiling deep in thought. "Oh my! *That* Knight!"

Breca looked to his ealdorman. "What do you mean? *That* Knight?"

Hereman said one word as he looked back to Ruari. "Gavra?"

"That's the one," Ruari confirmed, then continued for Breca's benefit. "Do you remember that we used a lure to distract the DeÁine while I moved the DeÁine Gorget out of Brychan? Well the lure was Talorcan.

The Covert Brethren found him in the most appalling circumstances as a child and brought him out of New Lochlainn. It wasn't just out of compassion, although how anyone could leave any child in those conditions would be beyond most men. Talorcan's mother is now the queen regent of the pure-bred DeÁine in New Lochlainn. The son everyone knew about, up until Gavra, was Ruadan and he's now king by title even if it's his mother who does the ruling. This woman is Eriu. We've never been able to understand why she had an affair with an Islander, but what we do know is that almost as soon as Talorcan was born she was trying to hide him and dissociate herself from him. It seemed to work, because shortly after she made her return into DeÁine society, the Covert Brethren found out that she'd caught the eye of King Nuadu and hasn't looked back since. Didn't look back, that is, except to have Talorcan's foster mother tortured in front of him and taken away and killed pretty gruesomely."

"My, my, that's some story!" Breca breathed. "Isn't it ironic that the one person he might have most in common with is Ivain!"

"Isn't it just!" Ruari agreed. "Now once Talorcan had grown to be a man and had trained for years with the Order, he agreed for his past to be dangled as bait to the DeÁine. The Covert Brethren spun a tale of Eriu's long-lost son returning to New Lochlainn with a small army of dissident Knights. The bait we wanted to hook – and caught – was King Nuadu's dim-witted brother, Bres. Having disabled Nuadu by means of a rather nasty poison which left him writhing in his bed, we told Bres that he could bring this new army into the embrace of the DeÁine, and then they would have a force they could infiltrate the Order with."

"Flaming Trees! He must've been a bit thick if he really thought that would work!" Breca laughed. "I remember hearing of a deception which was being run, but I'd never have guessed that was it."

"Oh, he was spectacularly dim!" Ruari conceded. "But that's what made him such a prime target. Unfortunately the Abend thought so too! That's how we ended up with the mess we did at Gavra, with Talorcan's mock army suddenly finding themselves face to face with an armed force of even greater size, and with Abend amongst them to boot.

"Although the Celidon Knights were just behind them, Talorcan was a hero that day! When the warnings of the approaching DeÁine came through, I've heard eyewitness accounts of how he gave Maelbrigt's men time to catch up by riding out in front of his own men and issuing challenges, or feigned willingness to negotiate with anyone of pure blood but not the Abend. He rode out alone, in full view of both armies, and had to dodge a few bolts of Power-fire in the process! So, gentlemen, how could I throw him into the cells for punching out your young king for what he sees as good reasons? He has to understand that he's wrong. Of course he does. But Talorcan in battle is far too useful to discard – and battle is coming whether we like it or not."

Hereman and Breca both looked uncomfortable. It was a mess and no mistaking.

"And I'm afraid it gets even more complicated," Hereman added. "When Swein and Talorcan's lance got here with the Arrow – after you'd left, Breca – they told me of something the Arrow's Guardian said to them. According to the Guardian, if you manage to bring any of the DeÁine Treasures out into the world, we should think about letting Talorcan try to use one of them if it becomes absolutely necessary. The Guardian thought that Talorcan might be able to bend one of them to his will, although I must admit I'd hesitate to try that with the Helm – that's supposed to be the most aggressively DeÁine of all the pieces. But the Gorget might just be possible, or even the Scabbard."

"Sacred Root and Branch!" Ruari gasped. "The next time one of the ancients puts in an appearance, I think we must let Masters Brego and Hugh know about that one! I have to say, though, that given the way the ancients have rather misinterpreted the consequences of their actions, I'd be very reluctant to let Talorcan do that except in the direst of circumstances. You only have to look at how they totally missed all of the implications for the squints to see how badly wrong that might go."

Hereman grimaced. "I know what you mean. It doesn't exactly fill you with confidence, does it?"

Confidence was not something Ruari was feeling the next morning when he went to tackle Talorcan. The younger Knight might have had chance to reflect on things, but going on what Ruari knew of him, the chances of him having come to the right kind of conclusions all by himself were pretty slim. His formal uniform having been unpacked and hung up to let the creases drop out, Ruari had donned it before setting out for his confrontation. It might seem a little overdone, but he wanted to make it plain to Talorcan just what rank he held now. When they had last met Ruari had still been the senior, but now the gulf had widen even more. If Talorcan continued to rail against Ivain and forced Ruari into ordering him to desist, Ruari wanted to give the notorious rogue Knight no opportunity for saying he had had no idea of who was giving him the order, and therefore maybe feeling free to ignore it.

Passing the guards, Ruari let himself into the chamber high on the west side of the keep. He was not really surprised to see the whole of Talorcan's lance in there with him. They were renowned for their loyalty. However he was surprised to see the burly sergeant, Barcwith spring to his feet and gesture him back to the door before Talorcan himself had seen Ruari.

"A word if you would, please sire," the veteran sergeant breathed softly.

It was a request couched in the politest of terms and Ruari had always had a great deal of time for veterans like Barcwith – without them, men like himself would have found running the Order next to impossible. So without saying a word, Ruari led the way back to outside the door and gestured for the guards to back off to the top of the staircase.

"What can I do for you, sergeant?" Ruari asked quietly. The door was very thick, but it did not do to underestimate how sound sometimes travelled in these big old castles. "I'm guessing you want to plead some kind of mitigating circumstances?"

"Sort of," admitted Barcwith ruefully. "How much do you know of Mister Talorcan's private life? If you don't mind me asking, that is?"

Ruari smiled. "Quite a lot, as it happens. Don't worry, Barcwith. I know all about Talorcan's past, who his mother is and how much he's done for the Order. You wouldn't know this, but I was in charge of the party moving the Gorget when you and Talorcan were at Gavra Pass. I briefly met and spoke with him back then. I've also spoken at length with Maelbrigt – the man who led the Celidon Foresters in support of Talorcan. He speaks very highly of your leader, and I'm not such a stickler for rules and regulations that I'd let a misjudgement cloud my opinion."

Barcwith's relief was plain to see. "Oh good! Then you won't mind, sire, if I add something to your knowledge?" Ruari gestured for him to carry on. "It's like this, you see. When we got this assignment, Mister Talorcan was dead set against it. Dragging some wee lassie halfway across the Islands on some half-baked treasure hunt seemed like the worst kind of nightmare to him."

Ruari had to smile at that. He could just imagine the response to Brego's order once Talorcan had left the Grand Master. In fairness it would not have been that far removed from his own in similar circumstances. But Barcwith had not finished.

"The thing is, the longer we were with her, the more she sort of grew on him. She was downright brave, sire. Even when she was chucking her guts up every dawn with morning sickness, she never made herself a burden to us. And some of her suggestions really helped us no end. But what really made the difference in the Boss' eyes was when we had to go to Brychan."

"Brychan? What in the Islands were you doing there?"

"Ah well, you see we didn't think it sensible to sail straight into Temair in case Magnus had any of his men there. So we had the *Craken* sail us to Farsan, so that we could get some up to date intelligence about how active the DeÁine had been on the opposite coast. Of course, once we got there we heard that things had gone base upwards in a hurry. That's where we met Swein for the first time with a young lady called Cwen. But more importantly for the Boss, we met someone from his past. A young chap he was what you might call 'fond of'.

"At that point we were really trying not to draw any attention to ourselves and what we were about. So we were really unlucky when it turned out that the lad's miserable old sod of a father wasn't far behind. Alaiz was a bloody marvel, sire! You should have seen her stand up to the old bully! She got the young lad out of trouble and saved us from being sucked into a fight.

"Since then she's been solid gold in the Boss' eyes. He hasn't had many women ever stick up for him in that kind of way. And it went against everything he believes in to let her go to Mad Magnus' court. He's been as worried sick about her as the rest of us have. It just really stuck in his craw to see her twat of a husband strolling off the ship when she might be dead for all we know. …Does that help make sense of things, sire?"

Ruari sighed. "Yes it does, but there's more going on than you're aware of, Barcwith. Thank you for explaining that. I think you'd better come in and hear what I have to say."

Turning on his heels, he led his way back into the room to find the rest of the lance standing protectively on either side of a very battered-faced Talorcan. Ivain had not done so badly after all, Ruari reflected. He must have landed a fair few punches of his own against a vastly more experienced opponent. Breca and Pauli were right, he did learn fast.

"Sit down, gentlemen," Ruari said firmly but in a neutral tone. The men of the lance looked to one another. This was not what they had expected. Cautiously they resumed the seats they had been in when Ruari had first entered. Talorcan, however, remained standing, chin in the air and obviously preparing himself to take whatever dressing down Ruari was about to hand out. The practised air with which he fixed his gaze on a spot somewhere around Ruari's hairline so that he did not quite meet his gaze, was a worrying indicator of how many times this must have happened. Getting bawled out was nothing new to Talorcan.

Recalling a private meeting with Brego, Ruari remembered being told that the old Grand Master of Celidon had been a Forester first and foremost. That had meant that the Foresters had come first every time, and the ordinary knights a poor second best. Brego had confessed that by the time the Celidon sept had been mothballed, and Talorcan had come under his own command at Lorne, the damage had been done. As an ordinary Knight, he had been used mercilessly without thought for the cost to him. And without the time or capacity to be spending all his time trying to unravel the younger Knight's troubled past, Brego had been struggling to redirect his most troublesome if talented Knight. *What a waste*, Ruari thought, *he should've been a senior captain at least by now, if not a commander. What's gone so wrong for you, Talorcan? Where's the man I met? How do I reach you*?

"Sit down, Talorcan. I meant you too," Ruari said lightly and was rewarded by Talorcan's bloodshot and bruised eyes snapping down to meet his own in surprise. *That got your attention didn't it*! Ruari thought. *I just stopped playing the same old, worn out game, didn't I, and so you have to step out of your tried and tested role of playing dumb to the superior who hasn't a clue about the real you. Good! Let's keep you on your toes!*

"Now then, gentlemen, I know that you are *all* worried about Alaiz and Cwen, and wish that you were with the men Ealdorman Hereman has already sent across to Kittermere to begin marching towards Magnus and Rathlin. I also appreciate that you've been kicking your heels here with nothing to do but wait for far longer than you are used to doing because of Swein."

"Beg pardon, sire," Tamàs said deferentially, "but we knowed that weren't Mister Swein's fault. 'T'weren't anything we held against him. None of us did."

It was carefully couched, but Ruari was astute enough to hear that he was being told that Talorcan had not been difficult with Swein. Well that at least was a blessing and one less thing to sort out.

"Good, I'm glad to hear it." Ruari's response was firm but calm, re-establishing his control of the situation. "Now there's something I want *you* to hear, and I hope you'll keep an open mind until I've finished speaking." He paused and looked at each of them in turn, coming to Talorcan last and holding his gaze for several heartbeats. *Don't push me*, he willed in that glance. *I'm not your enemy, but I'll do what I have to do if you leave me no other choice.*

"Firstly, Talorcan, you have to be aware that Eric thought you were a DeÁine attacking Ivain." That really made everyone sit up and take note. It certainly was not what they had expected him to start with. "I don't know if you've observed this with Swein and Dylan, or if there's been no situation where it would've become apparent, but Ivain and Eric are bonded in a way that means that they're now intertwined emotionally. You prodded Ivain and hit a nerve and Eric picked up on it. He sensed your DeÁine blood and thought he had to fight you. That got fed back to Ivain and look what happened."

"Flaming Underworlds!" Barcwith swore.

"Shit, that could've got serious in a hurry!" Galey agreed, as all the men of the lance, including little Ad, frowned worriedly.

"Indeed," Ruari agreed, glad that they all saw the wider implications without him having to labour them. "So whatever you think of what I'm going to say next, gentlemen, if you can't look at Ivain without wanting to smack him one, you *will* stay clear of him! Do I make myself clear?" There was a chorus of 'yes, sires' immediately – even from Talorcan, who had stopped looking belligerent and was sitting up and looking alert. Things were starting to look hopeful.

"Now then, I hope you're all grown up enough to understand that there's more than one side to an argument. You've heard Alaiz's, and while I'm not saying that she was wrong, I am saying that there's more to this than you know. For a start off, Talorcan, Ivain thought you'd *raped* Alaiz and that *you'd* got her pregnant."

There was a stunned silence for a moment, then Talorcan spluttered, "Me? *Rape* her?"

"Fucking Underworlds, he doesn't know much about you, does he?" Barcwith guffawed, showing a familiarity with his leader that was further reassurance to Ruari that he was not dealing with a mindless thug. If Talorcan of late had just become hardened and bitter, it was unlikely that he would tolerate such leg-pulling from his men, however closely they might work with him.

Ruari held up a hand to halt the shocked mirth. "No he doesn't. In fact he knows virtually nothing about you except what I've briefly told him since you tried to rip his head off. Now what you have to take on board is that *he's* been worried sick about Alaiz too. From all that he's told me while we've been travelling back here from Ergardia, I can see how it would be possible for Alaiz to have thought he was sowing his wild oats amongst the ladies of the court at every turn. I'm afraid the truth is far from that and actually rather sadder too. Ivain found himself pursued at every opportunity by the women of the court. Some of them may well have thought that since Alaiz hadn't produced an heir, that she could be removed and that they might take her place. Others, I'm sure, simply wanted him as a trophy to boast about. He told me himself that he never did anything with any of them, and Pauli confirms that he's said the same to him, and when he was roaring drunk at the time."

"You don't mean he's still a v...," Galey gasped as Ruari cut him off,

"...Yes he is! And no leg-pulling about that or making it common knowledge either! I know it's hard to do, but you have to imagine that from the time you barely enter your teens, women of all shapes, sizes and persuasions start trying to jump on you. It would take a strong-minded young man not to find that pretty intimidating – especially from the older ones! And from what Pauli told me, some of them were pretty raddled with the pox and far from in their first flush of youth. Some of them – Trees save him – had bedded his grandfather, and wanted to add the next generation to their list of conquest."

"Lost Souls!" Galey and Decke muttered together, clearly having a mental image of what such a woman would be like.

"Poor little bugger!" the ever sympathetic Tamàs added. "You'd be off women for life after a few shocks like that. Anyone would. It's a wonder he didn't cross over to your side of the fence, Boss!"

That really made Talorcan blink. "Is he?"

"I have no idea," Ruari confessed, "and I don't think he does either. However, that's by the by. What I hope you're beginning to see is that because of the very isolation Alaiz told you of, she only saw part of what was going on. What she told you is undoubtedly the truth as she knows it. I wouldn't disparage her by implying anything else. But it's not the whole truth. From Ivain's point of view, he found himself married to a girl he thought of as his sister before either one of them knew what marriage would mean. All that staying away from her was his awkward way of trying to deflect some of them worst scrutiny of the court away from her. He thought that if he steered clear of her for weeks on end, then at least they wouldn't have to go through some charade of being in love. He does love her, but as a sister, not a wife."

"Oh shit! What a mess!" Talorcan breathed. "Now you say that I can see how it could happen." Then his expression hardened again. "But that doesn't excuse his cowardice in the face of a conflict!"

"Cowardice?" Ruari repeated. "Oh no, Talorcan, you've got that wrong! Very wrong! Master Hugh himself told me what they never told Alaiz. About how close Ivain nearly came to being killed by Calatin the first time the war-mage took him prisoner. They didn't want to frighten her apparently."

"*Woah*! Hold on a minute!" Barcwith interrupted, forgetting Ruari's rank in the heat of the moment. "Ivain got taken prisoner by one of the *Abend*? When did this happen?"

Ruari let the lapse go, for this was more of the reaction he wanted. "Right at the beginning of the civil war here on Prydein. Ivain was in the east already, and Duke Brion asked Calatin to take Ivain prisoner for him. He very nearly succeeded in keeping and killing him too if it hadn't been for Haply and Grimston – so now you know why they're so close to him. But there's more. After Alaiz briefly saw Ivain at Quies Castle, Ivain went to Bittern. From there he was part of the army which got wiped out by Duke Brion's force. He did the forced march over the moors with Pauli to join Hereman, and since then he really has been trying to learn what he should be doing. He helped Breca take both Osraig and Draynes Castles over on Kittermere, and Breca's well impressed with the effort he's making – and I don't think Breca's impressed all that often!"

Talorcan slumped forward and buried his head in his hands with a groan as Barcwith asked,

"Has he really been in the thick of the fighting, then?"

"Yes he has," Ruari confirmed, "and doing well for someone who'd never held a sword in anger before. For what it's worth, having now been given the chance he's genuinely trying to work out where he's going in all of this. He doesn't want to be a martinet of a king like his late and unlamented grandfather. But he can see very clearly the dangers of being a puppet king. Nobody's had to beat him over the head over how the control the leading nobles had, through the years he's been the child-king, brought about the current crisis. In fact, he's talking about getting the Island back on its feet and then taking it back to having a Jarl with a body of counsellors around him, and it not being hereditary.

"And if you needed one more thing to confirm that Ivain isn't some worthless idiot being nursemaided by Pauli with Haply and Grimston, think on this. The Bow chose *him*! He didn't choose it. Everything the ancients have told us makes it clear that these weapons were designed to be just that – weapons. And they go to the person *best* suited to wielding them in battle. Do you really think, then, that the Bow would have chosen some pretty-boy prince who thought of no-one but himself?"

"I did hear from some of the archers that they thought right highly of the young king," admitted Tamàs. "It sounded a bit odd then, but I thought they must've only seen him off and on, like."

"Actually they were some of the few who really knew him," Ruari corrected him. "Hugh told me that the nobles were appalled that he would associate himself with the common men like that. He never did manage to do it in the capital or anywhere where the court held sway, but out in the countryside of the far east he was able to be himself, if only for a short while at a time."

"Shit!" Talorcan growled. "Shit, shit, *shit*! I got it so wrong, didn't I?" He looked up at Ruari. "If you'll let me, I think I need to go and apologise to Ivain. I got myself into this so I suppose I'd better start digging myself out of the hole."

Ruari smiled. "I'm glad you've seen that. Shall we go downstairs? I believe Ivain and Swein are in the courtyard with the squints getting ready to start working out how the two Treasures work together."

As the tall acting-Master led the way out Barcwith sidled closer to Talorcan. "So the next time I tell you you're being a fucking idiot and to shut up, will you listen to me instead of sticking both feet in your gob *again*?"

Talorcan laughed and then grunted with the pain from his bruised ribs. "Maybe…!" he said, slapping his friend on the back. "Maybe…!"

Rathlin & Kittermere, with the coasts of Brychan & Ergardia

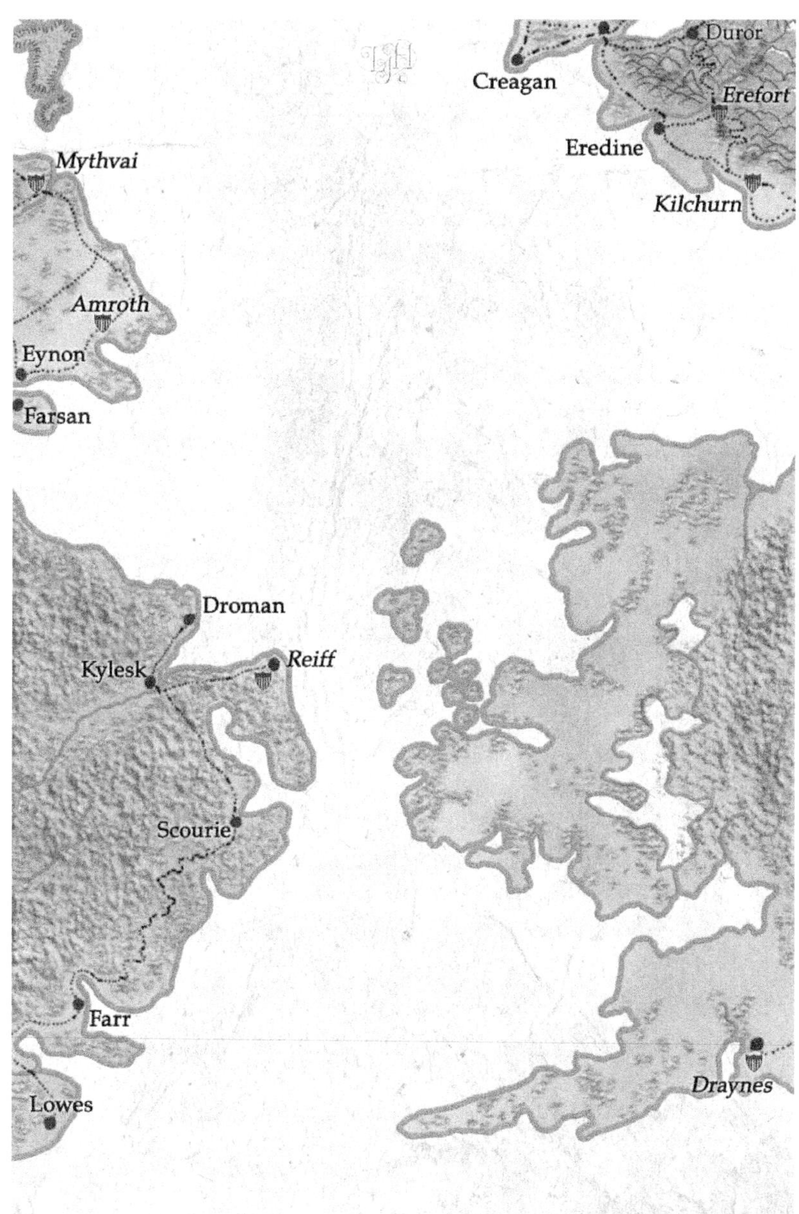

Chapter 11

Dire Warnings

Rathlin & Ergardia: late Spring-moon – late Earrach

Nearly a month earlier, Cwen stood shivering in the chill air after running for her life from Reiff Castle. All day she had fled with Scully's lance, dodging Magnus' search parties. At first Scully had led them in search of Warren and Mutley, Scully taking most of the weight of the great Spear with either Rolo or Brock while Cwen kept a restraining hand on it, with the alternate archer covered their backs. They had run straight into the two bulky sergeants returning to tell them that not a boat was to be found. Some small fishing boats were tied up down below the cliff, but as Warren said, there was little point in taking them when the locals could no doubt pursue such an inexperienced crew with ease. All that would achieve would be delaying their capture.

"We need to get down onto the rocks and shale," Mutley declared when he heard of the pursuit. "Somewhere where we won't leave an easy trail for them to see. Quick! Back this way!"

He led them on a frantic scramble down sheep paths, terrifying in the watery light by which they could just make out the great rollers pounding the rocks below.

"Tide's in," Brock puffed, as he caught Cwen before she slid too far, after losing her footing for the umpteenth time.

"That's good?" she gasped back, rubbing her grazed hand before diving for the end of the Spear, which was currently slung between Warren and Mutley. The combined strength of the two big sergeants was proving to be the only way they could get the Spear over such dreadful terrain with any speed.

"Could be," wheezed Scully breathlessly from up in front. "It'll wash away any tracks we have to make. Might get our feet wet on this stretch, but there could be a way around the headland at low tide without breaking our necks or getting killed."

At the bottom of the slope they found the narrowest of ledges where they huddled for a while. Above them was a sharp overhang which concealed them from prying eyes, and although they heard the jangle of horses' bits and a man calling back to others from just above them, they remained undiscovered. An hour later, freezing cold from standing still, they found that they could get down into ankle-deep water. The occasional big wave still splashed them right up their legs, but the great rollers were dissipating noticeably further out.

"Looks like there's some kind of stone shelf jutting out into the sea," whispered Rolo. "Probably two different types of rock on this cliff. The soft one's got worn away much faster, but the hard base is still there. Watch your step! There might be sudden hollows under foot."

For a moment they thought their time in the water might be brief when they turned a rocky shoulder, and saw a vast stone arch in the projecting cliff and beyond it a promising deep cleft cutting back inland. Yet they were scurrying backwards only a moment later when a man walked out on the top of the sea-arch. He was proceeding with great care, testing every footstep before putting his weight on it, and twice a chunk of earth and stones crumbled away into the sea at the touch of his foot. Unfortunately he did not fall, and he was soon out far enough to see along the coast. The six quarries huddled deeper into the shadows, getting soaked in the process. But the tactic worked, for the man was clearly looking for some kind of small craft on the water, not figures on the cliffs themselves.

"Bugger!" Mutley cursed when the man had returned to his fellows shaking his head. "Well that does it. We certain can't go inland up that gully. What now?"

Scully gestured them forwards. "Rolo, you scout ahead until you can see if we can make a dash across under that sea-arch. We'll try to hide in its shadows, then make another dash to the cliff on the other side. There's nothing for it. We'll have to carry on or wait out of sight until nightfall – and it's too cold for us to stand in the sea all day!"

Rolo crept ahead checking his every move until he was out of sight. He returned much more quickly to tell them that there was a slightly higher ledge which they could climb up on for a while. The bad news was that the distance to the arch was further than it looked from back where they were. Moreover, he had spotted Magnus' men on their shaggy hill-ponies riding along the inbound edge of the gully with the clear intention of coming back out along the other side to carry on down the coast. They would have to wait until the riders were round the next headland before they dared move.

After another long, cold wait, the Attacotti pirates disappeared from view, and the fugitives were able to make their crossing. Yet even this was not the passage they had hoped. By now the tide was low, exposing a clean sweep of sand beneath the arch – sand which would show their every footstep. However, there was no choice but to go on. They had to get off Rathlin somehow, which meant finding a boat, and that meant one of the villages down to the south, if not a big port.

Luckily they had stolen plenty of food when they had left Magnus' court, but cold water was no substitute for a hot drink, and the dried meat would go further if made into a warming soup. Weighing up the options, Scully led them across the sand right down at the waterline. It made for a longer run in the open, but Magnus' men were well out of sight for the moment and as soon as the tide started to turn back it would wipe away the evidence of their passage. Better to take a chance now than leave a clear sign which might still be there when the riders came back out onto the headland.

With chattering teeth they made it around two more headlands in short, frantic dashes, for the tide was on the turn by now and heading back their way. With some relief the wind had dropped so that the sea was no longer being whipped into a frenzy, but they still needed to get up out of the way of the waves by nightfall.

A series of small beaches all had caves, but none of them deep enough to go back sufficiently for the floor to rise above water at high tide. Several times they spotted the riders in the distance above them, and finally Scully decided that the only thing they could do was halt and let the riders get properly ahead of them. They had just sunk wearily onto some dry rocks when they heard voices coming back towards them and closely.

"Flaming Underworlds! They've got down on the beach!" Brock gasped.

Luckily they had just crossed the out-fall of a small river and had then been up on rocks, staying off the sand to stay out of the approaching tide. Just ahead was a proper large cave and Scully gestured to it. They had an ankle-wrenching scramble to get to it, for infuriatingly its entrance was surrounded with clear sand too, and they had to practically climb on the cliff to keep their feet off. However they made it, and dived into the gloom only moments before the nose of the first horse appeared silhouetted against the light.

Scully gestured to Cwen to keep her face down so that her pale skin would not show up in the gloom. He and the other men had their faces muffled by collars and scarves so that only their eyes showed. For a nerve wrenching few minutes the riders rode leisurely past, some gazing out to sea and searching the horizon, while others scoured the sand for signs of passage. Even after they had gone, the group did not dare move for a long time. Eventually the swiftly rising water forced the issue. With great care, Brock and Rolo edged to the mouth of the cave, bows at the ready with arrows nocked and waiting to fly. Looking out in small darting movements, they finally gave the all-clear and the rest sloshed out in their wake. By now the tide was washing their footmarks away almost as soon as they were made, and there was no sign left that they had been in the cave.

Hurrying up the course of the river, they found a place where they could scramble up onto dry land, at which point they could see why Magnus' men had come back this way. An Attacotti hamlet was tucked into the lee of a hillock and plumes of smoke from peat fires were rising into the air from chimneys, the smell of cooking wafting on the air as well.

Cwen's stomach growled hungrily.

"I know, lass, me too!" Mutley whispered. "Come on! Let's get somewhere where we can risk lighting a fire."

They edged around the cluster of shabby building until the wind would be blowing the settlement's smoke towards them to disguise any smoke of their own, then walked on until they were well out of sight. In the heart of a cluster of gorse bushes they made a fire pit, and got a small blaze going from wood they had gathered on the way. It was a meagre thing, but enough to put a pot over and heat some food on. Mercifully their packs had remained dry for the greater part, and Scully chivvied everyone into changing into what dry clothes they had. The damp clothing was draped over the bushes both to dry and act as a limited wind shield, although not much of one was needed that night.

With the gorse being dense and high enough to hide them, they stayed put for the start of the morning. Scully wanted to see if the riders continued on their search along the coast going south before he risked moving. The last thing he wanted was to set off at dawn, only to be overtaken by the very men they were trying to avoid. However, the riders seemed to have decided that they must have overtaken the fugitives, missing them on the way, and to everyone's relief they saw them appear up on a rise heading back towards Reiff.

Not that that solved all their problems. On the third day, the coast south of them suddenly dived around in a huge loch going back north-west. To follow its edge would take them back to a point between Kylesk and Reiff – the last place they wanted to be.

Their first true stroke of luck came when they discovered an old boat washed up on the shore as they wearily trudged along, having rounded the sea end of the loch. It was a pitiful thing, but the bottom was sound and, while nobody in their right mind would have set to sea in it, Brock reckoned it would get them across the width of the loch. Watching the currents closely, they shoved it out into the water when they guessed the tide was nearly at its highest. With nothing to steer it by except a couple of planks ripped from the already broken sides, they would have to rely on drifting for most of the way. As the one most used to tides, Brock's best estimation was that they should get part the way over before the pull back out to sea got too strong.

When they did try to steer it the whole thing wobbled alarmingly, for the one side was severely battered and lower than the other, unbalancing it badly. So they had to sit tight and hope for the best, just giving it a bit of a nudge every now and then. For a grim hour they all watched as they drifted sedately towards the inlet which led to the Attacotti port of Scourie – not a place they particularly wanted to land either. Then the tide turned and began to pick up speed. Another worrying few hours saw the first southern headland drift past, at which point they began to wonder whether they would have to jump out and swim before they got too far out to sea. But once a bit further out, the current pushed them land-wards once more as the sea swept round submerged rocks, and they heard the bottom scrape on some from a spur running inland. Piling out of the boat, they splashed through the shallows. The rocky bar stopped a couple of hundred yards from the shore itself and they had to swim then, although the side channel was not deep enough for the tide to be a serious threat.

Frozen to the marrow they staggered ashore.

"We have to have a fire and get properly dry," Rolo whispered to Scully. "Cwen can't take much more of this. If she doesn't get warm soon she's going to get sick."

Mutley nodded his agreement as they watched Warren and Brock trying to chaff some feeling back into Cwen's frozen hands so that she could hold the Spear for them to carry. "Not much point in saving this Spear-thing if she dies on us, and at some point we're going to have to risk contact with the ordinary people," he pointed out.

"I know," Scully sighed, "but we daren't risk the locals just yet. We're too close to Magnus' heartland."

Fortunately they stumbled across an abandoned sheep farm just in from the cliffs. Once a substantial building, its roof was still partly intact and the chimneys were sound. The wood from derelict sheep pens provided the fuel, and there was soon a huge blaze going in what had once been the main room. The well in the yard was still clean, and soon they were able to wash the salt out of their clothes in hot water and leave them hanging to dry about the place. Past caring about being seen, they decided there was little point in setting a watch. Anyone living close would spot the smoke from the chimney and raise the alarm long before any of them would know about it. But their luck held. When Brock and Rolo scouted around in the morning, they declared there was nothing to be seen for miles.

As a consequence they left the fire out during daylight hours, but stayed for another day, restoring their strength and trying to make some kind of a plan. In the end they all agreed that the only thing for it was to walk all the way down to Farr. Richert's maps were now looking very bedraggled, but the ink had not run so badly as to render them useless, and they showed Farr as a proper town further south.

"I reckon we should be there in ten days," Scully estimated. "We could do it faster if we take this proper road that's shown, but I don't want to risk that. We're too vulnerable to someone coming up on us fast on that. With the Spear we don't stand a chance of avoiding a bunch of horsemen."

And so for ten more days they trudged up hill and down dale across the Rathlin countryside. Lugging the Spear was a chore they came to dread, for its weight sapped the energy even of Mutley and Warren. Yet three days into their trek, Cwen suddenly gasped and keeled over in pain. Whatever it was soon passed, but while it continued the Spear also glowed a sickly blue-white light. It brought home to all of them in a forceful way just how much might be riding on getting this thing to safety, and quelled any thoughts of abandoning it until they could come back with reinforcements.

If the incident was worrying by its unexplained nature, what was reassuring was the deserted nature of the landscape. While there was much evidence of former occupation, it was all long abandoned. It was only when they were within a day of Farr that they began to guess why. Here the folk were very different. Gone were Magnus' scruffy raiders and pitiful cottagers, and in their place were small but neat little farms. Few could have been making much money, but they were clearly surviving well enough by exchanging goods with their neighbours. Farr itself had the same faded glory of Kylesk but, significantly, without the shanty town around it. Here the buildings had been patched and repaired, if not with the same level of high craftsmanship as the original, then with a fair degree of competence. The once fancy houses by the quay seemed to be occupied by whole extended families of fishermen, not left to go to ruin, and the potholes in the road had at least been filled in even if there were no more of the great stone pavers to make a proper repair with.

"I don't think Magnus' authority runs much down here," Cwen observed. "You know, we might even ask openly for passage out of here without being turned straight back over to him."

Scully was not prepared to take quite such a risk yet, but they did manage to secure passage on what appeared to be a weekly boat-run around to the market at the next town, Lowes. The folk must have been used to refugees from Magnus' territory, for nobody asked any questions as to why they came out of the north, filthy and tattered. The Spear was hard to disguise and so two of them stayed outside of the town with it at all times during the three day wait. Just before boarding the boat, they managed to wrap it in old sacks and tie them up with string. Thankfully nobody asked them what was in the strange bundle, although they had decided that the best cover was to say it was a piece of wood to splice into a ship's mast. With good quality timber hard to come by on Rathlin, it would explain why they were treating it with such care.

Lowes was very similar to Farr only a bit larger, and in the hustle and bustle of market day the six of them were blissfully anonymous. Some larger ships were tied up at the quays, and for the first time they hoped they might yet make it to safety.

"What have we got?" Scully asked, as they huddled together at the far end of the quays, at a spot where there was a solid stone wall to their backs and where there was little chance of them being overheard.

"Well there's that big merchantman at the end berth," Mutley said. "He's come all the way from the southern lands filled with fabrics, spices and dyes. He's headed for Rheged ultimately. The trouble is, he's going to call in at Farsan first, and then Belhaven on Celidon before he unloads more at Eredine on Ergardia. And really we'd want to stay on until he calls at Forres or Seaton on Ergardia, because they're a lot closer to the Knight's headquarters.

"The bad news is that he's twitchy about the troubles on Brychan. He's half thinking of cutting his losses and trying his luck in the far north-eastern lands beyond Rheged. He hasn't made his mind up yet. And look at the size of that thing! It's got all the speed of a lumbering whale! It'll take weeks to get anywhere. For him it doesn't matter because none of his cargo is particularly perishable, but I think we need a bit more speed."

Scully looked to Warren, who also shook his head. "The big fishing boat is about to go straight to the northern seas now that spring is on the way. No use to us at all."

"What about the ship with the blue figurehead?" he asked Rolo.

But the archer shook his head too. "Trading salt fish round the south coast of Rathlin to the old Attacotti territories in New Lochlainn. The last place we should be going!"

The Knights all looked at one another indecisively, and Cwen fervently wished that of all the people she had known that Berengar was here. Much as she had loved Richert with all her heart, this kind of situation was so far out of his experience that he would have been utterly lost, and she knew it. Richert may have wielded a great deal of power in some circles, but his experience in the field had been very limited – nobody risked the king's brother without very good cause. On the other hand Berengar had seemed very well versed in all forms of warfare, including the more covert ones. She felt sure he would have assessed the situation and come to some kind of a decision. Instead she found herself facing the awful realisation that she, of all of the group, had an idea of what was going on.

"We should wait around," she heard herself say. "It's only the fourteenth of Earrach, after all. This is just the start of the trading season. That merchantman's here precisely because he is slow. If he'd left it another few weeks, his faster competitors would've beaten him to the best bargains over on Ergardia and Rheged. He can take bigger seas than them, so he gets here early to make up for it. There'll be plenty of ships coming through soon, and most of them will have left their home ports long before the news of the invasion of Brychan got there."

The men all looked at her hopefully, then Scully nodded his assent. "Very well, we'll trust to Cwen. She knows more about trade around these waters than we do."

That was just what Cwen did not want. However, she smiled reassuringly and kept her fingers crossed behind her back that she was guessing right, and that a fast ship would come.

She was, but not for any reason she would have wanted. Over the next days more ships slowly passed by. All were fishing boats heading for the once frozen seas and the great shoals of fish they could now get to. Then on the twenty-ninth a fast vessel appeared, flying into port battered by the weather and with a haggard crew on board. A sleek, fast ship of the kind which carried small, expensive and perishable goods normally, this one had barely thrown the mooring lines to the quay before an exhausted young man appeared at the stern.

"Is there an Order fort near here? Any Knights anywhere?" he called urgently.

The locals shook their heads in confusion, but without grasping the young captain's desperation. Unable to stand by and watch, Scully allowed Mutley and Warren to shoulder a way forward for him.

"What's wrong?" he called up. Looking at the state of the ship he added, "You've clearly had a terrible voyage."

As the locals began to take notice, the young captain ran his hands over his face, then raised them in a gesture of despair. "Terrible voyage? Oh the weather wasn't that bad if we'd dared to take even one sail down. Oh Trees! I have to get to the Knights! I have to warn the Order!"

"Of what?" Scully demanded, his heart already sinking.

"We passed the route to the Isle of Arieda. Not called in – who would risk contact with them! – but a week's voyage away. We met a fast cutter running for her life. Her captain told us he'd spotted the biggest fleet he'd ever seen in his life. We should've been going the way he'd come, but he begged us to turn back. Once we'd heard what he had to say, I couldn't turn quick enough. …There's a *DeÁine* fleet on the high seas!"

Everyone gasped in horror. Such a thing had never been heard of – not even when the DeÁine had retaken the west of Brychan and made it New Lochlainn. Then they had come in smaller waves and remained unspotted. But the captain was in no state to be gentle in breaking the bad news.

"There's a DeÁine fleet," he repeated. "It must've put into Arieda by the end of Spring-moon. That means they had only two months' journey left before they could land in *Brychan*! Less if they land on Prydein or here. The only thing that's slowed them down is that they're filled to the brim with troops, and because of that they've had to stop to take on supplies – especially water – at Arieda. They're big! *Huge* ships! I know the type. They sail in the southern ocean. Slow, but what they can carry makes our biggest craft look puny."

He shook his head and slumped forward on the rail. "We've not slept or slowed since! Every man's worked double shifts trimming the sails to get the last drop of wind out of them. We must warn the Order! There can't be less than a hundred thousand troops on the way!"

Howls of terror rose from the quay as the locals began to panic.

"Quiet!" bellowed Mutley standing tall, as did the others. "We have a Knight here! Be quiet and listen!"

As a fearful hush descended on the crowd, Scully climbed on a bollard, resting his hand on Warren's shoulder to steady himself.

"Listen to me!" he called out. "I'm one of a group who came to try to bring a warning to Mad Magnus! Great danger is coming! The New Lochlainn DeÁine have already taken Brychan in the south!" A collective sob echoed around the quay, but he allowed no time for panic to set in and raised his voice a notch further. "Our leader is already co-ordinating a strike back, have no doubt over that. And he stands a good chance of winning.

"But this is dire news indeed. We were seeking a ship to get back anyway. If you want to do something to aid your chances of surviving, then help get this ship ready to sail again! Get her resupplied! And some of you younger men? Those of you who sail in the fishing fleets? I'll give you letters of mark if you'll sail with this crew and get us to Ergardia as fast as this ship can go! Her crew are exhausted. They've done their part. Now they need your help. All of the Islands need your help!"

Cwen clambered up on another stone bollard with Rolo and Brock's aid. "Magnus doesn't believe us!" she called out, using the skill acquired making herself heard over a noisy bar-full of drinkers. "He'll sit up in Kylesk getting drunk and leave you to whatever fate brings in on the tide! Your only hope is with the rest of the Islands. The Attacotti people can't live by ignoring this threat, and ignoring the rest of the Islands. You can't face this alone, and the DeÁine won't recognise the difference between you and Islanders from Rheged or Prydein."

"To the Underworld with Magnus!" someone called out from the back of the crowd.

"Bloody thieving pirate!" another cried. "He's never helped us before!"

And suddenly the quay began seething with people hurrying to and fro, but not in panic. Clearly Magnus was the bane of their lives, and nothing had secured their help quicker than the knowledge that Magnus was taking the view that there was nothing to bother himself over. Pushing their way through, the six refugees managed to get on board the ship, where Scully set Mutley and Warren to supervising the goods flowing on board, and took the young captain down below with Cwen.

"Where do we go?" the haggard man asked hoarsely.

"Draynes first!" Cwen declared without even having to think twice. "We can get there in a day or so. There might even be an Order warship there. Some others who were with us were heading to there. After that we go up the channel to Mullion or Bittern. They'll have birds there! They'll send messages out as fast as they can. We can't risk it all on just you and your crew. You've worked wonders as it is."

By the evening the ship was fully watered and supplied, the worst of the sails had been taken ashore to be patched and new ones fitted, all done on signed receipts by Scully in the Order's name.

"Cross of Swords, I hope Berengar approves!" Scully whispered in a moment of panic to Cwen. "If he doesn't, I'll be docked pay for the rest of my life to pay for this lot! I'm not senior enough to authorise such things normally."

"Don't be silly!" she whispered back. "Berengar trusts you. Even if it's a false alarm, he'll know you couldn't afford to take a chance on that."

On the early morning tide, long before dawn had broken, the *Flower of Millport* was slipping her moorings and heading out into the open sea once more. Sharing the only passenger cabin with Scully's men, Cwen sat on a sea-chest with the Spear in front of her. The cabin door was shut and the men were stood around her except for Scully, who was currently up on deck with the captain.

"Go on, have a go," Brock encouraged her.

Nervously Cwen reached out and grasped both hands around the shaft of the huge weapon. The wood felt like ash-wood, and the others agreed it looked like it. Taking a deep breath she recalled the Knights' prayer to the Trees which Esclados had taught her what seemed like an age ago now. Hoping she had remembered the section correctly, she cleared her throat and began.

"Great Ash, who links this world and the next. Make a bridge of your mighty arms for those who fall to the Summerlands. Protect their souls on their journey beneath the shade of your leaves. Great Ash in you we trust," she intoned clearly.

"Great Ash, in you we trust," the others immediately responded and the Spear went from a faint glow to incandescent in a heartbeat.

Terrified and yet unable to let go, Cwen cried out,

"Help us! Protect us now! Lend us speed to bring the warning to all the Islands! Help us, please!"

The air crackled like summer lightning was about to strike on a bone-dry night, and then a strange figure appeared in shimmering light. A warrior by the strange uniform he wore, although it was no suit of armour.

"I am Urien!" he declared. "I am one of the ancients! What are you doing?"

Yet before a petrified Cwen could unfreeze, another two figures appeared out of nowhere.

"For God's sake, Urien!" the first growled. "Be gentle with her!" He stooped to look Cwen in the eyes. "I'm Cynddylan, another of the ancient race, and this is Peredur. We bond with the Bow and Arrow. I believe a friend of yours has the Arrow."

"Swein," Cwen gulped.

"We sensed the connection, and you and I met at the chapel," Cynddylan reminded her.

"Oh! You were the big hound!" Cwen suddenly recalled.

"That's right," Cynddylan answered with a smile. "The things which are keeping us alive had begun to fail and we had to find ways of appearing which took less energy. Thankfully that's been addressed and day by day we're getting stronger again. Now tell me, what's got you in such a panic that you'd try to use the Spear without any help?"

"News! Bad news!" Cwen managed to get out. "In fact, the worst!"

Urien's face was a picture of irritation, but Peredur waved him to silence accompanied by a furious glare.

"Go on," Cynddylan encouraged her.

"This ship we're on came into the harbour where we were waiting," she explained, her voice wavering under such duress. "We'd got the Spear from out of Mad Magnus' hands and were trying to get it to safety. We had no idea he'd got it until we were at his court trying to warn him about the DeÁine being in Brychan already. He won't listen to that. But he bragged to one of the other women about the Spear. Her life and another of our friends are in great danger, but we had no choice but to leave them behind. It was them or the Spear."

"You see!" Peredur hissed at Urien. "There's intelligence and loyalty for you! You have a good person to work with if you'd give her half a chance!"

Cwen gave him a faint smile before continuing. "So we were at Lowes trying to get a ship, and then the captain of this vessel told everyone that there's a great DeÁine fleet on the way. He was told by someone who saw it heading into Arieda, and he came on to raise the alarm. He's up on deck with our Knight, Scully. He's nearly killed his crew trying to get here."

"A DeÁine fleet?" Peredur repeated, aghast, as if not sure he had heard right.

Cwen nodded. "A big one! They say the ships are from the southern ocean. Slow, but capable of carrying huge numbers of men." Her eyes began to tear. "They think there can't be less than a hundred thousand men on board."

All three spectres looked horrified.

"That has to be men from Elin and Sinut," Peredur gasped.

"Listen to me," Cynddylan said firmly to Cwen. "In a moment I want you to take your hands off the Spear – but not just yet, give Peredur time to warn the captain." And they saw that his apparition had already winked out. It must have manifested on deck going by the screams of panic they heard coming from above. "*We* shall carry the warning straight to the Knights. You mustn't worry about that. What *you* have to do now is bring that Spear north with all speed. We have to get all our old creations together as soon as possible. The others will be able to explain more when you see them, and we shall be with you too."

"Indeed we shall," Urien said in a very different tone of voice. The bitter sneer had gone from his face and he was giving Cwen an appraising look. "For someone without military training you've done remarkably well. And you've shown great presence of mind." He gave a funny little twisted smile. "I believe we shall do very well together – and if I'm too abrupt at times, I hope you'll forgive me. I'm sure Peredur and Cynddylan will be swift to chastise me if I am! And I have a squint you need to meet!"

"Now you may take your hands off …and please don't try to use the Spear again until we can prepare you better," Cynddylan added gently.

Seconds later the Spear was dark again and the three spectres had vanished.

The same three spectres appeared moments later at Lorne Castle to the astonishment of the assembled men eating in the refectory.

"Master Hugh!" Cynddylan gasped, gliding to the top table at speed. "I'm so sorry, but I bring you dire news. We've just located the Spear, which is good news of course. But its user was desperate to send you a warning. There's a DeÁine fleet heading for the Islands from their last place of exile with four times the number of troops you currently face on board."

"What?" Hugh exclaimed, dropping his knife and leaping to his feet as the shock echoed down the room.

"I'm afraid so," Peredur confirmed. "The person who has the Spear is Swein's friend Cwen. She seems a sensible young woman. Not the sort to make wild claims at all. The ship she's on sailed day and night, dragging every knot of speed out of it, to bring this news. We believe that these extra DeÁine are those whom we knew were in the last place of exile they lived in before coming back to New Lochlainn. Without the Abend's presence amongst them, we thought it unlikely that they would ever make a move against the Islands. Why they're doing so now is unknown, but we cannot afford to ignore the threat."

Sionnachan got to his feet and walked around the table to face the three ancients. "Just how many are in this fleet do you estimate?" he demanded with the calm of the professional soldier.

Cynddylan shook his head sadly. "I'm so sorry. I don't think you'd be overestimating by much if you said one hundred thousand."

Sionnachan looked to Maelbrigt and both fighters exhaled heavily. Amongst the few there who had fought such numbers at Moytirra, they knew only too well what kind of force they were now facing. So did Hugh. The ageing Master slumped back in his seat and covered his face with his hands.

"Oh Trees, this changes everything," he groaned. However, Hugh was never one to give in to despair. He took a long draught of the spiced mead before him and then sat up straight. "May we use you as messengers?" he asked the ancients, who all nodded – even Urien. "Thank you. I don't think we should tell Berengar just yet of what awaits him. We must think clearly. Let's focus first on dealing with those DeÁine already in Brychan. However, we have to consider where these new enemies will land. Do you have any idea?"

Urien volunteered the information for a change. "I believe they'll land either on the southern New Lochlainn coast or on Rathlin's southern coast."

Hugh looked to Maelbrigt and Sionnachan, received thoughtful nods, and declared,

"Then I think we have to make sure it's Rathlin they land on."

Mystified the three ancients exchanged glances of their own before Cynddylan asked, "Why? How is Rathlin any better than New Lochlainn?"

"Two reasons," Maelbrigt answered as Aneirin flicked into being followed swiftly by Vanadis and then Owein. "There are a lot of ordinary people living on the south coast of New Lochlainn. Ordinary Islanders – or at least Attacotti – and more than a few DeÁine slaves. Those slaves are the danger. We don't want them rounded up and thrown at us even if it is only as arrow-fodder. They'll still drain our resources. And we don't want innocent folk getting caught in the crossfire if we can help it. Let's not forget that the Abend will use Power-fire indiscriminately if pressed.

"The second thing is that we currently stand a chance of driving the Abend and the DeÁine from Brychan over the water to Rathlin. If we force them southwards rather than westwards, they're separated from any other pieces of Power which might be sculling about in Bruighean or one of the other palaces. We've learned a lot from Sithfrey."

"That we have," Sionnachan spoke up. "We should've thought of this earlier," *and so should you*, he thought, "but if the DeÁine made their Treasures, then it stood to reason that there'd be lesser pieces. You don't just whip something like the Helm up out of thin air on the spur of the moment. Not if you want it to work, anyway. Well there are more pieces, and they are what some of the acolytes can use. We can't avoid the fact that some will undoubtedly be in Brychan with the invading army. But not all of them. And we certainly don't want any more pieces coming on us unexpectedly."

Maelbrigt nodded. "And what's more, we can lure this new army to where we want to fight them on Rathlin. We can pick the terrain which will give us the best chance against those kinds of numbers. Rathlin's almost empty of folk. We don't have to worry about bringing sudden death onto half a dozen towns, as we've said, but it's more than that. We know what suits our style of fighting. The last thing we want is to fight the DeÁine on some big open plain where the weight of their numbers can overwhelm us. We need land where they won't be able to bring all their force to bear at once. The biggest asset we have is the DeÁine's own arrogance. They'll believe they can walk over us, so we'll present them with a nice tempting target right where we want them to come to us."

Urien shook his head. "That's a wonderful set of ideas. But will you have time to put them into action?"

"Well I guess that depends on when they'll get here," Sionnachan answered calmly.

"It could be as early as the end of Beltane," Cynddylan said sadly. However, before he could say another word he jumped as though he had been pinched. "Maker preserve us!" he gasped and winked out of view.

"What happened?" Hugh asked the others.

"Swein and Dylan just called to him," Vanadis answered as Peredur disappeared as well. "It sounds very urgent."

"Moments later Peredur flashed back into sight. "Two warnings of the same thing!" he announced without preamble. "Your friends at Mullion woke to find a DeÁine raven walking up and down the ramparts and swearing in Islander. It had a message attached to it from your other friends, Will and Oliver. I don't know all the details. Cynddylan is getting those now. But he told me to tell you that it confirms Cwen's warnings."

"Flaming Underworlds! A DeÁine raven!" Maelbrigt chuckled and Sionnachan grinned too. "I wonder who did that? That was a clever idea. They must've realised that messages must've been sent to Calatin when he was at Mullion."

"They did," a disembodied voice spoke, then Cynddylan appeared. "Your young Knight Oliver apparently worked with your hawks, so he, ehmm …dealt …with the raven." Even the sober ancient was clearly tickled by what he had heard. "Apparently they found it marching up and down the ramparts declaring that it was a 'fucking ugly duck'!"

Hoots of laughter greeted that.

"Oh Trees, that's Oliver's sense of humour, all right!" Hugh said when he had recovered.

"Well it did the trick," Cynddylan admitted. "The message they tied to its leg told Hereman and MacBeth that this fleet was summoned by Quintillean, no less. Apparently the arrogant bastard was so convinced that he'd get the Treasures this time, he summoned the others to help escort him back to the Emperor in style."

"Oh we can use that!" Hugh immediately declared. "Oh yes we can, indeed!"

"You can?" Aneirin echoed dubiously.

"Oh yes!" Hugh confirmed with a grin, even as Sionnachan and Maelbrigt also began to smile and Sionnachan added,

"It's just given us a very tasty piece of bait to dangle in front of these new DeÁine. …One their overconfidence pretty much guarantees they'll take!"

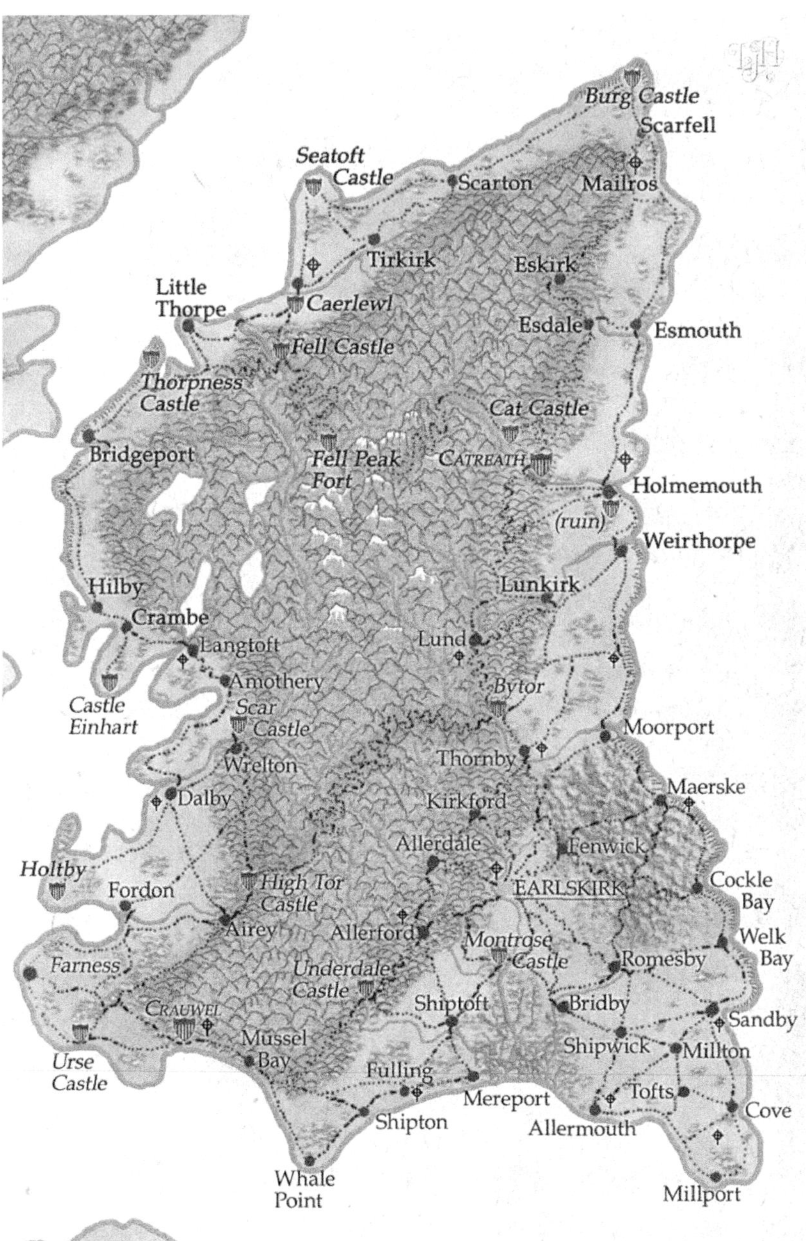

Burg Castle
Scarfell
Seatoft Castle
Scarton
Mailros
Tirkirk
Eskirk
Little Thorpe
Caerlewl
Esdale
Esmouth
Fell Castle
Thorpness Castle
Cat Castle
Bridgeport
Fell Peak Fort
CATREATH
Holmemouth
(ruin)
Weirthorpe
Hilby
Lunkirk
Crambe
Lund
Langtoft
Amothery
Castle Einhart
Scar Castle
Bytor
Moorport
Wrelton
Thornby
Maerske
Dalby
Kirkford
Allerdale
Fenwick
Holtby
Fordon
High Tor Castle
EARLSKIRK
Cockle Bay
Airey
Allerford
Montrose Castle
Welk Bay
Farness
Romesby
Underdale Castle
Shiptoft
Bridby
CRAUWEL
Sandby
Mussel Bay
Shipwick
Millton
Urse Castle
Fulling
Tofts
Mereport
Cove
Shipton
Allermouth
Whale Point
Millport

Chapter 12

A Matter of Heart

Rheged to Ergardia: Earrach – early Beltane

On a still chilly Rheged morning, Taise wrapped her cold hands around the mug of caff and met the equally deflated gaze of her friends. After arriving at the coast of Rheged on the first of Spring-moon she had travelled through the frozen landscape in the company of some tattered remnants of the Rheged army for more than two weeks to get here to Earlskirk. The reunion with Matti and Kayna had been joyful all round, but now, three weeks further on again and already into the month of Earrach, if she had had any hair she was pretty sure she would have been pulling it out in handfuls. Despite working closely with Foresters Elidyr and Aeschere, and those few who had known the Order of Knights of the Cross in Rheged, they had found nothing of the Spear. She had translated scripts, decoded messages and deciphered cryptic writings until her vision had blurred and her head had reeled. Yet not one word had appeared to give them the faintest hint that the Knights in Rheged had ever known there even *was* such a thing as the Spear, let alone where it was hidden.

Across the table from her, Abbot Jaenberht looked every bit as subdued. He had forced Edmund Praen, Gerard of Urse and Osbern of Braose to take over the restoration of order in the Rheged capital, freeing him to put his considerable intellect to use scouring all the church records for them as well, to no avail. The first meeting between Taise and Jaenberht upon her arrival had been wary on both sides, neither quite sure how to deal with the other. Taise had been worried that the profoundly devote cleric would see her as some kind of abomination. Particularly as he had obviously been struggling to give someone he saw as one of the enemy the benefit of the doubt solely on Matti's say so.

Yet within a week, her love of learning had won him over, while his willingness to explore unpalatable avenues of investigation had gained her respect, and they had formed a cautious friendship. However, none of this had furthered their cause one jot. As Elidyr and Aeschere had delved ever deeper in the wreckage of what had once been the Knights' headquarters in Rheged, tattered manuscripts had seen the first light of day in decades, if not in centuries, without a single clue appearing. Now there was nothing left to uncover.

Nothing, that was, unless they went and began hunting through the rooms occupied by the DeÁine mage, Tancostyl. This morning would be their first foray in that direction and nobody was looking forward to it.

"Come on," Aeschere sighed. "It won't get any better if we leave it," and got up, picking up his coat which had been draped over the table behind them in what remained of the Knight's refectory.

Without enthusiasm, Taise, Matti and Kayna joined Elidyr and Iago shrugging into outdoor wear. It was only a short walk to the old Jarl's palace but in this weather nobody was going to do it without extra layers.

"Blessed Martyrs, it's the ninth of Earrach," muttered Jaenberht, pulling his robes about him more closely, "you'd think it would start getting a bit warmer by now!"

"Well at least all that snow's gone!" Matti sighed thankfully. "This is just strong spring winds."

There had been flooding along many of the river valleys in Rheged for the last two weeks, which had caused all sorts of problems for the three friends dealing with the ordinary folk, and now Jaenberht was going to lend them a hand. As Gerard had pointed out, he, Edmund and Osbern had never been amongst the most senior of Rheged nobles used to large scale administration. Nor were they experienced at dealing with human tragedy on the scale they were currently trying to cope with. Bereaved families had come looking for news of men-folk killed in the storm which had wiped out all of the main army bases, then had been delayed returning home by the rising floods. Just feeding them had taxed the three men's ingenuity, and the previous night they had pleaded with Jaenberht to lend his authority at a meeting this morning in the main guildhall, to persuade reluctant merchants to start trading again.

"Good luck, Abbot," Aeschere said. "I don't know which of us has the worst job. Us with the wizard's lair or you with that bunch of self-serving and grasping old misers! You'll have your work cut out for you there."

Jaenberht gave a grimace. "The milk of human kindness got very diluted amongst our worthy guilds-men over the years," he admitted, "but they aren't actively dangerous. Petty and spiteful in great quantities, I'll admit, but if the worst comes to the worst Gerard, Edmund and Osbern will simply use what troops they have and take what the people need by force. I don't want that to happen – which is why I'm going to put the fear of the Maker into the tight-fisted, Spirit-forsaken specimens! But we can't let innocent folk starve because of a few men's greed. You, on the other hand, are going into a dangerous place, so be careful! And my blessings go with you."

A chill wind half blew them across the main square and through the propped open gates into the inner court. In a lonely single file, Elidyr led them up stairs and along corridors, until they stood at the base of the tower rooms which Tancostyl had occupied during his time in Rheged. Sergeant Iago took up position beside Elidyr at the door, and together they opened it quickly and stepped back. Nothing untoward happened. With great caution the two soldiers entered the room and flattened themselves against the walls on either side of the door, whilst they scanned the space in front of them. Aeschere appeared in the doorway.

"See anything? Feel anything?" he demanded tersely.

"All clear," Elidyr replied in a clipped tone, the bow in his hand still swinging to and fro.

"All clear," acknowledged Iago, his sword still at the ready too.

With measured steps, Aeschere entered the room and made a slow progress until he stood in the centre of the room. He quested about him, and then, satisfied that it was as safe as it was possible to ascertain, beckoned the three women in. Kayna was dressed similarly to the men in leather pants and, with a reinforced jerkin over her woollen jacket, looked formidable. She might never have undergone formal training as a Knight, but a lifetime of living and breathing the Order had made her as efficient a fighter as many of those entitled to call themselves a Knight. Matti would never have presumed to put herself in quite that category. However, the squire's uniform she had acquired reflected her capabilities well. She too was far from defenceless, and with Kayna she flanked Taise protectively.

Taise herself found it ironic that she, as the only DeÁine present entering rooms occupied by one of her own people, should be the one most needing protection. She was the only one who had little skill in the martial arts, but then that was not why they had brought her along.

"Right, let's search this room first," Aeschere commanded. "We'll do each room as we come to it. That way if there's a trap in any of them and we have to run for it, we won't be leaving something precious behind."

With painstaking care they took the room apart, Iago and Elidyr even using a heavy iron bar they had brought with them for the purpose, to prise the panelling away from the wall and check behind it. Two hours later they ventured into the next room. By the end of the day, weary and filthy, they had got through all four rooms and found nothing more than an awful lot of dead mice.

"Tancostyl – DeÁine war-mage and mouse killer extraordinary!" Elidyr grumbled with withering contempt. "By the Trees, I'm no lover of mice, but this is like the poor little sods were drawn to him and died in their hundreds."

"I think it's the Power," Taise told him sadly. "It does seem to draw some animals to it. It can't be because he was using them to feed his energy from. A mouse wouldn't be worth the effort. Not even in this number." She paused as they left, locking the door behind them with a master key which had been found in the housekeeper's room. "Do you know, I honestly don't remember ever seeing a mouse in Bruighean."

"What? Not one? In all that big palace?" Kayna was astonished. "I'd have thought with that many people all crammed into the space the place would've been heaving with them!"

Taise shook her head. "No, not one. And rats were very rare too. I was appalled when I first got out into the Islands and saw them for the first time in the villages. In Bruighean they weren't even in the secure cellar rooms where the other pieces of Power were stored."

Aeschere's head came up. "Cellars! That's the one place we haven't checked! Down where the Helm was stored!"

Matti looked dubious. "Surely they wouldn't have put the DeÁine Treasure down with the Island one?"

"It certainly wouldn't have been quiet down there," Taise said emphatically. "The two pieces would've quite literally struck sparks off one another. The signs would've lit up the night skies for folk to see miles away."

"No, I didn't mean that," Aeschere replied. "I was simply thinking that as the Helm was down there for safe keeping, if it came into danger then that's where people would go. And therefore that would be the place where you *would* see a message telling you where to get one of the pieces meant to counter its effects."

"Curses, why didn't we think of that before," Elidyr groaned. "Put like that it's obvious."

"First thing tomorrow, then!" Aeschere declared. "Come on, I'm starving! I hope there something other than vegetable stew again for dinner."

When they all left the refectory later that evening to go to their beds, Kayna noticed Elidyr following Matti. Over the last week or so the two seemed to have resumed their relationship and it worried Kayna. Her own feelings of attraction towards Edmund had cooled soon enough into pleasant, friendly banter and nothing more. She liked him well enough, to be sure, but Edmund was a little too practised at flattering conversations and winning smiles for Kayna. As she confessed to Taise, she was fairly sure he would also soon weary of her if he ever got her tied down to the domestic life, and he was attractive enough to find no shortage of women who would be willing to distract him from his boredom.

"And what an odd trio those three men are," Taise had laughed with her. "There's poor Osbern, whose wife turns out to have been murderously inclined towards him and who buried himself in religion. Then there's Edmund, the arch womaniser in the nicest way – if there is such a thing – who'll never be really happy in a marriage. And Gerard. Happily married, and as down to earth a man as you could ever wish to meet. How in the Islands are they friends?"

"Because they are so different probably," Kayna had speculated. "They never compete with one another for anything."

"Mmmm. You're probably right. Is that why you're worried about Matti? Do you think Elidyr is another womaniser?"

Kayna shrugged uncomfortably. "I suspect womaniser is putting it a bit strongly in his case," she admitted. "Let's face it, he was fighting in the salt marshes of the eastern lands with Ruari for three years. He can't have had much opportunity to practice his charms then! And Ruari certainly valued him as a soldier. No …it's more that I think they're two people who just now really need *someone*. Without degrading either of them, I'd say needing almost *anyone*.

"I saw the men who came back from Gavra Pass, Taise. The way some of them coped with the appalling losses of their comrades was to try to find some kind of normality at home. To try to find something that would make sense of why their friends had died. Something worth it. They made hurried marriages – not all of which turned out that well in the long run – and fathered kids like there was no tomorrow. I reckon that what's happening with Elidyr. He needs to feel that the vast loss of life he saw over in the east was all worth the sacrifice, and he's finding that justification in Matti. All the deceit and deception here, and the terrible sacrifices Jarl

Michael made in the east, weighed against something good. Something worth dying for – Matti! He's not being cruel, he's just battle-weary."

"And Matti? Don't you think she knows her own mind?"

"No, in an odd way I don't think she does. Oh Taise, it's such a mess for her! For years and years Will was an awful husband. He either ignored her or argued with her. So she made a separate life for herself and dreamed that she might've had Ruari instead of Will. But that Ruari was the young Ruari. A young man who read as much as she did, loved music and talked on every subject under the sun to her. But the man you've met is now as tied to his duty as any married man is to his wife, and she knows it.

"If anything happened to Will and they married, she'd be on her own as much as she's been with Will. And then that's been complicated by the fact that Will's suddenly taken notice of her, and she's been able to see a side of him he kept hidden for all those years. She's halfway to being attracted to him now, but she's scared to death that when all this is over, if they went back to their old home Will would just go back to how he was. It's all so complicated!

"Whereas Elidyr is easy. He's physically affectionate for a start. The one thing she's not had from either of the others! I fear she thinks she can take some comfort there and not worry about long-term consequences for a change. But I'm getting to know our Lady Matilda Montrose. Really know her beyond the mask she puts on to most people. She's just not the sort of person who can have casual affairs. She thinks too much and she cares too much. So my worry is that instead of being torn in two between Ruari and Will, she'll end up being torn in three instead."

"Oh dear," Taise sighed regretfully. "Now I can see what you mean. And he's awfully pretty isn't he!"

"Oh yes!" Kayna chuckled. "All slim hips, broad shoulders and flowing hair! Very easy on the eye! And apparently knows what he's doing in the bedroom too." She sobered swiftly. "And that's just not fair! How can I tell Matti she shouldn't enjoy something she's never had, and in a few months time might never have again?"

"You can't," Taise told her sagely. "None of us knows what tomorrow might bring, and you can't deny her some solace today on the off-chance it might lead to something worse. All we can do is be good friends and support her. As you've said, there'll be regret and sorrow whatever she decides …and *who*ever she decides she wants to stay with. But if she does wave Elidyr goodbye and goes home, at least she'll have some happy memories this way. …And if you're right about him, so will he when he goes back into the main force of Foresters."

They had reached Taise's door.

"Well let's just hope he doesn't remain attached to Ruari's men," Kayna wished fervently. "That would be too much. For her to see both Ruari and Elidyr regularly if she finds herself stuck with Will and reverting to his old persona. *Urgh*! Torment or what?" She shuddered, then hugged Taise and went to her own room.

The next morning was a hazy day of damp showers and gusting winds, which whistled mournfully through the largely deserted palace. When even this failed to wipe the smile off Matti's face, Kayna guessed that Elidyr had been more than usually active the previous night.

"For pity's sake stop grinning like that," she whispered playfully to her friend. "Do you want Jaenberht to know you two were at one another all night?"

Matti's shocked glance told her that the other woman had not realised her actions had been so telling. Then she grinned again widely before trying to compose herself a little more.

They reached the cellar stairs and as before Elidyr and Iago took the lead with Aeschere right behind them. At the bottom they negotiated the various locked doors of the wine cellars and other secure holding places before they came to what must be the right room, by virtue of it being the only one left. Elidyr placed his hand on the handle, and as Iago turned the key in the lock, turned it, leaning on it to push harder when it stuck a little.

He had just winked at Matti when Taise screamed a warning, but too late. A blinding flash and a clap like thunder stunned them all, Taise being the only one who reacted. Throwing up her hand she raggedly summoned Power of her own, and the ball of flames filling the doorway and coming their way was halted, although it continued to blaze with incandescent heat and they could hear the stone walls beginning to groan.

"Run!" screamed Aeschere, hauling Iago to his feet from where he had dived away at the last second.

Kayna had already turned and was trying to get Taise moving backwards up the stairs whilst she held her hand out controlling the barrier, when Kayna realised Matti was standing rooted to the spot, white-faced.

"Matti! Run!" Kayna screamed, drawing Aeschere's attention to the problem.

Then he and Iago saw what Matti had seen. From out of the sides of the door frame four metal spears had shot out impaling Elidyr where he stood. A pool of his blood was already forming at his feet from where one had pierced his thigh, and more was pumping out in a red jet. Even if they could get him free he had minutes left to live, if that. Iago looked down at his own calf and registered for the first time that he had a ragged wound along it. He must have missed one of the spikes by a hair's breadth, and that had been what threw him off balance.

"Get Matti!" he croaked to Aeschere. "I'll be alright. I can move!"

And with that he limped rapidly to Kayna and took up position behind her.

"No!" Kayna snarled. "You're slow! Get up the stairs out of our way!"

Iago flinched but nodded, recognising that when Taise got out of line with the doorway they would have seconds to get up the stair opposite it, and out of the way of the fireball which would pursue them.

"Elidyr!" Matti whimpered and made as if to go to him as their eyes locked in a final embrace.

"No!" Aeschere growled and bent to throw her over his shoulder. With Matti howling and reaching back with her free hand to the unconscious Elidyr, Aeschere pounded past the others and out of the cellars. As Iago stumbled to the top, he saw Aeschere dump Matti unceremoniously behind a great oak table which he kicked over.

"Keep her there!" the Forester ordered, then dashed back down the stairs.

Moments later a sobbing Kayna tore out of the stairwell and dived behind the table to cradle the keening Matti to her. In a flurry of movement Taise and Aeschere appeared together. The senior Forester was chanting furiously in an unknown tongue as he supported Taise and helped hold her hand up. The instant they were clear of the stair door he spun her and flung her flat, diving on top of her to shield her with his own body. A blast of flames flew out of the stairwell, driving scorched and shattered holes through thick stone walls, and immolating everything in its path as it spread outwards.

When it had passed, Aeschere gingerly eased himself off Taise.

"Are you alright?" he asked gruffly, coughing on the stone dust which filled the air and covered them all, until they were as white as ghosts from it.

Taise nodded weakly and gestured to the others, easing herself into a sitting position against the wall. As Aeschere hurried to help Iago to his feet, they became aware of calls of alarm and then Jaenberht appeared, robes flapping like some huge bird in flight as he ran at a speed belying his years. Gerard and Osbern were on his heels, swords drawn and nearly colliding with Edmund who flew in from another direction.

"Blessed Martyrs be praised! You're alive!" Jaenberht gasped with relief when he saw them. "Great Maker! What was that?"

"A summoning," Taise answered raggedly, gratefully accepting his proffered arm to lean on. "A fairly rudimentary spell for a war-mage, I'm afraid to say."

"But Tancostyl's been gone for months!" Jaenberht protested.

"Makes no difference," Taise told him as she winced with every step on a turned ankle. "That was the room the Helm was stored in. Over the years it would've absorbed enough of its Power that once Tancostyl put the spell into place, it would've sat there leeching all of the Helm's residual Power out of the room to feed it until someone triggered it. Poor Elidyr!" and she brushed the tears on her cheeks ineffectually as they began to fall faster and faster.

In horror Jaenberht looked back and saw Kayna with Iago, his arm over her shoulder and limping even more than usual, Gerard moving in on them and helping take Iago's weight. Behind them a distraught Matti was barely upright despite Aeschere's firm grip on her. He caught Jaenberht's eye and gave a minute shake of the head, but from his grim expression Jaenberht had no need to ask if there was any hope that Elidyr had survived. Osbern and Edmund ran over and linked arms to make a seat, and Aeschere hoisted Matti up for them to carry, hurrying close behind them to support her and make sure she did not fall backwards.

In stunned silence the ragged survivors staggered back to the refectory. Some of Jaenberht's monks hurried out with bandages and water to bathe wounds, for out in the clearer air it was possible to see that Taise and Aeschere had multiple tiny cuts from flying chips of stone. The most experience healer amongst them tended to the tear in Iago's calf, but nothing could mend Matti's wound.

Collapsed in Kayna's arms, she howled her grief without restraint until exhaustion took over. At that point Aeschere gallant carried her to her room and left her to be consoled by Taise and Kayna. Nobody pretended that there was any point in trying to do any more this day. When he took food up to the room, Aeschere did ask Taise if she thought any further danger remained in the palace, but she expressed a fair degree of certainty that nothing was left.

For the next few days, Aeschere and Iago went through the motions of continuing the search. However, Jaenberht finally asserted his authority.

"This is no good for any of you," he said firmly at the evening meal four days later. "It's blindingly clear that there's nothing left here to find – if there ever was! Aeschere, you have to take Taise back to Brego. He may yet have great need of her skill and there's nothing here that warrants her attention. The weather's clearer and you'll make the journey with much more speed. I shall stay here and try to do what I can with young Gerard, Edmund and Osbern to set this town to rights and then Rheged as a whole, but you have other duties to attend to. I've had a message from Brego at Lorne. Your Grand Master, Hugh, is there with him. I think you need to report back to him in person and tell him all that you've seen in some detail."

Aeschere's expression brightened for the first time since Elidyr's death at the news that Hugh was within reach. "Yes," he breathed with visible relief, "I would very much like to tell him what became of Amalric."

Another message had come from Aeschere's companions from Prydein, Saeric and Nazar, that the most recent Grand Master of Prydein was definitely back in the land of the living. He was recovering physically quite well down in the castle on the Rheged coast, but the twin brothers reported that his mind was shattered and that he was barely capable of looking after himself. There was no question of him ever being able to hold even the most humble of offices, let alone that of Grand Master – which they now regarded as a blessing, given the mess he had made of it. There could now be no objection to Hugh taking back the power he had once handed over to Amalric.

"And I think young Lady Montrose needs to get away from here too," Jaenberht added. "I'm not such an old fool that I couldn't see what was going on between her and that young Forester. I *am* too old to think I should be casting censure about for what they did, though," he said with a wry smile. "Let's just say that I think she'll recover much better away from the scene of such unhappiness. Take her with you to Brego, and her friend Kayna with her. He'll understand when you give him the letter I'm going to write – I won't ask you to explain all that on top of your own news."

The following day the monks packed them supplies, and with a small escort, Aeschere led the forlorn party back northwards. Their journey was as bleak as the ravaged Island they rode through. Everywhere folk were still trying to piece back together their lives after the destructive powers of the storm which had hit nearly five months ago. The dead might have been buried or cremated, but the gap they had left behind had not even begun to be filled. Nor had the sense of shock and horror disappeared, even if it had been dulled a little by the necessity of getting on with everyday life. To Matti it felt as if she had somehow fused with the Island of her birth, and that nothing would ever be quite the same again.

On the last day of Earrach, she once more stood at the ferry at Bridgeport – the same place where she and Iago had made their escape from Tancostyl at the end of the last year. For all that it was only months ago, it felt like a lifetime had passed in other ways. It was almost with relief that she saw the shoreline of Rheged slipping behind them and Ergardia coming closer. By the time they reached Lorne four days later she felt as though she could draw a deep breath for the first time without wanting to sob with it. Kayna and Taise watched her and breathed their own sighs of relief. She was nowhere near over the experience, but this was the first indication they had had that she was beginning the healing process.

"Let's just pray that she doesn't lose Ruari or Will," Kayna breathed softly in Taise's ear as they waited to be ferried across the loch. "If she did, I don't think she'd ever return to being the woman we've come to know."

"Sweet Lotus, that would be harsh!" Taise whispered back. "We must try to find out if anything's been heard of either of them as soon as we get to the castle. If there is bad news, we'll have to pick the time to break it very carefully if we're not to break her too."

However, when they got into Lorne, the news was at least positive. Ruari had been and gone and was still in one piece, while Will was still deep in New Lochlainn but apparently doing remarkable things and in rude health, according to the ancients who had watched him when they could.

Taise and Kayna had felt almost weak with relief at that, although Taise had a reunion which overrode even her concerns for Matti, for Maelbrigt was there to welcome her. The normally restrained Forester had swept his DeÁine lady into his arms and kissed her soundly in front of everyone at their meeting, generating a twinge of jealousy in Kayna and concern for Matti at seeing someone else so blissfully happy. However, Matti had managed a watery smile and declared herself genuinely glad that Taise and Maelbrigt were together once more. Only the tears swimming in her eyes gave away some of her deeper feelings.

"My dear lady, I'm so glad to meet you," declared a stranger coming to greet Taise.

"Where's Master Brego?" she asked, instantly worried that something had happened, but her concern was deflected by Aeschere hurrying forward to clasp hands with the slightly built, older man before her.

"Master Hugh!" he exclaimed in delight. "By the Trees, I'm glad to see you here! I've much to tell you!"

"Aeschere!" the Grand Master of Prydein responded with equal warmth. "Cross of Swords, we thought you drowned! When we heard you'd survived we were all hugely relieved, but didn't think to see you even this soon after what Brego told us of what's happened on Rheged."

"Where *is* Master Brego?" demanded Kayna considerably more forcefully than Taise.

Hugh quirked an eyebrow at Aeschere at her strident tone but replied evenly,

"He's gone to lead the troops of Ergardia and Celidon in battle."

"Battle?" Kayna gasped, utterly thrown. It was the last thing she had anticipated. "What in the Islands has happened?"

"Bad news, I'm afraid," Maelbrigt said, one arm firmly around Taise's waist. "It looks like every Grand Master received a warning from the man acting as Grand Master on Brychan. His name's Berengar and he's not the sort to send out hysterical messages. Rheged's warning must've got lost. A DeÁine army has marched into the heart of Brychan over the winter, with the Abend with them and in force."

The newcomers all gasped in horror.

"They're not having it all their own way, though," Hugh added cheerfully. "Their head Forester led the northern troops to a small but significant victory in securing the route to the north. Those DeÁine troops – about a Jundis and a Seljuq we think – were all wiped out without fatalities on our side. Since then they've been a bit hampered by the weather. If you think we've had flooding over here in the east, it's nothing to what Brychan's suffering. Our new friends, the ancients have been telling us of massive avalanches as the weight of snow becomes unstable as the weather's warmed a little. Currently we believe Berengar is very sensibly checking that there aren't any DeÁine at his back before he deals with the ones in front!

"But that's not all! We received a warning from a young lady called Cwen. Later I'll tell you what we know of her, but for now it's enough to say that she's in this as deeply as we are. She found out that there's another DeÁine army on its way here from another land."

"There are more of them?" Kayna moaned.

"I'm afraid so," Taise answered gently. "We were only the ones who came on from our last place of exile. Would I be right in thinking that this news concerns a force coming from Sinut?"

Hugh smiled at her kindly. "Yes I'm afraid it would, and I do appreciate that whilst there are other DeÁine who think as you do, Taise, and are to be trusted, unfortunately the ones who are coming aren't amongst them. They pose an even bigger threat than those who're holding Brychan at the moment."

The newcomers looked stunned, but Taise knew the full implications of what this meant and buried her face in Maelbrigt's shoulder with a sob.

"Don't cry, Taise," a new voice said, and she looked up to see Sithfrey smiling at her. Yet even in her distress she could see that something had changed about him. The intensely brittle air had gone, and if he hardly exuded confidence he did seem far calmer within than she had ever known him be before.

"Sithfrey's been quite the hero!" another familiar voice said, and Andra appeared, grinning hugely and also looking far from the meek priest she had first met.

"What have you two been up to?" she wondered as Andra went forward to hug Matti and look quizzically at her haunted face.

"Making me several years older by the minute!" a deep male voice said with dry humour.

Maelbrigt turned Taise in his arms to face the tall man behind him. "Taise, I want you to meet Sionnachan. He's the second-in-command of all the Foresters on Ergardia, and the one who leads them when they fight. He's been a good friend to me in the past."

Taise found herself in the rare position of having to look up to this man, and saw a weathered face with startling green eyes staring back at her.

"So you're Taise," he said with mock severity, "I've heard a lot about you." Then could not refrain from smiling. "…In fact at times it's been hard to shut Maelbrigt up about you! I'd begun to think it was something that I'd done that was stopping him from coming over and taking up the posts I kept offering him with the Foresters over here! Now I can see it wasn't that at all." He stepped forward and kissed her on her cheek. An action she was totally unprepared for and startled her. "Come on, let's get you inside. I don't want to be the one responsible for having you fall ill from wet and cold when you've only just got here. I'd never hear the last of it!"

And with that he turned and led the party indoors.

"He's not as scary as he seems," Sithfrey whispered in Taise's ear as he took her other arm, earning him another surprised looked from her. Sithfrey not scared of a Forester? What was the world coming to?

By the end of that evening Taise was even more bemused, although the surprises started almost as soon as they sat down to wait for dinner. For a start off she had swiftly discovered that wherever Maelbrigt went there was the strange figure of Squint not far behind. He seemed as disconcerted by her as she was by him. Every time Maelbrigt leaned in close to Taise, Squint whistled worriedly, clearly fully aware that she was a DeÁine and one who could tap into the Power, but not sure what to do about it. Maelbrigt told Taise that he thought Squint was aware of how he felt about her which confused the little alien tremendously.

In turn, Taise was less than sure how she felt about Squint, for she similarly could sense the way he connected to the Power. It was not the Power as she knew it, though. Yet she had studied it enough to know that the DeÁine had tapped into a far greater energy in a very specific way. It was this wider energy pattern which Squint was so deeply connected to, and she was adept enough to be able to feel it and worry about how it might draw Maelbrigt in.

Yet when Sithfrey and Andra had joined in with Sionnachan telling her their tale there was a further surprise.

"You have it here?" she said with awe. "The Gauntlet is here?"

"Yes it is," Sionnachan replied, "and we're hoping that you might be able to help Sithfrey figure out how it's changed. He's pretty sure it *has* changed, but it's also somehow bonded to him. It's clear to us it's changed because Maelbrigt's been chosen to use one of the Island Treasures, and it doesn't try to attack him when he's in close proximity to it. And he and Sithfrey can be together around the Island Sword without Sithfrey feeling like it's about to try to slice him open all by itself. We know – or rather Maelbrigt and Squint tell us – that object to object the Sword also makes no attempt to counter the Gauntlet now."

"How extraordinary!" This was something beyond anything Taise had ever heard of.

"It is," Maelbrigt agreed, "and all the more so because, when Sithfrey put the Gauntlet on and used it to heal McKinley, I wasn't here with the Sword but someone else was. His name's Ivain, and would you believe it, he turns out to be the young king of Prydein – Alaiz' husband! Ivain found the Bow and it's bonded to him. Master Hugh brought him here because he'd had word that Master Brego was looking for the Treasures. They were here at Lorne in the Master's office just at the point when Sithfrey healed with the Gauntlet, and the Sword and Shield were here too. They all glowed a different colour to what they had before, and Ivain said he felt under attack but then it changed. Shifted away from him. I felt it but less so, I suspect partly because I was on the sea at the time, away from the Sword, and I've been lucky enough to have Squint with me from the start. Without a squint of his own and in close proximity to three of the Treasures – one of which has yet to be claimed – Ivain got the full force of it."

"Can I see it?" she asked Maelbrigt. "Can I see this sword you've been joined to?"

Maelbrigt looked to Sionnachan. "Dare we risk it? I'd never forgive myself if it attacked her."

Sionnachan sniffed resignedly. "Look friend, unless you want to live in two separate houses, at some point you're going to have to have Taise and the Sword under the same roof. Better to find out now if that's ever going to be possible while you've got us lot around you to help pull it off her."

With great trepidation they led Taise up to an office. Hugh might have been left in command of Lorne, but he drew the line at using Brego's own office and had had another prepared for him just down the corridor. It was this one that they went to and Maelbrigt went to fetch the Sword.

"No point in subjecting you to the Sword *and* the Shield," Sionnachan said kindly. "If you get on with the one, we'll try you with the other one on its own, and only then, if all goes well will we let you into the room with the two of them." He gave a rueful grin. "I'm afraid to say that I'm more than a little curious to know what's going to happen. You're the first DeÁine we've been able to bring near them aside from Sithfrey, and we now have to consider him a unique case. I'm sorry if that sounds a bit callous, but it's something we have to know and there's no way we can simulate such contact with a substitute."

"That's alright," Taise answered faintly. She understood his academic curiosity. It was something which she herself had felt so often in the past.

What was more disconcerting was the realisation of how callous it could sound to an outsider, and it brought home to her why some of the things the DeÁine had done in New Lochlainn had so appalled the local Islanders. At least Sionnachan had gone to fetch some strange pouches which were set out on Hugh's desk and he was checking them over, clearly hoping that whatever he intended to do with them might protect Taise if things went wrong. She was humbled by the realisation that she had never taken such precautions while an acolyte.

Moments later Maelbrigt walked in lugging the biggest sword she had ever seen.

"Bit of a monster!" he said with a grin, hoisting it upright and putting the point onto the floor from where he was able to lean on the cross-guard at chest height.

"Feel anything?" Sionnachan demanded of him.

"No, not a thing."

"No strange tingling? Faint queasiness?"

But Maelbrigt continued to shake his head. Then Squint came in. The little creature looked from Maelbrigt to Taise and then very gingerly reached out a paw and placed it on Maelbrigt's arm. The Sword began to glow faintly.

"*Woah*! Now it's tingling!" Maelbrigt exclaimed swiftly tightening his hold on the grip.

In a clatter of feet Raethun, Ewan and Tobias rushed in with Arthur, having heard what was about to happen.

"It ain't glowin' all spooky!" Arthur observed excitedly. "This ain't nothin' like it did when Ivain was here."

"How's it different, Arthur?" Sionnachan asked, bending down close to the boy, who was now standing in front of Maelbrigt and watching the Sword intently.

"Well when you must've been doin' things up on the mountain, it first started glowin' all bluish," Arthur told him earnestly. "Then when you sez Sithfrey changed it, it went whitish. Now it's white but it's got more yellow to it. Not a real bright sunshine yellow like when that lady found the Spear, though."

Kayna jumped like she had sat on a thistle. "The Spear's been found?"

"Ah ...yes," Hugh murmured apologetically. "We were coming to that. Please bear with us for just a bit longer."

Kayna scowled so furiously at him that Hugh was put on his guard. From all that Maelbrigt had told him of Kayna, she had a tendency to be fiery, but she was not given to childish tempers. It must mean that something had happened for her to be so angry. Then he saw her go and put her arm around Matti's shoulders and saw the tears in the other woman's eyes. Oh yes, something had clearly happened and he must tread very carefully round this not to cause further upset.

However, Aeschere had come to stand by Sionnachan and Arthur, and was asking,

"Can he feel it? Does this lad have a connection to the weapon too?"

The two Foresters exchanged glances.

"I wouldn't say he's bonded to it like Maelbrigt is," Sionnachan answered cautiously. "But Arthur does seem to have a feel for *all* the Island weapons. He picks up on changes in them far quicker than the rest of us do, and I don't think it's just because he's younger." The senior man straightened but kept an arm around Arthur's shoulders. "My first thought was that being younger, Arthur's head wasn't cluttered up with all the everyday stuff adults have, and so that's why he saw things more clearly. But it seems to run a bit deeper than that. When he's not with Raethun and Ewan over there, I've run a couple of the tests I'd put recruits to the Foresters through, and he's done better than anyone I've ever seen."

"Except you," Hugh added pointedly. "What he's not told you, Aeschere, is that he passed to enter the Foresters with higher entry grades than anyone in over a generation. Over several, actually." As Sionnachan rolled his eyes in dismissal of such compliments, Hugh added mischievously, "I just wonder whether Sionnachan was on Prydein some years ago."

All but Arthur realised what Hugh was implying, although given that Sionnachan must have been twice Arthur's height at a comparable age and as redheaded as Arthur was dark, it was highly unlikely he was Arthur's father. Chuckles echoed around the room as Sionnachan gave Hugh a withering glare even as he ruffled Arthur's hair.

"Soon have you in uniform, won't we?" he said to the small face looking up at him. "The youngest Forester ever, that's what you'll be!"

"Great!" Arthur beamed.

"What do your parents say?" Taise asked worriedly. These men seemed to be taking it for granted that they could do what they wished with this child.

"Parents?" Arthur said turning to her with a blank expression. "Ain't got none of them! Never did have."

Taise felt her blood run cold. An orphan! "But surely whoever looked after you – the people who brought you up and cared for you – they must be concerned that you're caught up with soldiers."

"Nobody brung me up!" Arthur denied, clearly confused by the whole idea. "I looks after meself!"

"But when you were very small…" an increasingly appalled Taise protested.

"I was wiv' the other kids in the city," Arthur told her as if it was the most normal thing in the world. "They looked out for me, an' then when they went into the big gangs, I took over and now I looks out for the little 'uns – when I'm not here that is!"

Hugh gently took Taise by the arm. "We weren't being irresponsible," he told her softly. "Please don't press Arthur any more. I'll tell you all you want to know later."

"I'm afraid I've offered Arthur a home for his fostering period already," Maelbrigt added with a sheepish grin. "It's normal for underage recruits to be with an older member of the Order until they're sixteen and go into be properly trained. I hope you don't mind. I thought between the two of us he'd get a real head start."

Taise sighed. When would she get used to Maelbrigt surprising her? Just like that he had included her in the training of a young Forester with huge potential, making it clear that he thought that she could be as important to Arthur as himself, and not just as some nursemaid. How could she refuse? Without thinking she walked to Maelbrigt and kissed him. As her hand went over his on the grip of the Sword, a huge burst of light shot from it, bathing the room in white light. Squint gave a startled shriek, but not of distress even as he skittered backwards away from her.

"*Woah*! Look at that!" she heard Arthur yell excitedly behind her.

"Stand still both of you!" Sionnachan ordered urgently. "Don't move your hands!"

He stepped up to them. "Taise? Do you feel anything? Maelbrigt?"

Maelbrigt smiled. "Yes, but in a pleasant way. It's like the grip's warmer. Not hot, though. Nothing dangerous. Just like it's body heat. And there's a faint …humming sensation …is the best way I can describe it."

The air shifted and crackled and suddenly Aneirin was in their midst, a ghostly presence who made the newcomers jump. "Great God's teeth!

What are you lot up to now?" he demanded in a voice filled with exasperation, then even he stopped in his ghostly tracks as he saw Taise still with her hand over Maelbrigt's. "Sweet Goddess, who are you?"

"This is Taise," Maelbrigt answered considerably more calmly. "She's my lady."

"She's *DeÁine*!" Aneirin spluttered.

"Oh, well done!" Sionnachan said witheringly. "I think we might have noticed that." Privately he was getting rather fed up with this particular ancient, who insisted on talking down to them all. It was good to see him caught off guard for once. "We didn't just let some random enemy wander in and stick their grimy paw on your precious Sword," he continued in a voice weighted with sarcasm. "This was being done carefully and with consideration. Taise is the one who translated the documents which allowed us to find your bloody Sword in the first place. So you can stop looking at her like she's the rat you just found in your bath! Like Sithfrey, she's vital to helping us understand what's going on. Get used to it!"

Inside Taise was stunned hearing this ferocious Knight defending her so forcefully. When Maelbrigt had said Sionnachan was a friend she had still doubted whether he would accept her. Clearly Maelbrigt's friends were as exceptional as he was. However Sionnachan was not done.

"Don't you think it's rather more significant that instead of trying to use its energy to kill Taise, it seems to have drawn in some additional kind of energy through her?" he demanded of Aneirin.

"Oh, Sweet Lotus!" Taise breathed, her awareness jogged by Sionnachan's words. "I can feel the Power through it! Not like when I used the lesser pieces in New Lochlainn. This is …cleaner, fresher …in a way lighter …like it hasn't been weighted down with some kind of taint."

"What do you say to that?" Sionnachan demanded of Aneirin.

Instead the ancient asked Maelbrigt, "Is it different for you this time?"

Maelbrigt nodded. "Yes it is. It's like having a strong single musical note that vibrates through you, then hearing another join it a bit lower, but feeling it on the outside. It's not quite like a chord but it's getting there. Not fully joined but somehow complimenting it."

Aneirin shook his head and threw up his spectral hands. "I have no idea what you've done! The Sword is designed to protect. I don't know why it hasn't killed this woman on the spot."

"I do," Maelbrigt said as understanding burst upon him. "All the years I've known Taise she's been a healer. I've never known her do a single thing that's aggressive. Even when Sithfrey first appeared and tried to take her by force back to the Abend, she never wanted him hurt. Don't you see? You said that we would all have to have the good of the Islanders as a whole as our objective. That we *must* be united in wanting to save others from harm to get the most out of the Island weapons. Well Taise is the epitome of someone who lives that way! Why would the Sword attack her? She's in complete alignment with it already!"

"Flaming Underworlds!" Sionnachan swore. "That's it! You've got it, Maelbrigt. And that's what Sithfrey changed about the DeÁine Gauntlet. He changed its orientation so it's more like one of the Island pieces. That's why we can have him here in the room and nothing nasty happens. Sorry to question your almighty wisdom and knowledge here, Aneirin, but just what did you create these things to do? Did you make them to specifically be *DeÁine* killers? Or did you make them in such a way that they would repel anyone who had malicious intentions towards the Islands? Because unless you made them to be DeÁine killers – tuned them in specifically to the DeÁine, their slaves and any others – then why would they respond to Taise on the grounds of her race?"

"And isn't it unlikely that you're predecessors made them purely anti-DeÁine?" Maelbrigt added pointedly. "I mean, what point would there be if, say, the Sword only went after pure DeÁine? They'd only have to conquer another race and then send them in as the first wave of a conquering army and it would all be for nothing, because the Treasures wouldn't recognise the threat! That'd just be plain daft! You'd never be able to predict which of all the peoples on this earth would end up in a DeÁine army, and who might unexpectedly be our allies. So of course the Treasures would be focused on intent not bloodline. Had you not thought that out?"

"Oh Great Goddess!" Aneirin groaned. "I've got to tell the others about this! Even Vanadis is going to get a headache over this one!" and he disappeared again.

"Lovely!" Sionnachan snorted. "Now old grumpy's gone, shall we see about getting you two apart without blowing the castle up?"

He reached out and carefully put his hand over Taise's. When nothing happened he slipped his fingers under her hand until he was holding it. "Aeschere? Come here and slide your hand under mine and over Maelbrigt's. Let's break any physical contact completely first."

Aeschere did as he was told and once he was in position, Sionnachan carefully lifted Taise's hand away, his other resting on her shoulder to pull her out of harm's way just in case. Nothing happened.

"*Phew*!" Raethun sighed with a grin. "That was more excitement than I was expecting tonight!"

However Aeschere held up his free hand. "Hold on a moment." He clamped both hands over Maelbrigt's but nothing happened either then or when he let go. "That's interesting," he told the others who were all watching him. "My grandparents were all Attacotti, and so not the race the Treasures were aimed at defending. I think that might prove your point Maelbrigt. What's even more interesting is that I didn't feel a thing, and unless I'm very mistaken the Sword didn't either."

"No, it did nothin'," Arthur immediately replied solemnly. "I was lookin' at it and it went all flat and grey, not a bit of a glow."

"Can we try something?" Sionnachan said tentatively. "It's up to you, Taise. If you don't want to do this, then I won't push it and I wouldn't blame you."

She looked at him askance but cautiously nodded.

"Lean the Sword against the desk, Maelbrigt, and step aside," Sionnachan suggested, and Maelbrigt's expression suddenly registered his understanding of what the other Forester was about to do.

"Squint? Would you come here and put your paw on the Sword?" Sionnachan asked gently.

The small creature trotted forward and placed his paw on the hilt of the Sword. For his part Sionnachan came and stood beside Taise.

"We're going to walk towards it together," he said calmly. "If it so much as starts to glow we'll turn round and I'll put myself between you and it, alright? Arthur, you watch it very carefully with Maelbrigt. If you feel anything out of the ordinary, you shout out."

With great caution, Sionnachan led Taise forward until they stood right in front of the Sword. A faint hint of a glow within had appeared, but Maelbrigt was keeping up a commentary assuring them that he felt nothing untoward. It was just the same as when he held the Sword and it became active.

"Do you want to risk reaching out to it?" Sionnachan asked Taise.

"One moment," she answered. "Before that, shall I try tuning in to the Power as I would've done with one of the small healing devices I used in New Lochlainn? We used to tap into the Power first before handling one, so should I do that now?"

"Excellent idea," Sionnachan responded. "Yes, if that's the safe practice you're used to, then we should use what you know. Alright, go ahead."

As Taise breathed deeply and went within herself to reach out, the Sword's glow swept up it from the point to the hilt but white again, not yellow as when Maelbrigt held it. Squint whistled in alarm but kept his paw on the Sword, then trilled excitedly.

"Could Taise use the Sword?" Raethun asked him.

Squint's answer was clearly 'no'.

"What about if she used another one of the DeÁine Treasures?" wondered Raethun. "If she changed one like Sithfrey did the Gauntlet. Could she use it alongside Maelbrigt and the Sword then?"

This time Squint's response was a very emphatic 'yes'.

Everyone began laughing and clapping as Taise took a few steps back and the Sword went quiet again.

"Then I think that's quite enough excitement for one night!" Hugh declared, ushering everyone out and off to bed.

After all the excitement of the previous evening, the women's first morning back at Lorne was a much more sombre affair. At the official debriefing, Kayna laid out before Master Hugh and the assembled men just what had happened on Rheged. Everyone was appalled at the overwhelming loss of life which had taken place at the turn of the year, and nobody disputed that Rheged might well turn out to have suffered greater numbers of casualties than even Brychan when the final count was made. Her narrative was interspersed with additional information from Aeschere, since he was best qualified to talk of the situation in the west of Rheged, although nothing he said softened the blow. And once everyone realised the depth of the absent Master Amalric's involvement in the whole mess, few had much sympathy with his current condition.

"I think it's probably a good thing that he's in the state he's in," Aeschere said bluntly. "There's absolutely no way anyone in their right mind would think him capable of remaining in the Order even as the humblest Knight. You're the Master of the Prydein sept again, Master Hugh, and there can be no disputing it. Which I personally think is a blessing. The nobles back at home can huff and puff to their heart's content, but there's no way they could offer support to Amalric – no matter how much of a favourite he once was with them – and that means they can't split the sept in a leadership contest. The Order is healed rather than divided, and it couldn't have come at a more opportune time."

Hugh smiled and thanked Aeschere, but without any great satisfaction. For him it had all come at far too high a price, and thinking of prices he looked back at Kayna who clearly still had more to tell. The eye contact with him was all the encouragement she needed to continue her tale and she launched into the search for clues about the Spear.

"You might've sent us a message that the cursed thing was found," she added venomously, having got as far as recounting the realisation that there was nothing to be found in any of the Knight's buildings within Earlskirk.

"What happened?" Maelbrigt asked, picking up on her need for someone to prompt for what was surely going to be one of Kayna's more explosive outbursts. Knowing her the way he did, he was amazed that she had lasted this long without savaging someone for something she clearly saw as a grave mistake. Kayna's temper had always been short, and in the past she would never have been able to contain herself this long.

"Elidyr's dead, that's what!" snarled the dark-haired fury, her self-restrain snapped. "He died in what we now know was a bloody futile attempt to get into the place where the DeÁine Helm was kept for centuries! A fucking pointless waste of a good life! He died painfully from a trap set by that *fucking* war-mage! And if I get my hands on him, I'm going to rip his nuts off and feed them to him piecemeal for starters! I'll think about what else while I'm doing it!"

Hugh looked startled at Kayna's brutal language as did one or two others. Maelbrigt, on the other hand, recognised that for her to get this mad she must have been badly shaken by the event.

"A DeÁine trap?" he asked carefully. "What sort?" He knew Kayna would vent her anger further, but wanted it to be at him rather than any of the others.

"What sort?" she echoed, but three times louder. "The kind that leaves men bleeding to death before a fireball consumes them, you fucking idiot! The kind that someone doesn't stand a snowflake in the Underworld's chance of surviving!" She was on her feet and pacing up and down like a caged animal, unable to keep still in her agitation.

Hugh's eyebrows would have been up by his hair if he had had any left at the front, and Raethun and the other young Knights were looking troubled, while Sionnachan wore a concerned frown. Only Arthur seemed un-shocked. He seemed to take it as normal that someone in great distress would behave this way, which bothered Hugh even more when he looked to the child, expecting to be able to use him as a reason to demand that Kayna moderate her behaviour.

Before Hugh could think of some way of chastising her, Maelbrigt was on his feet and moving close to Kayna who was still swearing like a fishwife. Reaching out he pulled her into his arms, at which point her anger evaporated and she collapsed against him and began sobbing.

"That's the first time she's let herself grieve for him," Taise said sadly. "She's been so strong for Matti and me. Matti especially."

At her words, everyone realised that Matti had been sitting silently but with tears streaming down her face, a haunted expression fixed there.

"It wasn't anything like a grollican or a bansith," Aeschere added wearily. "Not that kind of summoning. Not active. Not the kind of thing whose energy would gradually give out if not replenished by its master. This was a trap which would've sat there for a century if necessary, waiting for some poor innocent to walk into it. Tancostyl must've had workmen install the basic spikes which pinned Elidyr in the doorway. But the mage himself must've created whatever shot them out with such force." He looked pained as he gave the details, knowing that they would be desperately hard for the three women to relive. "The spikes nearly went through Elidyr. Even if the ball of Power-fire hadn't been rolling towards us, he wouldn't have lived more than a minute or so with the way he was bleeding."

"Power-fire?" Sionnachan demanded. "How did you not get caught by that?"

"Taise," Aeschere said simply. "Without her we'd all be dead. She summoned Power of her own to protect us all." He smiled down at her gratefully then looked back up at Maelbrigt who had spun in shock towards his beloved. "You've one amazing lady there, Maelbrigt! She may not be used to using her powers but she certainly doesn't lack courage. She couldn't have held it off for long, and I had to use the little I know to assist her so that we could get out ourselves, but it gave the others time to get out of the direct line of it."

Maelbrigt almost bodily lifted the still crying Kayna closer to Taise, so that he could pull her close to him on the other side. It had shaken him more than he would have believed possible to know that he might have lost not only his adored Taise, but also the girl he thought of as his sister, in one blow. Meanwhile Aeschere had gone to stand by Matti's chair and put a comforting arm around her, although Andra was already sat beside her and now hugged her tightly from his side.

"Matti was particularly good friends with Elidyr," Aeschere explained tactfully.

With sudden insight Hugh understood that all three women had witnessed this brutal act, and that however brave they might be, it had shocked them to the core. Nothing any of them could possibly have seen in the past would have prepared them for that. It made him very glad he had not had the chance to say anything to Kayna. Her reaction was now only too understandable. He looked across to Sionnachan and saw the senior Forester raise his eyebrows back, clearly as appalled as himself. He took a deep breath.

"I'm so very sorry," he said carefully. "So very sorry that you all had to go through that, and for the loss of someone who had a bright future ahead of him. Please believe me, Kayna, when I say that we couldn't have sent you a message about the Spear in time to have saved Elidyr. You left Earlskirk when?"

"The fifteenth of Earrach," Kayna sniffed, searching desperately for a handkerchief in her pockets.

"Here you are," Tiny Arthur said, walking over and proffering a slightly grubby but unused one. "You'd better have this. Master Hugh gets real upset when you use your sleeve!"

The tension in the room evaporated, and even Kayna managed a wobbly smile at what she guessed was behind that statement.

Hugh exhaled deeply, silently blessing Arthur for his unwitting charm. "Indeed," he agreed with a wry smile, "I do keep trying to impress on Arthur the importance of a clean handkerchief!"

"You be careful, Arthur!" Matti managed to regain her composure. "My youngest brother always used his sleeve and our nurse sewed buttons on his cuff to make him stop it. The first time he forgot, his nose got cut by a sharp edge on one of them, and he had to sit still for a whole day while it stopped bleeding!"

Arthur looked horrified. Sit still for a *whole* day? By now everyone else was smiling and Hugh felt able to continue.

"You see, the ancients told us that the Spear had started moving some time about the end of Spring-moon, but that was all. Without a squint to help they couldn't trace it. Poor Finn is in no state even now to do something like that." Arthur had named Hugh's squint by message, yet

Owein had paid Arsaidh a visit and reported back that the wounded squint had surprisingly responded to his new name. "Nor were they alerted to it by it suddenly starting moving, because it wasn't in its chapel anymore. We still don't know what happened to that, although Cynddylan and Peredur told us that a landslip destroyed the chapel connected to the Bow, so maybe something similar happened centuries ago to the Spear. Whatever it was it weakened their tie to it. All they could tell us was that it *probably* wasn't on Rheged. However, the Bow had more clues as to its whereabouts written by our distant ancestors who moved it. So we had to hope that you might find another similar clue, because that would at least tell us where it was *starting* to move from.

"It was only on the thirtieth of Earrach – when you were already nearly here – that Cwen tried to use the Spear, and Cynddylan, Peredur and Urien were able to swoop in on her. You'll like Cwen by the sound of her, Kayna. She seems very like you! Apparently she was only able to try to recover the Spear when she heard that it was being hidden by the Attacotti leader, Mad Magnus. It was more than a bit of a shock for her when it bonded with her.

"Even worse, she and the lance who'd gone to protect her had to go on the run from Magnus. Yet even that has oddly worked out for the best. You see, she was waiting to find a ship which would get her from Rathlin across to Prydein, when one came flying in from the southern seas. Her captain had come to bring a warning that a vast DeÁine fleet is on its way here."

The shock for the newcomers from Rheged was not as great as it had been the previous night, and so Hugh was able to move on to tell them,

"Cwen immediately thought to use the Spear to try to send a warning."

"The lass has considerable presence of mind," Sionnachan praised her. "It was an original bit of thinking and it worked. The ancients felt her instantly and went to her. We got the warning within the hour and we've been working on the basis of that ever since. As luck would have it, Master Brego was already on the road to lead men in defence of Brychan. We've had to adapt our plans a bit in the light of this new information, though. The reason I've been here with Master Hugh is that my Foresters will be the last to leave Ergardia in the fourth shipment of troops. Sithfrey, Andra and myself only got back here on the twenty-sixth of Earrach with the Gauntlet anyway, so we'd missed Brego in person. It's a good job we've got these ancients, although they do seem awfully touchy about carrying messages back and forth!"

"Very touchy!" Maelbrigt confirmed. "Aneirin, whom I work with for the Sword, stands on his dignity rather a lot, and I pity poor Cwen because Urien is a right awkward character – and that's who she's saddled with for the Spear. Thankfully Cynddylan, Peredur and another called Owein are much more understanding. They recognise that until we have everyone who'll use the Island Treasures there's a limit to what they can do anyway, because whoever gets to use the Shield will only have to catch up with what the rest of us know. So they're willing to do a lot to help us help ourselves. They've relayed messages on tactics to and fro between us and Brego, so we're all working to the same plan now.

"Ruari went with Ivain and the Bow to meet with a friend of Cwen's called Swein, who has the Arrow and is with Talorcan on Prydein. Talorcan and his men are all well, by the way. They survived their exploits unscathed!" He noticed that that also brought a smile to Kayna's lips at least. "Now that Cwen's on her way to meet them, that means that the Bow, the Arrow and the Spear will all travel together to Kittermere, and then on to Rathlin with the full force of Master Hugh's army from Prydein. Let Magnus try to argue with that!"

Sionnachan grinned. "Oh yes! He'll have to watch his step, and ever serve him right! I'll be joining them with my Foresters directly on Rathlin. That's why we've delayed our departure until now. Master Brego is leading the main Ergardia force to free Brychan even as we speak, and there'll be enough of them that they won't need our help unless the Abend get really snitty and start throwing the Power around."

"That may well happen," Taise warned. "They won't just sit back and let you take back what they've seized so easily."

"Maybe, maybe not," Sionnachan said. "You see, on the twenty-ninth of Earrach, Talorcan and Hugh's ealdorman at Mullion, Hereman, found a second warning about the DeÁine fleet. This time it came by bird all the way from New Lochlainn! Quite a feat in itself! It turned out to be from General Montrose and one of Hugh's bright young officers – a lad named Oliver."

Matti, Kayna and Taise all beamed at one another. For Kayna and Taise there was the almighty relief that Will Montrose was well and clearly doing great things, so averting any further pain for Matti for the moment. On top of that Matti herself was glad, along with her two friends, that the love of their other friend, Alaiz, was also likely to be alive. Where Oliver went Hamelin was not going to be too far behind, and if one was well the other was sure to be.

Slightly confused at the sudden outburst of joy, Sionnachan shrugged and ploughed on. "It transpires from their message that it looks as though this fleet was summoned by Quintillean alone. We've talked this over with the more obliging of the ancients too, and we all agree that if the other Abend think that Quintillean is stealing a march on them, they'll try to stop him in some way. We think that they'll know that the fleet is coming by now, and so if they're confronted with a fight for Brychan, they'll let it go and focus on presenting a united front to those who are coming. I don't doubt that the Donns will put up a spirited fight. They have more to lose by going back to New Lochlainn with their tails between their legs. But the Abend? No. We're fairly sure that they'll focus on grabbing what they can to make sure they look good to whoever is coming."

"Who would be coming, Taise?" asked Maelbrigt. "Sithfrey thinks it'll just be more of the highborn ordinary DeÁine."

The other DeÁine scholar nodded his head to confirm that.

Taise, however, dropped her head and thought carefully. "There won't be any more of the Abend themselves, if that's what you're thinking," she said carefully. "There are only – and only ever can be by divine law – nine of them. But …and it's a big *but* …there were some very senior acolytes amongst us who got left behind at Sinut. The royal family there – of whom the likes of Bres, Nuadu, Ruadan and Eriu were simply the junior line – would never have consented to be left without some who were very skilled in the Power. If for no other reason than that they'd want plenty of those who could use the healing objects of greater strength. They wouldn't risk their own kin for want of a healer just to please the Abend.

"After all, it was the Abend who got them into this mess! The Abend caused the Exile in the pure-borns' eyes. Ever since then, although the Abend are very, very powerful in the Power, they still need access to the pure-breds to recruit new acolytes from, because without acolytes the Abend would sooner or later cease to exist. It's a conundrum which keeps the Abend in the awful position, from their point of view, of having to keep in the good books of the royal family. So no, no Abend, but you could find some acolytes who aren't much lower in Power."

"Bugger!" Sionnachan muttered. "Oh well, I suppose it was too much to ask that we'd have a clear run in from the east. The sooner we can assemble the Foresters and have a good planning session, the happier I'll be."

"Could *you* not use the Shield?" Kayna wondered. "If the Sword chose a Forester in Maelbrigt, have you tried with the Shield, Sionnachan?"

"Oh I've tried. Absolutely nothing! Not a glimmer of a glow. But we should try you, Kayna."

The young fiery woman jumped in shock. "Me?"

"Well why not? The Spear chose Cwen. Clearly being a woman is no barrier to being selected."

Maelbrigt looked to Squint. "Do you have any idea?" he asked his constant companion. Squint gave an ambiguous whistle. "Does that mean you don't know?" Another dubious trilling. "Or is the person in the room, but you don't know who?" This time Squint's reply was more encouraging, although still not positive.

"I think we'd better take everyone up to Master Brego's office," Hugh declared.

In a solemn procession they all trooped along the corridor and up a half floor to reach the great dragon-doors. With great ceremony, Hugh swung them inwards and everyone assembled in a curve around where the Sword and Shield lay on either side of the fireplace. At Hugh's request Squint called to Owein and Moss and the two shimmered into view.

"Thank you for coming," Hugh said courteously. "We think Squint believes the Shield's user could be in this room. Moss? Would you care to take a look?"

The final squint drifted on pattering feet along the line of people, his nose twitching and bright eyes staring hard at them as if he were trying to look into their souls. Suddenly he stopped in front of Matti and gave an excited chirp. Before anyone could say anything he had flung himself at her, nearly bowling her over.

"*Aaagh*!" shrieked Matti as the contact blasted her with the Shield's energy.

Moss also shrieked in pain but there was an undertone of immense relief with it as well. It highlighted only too clearly the anxiety he must have been feeling as the last of the squints in the in-between world, Daisy having been taken off by Urien to meet Cwen already. As Maelbrigt and Squint helped the shaken Moss up onto his back paws in his new reality, Hugh sat on the edge of Brego's desk and looked about him with satisfaction. Everything anyone had said about Matti had led him to believe she was a stable and reliable person. Personally he had been hoping against hope that it would not be Kayna. She was undoubtedly courageous, but he could not find any way of imagining her working as a unit with the other users.

"Well, well," he declared out loud. "So there we have it! All the Treasures have been paired up as far as we can. Brego has Sooty with him, so I shall just have to do the best I can with poor little Finn. Maelbrigt has Squint with the Sword, and now you, my dear, have the Shield with Moss. You two must think about leaving soon to go down to join the others, as Maelbrigt and Sionnachan suggested."

"Not on their own they're not!" Kayna declared fiercely. "If you think Taise and I are going to sit up here waiting for the gates of the Underworld to open up beneath us, you've got another thing coming! Anyway, you can't parcel Matti off in a whole army of men on her own. Taise and I will be there to support her like Sionnachan and Aeschere will be for Maelbrigt."

Maelbrigt looked as though he was about to protest at Taise going into danger when Sithfrey spoke up. "Yes, I think Taise has to come, because I think I need to be with you too. That way, the two of us can work on how this Gauntlet will fit into things if we get chance to use it."

"Well if you're going so am I!" Andra announced. "I've been left behind once before and I'm not doing it again!"

Hugh looked about him. "Then I think I may be the only one left behind," he sighed.

"No, Master Hugh," Aeschere spoke up. "You're my Master, first and foremost. With none of the others from Prydein here I'd like to stay with you, if I may. And while we're waiting I can be learning a good deal from Master Arsaidh. It's about time the Prydein sept of Foresters caught up with the others!"

"And we've got all our squints!" an excited Arthur added. "You promised! You said you wouldn't leave me this time. You promised!"

"Yes we did," Maelbrigt reassured him. "For good or bad you'll stay with me and Squint and Taise."

Sionnachan moved to stand in front of the arc of people. "Then I guess it falls to me to lead this expedition, since Maelbrigt will have his hands full dealing with the Treasures – of all descriptions. We leave in four days, people. Take what time we have to prepare. We may not be back this way for a very long time. We're going to war."

Chapter 13

A Shortage of Choices

New Lochlainn: mid Earrach

On a cool but bright New Lochlainn morning, Will and the men from Prydein scanned the walls of Kuzmin Palace from a short distance away. So far so good. They had crossed the Salu Maré unseen, as far as they could tell, and currently the vulnerable civilians they had brought with them were safely hidden on the last island along the chain-ferry's route. In the end, three hundred men had been brought to the banks of the huge sea-loch, after Will and the Knights had weeded out those who were unfit due to age or physique for this venture. Those precluded by age had come from the ranks of the slaves they had liberated, while others amongst the makeshift army had proven inept at moving stealthily, or just plain lacked stamina. However, those left behind still had a vital role to play in guarding the young women Will and Sioncaet had liberated from the temple at Tokai, plus the families of the slaves.

"It all looks quiet," Oliver observed from beside Will.

"Hmmm…," Will hummed noncommittally. "That doesn't mean anything. That bastard wizard could have all manner of nasty surprises up his sleeve that we'd know nothing about until the ground started shifting beneath our feet, or the dead started walking!"

"What do we do, then?" asked Hamelin. "I mean, how long should we wait until we're sure it's safe, if we can't ever know it's safe …if that makes sense?"

Will turned to him and grinned wolfishly. "Ah! That's the fun, young Hamelin! Running into battle never knowing what's going to bite you first! Come on! We're just going to have to jump in the water and then hope we can swim."

"Shit! He's as bad as you!" Labhran muttered darkly to Oliver, as they followed Will down off the small rise they had been watching from. "Do all you Islanders have some kind of lurking death-wish?"

Oliver turned and grinned back at the former spy. "*You're* asking? I thought you were an Islander yourself!" he responded with amusement. "Don't you remember your own home?"

Labhran rolled his eyes theatrically. "Oh please! That's so long ago it's a different world. And yes, I may be an Islander by birth, but there are times when I feel as out of place as any of these slaves from far, far away. And this is one of them!"

Oliver chuckled. "Nah, it's not us with the death wish. You're just gloomy by nature, I reckon! Too much rain and mist as a kid must've given you a touch of the Island glums. Water in the ears! That's what does it! Puts a dampener on everything! Every family has one. The old granny being the prophet of doom all the time. Or the brother who sees disaster even on a bright summer day. You must've been a real ray of sunshine to grow up with!" he teased lightly, but as he had hoped it did bring a wry smile to Labhran's lips.

Down in the shaded hollow behind the low ridge, Will was passing the word amongst his makeshift army. The actual orders had been repeated and repeated until everyone knew the details by heart before they had ever set foot on this shore. Will was taking no chances with his men's inexperience, and so now all that needed doing was passing the prearranged signals. When Will gave a nod, Oliver, Hamelin, and the two young Ergardian Knights, Kym and Teryl, went to their men and drew them off to one side. This hundred would be last to depart, for they were needed for the assault on the inner citadel. And as arranged, the twelve enlisted men of the Order were going with Oliver's party to aid the climb.

Meanwhile the rest drew up in columns behind Will, the other Ergardian Knight, Lorcan, and the three other Prydein Knights, Theo, Friedl and Bertrand. These five columns of around forty men each were going to make the first attempt at getting into Kuzmin. Silent as ghosts, Will led his men forward, hugging every hollow and dip in the ground and keeping to the shadows as much as possible. The good thing about attacking this early was that the sun was as yet still low in the sky, and blazing straight into the eyes of any sentry on the walls who happened to be looking eastwards across the short stretch to the shore – which was the land over which the covert attack was making its approach.

Yet Will could not see any sign of anyone making any real attempt at keeping guard. That worried him. Had Quintillean set some mystical trap? Was he so confident in not setting any guard because he knew that nobody could get close without tripping some kind of alarm, or waking some fell summoning? *Flaming Underworlds, what I wouldn't give for a few good Foresters now*! Will wished fervently. Anyone with a fair grasp on the arcane would be welcome. As it was he was probably the most sensitised of all of them, and that was why he had insisted that he be at the front, despite refusing to let Labhran or Sioncaet be there. If the worst happened, he had to trust that those two would lead the men out again and get them across enemy territory to safety.

They made it to the walls in one piece and began to sneak along them towards the gate. Just as Sioncaet had promised, this was identical to Tokai in every respect so far. Will's party had crept close just as the oval circuit of the wall began its sweep around to the south, and were now clinging to it, sidling up the eastern straight stretch towards the gates. If there was one good thing about the massive gateway it was that it had projecting walls of its own.

When they had practised at Tokai, Will had found that unless a gate-sentry stepped right out away from those two great bastions, it was impossible to see someone approaching when they were this close to the wall. Similarly, nobody up on top could easily see anyone down below. The chest-high parapet aesthetically made for beautiful symmetry, but defensively it was a nightmare, for there was nowhere anyone could lean out to look downwards. The only view the wall-sentries had was straight out.

Will and his leading men got right up to the corner between the wall and the gateway, and then halted to listen. However, strain his ears though he would, Will could hear nothing at all. Either any guards were being incredibly silent; were expecting an attack and so playing cat to their mouse; or there was no-one there at all. Shrugging to Friedl, who was watching further back along the wall with his own contingent, Will edged stealthily out, sword drawn and ready to have to fight for his life.

The reason they had heard nothing was partly due to the fact that their nearest half of the gate was shut, and when Will leaned on it it failed to move even an inch, suggesting that it was bolted on the far side. The other half-gate was almost closed, with only a slim gap showing open by the way a shadow played across the surface. A gap Will could not see through. He slid silently along the closed gate and paused right by the edge of it, trying to detect any movement beyond. For a moment he thought he heard a faint rustling, but then Bertrand appeared from the opposite direction around the other bulwark of stone with five of his men and edged up to the gap. At Will's gesture Bertrand inched up to the hinge of the gate and made a darting glance in. Flattening himself back against the stone he shook his head. Nobody was there as far as he could tell.

Will took a deep breath and thought. Perhaps because this was following the design of a palace and not a castle, he knew there was no portcullis beyond the outside gates, only a strange sort of bridge part way through the deep, arched gatehouse. That bridge was useless for defence, though, for the only openings were too small to fire through, and Sioncaet had told them that they were there for heralds to play their trumpets through to announce the arrival of important guests. At Tokai the inner gates had been wedged open and had presented no barrier.

Now Will mouthed, "Inner gates?" to Bertrand. The Knight blinked, then edged forwards once more. With great care he sidled along the gate being very careful not to touch it. At the opening he risked a fast, darting glance, then gestured to Will – who was almost close enough to reach out and touch him across the gap – that the inner gates were the other way round. The one straight in from Will on the left of the gate was ajar and the right one shut.

However Bertrand was not waiting for Will to decide. Having nimbly retreated back to the hinge of the gate he used the flat of his sword to put pressure on the gate. It moved a few inches. Enough that if anyone had been stood behind it they would have noticed. No-one sounded the alarm and all was silent. Barely able to believe his luck, Bertrand now applied his shoulder to the edge of the gate and it swung in with a faint wheeze of un-oiled hinges. In the gloom of the gateway not a thing stirred.

Will raised his eyebrows in surprise and Bertrand shrugged back. Neither could understand why the gate would be undefended. Bertrand was just about to enter when Will beat him to it. Every nerve on edge for the slightest whiff of someone or something using the Power, he edged forward until he was at the inner gate. Behind him the men slid in like ghosts, mere flickering shadows in the unlit stretch between the two sets of gates.

When both Will and Bertrand's men had jammed themselves into the tight space, a signal came forward that Freidl and Theo were lined up outside on the one side, and Lorcan on the other. It was now or never. Trying to steady his pounding heart, Will edged around the gap in the gate and surveyed the inner space. Just like at Tokai, there was a short alley straight ahead, which went nowhere except straight to the vast bulk of the mound on which the inner court sat. Risking stepping fully out into the daylight, Will paused to allow time for his senses to adjust. Now that he knew what to feel for, he recognised the same vague itching at the back of his mind caused by the Power-filled room up above in the temple. There was also something else niggling away as well, but whatever it was it was not any closer either, and it certainly was not focusing on them.

Gesturing Bertrand in, Will and his men stood guard over the small open courtyard while Bertrand led his men off to the right. A couple of twisting turns further on around the circuit there should be a narrowing. In a dingy right-angled corner at Tokai they had found a metal gate closing off the single street and Will wanted the duplicate here held by his own men. He had taken a liking to Bertrand, and while he could have wished to have the calm and experienced Knight covering his back, he also knew that Bertrand was the best man to leave to command this bottleneck. If they had to beat a retreat they would go that way, since they could block the passage against any pursuers and gain precious time, and that was when Will would need Bertrand's cool head.

As the last of Bertrand's men slipped along the narrow street and took up position to watch, Theo led his men into the open. With great care, Will now led the advance along the street to their left. Theo and Lorcan led their men in support of him, while Freidl began to tally his men off to check the walls, since there were small chambers let into the thickness just big enough for a couple of men to take cover from the weather. There might not be an open show of manning the walls, but it would only take one man to start shouting – one man who had been idling unseen in the shade – and they would be exposed.

It tore at everyone's nerves to be marching through this warren of seemingly deserted quarters. Everyone was jumping at shadows, even Lorcan who, aside from Labhran and Sioncaet, had seen more of the DeÁine than any of them except possibly Will. Men repeatedly changed hands on their swords, spears or bows as they wiped the nervous sweat from their palms. Once they had rounded the southern end of the loop and found no-one, Will could only think that, as at Tokai, these lower quarters were seldom used except when there was an influx of the highborn and their servants.

However, when the street suddenly narrowed and Will guessed they were almost at the flights of steps up to the inner court, his senses began to jangle in warning. Signalling everyone to halt, Will slid past the last empty set of suites, flattened himself against the wall and crouched down. Peeping furtively around the edge of the wall he hoped he was low enough down so that if he was observed the watcher would think it nothing more than a glimpsed movement of a stray cat. There had been the odd feral feline in Tokai, so hopefully there were some here too.

What he saw confirmed that Quintillean had to be there, for a triad of Hunters stood like statues at the base of the twin flights of steps. No slave guards this time! Sitting back on his haunches, Will mouthed to Lorcan the word 'Hunters' and held up three fingers. Leaving Lorcan to bring the archers forward, Will risked another glance. It was worth it. One of the Hunters sniffed and wiped his nose on the back of his hand – a sure sign, Sioncaet and Labhran had said, that a Hunter was due for another dose of his narcotic herbs. As he watched he noticed another sway slightly. These must be the ones who had stood the night watch and had not been relieved as yet. Mentally offering up a prayer of thanks to the Trees for dulled senses on these formidable enemies, Will eased himself to his feet and turned his attention to the archers who were now congregated beside him. Holding his arm up to catch their gaze he then signalled that they should make a shot, then run for all they were worth for the other side of the steps to where they could cover the steps, which he knew turned back on themselves to more steps rising above where they were now. A soft bird call indicated that word had been passed that Oliver and his group were ready to assault the inner wall from the gate end, and suddenly there was no more waiting.

Silently counting down, 'three …two …one!' with his fingers in the air and then launching himself out into the open, Will led the attack. He kept low and to the right as arrows flew out of the shadows and found their mark. These first archers had been chosen for their ability to hit accurately, and at this range they could hardly miss. The far Hunter staggered as five arrows imbedded themselves in him, while the middle one took three. The closest was unscathed but he had seen Will and stepped out to confront him, thus presenting a target to the next wave of archers who came to the front and fired. Even so, despite having multiple wounds and being in need of their drugs, it was not enough to bring down any of the Hunters completely.

The central figure turned on his heels and began to try to run up the stairs to sound the alarm. Will frantically gestured to the archers to bring him down even as he exchanged blows with the Hunter in front of him. Men swarmed past him dragging down the Hunter he had engaged plus the furthest one by sheer weight of numbers. It was neither elegant nor skilful but it did the job, and given the inexperience of the men around him that was all that Will could ask for. Dodging flailing limbs, he ran to the base of the stairs and saw archers, already up the first flights at the turning landing, shooting back towards the point where the twin flights joined at the centre to become a single flight to the highest level. Tearing past them, he saw the final Hunter crawling like an ailing hedgehog up onto the next small landing. Bounding up the steps two at a time, Will reached him and drove his sword straight down through his spine at the neck. The Hunter shuddered and then lay still.

Standing over the body, Will frantically gestured down for the men to be quiet. In the excitement of the attack the novice troops had begun to chatter to one another, but Lorcan was quickly stamping on the heady rush of euphoria at this first victory. They were not done yet. Mentally blessing Lorcan for needing no prompting to act, Will once more took the lead and slid snakelike up the final set of steps. As expected there was an open garden in the centre, but no subversive Islander had tended these plants. A rather sickly-looking pine of some foreign kind clung to life in front of the steps, while opposite, a spindly tree of unknown variety drooped listlessly. The two trees which should have stood to the north outside the temple, and to the south outside the palace, had apparently given up the fight against the harsher Island climate as soon as their canopies had risen high enough not to be sheltered by the buildings. Both stood stark and desiccated, not the slightest sign of spring leaf buds on either.

However, this was a blessing, for Will could see through the bare branches that Oliver's party by now had scaled both the high bank and the walls of the inner compound, and were currently crouched along the ridge tiles of the buildings which backed onto that area. Like a bunch of malevolent gargoyles, they lurked with drawn weapons waiting to pounce on the unwary below. Except that there were no unwary.

Where the fuck is everyone? Will thought as dread and doubt welled up inside. Had he totally miscalculated? Was something they had not foreseen going on? With Hunters on guard surely there had to be *someone* of importance here? He risked stepping out onto the open surface and signalled questioningly to Oliver. Yet the young Knight gestured back that he could see nobody either. Waving his hand to the left, Will sent Oliver's group off on a pre-planned foray into the living quarters attached to the temple. They had strict instructions not to go into the temple itself under any circumstances, but at least they all now knew that there were two inner courtyards in the priests' living complex, which the attackers could drop down into without going through the temple. This was where Oliver was now heading, with orders to clear the living quarters and then return as many men as possible to the roofs, leaving only a skeleton crew to watch the lone doorway from the temple and the stairs up to the levels above.

Meanwhile Will, with all of his own men plus Theo's and Lorcan's, hurried to the door of the palace. Vividly remembering how the strange place muffled and distorted sound when he had been at Tokai, Will was taking no chance of small groups of men getting cut off and killed where nobody could hear their cries for help. It was just as well. As he entered through beaten copper doors identical to the ones he had seen before, Will instantly knew something was different. There were noises. Muffled by the inner doors to be sure, but that low hum was the sound of voices. He leaned his ear to the crack in the double doors, being very careful not to put any weight on the doors in case they swung open and dumped him on the floor in the middle of an enemy force.

If anyone could have heard his thoughts they would have made a fishwife blush, for in his mind Will swore every curse he could think of. There was no doubt about it, there were Hunters beyond the door. He could tell that by the dreadful internal itch he was getting somewhere in his inner ears from their low grade, but still tangible, link with the Power. And knowing that the Hunters shared space with nobody, not even the most elite of the Jundis veterans, that meant that every voice in the great central room had to belong to a Hunter. Frantically waving the men back outside, Will pulled the copper doors to before turning to his two second-in-commands.

"Bloody hall is full of Hunters!" he hissed. "No wonder there were no flaming guards on the gate! With everyone this side of the mountains scared shitless of them, even Quintillean wouldn't expect to be attacked here. There must be dozens of the bastards in there!"

Lorcan winced and looked involuntarily to the sea of expectant faces watching the three of them. Will knew what he was thinking because it was in his own mind too. Even with just over a hundred men, given the desperate inexperience of those troops there was no way they could hope to take on that many Hunters and not suffer dreadful casualties.

"Get those dead trees down!" Will ordered, as inspiration came. "They must be brittle as anything! And dry, given that all the snow went east."

As he and Theo watched the door, Lorcan got the men pulling the trees apart. They could not hope to chop the trunks down and still be quiet, but all the top growth virtually snapped off in the hands of the men who climbed up and began throwing the lighter branches down to their friends below. When they had a great pile, Will eased the copper doors open again and gestured the men to start heaping them up against the inner doors. A respectable bonfire's worth was soon packed right up to the doors, with all the Island men lined up in ranks outside the copper doors at a decent distance near to the central pool in the garden. One enterprising soul had spotted a lamp, and had brought it over for Will to empty the oil over the wood, except for a long trickle back to outside that he left to take the igniting flame which he struck from his tinder box.

Flames leapt hungrily across to the oiled wood, and Will jumped back and pulled the outer copper door shut behind him, leaving just enough of a gap to allow a draft to fan the flames. Within an astonishingly short time, the roar of a good blaze could be heard and then cries of alarm. There was a sudden *whoosh*, by which the attackers guessed that some fool had opened the inner doors and the flames had billowed inside, a conclusion backed up by some dreadful howls of pain. Even a Hunter was not immune to being burned to death. Then one of the men pointed upwards and they saw wisps of smoke beginning to rise from the roof. The great central space was clearly acting as one great funnelling chimney, especially if the upper windows had been opened to take advantage of the fine spring morning. It was also a fair bet that the long drapes running down from the balcony had caught fire, and that the flames had already made it to the upper storey without further need for Will or his men to do any fanning or stoking.

If any Hunters were going to emerge now it clearly would not be en masse, and Will felt more confident of his men's ability to pick them off piecemeal. It was just a pity there was not a way to lock them in and leave them to cook at no risk to his men.

"Lorcan? Take your men and make a sweep of the side quarters," Will ordered, becoming aware of other cries of alarm. "Sounds like they brought some grunts along to do the dirty work, but don't assume they're slaves!"

The Ergardian Knight gave a terse nod of acknowledgement, and took his men off through the gazebo area to clear the apartments in the other wing from where Oliver had gone. In all of this Will had not forgotten the temple opposite, and Theo had been detailed to keep an eye on the two sets of doors on that side of the garden in case anyone emerged from there.

The only good thing about it was that there were no windows looking down on this garden, and so it was unlikely that anyone within the temple would even have smelled smoke yet.

Then the palace doors sprang open and the blazing figure of a Hunter shot out, arms waving as he dashed for the pool. He never got that far, going down in a welter of blood as those in line with him shot him with arrows, and slashed at him while trying to keep clear of the flames which licked about his person from his lighted clothes. Whether it was heroism or simple panic which had made him make the run for the outside was immaterial. He had opened the way for others to make an attempt to escape the blaze and they took it.

Will could only think that an early morning lack of drugs made the Hunters stupid, because although they were far less affected by the pain from their burns than ordinary men would have been, the damage was no different. Yet on and on they came. Many were already blinded by the smoke and heat, and although they struck out wildly, their blows were unfocused. It was simple misfortune which brought some of the attackers in contact with those cuts and blows, pressed too close by the mêlée which was going on in the garden by now. Eighteen of the Hunters finally lay smouldering on the grass and paths, the men seeing no reason to risk themselves by trying to put out the burning clothing. From within there still came the sound of more, but those voices were fewer by far and Will doubted that more than half a dozen remained. Those few were unlikely to risk trying to emerge before the flames had died away, and so he set a substantial guard and went to look for Lorcan.

He met the Knight emerging from the small door into the suites beyond the palace, wiping his bloody sword on a piece of cloth which must until recently have been a curtain.

"All clear," Lorcan reported calmly. "Five men with nasty sword cuts and a few minor bumps and bruises, but nothing worse."

"How many?"

"Oh, only about twenty, but you were right, they weren't slaves. We had the advantage of surprise but they had the edge in terms of experience. The close quarters worked in our favour, though – especially after you gave the lads those practice runs through Tokai." He smiled. "That was worth it, General Montrose! Worth waiting a couple of extra days to do! It made all the difference in there."

Will felt some of the anxiety lift from his shoulders for the first time in weeks. The first hurdle was over. The thing he had dreaded was finding the place far more guarded, even by half a Jundis. Against such odds his makeshift army would not have stood much of a chance, and he would have had to try to find yet another way to rescue the two boys. Even as he was walking with Lorcan back out into the garden, Oliver shinned down a stone drain pipe from the roof, and reported that the living quarters for the priests was clear.

"What you'll be glad to hear is that there clearly haven't been anything like the number of priests you encountered at Tokai here for ages," he told Will, as Lorcan and Theo listened in. "Some of those rooms had dust an inch thick on the floor. Just opening the door swept a great pile up behind it and filled the air with clouds of bits." Then even the ever-cheerful Oliver's face fell. "But the bad news is that something's going on! Not in the temple itself. That was so quiet we risked a quick look – although we obeyed your orders and never went in. It's like a tomb in there. Not a soul. Whatever it is it's going on upstairs. Maybe in the Power-room or in one adjoining it. We'd better hurry because they sound like they're working themselves into a frenzy. It's scarily like what went on in the temples at Bruighean. Trees, that gives me the shudders just thinking about it! I don't even want to contemplate the possibility that we might've got here too late."

Will turned to Theo. "I want you to keep watch out here. I'd have preferred it if we could've dealt with all those Hunters first, but by the sound of it we don't have time to wait. No heroics!" he said sternly. "Those bastards are dangerous! I'll leave you mainly archers, so use them. Don't get into a hand to hand fight with even one of the Hunters if you can avoid it in any way. I mean it, Theo! Not even you – with all of your training you still wouldn't stand a chance. Even experienced Foresters like Maelbrigt don't go one on one with them if they have any kind of choice about it. I need you to keep calm and do a job, not have to worry about whether you're being chivalrous about it. You're watching *all* our backs for us." He liked the young Knight, but of all of the inexperienced young Knights, Will feared Theo might do something impulsive.

The naïve might have thought Will's caution excessive as the men edged their way into the temple. Sending Oliver and his men back over the roofs to watch for any disturbance from above, Will sent Lorcan and his men in through one set of temple doors while he and his contingent took the other. For a moment it was as if they had entered the Underworld itself. After the fresh spring morning, the interior was dark and felt hot and stuffy, and it stank of sulphur and incense from the direction of the central shrine.

Taking a moment for their eyes to adjust to the gloom, the men then began to check the temple in the way Will had made them practise several times over at Tokai. However, Oliver was proven to be right, this place had hardly been used in recent months. The secondary shrines to their left and at the far end were all coated in the dust of time from far longer than just a month or two. Only the central shrine had seen any observances made within the last few days.

"Up?" Lorcan asked Will and got a terse nod for an answer. At the door out of the temple into the priests' quarters Will called out softly before opening the door. He had no intention of getting skewered by his own men on the other side. Someone on the far side opened the door for him and gestured up the stairs. Turning left and beginning his ascent, Will now saw that Oliver was crouched at the top step waiting for him.

"Can you feel it?" Oliver whispered to him as he came level.

"Feel it? It's like the Power's crawling all over me like ants!" Will hissed back.

"Thought you might," Hamelin added from the step below. "Even I can feel there's something going on up there. But is it on this floor, or up on the top one with the Power-room?"

Will thought for a second and tried to analyse what he felt. "I can't be completely certain, but I think it's up a floor again. Although it feels like it's a room back from the one with the big pool in." Then he stopped and shuddered. "*Aach*! But then again it's like it's closer."

"We'll start searching," Oliver sighed, and gestured Dusty and Jens forward with Colum at their backs, his bow strung and ready to watch for attacks.

The two experienced men-at-arms took searching the rooms far more in their stride than the novices who Will had led at Tokai had done. Lorcan's sergeant, Evans, rejoined his leader and together with Waza, the remaining archer of their original lance, they peeled off to the other side to search the rooms which at Tokai had housed the women. Will let them go, with Teryl and his two archers, Cody and Trip, on their heels. They had decided that someone must secure the message room and any valuable intelligence they might find there, and that it was not a task for the novices.

If something vital was there, then it had to be got out to the rest of the Islands no matter what else occurred. Of the Order men, that left Kym with his two men-at-arms, Newt and Busby, plus his own archer, Toby, and the two lance-less archers, Topher and Mitch, who now followed Dusty and Jens.

Will wanted any clearing done with stealth, and that meant he had to risk the few fully-trained men at his disposal. But even worse would be a clumsy search tipping the hand of the Abend members within that their sanctuary had been broken into. It felt like forever, but then Kym reappeared, gesturing Will back into the recess of the stairwell so that he could speak properly to him.

"It's weird," the young Knight whispered carefully. "Some of the rooms around the Power room are sealed off. And I don't just mean the doors are locked. They've actually been bricked up, and my men reckon it's a recent job too. Something to do with the mortar, according to Newt. We can get all the way around this floor in a great loop. That's not a problem. There's not a soul about. We met Lorcan on the other side. He says to tell you that this is very different to the palace rooms he's just cleared over the way. There, he said it was like folks had been there as recently as late last year, had packed up and gone, but intended to return. Here it's actually disused. He says the message room is the one place which looks like it's had any use, but even there he thinks someone brought birds with them when they were needed and the place was in use. He doesn't think there was a regular rookery like at Tokai – maybe not even since the DeÁine came back to the Islands."

"Is there *any* way into those central rooms on this level from this floor?" Will asked.

Kym shook his head. "We can't find it if there is."

"Go and fetch the others," Will sighed, "we'll have to go up and do it the hard way."

With everyone as nervous as pigeons in a house full of cats, the men made their way up to the second floor. By now everyone could feel the crackling of Power in the air and it scared every last man. There was no mistaking the magnitude of what was being channelled somewhere nearby, and Will took pity on his new recruits waiting on the stair and below. Detailing Kym and Teryl to take charge of them, he sent all but the Order men back down to the ground floor with strict instructions to stay clear of the area below the Power room.

"If either Quintillean or Masanae shows their face leave them be," he ordered the young Knights. "Don't waste lives trying to take them down. These men aren't experienced enough for that. The only time you should attempt to get close is if we die and *if* they have the two boys with them. Anyone else, let them go. I don't want a massacre on our hands."

With just the Order's twelve enlisted men plus Lorcan, Oliver and Hamelin, Will turned once more to the inner rooms of the temple complex. Making a complete circuit of the central block of rooms surrounding the Power room, he then drew his small war band out onto a balcony above the deserted rookery.

"The room at the other side?" he murmured very low.

"Agreed," Lorcan breathed softly, and Oliver and Hamelin – the only other ones close enough to hear – nodded.

"We open the door just a crack. See who's on the other side."

He led them back around to a room where the double doors showed the glimmer of a nearby oil lamp in the crack between. As his hand went to towards the handle, Waza slid forward with Evans beside him. At Will's questioning glance, Waza held up his hands and Will saw in the gloom the metallic glint of a garrotting wire. Evans' tiny nod was enough to signal that he too was prepared. Will stepped back and let Newt and Busby come forward to either side of the doors. Experience was everything here, and Will knew when to get out of the way and let other professionals at close-quarter mayhem do their stuff.

Newt drew a tiny tin out of his inside pocket and dripped a minute amount of oil onto the latch on each side. Just enough to ease the movement. Then watching each other closely, the two men-at-arms silently drew the doors open back towards them. A pair of Hunters stood with their backs to the doors but they had no chance to call out. Like a pair of striking snakes Evans and Waza were in and looping the wires over the two heads. The act was hardly clean, with blood from the slit throats covering the attackers and the walls and floors, but it was virtually silent. As the Hunters grappled in a frenzy for the razor-sharp wires sawing through their vocal chords, Newt and Busby were in and plunging knives into vital organs, swiftly followed by the other Order men. The Hunters might have fought hard to hold onto life, even as their life blood sprayed out, but once others could get close enough a long knife through the eye into the brain finished the job.

The Hunters never even hit the floor. Their bodies were caught and hoisted between men and lugged out of the room to one opposite which was known to be empty. As the evidence was removed, Will slid in with the rest of the men at his heels, and pulled the doors closed enough to avoid any light spilling in – not that much would come from the blackness of the corridor beyond.

To their astonishment they found that they were looking across the small room to a hole where the back wall had once stood. Edging forward, they were able to see that beyond it in the next room another wall had been removed, allowing them to see into the Power-room. However, in between, what had been the central room was now just a hole in the floor except for a small walkway left all around the edge by the walls. The Power hit Will like a hammer and he doubled up, being caught as he fell to his knees by Lorcan. His head was reeling, his stomach churned, and even his vision felt distorted. The DeÁine must have paused in whatever they were doing when he had walked in, for although he had felt giddy and nauseous he had still been able to function, unlike now.

On his hands and knees in the gloom, he made it carefully around the sides of the room to the hole in the wall, seeing blurrily that Oliver and Hamelin were crouched on the opposite side of the gap. Shadowy figures behind the two Prydein Knights told Will that all the Order's enlisted men had rejoined them, and that he probably had some behind him. He dared not turn to look, though, for fear of falling over. Fighting to keep some kind of control over himself, Will gritted his teeth and took another look into the room beyond, forcing himself to look downwards.

What he saw chilled his blood to the marrow. Wistan and Kenelm stood in what appeared to be a small pool made from black obsidian, each facing in to the centre and with their backs to some kind of strange platform with channels in it, also in black. He blinked hard, screwing his eyes shut and then forcing them open again to try and clear his vision. A third figure was just visible in the centre, who, going by the appalling state he was in and by his height, Will guessed might be the former king of Brychan, Edward. As he watched, Kenelm glanced to his right, leading Will to believe that at least one other figure stood where he could not see them.

Lorcan leaned over Will and looked down, and Oliver, seeing Will's horrified expression, also risked peering out briefly. Will saw him lean back and mouth a silent prayer. This was not looking good. On the plus side the two boys were still alive, but for how long was debatable. The strange ritual was already in progress and there was no more time to fret and plan. An ear-wrenching, high-pitched note suddenly pierced the air and then another. Not a scream of pain as Will thought for one horrible second. This was sung, as became apparent as more followed, modulating up and down in some fearful sequence. It all but knocked Will out, and once Toby and Busby had hauled him backwards out of the way, Lorcan could see why. The singer was Masanae.

It should have been erotic, for the leading female of the Abend was dressed in only the sheerest of shifts, and little was left to the imagination. It was anything but. There was nothing feminine about Masanae, and such exposure only served to highlight just how alien she was compared to the normal women the watching men had known. She was stood in the ripped gap in the wall opposite to them across the gaping hole, looking down at four quarters of the black pool with Edward in the centre. Lorcan urgently gestured the men back to the sides and offered up a prayer of thanks that she had been so absorbed in her own ritual that she had not noticed them. Behind her Quintillean then appeared out of the gloom, although the watching men thought that the Power-room was actually getting brighter. Not from any natural light though. An eerie, sickly red light seemed to throb within the space rising from the pool, and by its pulsating glow it was possible to make out four other forms.

"Acolytes," Lorcan mouthed to Oliver, but saw Evans at the young Knight's side nod with more understanding.

Masanae's caterwauling was showing no sign of abating, but to their astonishment she stepped off the side of the pit and began to move as if she were descending invisible stairs. It had to be some summoning of the Power which remained unseen to the others, although Quintillean came to the edge and stood staring downwards with a hungry, maniacal gleam in his eyes. Two of the acolytes followed Masanae down, bearing a pair of glittering knives each. Whatever the knives were made of it was not metal. Oliver found it hard to take his eyes off them. They could be glass or some kind of pure quartz he speculated, then saw the channel in each and realised that these were no mere ritual ornaments. The other two acolytes descended and disappeared from view.

When they reappeared it was to lay Edward back onto one of the sloping spurs of obsidian, but with his head downwards.

"Shit! They're going to drain their blood!" Toby hissed urgently, breaking the silence in his desperation.

No-one doubted him, for Toby had enough experience of butchery to know what he was talking about, although this suspicion was confirmed when Cody suddenly began jabbing a finger downwards and they realised what he had spotted. Clear goblets made of the same substance as the knives were sitting on the side of the obsidian pool. Even the hardened Ergardian men gulped, feeling their stomachs churn as the understanding bludgeoned its way in that the two Abend meant to drink the victims' blood.

Mercifully Masanae was still howling up a storm of Power below, and Toby had remained unheard by any of the DeÁine. However the veteran archer was now frantically gesturing upwards, even as he grappled for a particular arrow out of the quiver strung over his back. Lorcan saw what he meant. The original plastered ceiling must have been brought down over the great hole, possibly if Masanae or Quintillean had used Power to blast the floor out of existence. Now the roof beams of the great temple building were exposed in the eerie light. Without any need for further words, Cody and Trip began sorting out arrows to find the ones they wanted too, and Dusty and Jens each undid a loop of fine rope they had slung over their shoulders. Catching on, Topher and Mitch also began preparing to shoot, while Colum began threading rope from Evans and Waza into eye-holes cut into the special arrows. At this range there would be no problem imbedding the arrows into the roof beams deep enough for the ropes to take the weight of a man.

"What're you doing?" a groggy Will asked urgently, gradually coming round now that Masanae was no longer in direct line with him.

Lorcan leaned over and whispered in his ear. "We're going to fire rope lines into the roof beams. Then we'll drop down and grab the boys while the archers provide covering shots. It's not perfect as plans go, but it's the only option we've got left. We'll drop three men, each with one extra line just in case one gets fouled. Dusty, Jens, Busby, Newt, Waza and you will man the ropes – two to each. The six archers will shoot like mad to cover us, and then three of them will join you hauling the rescuers up. That'll be me, Evans, and one other."

Oliver was immediately gesturing that that would be him, for Hamelin was the heavier of the pair but also the stronger man to have on the ropes. Will shook his head to try to clear it. This was not how he had intended the rescue to go. To plunge three men right into the path of the Abend was insanity – but what other choice did they have left?

"You'll get blasted!" he growled softly in protest.

"What choice do we have," hissed Oliver in despair. "At least we signed up voluntarily, knowing that one day we might have to make a choice like this. Wistan and Kenelm didn't! We might just survive. They certainly won't if we don't act now!"

Chapter 14

Too High a Price

New Lochlainn: Earrach

"Hang on," Will croaked to the others desperately. "Are there any others down there? …Victims, I mean? What's going on with them and the boys?"

Oliver risked a snakelike slither to the opening and made darting glances downwards. "Whatever's going on," he reported when he was well back within the room's darkness again, "it's happening to Edward first. The boys are pretty terrified but there's no sign of them being prepared immediately. There are two other young men at the other shelves whom we can't easily see, and two more in chains whom the acolytes seem to be bringing round to where we'll see them in a second. All of them look older than Kenelm – but then he looks far younger than his age. They're certainly not boys of Wistan's age. They've moved Wistan out of the way to do whatever it is to Edward. At the moment he's right by Kenelm. There's no better time than now."

"Other innocents?" groaned Will, fearing that their rescue attempt had once more become complicated. In all conscience there was no way he could seize Wistan and Kenelm and leave others equally as undeserving to such a fate.

Lorcan now risked a covert glance down and retreated with a frown on his face. "I'm not sure," he whispered back, "but I think those others are Edward's cousins." He screwed his eyes up in concentration as he desperately tried to dredge up the memory. "Yes, I'm sure they are. I saw them once when I was on patrol over in Brychan. …Ah yes, I have it now! The two outside the pool are Uriah and Godber! Edward's supposed right-hand men in the north. How in the Islands they got to be here is anyone's guess, but we don't need to worry about abandoning them. They're complete and utter bastards! As are the two trussed up with our two lads.

"All of them are suspected of committing several murders within the royal family, and from an age when no normal child would think of such things. Even though I'm only going on descriptions, I'm certain they're also cousins of Edward – which is no doubt why they've become so twisted!

The ones in the pool are younger and identical twins – so I guess that's why they're being used first. That's why they're unmistakable. The older two must be there as spares."

"Twins," Will breathed, wishing his groggy head would clear, "and royal at that! That must be potent! But it explains why Masanae didn't bother hunting you lot too hard when you stole the girls out from under her nose. She had spares with her! Or given that you didn't think they travelled to Bruighean with your lot, maybe they'd already been captured, were sent on ahead, or came after. Not that it matters now."

Hamelin nodded. "It makes sense. For choice, two females to match Quintillean's two males. Ideally she must've thought that would keep the balance. Not let Quintillean have the ascendancy over her. But in the event of an emergency any royal would do." He looked to Lorcan. "Are the twins any more innocent than their older cousins?"

Lorcan snorted softly. "Lethi and Wicga? If anything they're worse than the older two. If those two Abend think they've got purity down there they're in for a nasty shock. It's said those two killed their two baby brothers when they were mere children themselves – and I mean only six or seven years old, not teenagers! Shed no tears for them! No-one else will! Edward was grooming them in his own image. The four of them could've been in Arlei to see him when the Abend got there, or were somewhere in the south closer to the border earlier in the year and got taken then. Maybe Edward even set them up!"

"I'd bet, from what I've heard, that Edward gave them up in a heartbeat if he thought it'd save his own skin, or curry favour with his captors," Evans added drily. "Mind you, I'd reckon it'd be a safe bet that the cousins would equally have changed sides in an instant if they thought it would save them from Edward's fate. Especially if they knew he'd betrayed them. Loyalty isn't a family virtue! They might even have come here willingly if they weren't aware of the whole plan for them. Maybe that's why we never heard of them being tortured?"

"Aye, but they won't have any DeÁine blood in them. Not like Edward!" Toby pointed out, coming forward with his bow all ready and taking aim carefully. "That might make them even more valuable from the Abend's point of view. The Maker only knows what it is they're doing down there, but if they realised Edward is part DeÁine, maybe that makes him redundant as far as the main ritual goes?"

Will acknowledged the information but did not stop to think much about it now. All that mattered here and now was getting their own two lads out of there, especially since they knew there were no others needing their aid. Gritting his teeth, Will inched his way to where he could see downwards. Right behind him he could feel Cody and Trip kneeling, pressing against his legs on either side to get the best angle as they took aim.

"Wait!" he hissed urgently. "They're going for Edward first, so let them get into what they're doing. Let's let them get really engrossed. The surprise will be all the greater for that."

With all the participants now down below where they could not look across into the men's hiding place, there was less need to be covert, and the men edged forwards to watch for the right moment. In ululating tones Masanae was swaying in front of Edward, an ordinary dagger raised high above her head in both hands. From above, the men now heard a gloating Quintillean hiss in Islander at the terror-stricken king,

"Now you pay for your insolence! You …*DeÁine*? You have enough to bind this spell and that's all! You've saved us sacrificing one of our valuable own! Die, you Island cur!"

And Masanae brought down the blade in a vicious arc to plunge it straight into Edward's neck. The arc of blood shot into the pool and the four acolytes immediately began chanting and spreading it around the walls of the pool with their hands. The screams of all the intended victims rent the air as they got a vivid view of what was in store for them all too soon. The twins Lethi and Wicga had less time to fret than the others. No sooner had Edward's initial gush of blood been smeared about, than the four acolytes took an arm each and held the two boys fast at their respective stations. Edward's body was thrown into a corner, but Kenelm and Wistan were still huddled together at the point where Kenelm had been stood. The two spare victims by now were chained to bolts in the walls and unable to move at all, apart from thrashing in panic. Even if Will's party had wanted to rescue them, there was no chance of being able to now.

Lorcan looked to the archers, and gave a nod while holding a hand up with three fingers extended. The bow strings were pulled back and aim was taken before their eyes swivelled to Lorcan's hand. He leaned out and watched as the acolytes manhandled the twins into position. One of the crystal knives had been placed by each shelf, but it was not Masanae who made a move towards them. She now stepped into the black pool along with Quintillean, who carried the goblets. Extending her hand, the air about her seemed to shimmer unnaturally as she cast her hands about, forming the smeared blood into a smooth, reflective coating on the basin. Then she loosed a bolt of the Power straight into the one boy. He appeared to resonate with it until he was almost glowing from within, at which, upon a triumphant screech from Masanae, an acolyte seized the crystal knife. As the boy gave a gurgling scream and died, the knife was plunged straight into the artery in his neck, and Masanae and Quintillean lunged forward to catch the blood in the goblets. The air around them was almost incandescent with Power, but it also muffled the sounds to the watchers above.

Seizing the moment, Lorcan's fingers counted down …three …two …one, and the great bowstrings thrummed with their own power, embedding the special stumpy arrows deep in the high beams. Fine lines snaked aloft with them, and in an instant the men were pulling them through the arrows' eyelets, and doubling up the attached ropes for the rescuers to use. Lorcan, Evans and Oliver already had their ropes in their hands and were preparing to leap when Kenelm moved. What possessed the young monk to act now of all times was never discovered, but something seemed to snap inside of him. With a howl, he sprang towards Masanae as she summoned her Power for the other twin, and he tried to grasp her arm. Furious, she brushed him off as though he was no more than a fly and spun her hand towards him. Above them, the three rescuers tottered on the brink of the drop and reached back to their fellows to halt their swing outwards. All knew it was pointless to attack Masanae herself – which was when it happened.

Kenelm was thrown backwards and fell supine on the blood-sticky obsidian, from where he suddenly saw the rescuers high above. His eyes flashed recognition and the words 'help me, brother' appeared on his lips. Masanae never noticed what he was looking at, no doubt assuming he was making some feeble prayer. Not the watchers above, though. As Masanae raised her hand and the glow around it rose to dazzling brilliance and she aimed it at Kenelm, instead of the remaining twin, Hamelin shoved Oliver aside and launched himself out into the void, dropping between Kenelm and Masanae as the ball of Power left her. The Power scythed into him and rent him in two even before he hit the basin, his blood showering the Abend and their victims alike, blinding them.

It saved Kenelm, but far stranger, something beyond the ken of the rescuers caused a reaction in the Power, for some of it seemed to ricochet back into Masanae, knocking her over. The rest of the Power then flattened itself out into layers and splatters, made visible by the blood upon it. Edward's Power-drenched blood turned as black as the basin it coated, but the flying shattered remains of Hamelin and his blood sizzled and sparked intense white as they landed on it, as though some incredible heat was made upon contact. As the ensuing vapours and particles shot upwards once more and collided with more of the Power, they appeared to shatter Masanae's summoning into shards, becoming a lethal shower beyond anyone's control. The Abend stood in the middle of a fire storm of energy, barely able to defend themselves much less control anything.

Much later Oliver was to speculate that Hamelin's response had been triggered by that fatal word 'brother'. The death of his brother Lucas had remained with him throughout the last few months, with no time to grieve – an innocent, much like Kenelm, whom it had been impossible to save. Kenelm had no doubt meant 'brother' in purely monastic terms, but it had hit the raw spot in Hamelin's soul.

Now though, as Oliver screamed in horrified shock, the archers swallowed their rising bile, seized the moment, and began raining down arrows on the DeÁine below, regardless of rank. Stunned and appalled, their training nonetheless kicked in, and they took advantage of the opening Hamelin's death had given them. Newt and Busby took the strain on a rope as Lorcan launched himself out, with Dusty and Jens doing the same for Evans as he too plummeted ground-wards. Waza tore the rope from Oliver's stunned grip and threw it to Toby, as Topher dropped his bow and leapt to aid Waza in swinging Toby down. The archer had his bow in one hand and no sooner had his feet touched the basin then he nocked an arrow and swung it to take aim for any threat. Lorcan had knotted his rope around Kenelm's waist already and was signalling for the monk to be hauled to safety, while Evans had Wistan nearly roped up too.

While Cody and Trip continued in their murderous onslaught from the edge of the hole, Mitch and Colum joined in hauling Kenelm upwards. The young monk was a dead weight, too shocked to even begin to try to help himself. Evans had much the easier task with Wistan. Despite shaking like a leaf the boy was obeying instructions, was resolutely not looking at all the blood but upwards, and was holding himself upright along the rope so that he at least did not swing about like a leaf in a gale. He also had his hand out ready and waiting as soon as he got near to the ragged edge of the hole.

By now the acolytes were dead, each punctured by many arrows but also by the Power. Power which had been thrown into convulsions, for Quintillean, the rescuers realised, had been blasting the second twin as Masanae had refocused on Kenelm. Both drawings had begun the same, but then had shot off charged shards of Power as though they had been exploded from within when Hamelin and Lethi had died simultaneously within the Powered confines of the basin. Shafts of needle-fine Power appeared to have been drawn to the acolytes as the summoning blasted erratically outwards. Ricochets off the walls were flung back into Masanae and Quintillean, who seemed to be magnets for the rebounding fragments. Now, having dropped between the two Abend, it saved the Order's men from stray rebounds, as the pair frantically tried to shield themselves with what little they could summon without making the fireworks worse.

The two of them were too battered to make much in the way of a focussed assault on the three men before them, although they had enough of their abilities to still make it impossible for the Order's men to kill them. Lorcan's sword seemed to be hitting an invisible barrier however he angled his blade at them, while arrows clattered uselessly to the floor half an arm's length away from the Abend's bodies. There were still murky swirlings of what looked like black vapour swirling low in the room, and there had been a brief flash of pure gold at the trigger point with Hamelin, but the remaining Power had become almost tangible, opaque, air-born strands, which refused to coalesce again no matter what Quintillean or Masanae did.

With the Power diffused, Will had managed to stagger to his feet to get to the edge just as Wistan appeared. Grabbing his hand he pulled his former ward into his arms and hugged him swiftly before untying the knotted rope. With a gentle shove he sent Wistan back into the gloom, as he reached out and helped the others drag Kenelm into the upper room. As the ropes were sent back down to the rescuers, Will had to drag Kenelm by the scruff of his clothing out of the way. A sharp backhanded slap did nothing to rouse the monk out of his stunned stupor, and Will left him to turn and add his strength to the ropes alongside a still sobbing Oliver – determinedly helping even if he could barely see what was happening beneath through the tears.

Moments later the three men from below appeared back over the edge. Ripping the ropes out of the arrows above, the men grabbed what weapons they had and fled the room. For the moment the staggering and disorientated Masanae and Quintillean were trapped in the sealed room they had created, but that would only last as long as they were incapacitated. As soon as one or other of them could summon enough Power to create the invisible staircase again, they would be out and hunting. Dusty had hoisted Kenelm up over his shoulders and was running bent almost double, with Jens and Waza on either side supporting him, while Topher, Newt and Busby scouted ahead. Will had Wistan in his arms, and was running for all he was worth with Oliver beside him, leaving Lorcan with Evans, Toby, Cody and Trip as the rearguard to watch for pursuit.

They had got down the first flight of stairs, and were just at the top of the stairs down to the temple, when an explosion sounded like thunder right behind them.

"Run!" screamed Lorcan.

Rather than walk out, Masanae or Quintillean had decided to simply blast the nearest wall out of the way to create an exit. Another resonant thump and the sound of falling masonry announced that the Abend were almost certainly now clear of any blockages and on their way for vengeance. The men practically fell down the stairs and into the temple, then pelted out into the courtyard garden. Blinking in the sudden bright daylight, they nearly cannoned into Kym and Teryl with a band of archers, all aiming their way. Without any need for explanations, Kym and Teryl shoved them to the right and the way out, and began a fast but ordered retreat with the archers covering them all the way.

They only just made it. As the last men reached the first landing of the steps down to the lower level, a jagged ball of Power-fire annihilated the balustrade above them. At the bottom they all streamed right again, heading for the bottleneck which Bertrand guarded – now praying the Abend would fall for the ruse in their befuddled state, and not expect them to retreat that way. If they did not this could get bloody very quickly!

A hefty young soldier took Wistan from Will, allowing him to resume control of the force, and turning, he was relieved to see that the experienced men of the Order had already spread themselves amongst the novice fighters. There was no panic and even a sense of purpose in the way the groups were moving. With any luck, Will prayed, they would not have too many casualties. Since that last ball of Power-fire in the garden there had been no sign of the Abend using it again, and he hoped like mad that they had exhausted themselves, or were too damaged after the backlash, to summon any more for a while.

At the narrowing of the passage they shot past Bertrand, who gave a piercing whistle as the last man fled through, and a rumbling thump, along with the descent of temporary darkness until they emerged from under the arch, told of the way being blocked behind them.

"Everyone else is clear!" Bertrand informed Will as he ran up behind him. "The other way's blocked already."

"Great! Let's get out of here!" Will gasped.

They brought up the rear with a few men, and were heartened to see that Friedl had been busy too. As they ran through the inner gates these were swung closed behind them, but only after two waiting carts filled with hay and rags were dragged across to block the way and set alight. Heavy bars were dropped in the gates' sockets, and for the first time Will had cause to bless the DeÁine's taking of slaves, for it meant that they had had reason to want to prevent escape as much as attack. The inner gates were there to keep slaves in and as such were barred from the gatehouse side, not the palace's, and were therefore able to be barricaded against pursuit.

The retreating force did not stop running until they reached the Salu Maré. There they streamed onto the rafts and began hauling themselves out to the safety of the first island. The water of the great loch was hardly as salty as the sea, but it was brackish enough that Will hoped it would offer some protection from the Abend too. As willing hands winched them across, Bertrand and Friedl looked about them.

"Where are Hamelin and Theo?" Friedl demanded in a voice weighted with concern at what he saw. Oliver was sat on the deck with his head between his knees, shaking.

"Hamelin's gone," Will said sadly. "Masanae killed him." As the two Knights stared at him in horror he could only add, "but without him Kenelm would've died and possibly Wistan too." Then it registered what they had said. "But where's Theo? Isn't he here?"

Kym touched him lightly on his sleeve to draw his attention to himself.

"I'm so sorry, sire," the young Knight said. "When Teryl and I took the men downstairs, we found a right commotion going on. I'm afraid Theo disobeyed your orders. He took about half the men and went in after the remaining Hunters in the palace."

Will and the others groaned in dismay.

"Stupid fucking idiot!" Will swore, more in grief than anger. "What possessed him to do that? Didn't he think there was enough glory or something?"

Teryl joined his friend. "No, sire, not quite like that. At least he disobeyed you with some reason. Some of the men we spoke to said they saw the remaining Hunters trying to get out of upper windows in the palace. It looked like they'd worked out that the temple was under attack, and were trying to come your way by following the route over the roofs which we and Oliver took earlier. Apparently Theo was worried that they might make it round to the rooms with windows overlooking the temple gardens. He led men in to try and stop them."

Kym nodded. "The men who were just coming back out when we got to them said that the remaining Hunters were all dead, but we lost about twenty of our men in the fight. Theo was one of them."

Will bowed his head. "I understand," he sighed. Then he looked about him again. "Aren't we short even more than that?"

Kym gave him what he hoped was a reassuring smile – although the way he felt at the moment it was unlike he was succeeding. "That was Labhran and Sioncaet's doing, General. They saw Theo's fight up on the roofs, and apparently there was this strange swirling going on in the air above the temple which Sioncaet recognised as some major nasty summoning going on. They tore up to the gatehouse, and told Friedl to block the main way and then get all of his men out of there straight away. They also sent a man up to what remained of Theo's men and us, and got all but the few men you and I took out of the temple down and out of the palace complex. Bertrand sent most of his own men off when he heard the first explosion – that's why the ferry was just coming back when you lot ran down onto the beach."

Bertrand himself came up to Will, grave-faced at the loss of his two friends but still in control. "May the Ash guide the fallen to the Summerland, but we've had far fewer losses than we might have. Twenty three went down with Theo, and we've about forty or fifty with nasty wounds, but none of those are likely to prove fatal unless they fester."

"Twenty-five dead in all," Sioncaet said, appearing from the other side of the crowded ferry where he had been helping tend the wounded. "That's remarkably good considering you've just taken novice troops up against two of the most powerful Abend." He took pity on Will's haggard expression. "I know every man down is a man who won't go back to his family, Will. There's never a way that that's good. But think back to other battles you've fought. When was the last time you went in with the odds so heavily stacked against you and came out of it this lightly?"

Will exhaled heavily. "I know." He looked over to where a distraught Labhran was now being comforted by a still-grieving Oliver. "But I can't help but think that maybe we paid too high a price this time."

Bertrand stood by his side nodding grimly. "I know what you mean. We'd just thought we'd got Labhran convinced that everything would be better this time. And much of that was due to Hamelin refusing to let him sink into despair. They may not've known one another for long, but I'm thinking that Labhran may miss Hamelin even more acutely than we do. Except maybe Oliver. For him Hamelin was the older brother he'd never had as well as his best friend. But at least we all have happy memories of him to hang on to, as we do for Theo. I don't think Labhran has a single happy thought left in him now."

By now Oliver and Labhran were united in the depths of their grief, and a small space surrounded them even in the cramped conditions on the ferry as the men tried to give them some room to themselves.

With everyone safely evacuated to the island, for most of them it was time to collapse into an exhausted sleep. No matter how much Will had tried to prepare his fledgling army, no spoken word was the same as encountering the gut-wrenching fear of coming up against the Abend and Hunters in the flesh, and as a first time experience of combat it would have been a severe challenge even for better-trained troops than these.

Despite still recovering from his earlier ordeals, Jacinto felt guilty beyond belief that others had sacrificed their lives while he had remained behind on the shore with Saul at the ferry. Nor was he unmoved by the grief amongst the Prydein Knights at the loss of their two friends. He doubted that anyone had mourned his disappearance from the Knights a few months ago in anything like the same way.

However, with his new found insight he realised that maybe the one thing which he could do to help was to take some of the burden of command from the grieving Knights. With that in mind, he spent all of the rest of the day doing things he once would have scorned to descend to. Walking amongst the novice fighters, he showed man after man how to clean their bloodied weapons, or chivvied others into preparing campfires so that an evening meal could be made. Others he sent to draw water to be heated on the growing fires so that the minor wounds could be washed clean. Belatedly it was impressed upon his conscience how much hard work it took to be constantly supervising someone, and he thought back to how much effort he had cost the likes of Esclados and shuddered within. No wonder they'd become exasperated with him!

Yet also for the first time his efforts were appreciated, and he felt a rush of happiness when Will came over and thanked him for taking care of the men. Praise had been understandably absent for much of his career, and it was a novel pleasure to discover how gratifying it was to have earned it. Mercifully Saul took charge of cooking for the Knights – Jacinto had no illusions of what kind of disgusting gloop he might have created! But once they had eaten, and Oliver, Bertrand and Friedl had clustered around Labhran and Sioncaet for mutual consolation, he dared to broach a worrying subject with Will and Saul.

"What do you plan to do now, General?" he asked cautiously.

Will scrubbed his hands through his hair and sighed heavily. "Good question! …We can't remain here for long, that's for sure."

Saul took a long draught of the hot brew he was clutching in a battered mug, before saying, "I'll go and scout for you tomorrow." As Will made to protest he waved him to silence. "Don't worry, I'm not going to go by ferry. We found a battered old rowing boat pulled up on the shore while we were waiting for you. We brought it across here towed behind the ferry coming back. I'll row across just before dawn and have a look around. One man won't be noticed."

Will frowned. "Very well. But not tomorrow! You can go the day after. Give Masanae and Quintillean chance to get out of there. It'll be safer."

However Saul had other ideas. "No, I'm sorry I don't think that's the case at all. They'll go back to that Power-filled room and probably use it to summon assistance from Ralja. What I want to do is make sure they're still *inside*! Make sure the gates are still barred and that they haven't blasted a hole through the outer walls somewhere. The best thing we can do is get away *right now*. Now, before they have chance to recover their strength. You got lucky in there, because they have to channel the Power in specific ways to perform sacrifices, and having drawn it one way in order to work their ritual, it was difficult to turn its nature to what they need in order to go on the attack.

"But if you wait, you'll find yourselves up against a war-mage with his Power all purposely lined up to be used that way. Quintillean was always weak in the rituals and subtle uses – as are most of the male Abend, which is why they need the witches. Give him something to fight against, though, and you walk straight into his strongest abilities. And after what you've just done he won't underestimate you again."

"What do you think we should do?" Jacinto asked Saul. "After all, you've had more time to watch this lot than any of us."

Saul hardly needed to pause for thought. "Go back across to Tokai!" he said firmly. "If anyone's come there since we've been gone at least it'll be only ordinary mortals!"

"Good point," Will sighed, "and in a way it fits with what I'd sort of half-planned anyway." He looked to Jacinto and Saul, and then over his shoulders to the others and to where the sleeping forms of Wistan and Kenelm lay. "I want to send those two back home as fast as I can. But that can't be via the southern route. Not with a whole DeÁine army sitting in the way. So I'm going to send them with Sioncaet and a stout band of bodyguards back up to Borth Castle. For speed we'll give them all the horses, except the ones we need for the pregnant women – at least the beasts should still be out in the fields where we left them."

"What about the rest of us?" Jacinto wondered.

Will answered with a question. "How well do you know the ways south, Saul?"

The former spy gave a slow dip of his head. "Fairly well. I know the main roads. I wouldn't guarantee to lead you true on some of the local routes around the maze of rivers beyond the Eldr Forest, but I could find the major ports if you wanted."

"The bigger towns?" Will asked.

"Yes, most of them, I think. I haven't been there in many years, but it won't be like the places will have changed much. There's no incentive to build under the DeÁine."

"Good!" Will drew a crude map in the soft earth at his feet. "Remember that message we found? Another fleet is on its way here. I want to raise the countryside in the south. If we do nothing more than deny them a landing place on the south shore, it'll be a help to the others. Cross of Swords! I hope that bloody raven Oliver sent out found someone! That's another reason to send Sioncaet back. He'll be believed if he has to break the bad news."

Saul nodded in agreement again. "In that case, I think Tokai is even more of a good place to go to, at least to start off with. We can march around the coast of the Salu Maré and pick up the main road going south. It's got the advantage that it crests a long ridge just before it comes down to meet the road from Ralja. That way we'll be able to see quite clearly if Quintillean and Masanae are coming along that road. If we went by the road from here at Kuzmin and passed Ralja Palace, we'd have to have scouts out at every hour of the day and night for fear of those two bastards coming up on us from behind. The men would be jumping at their own shadows by the third day.

"They'd be no good for anything by the time we reached the south, and if we have the Abend snapping at our heels, they'd also soon know if we've turned off. They wouldn't have to bother scouring the countryside looking for us, and we could find we have the remnants of the Bruighean army coming after us faster than we need. And another thing, if we go the Tokai route and it is belatedly discovered, I'd bet good money on the Abend assuming that we'd try to go south-east straight back into Brychan – and they'd be convinced of that south-eastern route because that's the way runaway slaves always go. So they would then hunt for us in that direction once they get more Hunters and troops, not the road to the south.

Will nodded. "Good. That's the kind of information I needed. Tokai it is, then."

Come the morning most were only too glad to be going away from Kuzmin again. However, Sioncaet had rumbled that something was afoot and was none too pleased when Will told him what.

"What about Labhran?" he demanded in a furious whisper, as he and Will chivvied folks onto ferries. "Don't you think he's suffered enough? He should come back with me!"

But Will shook his head firmly. "No! …Oh don't get me wrong, Sioncaet. My heart goes out to him. More than most I understand what he's been through. But don't you think it would be worse for him to go home now, and have nothing else to do all day but replay the whole ghastly tragedy over and over again in his mind? I think that's been half his trouble all along.

"You've heard Oliver and the others. Time and again Labhran assumed the worst, when in fact they were able to achieve an awful lot. Now he needs to see for himself that Hamelin's sacrifice wasn't in vain. See it with his own eyes. And if not, then to at least die trying. You said yourself he couldn't go on as he was, dying a little death inside every day. No. He's coming with me. This time he can play the DeÁine Donn without any of the grief, and I'll be the second-in-command pushing and shoving every recruit into shape. He'll be better for doing something. It's for his sake I'm doing this, not mine."

"Well, then I'll stay too!"

"No!"

"*No*? …I'm not one of your men to be ordered around, Will!" Sioncaet pointed out firmly.

Will blinked. "Flaming Trees! I didn't mean it like that, Sioncaet! I'm sorry, I'm just too bloody tired to be thoughtful or tactful that's…"

"…No, no! I'm sorry! I'm tired too, and I've done nothing like the fighting and organising you've done! I should've known you wouldn't…"

"…it's just that…,"

The two friends stood in silent sympathy and exhausted confusion for a second, before Will tried again to explain.

"I need your authority to raise the warning," he said more gently. "If Brego doesn't know what's heading our way, I daren't send someone from the Order who might get sidelined by an officious commander on the way. None of the men here are senior enough to make themselves heard, but you've just put your finger on why you can."

Sioncaet nodded in comprehension. "Because since I'm not from the Order they can't make me stay where I don't want to, or order me off somewhere else."

"Exactly!"

"Very well, I'll go then. But I'll think of some dreadful fate for you if Labhran comes back with what's left of his sanity in tatters!"

Will solemnly stared Sioncaet in the face. "If Labhran comes back in that state, it'll be because I'm already feeding the crows. I won't fail him while I have breath in my body. I *promise* you I'll give him something to channel all that grief into – and young Oliver as well. Just take the boys back out of harm's way for *me*! Please!"

When they got back to Tokai, though, there was resistance from an unexpected quarter. Wistan refused point blank to go with Kenelm, and no amount of cajoling from the Knights or Will would shift his resolution.

"Please, General Montrose! Let me come with you," he begged.

"Why?" a perplexed Will asked, desperately trying to grasp what had changed, and after his encounter with Sioncaet not wanting to act too heavy-handed with the lad. "I thought the whole reason you ran off from Abbot Jaenberht was to be with Kenelm? Andra said you always wanted to be part of a family and have brothers and sisters. Well Kenelm's your cousin, at least."

The young boy met Will's eyes gravely. "I know. And I did. …I do! …But Kenelm …" he sighed. "It's more like *me* looking after *him*!"

Will had to admit the lad had a point. At every turn Wistan had done all he could to get away from Quintillean, but Kenelm had proved to be dangerously slow to catch on as to what was going on around him. It had not occurred to Will that Wistan might feel responsible for his older cousin, but now the idea had been voiced, he could see what a strain it must have been for him. The poor lad had gone from being tied to his mother, to learning how to survive not just alone, but with someone even more naive than himself to watch out for. He had been doing some very fast growing up in a fearsomely short space of time.

"Can I make another point?" Labhran interrupted. He and Oliver had joined in the morning briefing despite being red-eyed and looking exhausted in both mind and body. "Masanae probably has a good sense of what Wistan and Kenelm feel like to her through the Power. If you keep the two of them together, if she isn't too wounded from yesterday you may be giving her a nice easy target to track. But if you separate them, and especially if she's a bit woozy, then she may find it much harder to pin down what direction either of them is going in."

Will made a growling noise in the back of his throat and then fixed Wistan with a feeble attempt at a stern gaze. "Your Uncle Ruari's going to have me in the stocks for the rest of my life if I let anything happen to you, you know that, don't you? I'm going to be a very old man who permanently stinks of rotten eggs and mouldy fruit!"

He was rewarded with a rather wobbly giggle from Wistan, but it was the first time the boy had even so much as smiled since being rescued. Belatedly Will realised that he and Matti might be the nearest thing Wistan had to go home to, and that made him swing the lad up and hug him. Against the odds, Wistan had somehow managed to put on a spurt of growth over the last months, and Will realised that if the boy was way too thin, he was also several inches taller than the last time Will had been this close to him. Wistan was definitely growing up.

"Alright, then! You'll come with us. Kenelm can go with Sioncaet, and be handed over to the first monastery he comes to for safe keeping." Privately Will thought Kenelm had possible always been a bit addled in the wits, and he held little hope that the would-be monk would recover much after this ordeal. A monastery was probably the safest place for him for the rest of his life.

Wistan, on the other hand, was showing signs of some of his father's fire and strength, not to mention his Uncle Ruari's. Will was far from convinced that being bundled off to a bunch of religious innocents – who might have him saying prayer to ask for forgiveness for sins beyond his control – would be a good thing. And where else would he go in these troubled time that was truly safe? Unless they stopped this coming threat, even Ergardia was unlikely to escape harm. Viewed that way, it did not seem so very wrong to keep Wistan where he wanted to be.

When he divided his force up, Will still sent as many men as they had spare horses for to go with Sioncaet and Kenelm. Labhran had made him think that sending a track-able trail north in the form of Kenelm, might be tempting to one of the Abend even now. And although it could prove useful to lure one of those into the arms of the Knights at the bottleneck around Borth, Sioncaet was too valuable an asset to risk him being taken on the way. Speed was of the essence.

"Get Kenelm out of New Lochlainn, but after that leave him wherever you think he'll be safe for now," Will instructed Sioncaet. "Any monastery in northern Brychan will have to do. I know that sounds callous, but I don't think he's exactly taking notice anymore, and if we don't turn back this coming invasion, it will only be weeks before everything we know is gone anyway. If you can shove him onto a ship to Ergardia, then well and good, but if not, then getting word to the Order and Brego is far more important."

Sioncaet had gravely embraced him before mounting up. "You take care of yourself, Will. And you Labhran!" he said to his friend standing on the other side of his horse. "Don't you dare do anything foolish! I'll be back as soon as I can, and with Brego and the whole Order if my powers of speech haven't deserted me to sway an argument!" He gripped Labhran's hand tightly for a second and leaned down to whisper softly. "I mean it, Labhran! Don't you dare go giving up! If you want to honour Hamelin's memory, then remember how he tried to turn everything to positive effect when you felt the blackness engulfing you. Keep his memory as a candle in your soul against it!"

Labhran raised his haunted gaze to Sioncaet's, and the minstrel saw something of a flicker of understanding in the sad eyes. Meanwhile, a few paces back Friedl and Bertrand were standing holding the head of Kenelm's horse while his escort mounted up.

"By the Trees, I don't envy Sioncaet!" Friedl sighed, flicking a glance up at the catatonic Kenelm.

Bertrand nodded. "It could be a very long ride. But I envy him even less if he's the one who has to break the news to Alaiz that Hamelin's dead."

Friedl's agonised gasp was enough of an indication that the young queen had temporarily been absent from his mind. Now, though, the possible complications battered their way into his mind, and he cringed at the thought. However, given where they were at the moment, neither Knight could do much to help. Instead they waved the mounted party off with the rest, and then went to help with the preparations to march.

For the first part of the journey, the women from the temple would be travelling with the main party under Will's command, along with the slave families. Saul had suggested that the safest place to leave them might be the ancient palace at Wyrdholt, on the western edge of the Eldr Forest. Unlike Mereholt, it had never found real favour with the Abend or the DeÁine nobility, perhaps because it was largely built of wood rather than stone. Whatever the reason, there were likely to be only a few household slaves there. Those who wished to join the rebels would be welcome, and the others would be taken onwards as prisoners when Will and the main force left for the south coast. Will and Labhran had agreed to this plan after Saul had pointed out that, should any attackers come to Wyrdholt, the easiest thing to do would be to evacuate into the forest and then come back out once any danger was gone. The undergrowth was too dense for easy hunting, so they would not have to go far, and even for the pregnant women this should not prove too arduous as long as it did not happen within days of a birth.

However, like Wistan, Heledd and Briezh refused point-blank to be left behind, albeit at a later stage. Both sisters declared that they were more than capable of keeping up with the army, and so Will decided that they should be in charge of looking after Wistan. As the long procession of men and families wound its way south out of Tokai, Will and Labhran took the lead, leaving Lorcan and Bertrand to take care of ensuring that nobody got left behind. It was the twenty-first of Earrach, and Will hoped to be at the cross-roads with the east-west road in eight days time.

When they got there on schedule, it was to see signs of a troop of riders having passed by at great speed only a couple of days previously.

"Sacred Trees! You were right, Saul!" Will said to the former member of the Covert Brethren. "If we'd done as I planned, they'd have ridden us down as we marched. As it is, they'll have passed here and not seen any sign of us coming down this road. So as you said, they'll think we went straight east. They must be hoping to cut us off at the Brychan Gap."

"Then they might be in for a nasty shock," Labhran said with as much optimism as he could force. Sioncaet's words about hanging on to Hamelin's memory were all that was getting him through each day at the moment, but for the first time he felt like it might just be possible to put it into practice. "You remember what Sioncaet said? About the snow all being up in the mountains of Brychan? Well look how much warmer it's got already! Those are daffodils nearly in bloom over there, and look at the trees way over in the forest!"

"Sacred Root and Branch!" Friedl exclaimed. "They're turning green! The trees are coming into leaf!"

"And that means a melt must be well underway," Bertrand added with a spreading grin. "You've got it, Labhran! They may be riding straight into the worst floods in living memory!"

"Let's hope so!" Will said with a grin of his own and a wink to Wistan, who was perking up remarkably well considering what he had been through. "Come on you lot! Four or five days should see us to Wyrdholt. We'll get the non-fighters settled there, and then we'll be off again."

"Where are we going to first?" Heledd asked, as she walked beside Will with Wistan between her and Briezh.

"Saul says we should skirt west of the Eldr Forest and come down to a small town called Curug," Will told them. "It's on one of the lakes that's part of the Sava River network. Not one of the biggest towns, but it's the furthest one east. That means we can work our way westwards and keep an eye on the coast. That way we'll be able to spot if the DeÁine fleet starts coming in towards the land. With any luck we'll get there by the tenth of Beltane."

"And what then Uncle Will?" Wistan wanted to know.

"Then, my lad, I start raising an army!" Will declared. "Even if there are DeÁine troops in the area, it's no place for a big set battle, and that's in our favour. We'll pick them off one bit at a time if necessary, but I'm betting that once the locals know that they have a choice, it won't be in the DeÁine's favour."

"And then what, Uncle Will?"

"Then? …Then we go and find what your Uncle Ruari's been up to, and whack the stuffing out of these bloody DeÁine once and for all!"

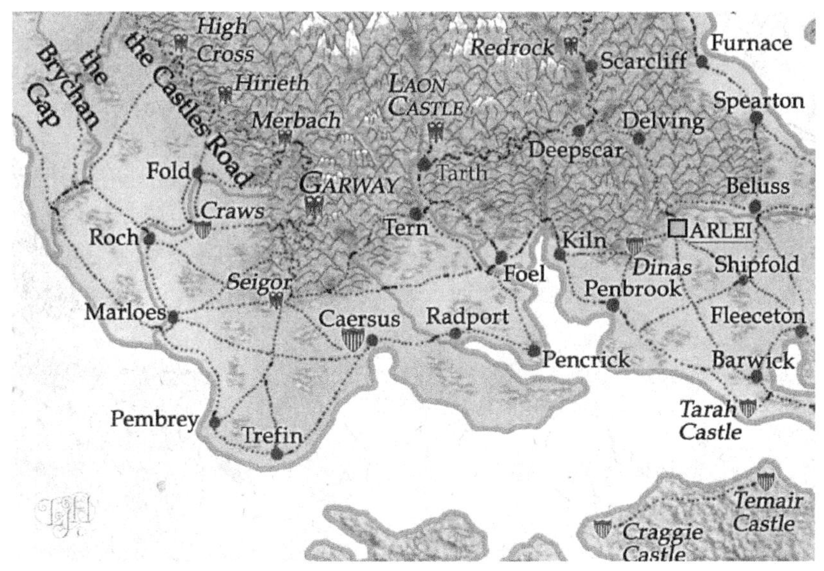

Chapter 15

Flood Defences

Brychan: mid-Earrach – early Beltane

Berengar and Warwick stood side by side on the battlements of Laon staring up at the snow-smothered mountains. A warm, soft wind was blowing up from the south-west, clipping the peaks and valleys in that direction as it blew towards them. Around them everything was dripping as the longed for thaw set in.

"Pray to the Trees that this wind stays gentle," Esclados observed from behind them. "That lot up there looks mighty precarious to me."

He was looking at the mountain range to the south-west of them which separated Laon from Garway. Garway had nothing to fear from this wind, since all its mountains lay to the north of it so that the wind was blowing the snow away from it, but Laon was right in the path of any avalanches a strong wind might bring.

"I'm glad now that I told Jonas not to take any chances, and get the Merbach men into the tunnels," Berengar agreed.

Aside from Laon and Redrock, Merbach was the only other Order castle with so much snow in a position to be able to roll over it if the wind proved fickle. But Merbach was by far the smallest of the three and the least likely to stand the weight of so much frozen water, hence the evacuation. A deep vibration suddenly shook the stones beneath their feet, and before they could turn and run for the stair, a great sheet of snow broke loose of its anchorage and began sliding down towards the river. Mercifully it was from the western slope of the east range which had been basking in the spring sunshine, and so it slid past Laon, although not by much.

"Sacred Trees!" Warwick intoned hoarsely, as he watched the great white tidal wave go past them, the top of it at the same level as them, despite the great height of Laon's walls. Where its edges briefly brushed the walls they could hear a scraping and grating, the very earth seeming to groan under its weight.

"I hope that fox you two have seen is watching out for us," Berengar said with feeling. "We might need some of his special powers to avoid disaster if this thaw happens too fast."

"I think he'll be there, never fear," Warwick consoled his friend, "but if he does come it'll mean that things really are bad, because I don't think he'll waste his energy on a social call, if you see what I mean."

Esclados had returned to the edge of the wall and was looking down.

"It's taken quite a bit of topsoil with it," he observed, looking at the side of the valley where the greatest height of the avalanche had now passed. "The ground's scoured down to the rock now, and there isn't a plant left in sight. I'm glad we've also got the folk of Tarth up here, because the town won't have much left standing at this rate. Do you think Tern will have evacuated to the south-west like you told them to?"

Berengar shrugged regretfully. "Who knows? It's too dangerous to send anyone out now to double-check. As long as they went part of the way towards Seigor, they should be safe from both the floods and the DeÁine, if they stay out of line of sight from the main road."

"There was still traffic heading back and forth to New Lochlainn when I was at Garway last week," Esclados confided.

"Well that won't last," Warwick said confidently. "I give it a week at the most before they're cut off and isolated from the homeland, and all the Hunters and Jundises in the world won't be able to help them then."

He paused as they walked around the circuit of the battlements to the opposite side to look down the valley. In the distance they could see a swirling mist of white as the avalanche continued its unstoppable journey downwards, throwing fine particles of snow into the air above it. To the west, the other side of the valley was still in comparative shade, but all three knew that once the avalanches undermined the weight of snow up there from its base, it would soon start moving too.

"Best get indoors," Warwick voiced all of their thoughts. "I think I'll issue an order that nobody is to use the top floor unless by express order. That way, if we hear the roof timbers starting to go, it'll give us time to get into the tunnels."

Berengar nodded his agreement, and the head of the Foresters hurried off to see to the welfare of his castle, leaving Berengar and Esclados to make their way to Berengar's new temporary office just inside the tunnel.

"When are we going to make our first strike?" asked Esclados, once they were in private.

"Soon, old bear, soon," Berengar said soothingly. "I want to start as much as you do, but I want the DeÁine to know that they have no choice any more. I want that sense of panic amongst their troops. As for when …well as soon as the worst of the avalanches have come off the south-facing cliffs of the mountains. I want to be able to march our men down the road here to whatever remains of Tarth, then eastwards on the mountain road towards Deepscar. We'll drop down on the fork which hits the coast between Foel and Kiln. Although the small river does drain into the sea there, I think on the whole the land is too high for much flooding at that point. That's where it's narrowest, and that's where it'll be hardest for their weight of numbers to be felt. It's where we can make them pay and pay for every inch of ground."

"What if they don't fight there?" Esclados worried. "The south-east has few rivers and so the low land there won't flood much. They could retreat down towards Mythvai or Amroth or Tarah, and once on the flatter countryside we'll have far less of an advantage. It could get bloody."

He did not need to say what he knew Berengar feared the most. They had had no news from the far south-east and that was where Cwen was. Esclados would be distraught if the girl (who was everything he would have wished a daughter to be) came to harm. But he knew what a mortal blow it would be to Berengar. To have waited so long to find someone he cared so deeply for, and then have her ripped away from him was harsh enough. If she then died, Esclados feared his oldest friend might never fully recover from the blow. Being Berengar he would carry on with his duties, but the man inside the uniform would only be a hollow shell of what had once been. And it would be all the worse if Berengar blamed himself for driving the DeÁine army straight at her.

Esclados was finding himself on his knees in the chapel on a nightly basis on all their accounts these days. The only relief was in finding Warwick's second-in-command, MacSorley, in there with him, and the two old soldiers shared their fears, both glad of finding someone else of a similar mind to confide in. MacSorley's firebrand of a daughter, Hawise, was a captain in charge of female Foresters, and would fight wherever Warwick sent them. As a father, MacSorley was torn between a fierce pride and fear that he would never see his only child again. A fear he found some solace in sharing with the understanding Esclados when he dared not voice it anywhere else.

However, battle was not upon them just yet. For four more sickeningly anxious days, they watched as wave after vast wave of snow broke loose from the slopes of the snow-laden mountains and thundered down towards the valleys. At one point Warwick moved the entire garrison of Laon into the tunnels for safety's sake, when it seemed like even the great castle of the Foresters would become engulfed. Yet by a whisker the worst passed them by. A wall of snow even higher than Laon's roofs ground it way down towards what had once been the town of Tarth – a wall which diminished for a brief while, then rose in strength again as snow, which had built up behind that which had already gone, broke free further up the River Tarth's valley.

For six long hours that day, an unending deluge swept past, rising and falling like the tide, but never halting. The very foundations of what was one of the most solid of the Order's castles felt like they were vibrating, and only waiting for one more rumble to shake themselves loose and follow the snow's decent to the sea. Only in the evening did the snow cascade slow and then peter out.

Mercifully, though, that was the worst of it. While a huge weight of snow still remained deeper within the mountain ranges it was not unstable, and there were mountain ridges between it and Laon. The danger from that would come if there was a sudden major thaw from the sheer weight of water, which would cascade down the river's course.

"We could end up with a whole new valley," Warwick observed. "That much water will carve its way even through rocks. It'll find the weak points and sheer boulders off, and gouge its way deeper into the river bed."

"Will the road hold?" Berengar asked, suddenly painfully aware that he had blithely assumed he would still be able to march men down to confront the DeÁine. Yet if the road got washed away, it could be a slow process even getting to a point where they might be able to find a place to fight.

"Pray!" was all Warwick could suggest, and they did.

A week had finally passed before they dared to send out scouts. The river was turbid and turgid, still excessively high and churning a thick, viscous brown with scoured rocks and soil tumbling through it. They blessed the road-makers of old then, for the road out of the castle clung part the way up the valley wall not down beside the river. Had it done that they would have been well and truly stuck, for the river was three times its normal winter depth, even in flood. Tarth was barely a day's ride away in normal weather, and so when the scouts did not return the following day the leaders became concerned. However, they were just about to send a larger party out to look for them, when the group of five riders pounded back into Laon two days overdue.

"By the Trees, sire, it's a mess down there!" the young Knight called out cheerfully, as he leapt from his horse and threw the reins to one of his men. "Tarth's gone for the most part! Anything built of wood must've been swept away in the first rushes of snow, because there's not a stick standing. Even the larger stone buildings have no roofs and the walls are battered about. But if there's a good thing it's that the snow took everything. There's hardly any debris on the road! What little there was left must've washed off with the melt, because it's gritty underfoot but not much worse than that."

"Thank the Trees for that!" Berengar breathed from the heart. "Why did you not come straight back?"

"Well, sire, it took us so little time to get to Tarth that we decided it might be worth carrying on. We talked it over, and my sergeant and one of my archers rode a bit of the way along that east-west rift-valley road towards Deepscar on what was the high road. That's bad news I'm afraid, sire. The first bit's alright, but they saw beyond there that there are other sections where whole lengths of the road have been swept away. Just sheared off rocks, not even the foundations of the road left which we could use.

"On the other side of the valley, where there were natural defiles already cut into the south face, the snow must've driven straight through them. The lads said that there're places where you can see right down to the main plain now where you never could before. And not all the snow's gone from those slopes by any means. All the rivers are up, but that east-west way is turning into a huge river all of its own. This must be how it got formed in the first place – perhaps with an ancient glacier when the mountains shifted – because no river's ever run across the mountain range's slopes like the way that irregular valley goes. ...Whatever that means for the future I don't know. ...What I do know is that nothing, and I really do mean *nothing*, is coming along the Deepscar road. But then that means we won't have to watch our backs, am I right?"

Berengar smiled. "Yes, you are, and for that I'm glad you used your initiative. You've saved me sending out another patrol to check that way. What did the rest of you do?"

"Went down to where the Tern bridge was," the young Knight answered and stopped to shake his head. "Lost Souls, if Tarth was bad Tern's bad in a different way. The rivers draining off the south face of the mountains already have the River Tern way up. If you want to march to Foel, sire, you're going to have to go prepared to make new bridges – or at least make extensions to get to the footings of the old ones. All the stone bridges still stand, but the water's washing right up to the arches with only the central spans still showing, and you can't get to the foot of them on either side by a long way. There's no way I reckon you'd dare march more than single file over them anyway, because any real weight on them – like a whole column of men marching four deep across – might be the end of what they can take. In fact I suspect within a day the water might be *over* those bridges! And the level's rising all the time, because the Tarth is draining into the Tern faster than it can all get to the sea. If we have any freak high tides it'll be disastrous, because the salt water will flow inland on the flood water. The land will be ruined for a generation."

Berengar looked to Warwick whose face mirrored his own dismay. This was as bad as they had feared and then some, for they had always hoped they could march out of Laon. Now that hope was dashed.

"Curses," muttered Warwick, "we're as stuck as the DeÁine! That's no good!"

Berengar rubbed his aching temples. "No, no! This won't do! We have to *think* our way out of this," he insisted. He turned again to the young

Knight. "Tell me, in your opinion could anything cross the rivers even now? Is the whole line of the flood plain really that? One big flood?"

Somewhat in awe that his Grand Master would ask his humble opinion, the young Knight gulped. "Well …yes, sire. …I think it *is* that bad, to be frank. …Unless it's a fish – and a big one at that – I don't see how *anything* would get across the River Tarn between what the DeÁine left of Foel and the ruins of Tern itself. And after that you're in the mountains …and you don't need me to tell you what they'll be like!"

Berengar was looking into the distance. Absentmindedly he dismissed the young Knight. "Thank you. That will be all. You've done very well, very well indeed. Draw your men extra rations of beer."

With Warwick and Esclados trailing in his wake, Berengar walked from the inner court of Laon and headed back for his office.

"This is going to be one Underworld of a plan," Esclados muttered quietly to Warwick, as they let Berengar have some space by hanging back and fielding those who sought the Grand Master's advice, or permission, for things which hardly warranted his attention.

"You think?" Warwick quizzed the older Knight. If anyone could tell what Berengar would do it was Esclados after all the years he had spent by Berengar's side.

The grizzled old warrior nodded confidently. "Oh yes. When he goes all distant like this it's a sure sign that he'll come up with something you never expected."

"Well I certainly hope so," Warwick wished fervently, "because we're running out of options here."

When they got back to the Grand Master's office in the tunnel, Berengar was staring down at the map of Brychan which lay permanently open on a table, a lantern suspended above it and another in his hand as he stared closely at a detail.

"Humph!" he breathed cryptically to himself.

"Here it comes!" whispered Esclados to Warwick, who looked back askance. How Esclados could know that was beyond him, but a moment later Berengar turned to face them, all indecision gone.

"We shall launch a pronged attack!" he declared. "We'll keep the fake letters coming out of the north, but in the meantime we'll sweep the road southwards clear of everything DeÁine until we reach Spearton as our marker on the east coast. At that point more of our men will come out of Redrock. I want it to look as though the whole of that garrison and a large number of survivors from the plain around Arlei are coming back to fight. We'll need to be a goodly number. Enough that the Donns won't just be able to send a token force this time. Enough that they'll get all their force up and out of Arlei to confront them. I don't want them to have chance to get into a place where we have to conduct a siege. The Redrock men will be the open show of force from the north-west of Arlei to tempt them. The Bere men from the north will sweep in westwards behind the DeÁine as they ride to confront the Redrock men, and trap them."

"Do we have time to manoeuvre everyone into position for that?" fretted Warwick. "And what of the river? I know fewer tributaries lead into the River Lei, but it rises further back into the mountains, and drains a greater volume of melt than the Tarth. It could get every bit as swollen. It won't do any good if I'm on this side with you, and the DeÁine are just sitting on the other bank at Arlei waving at us. Or even worse, with the Abend throwing balls of Power-fire at us."

"I know," Berengar said with a smile. "That's why we're not going to do it straight away. We have to have time to see just how bad these floods are going to get. The size and speed of them is now really starting to worry me, and nothing would be more catastrophic than to have freed our men from the snow only to have men we desperately need cut off by floods! So, …our first job, while we're waiting for the waters to peak, will be to clear the way west, because hopefully we'll be close enough to one or other of our castles to make a hasty retreat to if necessary. Therefore we shall ride in the opposite direction tomorrow, back to Garway through the tunnels. We'll then ride out and clear between the Tern and the Mer.

"Anything west of the River Mer is dead soon anyway, unless it goes higher through either High Cross or Hirieth. The lower reaches between the Mer and the Blane Water will become an impassable labyrinth of channels and isolated islands, and while the few locals will no doubt know the safe ways between them, I feel I'm not being too optimistic to think that the DeÁine and their minions won't! They'll be caught – trapped on pockets of higher ground! So I want all our men out on the high moors rooting out every last renegade slave and soldier.

"And not just for that tactical reason, either. I want the men alert and raring to go come our main attack, not sluggish from sitting on their arses in a castle all winter! And I want to hear from the castles at the west end of the Castles Road. To see if they've got into New Lochlainn. That way we'll know what we've got to deal with once we've driven the DeÁine out of

Brychan. This time, gentlemen, we're not stopping until we've driven the DeÁine into the sea!"

On the fifth day after Berengar had laid his plans, he sat on a frisky charger at the head of a great column of mounted men, all ready and waiting to ride out of Garway. As he dropped his raised hand, the trumpets rang out from the castle walls, and he led them in a steady walk out over the first drawbridge to the wide rock platform and over the second drawbridge. The Knights might only have been going out to clear the area, but Berengar had every man in full uniform with hawks before them where appropriate. He wanted the people of Brychan to know that they had not been deserted by the Order at this time. This was the first time the Order had managed to get out of their fortresses, and Berengar was determined that it would be as a show of force to instil confidence at this desperate time.

Rather than going straight down to Seigor, he turned them right onto the road towards the blackened and ruined fortress of Craws. Their first job was to make sure that no contingent of DeÁine had holed up there and taken over the great fort behind their backs. It was also a good chance to check on its bridge. That would give them a fair idea of how bad things would be lower down on the plain, but also going west back into New Lochlainn. Men from Merbach Castle had already reported that the evacuated town of Fold had suffered as badly as Tarth from the avalanches, and the high waters which had come in their wake. However, from there the river went in a long loop to get to Craws, and with plenty of lowland for the river to burst its banks over to ease the torrent. Berengar therefore had high hopes that the bridge at Craws might yet hold and allow them to get to the hopefully evacuated town of Roch.

As they descended from the foothills on the shorter run to Craws than the ride to Seigor, the flood water spread out before them like a great inland sea, sparkling in the spring sunshine and concealing the devastation which had already taken place. For as far as the eye could see there was water in one form or another. The greatest swathe was collected around the original river, but huge lakes had developed in every low lying pocket of land, and trickles ran between them making new water courses as they did so.

"May the Oak protect us!" Esclados wished fervently. "We need boats not horses!"

"There's the first Mer bridge," Warwick pointed out, extending his arm to the right to where the top of the bridge's centre span was just visible. Where it had come from and where it was going to, however, was only conjecture for water surrounded it on all sides. "I don't think we'll be crossing there any time soon."

"By the Trees that's come up quick!" someone behind them commented.

"Aye, and it's got a way to go yet," another voice responded. "Could come up to double that height if it's a fast thaw."

"Flaming Underworlds!" a third voice gasped, appalled at the thought of how much water that would mean.

"Gentlemen," Berengar spoke up, "I think you're missing something!"

As those around him turned to look at him instead of at the water, they realised that he was pointing in the opposite direction, off to his left. Following his outstretched arm they too saw what he had spotted. There on the plain on their side of the inland sea was a sizeable contingent of DeÁine. They had to have come through from New Lochlainn, for they were clearly in confusion as to where to go now. Having unwittingly crossed at the last possible moment before the flood cut them off from the homeland, they then must have realised that the way in front was closing fast and had tried to turn back, only to find that they were already too late for that as well. Grins began to break out on the faces of the men at the front, and as the word spread backwards, Berengar could hear the excited hum of voices rising. This was more like it! This was what the Knights trained for!

Three thousand rode behind Berengar on this morning, and down on the plain there were the same number. The difference was that there were two Seljuqs of slaves and only one Great Jundis of veteran troops. Against them were a battalion of seasoned Foresters whom Warwick had insisted upon bringing, plus half the men of Garway and reinforcements from High Cross and Hirieth, since both the latter castles were utterly isolated now by the floods and in no danger of attack whatsoever, and veterans all.

"I think someone thought they were coming to join the party," Esclados said with a chuckle. "Now they've got their feet wet and they don't know what to do."

"It certainly looks like one of the lesser families decided to throw their lot in with the Abend after all," agreed Warwick.

"Well I think they need to know the price of that," Berengar said resolutely. "Fan out, gentlemen! Make your way down onto the plain through as much of the highland as you can. Let's break up our outline as much as we can so they don't see what's coming. Warwick? Will you lead the right wing? Take them as far over as you can and sweep round. We'll steady our progress to give you time. I don't want them running south towards towns like Marloes if they break and scatter. I want them all in the net!"

With the ease born of practice, the Knights fanned out and began moving with orchestrated precision. They had been riding steadily downhill for the best part of an hour before any of the DeÁine caught sight of them. Once they did, however, the panic began to spread. The Knights observed the slave-masters using whips and thundering amongst their charges on the fell beasts they habitually rode. No longer needing concealment, the Knights let their hawks loose into the air, and above the riders there rose a wheeling mass of feathers, as the birds of prey rode the thermals high enough to prepare to hunt. The horses caught the mood of the men, and it became harder and harder to hold the chargers back from rising to the gallop. Almost by default the whole force rose to the trot, struggling to refrain from breaking into a canter.

In the lead, Berengar at last caught sight of Warwick and lifted his arm with a pennanted lance raised high in his fist, then swept it downwards in an arc. It was seen across the line. Like a hound after a hare, the whole right flank of the Order sprang forward as one, the huge, muscled horses devouring the space between them and the DeÁine at speed. As the whole force wheeled to drive the DeÁine force eastwards, rank after rank rose to the canter in a fluid arc to join Warwick's men, until everyone was on the move at the same pace. At that point Berengar let his horse have its head, and it shot forward at a full gallop. That was all the signal anyone needed. Every horse eagerly sprang to full speed, and their riders lowered the spears they carried in readiness for the first attack, after which they would use the swords at their belts.

Someone in the DeÁine camp at least had the presence of mind to draw the Jundis up into a square, but the Seljuqs were too panicked by now for such precision. Instead their slave-masters simply turned them in a great seething mass and drove them towards the Knights. It was designed to unhorse many of the riders bearing down on them, for once the Knights were on the ground, the slaves would hack them to death with little technique but much ferocity. Or so they hoped. But this time they were not facing the incompetent King Edward. Berengar and Warwick had seen this move before and were ready for it.

The riders of the Order split themselves into two wings, and swung outwards instead of simply ploughing into the milling slaves. As they pounded past, the earth shaking beneath the chargers and divots of turf flying into the air from the hooves, the riders launched their spears at an angle into the mass of bodies. There was no way that they could fail to find a target. Then for the wounded a new horror fell from the skies. The hawks plummeted down going for the eyes with their talons, striking unprotected flesh and ravaging it, even as they swooped onwards and upwards to strike again. The sheer force of a huge bird impacting on their heads knocked others to the ground who had broken from the mass to flee, where they cowered and screamed in terror.

As rank after rank of the slaves fell, and the Knights streamed past to turn and come back again, they were observed from afar. Riding down from Seigor, Tancostyl was appalled to see what was happening. He was furious already. Where had all this water come from? Helga, he thought savagely. The infernal fool could not just have snowed-in the Knights. Oh no. She had overreacted in her pique and brought too much snow to the mountains. He ground his teeth. And now this! Immaculate Temples! To find the Knights out of the first of their castles just at this precise moment was bad luck of the worst kind. He should not risk taking the Helm too close. Yet he dared not risk having to make the run back east, with only the bodyguard of forty men he had brought with him, if the Knight were at his heels in such force.

He looked at the mess going on ahead, and began drawing Power into himself. There was nothing for it. He would have to aid the idiot leading the DeÁine troops then commandeer them for himself.

"Looks like the Ertigun family," a man at his side observed. "That's their gonfalon flying at the head."

Tancostyl stared at the banner and when the wind blew the attached streamers away he saw the camelopard emblem, the creature's spots shining distinctively. It was the Ertiguns – which explained a lot. Not one of the great families, they had to be cautious over whom they showed open support for. The Monreux and other top rank families could afford to take the odd disaster in their stride, but lower down the scale the fight to climb the social ladder was conducted more circumspectly. The Ertiguns had evidently thought things were currently moving the right way enough to risk joining in, since there had been so little resistance. Yet now they were the first to feel the backlash. However, they were not in a position to buy the best fighters who came out of the great training camps for their family's army either, which was why it was turning into a debacle up ahead.

"Phol's gonads he's making a mess of that!" Tancostyl swore as he watched the leading Donn give conflicting signals. "Behind me!" he called to his men, and kicked his horse into a gallop.

The moment he got within effective range, he unleashed a ball of Power-fire and watched it plough into a mixed mêlée of men. He had probably killed more of the Ertigun's slaves than he had Knights, but no matter. It had the desired effect. Even if the Seljuq still panicked, the men of the Jundis steadied, suddenly surer of what they should be doing now that a war-mage was with them, despite the garbled commands of the inexperienced Ertigun Donns. They ignored the Donns and formed up in the way they had been trained in the camps, and began retreating towards the war-mage in something more like a professional show of force. Their opponents, on the other hand, were suddenly pulling back.

"Where did that bastard Abend come from?" bellowed Berengar in disbelief to anyone who might be listening and capable of answering.

"Came in from the direction of Seigor, sire," someone yelled back in answer.

"Only had a small escort," another called across.

"Flaming Underworlds, what bad luck," Esclados growled as he galloped beside Berengar. "He must've been heading for New Lochlainn and got here at just the wrong time for us."

Overhead the hawks had disengaged and now watched their handlers from far on high, waiting for the signal to fight once more. As Berengar halted his men and wheeled them back to face the enemy, from a distance which the Power-fire could not reach, a rider tore up from Warwick.

"Sire," he panted. "Master Warwick says that if you'll follow his lead he thinks we can do something to counter the war-mage. It's not a lot but it should help."

Berengar trotted his horse a little out of line with his men so that he could be seen by Warwick, and gestured him to lead on. Up on the right flank, Warwick turned his men and rode on further southwards until a shallow channel of floodwater lay between the Knights and the DeÁine. The Foresters dismounted and most went to stand in a line beside Warwick while a few squires acted as ushers, gesturing the other Knights to take their lances on until they were all drawn up in lines behind the Foresters. Then as one the Forester Knights began to chant. The language was old and unknown to the others, words rising and falling in a singsong rhythm, almost like a spoken song. Not a high note was heard, but within the lower registers the men were still displaying a remarkable vocal range. On each side of a Forester Knight, the men of his lance placed slender wooden staves into the soggy ground, and the wet and glutinous soil began to vibrate in sympathy with the deep bass notes.

"Sacred Root and Branch!" Esclados whispered in amazement as the water began to move, and several other men could be heard expressing their shock along the line.

It was if the wet land was being squeezed like a sponge. The water shook itself out of the land at the Foresters' feet and moved away from them. Away from them and towards the DeÁine troops. When a couple of feet had been covered one man from each lance stepped forward and stuck his stave into the soil at the edge of the retreating water. Then another would come a few paces forward of him. As the vibrations built, Berengar realised that the water was coalescing ahead of the staves. While the ground he was following the Foresters on was soft but passable, the ground towards the DeÁine was getting more and more liquid.

"Those staves are one of each Sacred Tree!" a sharp-eyed young Knight nearby suddenly spotted. "The Forester has the Rowan and the others have one each!"

Berengar turned to look at Esclados, the anger in his eyes changed to fiery understanding, and he grinned wolfishly then stood in his saddle and gestured for silence. The faint murmur of voices along the line died away completely.

"The prayer!" Berengar called out loud enough for all to hear, at which Warwick flicked a look back over his shoulder and gave a strained but positive nod. The word passed along the line and the men drew in a preparatory breath.

"Great Oak," Berengar began and all those of Knightly rank joined him. "Give us this day your strength in body and spirit. Lend us your power in defence of this land. Great Oak in you we trust."

As one the men of the lances responded, "In you we trust."

It was said from the heart, and at that they all felt the land give a mighty shudder, as if some subterranean beast had woken from its slumbers. The DeÁine felt it too. Normally the slave-masters on their strange beasts would have kept the slaves at least in a group even so. But first one, then another, hideous beast began to paw the ground and snort in terror, until all of them were fighting their reins and their riders in their own panic. One beast of the kind with overlapping rows of armoured scales and a long snout suddenly squealed, threw its rider and turned tail to run, trampling several slaves who had the misfortune to be behind it. Others of its kind flung themselves about until they could chase after it. The other beasts with the horns and great plates of hide, although clearly having less of the herding instinct, nonetheless showed their discomfort by backing and thrashing about individually. The wicked double horns tossed and gored several unfortunates as they threw their heads about wildly.

Warwick's men by now had moved forward several paces on, but the water had made a leap ahead. Even so they were still at the limit of the range of Power-fire, but Berengar saw Tancostyl raise his hands again.

"Both hands! Fuck! This is going to be a big bastard!" a veteran sergeant swore behind Berengar, who silently agreed.

However, Tancostyl knew he needed to be just that bit closer to really do damage. He urged his horse forward, and although the terrified animal rolled its eyes in panic, he fought it several steps onwards. Then suddenly it sank. Its front hooves had reached the edge of the water and it dropped as if it had stepped off a ledge. Up to its belly in mud and sinking fast with Tancostyl's weight on it, it was unable to pull itself free let alone move anywhere. It threw its head up wildly and smacked Tancostyl in the face as he pitched forward. All control gone, a huge blaze shot out of him but dissipated long before it made contact with anything ahead of it, having nothing to control it. But Berengar had already begun again as he saw Warwick's men take another step.

"Great Birch, tree of air and water. May the wind that passes through your branches heal us from evil spirits, and drive away the malignancy summoned against us. Great Birch in you we trust,"

"In you we trust," all the men intoned and the earth convulsed once more.

In a massive, shivering, slurp, the soggy ground consumed the unfortunate horse, and Tancostyl found himself up to his waist in the gelatinous gloop before he knew it. Neither Berengar nor Warwick ever knew what he did to get himself out, but it had the desired effect of forcing him to divert all his powers to his own defence instead of against them.

And with his arcane charms on the slaves loosened, they finally broke free and fled screaming back the way they had just come, although they were heading away from the only home they knew. For now it was enough to put as much distance as possible between themselves and the ravenous ground. Suddenly something was expelled up out of the sodden soil. It shot upwards as if a great hand beneath the surface had thrown it back, and Tancostyl pounced on it, raising it shaking dripping water from it and placed it on his head.

"The Helm!" Esclados cried out in warning to both Berengar and Warwick.

"Great Maker! The earth of the Islands wouldn't have it!" Berengar whispered, appalled.

Warwick's Foresters began again with more force and at greater volume, which Warwick himself broke off from to call back to Berengar,

"Yew!"

Berengar did not bother to question why Warwick wanted him to skip the verse concerning the Ash, which would normally follow the Birch. He simply raised his voice and led his own men as they chanted,

"Great Yew. Symbol of eternal life and rebirth. May the earth at your feet protect our bodies from those who would summon them for evil. Great Yew in you we trust."

They barely got the words out in time, and even as the men chanted "in you we trust," Tancostyl let fly with the Power he had summoned through the Helm.

From the visor of the Helm a sheet of light shot out and spread out like an ever expanding blade. It shone with a sickly blue-white light and practically seared the air itself. Few of the Knights would survive if they stood their ground, for it was wide enough to encompass most of their force and came at them at waist height.

"Great Ash," someone began and impulsively the men began to pray,

"Great Ash, who links this world and the next. Make a bridge of your mighty arms for those who fall to the Summerlands. Protect their souls on their journey beneath the shade of your leaves. Great Ash in you we trust,"

"In you we trust."

Yet even as men prayed and dived for the ground in an attempt to avoid the cutting energy, the earth beyond them surged up in a great high wave. The thick and gritty mud rose several feet into the air and dulled and fragmented the sheet of scything Power, even if it did not quite stop it.

Men pulled horses down and the well-trained beasts lay down, so avoiding the worst of it with their riders. Many amongst them suffered painful cuts where shards of the Power had sparked off at angles. Cuts which, it transpired, bled for far longer than they should have and healed awkwardly, but which they survived. However, seeing the Knights all on the ground and hearing the faint moans of those who had more serious cuts, Tancostyl must have thought he had won the day. Cuffing a Donn from a horse, he mounted up and turned back towards the crossroad, the DeÁine soldiers hurrying in his wake.

"Do we follow them?" Esclados asked, as he hauled himself stiffly to his feet, and tried to get the worst of the wet soil from off his cloak and breeches.

"No," Berengar said thoughtfully. "Let the mage think he's won for now. I want him out of the way." Warwick squelched his way up to them. "And that was impressive!" Berengar told his head Forester with genuine respect and admiration. "I do hope you've more tricks like that up your sleeve!"

"Not many," admitted Warwick ruefully. "We were lucky. If the ground had been hard we'd have been in trouble. Just thank the Trees that it wasn't high summer and the soil baked like bricks!"

"I think we'll *all* be doing some thanking of the Trees!" was Esclados' heartfelt response.

"That we will," Berengar agreed.

"Back to Garway for now, then?" his old friend wondered, expecting Berengar to need time to think again, but he shook his head.

"No. We're out now and I want to keep it that way. If there'd been more of the Abend nearby we'd have known about it, I think. Do you agree, Warwick?"

"Absolutely! To have got off so lightly there had to only be one within many miles of here, or they'd have joined up and given us a real thrashing."

Berengar gestured southwards. "Then we'll ride towards Marloes, or as near as we can get to it, then go and look at Caersus. That was one family's army coming east who got both unlucky in being trapped by the floods, and lucky in finding a stray war-mage. There may be other families who've decided to come and take their pick of the Abend's leavings, and who think they're nice and safe. We may not be able to fight the Abend yet, but we can give the flesh-and-blood troops a bloody nose, and I intend to do so if they're out there."

Over the next four days the men of the Order rode southwards, every day torn between awe and desperation at the extent of the flooding. In the far distance they would sometimes catch glimpses of knolls of land above the water. Beyond that they found a truly vast new sea to the west of them.

"What of the livestock?" one Knight wondered aloud. "There must be thousands of animals drowned."

"There are sanctuaries even with the water this high," another reassured him, being a local man. "There's even a spine of high land between the Mer and Blane Water which can be used as a kind of corridor to the mountains. High Cross and Hirieth might find themselves inundated with cattle and sheep, but enough should survive to keep the flocks and herds going."

"That's good to hear," Berengar commented, having overheard the conversation. "I feared we might be having to drive breeding stock down from the north to avert disaster."

"I doubt it'll come to that, sire," the local man assured him. "We're used to flooding down here. I know this is worse than any within living memory, but the sensible folk would already have had their stock up on high ground expecting flood water, given that the snow was due to melt soon anyway. It's not like they'd have had to round them up from scratch, and these lands were never as densely farmed as where we're heading because of the DeÁine. Once upon a time all this rich farmland was filled with farms, although the fertile soil meant they were more arable than pastoral. If it'd been like that now it would've been a tragedy of vast proportions, no mistake, but the few hardy souls left will cope."

However, east of there the farmlands were wet but not sodden, and they began to see farmers out with plough teams on the higher, drained fields, anxious to get early crops sown. On the thirtieth of Earrach they halted at Trefin to join the town in the celebrations to welcome in the month of Beltane – the sign that spring was officially in full flow and summer only just around the corner. In the midst of the celebrations, Berengar stepped outside to find the nearest privy to the guild hall and found a fox in his path.

"I must be fast," the fox hissed urgently. "We have no wish to alert the Abend that we're around and aiding you, and all of them are on edge at the moment. This is just to tell you that you're not alone! Hold the line! Hold the faith! Help is coming!" and he disappeared.

Returning to the heaving guildhall, Berengar elbowed his way to the bench against the wall where Warwick and Esclados had saved his seat.

"Well that was odd," he had to bellow to them to make himself heard. "I've just had a message from the fox. What in the Islands it means is anyone's guess, but he says help is coming."

"Maybe it's the ancients?" Esclados wondered.

"Bit unlikely since they can't even hold human form," Warwick managed to yell back.

"He said they don't want the Abend to know they're about the place," Berengar added. "Doesn't sound too hopeful to me, if they daren't openly confront their old enemies. Still, he said hold the line, and that's what we're doing with our original plan, so all we can do is carry on and hope for the best."

Turning north once more from Trefin, all was still peaceful and blessedly un-flooded. Only when they got to Caersus on the fourth did they see signs once more of devastation, and that from war not acts of nature. The land around the walled city was a mess, but clearly no great DeÁine force had come its way to try the strength of those walls, and certainly no member of the Abend or their acolytes.

Berengar sat on his horse and tried to maintain his composure as the unctuous Prior Poer – the very man who had done his best to have Berengar and the others killed when they were last here – grovelled with other town worthies for protection by the Knights.

"You must protect us!" demanded the mayor in outraged fear. "This is a valuable town! We have special privileges from the king!"

"Then I should tell that to the king!" Berengar said acidly. "Oh no, you can't can you! And why's that? Because he invited the DeÁine in in the first place!"

As that sunk in, the bombastic guildsmen and officials visibly deflated.

"As for the abbey," Berengar went on with silky venom, "You should spend your time contemplating the price of deceit. The ordinary brothers weren't at fault, I know, but you Poer, you have much to answer for!" The fat prior wobbled in shock at the fact that this fierce armed warrior should know his name of all the folk. He had only just recovered from being throttled by King Edward! He did not want any more punishment.

"Do you not recognise me?" Berengar lifted off his mailed helm and Poer fell to the ground, horror-stricken. Never had his actions come back to haunt him quite so forcibly.

Berengar grinned with lupine ferocity. "I think you should leave ... *now*! Start walking eastwards. By the time you get anywhere you'll be considerably thinner, and you can spend the time in contemplation of the vows you seem to have treated so contemptibly over the years. If you're lucky, one of the monasteries which still stand *may* take you in, but the price of the Order's protection for the brothers of any such place is your demotion to the lowest rank of lay brother, and the permanent exile from this abbey."

The locals practically tore Poer's chain of office from his neck and his fine robes from his back. As Berengar sat watching like immutable stone, a smock of sackcloth was found and dragged over the quivering bully, who was dithering half from terror and half from being reduced to his underwear in less than warm conditions in the great open square before the town gates. A few humble folk who had suffered at his hands even rustled up a few rotten eggs which they pelted him with, and none of the Knights made a move to stop them. With a crude walking staff thrust into his hands, Poer was chivvied on the road eastwards by jeering poor folk who lined the side of the road. For once the malevolent prior had truly reaped the harvest of the ill he had done over the years.

However, once the basic security of Caersus was attended to, Berengar could not afford to let himself get distracted by local events. The key issues took barely a day to sort out and then he turned his men north once more. Passing deserted Seigor, with its Power-fire blackened walls, brought everyone back to reality from the brief respite of the peaceful south. By the time they were back at Garway, the men had steeled themselves for what was to come. There was an enemy in their midst and now it was time to do something about it.

Chapter 16

Selecting Candidates

Brychan: Earrach

The wind was whistling through the castle at Arlei and it was doing nothing to improve Helga's health and temper. She had arrived back only the night before and this was the first chance she had had to observe what remained of Geitla. If the two of them had been at loggerheads for the entire time they had known one another, it still did not mean that she felt any more comfortable looking at the strange thing before her. It was Geitla on a superficial level. Enough for her not to even consider that Magda had tried to dupe her with some other body. And yet it was not Geitla as she had known her either. Her old adversary's soft, plump and feminine features had somehow coarsened into something more masculine without being wholly male. Even stranger was the glowing ball of Power residing in the former witch's womb, whose presence she had been able to feel as soon as she had entered the tower where the body was kept.

"Do you have any idea how something like this might happen?" Barrax had asked her when she had had chance to observe it for a few moments.

There was nothing she would have liked better than to be able to cut him down with a sharp observation, even though he had been careful in the tone and phrasing of his question. Helga was less than happy about having been cut out of his selection, but, having given her assent for Magda to go ahead on everyone's behalf, was now in no position to complain. To add to her ire she had not achieved what she had set out to do in going to Rathlin, either, which rubbed salt into the wound. Had she been able to sweep through the island and take a seaport heading east, she could have written it off as bad luck that she was away when the selection of a new member had become all the more urgent, but it was beyond misfortune to be so totally adrift from the centre of things. The only consolation was that Quintillean and Masanae had been even more sidelined in all of this, despite their position as heads of the Abend.

Gritting her teeth at having to cede ground to the newest member of the Abend, Helga admitted to Barrax,

"No, I've never seen anything like it in my life. …Do *you* know what it might be?"

"Know?" the tall, athletic young DeÁine mused. "I wouldn't go as far to say 'know' by any means. I think 'suspect' might be as far as I would venture as yet, and that very cautiously. But what Magda and I *suspect* is that the one you knew as Othinn – and who of late has been presenting himself as some kind of incarnation of Jolnir – wants to return to the real world. To the world where he can have a flesh and blood body. *How* he's managed to do this, though, is a total puzzle."

"Oh that must delight you!" Helga purred sarcastically to Magda, who at present was standing back by the chamber's window to allow Helga and Barrax an uninterrupted view of the recumbent Geitla. "Another of your little pets to play with again!"

"Hardly," Magda responded frostily. "There's a strong possibility that he's doing this in order to be able to properly *die*, not to live."

She had failed to tell Helga that that side of it had been Barrax's discovery, and that until then she had been too blinded by joy to spot the emotional black despair which pervaded the weavings of Power. There was no way she was going to give Helga any sort of opening to lord it over her. Luckily Barrax was also presenting a united front alongside Magda, and so far it seemed to be working.

"So, he'll do what? Wait until he's fully melded with what remains of Geitla and then commit suicide?" an astonished Helga asked.

Barrax shrugged. "Your guess is as good as ours," he responded, still keeping his tone neutral, neither antagonising her or becoming subservient. "I'd welcome you examining her. From what Magda's told me of your experiments back in New Lochlainn, you may be able to sense something which eludes me."

It was cleverly put, and Helga now found herself put on the spot. Normally nothing would have persuaded her to make an internal examination of another female except in the course of torturing. However, to decline now would be to lose face before Magda and a *junior male* – not something to be even remotely considered! She was also smart enough to realise that once she did this, there would be no way for her to claim that she had not known the full extent of what was going on – maybe blaming the other two if something went badly astray – but there was no getting round it.

So she rolled up her sleeves and proceeded to the bed. Before her fingers even got close to the weaving of Power she could see what Barrax meant. Any halfway trained and talented acolyte would have been able to spot the male nature of the weaving. That required no great skill. But had she not been forewarned she might have missed the more subtle undercurrent of the death-wish, and she had to admit that Barrax had skill if he had spotted that straight away and not gone blundering in. And she was pretty sure that it was Barrax who had picked up on this and not Magda, because although Magda was senior to her and had vastly more experience, the second oldest witch had been losing her analytical faculties for some time now.

Probing ever so gently now, she could feel the subtle shifting of the ward and withdrew her hand before it could do her any damage.

"Curious!" she admitted to the other two. "As you say, there's a real sense of wanting to end it all, but not yet. It's as though whatever, or whoever, it is is waiting for something."

"I've spoken to Eliavres and Anarawd again," Magda said, coming forward now, "and they've agreed that if you confirmed our suspicions, then we should start recruiting for another to take Geitla's place in the Abend. She's never going to be the same again, even if by some miracle she lives through whatever it is this life-force has planned for her. And we all agree that even if this *thing* proves useful to us, it won't be as one of us."

"No," agreed Barrax. "I feel that it's taking all that spirit's strength in the Power to do what it's doing. There's no way that it would be able to wield Power in concert with the rest of us. It will be a useful appendage if we need to confront the Islanders, nothing more."

Helga felt trapped by his logic. There was no way she could deny that he had summed the situation up flawlessly. On the other hand, she wished that she was in a position to bring her own favourite acolyte into the nine. However, just at the moment the rest of the Abend were still seething over Helga's using Dagmar to dispose of Geitla's lovers. There was absolutely no way that any of them would even consider that bright young acolyte for the foreseeable future, even if, in Helga's eyes, she was the obvious candidate for the vacant seat.

"Who have we got?" she asked the others, as they exited the room and headed for the solar, where Magda had told servants to prepare breakfast for them.

Magda scowled at her. "Don't say it like that, Helga! We're not deciding what to have for lunch! It's not just a case of picking one from the top few acolytes. I selected Barrax on the basis that what we needed first and foremost was another war-mage. Someone who would be compatible with Quintillean *and* Tancostyl – who isn't the easiest of us to partner – as well as Eliavres. If such matters had been thought through a little more carefully in the past, then we might not have ended up with either Anarawd or Calatin as part of the nine. And let's face it, Geitla might have been very strong in her ability to direct quantities of Power, but she was never willing to put the effort into learning how to control and direct it. She was well on the way to becoming a liability even before this happened."

For once she caught Helga out, and the younger witch whipped round to look at her in surprise. Helga and Masanae had discussed Geitla's unsuitability in private, but had thought that it had gone unnoticed by the others. Ruefully Helga now thought that maybe they had vastly underestimated their fellow Abend, for they had planned to elevate Dagmar as an automatic thing once they had arranged a suitable 'accident' for Geitla. Evidently that would not have gone as unchallenged as they had supposed, and Helga quietly breathed a sigh of relief that she had not ended up being the one doing Masanae's dirty work. The responses over Dagmar this far had been bad enough. No, she must re-evaluate her position and loyalties as a matter of urgency, for it was clear that Masanae's absorption with whatever scheme was going on between her and Quintillean had caused her to miscalculate badly. At this rate it could end up with Magda as the senior female Abend, on the basis that none of the males apart from Quintillean would work with Masanae.

Moreover, Magda was right, she realised with a jolt. If the senior royal family were indeed coming from Sinut, already believing that they were about to return home to the Emperor with the long-lost Treasures, then there could be some very advanced acolytes amongst them. And all well-trained and developed enough to exploit any signs of disunity amongst the nine, if they thought it possible that they might ride home with the royals in a cloud of glory, leaving a disgraced Abend to moulder in the Islands. Not that Helga wanted to go back to the ancient homeland of Lochlainn. Far from it! But there was a world of difference between choosing to remain here – with all the trappings of power she was used to, and with a goodly number of Power-talented pure-bloods from whom to select new acolytes – and being abandoned with no slaves and no army to defend herself with.

No, Magda was right, they must have someone who would work with them, not be drifting off on their own as Calatin had done for so long. Or be endlessly following their own schemes and agendas, as Anarawd had done up until recent events had forced him to see things differently.

By now they were in the solar and securely alone again, and as Helga helped herself to a glass of the freshly squeezed fruit juice and took one of the sweet cinnamon buns to nibble on, she carefully asked,

"What do you see as our priority now, then?"

Magda sipped at her mug of scalding hot caff smothered in cream before replying. "I think that depends on how much fighting you think we're going to have to do in the near future, don't you? If we need another war-mage then we're going to have to spread our net a little wider than the acolytes we have here. Maybe summon more from Bruighean. Barrax was the clear choice the last time, but I have to say that as a war-mage he already stood out head and shoulders above the other candidates, *and* according to those I spoke of concerning those back at Bruighean. There's nobody else here anywhere near his quality, and we might be struggling to select one from amongst those left behind too."

Helga turned to look at Barrax but caught no sign of him preening himself in the face of such praise. That was something, at least. No overweening pride on show as yet. It might come with time, of course, when he got used to his position. But they were not worrying about the next century just yet, it was the here and now which was causing concern.

"On the other hand," Magda was continuing, "if we're thinking about someone with Geitla's kind of talents but more stable, then I think we might have a few worth looking at. Not least because we have more female acolytes here than males at the moment."

"Mmmm," Helga mused. "It would certainly be useful if we could find someone with an affinity for working with the weather, like me. Attaching that glamour to the summoned storm was villainously hard work for me, even if the rest of you were channelling Power through me. If we want to fight in that sort of way again, it would be better to have another who could work with either you or Masanae, while the other one of you channelled through me. One to one is a lot easier to control."

Barrax cleared his throat. "Excuse me for asking, but as I wasn't there I don't know. Do you think Geitla's unpredictability made it harder for you? What I mean is, each one of us has a very individual way of weaving our Power. You must have been trying to tie those other strands into yours to do what you did. Now if one of those was very powerful, but bouncing around all over the place, then that must have made your job even worse, surely? Harder than if you had had three very controlled weavings, before you even start considering compatibility."

Once again it was a very perceptive comment, and Helga began to think that Magda might have actually made a very good choice in Barrax. The more she thought about his words the more sense they made and she nodded.

"Yes, I think you could be right about that. For all of Geitla's strength, it only helped us when we could let her unleash it by herself. When we had to work in concert it wasn't much of a benefit at all."

Magda sighed. "That's what I've been thinking. You wouldn't remember this, Helga, because you're too young. But back when I was in training, the ancient and very powerful Abend of our homeland only ever worked as a mix of staunch individuals, because most of the time they worked alone with their own acolytes. There was no need for the members of the Abend themselves to work together unless the Emperor was orchestrating things.

"But I remember how those of us who were acolytes together under one of the Abend all linked together. Everyone who trained with me under Escobar had a similar way of doing things. …Oh, it was lovely! The way it felt when you all tapped into a strand of the Power together and worked on it. …I've not sensed that when working as an Abend myself. Not ever! The nearest I've come to it was working with Othinn and Eliavres together, and back then they were both very inexperienced. That's why it feels so right to have Barrax here. He's worked with Othinn in his early days and then with Anarawd, and when he joined with me to talk to Eliavres and Anarawd just before you got back, it was almost like old times. Together we were more than our separate parts!"

Now that was an interesting concept, Helga thought. Not something which Masanae had ever put forward either. But maybe that was because Masanae was too busy making sure she stayed at the top. Underlings working in unity might just have proved a challenge. Well, well, so the self-elevated queen of the witches was fallible! And maybe disastrously so, Helga thought, as she realised how much Masanae was the outsider at the moment. If they continued to follow Masanae and Quintillean's lead they might end up by losing everything. Whereas what Magda was suggesting was not particularly palatable to her, but it did seem to have some guarantee of delivering what she wanted when they finally got out of this mess.

"I can see the value in that," she declared, taking the plunge. "Then I think we need to find someone who will best work with us. Someone to augment our powers. I think you were right, Magda. Last time we very much needed a war-mage. But this time I think we have other criteria. …So …Who have you got?"

Now Magda spoke obliquely. "Did you feel anything three days ago?"

"Three days ago? Why?" Helga was thrown by the switch.

"Well something very odd happened," Barrax elaborated. "At first it was like someone was drawing a lot of Power in. Nothing particularly unusual in that, given that we felt it in the direction of the Houses of the Holy. So at first we assumed that the priests were working on one of their archaic observations."

"But it wasn't?" Helga guessed.

"Oh no, sweetling," Magda declared emphatically. "Definitely not the priests! We suddenly got the feeling that it was probably Quintillean and Masanae. Then we got a frantic sending from Tancostyl. He'd picked it up too, and he said the Helm was getting very peculiar."

"The Helm?" Now Helga was beginning to understand their concern. "By the Lotus, what could have affected the Helm?"

"That's what we wondered," Barrax said dryly. "Didn't take much imagination to figure out that they must've been trying to do something to get control of the Treasures. The bigger surprise, though, was the way it ended. It was like the Power erupted and dispersed. Like one of the water geysers we've seen out on Areida. And it felt tainted too – as though something had got into it and flowed back into the Power. Very odd! Very odd indeed!"

Helga shook her head and thought furiously. "Three days ago… That would've been just as I was landing. Now you mention it I did feel quite disorientated. I put it down to the sea voyage, but that surge sounds familiar."

Magda inclined her head in acknowledgement. "Eliavres and Anarawd said they felt nothing specific either, but like you they were aboard a ship, so it's hardly surprising. All of your senses were adrift, so you wouldn't have been able to pin it down as we did. We think that whatever the two of them were conjuring up failed."

"More than failed," Barrax added. "I think was 'stopped' would be a more accurate assessment. By whom we can't say. It's just possible that they overstepped the mark with the priests and they joined forces to stop them."

"Would they dare?" a shocked Helga asked. "I mean, this is the two leading members of the Abend we're talking about here!"

But Magda was nodding her head. "Oh yes, poppet, they'd dare! You must remember that the priests see themselves as the ones preventing us all from becoming savages. Guardians of the purity of the Power – or what's left of it! If they thought that what Masanae and Quintillean were doing amounted to sacrilege then, yes, they would unite and do everything in their power to halt it. And if they got all their novices working in unison they might well be able to do it too. Don't forget, it's a very different thing shattering a summoning to having the strength to draw it up in the first place. They could be as brutal and crude as they wanted, or were able, to be. They didn't need the control necessary for finesse."

"Great Mother Seagang!" Helga swore.

"Indeed," Barrax agreed wryly. "And who else would stop such a flood of Power?"

"Unless the ones from Sinut are here already?" fretted Helga.

"No, I don't think so!" Barrax instantly rejected that suggestion. "Not because they wouldn't be capable, of course. No, I just don't think they've had time to get this far, and anyway, I'm sure we'd have felt *their* presence much sooner if they were this close."

"So you see, poppet," Magda continued smoothly, "we feel that it would be no bad thing to have someone who's spent sometime within the Houses of the Holy amongst us. Someone who might know exactly what sort of powers the priests might possess when combined. One priest alone, of course, would be incapable of hurting the weakest of us. But all together?"

She left the suggestion hanging, but Helga was more than capable of filling in the gap.

"Do we have such a candidate?" she asked when her composure had sufficiently returned.

"Actually we have four," Barrax told her with a grin. "We were about to start interviewing them today anyway. We haven't told them why, but it seemed a sensible precaution to start the whittling process and at least find out exactly what their strengths and weaknesses are."

"Then I think we should begin, don't you?" Helga said, trying not to show her relief.

They were still working on their potential recruits three days later when a frantic sending came their way from Tancostyl. Dismissing the recruits abruptly, they focused back on him.

"*What's wrong?*" Magda asked with none of her usual sweetness, for it was clear that something had severely rattled the war-mage.

"*The bloody Knights are out!*" his thoughts snarled, "*and you really fucked up!*"

Helga could feel her usual frigid calm evaporating. "Typical Tancostyl," she sighed to the others. "Always someone else's fault!" "*And in what way did we fail you this time?*" she sent back to him with poorly disguised impatience.

"*The snow!*" he shot back.

"*What was wrong with the snow?*" Helga growled. "*Too white for you?*"

"*It's melting!*"

"*Well of course it's melting, you idiot! It's springtime! What did you think it was going to do?*"

"*There's too much of it!*" was Tancostyl's acid reply.

"*<u>You</u> wanted the Knights to be snowed-in! That was never going to happen with just a few flakes! I told you at the time when you asked me to do it that I wouldn't be able to control it once it was there.*"

"*That's true, she did,*" admitted Magda, silencing Tancostyl's psychic spitting for a second.

"*Well we're well and truly cut off from New Lochlainn now,*" he announced huffily. "*The floods are beyond anything I've ever heard of outside of the Mother Seagang in the homeland! It's one huge inland sea where we marched through! We'd need a fleet of ships to get back to Bruighean at the moment! And it's only going to get worse. This is only the start of the melt! All the mountains are still covered in white for as far as the eye can see. And then to cap it all I ran into a troop of the Knights on the last of the dry stretches I found. They had some of their bastard Foresters with them, too! I'm coming back with the Ertigun contingent. The useless idiots were well on the way to getting wiped out, so I had little choice but to save them since they'll be the last of the replacements we'll get for some time – so don't squander what we have!*"

"*We have the Kolacz, the Deipners, the Dzoshuns and the Norainne families here now too,*" Helga quickly added, refusing to give in under Tancostyl's tirade. "*That's half a Seljuq and half a Jundis for each of them. Did you not pass them on the road?*"

"The Dzoshuns and the Norainne I did. I think maybe the others were close enough to you for me not to have acknowledged them as separate from our existing force. So the Norainne and the Kolacz decided to come after all, did they? Remembered which side their bread was buttered on, eh?"

The others did not bother rising to Tancostyl's bitter sniping. They all knew that the minor families walked a much finer line than the major ones, and could little afford to be reckless in their promises of support. Magda had tactfully welcomed the newcomers with open arms and profuse thanks for coming, with no hint of censure over why it had taken them so long to appear. That they were here at all was confirmation that the pure-bloods were taking the Abend seriously for the first time in nine years, which was not something to be brushed aside unappreciatively. As it was, Tancostyl's carping was reinforcing what Magda had said, and Helga was further convinced that what they needed was a new member of the Abend who did not just barge in like a bull at a gate at every new obstacle.

"*I presume you're coming back here, then?*" Barrax was sending to Tancostyl. "*You'll not be wanting to risk the Helm's safety to inexperienced guards in case the Knights plan a truly large-scale ambush, will you?*"

It was cleverly put, Helga thought. Not actively saying that Tancostyl was not yet up to taking on a full-frontal attack by blaming his weakness onto those he clearly already despised. When Tancostyl's snapped confirmation came back, Barrax asked him when they might expect him.

"*For I feel it would be well for me to learn how you do things if I'm to back you up should it come to outright confrontation,*" the newest member of the Abend lied smoothly.

"*Probably by early Beltane,*" was the curt response before Tancostyl broke contact.

"Good," Barrax smiled to Helga and Magda. "Then I think we should be thinking of having someone all lined up, if not actually sworn in, by the time he gets back, don't you? Because I don't think he's going to grasp the importance of a united front, or of the more subtle ways of fighting." He turned and walked to the window before turning to look at the two witches again. "However, I have a question of my own for you. Are we only confining our search to women this time? The four we're looking at are all very worthy, I'll grant you that. But a male candidate who wasn't a war-mage? Would that interest you? Would that be acceptable?"

It was an interesting point.

"Do you know of such a male?" Magda asked tentatively. Was this when Barrax showed some partiality to raising someone who would side with him in a crisis? Part of his attraction had been the lack of any alliances she could detect.

Barrax nodded but without any show of eagerness. "I've observed someone. He's not someone I've ever worked with because his talents and mine are so very different, and as Magda said before, as an acolyte you tend to work with like-minded students. It's rather that when I've been in the vicinity of him, he's been the person I've felt very clearly if he's been working with one of the objects of Power, or on exercises. Someone with a distinct and powerful signature. I can't tell whether he's right for what you want based on that. But he might be another you'd want to look at and decide if he would work well with your kind of talents."

Not a friend, then, Magda breathed a hidden sigh of relief. "Very well. Let's send for him and see what he's made of. I presume you have seen him since we've been here? He's here and not at Bruighean or somewhere else?"

With a nod of confirmation Barrax left them. Once alone Magda turned to Helga whose face had become even more mask-like than normal – a clear sign that something was bothering her.

"You don't have any deep-seated objections to another male, do you?"

The icy blonde glided to a window seat and reclined before answering. "Purely as a male? No…"

"…But?"

"…But it would mean a very unbalanced Abend. Six to three! I won't pretend that that doesn't make me uncomfortable. There are times when a female perspective is vital, and with such a weighting we'd be very lucky to override the war-mages if two other mages joined them. I'm concerned for those times when patience is a virtue. When there's more to be gained by playing a long game." She paused, considering her words. "You did an excellent job in finding Barrax. He's more a true war-mage than ever Calatin was – even I can sense that. But that may mean that in the heat of the moment he's more inclined to Tancostyl's impetuosity."

As Magda quirked an eyebrow in surprise at that, Helga modified her statement. "Alright, maybe not that bad. But you have to admit that even your beloved Eliavres can be quick to leap in at times. Granted, he's led us into Brychan with barely a blow being struck, but it could have gone badly wrong for us. Where *is* the Gorget? The promise of which was what got us on the road in the first place. You can't ignore the fact that he messed up badly over that. He *assumed* …and that's very much a war-mage characteristic.

"So currently we have Quintillean, who's a mighty presence but at the moment is up to who knows what. Then Tancostyl – the ultimate war-mage. Our best for many generations, and who may yet be our greatest asset if we have to show the ones from Sinut that we still have muscles to flex. Eliavres, a much more balanced war-mage but still very useful, and now Barrax, who will work very nicely with the existing mages. And if that was it, Magda, I'd be quite happy to have another male.

"But there's Anarawd. As you rightly said, he maybe wasn't the best choice for elevation with hindsight, but we're stuck with him. And he seems to have struck some sort of deal with Eliavres and is working with one of us for once. Against that there's you and me and Masanae – and if the Great Volla knows what she's up to then he's probably the only one! I won't lie to you. I'd feel a lot more …secure …if we had another witch whom we stood a chance of getting around to our way of thinking every so often. Even Geitla managed that occasionally!"

Magda had been nodding in agreement, and it occurred to Helga that she had been far less distracted and disjointed mentally since the Power-based being had attached itself to Geitla's body. Had it been trying to find such a way into Magda prior to that? Was that why Magda had seemed to be losing her mind so much in the last few years? Helga mentally noted the need for them to conduct much more research into such things when the current crisis was over. It was something they knew far too little about, and if a psychic attack though the Power was something they were vulnerable to, then they needed to be much better prepared in the future.

This sharper and shrewder Magda had her pretty face screwed up in thought. "I find myself in agreement with you, sweetling. Let us agree, then – just between the two of us – that the only way we shall approve this new candidate is if he turns out to have such a prodigious talent that his elevation is unavoidable. If he is of anything like the same quality as the four we've already looked at, he will not be the first choice."

"Agreed."

"Good."

Within the hour Barrax had reappeared with the new candidate. Whereas Barrax was a man of good stature and build, the new male entering the room was positively cadaverous, even for one of the Abend.

Magda's initial instinctive response was that here was another Calatin. One who became so immersed in his work that he rarely looked up to the real world. She looked to Helga and saw the minutest of head shakes. Helga was obviously not liking what she saw either.

"This is Nicos," Barrax introduced him. Yet as the potential recruit came to face Magda and bow before her, she caught eyes which were chillingly in the here and now. Something about him made a shuddered run down her spine, and when he turned to Helga there was the faintest stiffening of her stance which told Magda she was not alone in her revulsion. However, they had promised Barrax to give him a fair review, and so they sat him in one of the solar's window seats and had him go through the same exercises they had asked of the others.

The shock came when they asked him to perform a communication summoning. Instead of reaching out on the Power-currents they expected, he instinctively dove far lower and began reaching out in wholly different manner. Helga was shocked and perplexed, but this was where Magda's long years of additional experience paid off.

"Sweet Lotus! You're a Spirit-walker!" she gasped.

Not only Helga but Barrax too blanched at this. Spirit-walking was an exceedingly rare talent, and one which sat comfortably with only a very few of the talented. Communicating with the dead was hardly an everyday occurrence even amongst the Abend. No doubt this was why this acolyte had found nobody yet who was prepared to truly cultivate his gift, and why he seemed to have been overlooked. One look at Barrax's face told Magda that he was no longer anything like as keen to include Nicos in amongst the nine Abend either. Close contact with such a mind on a regular basis could have all sorts of unforeseen consequences.

"I have to tell you, poppet, that there has never yet been one with your talents elevated to the nine," Magda told Nicos solemnly. "And for very good reason. Close contact with one another's minds, as we have on occasion, becomes very dangerous with one such as you amongst the group."

A flicker of bitter resentment blinked behind Nicos' eyes, but Magda gave him no time to let it build. "But tell me, sweetling, why were you never taken into the priesthood? With a talent like yours you could have risen very high in their ranks, very high indeed. Surely it would have been no disgrace to you to change across if it let you show your true worth?"

"I *was* with the priests," Nicos responded in his dry voice, which carried more than a little of the graveyard in its tone. No hiding the bitterness there either. "All they wanted me to do was fetch and carry messages to the great who were in the beyond. You think the pure-bloods are irritating in this life? You should contact them in the next! Petty, *mean* little minds! Still wittering on about everything and nothing! Being dead doesn't make you any smarter!"

"You *began* with the priests?" Helga checked and got a terse nod. "Then what in the Immaculate Temples did you do to get sent away?"

Nicos gave a short bark – which must pass for his laugh, Magda thought.

"They said I aimed too high! I was too impertinent in my ambitions."

"What *did* you do?" Barrax repeated, fascinated and repelled at the same time.

"I tried to contact Volla."

"Great Mother Seagang!" Helga gulped, as Magda clasped her dainty hands to her mouth and whispered, "Sweet Lotus!"

"Volla? Our most potent *god*?" was Barrax's strangled gasp. "Why in the name of the Immaculate Temples? Why?"

Nicos looked back at them with no hint of emotion. "Because everyone keeps doing things in his name, and I wanted to know if that was right or not. He never wrote anything down, as far as I ever learned, anyway. So who decides what he meant or wanted? I thought it was about time someone actually *asked* him!"

The three Abend stared back at him, too stunned for a moment by the cold logic to speak. Barrax finally managed to croak out,

"And did you?"

"Ask him? No. I haven't reached Volla yet." Internally, the three Abend breathed huge sighs of relief, while struggling to maintain an outward calm. Clearly Nicos was teetering on the brink of madness, and the last thing the DeÁine needed was some manic Power-wielder wandering about the place claiming that he had a direct contact with Volla. Who knew where that might lead! "I did reach others though," Nicos proclaimed with a satisfied, tight-lipped smile."

"Like who?" Helga asked faintly.

"Your former acolyte Othinn for one," Nicos said, as though it was the most normal thing in the world to be conversing with the one acolyte who had managed to rip himself out of his flesh and blood form and into the Power.

"Marvellous!" Magda said with shaky enthusiasm, seizing on the opening like a drowning woman grasping at a passing branch. "Then I think we have just the job which will appeal to you! Maybe you'd like to ask him what he's doing with Geitla? Tomorrow morning meet us at the east tower."

When he had gone they all sat in horrified silence for a while.

"Mad as killer bee!" Helga finally sighed, when she felt she could speak without screaming.

"My sincere apologies!" Barrax added quickly. "I *truly* had no idea that he was like that! All I knew was that he seemed very strong in the Power, and in a very different way to what I was used to. I wouldn't even have suggested him if I'd had a hint that his talents lay *that* way."

Unclasping her hands now that they were no longer shaking, Magda waved his protestations down. "No, no, poppet, it's not your fault. No reflection on you whatsoever. …And indeed, if he can communicate with what ails Geitla, you may have done us a favour by bringing him to our attention. …But when we next speak to Eliavres and Anarawd, I think we can safely say that there are *no* suitable male candidates, don't you?"

The hasty nods all round confirmed the others' agreement, and they went back to studying the merits of the original selected four. By now they were well on the way to finalising their decision, and all were motivated by their brush with Nicos to be decisive. Two of the women were very talented in Helga's way but nothing exceptional in other ways.

"I'm glad we did this," Helga declared when they broke for the evening meal. "I shall certainly be keeping Ljota and Visna very close to me for the foreseeable future, but as my acolytes and supporters. That way if we need any weather controlling, or other natural barriers raised or destroyed, they can aid me."

"You don't think Ljota's the one, then?" Barrax checked.

"No. …Great talent, but it needs someone else directing it. She could be as much of a liability as Geitla was becoming. No initiative! We don't want someone who sits around while we do all the work. It's one thing for an acolyte to just be a tool for us to use, but not one of our own."

"And the same goes for Hirmin, but with less talent," Magda said of the third candidate, as she speared a dainty morsel of bloody meat and squished it in her mouth. "Mmm, this is very good. What do you think it is?"

"Cat, I suspect," Barrax answered with little interest. "There aren't any chickens left." Barrax ate with great efficiency but with no sign of enjoyment, merely of providing fuel for his body – very like herself in that, Helga noted with approval.

"No, I suppose there aren't, sweetling," Magda mused, taking another piece and dipping it into the sweet sauce on her plate. "Most tender, though. Maybe we should ask for it on the menu more back at Bruighean?"

"So that leaves Laufrey," Barrax concluded, hurriedly changing the conversation before Magda could get too distracted. "Unless, that is, you want to spread your search even wider?"

"No, I think not," Helga declared. "We shall ask her to perform the final test, as we did with you, but I have high hopes of what she might achieve with her new gifts."

The final test involved channelling Power through an ancient device which went everywhere with the Abend. A peculiar kind of double bracelet, it locked the candidates hands together and once on could only be released by the candidate becoming one with it. It was only risked when the final selection had been made, for it was a radical procedure. Successful candidates made the complex succession of weavings to make the connection, and then found the device opening up something within them. New neural pathways which allowed them to function on a higher plane than before. However, make one mistake, or fall below the precision required, and it was instant death. The wormhole which broke down psychic barriers could also devour whole sections of the brain with one wrong turn. Nobody half made it into the Abend!

It was therefore a tense moment when they summoned Laufrey before them first thing the next morning. If she was at all borderline in her abilities, they could end up killing a very talented acolyte who might have given them many more years of useful service. However, the smouldering young woman showed none of any inner fears she might have been having. Well-suited, Barrax thought, and physically too. If Helga was an icy blonde version of the dark, frigid and menacing Masanae, then Laufrey had the promise of being a younger, fairer version of Magda's subtle, intuitive and sultry feminine talent. She might even share Magda's tastes, he thought even more hopefully. Might even like the idea of forming a threesome with them to while away the winter nights? That was an encouraging thought! However, only if she survived the next turn of the hour-glass.

As she focused deeper and deeper within herself there was a tense air of expectation in the room. At the moment the device returned her contact it was like being in the eye of a great and terrible storm. The constant tides of the Power which they were all constantly aware of stilled, then suddenly there was a surge. And what a surge! They could almost see the strands of Power swirling about Laufrey as her mind was peeled open with each new working, her eyelids closed but the eyes beneath them were making rapid movements beyond any dream state as her body quivered in a Power-drenched limbo. Then Laufrey's eyes flew open and she smiled.

"*Hello*!" she sent on the Power, with a confident sure touch, and the newest member of the Abend had arrived amongst them.

Chapter 17

A Tougher Acquisition

Kittermere: Earrach – early Beltane

Anarawd and Eliavres for once were in complete and total agreement – neither had ever felt so dreadfully ill in all their long lives, except for making the trip from the Isle of Areida to what the DeÁine had made into New Lochlainn upon their return to the Islands decades ago. The first leg of their current voyage from the port of Janja in southern New Lochlainn had given them false hopes. It had been far from pleasant, for the nausea at the ship's motion was accompanied by severe muscular cramps, headaches, and a most unpleasant sensation of being disconnected from the Power. However, their captain knew his business and also their wishes, and kept as close to the shore of Rathlin as its ragged cliffs would permit. Neither mage wanted to be close to the Brychan shore, despite it being navigationally the safer one of the two. That was just inviting Masanae or Quintillean to command them to return to Brychan and await their pleasure – something neither mage had any intention of doing. If it was possible to get their hands on another of the DeÁine Treasures, then by hook or by crook they were going to do it, before Quintillean scooped them all up for himself.

Briefly landing at the site of some kind of ancient Islander defence-work, they spent two nights ashore to restore their strength. Neither wanted to rush this job to the extent that they might land on Prydein in such a state that they would be unable to blast the pestilent Islanders holding the Scabbard straight to their pagan Underworld. The fortification showed signs of having been used fairly recently, and the pair deduced that it must have acted as a refuge for some escaping Islanders – no doubt running in fear of the might of the DeÁine army. Neither was particularly bothered by that, especially when they found traces of Helga's Power-weavings when they got to an upper chamber. There would soon be time to mop up such ragged resistance, and it was hardly as though there was any sort of army who could be recruited in this desolate land who might threaten the mainland. And so, feeling relaxed and confident they set sail on the day that Magda informed them of Barrax's selection – something which Anarawd in particular felt very smug about, given that Barrax had once been his acolyte.

However, when the sea-way opened up as the last of the Brychan coast fell away to their left, they realised how badly they had miscalculated. What they had experienced so far faded into nothing compared to the agonies they suffered as the ship bucked and rolled its way across the empty space between Rathlin and Kittermere. Had they known it, it was largely because here the sea floor fell away to immeasurable depths. This was where the scouring seas from the frozen north around Taineire surged through on their way to the great southern ocean. Most of this great tide took the broad sweep around Ergardia, and plunged southwards along the east coast of Rathlin, while the waters surging northwards from the warmer ocean swept up past the western coast of New Lochlainn, bringing with them the balmier climate which graced the land west of Brychan's mountains. But this narrow funnel made a short cut for whichever current was dominant in any given month. The Island sailors used it to their advantage, and skilfully cut days of tortuous sailing off journey times when the tides were right, and adjusted their routes accordingly when they were not.

Unfortunately Anarawd and Eliavres' captain had no such local knowledge, and all he could do was point his ship in the right direction, fight every wave as it came at them, and pray that the wind would not suddenly desert them. Wrecking would be inevitable without functioning sails to control their passage. By the time they had clawed their way to the first sighting of land six days later, the captain was so terrified that his august passengers were dying, if not dead already, that he put ashore. He had his men carry the two Abend as far inland as he dared, and posted guards about them. He had no idea what, if anything, he should do for them, and so he had to wait for them to regain consciousness on their own. Even then, the pair of them were clearly delirious and could tell him nothing he could make any sense of. Five days beyond that they were finally awake, coherent and recovering, neither overly pleased at the amount of time they were losing, but unable to complain too hard since it was they who were holding everything up.

"We cannot risk being so incapacitated again," Anarawd fretted to Eliavres, out of the hearing of their servants. "We lost consciousness for seven whole days!"

Both were also stunned to realise that Magda and Helga had been trying to get in touch with them with increasing anxiety as the days went by. To then find that it had been to tell them of Laufrey's elevation to the Abend made it all the more regrettable. She must be thinking that they were hardly the stuff legends were made of in the circumstances, yet neither of them wanted to make contact with her in the state they were in either. First impressions could only be made once, and both wanted to make sure she was well aware of their seniority, and where she stood in the pecking order. In time she would begin to jockey for power and influence, but that should not be starting straight away in the face of their perceived weakness. The only consolation was Magda's tale of how they thought Masanae and Quintillean's ritual had been broken. Nobody had made contact with the two senior Abend yet to inform them of Laufrey either. So hopefully she would think their own silence the normal thing to happen.

Stranger still was the report of Nicos' contact with Geitla. The strange Spirit-walker had confirmed that it was indeed the essence of Othinn which was taking up residence in the unconscious witch.

"*Nicos says that he can feel Geitla's essence is still there, but she's not in any way alert to him or anything else*," Magda reported regretfully. "*There's absolutely no way to communicate with her at all. She's not alive in the real sense, but she's not dead either. Not even in the way that Othinn is, because if she was, Nicos would be able to talk to her too. As it is he's managing to make some headway with Othinn*."

"*Is he*!" Anarawd exclaimed. "*And? Has he made any sense of what he wants*?"

Magda sniffed. "*I hesitate to call it sense! ... Let's say rather that he's deciphered some of the ramblings. It seems that it's all very well believing you're Jolnir, but without a little assistance from this side of the veil, it turns out it's not that easy to interact with living things. He thought he was going to create mayhem. Instead, he barely managed to raise a few ghosts until Helga worked her talents and made the glamour. It was that which made him realise that he needs us. In that night of wild rampaging across the Islands he got a taste for what he might achieve*."

"*Is there any way we might use him and his ghostly army*?" Eliavres pondered, and Magda picked up on the inferences swimming around in his thoughts which focused on graves, and other necrophilic and necrotic ideas.

"*Oh you wicked boy, poppet! That's so naughty! ... Oh yes! ... Oh yes! I think you might have something there*!"

"Sweet Lotus, she sounds almost orgasmic!" muttered Anarawd.

"She does love a bit of mayhem and slaughter to get her juices going," Eliavres chuckled. "*Now, my dear heart, when you've finished getting quite so excited, do you think that you might suggest something of the sort to Nicos? See if he can prompt and prod our lunatic spirit into doing something useful for once?"*

Her excited giggle of a sending affirmed this, and she disappeared to be replaced with a very subtle, narrow and quiet sending of Helga's. One deliberately designed for Magda not to hear, nor either of the newcomers. For once the iciest of the witches was not trying to play games with them or strike points against them. "*I have a worrying thought for you,*" she began. "*I know Magda has always had stranger bedroom tastes than some of us, but that aside, how do you think she is of late?*"

The two exchanged glances and thought about it for a moment. It was Eliavres who answered, but with one eye on Anarawd, who was nodding in agreement as he listened in on the sending.

"*Now you mention it, I'd say she was almost back to being the Magda who was such a formidable teacher to me. She's much more alert and focused, isn't she?*"

"*Good. I'm glad you could feel that. It's even more noticeable when you see her in person. The thing is, Nicos has confirmed something I had begun to think even before he appeared on the scene. I think Othinn has been trying to get back for longer than we think. I suspect his sense of time has been very skewed in his altered state. I also strongly believe that since he sucked additional Power from Magda in order to convert himself into Power, that he thought he could do the same to get back.*"

"*Great Dragon of Death!*" Eliavres was appalled. "*Does that mean you think that what we saw as Magda's decline into senility was really because she was being attacked from within the Power? That he was trying to make unnatural connections with her time and time again?*"

"*That's exactly what I think.*" Even Helga could not quite keep her emotions at this thought hidden. It struck at the very heart of what it meant to be an Abend. Whilst connected to the Power, they were used to thinking that they were invulnerable. Attacks might come from without, but the actual flows of energy had never been turned against them from within. The Power was sacred and as such was a sanctuary as well. To realise that this was far from so was deeply unsettling.

Suddenly they both felt Anarawd start, then the warm glow of returning positivity.

"What?" Eliavres asked, but Anarawd was already sending to both of them.

"*We might be able to turn this to our advantage, you know?*"

"*How?*" a wary Helga wanted to know.

"*Well we've been ... concerned ... about the potential number of gifted acolytes who might be coming with the Sinut fleet, haven't we. It would be ... undesirable ... if they got the idea that they didn't need us. That maybe a grateful Emperor might decide to create a brand new Abend back in the homeland if they return with the Treasures, leaving us behind. But if we were to tell Othinn that they wanted to take him back shackled within the Power for Emperor's amusement too, how do you think he would react?*"

"*Like a beast in a trap!*" Helga supplied without a pause. "*He'd go on the attack!*"

"*My thoughts too,*" Anarawd agreed. "*And if we showed we could control him – we don't need to in any way let them know that it would be by destroying his vessel in the form of Geitla, nor that it's something we could only do once. Imply that we, as the higher authority, know a few things even they don't, well I'm sure they won't be quite so keen to confront us.*"

For once even Helga was in awe of the convoluted way that Anarawd's mind worked. It was a brilliant idea, though. Sneaky and conniving, and just likely to save the day if things got nasty. Offering thanks which for once were genuine, she left them to go and relay the idea to Magda. Her natural caution made her not include Barrax and Laufrey just yet, for she knew neither well enough to know what their instinctive reaction might be. It also struck her that Tancostyl might be easier to handle if he was offered some morsel which allowed him to keep an outer show of his seniority. By telling him before the two newest members it would allow him to feel superior, and might just stop him from trying to lord it over them in some other way. Strangely enough, she was sure that Barrax would handle the cranky war-mage far better than Laufrey would. Too much of Tancostyl's confrontational, male aggression might make the younger woman feel she had to strike back to protect herself, and that would not be a good start!

For Eliavres and Anarawd, the next day it was back to the boat. They dared not linger longer, but at least now they could put ashore for the night on alternate evenings to give them recuperation time. On the last day of Earrach, their ship put in at a tiny bay just before the headland which protected Boddigo on the north Prydein coast. This was the headland where the priests' map had shown the Scabbard resting, even if the two Abend had no idea of what its name was and cared even less. In the depths of night, when what little local shipping there was was tied up, they slipped past the port with no lights showing, and crept two bays further into the broad estuary. By now both Eliavres and Anarawd could sense the

Scabbard, and could have homed in on it on the blackest of nights and blindfolded.

Getting ashore at first light with their triad of Hunters, they expected to make a clear crossing of the countryside at least, before they had to encounter any resistance. Yet to their horror the entire countryside was heaving with troops. And not just any old army. These were Knights. The men of the Order were everywhere. Enlisted men cared for horses in the fields, and the roads had rows and rows of tents lined up along them.

"Surely all this isn't to guard the Scabbard?" a bemused Anarawd wondered. "They can't possibly have known we were coming!"

"No, this must be for something else," agreed Eliavres, as they hid in the lee of a clump of stunted hawthorns. It was a new experience for Anarawd, and one he really did not like. For Eliavres this was far too much of a reminder of the months he had spent creeping through the Order-infested landscape of Brychan when he had thought he was tracking the Gorget southwards. Now he could feel the Scabbard, he realised only too well how wrong he had been then. The resonance the Scabbard was putting out on the Power was unmistakable, and had he been anywhere near the Gorget he realised he should have been feeling the same. But then how was he to know? He had not even been born when the Treasures were lost, and had never worked with a major object of Power. All he had had to go on was what Abend like Quintillean and Magda had told him. It was hardly his fault if they had failed to explain it properly.

However, the Gorget was not here and the Scabbard was, but getting to it was going to be another thing all together.

"We're going to have to go back to the ship," he told Anarawd. "There's no way we can get through this lot. Even if we summoned Power-fire and blasted this first batch out of the way, we'd have to keep it up for hours to get through all that lot up the hill and beyond. And I don't feel up to that, do you?"

Even to an Abend with such little interest in military things as Anarawd, it was blindingly clear that the men were loitering here because there were so many more up ahead, there was no room further on to accommodate them. Suddenly, though, there was a flurry of activity and the men began to prepare to move.

Had the two war-mages but known it, the first wave of men had embarked onto ships in the grey hours of dawn at Mullion, and were currently on their way to Kittermere. This was the muster which Hugh de

Burh had called for, and which by now had congregated along the road between Mullion and Bittern. The Order men whom the mages were observing had remained on the headland to allow the huge contingent of archers from the east to march past, brought up under the leadership of Commander Instone of Rosco. It was Ealdorman Hereman who had decided that the archers would be better off in the middle of the shipment – not wanting them to be the first to land in case of resistance when they got to the Rathlin side of Kittermere, but equally not wanting to leave them until last, when they might be of great strategic use before then. Now the archers were past the bottleneck on the road and marching onwards to Mullion and the ships, and there was room for the second half of the Order's men to begin to head that way too.

From the side of the ship, which had been hung with some tattered sails to make her look as though she had suffered some damage and was simply making repairs, the two Abend watched for the rest of the day. The captain managed to get rid of annoyingly helpful fishermen who kept coming up in small boats to offer assistance, but clearly for them to linger longer would invite far too much comment.

"Can you take us back out to the bay this side of the one where we waited for nightfall?" suggested Eliavres. "That looked quieter! If you put us ashore there, you'll be able to wait without all these pestilent Islanders bobbing up every hour of the day." It was clear that the Scabbard was not right here but further inland, and that would mean a search – something they could not do just yet.

It also had not occurred to any of them that in reality there was a distinct lack of any shipping of any size in these waters. Unused to the bustle of a busy Island port, they had accepted the quiet as normal. In fact, every ship of any size had been commandeered and was currently involved in the movement of troops – hence those fishermen left with only rowing boats' helpful intentions. Islanders going from Prydein to Kittermere might not have aroused curiosity in the DeÁine, for the comings and goings of a people they looked down upon so deeply were thought of as being of little consequence. However, a little more thought might have had them wondering why so many were needed, and whether these soldiers were going anywhere beyond Kittermere. It was a thought which would return to haunt Anarawd and Eliavres later, and forcibly at that.

For now, though, they had only one thought, and that was for the Scabbard.

"After all these years," breathed Anarawd with barely contained excitement.

It was three mornings on from their first, abortive attempt to land. This time they had come ashore on a deserted beach and had made the day-long walk across the headland, and now they were looking at a castle further inland than the small port they had first try to land at. Anarawd had been somewhat disgusted at this sneaking around, but Eliavres was the one with experience of getting through enemy territory, and so he perforce bit back his natural inclinations to summon servants and horses by overwhelming peasants with the Power. And Eliavres' tactics had paid off. They were sitting on a small knoll with the triad of Hunters, hidden from the castle's view by dense woodland but able to see out.

"May the Mother Seagang rot their bones!" Anarawd muttered disconsolately, "Cursed soldiers all over the place still!"

"Yes," hummed Eliavres distantly, taking little notice of Anarawd's wittering and focusing his tactical mind on the matter. "Must be twenty over in that tower at least, and the same in the other one. …Hmmm …Must allow for at least double what we can see as well. …Mmmm …I doubt there are less than a hundred men in that castle, so that rules out a direct attack."

Anarawd shot him a quizzical glance.

"Oh come on!" Eliavres said witheringly. "Reach into yourself! How much Power can you hold at the moment after that voyage?" He felt the other mage go through the motions, and then his rising panic as he realised that he was feeling only a fraction of what he was normally used to doing. *Great Lotus, no wonder Quintillean ruled him out of being one of those to go in search of the Treasures*, Eliavres thought to himself scathingly. *The bloody fool would have got himself trapped within a week! He may be a wondrous schemer but he's useless in the field.* However, his own natural conniving kept his tone civil when he spoke again, for he still needed Anarawd, and he knew only too well how touchy his fellow Abend could be.

"So …with just three Hunters and both of us under-powered in every sense of the word, we're not going to be blasting our way into a castle stuffed with well-trained Knights, are we? So let's focus on pinpointing where the Scabbard is. My feeling is that it's deep in the ground." He gestured to the great mound of packed earth and stone upon which the castle sat. "I don't think the Scabbard is so much *in* the castle as *under* it."

Anarawd frowned, but Eliavres could feel him reaching out and confirming his own findings.

"So how do we get to it?" Anarawd fretted.

Eliavres grinned. "We make a tunnel!" Anarawd's expression told him that he was again thinking simplistically, and was visualising the five of them with picks and shovels getting very dirty and sweaty. Struggling to keep his smile in place in the face of such blindness, Eliavres elaborated,

"Tonight we are going to make a tunnel with the Power. Or rather, you'll make the tunnel, and I'll be using my Power to remove the soil and rocks as you sear your way in. It doesn't have to be a big tunnel! Just large enough for one of these to crawl down." He gestured to the Hunters and suddenly Anarawd brightened. Neither of them would be risking life and limb down the hole, and a Hunter could handle one of the great pieces of Power for long enough to bring it out to them. What neither of them said either, was that if the Hunter got killed, it was of little importance as long as he had turned around, and was holding the Scabbard in front of him on the way out. If he died, then at least his body would be blocking the way for the defenders, and one of the other Hunters could crawl in and drag the Scabbard the rest of the way.

"Tonight!" Anarawd said with new-found satisfaction and Eliavres echoed him.

They retreated a little way off, and while the Hunters kept watch the two mages slept, building and conserving their strength. With nightfall came a persistent drizzle, enough to dull visibility and ensure that they were unlikely to be seen by any sentries, but not enough of a deluge to turn the earth to mud. The two rested Abend easily found a good spot which allowed for the shortest possible tunnel and began work. Even then, Eliavres had to pull Anarawd up sharply with the first channelling.

"Great Volla, give me strength!" he growled through gritted teeth as he broke Anarawd's first weaving. "Not like that! Do you want them to empty the castle onto us! Even the densest guard will feel it if you start throwing Power around in those quantities. When I said a *tight* beam, I meant it! Like *this*!" He demonstrated, creating a thin, lance-like beam which entered the soil and began to steam as it vaporised the solid matter before it. "Now you take over while I enlarge it behind you!"

Anarawd's sullen expression told Eliavres that he did not appreciate being lectured to like a newly recruited acolyte. However, even Anarawd had enough sense of self-preservation not to start throwing temper tantrums out here in the wilds. Instead he did as Eliavres had shown him, venting his anger instead by channelling hard so that his beam of Power was soon diving deep into the ground, and Eliavres was struggling to keep up.

"Wait!" Eliavres suddenly panted. Anarawd turned to him with smug satisfaction thinking he had outpaced his colleague, but that was not why Eliavres had made him pause. "We must get the tunnel completed before we make the final cut through into the castle itself," Eliavres pointed out. "No use blundering through and giving them advanced warning before we're ready to go in and get the Scabbard."

Anarawd's smirk disappeared and was replaced with the sullen frown again. The fact that Eliavres was right was doing nothing to mollify his dented ego. All that was keeping him from turning on his heels and leaving, was the memory that Eliavres had promised that he would be the one to wield the Scabbard once they had it. And having one of the Treasures took him one step closer to achieving his goal of having control over all of them. He had had a momentary surge of fear when Magda had told them about the strong possibility of the priests disrupting Masanae and Quintillean's plans. Had the priests also caught on to what he was doing?

Then he got a grip on himself again. No, of course they had not! He had been far more subtle than the two senior Abend, and he had made very sure that the priests saw him as no kind of threat to their own position – either morally or physically. No, his harem would still be there when he got back, and if this was an annoying interruption then that's all it was. When playing as long a game as Anarawd had planned, and begun executing, it was possible to take a few months out if it meant that everything went more smoothly thereafter. It was fools like Tancostyl who did everything in a rush, and then blamed others when they failed to allow time for unforeseen interruptions.

And so, keeping a mental image of a much humbled and chastened Eliavres as consolation, Anarawd did as he was told. It took until well after midnight before Eliavres was satisfied with the state of the tunnel, but as he emphasised to Anarawd, even that was not a waste of time for it meant that the garrison were all fast asleep except for a few sentries. All the less likely that someone would be in a room close enough to the Scabbard to realise what was happening. With one fine blast of Power they broke through into the dank hole where the Scabbard was housed. Not exactly quietly, for the last barrier was a massive, solid, stone block. One of four which made the walls of the hole at the bottom of the dungeon, which had been made that way with the express intention of making it impossible for a prisoner to tunnel out.

The low deep *crump* of the stone vaporising was followed by a puff of dust coming out of the hole, but the first Hunter was already at the entrance and dived in regardless of the choking bits in the air. They saw his legs disappear and followed his progress with their senses. What they did not know and had not registered – because they had not bothered to check – was the presence of sentries higher up in the dungeon. Ealdorman Piran had taken his new posting very seriously. If Master Hugh was going to entrust him with guarding a weapon of the enemy, then he was going to guard it! Nobody could stand being too close to the dreadful thing for long, and for that reason alone, Piran had relented from posting men in the dungeon cell itself. Being directly above the hole, everyone he had put in there had come out jumping at their own shadows after a two hour shift. However, the guardroom above that seemed to have sufficient distance, given that the Scabbard was encased in a lead-lined box made of sacred Rowan. And usefully, the room had a small fireplace and its own latrine, which meant that there was no reason for men to ever leave without a replacement being there to hand over to.

It was also the war-mages' misfortune that the men left behind at Bittern were the truly old veterans. Like all the others left behind to guard Order castles and preceptories, they were men only a short way off retirement, or ones who had actually retired and willingly come back at the signs of trouble. Too old to fight in the field except under the direst of circumstances, yet also with years of experience and the level heads which came with them. Men who could be trusted to act with initiative and consideration. All of them had seen action against the DeÁine at Moytirra and elsewhere, and they knew the feeling when Power was being channelled, even if they lacked a grain of talent for it.

"Do you feel that?" an elderly man-at-arms had said to his companions as they played dice to while away the hours.

The old archer to his left looked down at his grizzled forearm and the way that the hairs were beginning to stand on end. "Ants!" he muttered, not needing to say any more. Anyone of their age who had served for as long as them knew it was the way everyone described the feeling of Power on the air. It was as if ants were crawling all over you, and that was just how the men were feeling now. A younger man might have put it down to the chill down here, and the itchy bedding they had all been forced to make out of old bracken to allow the bedrolls to be taken with the men going on campaign. A younger man might have put it down to being dog tired after the long march to get here, and then running around to get sorted in time to relieve all of the garrison who were going. But these were not young men.

Without another word, the second man-at-arms got up and went out. On rheumatic legs, he hobbled as fast as he could and still be quiet up to the next guardroom. In a hushed voice he alerted the men there and then returned to his post, taking the opportunity to grab an extra quiver of birch arrows on the way, just in case. One of the second group of guards hurried out and ran as fast as he could for the senior office of the watch, who in his turn roused Piran. By the time the stone block exploded inwards there were twenty men crammed into the dungeon space above. The unexpected cloud of dust had them all coughing and spluttering and wiping streaming eyes, but they did not move away.

Then one gestured furiously down into the hole. They had already removed the iron grill which had covered the hole, and so ten archers all took an uninterrupted aim down into the swirling mist of stone dust. Nobody could see anything precisely, but the man had caught a hint of what he thought might be soil being pushed outwards into the hole. A darker spot, nothing else, but it was enough. Ten yew boughs strained into curves and goose feathers brushed cheeks. Every man in the room felt their senses swimming as the Power from the two mages established a connection with the Scabbard, but there was little need for accurate aiming in such a confined space. Waiting until the Hunter had hauled himself out into the hole, the ten let fly and the Hunter was impaled, several arrows going through him and virtually pinning him to the Scabbard's casing.

Yet he had only recently taken more of his drugs – taken them earlier than he might have done, or was ideal, at the mages' insistence. They had wanted him working to the full peak of his potential, and now the wisdom of that paid off. Hauling himself off the Scabbard and disregarding the tears in his flesh which resulted, he turned in the cramped space, breaking the shafts off arrows against the walls as he did and splattering them with his blood. His body shuddered again with the impact of more arrows, yet he managed to stuff the Scabbard into the hole even so. A third volley finally killed him, but his fellow Hunter had already grasped the Scabbard and was now crawling backwards as fast as he could.

It had also taken Eliavres and Anarawd those brief moments to respond, and to realise that their activities had not gone as unnoticed as they had hoped. Yet they were not members of the Abend for nothing. Anarawd attached a tentacle of Power to the ankles of the reversing Hunter and yanked him out with vicious speed, while Eliavres projected his weaving beyond the Hunter and created a shield at the tunnel's entrance. As the first man-at-arms jumped down into the pit it was just as Eliavres was doing it, and the man's legs were sheared off at the knees, the jolt of Power also stopping his heart.

"Bastard Abend!" the captain above swore, but recognised the futility of sending more men to their deaths when the problem was something so far beyond their control. "Runner! Go and tell the Ealdorman they have it!"

Piran himself had realised that although the chances of the Abend being within the castle were very remote, they were undoubtedly nearby if not almost up to the walls. Consequently he had rallied squads of men, and now had them quartering the land outside the bailey. It was a miserable task, for beyond a narrow patch of cropped grass surrounding the castle's motte, there were dense woods and thickets of shrubs where the trees left gaps. Difficult to search under any circumstances. In the night's soaking wet, the torches guttered and spat, failing to illuminate some places and casting brief but peculiar shadows in others, and making their searching even harder. Nor did Piran want to risk making straight for the far side of the castle, where he was sure it was most likely that the Abend would be. It was just possible that they were counting on that, and had some plan to get into the castle to get hold of horses for a swift escape, or something equally daring. Bad enough to lose the Scabbard, but even worse to hand them the castle as well.

Swearing fluently under his breath, Piran sat on his horse, flaming torch held aloft as he followed the double line of men making their way round from the east. A second group were working westwards under his second's command. He had had no time to even don a cape and the rain had plastered his shirt to him, and he had trickles of water running down the inside of his breeches as well the outside. Backhanding the wet out of his eyes as it ran down from his drenched hair, he strained to see out into the gloom.

"Where in the fiend-infested Underworld are you?" he snarled to himself. "Even you bloody Abend can't vanish into thin air!"

"Sire!" a voice called urgently, and looking in the direction of the call, he saw a man frantically gesturing towards a clump of trees.

For a moment Piran could not see a thing which would warrant the man's warning, and then he spotted it! The air in front of the trees suddenly shimmered in a flicker of torch-light, as if reflecting it back. A shield! That had to be where they were! Already the old veterans were exchanging hand signals and sweeping round from a line into a horseshoe shape, at the same time carefully questing closer to the spot.

For Anarawd, the jubilation of getting his hands on the Scabbard had made him relinquish his control over the weavings he had.

"By Volla, Fano and Esras!" Eliavres choked out. "You're a Temple-forsaken nightmare, Anarawd! Stop drooling over the thing and focus on helping me get out of here, or we may all die before you've even had a chance to handle it!"

Anarawd looked up dizzily.

"Get the shield back up properly!" Eliavres fumed as he pulled on his war-mage's gauntlets. With these on he could throw balls of Power-fire all day if he had the energy to summon them for that long. Without them he risked peeling the skin off his palms, but they also had weavings built into them which aided a war-mage with focusing and aiming. Not quite as good as the great Volla's Gauntlets, he had been told, but since nobody had seen them in action in over half a millennium and one Gauntlet was gone to dust, he was quite content with what he had.

He was waiting for as long as he dared before he began striking back, for they were still a long way from the coast, and it could be a wearing retreat if he had to fight all the way back for them. However, the cursed Knights were getting closer by the moment, and he reached deep down into the Power and began sucking up all the Power he could hold. His first blast was a small controlled one. Just enough to wipe out the men who were an immediate challenge to them. Luckily the two remaining Hunters were in their peak and had experience as well. They formed up on either side of him and guided him with a hand each, even as they had their swords up in the other hands ready to cut down any who got through the shield.

Eliavres hardly had time to be gazing about him, but a rapid, darting glance towards Anarawd nearly had him weeping with frustration. The other mage was busy fumbling with the casing on the Scabbard, tripping over roots and blundering into branches as he tried to keep up at the same time. Even if the Knights could not see them they would be hearing his clumsy passage.

"If he drops it, grab the infernal thing and leave him!" Eliavres hissed to the Hunters, and he felt the faint squeeze of acknowledgement in their grips as he launched another Power-ball. If Anarawd was going to be so unremittingly stupid, then Eliavres had better things to be doing then hauling his arse out of the fire all of the time. From what Magda had said this new war-mage, Barrax, was far more use, so why not think about finding another such as him? One who would not be such a Seagang-rotted liability all the time. He launched another fireball and had the satisfaction of hearing many men cry out in agony. Could it be any worse going into battle with an untried war-mage when the ones who were supposed to be experienced were as useless as Anarawd?

However, either Anarawd finally woke up to the very real danger amassing around them, or he had actually been thinking more than Eliavres had credited him with. With a triumphant yelp he pulled the Scabbard free and held it close to his chest, dropping the Knight's heavier casing and abandoning it. Without any hesitation he began to channel Power into it. For a moment Eliavres thought it would be something which would take hours just to charge it fully, but Anarawd clearly knew what he was going. Suddenly the flow of Power reversed and it began to spill out of the Scabbard in increasing quantities. Moments later Eliavres could feel Anarawd weaving it into the most effective shield he had ever come across. It was not just protecting, it was hiding them too.

This was confirmed by the sudden cries of dismay coming from the men hunting them. From their perspective the fugitives had simply vanished into thin air. Before Anarawd could say a word, Eliavres was already lowering his arms. The very worst thing he could do just at this moment was continue to fight back, for that would reveal their location all over again. Even more surprising was the fact that Anarawd was able to turn and run with them now. The Scabbard seemed capable of holding the concealment spell without any great input on his behalf.

In this way they got well beyond the perimeter of the soldiers and were able to slow to a brisk walk. From then on it was simply a matter of keeping walking back to the bay where the ship waited. A terse summoning meant that a boat was ready and waiting for them even as they slithered down the face of the dunes onto the beach, and half a turn of the hourglass later they were back on board ship. Taking advantage of the cloaking spell, they got underway and out of sight of land before the salt water got to the mages, and even the Scabbard could not save them from that!

The one thing they were able to do before resigning themselves to the crushing sickness once more was to contact Magda.

"*We have it!*" Eliavres told her, and relayed how Anarawd had managed to use it too. This time, however, he kept the news on a very quiet and controlled sending. None of them wanted a repeat of Masanae's party crashing from when the Helm had landed in Brychan. This time they would hold onto the Treasure they had!

Chapter 18

Falling Out

New Lochlainn – Brychan: Earrach – Beltane

Quintillean and Masanae staggered through the warren-like street of the lower tier at Kuzmin Palace. Both felt like they had been hit by an avalanche of Power when the strange man had fallen in the way of Masanae's summoning. Two things had happened almost simultaneously at that point. The careful weaving they had created had been infused by the essence of the first sacrifice and the one Quintillean had been charging with Power, but instead of providing a pure and untainted conduit, the sacrifices' essence had been something very different. Corrupt and perverted, the essence had been a stunted and twisted thing which caused the Power to buck and cavort in unexpected ways, testing both Abend's control skills. In that instant, both Abend had felt a moment of panic, for this perversion, this very strong link to things murky, earthy and knowing instead of being a blank sheet of unawareness at such a young age, was something they had never expected.

Yet that had been nothing to what happened mere seconds later when the unexpected figure had fallen in between Masanae's hurried, second, killer-blast and its intended victim. At the moment of impact between the Power and the man, something beyond the experience of either Abend had occurred. Here was the unsullied essence they had sought, yet from such a wildly different source and one they would never have dreamed of looking at. He was a mature man not a babe, and even more disturbing, what had fed back into the Power weaving from him was a purity of a whole different nature to the malleable, blankness of a child's.

Moreover this was white, not a clear void. Pure, unflinching, white essence, strong and unwavering. Not even a soft white but a painful, blinding intensity that had the qualities of a close lightning strike in a dark night sky. It blasted its own signature back at them with a vibrancy which was potent beyond their experience, and to their utter astonishment it somehow called to, and was answered by, a whole new thread of the Power that they had never known. It fed this new blast, charged and invigorated it, and sent it straight back into their minds where it burned into them like searing shafts of sunlight. Moreover it had caused the freakish black summoning to shatter into shards. Shards that they could control no more than the original, shocking perversion. Shards which exploded outwards in a star-burst, killing not only the acolytes, but also the two spare victims whom Masanae had had waiting in the room as reserves, in case more blood had been required to cement the ritual. Only vaguely were they aware that they were also under attack from men, and that the last two sacrifices had been whisked away, yet it just about registered that they must pursue them.

Horrifically, the spare victims' death had released more of the dark contaminant, maybe even calling to the shattered essence too. Malevolence of itself was no obstruction to the Abend, nor was it something which normally repelled them, for it was inherent in their very beings, had they ever stopped to examine themselves to see it. This, however, was a wholly different variation on what they were accustomed to, for this Power failed to unite despite all the normal coalescing tactics. It was exceedingly powerful, and yet it scattered about the room like flying splinters of glass which had flown out from a broken decanter, yet were unable to settle to the floor. To ones with the sight to see the Power, it was like trying to dodgy ethereal, black, poisoned darts.

Dodging the random ricochets, Masanae found that shutting down the strands she had been trying to weave for the ritual, and summoning something cruder to remove a section of wall, also further fragmented the black weaves in its wake. Now needles of inky corruption were all over the room. When, with an equally dazed Quintillean, she pointed that Power at one wall, they had to throw themselves flat to avoid the flying rubble both material and Power-based. Having managed to scrape together enough energy to blast their way out of the room of sacrifice, they were barely able to escape the black, piercing shards, and had to rely on the physical barrier of the walls to protect themselves. Once outside the room they also found they had nothing left within themselves to make any further summoning of any size with.

Sheer fury and disbelief kept them on the trail of the escaping last sacrifices, but neither could hear a thing, and they were working blind, since it was impossible to see more than a few yards ahead in the twisting mass of buildings. The weird backlash of Power had their mental powers in a numbed state, and the blasts which they had used to free themselves – both from the room and from the dangerous overspill of Power – had also deafened their physical hearing. All of which meant that they could not hear the retreating troops, and sound was the only way they would have known it in such enclosed spaces.

"Wh're've they g'ne?" slurred Masanae, cannoning off a wall as they exited the temple and she tried to move faster. When Quintillean failed to reply, she turned round in time to see him trying to rise from his hands and knees where he had clearly been voiding his stomach. He just about managed to unleash a weak blast of Power-fire in the direction of the garden stairs with an unclear wave of his hand. He could not make it further, though, and proceeded to come after her on all fours for a few yards before collapsing unconscious in a heap.

Trying to shake her head, Masanae swiftly realised that this was not the way to try to clear it. The world span violently and she too ended up on her knees, vomiting up what little precious Power-infused blood they had managed to consume. Furious with herself for wasting it, she tried to push herself onwards but to no avail. She made a few more yards and then joined Quintillean in oblivion.

When she came to again, it was to find herself propped up on cushions in what she assumed must be one of the servant's quarters in the lower level – somewhere she had never visited before. For a moment she could not work out how she had got here either. If some house slave had found her, brought her here, and then left her in this state, she would have them flogged to death for their negligence. Then a ragged cough to one side made her look into the gloom and she saw Quintillean. The war-mage looked as rough as she had ever seen him. He was feeding bits of wood into a small fire on the hearth and seemed to be trying to heat some water up.

"Where are the slaves?" She had meant it as an imperious demand but it came out as a feeble croak.

Quintillean hawked up a gob of phlegm and spat into the flames before answering her.

"We're alone, dear heart. …Just you and me."

Belatedly Masanae realised that Quintillean himself must have brought her inside, and bit back the string of invective she was about to let rip. Going by the state of him it must have cost him dear, and he could have left her where she fell. Then he spoke again, and she realised he had paused as much to get his breath as to give her time to answer. That strange noise she had been vaguely aware of was him wheezing!

"Those Knights ...they blocked both ways ...out to the gates." He drew a deep breath in slowly.

"Surely you didn't walk to find out?" Masanae was more shocked at his state than she would have thought herself capable of feeling.

"This way ...yes. ...The other way ...I was able to make a small sending. ...Just a feeling. ...They brought down an arch ...totally blocked. ...Gate's barred anyway. ...Can't get out. ...Not without being able to blast..." And he dissolved into a paroxysm of coughing which left him purple in the face.

Forcing herself to her knees and then to her feet, Masanae managed a wobbly walk over to his side, where she slid rather ungracefully onto a large floor cushion. She had intended to reach into the Power and try to heal him. However, even extending her senses brought the sharpest pain she had ever known inside her head.

"Ooah, ouch!" she whimpered, and clutched her splitting skull with both hands. "Oh Sweet Lotus, Quintillean! What's happened to us?"

"Backlash of Power," he answered, having eased his coughing with several sips of the warm water. "Happened to me on Ergardia too."

Suddenly Masanae felt uncharacteristically guilty for having acted so superior when Quintillean had contacted her following his narrow escape from the enchanted Island. It suddenly was not so funny anymore. If he had felt this bad, it was little short of miraculous that he had made it back at all, let alone bringing two of the valuable sacrifices with him.

"How long will it take to recover?" she asked, dreading his reply.

He shrugged. "Took me weeks ...but then I was on that Lotus-forsaken Island for some time ...then on the sea. ...All knocked the guts out of me!"

Masanae felt her stomach lurch involuntarily at the thought of making a sea journey when in this state. In a rare rush of feeling she reached out and wrapped her arms around him, reminding herself that his extraordinary strength and resilience had been what had formed the original attraction to him. He responded by wrapping an arm around her shoulders.

"Checking the place out ...knocked me out for an hour ...no, several. ...But then I made a ...sending to Ralja. ...Hunters are coming!"

Great Mother Seagang, Masanae thought, *he actually managed a sending? I can't even reach out on the Power, much less make any contact with anyone*! Forcing herself to get up again she went in search of any stores which had been left behind. There was not much, but she did find dried fruit in one stone jar, and some flour which she was able to turn into rather disgusting flat-breads on an old metal pan. It was pitiful fare, but at least she felt she had contributed something to their survival and had not left it all to Quintillean.

When the Hunters appeared the next day and dug them out, she was horrified to realise that she must have been unconscious for two whole days. Quintillean's efforts had taken him longer than she had thought, not that she had any intention of criticising, for without him she would still be mouldering in the rubble. Someone at Ralja had shown initiative, and the Hunters were accompanied by priests and acolytes bearing healing devices. It was bliss to have the blinding headache gone, and by that evening both felt capable of eating a substantial meal prepared by their rescuers, even if they had to eat in the servants' rooms. It had been a shock to get back up to the Palace suite and discover the fire-blackened rooms still smouldering. Nobody would be sleeping there for some time.

By the time they were back at Ralja, Masanae had recovered most of her normal frosty calm. A calm only disrupted by a building fury towards those who had done this to her. A final session of healing at the hands of the head priest himself had her fit to take command once more, and her first demand was for the Hunters to give her an assessment of where the renegades would be now. Along with Quintillean, they agreed that whoever had been responsible for the sacrilege at Kuzmin must be riding with all speed for the Brychan Gap. Not that they had come past Ralja, that the Hunters were sure of, especially when Quintillean spoke of the number of men the terrorists had had with them. They therefore had not taken boats in the short cut across the arm of the Salu Maré as a short cut to Ralja and must have gone by road. Believing Tokai was still held by the priests, they never even considered the terrorists might have gone that way, and there was no way that they would consider contacting those priests on the Power anyway, for that would reveal that they had been bested by mere mortals!

"East," Masanae growled venomously, "we ride east first thing in the morning. Be prepared!"

Allowing these miscreants to escape was not an option. They would be caught and punished for all to see what happened to those who so dared to challenge the might of the DeÁine.

Yet no matter how hard they rode they couldn't seem to catch up with the rebels. By the time their exhausted horses were replaced by new mounts brought south-west out of Bruighean to meet them, there was still no sign.

"Curse them! They fly as if the very fiends from their Underworld were at their heels!" a frustrated Quintillean snarled.

He and Masanae had been venting their frustrations in passionate couplings at night, which had guaranteed that the rest of their force gave them a very wide berth indeed, but had had the unexpected bonus of awakening some of his lost abilities in the Power. His private fear had been that his experiences on Ergardia had done him some permanent damage, for despite having been healed in most respects there had been certain things which had refused to function. Now, having joined minds with her in the Power as they had joined bodies, the flood of her ecstatic state washing through him had done something all the healing devices had failed to do. They had re-established the lost pathways in his mind. *I'm back*! he thought jubilantly. *The greatest of the war-mages and still in my prime! Just wait 'til I get my hands on those rebels*! It was a glorious thought but one destined not to happen.

Only a couple of days later, as the Islanders celebrated the first of Beltane with feast days across towns and villages, the vengeful Abend encountered a rider who brought them staggering news. Abasing himself in the dirt at their feet and hoping that they would not strike him dead for his efforts he told them,

"The road ahead is closed, oh Great Ones."

"Closed?" spat Masanae.

"Yes, oh Great One. With flood water." He cringed and dared not look up to see how they were taking this. "All the snow, Great Ones. It's all melting. The southern slopes were the first to go. That started the floods. But now spring is even starting to come to the deep mountains. There is no southern route around the mountains anymore. None! Nothing for miles and miles. Just a huge inland sea!"

Quintillean unleashed his new-found powers and really stretched them for the first time, questing ahead of their position and what he felt shocked him to the core.

"He speaks the truth," he said just in time to stop Masanae blasting the man to cinders.

"What?" She was aghast.

"The whole of the valley, it's flooded. And not by a small amount, either. This man said the truth. It truly is submerged under water many feet deep, and it's cold. There's no way even a horse could swim through those icy waters for the distance it would take to find dry land. We can go no further this way."

Masanae strode off grinding her teeth. When she and Quintillean were alone she snarled,

"Then where are our rebels? Where are the terrorists who attacked us in our own stronghold? Did they sprout wings and fly like birds across this *sea*? Or are they holed up somewhere ahead waiting for the water to subside?"

"They are not ahead of us at all," Quintillean told her calmly. He was rather enjoying the fact that he was the calm one for once. "They must have eluded us and gone south at some point."

They left it at that with all their force around them, instead announcing that they would camp, and then sat in stony silence while frantic activity took place all around them. Only when they were alone did they confer, and even then using the Power not speech.

"*What do you want to do now*?" Masanae sent to Quintillean as they ate their meal in solitude. Indecision in the face of lesser beings was something never to be even hinted at, and that was why she spoke on the Power rather than aloud, knowing servants hovered attentively at the tent's flap.

"*We should ride south*," Quintillean answered firmly. "*Since I cannot feel Tancostyl on this side of all that water, we must assume he and the Helm have been prevented from coming west, just as we cannot go east this way. I feel we must focus on that now. Delightful though it would have been to exact our revenge on our attackers, I fear that will have to wait. Do you not think it odd that we have had no communication from the rest of the nine? For two weeks or more we have been out of communication with them in every way. Surely they should have remarked upon that and thought to try to reach us*?"

With a jolt Masanae realised that he was right. Being out of touch with Quintillean was one thing. He had been insistent on them not making too many contacts while he went after the Treasures, and so they had probably been waiting for him to get in touch with them. But the other witches? Why had they not been keeping her appraised of what was going on? Summoning her skills she wove a sending and reached out along it in the direction of Arlei. When she made contact the surprise nearly made her cry out loud in shock.

"*Greetings, sweetling! So you've decided to stir yourself again have you*," sent back a very clear and controlled Magda, not a flicker of madness anywhere. A Magda worryingly like the one of old who had been Masanae's equal in every way. Back then it had only been the fact that she was Quintillean's partner that had given Masanae the edge, which had made it possible for her to act as the leader of the witches. She thought she had moved far beyond that. But to make matters worse there was the sensation of others instantly linking with Magda. One of them was clearly Helga, and she was not rushing to Masanae as she had done up until Masanae had left to return westwards. But who in the Immaculate Temples was this other female? And a very strong female at that!

"*This is Laufrey*," sent Helga with remarkable insolence. "*She is the replacement for Geitla.*"

"*Geitla*?" both Masanae and Quintillean sent together in shock.

A terse report followed from Magda and Helga on the reasons for selecting Laufrey, though at no time was any sort of apology offered for not contacting or including the senior pair. As Quintillean was about to stamp his psychic foot in anger, Tancostyl's 'voice' plunged in in defence of the two witches.

"*Don't even think about getting on your high horse, Quintillean*!" he threatened. "*You've put us all in jeopardy*!"

"*In what way*?" blasted back Masanae in her lover's defence.

"*Oh, don't you know, sweetling*?" Magda asked with sickening sweetness. "*Oh Quintillean, you silly boy, fancy not telling Masanae that you've summoned the others from Sinut*!"

Masanae turned to Quintillean reeling from the shock. "You did *what*?" she hissed in disbelief.

Quintillean himself felt his new confidence draining through the soles of his shoes. How could he have forgotten that he had done that? How could he have been so arrogantly confident that all would just fall into place? His mind frantically scrambled to work out how long he had left before they were likely to turn up. However, Magda was there supplying the answer to Masanae before he had chance to finish working it out.

"*You see my precious ones, they'll have arrived in Areida about …oh, how about …a month ago… today*!" The last word was snarled with dreadful focus and it made Quintillean wince. "*Yes, poppets, they've probably taken on water and are making ready to set sail if they haven't already, and we have probably all of two or three weeks before they're standing right here in front of us. So what were you planning on telling them, Quintillean? Have you got all the Treasures? No! We've felt a jolt from the Gauntlet, but not from one of us moving it. The Great Lord Volla alone knows where the Gorget is nowadays, but do you have it? No you don't! So all we have is the Helm, which dear Tancostyl has here with us, and here it's going to stay! You've had your day of demanding that it comes to you for your little schemes. We're not playing by those rules any more. Because, you see, dearest Anarawd and Eliavres are very close to getting the Scabbard. Aren't they clever boys? So if you don't want to be left out in the cold I suggest you come to us!*"

"*How dare you*!" exploded Masanae and got another dreadful shock in response.

"*Oh we dare,*" another new voice on the Power said. "*Get off your dignity, Masanae*!"

"*Who are you*?" Quintillean asked before Masanae had recovered enough to ask for herself.

"*Me? …I'm your new war-mage! …Oh don't act so surprised Quintillean. What did you think would happen? You disappeared off into the wilds and put all the other war-mages into dangerous positions too. We might be good, but alone against a whole land full of Islanders? That was odds even you couldn't guarantee to come out of unscathed. And Calatin didn't survive those odds, did he? But what did you do when you knew he was gone? Nothing! You thought of yourself first and left the others in limbo, despite the impending crisis you created with the exiles from Sinut.*

"Even when the others told you they were going ahead and recruiting a new member, you didn't bother that much. Did you think they were simply bluffing? That they wouldn't actually do anything for fear of upsetting you? Well you were wrong. Magda found me and elevated me, and the others agreed. So it wasn't the huge jump to decide to find someone to replace Geitla and act upon it, now was it? And do you know what? When Tancostyl rode in this morning we went off and had a nice little man to man chat over some mulled wine. All very civilised like. Turns out we're getting on just fine, so I don't think you'll be playing your games of divide and conquer again for a very long time – not either of you!"

Masanae turned to look at Quintillean, utterly appalled. What could they do in the face of such unity amongst their fellow Abend? A unity which was virtually unheard of before. The nominal leader of the nine looked seriously worried in person, but his reply on the Power was a masterpiece of control.

"*So do you intend to sit there in the middle of your icy puddle just waiting for the Knights to come out of the mountains*?" he demanded with withering sarcasm. Unfortunately the response it elicited was far from the panicked dawning of realisation that he had hoped for.

Barrax's telepathic snort of derision sent a shiver down his spine.

"*Great Volla! What kind of fools do you think we are, Quintillean? Tancostyl has been one of the Abend for nearly as long as you have, and a war-mage for even longer. He would hardly have survived this long if he blundered through his conquests so blindly*!"

Back in Arlei Tancostyl exchanged a smile of pleasant surprise with Magda. To have the newest recruit supporting him even as he was cutting Quintillean down was a novel experience, but one he would not mind more of. The only one who had ever acted remotely like this had been Eliavres – and in the past he had never had quite such assurance because of Calatin's random changing of loyalties, let alone Anarawd's convoluted scheming. But with Eliavres and Anarawd firmly behind them for the foreseeable future, Barrax could speak his mind, confident in the knowledge that Quintillean was isolated unless one of them foolishly gave him reason to think otherwise.

"*We have discussed the situation*," Laufrey added with confident serenity. "*We shall leave a substantial contingent of the army here under the command of several senior Donns. They can mop up the pockets of resistance as they appear. There is hardly any need for us to stay and do such work. After all, the insolent Islanders are unlikely to appear in any great numbers at one time. The road to and from the north has been in our hands for some weeks now with reports of minor skirmishes – nothing more. The Knights will only be able to come out of the mountains when the snow lets them, which will be a bit at a time. And those closest to New Lochlainn will inevitably be just as restricted in the area south of the mountains by the floods as we are. We may not be able to get back to New Lochlainn that way, but neither can they ride out and attack us. Therefore we may regard them as an ongoing but minor problem.*

"*More urgent is the need to decide what will be done in the face of the ones from Sinut. We have decided to move south and secure the southern island. Helga has made a foray in that direction and reports wild tribes but nothing more. Hardly the kind of resistance to prove a challenge to our army! Therefore we shall secure that island and annex it to New Lochlainn, enabling us to greet the fleet you so unwisely summoned in haste. We suggest you join us there*!"

Her tone virtually bordered on making it an order and both Quintillean and Masanae bridled at it.

"*Too late for that now sweetlings*," Magda sent, her words tinged with amusement. "*Time to control that touchy dignity of yours! I would suggest you hurry and find a ship to bring you to us. If you don't, who knows what we might say in your absence when we greet the high royal family and all those acolytes they'll have with them?*"

The contact was broken leaving Masanae and Quintillean quivering between rage, disbelief and fear. Magda had not needed to say more. They knew just what she was threatening! When the Sinut fleet landed and found that the Treasures were not there waiting for them, who would be blamed? Especially as the others would have at least two of the long-lost quartet there. Any venom and ire could be neatly deflected Quintillean's way, and Masanae was furious to realise that she had hitched herself so securely to him and his plans, that this time she would share the fallout with him. There was nothing for it, they would have to be there if only to exercise damage limitation.

However, looking at the stiff way in which Masanae marched away from him, Quintillean guessed that it would be a very long time before he enjoyed another union with her. Rather a good job, then, that he had got his unconventional healing when he had, because to be in this situation and yet be as crippled in the Power as he had been up until only a week or so back was too terrifying to contemplate. Great Dragon of Death! If they could not only contemplate, but actually act upon replacing Geitla before she had even died, then what other kind of decisions might the others be capable of with these two unknowns in their midst?

Four days later the pair of them had ridden hard, and were already past the old palace of Mereholt when they were curtly informed by Laufrey that Anarawd had the Scabbard, having rescued it with Eliavres. It should have been something to rejoice over. To have even one of the pieces which had been captured over five hundred long years ago was a substantial achievement, and something their predecessors had signally failed to do. But the pair's enthusiasm was wilted in the face of their loss of status. A loss heightened by the fact that, in comparison to previous leaders of the Abend, their time at the top had been relatively brief. To have to be fighting to retain their influence was a battle neither one had thought about as needing to be fought for several centuries yet. It forced Masanae to swallow her bitterness towards Quintillean, her self-serving nature recognising that she needed to present a united front with him until they could determine what would happen with the Sinut contingent. They might be in the minority, but alone they were even more powerless than as a pair.

A further five days found them on the quayside at the former Attacotti town of Pahi. Imperious commands sent on the Power had already alerted Hunters in the area, and they in turn had summoned the two nearest pure-bred families. The pure DeÁine of the south were anomalies. Not of quite the venerable lineage as those who formed the court at Bruighean or the royals of Sinut, they were still a substantial step up from the minor ones who had so lately joined in the conquest of Brychan, or the crossbreeds who made up the bureaucracy and higher servants which kept the systems working.

Just as families like the Monreux had once been warlords in distant Lochlainn, these families had been the ones controlling the trade routes out of the Empire, the Souk'ir traders. Like the others, they had bid for a chance to expand trade in the same way that the warlords had first vied to come to the Islands, to claim territory in the Emperor's name. Later both had shared the fate of Exile for being with the previous Abend when the Treasures had been taken and destroyed. In the long years of the Exile, they too had fought to retain what they had, and to reclaim their place in the homeland amongst their own people once more.

When Quintillean had brought the Abend back to the Islands this time, along with the minor members of the royal family in Exile, many of the Souk'ir had also accompanied them. New markets were new markets, after all, and the best woollens in the world came from these ghastly cold islands. Not a cloth that the DeÁine themselves had ever expected to have a use for, but it was a commodity which they traded for vast amounts of money in many lands. Money which bought slaves, and slaves were the lifeblood of the DeÁine civilisation. They toiled in the fields to provide the pure-bloods with food. They filled the massed ranks of the army – the Seljuqs of slaves thrown at any enemy to weaken them – and from those ranks came the recruits who went on to be trained for the real fist of the DeÁine – the Jundises of shock troops.

Not surprisingly, then, the Souk'ir were a force to be reckoned with, even if their blood was a touch less pure than other highborn DeÁine. They demanded and got concessions which other families were denied, the prime one being a double quota of troops for their personal armies. In part this was tolerated because they ran the training camps from which the others purchased their slaves and militia, and in part because they undertook perilous but inglorious missions to capture new blood. Missions regarded as dirty and below the dignity of the warlord families.

Now, though, Masanae and Quintillean had called upon leaders of two of the six prime Souk'ir families, who controlled the south and the substantial levy of men which went with them. The Tabors were the leading family of the Souk'ir and currently Maj'ore Tabor (the senior male) was standing before the two Abend with his friend, the leading man of the Dracmas, Maj'ore Dracma. Both men had the typical DeÁine height but in common with all of the Souk'ir, had kept the dark hair colouring and jaundiced skin tones of the ordinary folk of the northern DeÁine homeland. Hawk-featured and dark-eyed, these men were suitably courteous but not subservient, both fully aware of the positions they commanded from. Now both nodded in agreement.

"Very well, Great Ones," Maj'ore Tabor said, making it sound like he was agreeing with them rather than taking a command from them, "our family ships will be here within the day. I shall personally see to your comforts for the journey."

He had been at pains to point out that the Indiera family and the Chowlai were equally loyal, but too far away to be capable of arriving in time to depart with them. Those two families controlled the long network of New Lochlainn lakes and tributaries which formed the Drina river system, which rose in the Eldr Forest and flowed straight southwards to the coast. Beyond them the Sava river system was controlled by the Inchoo family, but they were away anyway, negotiating for more slaves deep in the southern ocean, and not likely to return for three months yet. Only a token of their force remained behind to keep order in their lands, as was the case for the last family, the Bernien – also on a long voyage. But then the Bernien were only a minor family, and held the Assynt Highlands by virtue of nobody else wanting them, and had only as many ships as were needed for essential trading voyages.

Not like the Dracmas and the Tabors, his unspoken words implied, as he smiled silkily while reporting that they would be able to transport the three Seljuqs and the Jundis of requisitioned men in one sailing. No waiting would be necessary for the Tabors and the Dracmas, he informed them with quiet confidence. They would be landing alongside them, ready to defend what they had achieved in the Islands in contrast to the Sinut Souk'irs indolence. No DeÁine army would fail for want of men when the Tabors and the Dracmas were around!

With a deep bow which still failed to be obsequious, he turned and departed to be followed by Maj'ore Dracma. To her self-disgust, Masanae found herself understanding why Geitla had so often come down here to satisfy her physical cravings. These DeÁine were more overtly male than almost any of those who hung about the royal court in Bruighean, perhaps because it was so much rarer to find any who had a talent for the Power from amongst these families. She sighed as she left Quintillean to go and enjoy the delights of a hot bath. Maybe it would be necessary to indulge her body with one of them, for to her irritation, having begun by satiating her frustrations by using contact with Quintillean it was not so easy to simply stop.

Walking past the male bathhouse in the inn's courtyard, she saw one of the younger Dracma emerging from a steam room, his long dark hair hanging in a polished sheet down his back. He returned her stare with one every bit as frank, and before she knew it she had slipped out of her robe and walked in to join him. When the inn shook on its foundations a moment later, Quintillean swore viciously. This had to stop! If not, Masanae was likely to have them dead at the bottom of the sea instead of floating off to fight on it!

The following morning when he raised the matter with Masanae, it was far from the simple demand he had thought it would be. The leading witch promptly took umbrage and retired to her room, refusing to leave. Even worse, she seemed to have had some contact with the Dracma of her own, and Quintillean found himself faced with going on alone with the Tabors or having to cajole Masanae. Grinding his teeth with fury and frustration, he eventually went to speak to her in person rather than trying to get through on the Power, which she was ignoring. She sat there and let him speak his piece before saying acidly,

"And when were you going to tell me about the families from Sinut? You have the gall to tell me I'm jeopardising things! *Phaa*! Without you there wouldn't be a need to hurry to make this crossing. Have you bothered to look at the water? No! The Tabor and Dracma are confident because they could sail in the teeth of a gale and not feel it! But what of us, eh? We shall arrive on that desolate rock as weak as babes at the Great Ama's teats.

"May the Seagang rot you, Quintillean! We could have got the Souk'ir to fetch the Helm and the Scabbard and thought ourselves well pleased. With those two pieces we could have waited for the floods to subside, and then blasted our way into the other Islands to get the Gauntlet and the Gorget. All that needed was a little patience. But to summon the others? That's a trick even Calatin or Anarawd weren't stupid enough to do, yet you, our supposed leader, went and thought of nothing but yourself! Next time go and smoke the Lotus until your brains curdle! If there is a next time!"

"You were fast enough to agree to sideline the other Abend when it suited you," he snapped back.

"Fanu's arse! That's not the same thing! That was an agreement to get *control.* To keep our ascendency *within* the nine! To be able to regain the lost Treasures by one means or another. *You* were the one who found the ritual, who was convinced it would work, and for some unfathomable reason I believed you. I did it believing that if we failed, we would be no worse off than we've been since we got back to this Lotus-deserted, sodden wasteland! Instead, we're now going to be eating dirt just to get back in with the rest of the nine. Or had you not thought about that? Are you still deluding yourself that they'll just cow down when you appear in person?"

That rattled Quintillean more than he hoped showed. He had been so sure of his position for so long that it had not entered his head that when the Abend were reunited that the power balance might have shifted. Now, though, he saw what Masanae had seen first. That made him angry and tetchy.

"So? And what does that have to do with you throwing a fit and taking to your room?" He was not about to argue the other point with her until he had had much more time to think things through. However, Masanae was not about to give him the chance.

"What it's about, you arrogant spawn of Esras, is me wanting to know what you propose to do when we meet the others? Because I'm not having you suddenly turning around and shifting the blame onto me for it all! You need me, Quintillean!"

"I need you? *You'd* be still sitting in the rubble with a headache if it wasn't for me?"

"If it wasn't for you I wouldn't even have been there in the first place!"

"Ha! You weren't so slow when you thought you were getting something the others weren't!"

And so it went on. The two Abend arguing the toss, and the whole area around Masanae's inn so full of flickering ripples of Power that nobody could think straight, let alone work. On into the night it went, and the Souk'ir sat on their ships and waited, quietly cursing the temperamental Abend, and the fact that water and food for the troops was being used up getting nowhere. Eventually the two came to a convoluted agreement and word was passed that they would depart with the morning tide after all.

Come the morning, the waters around Pahi were filled with the Souk'irs' deep-draughted ships, and once Masanae and Quintillean joined

Maj'ore Tabor on board his own craft, signals were passed and the sails on every boat rose in concert. Less pleasing to the two Abend was the Souk'irs' own revelation that they would have to sail south a way first.

"It's what makes Pahi such a safe harbour," Maj'ore Tabor explained, just falling short of implying that such knowledge was common to any fool. He was quite enjoying the fact that both mighty persons were already looking a little green and they had not untied from the quay yet! It was small revenge for the messing about they had endured from their august passengers, but worth savouring.

"The great bars of silt and sand have become a natural breakwater over centuries," he said in the unctuous tones he normally reserved for difficult clients – like the petty warlords whom he bought slaves from, who were nothing but thought themselves very grand. "Behind them we have little to fear from the great winter storms which can come ripping up from out of the southern ocean. Have no fear, it will take little more than a few hours to clear them and we shall be on our way by late morning." Privately thinking that he could carry these two to the frozen Underworlds and they would be incapable of doing a thing to him once the salt water got to them. It was a short-lived period of having the upper hand, but worth relishing.

He clearly knew his trading waters well, for as the sun rose towards midday they were clipping the waves briskly – not that Quintillean or Masanae were appreciative of the fact. At the first hint of sickness they had retreated swiftly below and stayed out of sight, leaving their Hunters to maintain a visible reminder, should one be needed, of who was on board. Maj'ores Tabor and Dracma might not know the details, but they were astute enough observers from experience in trading to be alert to the import of the situation. The Abend were uniting to face something, and woe betide the captain who failed to get the powerful ones to where they needed to be and in good time. After all, there were others of the Abend waiting for them to get there. Abend who had not been weakened by a sea voyage, and who might smite anyone who failed them. And if there was to be such an unfortunate soul, the Maj'ores were determined his name would not be from among the Tabori or Dracmas.

Chapter 19

Bows and Arrows

Rathlin & Prydein: late Earrach – early Beltane

As Earrach turned towards Beltane, Eldaya edged her way around a door with a plate in one hand and a mug of camomile tea in the other. It was well over a month now since she'd been back at Magnus' court, but in that time much had changed. If she had been worried for their safety the first time she had come here, she was now worried for very different reasons. Lying on adjoining beds were Gillies and Alaiz, both mercifully fast asleep for now, for of late it was the two of them who had plagued Eldaya's dreams. It had seemed quite straightforward when she had promised Cwen that she would remain with Alaiz to oversee her pregnancy. What she had never foreseen was that she would end up with sole responsibility for two women who were having far from normal confinements.

She sighed and sank down into the cushion-piled chair which was placed by the window. It had been a balmy spring on this side of Rathlin, for which she was very grateful. It had enabled her to have the window shutters at least partially open every day, even on those days when it had rained and they could not be thrown wide open. Today, however, it was bright and sunny, and she had the shutters flung right back, allowing in the gentle fragrance of the climbing plant which was swarming all over the house walls. She had managed to persuade Magnus that the rowdy confines of his court was doing nothing for the health of his mistress, and so this old merchant's house had been swept out and handed over to her. Putting her feet up on the small stool, she munched on the warm rye bread and honey she had brought up with her, and sipped the sweet camomile and apple tea. It had been another long night with Gillies and she was shattered.

She was just beginning to doze when the door opened and Magnus himself walked in. The man before her had visibly changed since their first meeting, and she was able to smile at him with genuine warmth.

"How are they doing?" he asked softly, coming to take over the stool, but lifting her aching feet back onto his lap and began massaging them for her.

"Oh Trees, Magnus," Eldaya groaned, although partly in pleasure as his strong fingers eased the discomfort. "It's hard to say. With Alaiz nothing's changed that much. She was on the road for far too long for someone in her condition. I think that if she stays here and rests for the remainder of her time, she's in with a chance of everything going well and having a healthy child."

"You don't think it is twins, then?" he wondered.

Eldaya shrugged. "It's very possible. She's much bigger than I'd expect for someone having their first child – especially as she's not a big person herself and neither, apparently is the father. But that's a long way from knowing whether she's carrying two or not. If her baby was moving more I might feel if there were two in there or not, and so might she, but it's a quiet little soul. On the other hand at least it does move about a bit, and in a way that seems to me to be within the bounds of normality."

"Not like Gillies," Magnus said with a hint of despair.

"No, not like Gillies."

Eldaya's heart went out to Magnus. She had become convinced that his supposed madness had come from handling the Spear, for now that Cwen and the others had taken it far away, he was becoming more grounded by the day. But one thing had not changed. He was clearly desperate to become a father, and with his sanity returning he was only too aware that things were not well with Gillies and his child.

He had recently confessed to Eldaya that he had taken the narcotic herbs to ease the pain in his head, and clearly that pain had prevented him from becoming truly addicted to the effects of it. Magnus hardly ever touched the stuff now, and when he did it was more to remain sociable with some of his men who enjoyed using it. He smoked it in very small quantities, often passing the pipe on having taken hardly a puff. The same could not be said for Gillies. Until Eldaya had brought her away from the court it had proven impossible to keep her away from the narcotics, revealing her to be a true addict. Now Eldaya was deeply worried by the lack of movement in the child, especially given that Gillies could not be more than a month from her due time. It was as though the child had absorbed the drug with its mother to the extent that there might be something severely wrong with it.

At first, when she had suspected this, Eldaya had been reluctant to confide her fears to Magnus. She had been worried that he would separate her from Alaiz in order to have her nurse Gillies full-time. Yet when he had returned from his brief but disturbing fight with the DeÁine troops, it was as though that had been the final wake-up call he had needed. Far from blaming the women for bringing one of the Abend down on to Rathlin, or dismissing their fears, he now wanted to know everything Eldaya and Alaiz could tell him. As a consequence he often came to talk to Alaiz, whenever he was back in Kylesk in between scouting his territory for enemies, and was treating her with nothing but kindness and respect. That in turn had meant that Eldaya had felt that she could no longer, in any conscience, keep her fears for his child hidden. She had explained it to him one night when he had come to her bed, closely watching his expression, fearful that he might still take his disappointment out on her. Instead he had just looked extraordinarily hurt, which was when she had gone to him willingly for the first time.

Since then her feelings towards him had strengthened, and she was hoping that she was not deluding herself in thinking that his affections were slowly transferring from Gillies to herself. Gillies certainly was not helping matters. For whatever strange reason, for the most part she had been relatively quiet during the days, but at night she would try everything to get out and go in search of some herbs and the water-pipe they were smoked through. In the last few days, though, as her cravings had begun to really bite, Gillies had taken up all of Eldaya's time in the day too. Yesterday she had needed help restraining Gillies, and her calls for help had brought Magnus himself later in the day when the news had reached him. Now he was watching Gillies with a mixture of distaste and worry, and Eldaya did not need any magical skills to know that the distaste was for Gillies and the worry for his child.

"Will she make it to her time?" he asked aloud, although it sounded more as though he was talking to himself or some higher authority than to Eldaya.

She paused for a second before answering. "Maybe. …But I would caution you to be prepared for her not to. And before you ask, I honestly don't know if your child will live or not – and any midwife who promises you better odds than that will be lying through her teeth! It's just not possible to know what's been going on inside her."

Magnus nodded thoughtfully. "I know. …I mean, I understand what you're trying to tell me." He stood up and sighed. "I came to tell you that I shall be leaving tomorrow at first light. I've called a muster of all the men I command, but we cannot assemble here or at Reiff – there simply isn't enough room." He sighed again. "I thought things were bad enough with that skirmish we had with the DeÁine – that we'd been fighting the tail end of a force attacking the Knights and just about holding our own. But now we've had a new and very disturbing report come in."

He bent and kissed her. "Thank the Goddess you came and woke me up, because I'd never have believed this before. Apparently a ship sailing the southern seas spotted a whole new DeÁine fleet heading our way." As Eldaya gasped he shook his head. "No. Not from New Lochlainn or Brychan – that would have been bad enough, but at least we could have estimated how many there might be. No, this is a new threat! The word is that the DeÁine in New Lochlainn have sent for massive reinforcements to some others of their cursed race, and these are them."

"Oh Lost Souls!" Eldaya moaned, clasping her hands to her mouth in shock.

"I know, it's as bad as it could be! Since you never mentioned it, I thought right away that you and the Knights couldn't have known of this." Eldaya shook her head mutely. "So I'm going to take a risk. I'm going to leave Kylesk Bay undefended. I can't fight on all sides. I don't have enough men for that. Come to that, I can't fight any great DeÁine force with my few men. So I'm going to do something I thought the Underworld would have to freeze before I'd even consider it – I'm going to try to join with the Order! I have to believe the Knights will behave honourably, and that any of those who come here are coming to our aid and not to conquer, because that way I can ignore everything to the east. Before I do, though, I'm sending some of my men up to your friends in the north at Craggie, because they need to know about what's coming. But most of the men will ride with me into the south. In part, it's because I fear I shall still have to have something to negotiate with with those Knight friends of yours before they'll believe my change of heart, and the one thing which might make them look more kindly upon us is the chance of new intelligence. And even without them, for ourselves we need to know if these new, strange DeÁine have landed – or are likely to land – here on Rathlin."

"And if they don't come here?"

"Then the Goddess will have looked after us more than we deserve, and we shall go to the aid of those in the north. You were so right, you and your friends. This time there's no way I can hide it out thinking we'll be overlooked in Rathlin if the other Islands fall. …But somehow I think that if the DeÁine have any maps left at all from their first invasion all those centuries ago, they'll know that they can't land on Prydein with ships that big. And if they don't land there then where will they land if not here? We're the first and only safe landfalls for huge ships along all of the southern coasts."

Eldaya nodded. It made horribly good sense, but now she feared that it would be Magnus' warning which would be disregarded despite the circumstances. "Let me send a letter to Cwen and the Knights with the men you send north," she begged Magnus. "That way they'll know that you're not just trying to deceive them."

"Would they think that?"

"Hmm... Given the way you behaved the last time any of the Order saw you, I'm sorry Magnus, but it is possible."

"Was I that bad?"

"You don't remember?"

Magnus shook his long dark mane and frowned. "No, not really. So much of the last few years is blurry at best. Some bits have completely gone."

Eldaya once again felt her heart go out to him. "You were erratic, to put it politely..."

"...and if you aren't? ...Putting it politely, that is..."

"...You were a brute who followed your own whims and nobody ever quite knew what you'd do next," Eldaya told him sadly.

Magnus hung his head in shame. "What in the Islands happened to me?"

"My best guess would be that when you took the Spear you had no idea of what its powers were."

"I still don't!"

"And maybe you don't want to," Eldaya cautioned him. "If what I've heard is a fair indicator, the Island Treasures will work for a specific type of person. But more importantly that person has to be a pure Islander from amongst those people who came in centuries ago. I know your people were the original inhabitants, but no-one of Attacotti blood will be able to handle these things. And that was your downfall. The only time it helped you was when you were fighting against the DeÁine, and that was because they are the foe the Treasures were built to defend against. But when you turned against the Islanders, then it turned on you. ...It might even be that by taking the herbs to dull the pain, that you actually stopped it from doing even more damage than it did. I'm no expert on these things, but it seems possible that you could have ended up being completely and irrevocably mad."

That really shocked Magnus, and he sat in silence for a while digesting this information. Their reverie was broken by a cough and moan from the beds. On the nearest bed Gillies woke and stared about her wildly.

"What're you doin' here," she demanded fuzzily of something only she could see in front of her. "Go 'way! …Shoo! …Go '*way*! …*Aaaagh*!" And she began screaming and thrashing about on the bed, fending off her unseen assailant.

Magnus joined Eldaya in trying to hold her down and prevent the worst of her contortions, but even with Magnus' strength they were struggling, for they were constantly hampered by not wanting to put any pressure on her distended belly.

"Let her go," Eldaya finally gasped to Magnus. "We're only going to do her more harm carrying on like this." And the two of them stepped back from the bed to leave Gillies to her nightmarish reality.

"She's lost her mind, hasn't she," a weary little voice said from the other bed, more as a statement of fact than any query.

They turned to see Alaiz lifting herself into a sitting position. As they hurried to her side to help her, Eldaya confessed,

"Yes, I think so. Although whether it's permanent or not, only time will tell."

Magnus sat on the edge of Alaiz's bed and gently reached out to place his hand on her expanding bump just as Alaiz grunted.

"By the Goddess! I felt that!" he exclaimed, his face breaking into a broad smile for the first time in days that Eldaya knew of.

Alaiz smile shyly back. "Yes, he or she has been doing that off and on all night! Oooof!" as another kick clearly happened. "Oh Trees! I really need to piss! *Again*!" she gasped and began struggling to get out of bed. "I don't know how I'm going to cope with another three months of this!"

What Eldaya did not want to tell her was that with twins she was unlikely to go that long – Alaiz had enough stress and worry without adding that. With Eldaya's help she hurried to the privy in the adjoining tiny room leaving Magnus alone with Gillies, at which point he became aware that she was now grunting, as if in pain. Walking back to her bed he stood looking down at her, and then ripped the bed clothes back to expose her as he guessed what was happening.

"Eldaya!" he roared. "Quickly! Come here!"

As Eldaya ran out she saw what he had seen. Gillies' waters had broken, but there was also an awful lot of blood soaking into the sheets. "Take Alaiz into my room next door!" she ordered him, and ran out to call for help from the two women she had selected to assist her when the time came.

When Magnus returned it was to find the room a hive of activity, and he had the sense to stand back against the wall until Eldaya came to him.

"It's too soon, isn't it," he said flatly, and not wanting to give him false hopes Eldaya simply nodded. "Well by the time I leave tomorrow, I suppose I'll know whether I'm going to be a father or not," he sighed and turned on his heels.

When Gillies had come back to him, and then he had discovered that she was carrying his child, he had thought that he would want to be there when it arrived. That he would want to be the first to hold his child in his arms, come what may. Now, though, he found he could not bear the thought of being handed a small corpse. Better not to see it. Better to keep his own imagined image of a tiny perfect babe, if very still, than anything which Eldaya might come to him holding. Then he revised that thought. No, Eldaya would not subject him to that, she was too kind, but to the other women he was still Magnus the war leader, tough and strong. He could not be seen by them weeping for his dead child.

Stranger than that, he was beginning to see that Gillies had been the love of a young man. A young man he no longer was. Oh he had had many sexual encounters in the intervening years, but there was a world of difference between casual coupling and being with one person all the time, and now he was back to his senses, the idea of a different woman each night no longer appealed. The older, more mature Magnus wanted a woman he could talk to, someone whom he did not need to keep the image of leader in place for all the time. And increasingly he had come to realise that that person was Eldaya, not Gillies. Gillies may have fired his lust, a lust which he had done nothing to curb, but was it really going to win him the respect of his people to take his woman in front of all of them? The flame-haired girl of his youthful passion had turned into a shameless and self-indulgent woman who cared little for such niceties. But the new, sober Magnus found himself inwardly blushing as he recalled some of their exploits over the last few months.

No wonder other, more respectable Islanders had never taken him seriously as a leader. He had never behaved like one! And what Eldaya had said about him leaving the more far flung Rathliners to their fate, instead of defending them to the best of his ability, had also stuck in his mind and refused to go away. How could he call himself a leader of the Attacotti if he only bothered about his own clansmen?

Upstairs, Gillies' exertions were beginning to fail and Eldaya could already see the pulse in her neck beating more erratically.

"We're going to lose her, ma'am," the one helper, an experienced midwife from the town, muttered sadly as she bathed Gillies' sweat-soaked forehead.

"I know," Eldaya sighed, "but let's see if we can at least save the child."

However, when the tiny figure appeared it was clear even before it had fully emerged that it had been too late for the child for some time.

"Been dead for days," the older midwife declared sorrowfully. "Poor little mite. Perhaps it's for the best, though. Look at the state of it! It would never have led a normal life."

Not wanting to look and yet feeling that she had to, if only for Magnus' sake, Eldaya made a cursory glance towards the child. That was enough. She did not want to see more. "A boy?" she asked, having been more preoccupied with Gillies.

"Aye, and that'll make it harder for the master to bear," the midwife observed philosophically.

"She's gone," the other said before Eldaya could reply.

"Clean them up and put them in winding sheets," Eldaya said wearily, getting to her feet. "I'd best go and break the bad news."

"Rather you than me, ma'am."

However, when Eldaya found Magnus out in the garden, one look at her must have told him all he needed to know.

"Neither of them?" he asked flatly.

"No, I'm sorry." Eldaya took a deep breath. "Your son wouldn't have made it anyway. He wasn't …right." As she got close to him she could see that Magnus must have already given in to his grief in expectation, and went to wrap her arms around him. "You could still have children, Magnus. It was her, not you. All those herbs …and she was old to be bearing another child even if she wasn't an old woman."

"I know," he replied, his words muffled in her hair as he held her tight.

Later, when he had left and she had rejoined Alaiz in a different room, she sank onto the bed and lay back with relief. "By the Trees, I'm exhausted!" she sighed.

"Mmmm."

Eldaya opened one eye and looked at Alaiz. "That was a very cryptic 'Mmmm'! What did you mean by that?"

Alaiz gave a smug smile. "Well I know you've been running round a bit after Gillies. But don't you think you've been rather a bit *too* tired? Oh don't look at me with that wide-eyed innocence! I've heard you with him in your bed at night. And you were clearly at one another in the garden just now!"

"I was comforting him!"

"Of course you were! …You didn't think bedding a lusty man like Magnus would come without consequences did you?"

A stunned Eldaya looked down at her own stomach and did some rapid calculations.

"Looks like Magnus might get a son yet!" Alaiz chuckled mischievously, then sobered swiftly, "although what kind of world we'll be welcoming our children into if the DeÁine overwhelm us terrifies me beyond belief. I never, ever dreamed I'd be starting a family with death all around me, Eldaya. Is Gillies just the first of us to die? Will we be next? Not dying in our beds but at the hands of some outlandish monster? Oh Blessed Martyrs! It overwhelms me so much, all I can do is pray that Hamelin comes home safe to me, and that we all survive the next few months."

"Hush," Eldaya comforted her, coming to wrap her arms around the younger woman. "We'll survive! We have to believe that. We have to…" Yet it was no consolation to have to sit and wait.

In the two weeks he spent kicking his heels at Mullion, Ruari had time to become infinitely more sympathetic towards Talorcan and the Knight's sense of frustration. As the leader of the movement of Prydein troops he should have been in the vanguard. However, as the man also in charge of those destined to wield the Islands Treasures, he was at the same time in a very different position. Having landed on Prydein on the twenty-third of Earrach, he had hoped to be amongst the first to leave again. Hereman had only been waiting for the news that all of the muster was nearly upon them, to start shipping the men he had assembled across the narrow sound to Kittermere. Experienced in such manoeuvres, Hereman had no intention of letting the leading shipments get so far ahead of the others that they became in danger of being cut off and isolated.

The east coast of Kittermere might be completely under the control of the Knights, but there was no telling what they might find on the west coast. Mad Magnus might have a whole settlement of Attacotti warriors hidden there, for all they knew. For although there had been many scouting missions, nobody knew the lie of the land that well over there. Far too much of the rolling countryside had hidden valleys for Hereman's liking.

Ruari agreed with such sensible caution, and used much of the first week taking over the organisation of the first wave of men, to allow Hereman the chance to devote more time to sending messages back and forth to the other ealdormen on Prydein. Ruari also continued doing his best to continue Ivain's education. Yet in one thing none of them could help Ivain much – the Island Bow was something he was having to figure out for himself. Luckily, Swein and Ivain had instantly taken a liking to one another. This made life much easier than it might have been, for the two of them compared notes and readily discussed their individual responses to situations. Swein had also gladly joined up with Ivain for Ruari's teaching sessions, and Ruari welcomed the second pupil since it made it far less lonely for Ivain.

As for Ivain and Talorcan, after their bloody fight, gruff apologies were made on both sides, and then they avoided one another for several days. However, with Talorcan's archers Tamàs and Decke having already taken Swein under their wing, Ruari had thought it no bad thing if they continued supervising the archery side of things. Once the ferocious black eyes received from Talorcan had receded enough for Ivain to be able to aim a bow again, Tamàs had declared himself very pleased with Ivain's ability with bows of the ordinary variety. Like Swein, he had a natural talent, instinctively picking up on things and only taking one telling to pick up on the expert tips Tamàs was passing on.

All of them agreed that it was a good thing that it was Ivain who was handling the great Bow, though, as slender Swein could not even move the bow string, let alone pull it back enough to aim it. Decke mocked up a replica for the huge empowered arrow, and in the practice sessions Swein shot this through his lightweight hunting bow. Meanwhile, Ivain shot an ordinary arrow through a monster of a bow which a Prydein blacksmith and archer had been persuaded to part with for the time being, which was the nearest they could get to the Island Bow in size and weight, and in this way they achieved something like co-ordination. Nobody as yet wanted to risk using the real things – at least not until they were much surer of what the outcome might be!

By the end of the first week, Ruari had spotted Talorcan lurking in dark corners watching the training sessions. Given that his sergeant, Barcwith, and his other man-at-arms, Galey, had also come forward to offer their services for Swein and Ivain to spar with, Talorcan was clearly feeling somewhat abandoned. For Ruari, having the two expert swordsmen join him helped hugely. With them running through the exercises with the two novices, it allowed him to walk around the sparring pairs and observe them and offer advice. The remaining member of Talorcan's lance, the young lad Ad, made himself useful keeping them supplied with drinks and food and other things, and when not doing that sat on the sidelines calling encouragement and looking after the squints. Nothing would persuade Dylan and Eric very far from Swein and Ivain, even if they spent most of the time basking in every warm patch of early summer sun they could find.

"It must've been real cold over in that in-between place," Ad observed quietly to the lance and Ruari as they paused for a break.

"I know just how they feel!" Ruari said with feeling. "After years spent sloshing through the marshes in the eastern wetlands, and then running round Rheged in the depths of winter before going to icy Taineire, I thought I'd never get warm again!"

"Is Taineire really all ice?" Ad wanted to know. He had taken a deep liking to the big, rangy acting-Master of the Rheged sept, who seemed a very different kind of man to the leader of the Ergardian Knights, Master Brego. For a start off, Ruari was noticeably younger – even to someone of Ad's age where everyone over thirty was heading towards being ancient. It made Ruari more like the ordinary Knights Ad knew, rather than distanced by decades of holding the highest rank, and he seemed not to mind Ad's questions either.

"Ice as far as the eye can see," Ruari told him. "So white it hurts your eyes when the sun comes out. The ancients said that it was a place like any other in the Islands once upon a time, but that hasn't been the case for hundreds of years."

"Speaking of the ancients," came Talorcan's voice from behind them, and they all turned to meet him. The errant Knight was also still sporting the bruises from his fight with Ivain, and his usually ferocious appearance seemed even worse at the moment because of them. The Knight came bearing piping hot pasties from the castle's kitchens for their lunch break and handed them out. That done, he addressed himself to Ruari.

"When the ancients next put in an appearance, do you think you could ask them to talk to the squints?"

"What for?" Ruari asked, slightly puzzled.

Talorcan shifted uncomfortably. "Look at the two squints," he said. "They were totally relaxed when I saw them from the top of the wall on my way down here. Now look at them! They're as tense as can be. Dylan used to be alright with me, but since I came to blows with Ivain he's picked up on Eric's nervousness, and they both start twitching their whiskers whenever I'm anywhere near them. Can we get the ancients to explain that I'm no threat to them or Ivain and Swein? ...Please?"

Ruari turned his attention to the opposite side of the castle's lists where they were currently training. Now that Talorcan mentioned it he could see the difference in the two squints. They were definitely on edge compared to the way they had been only moments ago. That Talorcan should be the one to pick up on it briefly surprised him before he remembered the lance telling him that, however brusque Talorcan was with people, he was deeply fond of animals and could not bear to see one mistreated. He turned back to the Knight, and realised that Talorcan was genuinely disturbed by the effect he was having on the squints. Whatever Talorcan privately thought of Ivain, it clearly did not extend to his strange little companion.

Ruari nodded. "I think that's a reasonable request. I'll mention it to the next one who shows up. After all, you'll be travelling in fairly close proximity to them once we start moving. And if they're that sensitive to DeÁine blood, then I'd rather they were signalling a real threat when we encounter one, not just jumping at every turn because you're there."

Luckily the next ancient to show up was the amiable Cynddylan, who was linked with the Arrow and therefore with Dylan and Swein. He quickly caught on to what was needed, and proceeded to take the two squints and their humans aside for a long chat. Eventually he signalled to Ruari to bring Talorcan in, and the dark-haired Knight walked cautiously into the chamber which the senior men had turned into their dining hall. At first Talorcan kept to the other side of the long oak table, waiting to see what the reaction would be.

"Come closer," Cynddylan called encouragingly.

With great care, and keeping his gaze very carefully on the squints, Talorcan walked around the table until he was within a couple of feet of the little group. At that point he went down on one knee and held a hand out, palm upwards, as he would have done for a nervous dog.

"Hello again, Dylan," he said gently. He had never tried to handle the squint in the past, understanding that his DeÁine heritage might make it painful for the odd creature of the old world. Now he was just hoping that Dylan would sniff at him. However, Dylan had other ideas. He waddled forward on his chunky back paws and reached out delicately with one of his dainty forepaws. A soft, velvety pad made contact with Talorcan's palm and everyone held their breath. All remembered only too well how painful it had been for the squints making first physical contact with people, and were worried that touching someone who was half-DeÁine (and a very pure half, to boot) might be equally as harsh.

Instead it was Talorcan who flinched a little.

"Are you alright?" Ruari asked him, bothered by the way the younger Knight had gone rather pale.

"It …tingles!" Talorcan tried to explain. "And it feels a bit disorientating. Nothing really bad. More like being a bit drunk but without the beer! …Actually it's getting better now. The room's stopped swimming about! …Thank you, Dylan!"

The squint gave a cheerful whistle and then chirruped something to his companion. As Dylan moved back, Eric edged forward. With even more caution the squint crept closer to Talorcan's outstretched hand, but this time there was no extended paw to meet it. Instead, Talorcan leaned a little further so that his fingertips could brush the thick fur of Eric's front. Eric was almost going cross-eyed looking down his long nose at Talorcan's fingers, but he did not run away. As they touched, he gave a long and rather mournful whistle, his breath wafting over Talorcan's hand and making the Knight smile.

"There, that wasn't so bad, was it?" he said softly. "You've been very brave, Eric. I'm so, so sorry I frightened you when we first met."

The squint now looked up to meet his gaze, and the head went on one side and the feathered ears twitched, as if he was seeing something beyond the outer shell of skin. Then he gave a surprised little whistle and moved closer to lean his furry forehead against Talorcan's – almost as if he was making a show of sympathy.

"Well there's a turn up for the books!" Barcwith muttered. "It's almost like the little fella' could see inside the Boss."

"In a way he can," Cynddylan replied drifting around to the men. "Or at least he can sense what's in someone's heart." A surprised chirruping exchange was now going on between Eric and Dylan. "Eric seems to think that your captain is in pain in some way. Yet he looks fine to me. Do you understand what he means?"

"Oh yes," Barcwith confirmed, "there's a lot of pain going on inside him. He makes a point of not letting it show for the most part. But those of us who've been around him for years know about it."

"And even some of us who haven't," Ruari added pointedly. "It's certainly on Talorcan's service record. For now, though, I'm surprised but very pleased that Eric picked up on it all by himself. It certainly shows that the squints have quite a sophisticated understanding of what DeÁine are, and that not all are evil. However, since you didn't know that we were going to ask you to mediate for us, I'm guessing that you had some other reason for wanting to see us, Cynddylan?"

"Indeed. I came to tell you that Cwen will be here within the week providing the weather holds."

Ruari felt his enthusiasm sink. The first men were leaving at the break of dawn the next morning, but it looked as though they would not be going with them.

"I suppose we should wait for her," he said with as much good grace as he could muster.

Cynddylan gave a sympathetic smile. "I'm afraid so. She'll really need all the help you can give her. If her ship was to put her ashore on southern Kittermere, and she was to ride to meet you it might take even longer before she caught you up. That's time she really doesn't have spare to be wasting like that."

Ruari nodded. The plan was to ship men straight across to Kittermere, and then have them march across a long ridge of high ground between the vast sea marsh of the island's north and its lesser one to its south. This would lead them right into the highlands of Kittermere, which they would march over to the far north-west coast. There they would meet the ships Brego was sending from Ergardia – once the fleet had transported the Ergardian men to Brychan – and they in turn would be shipped across to Rathlin. The fishing boats of western Prydein were all doing their best in taking the men from Prydein to Kittermere, but were far too small to use for the wider crossing from Kittermere to Rathlin. They could cope with the summer seas, but could not take men in sufficient numbers to guarantee their ability to fight against Magnus' men should they encounter resistance. Back in the planning stage at Lorne Castle, all had agreed that the first wave of Order men landing on Rathlin should be a substantial one. For Ruari and his party, however, this meant that there was nothing to be gained even by Cwen landing at Draynes, since she would still be left with a long ride north to intercept the army.

"We'll wait," Ruari said with more calm than he was feeling in his heart. Once Cynddylan had gone, though, he sank into a chair with a groan.

"More waiting!" Talorcan bit out.

"More waiting before we can find out if Alaiz is alright," moaned Ivain, his worry oozing through every word as he sank onto the bench, and with his elbows on the refectory table, leaned his head in his hands. Ivain had eased some of his fears by telling Swein all about his young queen, whom he thought of more as his sister than a wife. Swein, for his part, had made an understanding audience, in his turn telling Ivain about the way Cwen had virtually adopted him into her family, becoming the sister he had never had or dreamed of having. In the gloomy silence which followed Ivain's words, Swein consequently felt guilty that the one woman he would have worried about was already on her way to meet them, and clearly others were equally wrapped in their own worries.

The quiet was unexpectedly broken by Talorcan. "If Magnus has harmed Alaiz, I shall personally take him to one of his dungeons and be pointing out the error of his ways," he muttered through clenched teeth and with such venom that Ivain looked up. He had not been able to work out why the strange Knight had taken such a deep liking to his wife, but there it was again, that heartfelt expression of caring.

"Well don't keep him all to yourself," he remonstrated. "I shall want to be doing a bit of error pointing myself!"

Talorcan quirked an eyebrow and then managed a sardonic smile. "Better hope he's been a good boy, then, or the Attacotti might be short of one leader by the time we've both done! Either that or they'll be having to lead his horse into battle, and get an interpreter for where we've knocked all his teeth out!"

Ruari found himself quietly smiling at the exchange. Thank the Trees for that! The two of them had finally managed to recognise that they had a cause in common beyond that of the Islands. With any luck they might even manage some kind of friendship before their time together was done.

His hopes were confirmed when a day later, a thoroughly bored Talorcan offered to take over the weapons training with Swein and Ivain for Ruari. It did not do much for Ruari's sense of feeling redundant, but he let Talorcan do it. He fervently hoped he himself was going to survive these next few months, but if he did fall, he wanted Talorcan to be able to take over guarding the three Treasure-wielders without there being any acrimony. It was a job he could hardly put onto Hereman or Breca, since both men already had their hands well and truly full, and once the fighting started the pair had important roles to play within the greater army. So he kicked about the castle, helping where he could and feeling like a spare part for far too much of the day.

In the second week there was a blessed break in the tedium, for Commander Instone of Rosco rode in at nightfall with the muster of the eastern archers marching behind him. When the sentries called their imminent arrival, nothing would satisfy Ivain but that he should go and greet them personally. It was a side of the young king which Talorcan had not really believed existed, even though he had been told by Pauli about the way Ivain defied his mentors at court by fraternising with these commoners. However, he saw enough proof of it in the next few hours.

Ivain hurriedly scrubbed off the sweat of practice and dragged out a halfway decent shirt, before going and positioning himself by the great gate. For the next five hours he stood there welcoming man after man by name. Not everyone to be sure, but far more than Talorcan would have believed he could have known. Even more shaking to the Knight was the genuine delight these rustic militiamen displayed on finding their king alive after all. Many of those Ivain greeted by name then proudly introduced nephews, cousins or friends back to him, and Ivain shook hands with them all.

When the last man had trailed in under the massive portcullis and the gates had been secured for the night, Ivain finally turned away. At that point he was startled to register that Talorcan was still standing behind him, but the Knight in mutual surprise saw that the young king was cradling what was clearly a very sore hand from all the handshaking. That had to have been hurting for the last hour if not longer, and yet Ivain had shown no glimmer of lessening willingness for greeting the last man from the first. Pauli had been stood beside Talorcan, and now he shot him an 'I told you so' look before putting a guiding hand on Ivain's shoulder.

"Come on, let's find something to soothe that," he said companionably.

"I'll go and make sure they save you both some dinner," Talorcan told them without any of his former cynicism.

By the time Ivain and Pauli made it upstairs, most of the others had eaten and gone, but they found Talorcan sitting guard over two heaped plates which were keeping warm by the side of the fire. It was warm during the day now, but by night it was still chilly enough to warrant a good blaze. Taking a thick cloth from off the back of the campaign chair he was sitting in, Talorcan used it to grasp the two hot pewter plates and brought them over to the table, where two large flagons of small beer were also waiting for them.

"Here you go, I think you've earned it today," he said equably.

Too tired to worry about potential hidden meanings in the Knight's words, Ivain sank gratefully onto the bench and got stuck in to the excellent rich stew, as did Pauli. Only as they were mopping up the last of the gravy with some warm, crusty bread did they realise that Talorcan had sat down opposite them and was still there.

"I seem to owe you yet another apology," he said as they turned to their beer again. "Obviously being king of Prydein isn't the same as the young noblemen I saw when I was a child in Brychan. I thought people like Breca were being charitable when they said you knew the archers. But you really do know them, don't you? I've seen more than a few spoilt sons of rich merchants, but even when they were putting on a show of knowing folk because their families demanded it, it wasn't the same. They couldn't have put names to faces for the most part. And nothing like the number of men I've seen you speak to. You have to *want* to know people to remember that number of faces and names. I've known ealdormen and commanders who couldn't have done what you just did, and that with their own men!"

Ivain had the strange feeling that there was a substantial compliment in there somewhere if he had not been too tired to work it out. Instead he nodded sleepily and then had to smother a huge yawn.

"Yes …I used to go out to eastern Prydein whenever I could. Those men saved my sanity, I think. It was such a blessed relief to just be me. Out there they didn't care if I was the king, or any other fancy nobleman. It was more important that I showed an interest in what they did, and for their welfare. When I started showing an interest in learning how to fire a bow they were delighted. I'd never been shown in what little weapons training I had at court, you see. Not a nobleman's weapon, my trainers thought. I could never understand why anyone who might have to lead the Prydein army *wouldn't* want to know about what the archers did. After all, they're recognised as being our Island's great strength. It just seemed like common sense to me, but it wasn't approved off by men like Amalric – our last Grand Master when Master Hugh stepped aside."

"Bloody fool!" muttered Pauli, clearly having little sympathy for his former leader despite his fate.

"Well your idea of common sense certainly brought its own rewards," Talorcan said with the first genuine smile Ivain had seen from him. "If I'm any judge of men, those archers would fight their way into the Underworld and back again for you! In fact, I was thinking of having a word with Ruari and Hereman. I think we should keep a sizeable contingent of those same archers right close to you and Swein. We'll have to work on it a bit, but I'm wondering if that bond to you might mean that when you and Swein use the Bow and Arrow, that it will somehow spread out to the volleys of arrows those archers will be laying down."

That woke Ivain up in a hurry. "By the Trees!" He looked at Talorcan in shock. "Do you think so?"

But Pauli was now nodding enthusiastically. "Oh that's a thought and a half! Yes, that's sort of an extension of what the ancients were telling you, Ivain. You remember? When they were saying that intention is everything? They told us all that it was important for the Treasure users to be of the same mind. That everyone acts from the same motivation – to save the Islands. To protect people! Well the archers will be feeling that alright. Their families are still in Prydein, so that's the obvious motive, but they have that bond to you too. Their loyalty is from the heart. It's not just because someone has told them to march here and fight for you. Talorcan has made an almighty important connection!"

Ivain looked from one to the other as if he could hardly believe his ears, and that was something else which mildly surprised but pleased Talorcan. There was no ego here. No accepting this new facet of the archers' loyalty as if it was his right and due. Ivain was looking abashed and more than a little overwhelmed by the idea.

"Don't look so worried," Talorcan found himself saying. "We're not expecting you to lead them into battle tomorrow! We have loads of time to work out just how that might work. Come on," he clapped Ivain on the shoulder with the friendly familiarity Pauli had seen him use along with

Barcwith and the others. "Time for a good night's sleep before you have to worry about that!"

Ivain's smile was a little watery. It felt very odd to have made this transition with Talorcan. If the truth were told, he had still been a little worried by the Knight once his initial fury had worn off. In part it was generated by his own honesty, for he knew in his heart of hearts that he had simply been lucky getting the first few blows in when they had fought. No doubt Talorcan had thought him such a total wimp that he had never expected Ivain to strike him let alone put up a fight. But once Talorcan had got him on the ground he now realised, with hindsight, that he had been well on the way to getting the pounding of a lifetime had Ruari and the others not broken the fight up. With his years of fighting in all kinds of conditions, in short order Talorcan could have made mincemeat of him, maybe even killed him, and Ivain knew it.

Yet for some inexplicable reason, neither did he doubt that Talorcan's expressions of worry over Alaiz were also genuine, even though Ivain now knew that Talorcan had no sexual interest in her or any other woman. It was all very confusing. Talorcan did not seem like the kind of man who would have female friends either, say in the way Swein felt about Cwen. He was too much the professional killer, at home in the company of fighting men but unlikely to ever want to set foot in a ladies parlour. Ivain yawned again. He was too tired to unravel the tangle tonight, but as Talorcan bade them goodnight, he realised that for the first time he was seeing the person who might attract others to him. What a complicated man! A thought which was still ricocheting around his head as he fell into bed, but not a second longer as sleep took over.

For the next two days he also fell into bed utterly spent, for Ruari, Hereman and Talorcan had swiftly conferred and then begun making trials. As each batch of archers was freed up after drawing additional stores for the onward march, they were brought to the lists outside of the castle walls. There they made practice volleys working with Ivain and Swein. Some worked better than others, but all worked better than an experimental group of archers made up of men pulled out of various lances of the Order. With the Order's archers the volley was a beautifully co-ordinated affair but nothing more. However, with certain of the militia archers there was positively a crackling on the air as they drew back their bowstrings and let fly with Ivain. In the air the arrows flew as one – far beyond anything attributable to human skill.

"Flaming Hound of the Wild Hunt!" Ruari breathed as a flight of forty arrows thudded into the soft soil as one. "That's awesome!"

"Isn't it just!" said Peredur appearing out of thin air with Cynddylan. "We could feel that something was going on even right up in Taineire! What have you found out?"

Once the ancients heard of Talorcan's bright idea they were full of praise, but added an idea of their own, which was to get the squints to pick out the closest linked archers as they fired with the two wielders. For the rest of the day the squints were run ragged going up and down lines of men, but by the end of the day Ivain and Swein had their men. Out of the three thousand archers who had marched in from the east, five hundred seemed to have a deep bond with Ivain. Another five hundred had a close enough link to make either a second file, if firing in lines, or as wings to the main contingent if firing on the move.

"A whole linked battalion!" Ruari breathed, feeling rather overwhelmed by the prospect even as he was delighted. "A whole battalion we can use as your bodyguards and personal fighters! I never thought we'd come to this!"

"Neither did we," confessed a rather bemused Cynddylan. "We've not had anything like it with any of the others yet."

"Maybe the weapon has everything to do with that," Talorcan mused as he massaged Ivain's aching shoulders for him. A whole day of pulling the massive bow had poor Ivain suffering the most awful cramps by the evening, and Talorcan had instructed his lance to go off and make a sweat lodge for him so that he could ease his muscles with some real heat therapy. In the meantime, Talorcan was standing behind Ivain, who had subsided onto a fallen tree trunk which acted as seating by the lists, and was doing his best to ease the muscular twinges.

"Fighting with a sword is a pretty individual thing, and Maelbrigt has been the most experienced of the chosen, so you're looking to him as being the model for the others. Don't forget he's also *used* to being a leader – a pretty individual thing again – but which Ivain and Swein aren't, so they're going to think differently. But while archers can fight alone, they more often work in companies. I think we should think about not only the Spear having this kind of potential, but also the Shield. After all, we have enlisted men make shield-walls in battles. Maybe we should be thinking of the Sword working with the Knife doing the directing of the power of the Bowl, but all the others working with our armies more directly."

Everyone stood in stunned silence for a moment. Then Ruari broke the quiet.

"Talorcan, you really are wasted just leading one lance, you know! If you can think up tactics like that I have better uses for you, even if your previous grand masters haven't!"

However, Talorcan found another use for himself, and one which had Ivain shaken by the Knight's courage. The next day Talorcan suggested that they locate himself right at the far end of the lists, several yards beyond the archers' full range to date, and then shoot at him. He thought it a valid trial to see if having a DeÁine in their sights made any difference. Ruari reluctantly agreed, but only on the condition that several large bales of hay were set up as protection in front of Talorcan, and that no more than ten men fired at one time. Ivain himself was far from happy at the prospect – firing at new found friends was not what he wanted to be doing at all, even if that friend was confusing the living daylights out of him at the moment. The sweat lodge had been as therapeutic as Talorcan had promised, but the teasing which the lance had given Talorcan had made him feel terribly naïve. Clearly Talorcan used commercial sweat rooms for more than he had told Ivain.

"Are you going in too?" Barcwith had asked with a mischievous twinkle in his eye.

"Going to expand the lad's education?" Tamàs had quipped a little later, and even Ivain had picked up on the inference of what sort of education was meant.

To make matters worse Ivain was finding himself having some very odd thoughts with that regard. Having been pursued aggressively by the women at court, he had put his lack of interest in things sexual down to a mixture of fear and never having the chance to make what he thought of as normal overtures towards anyone. He had barely had chance to say two words to any woman without someone else coming up and hanging on his every word. But now he was feeling something very different towards this new, approachable Talorcan. Something which felt very right for him, and yet was strange and rather unnerving. The massage last night had been the finishing touch, with his body having a mind of its own over its responses to having Talorcan's strong fingers kneading the sore spot between his shoulders.

Now he was standing in the lists with Swein and trying to aim at the distant haystack which hid Talorcan. He managed to take aim, putting an ordinary arrow in the Bow, while Swein lifted the Arrow aloft in one hand while resting the other on Ivain's shoulder – firing the real Arrow had been decided as reckless in the end, since once let fly there would be no way to get it back in a real battle situation. The flight of eleven arrows took off and streaked towards the hay bales as if they had a mind of their own, terrifyingly seeming to increase their range.

"Oh Blessed Martyrs, no!" Ivain gasped as they sailed over the hay bales.

"Jolnir's bollocks!" they all heard Talorcan's distant and rather shaky yelp, and everyone ran like mad down the grassy sward towards him.

They found him flattened back against the hay bales, a neat semicircle of arrows surrounding him. Luckily he had had the presence of mind to jump into the bales and not run from the arrows. Had he done that he would undoubtedly have been impaled.

"Flaming Underworlds!" Ruari swore. "Well we're not repeating *that* experiment again!"

"And that's when you fancy the target!" an amused Swein whispered softly to Ivain as they all trooped back again.

Ivain whipped round to stare at Swein who was grinning at him.

"Oh don't act the innocent with me," Swein chuckled. "I've seen the way you can't take your eyes off him. He's very handsome in a rugged kind of way. Good luck to you! I wouldn't mind a night alone with him myself, but somehow I don't think I'm his type."

Ivain's head whipped round in shock even if he did then wince at the pull on his muscles.

"I'm not.., not.., well like that!"

"Oh you *so* are!"

Ivain had gone pale. "But I don't know… I mean, I've never… Oh Blessed Mungo help me! …Is it that …erm…?"

"Obvious? …Yes!" Swein said baldly. Then an astonishing thought came to him. "You really didn't know you were…"

"…No. …No, I'd never even thought I might… Oh Trees! …Oh Spirits, is that why Amalric kept making those strange comments to me? I was so confused by that! I thought …I thought he was dealing with some frustration of his own. It never occurred to me that he might see something of it in me. …Shit! What a mess! …Lost Souls, I'm so bloody hopeless …I don't even know me …let alone someone else."

Now it was Swein's turn to be shocked. It had never occurred to him that someone might not know their own sexual preferences. He had known right from a small child what he was – might have wished it different in that it would have saved him a lot of grief, but never not known. But then the future of a royal dynasty had never hung on him producing an heir. Maybe Ivain had been so blinkered by those around him, so directed with only one option ever presented to him, that anything different had never entered his mind. The young king's agonising over Alaiz made even more sense if that was the case, and Swein felt deeply sorry for his new friend and the turmoil he was going through. He was going to have to help him, and do it now if Ivain was not to end up facing the enemy too confused to think straight. If nothing else, Swein silently vowed, Ivain would feel comfortable within his own skin before too long, and he was uniquely placed to be the much needed help.

"Hmm," Swein hummed tucking a friendly arm through Ivain's. "I think you need Swein's master class in seduction, my friend! There are many things in this world that I'm hopelessly in ignorance of – as I've painfully found out over these last few months! But how to get a man into my bed? That's something I know all about!"

However, they were soon disrupted by far more pressing worries. A hawk tore in late on the fifth of Beltane from Bittern, with Piran's horrifying news that the Scabbard had been taken. It arrived with the ancients hot on its heels. To Ruari's mixed feelings of disgust and amusement at their discomfort, they admitted that they had felt something, but had taken this long to work out what it was. Their inability to react quickly to this event reminded everyone, as if a reminder was necessary, that it would not do to depend too heavily on the ancients in this battle. They were still going to have to work out a lot for themselves. Meanwhile the ealdorman was clearly distraught and blaming himself (as Ruari privately wished the ancients might show more inclination to do sometimes), but had equally obviously done everything humanly possible to avoid the disaster.

"It's not Piran's fault," Hereman sighed as the senior men held a hurried conference. "If the bloody Abend managed to tunnel in using the Power, how could he stop them? He wouldn't have had time to do much! Not like ordinary men tunnelling in. And in the dark it's no wonder he couldn't track them. In the daylight he might have seen the distortions around the edge of the glamour hiding them, but not at night he wouldn't."

"I agree," Ruari said firmly. "And I won't have a good man beating himself up over something so far out of his control. We took every precaution. How could we know that one of the Abend would be so reckless of their own safety to come by sea? It was something even Hugh didn't consider. On the other hand, it means that there's now nothing to keep all those men up at Bittern for. Send a message back – will Cynddylan or Peredur do that, do you think? – that Piran's to leave the castle to the second-in-command with a basic garrison, and he's to bring the rest of the men to join us. At least if he has a chance to fight, he'll feel he's going to get a chance to redeem himself – in his own eyes even if it's not necessary in anyone else's."

It put something of a blight on the rest of the evening, but come the morning there were new reasons to start feeling more cheerful again. For a start the outriders of the main contingent of the Order's remaining muster came with the dawn. Thorold had come and they could start moving men in earnest. Using the boats, Hereman had already moved all his own men across to Kittermere, and then all those archer not awaiting Ivain. Only a skeleton garrison remained at Mullion, and the first of the new troops were marched straight to the quay and loaded on board.

Then to Ruari and Talorcan's delight, as well as Swein's, the sails of a tall ship were spotted coming up the sound. By the size of it it could only be the ship carrying Cwen, and so those who had been waiting for her were finally able to get their own gear packed and ready to go.

By evening time Thorold himself was at the gates of Mullion.

"I've left Wulfric looking after things in Trevelga," he announced. "After that scare we had with his heart I told him straight, no campaigning for him! And he must have still been feeling pretty rough, because for once he didn't complain!"

"Will he be able to cope on his own?" Hereman wondered.

Thorold grimaced. "I hope so. Let's put it like this, there's no resistance in the capital. Hugh had already spelled it out to the nobles and told them there would be no arguing. The Order will run the Island for the immediate future, and hand over to a civilian government as soon as possible. But that doesn't mean the same old faces will still be in power! He clapped the troublemakers in goal and there they'll stay until we see fit to release them. Wulfric has no qualms about that, so there's no way he'll release them. And with the worst of the rabble-rousers out of the way, few others have shown any signs of getting odd ideas. I think one taste of Duke

Brion, and another of Hugh's swift reprisals, have seen to that! Wulfric has plenty of the old and steady men left to help him too. No hot-headed youngsters who might go off on the rampage. It's just so long as he doesn't sicken any further. That's my biggest worry, but who could I leave behind with him? I'm not denying young Instone the chance to get valuable experience and Piran has the Scabbard to guard."

Then he saw the way the others' faces fell. In few words Hereman told him of the disaster at Bittern. "So you see, Piran will be joining us after all. On the other hand, with the cursed thing gone there's even less chance of Wulfric having to cope with a crisis, I suppose."

"A very cockeyed blessing," admitted Thorold, "but I take your point. What a strange day!"

The senior ealdorman had been overwhelmed with joy at meeting Ivain once more. Hugh had sent him news of the discovery that Ivain lived, but somehow it had not quite seemed real until he had been able to take his young king and shake his hand in the flesh. It had also been the first time Thorold had seen the fabled Island Treasures for himself, turning the day into something vaguely unreal as if legends were coming to life. He was just very glad that Hugh had appointed someone so thoroughly down to earth as Ruari to lead the Prydein sept in his absence. It was not a job he would ever have wanted, and he had been dreading the thought that he might get to Mullion and then be expected to take over full leadership of the mobilisation. It was a great relief to find that nothing of the sort was anticipated – second-in-command was a job he relished and was happy fulfilling with comforting familiarity.

As for Ivain, he had welcomed Thorold with genuine warmth, having known the gruff ealdorman for all of his life. But soon afterwards he had joined Swein down on the quay, where they waited with Talorcan and his lance for Cwen to arrive. No sooner had the battered ship thrown its lines to shore and been made fast, than a gangplank was run out and a delighted Cwen came running down onto the quay.

"Swein!" she cried with delight, and threw her arms around him in a huge hug.

Her squint, Daisy, came scuttling down the plank after her, and was immediately whiffled and snuffled over with great delight by Eric and Dylan.

"Oh bless 'em!" Tamàs said fondly. "Poor little beggars are so glad to see one another. How could anyone leave 'em in limbo like they was? Bloody cruel thing to do!"

"Very cruel," Talorcan agreed. He was still less than enthusiastic about the ancients in the light of their willingness to sacrifice others with so little thought as to the cost. It made him wonder whether they would be any more thoughtful over the human cost. Admittedly they had supposedly sacrificed themselves to save the Islanders the last time the DeÁine had threatened, but Talorcan had not lived this long by taking things at face value. However, he was pleased to see Swein looking so happy. It brought it home to him just how much the young man must have been worrying about Cwen, and if he could care that much for his friends he was the right sort of person in Talorcan's books.

Cwen was now formally introducing the lance who had cared for her in her traumatic travels to Ruari. Scully was the kind of dependable Knight Talorcan had met time and again in his years of service, and he liked him immediately. There were no hidden depths to men like Scully, you knew exactly where you stood with them, but this man had also shown considerable resourcefulness in protecting Cwen and then the Spear as well. With him were two huge sergeants, Warren and Mutley, who looked like they would be useful in a tight spot, and two older archers who were introduced as Rolo and Brock.

Already Rollo and Swein were engaged in an intense conversation about archery with Brock listening and nodding vigorously in places, and when Tamàs and Decke joined them there was much hand shaking and comparing of notes going on. Clearly there would be no problems in that quarter.

"Lucky Swein," Talorcan heard Ivain say wistfully beside him, and turned to see Ivain standing back a little looking rather sadly at the joyful cluster on the quayside. Ivain in turn suddenly realised that Talorcan was looking at him. "He has a way of making friends easily," he said as some sort of explanation. "I find that so hard to do. At every turn I was actively discouraged from letting anyone too close to me. 'It won't help you when you come to rule,' they used to tell me. 'You have to be impartial'."

"Pfff! What a load of bollocks!" Talorcan snorted. "Lost Souls! Even Master Brego has his friends! And you don't see him having any trouble with holding on to being Grand Master, do you?"

Ivain's sad face developed the watery start of a smile. "Well no…"

"Of course not!" Talorcan grasped Ivain's shoulder and gave him a small shake. "Look, it's just another example of that pile of crap they fed you from dawn to dusk to keep you in line! Let it go! Stop worrying that you're somehow cut off or condemned to be different. You're not! My lads like you, and believe me, if they thought you were an idiot they'd tell you to your face that's what they thought. They don't mince their words with anyone!"

And with that he propelled Ivain forward towards Cwen, so that once they stood behind Swein they were introduced properly. Cwen herself was full of apologies over her news that Alaiz had had to be left behind.

"I'm so sorry," she said time and again to Ivain, Talorcan and his lance. "I'd never have done that if she could have been moved without risking her life. It was horrible, but Eldaya and I both agreed that they stood at least an even chance of surviving if they just went back as innocents whom we'd used as hostages. And that ride back was nothing to what we'd have had to put Alaiz through if she'd come with us."

"But is she alive?" fretted Ivain.

"I can't promise you that," Cwen sighed sadly. "I guess we'll only know for certain when we get to Rathlin."

"Well look on the bright side," Barcwith said – he, Galey and Ad having joined the welcoming, even as Ruari hurried away with a relieved look on his face. "Now Cwen's here I doubt Master Ruari with be hanging about. Unless I'm very mistaken we'll be off and riding like the wind as soon as Miss Cwen's spear-wall men have been sorted out. In fact, I'd take bets on Master Ruari not bothering with that too much while our forces are split between Prydein and Kittermere, because what would be the point of picking a team only then to find that there were better men we'd never even looked at because they were ahead of us?"

His words proved prophetic. Ruari announced that night that they would delay their departure only by one more day, and that only to find the start of a proper bodyguard for Cwen.

"We must ride, and ride hard, now," Ruari announced to the assembled leading men in the refectory. "When those ships Master Brego sends arrive on the west coast of Kittermere, I want us lined up and waiting to embark, not spread out over the Kittermere hills like a bunch of lost sheep! Gentlemen, we are war! Now is the time we show the DeÁine what the men of the Order can really do!"

Chapter 20

A Return to Sanity

Kittermere: Beltane

With Cwen being amongst them at last, Ruari's party took the boats across to Kittermere as soon as the sun rose. The continued presence of a bodyguard, which Ruari had insisted she have, had not turned out to be half as bad as she had feared. Her experiences around Magnus had scarred her more than she had realised when it came to heavily armed strange men in close proximity, and she found now that she felt surprisingly uneasy about having unknown men quite so close. Instead, Scully had been delighted to be asked to remain in command, and Mutley and Warren also stayed with her, so she had familiar faces with her at least. A couple of new men equally as large as the two sergeants were with them too, but only as a temporary arrangement. For Rolo and Brock also sailed with them, although as part of Swein and Ivain's coterie for the time being, simply because as archers they were aiding Tamàs and Decke in tutoring the pair. However, Ruari had also been insistent that Rolo and Brock would return to Cwen's side soon, so that she had personal protection from archers once they were in more hostile territory. Not that they were short of those, for the battalion of archers attached to Ivain were all sailing in their wake.

It was a strange voyage, since the narrow strait between Prydein and Kittermere meant it was too long to be able to do much else that day, yet not long enough to make it worthwhile trying to do anything whilst on board either. What she did find a relief was to discover that Ruari and the other Knights had already given substantial thought as to how to transport the Treasures. Despite Ivain and Swein being physically able to carry their own weapons, Ruari had felt it important that they have regular rests from the Treasures' potent presence. Practising was vital, but once they had done for the day, Ruari insisted that the Bow and Arrow go back into specially prepared cases. To Cwen's amazement they even had a case waiting for her Spear thanks to the ancients giving Hereman's men the dimensions of the vast weapon. Each case was then put into a litter slung between two horses, and given a guard from amongst both the Order's men and the Prydein archers. It saved her from having to have a hand on the Spear all the time for others to carry it, and she had not realised how it had become such a burden until she was able to stop.

Having Daisy was another bonus, although she was struggling to understand quite how they were going to work together. She had got as far as working out that Daisy could help with preventing the Spear's bearers from feeling ill, but quite how that was supposed to work if she was using the thing was another matter. Much of her confusion came from Urien. The others might reassure her that he was becoming more reasonable and approachable with every day since the squints had been rescued, but Cwen still found the ancient abrasive and unpleasant. He had not been around much as she had travelled to Kittermere once he had delivered Daisy, declaring that he would start training her once she was more settled. He had been far from happy at Ruari taking her off on the road straight away again, and had spent most of the little time he had been around her at Mullion fulminating about how he was ever supposed to train a 'girl' to use a weapon if she was darting off here, there and everywhere.

Not having met Cwen before, Ruari was unaware that she was well on the way to becoming thoroughly depressed until the third night they spent in camp on Kittermere. Mercifully, in the south, Beltane was turning out to be a dry and fairly warm month, so they had dispensed with the raising of tents each night in the interests of speed. Here on this side of Kittermere there was also no need to set guards each night, and so once everyone had settled down to sleep, Cwen found herself wandering outside the camp to let out the emotions she was keeping a lid on during the day. That night as Ruari tried to find a suitable hollow for his hip to fit in, mentally cursing the lack of a comfortable bed yet again, he was vaguely aware of someone going past. However, he assumed it was just someone heading for one of the latrine pits out beyond the camp, and thought nothing more until Daisy came and sat beside him, whistling softly but mournfully.

"Hello, little one, what's the matter," Ruari mumbled drowsily, reaching out to stroke the fur just under her throat. All the squints seemed to have the same enjoyment of that as the big dogs Ruari had grown up with, and normally their eyes would gradually close in bliss as they were gently ruffled. This time, though, Daisy's dainty forepaw tried to catch hold of Ruari's much bigger hand. Both paws then clasped around it and she tried to tug at him. It was such an odd thing for her to do that Ruari sat up. Now he was awake again he could see that she was definitely in some distress.

"What is it, Daisy?" he asked again. Cwen could not be in any sort of danger, even in a camp-full of thousands of men – not because he thought every last man was respectful of women, but because Daisy was not showing that kind of distress. After the incident with Eric and Dylan, Ruari was pretty sure Daisy would have been whistling like a steaming kettle and making enough noise to rouse the whole camp if real danger threatened Cwen, not to mention the Spear glowing fit to light the whole camp and then some. Yet something was still very wrong.

"Do you want me to come with you?" he asked, and got a very definite nodding, with Daisy taking a couple of steps back and then pausing like a dog waiting to show its master where the game lay. Wincing as he got back onto his feet which still ached from marching all day, Ruari paused only to pick up his sword, just in case, and then followed his small, white, furry guide. Walking out he became more concerned when Daisy went nowhere near the latrines, but just kept going further and further from camp. He was just about to try and determine from Daisy what Cwen was doing out here when his ears answered the question for him. Someone, presumably Cwen, was sobbing their heart out.

Part of Ruari was touched by the fact that she clearly had not wanted to make a fuss and disrupt the camp with whatever ailed her, while the other part quailed at the thought of dealing with the matter. In a life spent in the army, Ruari had not exactly had much experience of sobbing women. Then he spotted her, a shadowy hunched figure in the lee of a large gorse bush.

"Cwen?" he said softly, not wanting to frighten her by his sudden appearance.

She started nonetheless and then tried to stumble to her feet, dragging her sleeve across her eyes.

"No, no, sit down," Ruari said gently, putting a hand on her shoulder and halting her rise, then plonked himself down beside her. He adopted what he hoped was his most comforting tone of voice to ask,

"What's wrong?"

"It's alright," Cwen sniffled bravely, "I'll be alright." However her voice trailed off faintly and sounded far from convincing.

"You're a bloody awful liar," Ruari responded before thinking that this might not be the best approach to a distressed young woman.

He got a startled hiccup from Cwen and hurriedly qualified his words with,

"It was Daisy who came and fetched me. If it was nothing, or just some …if it was a …ladies problem, then I assume she would have roused one of the women following behind."

The Prydein archers seemed to have a small coterie of older women with them, all carrying large quantities of herbs going by the pungent aroma rising from the large sacks slung across their backs. Ivain had told him that they would all be widows without young families who came along to treat the wounded, and so Ruari had given them an official place in his army, albeit very much at the rear.

His stumbling words at least raised a faint smile from Cwen, just visible in the clear night illuminated by a myriad of stars, but no moon yet. "No, it's not women's problems," she managed with a quaver in her voice which might even have been tinged with amusement.

"What then?" He pointed to Daisy who was now sat opposite them but watching Cwen with a very fixed stare. "I don't think you're going to get away with *not* telling me, and I don't know about you, but I'm knackered after all this walking."

This time Cwen really did laugh. It was actually rather nice that he was not trying to be cloyingly sympathetic – most men she had met did that so badly. It also reminded her of her lost lover, Richert, with his blunt, soldierly ways, and also of Berengar and Esclados, whom she was missing almost more than Richert these days. None of them would have pretended they had a clue as to what she felt, but they would all have been worried enough to be blunt in asking out of kindness not insensitivity.

"I think I'm the wrong person for this," Cwen said baldly. "I haven't a clue about fighting battles, and most definitely not about what in the Islands you do with a spear! I'm just an innkeeper's daughter. I'm not like those noble warrior-lady friends of yours whom Alaiz told me about."

Ruari snorted with laughter. "I suspect that's the first time in her life that Kayna has been called a warrior *lady*! I think Maelbrigt's usual term was 'pain in the arse'!" That at least elicited another hiccupping laugh. "And as for you being '*just* an innkeeper's daughter', I'm sorry but you'll have to do better than that to convince me after what I've heard from Swein. I don't think many other innkeeper's daughters decide that they're going to bring down a corrupt king, all by themselves if necessary! And I don't think many of them would square up to the Master of a whole Island sept and tell him he's an idiot right there in his own office, either."

Cwen turned her head away, but Ruari did not need to see her face to guess that she was blushing.

"So come on, then …what's the real problem?"

Cwen sighed and began falteringly. "Well to some extent what I just said. …I mean, …I've watched soldiers practising, …but that's not the same as actually knowing what's going on, …and I'm not daft enough to fool myself into thinking I can suddenly pick up on things it's taken those men years of work to perfect."

Ruari plonked an arm around her shoulders and hugged her. Bless her, she really was a gem, he thought, so like Matti! He also felt rather guilty for not having explained things better to her. "Sacred Trees, Cwen! We weren't expecting you to do anything of the sort! That's why I want to find you men who *are* experienced for you to work with. But also for them to be able to advise you, and *you* personally, when we get to a fighting situation."

"But I feel so alone! At least Ivain and Swein have each other. They can share things. Work things out between them. I feel like a spare part, stuck out on the side of the army, no use to anyone until the Underworld breaks loose, and even then I might not have a clue as to how to make this bloody Spear do anything. I *hate* the cursed thing! I wish I'd never laid eyes on it! Better that it had never been found then for me to take it into battle and then let everyone down."

She spoke with such fury and bitterness that Daisy began to whimper.

"Woah! Steady! Both of you!" Ruari exclaimed. "Daisy, that doesn't mean she hates you!"

Cwen's head shot back up. "Oh Spirits no! Oh Daisy, I'm sorry! No, I didn't mean I didn't want you!" She held her arms out and the white squint shot forward to be hugged.

"How much help have you had from Urien?" Ruari asked, a nasty suspicion beginning to lurk in his mind.

Cwen's snort was enough confirmation even before she said,

"Humph! Him? No *help* at all! All I get is complaints about how is he supposed to train me – and horror of horrors, a girl at that – if we're never going to stop and do training."

Ruari made a growling sound in his throat. So that was what lay at the heart of it! Urien was successfully undermining what little confidence Cwen had in the first place. No wonder she was upset!

"Right!" he said decisively. "Now listen to me, Cwen! For a start off, don't think for a minute that Urien knows all there is to know about this

Spear. In every case so far, we've found out more by working amongst ourselves than we ever have from the ancients. Daisy is your biggest ally, because she can tell you if you're focusing correctly for the Spear to respond. And because we've now got enough squints to have one for each Treasure, I think we can bypass Urien. If we need Daisy's words translating for something specific, we'll ask one of the three more friendly ancients. I'd rather do without Urien altogether if he can't be more help to you than this.

"And the other thing is, you're not alone, and you won't be alone – not just in the sense that none of us are exactly alone in this big force, either. I haven't been putting you through your paces yet simply because there's no point until Matti gets here. Just as Swein and Ivain will be working together, you and Matti will be working towards providing our defences. In a normal battle situation the shields interlock and then the spears poke out between them – rather like a hedgehog's spines. If a group of men hold firm and keep the shields overlapping, and use the spears to deflect attacks, then it's almost impossible to overrun them. If those men then advance all together, then they secure ground that other soldiers have taken. *If* you get to the point where you feel confident enough to push forwards with the spears that would be great, but if you don't it doesn't mean your presence won't be very useful – it will!

"So please believe me, I'm not expecting you to go into the heart of a battle and actively push forwards leading some attack, like a general such as Will does. You'll be with Matti, behind Maelbrigt, Swein and Ivain and watching our backs. Does that make you feel any better? Or would you like me to ask Peredur or Cynddylan to fetch Owein? He's the ancient who works with Matti and Moss, and he's quite friendly and approachable. I'm sure under the circumstances he'd be willing to do a bit with you in terms of taking messages back and forth, and translating what Daisy says."

Cwen's shoulders had stopped their quivering under Ruari's arm, which gave him hope, and then she said much more normally,

"Thank you. Let's not disturb Owein too much until we have to. I feel much better already knowing that I'm not going to be in the front row of the battle with men looking to me, and that I'll be with Matti. So hopefully I can ignore Urien a bit more now."

She allowed herself to be led back into the camp by Ruari, but was surprised when he went and picked up his bedroll and came to lie beside her. Daisy immediately wriggled between them, gave a contented sigh and went fast asleep, clearly feeling much less fraught now that Cwen was calmer. On the other hand, Cwen was less sure why Ruari had felt it necessary to be quite so close to her until Urien turned up as they were getting up in the morning. The ancient made no acknowledgement of anyone other than Cwen and began promptly issuing a string of instructions.

"Hey! What do you think you're doing?" Ruari said firmly, coming to stand by Cwen's side.

"I'm *trying* to train this girl," Urien snapped. "These are codes she should have known long before all of this, and there's a lot of maths she should have learned before trying to use the Spear."

"Maths?" Ruari was aghast. "Flaming Underworlds! We're going into a *battle* for our very existence, not teaching a bunch of acolytes! Let's worry about how these things work after we've survived the coming fight!"

"How can you use these weapons if you haven't a clue what it is you're using," Urien demanded almost petulantly. "Trajectories are *important*, you know!"

But Ruari, as senior Knight in the camp, was clearly taking no nonsense from any ancient, and he was more than a little annoyed that this had been happening behind his back.

"You can help us as we make our way westwards," he said firmly, "or you can go and sit back in the frozen waste, and we'll take what advice we can get from your more obliging colleagues! It isn't possible for Cwen to sit around here taking months to learn how to use the Spear in the way you're thinking of – whatever that is! – so stop taking it out on her because the DeÁine have set things in motion beyond all of our control. If you can't be kind to Cwen, then don't come here at all. Daisy is much more obliging, and she can work with Eric and Peredur, and Dylan and Cynddylan, so she can get what help your kind can give us without you putting her and Cwen through extra misery. Make your mind up! Cwen has enough troubles. She doesn't need you throwing rocks in her path and making her feel like dirt. But I warn you! You keep on like this and, if I survive, I shall come back to Taineire and pull every one of those funny tubes and metal strands out of your coffin until you die for good!"

Urien's ghostly eyebrows shot up and he winked out of existence before anyone could say anything else.

A few moments later Vanadis appeared, her beautiful face marred by a deep frown.

"What *are* you doing, Ruari?" she demanded imperiously. "This is no time to be testing us!"

Ruari drew himself up to his full and considerable height, and looked down his hawk-like nose at her, blue eyes as cold as ice.

"Madam, I don't need you to tell me how to run an army or a war!" he barked. "And my response will be the same to anyone else who upsets my troops, makes a nuisance of themselves, and fails to do anything to help us!"

Vanadis looked at him askance. This clearly was not the response she had expected.

"I rather expected better of *you*," she said with the air of a teacher chastising an errant pupil, but Ruari was not in the mood to be lectured to.

"Then maybe you don't know me that well after all," he retorted. "I'm not your pet! You may have watched me for years, but you did so with only yourself in mind. You needed me to get into that frozen tomb you all built for yourselves, and I did it for you. But I did it in the hope that we would get some real help against this vast threat we're facing.

"Instead, only half of you are any bloody use at all, and you're not one of them, and neither is Urien! So if you've come to tell me to be nice to Urien, you can forget it! I'm not in the mood to be pandering to some semi-senile being, whose idea of warfare is so strange as to bear no resemblance to fighting as we know it, and is therefore useless. …Now …if you don't mind, I have to get several thousand men across this island and over to Rathlin in under a month. So unless you intend to do something spectacular – like magic us to the west coast in an instant – I suggest you go away, and leave us to make a better job of dealing with the circumstances than you are!"

Taken totally off guard, Vanadis blinked in shock, half opened her mouth as if to speak, then clearly thought better of it and disappeared.

"Wow! That was impressive!" Ivain said as Ruari turned around, and saw Swein with his arm around Cwen's shoulders and Ivain standing on Cwen's other side. The men of Talorcan's lance were clustered around the trio along with Scully and his men, while Talorcan himself stood just a little apart but grinning widely.

"I'm so glad I'm not the only one to get a bollocking like that!" he chuckled with more humour than Ruari had given him credit for having.

Ruari could not help but grin back. "Well there's no point in having this smart Master's uniform if I don't get to flex my muscles once in a while," he declared somewhat sheepishly. "However, since you're here, Talorcan …as you've probably gathered, Cwen's been having more than a bit of trouble with Urien. So what I'd like is for Scully to take overall command of the bodyguards for our three chosen ones. That will free you up to take on some training with Cwen. I know we can't do much on the road since we all have to walk, but I'd like you to start getting Daisy to scan the men to pick out any she thinks are useful, just like Eric and Dylan did. I'll free up some of the packhorses for you so that, with Daisy still riding in her litter, the two of you can ride ahead a way and then wait while men go past. That way Cwen can at least start getting to know the men she'll be in closest contact with."

The grateful glance Cwen gave him was a good sign that he had got things right this time, which was a relief. Nobody was mounted at the moment, because getting horses across to Kittermere in any numbers had just not been feasible in the time they had, so every horse they could muster had been laden with supplies to allow the men a speedier march. However, taking a couple out of those numbers would not be so detrimental to the overall plan. So by midday Cwen was sat at the side of the road with her arm around Daisy, and Talorcan looking on, as the men marched past.

Breca was somewhere up ahead of them by a few days with the vanguard, and Hereman would cross to Kittermere with the last contingent to bring up the rear and deal with any unexpected problems, now that Ruari was too distant to have contact with the whole force. Thorold was currently acting as their anchorman on the Kittermere side, making sure everyone moved on swiftly to allow more men to land, but once everyone was across he would take over the rear, and Hereman would ride with all speed to meet up with Ruari. It was a plan, Ruari conceded, but plans and reality were often two very different things. He would be an awful lot happier once most of the men had reached the western shore, and they were within striking distance of Rathlin. At the moment they were too spread out to make a response if the enemy fleet beat them to Rathlin, or if Magnus went even madder than ever and attacked them.

Two days later, as they made camp for the night, Talorcan drew Ruari aside.

"This isn't going well," he confided softly. "Out of the men we've seen so far we've found one man who would do, but who Daisy was a bit cautious of, and about four who'd be good in an emergency to build up the numbers a bit. But I'm afraid that there's nobody here who really clicks into place the way they did with Ivain and Swein. In fact, I'm thinking that that's not because we haven't got good men here, but rather that we've got so many committed archers. I'm sorry, Master Ruari, but I think we need to spread our net wider."

Ruari grimaced. "Curses! …Oh not you, Talorcan. …I think you've very astutely put your finger on the reason why Cwen's not finding men for the Spear. It's just that I don't want to be splitting our three up. So either they need to dally around until more of the men catch up…"

"…Which isn't a good idea because, quite apart from the fact that you need to keep everyone moving forwards, we don't want you and the three weapons at the back of the force in case it all goes base up in a hurry."

"Quite!"

"So I think we need to find enough horses to get us and the three, plus squints a bit further ahead."

"Not to mention their bodyguards!" Ruari added. "Do you see Scully stopping behind? He might be under my command for the moment, but I don't need magic to know that he's worried to death about letting his own Grand Master down by allowing something to happen to Cwen."

"Yes, Master Berengar adores her by all accounts. I wouldn't want to be the man who had to tell him she was injured or worse."

Lucky Berengar, Ruari thought wistfully, to be in with a chance of having a life with a lady as worthy in every respect as Cwen, and without the complication of her husband being his best friend. He was unlikely to ever be in the same position with Matti, especially now that he had so many responsibilities, which was a rather depressing thought. Mentally shaking himself and forcing his mind back to the present, Ruari came to a decision.

"That's a good idea, though. Come on, let's go and find Scully. If we're going to put it into action, I want his men to get a few hours sleep, but then to get on the road long before us. You and I will ride with the three and the squints in the morning to catch up with them, while your lads can start with us and then march on until they catch up with us. This army is pretty stretched out all the way along the road, so I doubt there'll be anywhere where we're out of earshot of several dozen men if we get into difficulties. It might take us a few days of marching like that, but we should be able to catch up with Breca. He's eight days ahead of us, but that's with a normal day's march. We should be able to shorten that gap."

They put the plan into operation and spent a gruelling couple of days hurrying forward. However, they had a visitation from Peredur on the third day in which he announced that Breca and the leading men had made it to the west coast where they had found some ships already waiting.

"Master Hugh's men seem to have put the fear of the Underworld into some of the merchantmen of Prydein," Peredur divulged with some glee. "I don't think I've ever seen merchants quite so subdued! Mind you it was also rather fun taking Master Hugh's advice and appearing to them out of thin air to relay messages to them, just in case they had any ideas about not complying with his requisition!"

"We must be having a corrupting influence on you," Ruari said with mock innocence, secretly pleased that this ancient at least was finding some enjoyment in helping them, and getting some recompense for helping carry the load of communications.

Peredur assumed a similar caricature of innocence. "You? Corrupting? No I don't think so …but then again Vanadis has been in a huff for days. That couldn't be anything to do with you either, could it?"

"By the Trees! Caught out again!" Ruari laughed openly this time. "Yes, I'm afraid I told her she was being no help at all, and neither was Urien. In fact I've told Urien not to bother coming again until he can be more civil to Cwen."

"Ouch!" Peredur winced. "No wonder he's like a wounded bear at the moment! Oh well, we did warn him! By the way, Owein is keeping a close eye on the Abend for you, which is why none of you have seen much of him at the moment. It's a bit of a trial for him because the Abend know our signature energies in the Power, so he's having to be very careful. However, you'll be pleased to know that there's terrible flooding in Brychan which is stopping the Donns from moving west to go home, or getting reinforcements, and has five of the Abend marooned in Arlei with the Helm. Apparently Anarawd and Eliavres will land with the Scabbard at Temair this evening, and Quintillean and Masanae are also aboard ships and should land at the same place in three days' time. Owein said to tell you that the two leaders have recruited extra men, presumably to make an impact on those arriving from across the sea, since they don't know we're coming. He said he'll bring you a proper estimate of numbers when he can get close enough to observe them."

"Please thank him for us," Ruari said sincerely. "Tell him I just wish Vanadis, Aneirin and Urien would put as much effort in as you, Owein and Cynddylan are doing. Your efforts are much appreciated."

He felt it was not the time to be asking for someone to come and help hunt down a coterie to work with Cwen. Instead he decided to slow their pace a little. They would still get to the coast ahead of the battalion of archers, but there was now no point in exhausting those on whom they might end up depending on most when a substantial number were already on the sea.

Up at the leading edge of the force, Breca was busy detailing the last men onto the ships. He wanted them to sail with the next tide, but he was also determined to get as many men on board as possible. His biggest fear was that they had to land at Kylesk, Mad Magnus' home port, where they might get the Trees alone knew what kind of reception. It could be out and out hostility, and he wanted enough men to be able to respond in kind.

On the twenty-second of Beltane, with a fair summer wind filling the sails on their ships, they entered Kylesk Bay. All the archers were at the sides, armed and waiting, while the men-at-arms lurked just below deck but no less ready to spring into action if need be. However, if anything he was more shocked by what actually greeted them than the expected hostility. Magnus stood on the end of the quay, visibly unarmed, and with his men lined up but also clearly not bearing weapons. A tall dark-haired woman was the nearest person to Magnus, although several paces behind him, and she seemed to be speaking to him as if reassuring him, even though those onboard the ships could not hear her words.

"Steady everyone," Breca ordered loudly enough for his own men to all hear him. "Keep the bows down, don't make any gestures which they could take as threatening. Watch for ambushes, though!"

His lead ship drifted up to the end of the main projecting jetty, and the sailors nervously jumped ashore to secure the lines. No other ship would dock until Breca was much more certain of how things stood here, but they were close behind, and he knew that from where Magnus stood they would look a substantial force.

"Greetings, sire," Magnus said calmly, coming forward with his left hand extended and not a glimmer of madness in his eyes. Breca swept his eyes over Magnus and realised that the Attacotti leader was left-handed going by where his empty scabbard hung on his belt. No attempt to deceive, then, unless it was a very thorough and clever one. He stepped forwards and took Magnus' hand.

"I know we've had our conflicts," Magnus said without preamble, "but I hope you'll agree that we have a bigger threat to worry about just now."

This totally threw Breca. Did Magnus both know about the DeÁine and understand what it meant? His confusion must have been noticed because the young woman now came forward. She was tall enough to look him in the eye and seemed to be willing him to be calm.

"My name's Eldaya," she said with a smile, but an urgent undertone lurked beneath the apparent calm. "I was sent with Alaiz by Cwen to look after her. Have you met Swein and Talorcan yet?"

"Er . . . yes," Breca gasped, now utterly wrong-footed. "Swein should be coming along behind me in a week or so."

"Oh good!" Eldaya gushed with relief. "So you know how we've come to be here. Alaiz is well but resting. After Cwen left, I managed to warn Magnus of the DeÁine threat. He's got a lot to tell you!"

Breca in turn breathed a small, but hopefully imperceptible, sigh of relief. Thanks to Peredur and Cynddylan he knew that Cwen had arrived safely but had not wanted to mention her and the Spear in case it made Magnus wild. This was sounding much more as though the removal of the Spear had done much to lift whatever it was that had ailed Magnus' mind. However, he had every intention of proceeding cautiously.

"So you know about the coming DeÁine threat?" he asked Magnus directly, wanting to hear the leader's own view.

The dark shaggy head bobbed minutely although he never broke eye contact. "Indeed I do. At first I'll admit that I thought it some overblown fancy of the girls', here. But we had a warning from one of our ships that DeÁine galleys were going back and forth off our north coast. I don't have time to tell you all just now, but you should know that they had one of their witches with them."

Good, was Breca's first thought. At least there was no need to convince him that the threat was real.

"Please, bring the rest of your ships in," Magnus invited. "We have more room than people here, so they can hopefully find places to rest. But if you and your guards would come with me, I'm afraid we have intelligence of happenings in the north from many of my scouts which you need to hear!"

Chapter 21

Shifting Alliances

Brychan & Rathlin: Beltane

"*I would move if I were you*!"

Helga's warning on the Power jolted Eliavres awake with a start. He sat up on the hard, rough bed in the castle at Temair to see Anarawd also rubbing a hand over his face and blinking blearily.

"*Why*?" Eliavres sent back, keeping it short to avoid giving Helga any impression that he was less than fully alert.

Instead Magda's thoughts took over. "*Because, dear heart, Masanae and Quintillean are heading your way*!"

"*Our way specifically? Or are they maybe trying to reach you*?" suggested Anarawd, having had the vital few extra seconds to compose himself. "*It's not that I doubt you*," he added, taking a leaf from Eliavres' book for dealing with the other Abend, "*but in that palace you have both the Helm and two new members of the Abend whom our un-beloved leaders haven't had chance to stamp on yet! Is that maybe more of a draw …a lure …than us*?"

"*A fair point*," Magda conceded, "*but unfortunately not the one which those two seem to have decided to aim for. Barrax has been tracking them, and reports that from the maps of tides around these horrid islands, they must surely be aiming to land on the north coast of the southern island where you are now. We've discussed it and believe that they think you'll be the easier target. We suspect that they'll try and take the Scabbard for themselves – although we can't tell whether it's to then put them on a more even footing with us, or to be taken south towards the Sinut fleet*."

"*Have we any more news of the Sinut fleet*?" Eliavres asked. The others would surely know that he and Anarawd would have been unable to quest around while they had been at sea, but he would not openly admit it even if it was common knowledge.

This time Barrax answered for himself. "*Since they don't know Laufrey or me – or at least not our signatures now that they've been altered by the elevation rites – we've done a little scouting on the Power. We didn't get too close, but by the signatures we spotted, I would say that the fleet is still a good month away. They appear to be having trouble with a combination of tides and winds. If the dreadful maps we have in this hovel they call a palace are remotely correct, then we think they'll land on the south coast of your southern island, which is apparently called Rathlin. We thought they might sail directly for our own southern ports in New Lochlainn, but they've already had to alter course towards a cluster of rocky islands due to summer storms and, we assume, to take on more water.*

While we were watching they were actually driven back by two days by a ferocious thunder storm. It did us a favour, because the acolytes on board tried to use the devices they have with them to push the storm away. We felt them trying to punch at it, which was a big mistake. The storm wasn't of the kind they're used to on the desert shores. It was far more like the huge summer storms Magda told us happen back in the homeland. This monster must have been building clouds from right across the ocean! So when they lashed at it, instead of them pushing it away, they ended up ricocheting backwards themselves."

"*Did you get any sense of how many acolytes they have?*" Eliavres asked hopefully. It would be very useful to know just what they were facing.

This time it was Laufrey who replied in silky tones, but beneath the lightness Eliavres and Anarawd could detect a steeliness which would guarantee that she would be unlikely to ever be ensnared by Masanae the way Helga had.

"*In terms of Power there are a good many who have substantial strength. However, since you brought with you all those who needed closest training by full members of the Abend, although these acolytes have come on a long way in terms of development, they have very poor direction and control. In fact Barrax and I think that a lure to bring them to our side would be a display not of brute force, but of subtle skill. Something which would make them sit up and see that there's so much more they could learn from us. There were odd currents in their Power weavings which we couldn't quite work out at first, but then we realised that it came from the fact that they must be being used as almost slaves to the remaining Donns and Souk'ir and their families. They resent what they're being made to do! Give them a taste of being the masters for once and we believe they'll change allegiances in a heartbeat!*"

"That was cleverly done," Anarawd said aside to Eliavres.

"Yes, indeed! Magda did well in picking those two. They'll work with us but they think things out for themselves. What a refreshing change from Calatin and Geitla!" He refrained from saying from Anarawd too, but he had no doubt that Tancostyl, Magda and Helga had thought it just as he had.

"*Wonderful! And nice deductions too!*" he thought back. "*But numbers? I'm just a touch …concerned …that if these acolytes are being coerced, then they might be pushed to launch a Power attack against us. Not that they could truly hurt us, but rather that they might be used to keep us occupied while the Donns take the Scabbard. Are there enough of them for that to be a possibility?*"

"*An interesting thought, poppet,*" Magda now responded, "*and a genuine threat if Quintillean and Masanae threw in their lot with them out of pique. What do you two think?*"

Anarawd answered first. "*I think Quintillean and Masanae will jump whichever way they think will give them the quickest route back to being in power.*"

"*In which case, sweetling, do you think you two could fend them off just now if they decide to be brutal and try to seize the Scabbard from you?*"

"*You see, I think they might see you as tempting bait,*" Barrax added, "*and if you can't fight them off then you need to set sail pretty quickly to get clear of them.*"

Now Eliavres was in a quandary, but before Anarawd could chip in he had made his mind up and answered.

"*To be frank, this last journey has been a sore trial for Anarawd and myself. We got on board having had to use quite a lot of Power. Normally such drawings would scarcely have bothered us, but getting onto a boat without any time to recuperate left us much more at the mercy of the effects of the salty sea. I don't think we can set sail for another day or two yet. How long have we got?*"

"*Probably three more full days,*" Barrax estimated. "*After that I doubt you'll be able to get away at all. They have many ships with them, so once they start coming towards the coast, no other boat will be able to leave without being spotted.*"

"*Do you think the sea has been wearing enough on the two of them that they might not know it was us leaving?*" Anarawd asked, unable to keep the hint of desperation out of his mental voice. He really did not want to be putting to sea again just yet. Today he could just about stand up without the room spinning and him wanting to be violently sick.

Barrax's mental shrug was felt, even if the physical act could not be seen. "*If it was just you two? Maybe, although I wouldn't want you to regard it as a promise even then. But with the Scabbard? Not a chance! Just how bad is it for you?*" The last question was sympathetically put, and although both Anarawd and Eliavres knew it was almost certainly as much for the safety of the Scabbard, Barrax was at least allowing them to save some face, prompting Eliavres to be frank.

"*Honestly? Between ourselves, if Quintillean and Masanae are only marginally weakened then we're in trouble! We'd need them to be substantially incapacitated to be sure of holding our own. Quintillean was always stronger than me, and as I am now I'd be struggling to resist him if he decided to be brutal. ...Magda? How desperate do you think they'll be? You've known them longer than anyone else, and we've only ever known them when they've been in full control. How will they react?"*

"*I think they've been already having some kind of trouble we know nothing about,*" Magda said bluntly. "*At the time when we felt that strange surge on the Power six weeks or so back, we didn't know what it was, but it was in the direction Masanae and Quintillean have come from. And then there was that horrid backwash we felt two weeks later. I now believe that whatever ritual those two were up to was terminated in some way, and by someone or something unknown. Of all of you, I was the most tuned into the Power just at that time, and I can tell you that my continued observations make me fairly certain that they had to be healed after whatever happened. When they contacted us, Quintillean in particular felt as though he'd been healed ...his Power felt ...rearranged ...put back into place!*"

"*Great Dragon of Death! What have those two been up to behind our backs?*" snarled Anarawd.

"*Well might you ask, poppet! But you can then see why I don't think they'll want to let you carry on holding the Scabbard. Without it they are in a very precarious position if we choose to challenge their leadership.*"

"*Oh, I don't think now is the time to be challenging their leadership,*" Eliavres said dryly. "*If any bastard's head is going to roll for all of this, it shouldn't be one of us who's been newly elevated to the position of head of the Abend!*"

"*Who said anything about heads rolling?*" Helga demanded scornfully. She still was not willing to give Eliavres anything but the barest support.

However, Eliavres was not deterred in the slightest by her attitude. "*Oh I think we may reasonably expect that the Sinut families might have used those same acolytes to send a message back to the Emperor, don't you? After all, if we were in their place, and we thought that we were coming along just to provide an escort back to the homeland for the Treasures, wouldn't we want to get in first? Be the ones to tell the Emperor that his beloved lost pieces would be coming back? Make sure that he knew that we were actively taking part in this rescue instead of trailing in the wake of ...well, let's be frank, an Abend whom we know they've hated for the whole Exile! And they do hate us, don't they! Never mind that they, or at least their ancestors, were as keen to come to these islands and conquer them, and were as complicit as the original Abend in getting the Treasures lost. We've always shouldered the blame for the Exile happening from the generations we have with us now.*

"*Well we've got two out of four. But that's not what anyone is going to want to hear, is it? And even worse, we're the ones who have to sense the pieces, so if anyone's going to be left behind to carry on finding the Gauntlet and the Gorget, it won't be the noble-born. So I think that since Quintillean started this sorry mess, he can be the one who goes back to Lochlainn and explains why we didn't deliver what he promised. And then those of us who have no desire to be turned inside out and hung out to dry from the Immaculate Temples by the Emperor can stay here, as we've wanted, and set about putting our own plans into action.*"

He felt the collective psychic gulps of all his fellow Abend, and struggled to hide his amusement both mentally and physically from Anarawd stood next to him. So they had not thought it out, had they? A good thing they had him here, then, was it not?

"*Sweet Lotus*!" Laufrey murmured, with remarkable restraint for one so newly elevated and unused to the inner scheming which went with being part of the Abend.

It was the normally icy Helga whom he could feel shaking the most. Tancostyl was building up to a real rage, and Barrax, interestingly, was displaying similar war-mage tendencies. Not quite so controlled, then!

"*My word, sweetling! You have been thinking, haven't you*!" Magda finally spoke. "*And I do believe you're right! Yes, that's precisely what we should expect the Sinut families to have done. Well I for one am in total agreement with you, in that case. I think we make a point of telling Quintillean and Masanae that we have no intention of removing them from their positions, and why! Let them sweat a little! They deserve no better. And in the meantime we shall retain control of the Treasures. Or rather Anarawd and Tancostyl will continue to hold them with the rest of our backing and consent. But that makes it all the more important that you aren't taken captive by them. Set sail late tomorrow and get your captain to make for the port marked on the maps as Farsan. Helga has left men there, so you'll be in no danger from the locals no matter how weakened you are. We shall come to meet you, so once you've landed there you won't need to move for several days. We shall wait there for Quintillean and Masanae to come to us.*"

"*And then present our decisions to them while they're still recovering from their journey*," hummed Laufrey with the kind of amused undertone which made the others think that it would not be long before she was contributing schemes of her own to the group.

"*Well just make sure you get to the coast before they do*!" Eliavres warned.

"*Don't worry. It should take us not much over four or five days to get to you*," Helga told him, not confrontational for once, having had to admit that he had got it right this time. "*I doubt they'll turn straight around and come after you. Masanae at least will want to spend some time finding out just what's going on. If we leave here at the same time as you depart, we should still get to you long before the force Quintillean and Masanae have with them can get to you.*"

"*Force?*" Anarawd gasped. "*What in Volla's name do you mean? What force?*"

"*Oh, our dear leaders have coerced the Tabor and Dracma Souk'ir to rally their forces and accompany them,*" Barrax informed him with more than a hint of dry cynicism. "*Hence why we think they might be a touch desperate. They might have spun the Souk'ir any number of tales, but I would bet that beneath it all is their desire to have a substantial bodyguard, just in case the Sinut families get here faster than expected. And along with that, if you present them with a tempting target, then I suspect that they could physically overwhelm you. Of course they couldn't take you prisoner without displaying far too much weakness to mere traders, but once they've taken the Scabbard off you, they would have achieved their goal anyway. So if I were in your place I would be gritting my teeth and getting back on that boat!*"

As far as avoiding the two leaders went, Eliavres and Anarawd were successful, landing at Farsan to be greeted by a suitably deferential Donn Monreux, who promptly provided litters to carry them to a comfortable room. Litters which were desperately needed since both Abend were incapable of standing unaided by now. The accommodation was hardly up to the Abend's normal standards of luxury, but after what they had been through of late, it was more than satisfactory for the two mages. Hot baths were provided, and two plump feather mattresses ensured that they rested in less discomfort as they slept off the effects of so much time at sea.

For Magda things were nowhere near as relaxing. For a start, there was the question of what they were going to do with what they were still calling 'Geitla's' body. They could, of course, simply leave her at Arlei until they returned. Yet Magda was unwilling to do that, in part because despite their current helpful attitude, she did not wholly trust the Donns. More than that, though, was her gut feeling that they should be observing Geitla closely. If the Jolnir/Othinn personality chose to try to manifest while they were away, who knew what the result might be? Not that Magda was fooling herself anymore into believing that they had control over the being. Far from it. But she did want to be alert to what it was like when it came into their reality, and maybe, just maybe, with Nicos helping them they might contain it until it could serve a useful purpose at its passing beyond the veil. Taking out a few thousand natives with it would not be a bad start!

So with Nicos and Laufrey, she set about arranging a special litter to carry the comatose body. Only when this was done did she realise that there was substantial friction building between the other three Abend. The Donns were hardly hurrying to get their troops ready to march, and Tancostyl and Barrax were getting to the point of showing the younger Donns just what a war-mage could be like when roused. However Magda spotted instantly what the problem was. Helga, ever jealous of her rights and territory, was countermanding the war-mages' orders as soon as they were out of sight, and with Helga being the Abend the Donns were most familiar with, it was proving chaotic.

"Stop it!" Magda snapped as she marched into Helga's quarters without knocking.

"How dare you!" fumed Helga, but got no chance to remonstrate further.

"I said stop it and I mean it! I don't care what you feel about Eliavres, this is not the time to be playing games, Helga! You can't fool me, I can see right through your ploys and schemes. You want Eliavres to sweat. You want him to think we aren't coming, or won't get there in time. Well this isn't the time to score petty points! How ever wrong he's been in the past, here and now Eliavres is right. We have to respond to Masanae and Quintillean the way he suggested, or we might find out just how astute he was in predicting the scale of the disaster if first those two, and then the Sinut nobles, exploit the lack of unity amongst us.

"And think on this. What if we have to fight the Sinut nobles to prove our supremacy? Has that occurred to you? Because in that eventuality, the Donns will need to look to our war-mages for leadership, and a leadership that isn't undermined by doubts and worries fostered by another of the Abend. And if you haven't the wit to see how that saves your own skin, then I shall take steps to deal with the matter myself. Then you might find out just how close the leadership choice was between Masanae and myself!"

And with that she swept back out of the room, leaving Helga shocked and more than a little in awe of the sense of sheer contained Power she had felt coming off Magda. This was a Magda she had forgotten had existed, and certainly had never expected to reappear. For in her prime Magda had been immensely skilled and versatile, and it had been rumoured that she had held back at the final tests to see who was the strongest of the witches because she had no desire to lead, not because she could not have bested Masanae. And that prompted Helga to wonder if Magda's revitalisation might be almost a bigger shock to Masanae than discovering the seven of them working together. What Quintillean would make of it was not something she could anticipate, but she had a fair idea of what Masanae would think, and it was not a happy thought!

So finally, as Eliavres and Anarawd lurched pale and sickly off the ship at Farsan, the Donns finally grasped what it was that the collected Abend wanted and the DeÁine army drew itself together and began to move. Like an elaborate dance, the Seljuqs and Jundises of the minor families swept around to march into Arlei from the north, while five Jundises of the great houses fell in behind the litters of the Abend and were themselves followed by a similar number of slaves. Barrax had done a splendid job of scanning the ships bringing the two leaders, and reported that they had some six thousand men with them. It was therefore vital that the larger portion of the Abend also have a noticeably larger amount of men with them – not least to demonstrate to the pair that they had been observed and were not being taken on trust any more.

A day later and the expected fireworks started when a blasting thought came through from Quintillean.

"*What's going on?*" he demanded. "*Where are you, Anarawd? Where's the Scabbard?*"

In the warmth of the capacious bed in Farsan, Anarawd groaned, put the pillow over his head, and snuggled deeper beneath the quilt. He still felt rough and had no intention of responding to such bullying tactics. However, Barrax heard quite clearly and responded on Anarawd's behalf.

"*He's on his way back to us, as is Eliavres. Is there a problem with that?*"

Quintillean's mental snarl gave a fractional warning of the blast of Power which slammed at Barrax. A blast which he did not know Quintillean well enough to anticipate, but Tancostyl did and he had a shield up protecting them in the nick of time. A shield which he could hold for some time if he used the Helm too.

"Thank you," Barrax said with genuine gratitude as he rode alongside Tancostyl. The older war-mage nodded and gave a tight-lipped smile. He was beginning to think in the last few days that in Barrax he had someone whom he could really work with. The younger mage was quicker than him to gage responses and to make astute verbal ripostes, while showing him some deference over the art of being a war-mage, even going so far as to ask him for some guidance. Tancostyl liked that. He liked it a lot. Calatin had been just too strange all round for that to ever happen, and Eliavres had had such a rough introduction to the Abend by Quintillean that there had never been a point when he would have risked opening up to

Tancostyl afterwards. And maybe that had been the point of Eliavres' rough initiation, Tancostyl belatedly realised. Perhaps it had been done deliberately to ensure that the other war-mages never formed an alliance which might threaten Quintillean's leadership. Tancostyl barred his teeth in another grim smile. Well that had changed and this time it would be Quintillean who would have to adapt.

As he felt the Power-blast rebound and recognised Tancostyl's signature on the shield Quintillean swore vigorously. So that was the way of things, was it?

"May the Lotus eat their brains and the Seagang rot their bones!" he growled to Masanae.

"Indeed," she answered with icy haughtiness. "Well done, that's the first time that seven have gone against the two of us. You've just made history, Quintillean! Now what do you think you're going to do? Follow them again and then try to convince the Dracma and Tabor to fight the Donns? They've got the Monreux, the Corraine, and the Telesco at their head, do you realise? The three most high famili…"

"…Yes! I know! Shut up!"

"…I'm not your acolyte to command!"

The two faced one another with looks fit to kill, eyes flashing and their Power barely contained.

"We wait here and we negotiate," Masanae declared after they had both taken ragged breaths to regain control, for they were still aboard ship in the bay, and neither wanted to vaporise the wooden ship and get immersed in the brine.

"I negotiate with no-one!" snapped Quintillean.

"Oh I think you don't have a choice this time!" Masanae retorted. "This is your mess, Quintillean! The great Lord Volla only knows you've tried my patience this time. So if you don't want me to take the Dracma and go to join the others, you'd better start getting a grip on that temper of yours and let me handle this."

"*Phad*! You berate me then tell me to trust you? What kind of fool do you take me for? And just remember who pulled you out of the rubble at Kuzm…"

"…Be quiet! You can stop throwing that in my face at every step! If I hadn't been following you then I wouldn't have been in that mess. And as for trusting me, think on this. They'll never negotiate with you given what you've done in bringing the Sinut troops here, but we've still got to face those families and their army, and in only a few weeks or even days, Great Lotus protect us! So if you want to salvage anything from this dreadful muddle, then *they* have to see the Abend all together, and standing side by side, or they'll see the cracks in an instant and exploit them. Do you want that? …No, of course you don't! So we must negotiate with our fellow Abend, because they at least also have something to lose if they fail to impress the Sinut nobles. Together we are *the* Abend. Alone we're just war-mages and witches to be tamed one by one. Do you want *that* Quintillean?"

The leading war-mage seemed on the verge of exploding from the conflicting emotions raging within him. After several tense moments he said through gritted teeth,

"Deal with them, then!" and turned on his heels and stomped along the side of the ship so that he could be first down the gangplank which was just being lowered onto the quay at Temair.

Taking a deep breath and calming herself, Masanae then sent a controlled and unemotional thought across the water to Magda.

"*It appears we have a dilemma, my dear. What is all this about?*"

Magda's response rattled her and she was glad nobody saw her as the diamond-sharp response lashed back at her. "*Oh don't be coy, Masanae! You're in trouble and you know it!*"

Where had this Magda come back from? As bad timing went it could not have been worse. Just when she wanted the witches at least to be united behind her, she did not need Magda suddenly flexing her leadership muscles again. Then Magda's continued reply made her realise that it was already too late – Magda, not she, was controlling the other witches' choices. Her title of leading witch was a hollow sham – something now existing in name only – as Magda was demonstrating.

"*You can risk the sea crossing if you want to, but I should warn you that we'll be meeting the dear boys before you can cut them out and take the Scabbard for yourselves. So what do you propose to do? Undermine the symbolic strength of the Abend by letting all and sundry see us squabbling like children – or rather you two throwing tantrums like a pair of acolytes? Or will you face the Sinut fleet alone? In which case you'd better have a very good story as to why we're sitting here with the Treasures and you're standing on the shore empty-handed. Or are you prepared to climb off your high horses and treat us as equals and save some face?*" Masanae groaned in her soul. So it had come to this. "*Oh, and by the way, are you negotiating for yourself or for Quintillean as well?*"

Dragon of Death be merciful to me, Masanae found herself praying. What a cleft stick to be caught in!

"*I have persuaded Quintillean that we should discuss things with you*," she responded carefully.

"*How delightfully diplomatic of you, poppet*," Magda purred back. "*So our oldest war-mage is like a bear with a sore head, is he?*"

Masanae winced again. No fooling Magda, curse it! She knew Quintillean too well and in a way which only Tancostyl might rival, and Tancostyl had already made it clear which side he was on.

"*Very much so*," she sent back, injecting every ounce of apparently weary toleration she could into her response. "*He has totally failed to predict what the results of all this would be. I don't expect you to believe me, but I knew nothing of the Sinut summons until you told me.*"

"*Actually, dear heart, I do believe you. Quintillean has behaved very stupidly and extraordinarily selfishly, and with the kind of lack of planning which isn't your style at all. But that's not me complimenting you. Make no mistake, you'll have to pay for siding with him, but the question is, how far are you in with Quintillean? Will you sacrifice him if necessary?*"

"*Sacrifice? What are you talking about?*"

By the time Magda had finished telling her of Eliavres' extrapolations, Masanae had collapsed onto her bunk bed and was struggling not to scream. In Ganna's name, how had she not seen this? He was right; there was no doubt about it. Eliavres was right. Eliavres, who had never even known the Most High and Noble Luchaire, had seen what they had not and had made a very astute deduction too. The Emperor must know by now, and his anger would be awesome once he found out that he had been misinformed.

"*So, sweetling, are you prepared for the possibility that we may have to send Quintillean back to the Emperor as a sacrifice to appease him and choose a new leader?*"

"*Yes*," croaked Masanae, still stunned and too horrified to argue.

"*Very well. Then you must therefore appreciate that we wish for Quintillean to remain as leader in name at least for the time being. We have no intention of having one of us being sent back on the long trek to Lochlainn in disgrace for something he did alone. He will remain the leader as far as the Sinut nobles and the families here are aware, but – and it's a major 'but' – from now on he will make no decision without first consulting us all! If you agree to that, then you will stand beside us when we greet the Sinut fleet, and at least maintain the appearance of having a say in the deployment of the*

Treasures. After that, it will depend very much on what news the Sinuti bring with them as to what we do next."

"*You said Quintillean will remain leader for now. What about afterwards?*"

"*I think that depends. If some of us are going to take the Treasures back, then you'll have to find some consensus between yourselves.*"

"*What? What do you mean, 'some of us'? We shall all go home as befits the Abend and retake our place in DeÁine society once more!*"

"*Ganna's poisoned breath! Are you such a fool, Masanae? Go back to what? Do you really think the Emperor has made do without an Abend for all the centuries we and our predecessors have been gone? You and Quintillean always pressed this fiction on us and assured us that the priests at Tokai confirmed that our place was still secure. But Eliavres has proved himself a very able analyst. It was he who showed us how blind we were to believe that. He's also been putting what Anarawd saw in the Houses of the Holy into a rather different perspective.*"

"*Anarawd's been in the Houses of the Holy?*" Masanae was really worried now. Quintillean had assured her that the other Abend never bothered with the priests and so their experiments would go unnoticed.

"*Oh yes, we know about you using the Power-room to track Volla's armour,*" Magda added, giving Masanae no time to think of a clever misdirection – which would not have served any purpose anyway, she belatedly realised. "*But what they didn't bother telling you was that they've had plenty of communications from the homeland, and the Emperor isn't of a forgiving turn of mind. Aside from Volla's treasured pieces of armour, the only thing he wants from us is the elevation bracelets so that he can elevate a whole new Abend of his choosing. Eliavres made Anarawd repeat some of the things his female priest friends told him, and we all now agree that Eliavres is right when he says that it sounds as though the Emperor's welcoming us home will be the last thing we do. He's been training priests in Lochlainn to do many of the things our predecessors once did for him and his family. Our priests in Tokai think that, when we've been bundled onto a ship back to Lochlainn, they'll be given a pronouncement to make from the Emperor which will move them all fully up into our place.*"

"*The priests in our place! No! That's unthinkable!*"

"*But unfortunately, eminently possible, sweetling.*"

"*We were supposed to be forgiven!*"

"*And who actually said that? I can't ever remember being told that by whoever it was who faced the Emperor, and heard the exile pronounced from his own lips, that we would be allowed to resume our places. In fact, I seem to recall that the banishment was done through his chamberlain to make it all the more degrading. So, was it all just wishful thinking on our predecessors' part? And has it been fed by the priests? Because, now that I think hard about it, it doesn't sound much like the Emperor Luchaire I remember. I recall him as a vengeful and sadistic man who enjoyed watching tortures even more than Helga does*!"

Masanae felt her throat go so dry it almost choked her. "*What's the alternative*?" she sent back, hoping that her inner quaking was not revealed in the process. She found herself with her hands clasped over her face in prayer in a way she had not done since she was a mere child, hoping against all hope that the price for survival would not be too high. How had it come to this and so fast? From leading Abend to a feather adrift on the winds of fate?

"*Ah, the alternative*," Magda purred coyly. "*Well now, poppet, that's the thing, isn't it? What Calatin ever wanted is beyond me to guess and it's irrelevant now. But you see, the younger members of our nine never have wanted to go back. That's Eliavres and Helga, and once upon a time Geitla. They've never known the royal court and so they didn't miss it. And now we have Laufrey and Barrax they're in the same position. That leaves just you and me, and Tancostyl, Anarawd and Quintillean, with any iota of recall of the homeland, and I have to say that I'm now of a mind to stay and see what our new members turn out like. Tancostyl doesn't want to stay here, but has decided that he would quite like to lord it in Sinut, Elin, or at least somewhere warmer. Anarawd thinks he can let the Treasures go and then slip into the homeland unnoticed – something to do with one of his convoluted schemes I dare say – but somehow I don't think that will happen as he thinks. That leaves you two*!

"*For those of us who stay behind, though, there will have to be a new leader. If, against the odds, Quintillean isn't forcibly dragged off on a ship to Luchaire's deepest chambers, or insanely chooses to go, then he cannot remain as leader. I believe Eliavres will become the new leader, not because he's the strongest, but because he's shown his exceptional ability to protect our interests in these recent crises. If you can live with that, then we shall then discuss who will be head of the witches, but I regard that as being too far away to concern us just yet.*

"*You have four days in which to consider your position. If at that point you agree to our terms, then you and Quintillean can come to us and we shall prepare the story we shall present to the Sinut nobles. We shall also send these troops we will have accompanying us, along with your new allies, to start clearing a route through the countryside, so that we can greet the ships without any fear of rebels making us look even worse than we will already.*"

"*Rebels*?"

"Oh yes. Helga had a minor encounter with some when she was scouting on the island you're on. Nothing dramatic, but they would hardly enhance our appearance, so they must be eradicated. If necessary, we shall set the Donns and the Souk'irs' men to wipe out every inhabitant of that misbegotten isle. They've long proved useless even as slaves, so there's no reason to leave them at our backs. Bad enough to be seen as failing without adding incompetent to it, because remember that what these newcomers see is what the Emperor will get to hear of. Let's at least send them home with the idea that we can hang on to what we have, even if we'll never see the homeland again! …Four days, my sweet! Make up your minds! With us or on your own, it's your choice, but it will be a final choice!"

And with that Magda disappeared, leaving Masanae feeling as though the ground had disappeared from beneath her feet and was never going to come back. Four days! Upon the Immaculate Temples, how was she to convince Quintillean? It might take her that long just to make him realise that their dream had been all a lie. A fight, that's what she must give him. No use in fooling herself into thinking he would lie down and accept this as it was. She must find him a way to direct his warlike instincts, but not at the other Abend! Eliminating the population of this island of Rathlin might be a start. A way for him to face the Sinut nobility and wave his hand saying 'I did this', even if he did not have his hand on the Scabbard or the Helm on his head.

Yet most of all she must find a way to unite him with the rest of the Abend, if only in appearance, and that might mean that she dressed the news up a little differently. Since he would never accept another leader, why tell him? Let him think that the others would support his continued leadership and not mention the conditions – after all, he was not likely to be around to worry about the long-term ones if Magda was right. More important for her to save her own skin now if he was to be the sacrifice!

Four days of intense wrangling later, and with Masanae nursing the worst headache of her life as a result, she presented their decision to Magda. Quintillean was still fuming over the concessions she made him make, and had declined to be present at the meeting, going off instead for a day of mayhem and slaughter with the troops of the Tabor.

"*Is he willing?*" Magda asked, and when told gave her wicked laugh. "*You haven't told him he's to be the goat on the altar, have you poppet? Oh dear, he will have a surprise coming!*"

"*This is what will get him to a meeting with the Sinut nobles and standing alongside us,*" Masanae told her coldly. "*If he can't be saved, then I have no intention of going with him. Let's give them a warm welcome, hand over the Treasures, and wave them goodbye. The cursed things aren't worth dying for!*"

"*Smart lady!*" Magda agreed. "*Then set sail as soon as he's back and we'll introduce you in person to Barrax and Laufrey.*"

When the two stepped out onto the quay at Farsan two days later it was to find the seven others standing side by side along the quay in front of them. There was no sign of either the Helm or the Scabbard, and Quintillean's last hope of wrenching one free and rattling everyone's teeth until they cowed before him once again disappeared. Then he realised that Masanae was gliding forward to greet the others, and that, if he did not want to be left looking like he did not have an ally in the world, he had better catch up with her.

Barrax was something of a shock. He could not remember him as an acolyte and, belatedly, realised that this why Masanae had thought him foolish for not taking more interest in those coming along behind them. The youngest war-mage was the one of all of them who looked like a warrior. He was taller than Eliavres and almost on a par with Anarawd and Tancostyl, but was broader in the shoulder than any of them. Looking at his features Quintillean suddenly realised that Barrax was more than likely a Monreux. No wonder he had made a good war-mage! And it was clear that he had the Monreux self-confidence, because he was showing no nervousness at facing a senior war-mage who might display no little ire at being gainsaid.

As for Laufrey, she was stunningly beautiful. One of the lightest coloured DeÁine like Helga, she put the more senior witch in the pale, for she had a sensuality about her which made Helga appeared hatchet-faced and haggard. He reached out to her then jerked back with shock. He had had half an idea that she might be his next new ally if Masanae was going to be this unbending and vengeful. But even the lightest of contacts had blown that option into smithereens. She was not even trying to disguise the revulsion she was feeling on seeing him walking towards her. That finally hammered it home to him that Masanae had been trying to prepare him for this. She had not been scheming when she had said that the others would be expecting to have an equal say in what happened next. He really was leader in name only now!

"Quintillean, dear heart, what have you done?" Magda chastised him, standing there in all her old seductive splendour. "You really have been such a naughty boy! Come! We must make our plans now, because it could take us weeks to get across to the south coast, given the terrain we shall have to march our men through, and the Sinut fleet draws closer every day!"

Now go to *Unleashing the Power* for the final, exciting chapters of this series!

If you've enjoyed this book you personally (yes, *you*) can make a big difference to what happens next.

Reviews are one of the best ways to get other people to discover my books. I'm an independent author, so I don't have a publisher paying big bucks to spread the word or arrange huge promos in bookstore chains, there's just me and my computer.

But I have something that's actually better than all that corporate money – it's you, my enthusiastic readers. Honest reviews help bring these books to the attention of other readers (although if you think something needs fixing I would really like you to tell me first!). So if you've enjoyed this book, it would mean a great deal to me if you would spend a couple of minutes posting a review on the site where you purchased it.

About the Author

L. J. Hutton lives in Worcestershire and writes history, mystery and fantasy novels. If you would like to know more about any of these books you are very welcome to come and visit my online home at www.ljhutton.com

Also by L. J. Hutton:

If you would like to receive the first eBook for free in a new (slightly smaller) fantasy quartet, set in the same world as these books, but in a different location and slightly later in date, then all you need to do is to go to my web page, follow the link, and send me your email. I promise not to bombard you with random mail – this is just to be able to let you know when new books are coming out. Sadly I cannot provide free paperbacks due to the much higher production and distribution costs, but if like me you love holding a real book in your hands, then this new series is also available in paperback.

Menaced by Magic

A lost soldier, a duchy in peril, and a missing heir who alone can control its only defence. Can a stranger hold the key to everyone's survival?

Modern-day soldier, Mark, wakes up in a strange place only to find he's the double for the lost heir to the Duchy of Palma. Even as he struggles against the intense hatred his double has earned, Mark discovers a new danger is coming, and this one has a potent magical power he has no idea how to combat. How do you fight insane mages whose power you don't even begin to comprehend when they think you've stolen their kingdom? Totally out of his depth, and with no way to return home, Mark must help his new friends fight for the survival of the duchy and its people, or die with them.

~

I also write mysteries which are a kind of urban fantasy and have a paranormal twist. You will get one of these eBooks for free as well when you sign up! And if you love real history too, then look for the first trilogy in my retelling of the Robin Hood legend.You can get the prequel, *Heaven's Kingdom*, for free when you sign up. The first book is *Crusades* and is available from Amazon and other retailers.

Can one man change the fate of thousands? Guy of Gisborne tries, but he needs Robin Hood to succeed!

Forced to leave their home, cousins Guy and Robin are destined to lead very different lives. While Robin goes with the Templars to the crusades, Guy faces danger on the Welsh border serving brutal sheriff de Braose. Yet a chance meeting with rebel Welsh priest, Tuck, sets Guy on the path of covert righter of wrongs, even before a chance meeting with a prince returns him to Nottingham. And when Robin returns, too, the cousins launch a wider crusade to find justice for the people of Sherwood.

As Robin's spy inside the sheriff's castle, Guy risks being hung – or worse – if caught. Alone and often torn by the decisions he's forced make, Guy must act against the very class he was born into, but once his eyes have been opened to the plight of the ordinary people there's no going back. Yet it will be the infamous events in York in 1190 that will seal the fate of one famous outlaw, his cousin, and a legend!

Printed in Great Britain
by Amazon